"Readers won't be able to put down this dark and riveting tale of power and revenge." —*Kirkus Reviews* (starred review)

"With all the knife-sharp thrill of its cinematic predecessor . . . Fans of *Vicious* will be overjoyed to rediscover this exciting series." —*Publishers Weekly* (starred review)

"*Vengeful* picks up five years after the insane events of book one, ratcheting up the stakes and introducing two kick-ass women with extraordinary powers." —*Paste*

"Schwab does a masterful job in these two books, capturing all of the questions superheroes would raise in our reality and with nuance not often found in the genre at large." —*Book Riot*

"If *Vicious* is a blast to the chest, then *Vengeful* is a cold knife between the ribs, sharp and something that'll sit with you long after you reach the last page." —*Culturess*

"With each page, the story grows faster, denser, and more inescapable." —*Den of Geek*

"The long-anticipated sequel to V. E. Schwab's supervillain novel, *Vicious,* is finally here, and it's worth the wait." —*Bustle*

"V. E. Schwab showcases her prolific writing prowess in *Vengeful*. . . . An adrenaline rush." —*Hypable*

PRAISE FOR *VICIOUS*

Entertainment Weekly's 27 Female Authors
Who Rule Sci-Fi and Fantasy Right Now

"Fresh, merciless, and, yes, vicious. Wow."
—Mira Grant, *New York Times* bestselling author of the Newsflesh trilogy

"Schwab's characters feel vital and real, never reduced to simple archetypes. . . . In a genre that tends toward the flippant or pretentious, this is a rare superhero novel as epic and gripping as any classic comic. Schwab's tale of betrayal, self-hatred, and survival will resonate with superhero fans as well as readers who have never heard of Charles Xavier or Victor von Doom."
—*Publishers Weekly* (starred review)

"A fun, morally flexible revenge tale . . . *Vicious* methodically ratchets up the tension as Victor and Eli circle each other for the inevitable kill." —Daniel H. Wilson, *New York Times* bestselling author of *Robopocalypse*

"Schwab's artful chronology-bending plotting rivals that of any Iain Banks novel, and her writing is a sly, cynical treat."
—*Financial Times* (UK)

TOR BOOKS BY V. E. SCHWAB

Vicious

Vengeful

A Darker Shade of Magic

A Gathering of Shadows

A Conjuring of Light

VENGEFUL

V. E. SCHWAB

TOR

A TOM DOHERTY ASSOCIATES BOOK
NEW YORK

This is a work of fiction. All of the characters, organizations, and events portrayed in this novel are either products of the author's imagination or are used fictitiously.

VENGEFUL

Copyright © 2018 by Victoria Schwab

All rights reserved.

Edited by Miriam Weinberg

A Tor Book
Published by Tom Doherty Associates
120 Broadway
New York, NY 10271

www.tor-forge.com

Tor® is a registered trademark of Macmillan Publishing Group, LLC.

The Library of Congress has cataloged the hardcover edition as follows:

Schwab, Victoria, author.
 Vengeful / V.E. Schwab.—First edition.
  p. cm.
 "A Tom Doherty Associates book."
 ISBN 978-0-7653-8752-3 (hardcover)
 ISBN 978-0-7653-8754-7 (ebook)
 1. Superheroes—Fiction. 2. Revenge—Fiction.Ambition—Fiction. 3. Heroes—Fiction. 4. Ability—Fiction. I. Title.
 PS3619.C4848 V46 2018
 813'.6—dc23

2018289619

ISBN 978-0-7653-8753-0 (trade paperback)

Our books may be purchased in bulk for promotional, educational, or business use. Please contact your local bookseller or the Macmillan Corporate and Premium Sales Department at 1-800-221-7945, extension 5442, or by email at MacmillanSpecialMarkets@macmillan.com.

First Edition: September 2018
First Trade Paperback Edition: January 2020

Printed in the United States of America

0 9 8 7 6 5

*To Mum, and Holly, and Miriam,
the most powerful women I know*

While seeking revenge, dig two graves—one for yourself.

—*Douglas Horton*

GENESIS

SIX WEEKS AGO

THE MERIT SUBURBS

THE night Marcella died, she made her husband's favorite dinner.

Not because it was a special occasion, but because it *wasn't*—spontaneity, people insisted, was the secret to love. Marcella didn't know if she believed all that, but she was willing to try her hand at a home-cooked meal. Nothing too fancy—a good steak, edges seared with black pepper, slow-baked sweet potatoes, a bottle of merlot.

But six o'clock came and went, and Marcus wasn't home.

Marcella put the food in the oven to keep it warm, then checked her lipstick in the hall mirror. She freed her long black hair from its loose bun, then put it up again, teasing a few strands out before smoothing her A-line dress. People called her a natural beauty, but nature only went so far. The truth was, Marcella spent two hours in the gym six days a week, trimming and toning and stretching every lean muscle on her willowy five-foot-ten frame, and she never left her bedroom without her makeup expertly applied. It wasn't easy, but neither was being married to Marcus Andover Riggins—better known as Marc the Shark, Tony Hutch's right-hand man.

It wasn't easy—but it was worth it.

Her mother liked to say she'd gone fishing and somehow bagged a great white. But what her *mother* didn't understand was that Marcella had baited her hook with her prize in mind. And she'd caught *exactly* what she'd wanted.

Her cherry red heels clicked across the wood floor before being swallowed by the silk rug as she finished setting the table and lit each of the twenty-four tapers in the pair of iron candelabras that framed the door.

Marcus hated them, but for once Marcella didn't care. She loved the candelabras, with their long stems and branching limbs—they looked like the kind of thing you'd find in a French chateau. They made the home feel luxurious. Made new money feel old.

She checked the time—seven, now—but resisted the urge to call. The fastest way to kill a flame was to smother it. Besides, if Marcus had business, then business always came first.

Marcella poured herself a glass of wine and leaned back against the counter, imagining his strong hands closing around someone's throat. A head forced underwater, a jaw cracking sideways. Once he'd come home with blood on his hands and she'd fucked him right there on the marble island, the metal shaft of his gun still in its holster, the steel hard against her ribs.

People thought Marcella loved her husband in spite of his work. The truth was, she loved him because of it.

But as seven became eight, and eight neared nine, Marcella's arousal slowly turned to annoyance, and when the front door finally swung open, that annoyance hardened to anger.

"Sorry, darling."

His voice always shifted when he'd been drinking, slowing to a lazy drawl. It was his only tell. He never stumbled or swayed, his hands never shook. No, Marcus Riggins was made of stronger stuff—but he wasn't without his flaws.

"It's fine," said Marcella, hating the edge in her own voice. She turned toward the kitchen, but Marcus caught her wrist, pulling her hard enough that she lost her balance. His arms folded around her, and she looked up into his face.

Sure, her husband's waist had widened a little, while hers had narrowed, that beautiful swimmer's body bloating a fraction with each passing year, but his summer brown hair hadn't thinned, and his eyes were still the rugged blue of slate or dark water. Marcus had always been good-looking, though she wasn't sure how much of that was his tailored suits or the way he moved through the world, as if expecting it get out of his way. It usually did.

"You're gorgeous," he whispered, and Marcella could feel the press of him, hungry against her hip. But Marcella wasn't in the mood.

She reached up, nails dragging down his stubbled cheek. "You hungry, sweetheart?"

"Always," he growled against her neck.

"Good," said Marcella, stepping away and smoothing her skirt. "Dinner's ready."

∞

A bead of red wine slid like sweat down the side of the raised glass, tracing its way toward the white tablecloth. Marcella had filled it too full, her hand made clumsy by her worsening mood. Marcus didn't seem to notice the stain. He didn't seem to notice anything.

"To my beautiful wife."

Marcus never prayed before meals, but he always made a toast, had since the night they met. It didn't matter if he had an audience of twenty or if they ate alone. She'd found it endearing on their first date, but these days the gesture felt hollow, rehearsed. Designed to charm instead of being genuinely charming. But he never failed to say the words, and perhaps that was a kind of love. Or perhaps Marcus was simply a creature of habit.

Marcella lifted her own glass.

"To my elegant husband," she answered automatically.

The rim was halfway to her lips when she noticed the smudge on Marcus's cuff. At first she thought it was only blood, but it was too bright, too pink.

It was lipstick.

Every conversation she'd had with the other wives came rushing back.

His eyes start to wander yet?
Keeping his stick wet?
All men are rotten.

Marcus was busy cutting into his steak, and rambling on about insurance, but Marcella had stopped listening. Behind her eyes, her husband traced his thumb across a pair of stained lips, parting them around his knuckle.

Her fingers tightened on the wineglass. Heat was flushing her skin even as a cold weight settled in her stomach. "What a fucking cliché," she said.

He didn't stop chewing. "Excuse me?"

"Your sleeve."

His gaze drifted languidly down toward the bloom of pink. He didn't even have the decency to look surprised. "Must be yours," he said, as if she'd ever worn that shade, ever owned anything so tacky and *twee*—

"Who is she?"

"Honestly, Marce—"

"Who *is* she?" demanded Marcella, gritting her perfect teeth.

Marcus finally stopped eating, and leaned back in his chair, blue eyes hanging on her. "Nobody."

"Oh, so you're fucking a ghost?"

He rolled his eyes, clearly tired of the subject, which was ironic, considering he usually relished any topic that revolved around *him*. "Marcella, envy really doesn't suit you."

"Twelve years, Marcus. Twelve. And *now* you can't keep it in your pants?"

Surprise flickered across his face, and the truth hit her like a blow—of course this wasn't his first time cheating. This was only the first time he'd been *caught*.

"How long?" she asked icily.

"Let it go, Marce."

Let it go—as if his cheating were like the wineglass in her hand, something she'd just happened to pick up, could just as easily set down.

It wasn't the betrayal itself—she could forgive a lot, in the interest of this life she'd made—but it was the look in the other women's eyes that Marcella had always taken for envy, it was the stoic warnings of the first wives, the twitch at the corner of a smile, the realization that they all *knew,* had known, for god knows how long, and she—hadn't.

Let it go.

Marcella set the wineglass down. And picked up the steak knife. And as she did, her husband had the nerve to scoff. As if she wouldn't know what to do with it. As if she hadn't listened to all his stories, hadn't begged for details. As if he didn't go on and on about his job when he was drunk. As if she hadn't practiced with a pillow. A bag of flour. A steak.

Marcus raised a single brow. "What do you plan to do now?" he asked, voice dripping with condescension.

How silly she must look to him, with her perfectly manicured nails gripping the monogrammed hilt of the blade.

"Dollface," he crooned, and the word made Marcella seethe.

Dollface. Baby. Darling. Was that how he really thought of her, after all this time? As helpless, brittle, weak, something *ornamental,* a glass figurine designed to shimmer and shine and look pretty on a shelf?

When she didn't let go, his gaze darkened.

"Don't you turn that knife on me unless you plan to use it . . ."

Perhaps she *was* glass.

But glass is only brittle until it breaks.

Then it's sharp.

"Marcella—"

She lunged, and had the thrill of seeing her husband's eyes widen a fraction in surprise, the bourbon spilling as he jerked backward. But Marcella's knife had barely skimmed his silk tie before Marcus's hand cracked across her mouth. Blood poured across her tongue, and Marcella's eyes blurred with tears as she tumbled back into the oak table, rattling the china plates.

She still had the knife, but Marcus had his hand wrapped around her wrist, pinning it to the table so hard the bones began to grind together.

He'd been rough with her before, but that had always been in the heat of the moment, signaled by some unspoken pact, and she'd always been the one to signal it.

This was different.

Marcus was two hundred pounds of brute strength, a man who'd made his living breaking things. And people. He clucked his tongue now, as if she were being ridiculous. Blowing things out of proportion. As if she'd made him do this. Made him fuck another woman. Made him ruin all that she'd worked so hard to build.

"Ah, Marce, you've always known how to rile me up."

"Let me *go*," she hissed.

Marcus brought his face close to hers, ran a hand through her hair, cupped her cheek. "Only if you play nice."

He was smiling. *Smiling.* As if this were just another game.

Marcella spit her blood into his face.

Her husband let out a long-suffering sigh. And then he slammed her head against the table.

Marcella's world went suddenly white. She didn't remember falling, but when her vision flickered back she was on the silk carpet beside her chair, her head throbbing. She tried to get up, but the room swayed viciously. Bile rose in her throat, and she rolled over, vomited.

"You should have let it go," said Marcus.

Blood ran into one of her eyes, staining the dining room red as her husband reached out and wrapped his hand around the nearest candelabra. "I always hated these," he said, tipping the pole until it fell.

The flame caught the silk curtains on the way down, before the candelabra hit the floor.

Marcella struggled to her hands and knees. She felt like she was underwater. Slow, too slow.

Marcus stood in the doorway, watching. Just watching.

A steak knife gleamed on the hardwood floor. Marcella forced herself up through the heavy air. She was almost there when the blow hit her from behind. Marcus had knocked over the second candelabra. It came crashing down, iron arms pinning her to the floor.

It was disconcerting how fast the fire had spread. It leapt from the curtain to a puddle of spilled bourbon, to the tablecloth and the rug. It was already everywhere.

Marcus's voice, through the haze. "We had a good run, Marce."

That fucking prick. As if *any of it* had been his idea, his doing. "You're nothing without me," she said, her words unsteady. "I made you, Marcus." She heaved against the candelabra. It didn't move. "I will unmake you."

"People say a lot of things before they die, sweetheart. I've heard them all."

Heat filled the room, her lungs, her head. Marcella coughed, but couldn't catch her breath. "I will *ruin* you."

There was no answer.

"Do you hear me, Marcus?"

Nothing, only silence.

"I will ruin you!"

She screamed the words until her throat burned, until the smoke stole her vision, and her voice, and even then it echoed in her head, her last thoughts following her down, down, down into the dark.

I will ruin you.

I will ruin.

I will.

I—

∞

OFFICER Perry Carson had been stuck on the twenty-seventh level of Radical Raid for the better part of an hour when he heard an engine rev to life. He looked up in time to see Marcus Riggins's sleek black sedan peel out of the slate half circle that formed the mansion's drive. It tore down the road, a good thirty over the suburb-mandated speed limit, but Perry wasn't in a patrol car, and even if he had been, he hadn't spent the last three weeks in this shit-heap eating greasy takeout just to bust Riggins for such a minor infraction.

No, the Merit PD needed something that would *stick*—and not just to Marc the Shark. They needed the whole crooked sea.

Perry settled back against the worn leather and returned to his game, cracking the twenty-seventh level just as he smelled smoke.

No doubt some asshole setting a poolside bonfire without a permit. He squinted out the window—it was late, half past ten, the sky an inky black this far from Merit, and the smoke didn't stand out against the dark.

But the fire did.

The officer was out of the car and across the street by the time the flames lit the front windows of the Riggins mansion. Calling it in by the time he reached the front door. It was unlocked—thank god it was unlocked—and he threw it open, already composing his report. He'd say it was ajar, say he heard a call for help, even though the truth was he didn't hear *anything* but the crack of burning wood, the whoosh of flame sliding up the hall.

"Police!" he called through the smoke. "Is anyone here?"

He'd seen Marcella Riggins arrive home. But he hadn't seen her leave. The sedan had gone by fast, but not fast enough to leave any doubt—there was no one in the passenger seat.

Perry coughed into his sleeve. Sirens were already sounding in the distance. He knew he should go back outside and wait, outside, where the air was clean and cool and safe.

But then he rounded the corner and saw the body trapped beneath a coil of iron the size of a coatrack. The tapers had all melted, but Perry realized it was a candelabra. Who even *owned* a candelabra?

Perry reached for its stem and then recoiled—it was searing to the touch. He cursed himself. The metal arms had already burned through Marcella's dress wherever they touched her, the skin raw and red, but the woman didn't cry out, didn't scream.

She wasn't moving. Her eyes were closed and blood slicked the side of her head, matting the dark hair against her scalp.

He felt for a pulse, and found one that fluttered, then seemed to fall away beneath his touch. The fire was getting hotter. The smoke was getting thicker.

"Shit shit shit," muttered Perry, scanning the room as sirens wailed outside. A pitcher of water had spilled across a napkin, leaving it unburnt. He wrapped the cloth around his hand and then took hold of the candelabra. The damp fabric hissed and heat shot toward his fingers as he heaved the iron bar up with all his strength. It lifted, and rolled off Marcella's body just as voices filled the hall. Firefighters came storming into the house.

"In here!" he wheezed, choking on the smoke.

A pair of firemen cut through the haze right before the ceiling groaned and a chandelier came toppling down. It shattered against the dining room table, which split and threw up flames, and the next thing Perry knew, he was being hauled backward out of the room and the burning mansion, and into the cool night.

Another firefighter followed close behind, Marcella's body slung over one shoulder.

Outside, the trucks were splayed across the manicured lawn, and ambulance lights strobed across the slate drive.

The house was going up in flames, and his hand was throbbing, his lungs burned, and Perry didn't give a damn about any of it. The only thing he cared about right then and there was saving the life of Marcella Riggins. Marcella, who had always flashed a wan smile and a pert wave to the cops whenever she was followed. Marcella, who would never, ever snitch on her crooked husband.

But judging by the gash in her head, and the house on fire, and the husband's swift departure, there was a chance her position had changed. And Perry wasn't about to waste it.

Hoses sent jets of water into the flames, and Perry hacked and spat, but pulled away from an oxygen mask as two medics loaded Marcella onto a stretcher.

"She's not breathing," said a medic, cutting open her dress.

Perry jogged after the medics.

"No pulse," said the other, beginning compressions.

"Then bring it back!" shouted Perry, hauling himself up into the ambulance. He couldn't put a corpse on the stand.

"Ox-sat levels tanking," said the first, strapping an oxygen mask over Marcella's nose and mouth. Her temperature was too high, and the medic pulled out a stack of cold packs and began to break the seals, applying them to her temples, neck, wrists. He handed the last one to Perry, who grudgingly accepted.

Marcella's heartbeat appeared on a small screen, a solid line, even and unmoving.

The van pulled away, the burning mansion quickly shrinking in the window. Three weeks Perry had spent outside that place. Three *years* he'd been trying to nail Tony Hutch's crew. Fate had handed him the perfect witness, and he'd be damned if he was giving her back without a fight.

A third medic tried to tend to Perry's burned hand, but he pulled away. "Focus on her," he ordered.

The sirens cut through the night as the medics worked, trying to force her lungs to breathe, her heart to beat. Trying to coax life out of the ashes.

But it wasn't working.

Marcella lay there, limp and lifeless, and Perry's hope began to gutter, die.

And then, between one compression and the next, the horrible static line of her pulse gave a lurch, and a stutter, and finally began to beep.

1
RESURRECTION

I

FOUR WEEKS AGO

HALLOWAY

"I won't ask you again," said Victor Vale as the mechanic scrambled backward across the garage floor. Retreating—as if a few feet would make a difference. Victor followed slowly, steadily, watched as the man backed himself into a corner.

Jack Linden was forty-three, with a five-o'clock shadow, grease under his nails, and the ability to fix things.

"I already told you," said Linden, jumping nervously as his back came up against a half-built engine. "I can't do it—"

"Don't lie to me," warned Victor.

He flexed his fingers around the gun, and the air crackled with energy.

Linden shuddered, biting back a scream.

"I'm not!" yelped the mechanic. "I fix *cars*. I put *engines* back together. Not people. Cars are easy. Nuts and bolts and fuel lines. People are too much *more*."

Victor didn't believe that. Had never believed that. People were more intricate perhaps, more nuanced, but fundamentally machines. Things that worked, or didn't, that broke down, and were repaired. *Could be* repaired.

He closed his eyes, measuring the current inside him. It was already in his muscles, already threading his bones, already filling his chest cavity. The sensation was unpleasant, but not nearly as unpleasant as what would happen when the current peaked.

"I swear," said Linden, "I'd help you if I could." But Victor heard him shift. Heard a hand knocking against the tools strewn across the floor. "You have to believe me . . ." he said, fingers closing around something metal.

"I do," said Victor, eyes flicking open right as Linden lunged at him, wrench in hand. But halfway there, the mechanic's body slowed, as if caught in a sudden drag, and Victor swung the gun up and shot Linden in the head.

The sound echoed through the garage, ricocheting off concrete and steel as the mechanic fell.

How disappointing, thought Victor, as blood began to seep across the floor.

He holstered the gun and turned to go, but only made it three steps before the first wave of pain hit, sudden and sharp. He staggered, bracing himself against the shell of a car as it tore through his chest.

Five years ago, it would have been a simple matter of flipping that internal switch, killing power to the nerves, escaping any sensation.

But now—there was no escape.

His nerves crackled, the pain ratcheting up like a dial. The air hummed with the energy, and the lights flickered overhead as Victor forced himself away from the body and back across the garage toward the wide metal doors. He tried to focus on the symptoms, reduce them to facts, statistics, measurable quantities, and—

The current arced through him, and he shuddered, pulling a black mouth guard from his coat and forcing it between his teeth just before one knee gave way, his body buckling under the strain.

Victor fought—he always fought—but seconds later he was on his back, his muscles seizing as the current peaked, and his heart lurched, lost rhythm—

And he died.

II

FIVE YEARS AGO

MERIT CEMETERY

VICTOR had opened his eyes to cold air, grave dirt, and Sydney's blond hair, haloed by the moon.

His first death was violent, his world reduced to a cold metal table, his life a current and a dial turning up and up, electricity burning through every nerve until he finally cracked, shattered, crashed down into heavy, liquid nothing. The dying had taken ages, but death itself was fleeting, the length of a single held breath, all the air and energy forced from his lungs the moment before he surged up again through dark water, every part of him screaming.

Victor's second death was stranger. There had been no electric surge, no excruciating pain—he'd thrown that switch long before the end. Only the widening pool of blood beneath Victor's knees, and the pressure between his ribs as Eli slid the knife in, and the world giving way to darkness as he lost his hold, slipped into a death so gentle it felt like sleep.

Followed by—*nothing*. Time drawn out into a single, unbroken second. A chord of perfect silence. Infinite. And then, interrupted. The way a pebble interrupts a pond.

And there he was. Breathing. Living.

Victor sat up, and Sydney flung her small arms around him, and they sat there for a long moment, a reanimated corpse and a girl kneeling on a coffin.

"Did it work?" she whispered, and he knew she wasn't talking about the resurrection itself. Sydney had never revived an EO without consequences. They came back, but they came back wrong, their powers skewed, fractured. Victor felt gingerly along the lines of his power, searching for frayed threads, interruptions in the current, but felt—unchanged. Unbroken. Whole.

It was a rather overwhelming sensation.

"Yes," he said. "It worked."

Mitch appeared at the side of the grave, his shaved head glistening with sweat, his tattooed forearms filthy from the dig. "Hey." He drove a spade into the grass and helped Sydney and then Victor up out of the hole.

Dol greeted him by leaning heavily against his side, the dog's massive black head nestling under his palm in silent welcome.

The last member of their party slumped against a tombstone. Dominic had the shaken look of an addict, pupils dilated from whatever he'd taken to numb his chronic pain. Victor could feel the man's nerves, frayed and sparking like a shorted line.

They'd made a deal—the ex-soldier's assistance in exchange for taking away his suffering. In Victor's absence, Dominic clearly hadn't been able to keep his end of the bargain. Now Victor reached out and switched the man's pain off like a light. Instantly, the man sagged backward, tension sliding like sweat from his face.

Victor retrieved the shovel and held it out to the soldier. "Get up."

Dominic complied, rolling his neck and rising to his feet, and together the four of them began filling Victor's grave.

∞

TWO days.

That's how long Victor had been dead.

It was an unsettling length of time. Long enough for the initial stages of decay. The others had been holed up at Dominic's place, two men, a girl, and a dog, waiting for his corpse to be buried.

"It's not much," said Dom now, opening the front door. And it wasn't—a small and cluttered single bedroom with a beat-up sofa, a concrete balcony, and a kitchen covered in a thin layer of dirty dishes—but it was a temporary solution to a longer dilemma, and Victor was in no condition to face the future, not with grave dirt still on his slacks and death lingering in his mouth.

He needed a shower.

Dom led him through the bedroom—narrow and dark, a single shelf of books, medals lying flat and photographs facedown, too many empty bottles on the windowsill.

The soldier scrounged up a clean long-sleeve shirt, embossed with a band logo. Victor raised a brow. "It's all I have in black," he explained.

He switched on the bathroom light and retreated, leaving Victor alone.

Victor undressed, shrugging out of the clothes he'd been buried in—clothes he didn't recognize, hadn't purchased—and stood before the bathroom mirror, surveying his bare chest and arms.

He wasn't free of scars—far from it—but none of them belonged to that night at the Falcon Price. Gunshots echoed through his mind, ricocheting off unfinished walls, the concrete floor slick with blood. Some of it his. Most of it Eli's. He remembered each and every wound made that night—the shallow cuts across his stomach, the razor-sharp wire cinching over his wrists, Eli's knife sliding between his ribs—but they left no mark.

Sydney's gift really was remarkable.

Victor turned the shower on and stepped beneath the scalding water, rinsing death from his skin. He felt along the lines of his power, turned his focus inward, the way he'd done years before, when he'd first gone to prison. During that isolation, unable to test his new power on anyone else, Victor had used his own body as a subject, learned everything he could about the limits of pain, the intricate network of nerves. Now, bracing himself, he turned the dial in his mind, first down, until he felt nothing, and then up, until every drop of water on bare skin felt like knives. He clenched his teeth against the pain and turned the dial back to its original position.

He closed his eyes, brought his head to rest against the tile wall, and smiled, Eli's voice echoing through his head.

You can't win.

But he *had*.

THE apartment was quiet. Dominic stood out on the narrow balcony, puffing on a cigarette. Sydney was curled on the sofa, folded up carefully like a piece of paper, with the dog, Dol, on the floor beside her, chin resting by her hand. Mitch sat at the table, shuffling and reshuffling a deck of cards.

Victor took them all in.

Still collecting strays.

"What now?" asked Mitch.

Two small words.

Single syllables had never weighed so much. For the last ten years, Victor had focused on revenge. He'd never truly intended to see the other side of it, but now, he'd fulfilled his objective—Eli was rotting in a cell—and Victor was still here. Still alive. Revenge had been an all-consuming pursuit. Its absence left Victor uneasy, unsatisfied.

What now?

He could leave them. Disappear. It was the smartest course—a group, especially one as strange as this, would draw attention in ways that solitary figures rarely did. But Victor's talent allowed him to bend the attention of those around him, to lean on their nerves in ways that registered as aversion, subtle, abstract, but efficient. And as far as Stell knew, Victor Vale was dead and buried.

Six years he'd known Mitch.

Six days he'd known Sydney.

Six hours he'd known Dominic.

Each of them was a weight around Victor's ankles. Better to unshackle himself, abandon them.

So leave, he thought. His feet made no progress toward the door.

Dominic wasn't an issue. They'd only just met—an alliance forged by need and circumstance.

Sydney was another matter. She was his responsibility. Victor had *made* her so when he killed Serena. That wasn't sentiment—it was simply a transitive equation. A factor passed from one quotient to another.

And Mitch? Mitch was cursed, he'd said so himself. Without Victor, it was only a matter of time before the hulking man ended up back in prison. Likely the one he'd broken out of with Victor. For Victor. And, despite knowing her less than a week, Victor was certain Mitch wouldn't abandon Sydney. Sydney, for her part, seemed rather attached to him, too.

And then, of course, there was the issue of Eli.

Eli was in custody, but he was still alive. There was nothing Victor could do about *that,* given the man's ability to regenerate. But if he ever got out—

"Victor?" prompted Mitch, as if he could see the turn of his thoughts, the direction they were veering.

"We're leaving."

Mitch nodded, trying and failing to hide his clear relief. He'd always been an open book, even in prison. Sydney uncurled from the sofa. She rolled over, her ice blue eyes finding Victor's in the dark. She hadn't been sleeping, he could tell.

"Where are we going?" she asked.

"I don't know," answered Victor. "But we can't stay here."

Dominic had slipped back inside, bringing a draft of cold air and smoke. "You're leaving?" he asked, panic flickering across his face. "What about our deal?"

"Distance isn't a problem," said Victor. It wasn't strictly true—once Dominic was out of range, Victor wouldn't be able to *alter* the threshold he'd set. But his influence *should* hold. "Our deal stays in effect," he said, "as long as you still work for me."

Dom nodded quickly. "Whatever you need."

Victor turned to Mitch. "Find us a new car," he said. "I want to be out of Merit by dawn."

And they were.

Two hours later, as the first light cracked the sky, Mitch pulled up in a black sedan. Dom stood in his doorway, arms crossed, watching as Sydney climbed into the back, followed by Dol. Victor slid into the passenger's seat.

"You sure you're good?" asked Mitch.

Victor looked down at his hands, flexed his fingers, felt the prickle of energy under his skin. If anything, he felt stronger. His power crisp, clear, focused.

"Better than ever."

III

FOUR WEEKS AGO

HALLOWAY

VICTOR shuddered back to life on the cold concrete floor.

For a few agonizing seconds, his mind was blank, his thoughts scattered. It was like coming off a strong drug. He was left grasping for logic, for order, sorting through his fractured senses—the taste of copper, the smell of gasoline, the dim glow of streetlights beyond cracked windows—until the scene finally resolved around him.

The mechanic's garage.

Jack Linden's body, a dark mass framed by fallen tools.

Victor pulled the mouth guard from between his teeth and sat up, limbs sluggish as he dragged the cell phone from his coat pocket. Mitch had rigged it with a makeshift surge protector. The small component was blown, but the device itself was safe. He powered it back on.

A single text had come in from Dominic.

3 minutes, 49 seconds.

The length of time he'd been dead.

Victor swore softly.

Too long. Far too long.

Death was dangerous. Every second without oxygen, without blood flow, was exponentially damaging. Organs could remain stable for several hours, but the brain was fragile. Depending on the individual, the nature of the trauma, most doctors put the threshold for brain degradation at four minutes, others five, a scant few six. Victor wasn't keen on testing the upper limits.

But there was no use ignoring the grim curve.

Victor was dying more often. The deaths were lasting longer. And the damage . . . He looked down, saw electrical scorch marks on the concrete, broken glass from the shattered lights overhead.

Victor rose to his feet, bracing himself against the nearest car until the room steadied. At least, for now, the buzzing was gone, replaced by a merciful quiet—broken almost immediately by the short, clipped sound of a ringtone.

Mitch.

Victor swallowed, tasting blood. "I'm on my way."

"Did you find Linden?"

"I did." Victor glanced back at the body. "But it didn't work. Start looking for the next lead."

IV

FIVE YEARS AGO

PERSHING

TWO weeks after his resurrection, the buzzing started.

At first, it was negligible—a faint humming in his ears, a tinnitus so subtle Victor first took it for a straining light bulb, a car engine, the murmur of a television rooms away. But it didn't go away.

Almost a month later, Victor found himself looking around the hotel lobby, straining to find a possible source for the sound.

"What is it?" asked Sydney.

"You hear it too?"

Sydney's brow furrowed in confusion. "Hear what?"

Victor realized she hadn't been asking about the noise, only his distraction. He shook his head. "Nothing," he said, turning back to the desk.

"Mr. Stockbridge," said the woman, addressing Victor, "I see you're with us for the next three nights. Welcome to the Plaza Hotel."

They never did stay long, bounced instead from city to city, sometimes choosing hotels, and other times rentals. They never traveled in a straight line, didn't stay at places with any regularity, or in any particular order.

"How would you like to pay?"

Victor drew a billfold from his pocket. "Cash."

Money wasn't a problem—according to Mitch it was nothing but a sequence of ones and zeroes, digital coinage in a fictional bank.

His favorite new hobby was skimming minute quantities of cash, pennies on the dollar, consolidating the gain into hundreds of accounts. Instead of leaving no footprint, he created too many to follow. The result was large rooms, plush beds, and space, the kind Victor had longed for and lacked in prison.

The sound inched higher.

"Are you okay?" asked Syd, studying him. She'd been studying him since the graveyard, scrutinizing his every gesture, every step, as if he might suddenly crumble, turn to ash.

"I'm fine," lied Victor.

But the noise followed him to the elevators. It followed him up to the room, an elegant suite with two bedrooms and a sofa. It followed him to bed and up again, shifting subtly, escalating from sound alone to sound and sensation. A slight prickle in his limbs. Not pain, exactly, but something more unpleasant. Persistent. It dogged him, growing louder, stronger, until, in a fit of annoyance, Victor switched his circuits off, turned the dial down to nothing, numbness. The prickling vanished, but the buzzing only softened to a faint and far-off static. Something he could almost ignore.

Almost.

He sat on the edge of his bed, feeling feverish, ill. When was the last time he'd been sick? He couldn't even remember. But with every passing minute, the feeling worsened, until Victor finally rose, crossing the suite and taking up his coat.

"Where are you going?" asked Sydney, curled on the sofa with a book.

"To get some air," he said, already slipping through the door.

He was halfway to the elevator when it hit him.

Pain.

It came out of nowhere, sharp as a knife through his chest. He gasped and caught himself on the wall, fought to stay upright as another wave tore through him, sudden and violent and impossible. The dials were still down, his nerves still muted, but it didn't seem to matter. Something was *overriding* his circuits, his power, his will.

The lights glared down, haloing as his vision blurred. The hallway swayed. Victor forced himself past the elevator to the stairwell. He barely made it through the door before his body lit again with pain, and his knee buckled, cracking hard against the concrete. He tried to rise, but his muscles spasmed, and his heart lurched, and he went down on the landing.

His jaw locked as pain arced through him, unlike anything he'd felt in years. Ten years. The lab, the strap between his teeth, the cold of the metal table, the excruciating pain of the current as it fried his nerves, tore his muscles, stopped his heart.

Victor had to move.

But he couldn't get up. Couldn't speak. Couldn't breathe. An invisible hand turned the dial up, and up, and up, until finally, mercifully, everything went black.

∞

VICTOR came to on the stairwell floor.

The first thing he felt was relief—relief that the world was finally quiet, the infernal buzzing gone. The second thing he felt was Mitch's hand shaking his shoulder. Victor rolled onto his side and vomited bile and blood and bad memories onto the landing.

It was dark, the light overhead shorted out, and he could just make out the relief on Mitch's face.

"Jesus," he said, slumping backward. "You weren't breathing. You didn't have a pulse. I thought you were dead."

"I think I was," said Victor, wiping his mouth.

"What do you mean?" demanded Mitch. "What happened?"

Victor shook his head slowly. "I don't know." It wasn't a comfortable thing for Victor, not knowing, certainly wasn't something he cared to admit to. He rose to his feet, bracing himself against the stairwell wall. He'd been a fool to kill his sensitivity. He should have been studying the progression of symptoms. Should have measured the escalation. Should have known what Sydney seemed to sense: that he was cracked, if not broken.

"Victor," started Mitch.

"How did you find me?"

Mitch held up his cell. "Dominic. He called me, freaking out, said you took it back, that it was like before, when you were dead. I tried to call you but you didn't answer. I was heading for the elevator when I saw the light burned out in the stairs." He shook his head. "Had a bad feeling—"

The cell started ringing again. Victor took it from Mitch's hand and answered. "Dominic."

"You can't just *do that* to me," snapped the ex-soldier. "We had a *deal.*"

"It wasn't intentional," said Victor slowly, but Dominic was still going.

"One minute I'm fine and the next I'm on my hands and knees, trying not to pass out. No warning, nothing in my system to dull the pain, you don't know what it was like—"

"I promise you, I do," said Victor, tipping his head back against the concrete wall. "But you're fine now?"

A shuddering breath. "Yeah, I'm back online."

"How long did it last?"

"What? I don't know. I was kind of distracted."

Victor sighed, eyes sliding shut. "Next time, pay attention."

"*Next* time?"

Victor hung up. He opened his eyes to find Mitch staring at him. "Did this happen before?"

Before. Victor knew what he meant. Once his life had been bisected by the night in the laboratory. Before, a human. After, an EO. Now, it was split down the line of his resurrection. Before, an EO. After—this. Which meant that it was Sydney's doing. *This* was the inevitable flaw in her power, the fissure in his. Victor hadn't avoided it after all. He'd simply ignored it.

Mitch swore, running his hands over his head. "We have to tell her."

"No."

"She's going to find out."

"No," said Victor again. "Not yet."

"Then when?"

When Victor understood what was happening, and how to fix it. When he had a plan, a solution as well as a problem. "When it will make a difference," he said.

Mitch's shoulders slumped, defeated.

"Maybe it won't happen again," said Victor.

"Maybe," said Mitch.

Neither one of them believed it.

V

FOUR AND A HALF YEARS AGO

FULTON

IT happened again.

And again.

Three episodes in less than six months, the time between each a fraction shorter, the duration of death a fraction longer. It was Mitch who insisted he see a specialist. Mitch who found Dr. Adam Porter, a compact man with a hawkish face and a reputation as one of the best neurologists in the country.

Victor had never been fond of doctors.

Even back when he wanted to *become* one, it had never been in the interest of saving patients. He'd been drawn to the field of medicine for the knowledge, the authority, the control. He'd wanted to be the hand holding the scalpel, not the flesh parting beneath it.

Now Victor sat in Porter's office, after hours, the buzzing in his skull just beginning to filter into his limbs. It was a risk, he knew, waiting until the episode was in its metastasis, but an accurate diagnosis required the presentation of symptoms.

Victor looked down at the patient questionnaire. Symptoms he could give, but details were more dangerous. He slid the paper back across the table without picking up the pen.

The doctor sighed. "Mr. Martin, you paid quite a premium for my services. I suggest you take advantage of them."

"I paid that premium for privacy."

Porter shook his head. "Very well," he said, lacing his fingers. "What seems to be the problem?"

"I'm not entirely certain," said Victor. "I've been having these *episodes.*"

"What kind of episodes?"

"Neurological," he answered, toeing the line between omission and lie. "It starts as a sound, a buzzing in my head. It grows, until I can feel the humming, down to my bones. Like a charge."

"And then?"

I die, thought Victor.

"I black out," he said.

The doctor frowned. "How long has this been happening?"

"Five months."

"Did you suffer any trauma?"

Yes.

"Not that I know of."

"Changes in lifestyle?"

"No."

"Any weakness in your limbs?"

"No."

"Allergies?"

"No."

"Have you noticed any specific triggers? Migraines can be triggered by caffeine, seizures by light, stress, lack of—"

"I don't care what caused it," said Victor, losing patience. "I just need to know what's happening, and how to fix it."

The doctor sat forward. "Well, then," he said. "Let's run some tests."

∞

VICTOR watched the lines chart across the screen, spiking like the tremors before an earthquake. Porter had attached a dozen electrodes to his scalp, and was now studying the EEG alongside him, a crease forming between his brows.

"What is it?" asked Victor.

The doctor shook his head. "This level of activity is abnormal, but the pattern doesn't suggest epilepsy. See how closely the lines are gathered?" He tapped the screen. "That degree of neural excitation, it's almost like there's too much nerve conduction . . . an excess of electrical impulse."

Victor studied the lines. It could be a trick of the mind, but the lines on the screen seemed to rise and fall with the tone in his skull, the peaks in rhythm growing with the hum under his skin.

Porter cut the program. "I need a more complete picture," he said, removing the electrodes from Victor's scalp. "Let's get you into an MRI."

The room was bare save for the scanner in the center—a floating table that slid into a tunnel of machinery. Slowly, Victor lay back on the table, his head coming to rest in a shallow brace. A framework slid across his eyes, and Porter fastened it closed, locking Victor in. His heart rate ticked up as, with a mechanical whir, the table moved and the room disappeared, replaced by the too-close ceiling of the machine in front of Victor's face.

He heard the doctor leave, the click of the door shutting, and then his voice returned, stretched thin by the intercom. *"Hold very still."*

For a full minute, nothing happened. And then a deep knocking sound resonated through the device, a low bass that drowned out the noise in his head. Drowned out everything.

The machine thudded and whirred, and Victor tried to count the seconds, to hold on to some measure of time, but he kept losing his grip. Minutes fell away, taking with them more and more of his control. The buzzing was in his bones now, the first pricks of pain—a pain he couldn't stifle—crackling across his skin.

"Stop the test," he said, the words swallowed by the machine.

Porter's voice came over the intercom. *"I'm almost done."*

Victor fought to steady his breathing, but it was no use. His heart thudded. His vision doubled. The horrible electric hum grew louder.

"*Stop the—*"

The current tore through Victor, bright and blinding. His fingers clutched at the sides of the table, muscles screaming as the first wave crashed over him. Behind his eyes, he saw Angie, standing beside the electric panel.

"*I want you to know,*" she said as she began to fix sensors to his chest, "*that I will never, ever forgive you for this.*"

Alarms wailed.

The scanner whined, shuddered, stopped.

Porter was somewhere on the other side of the machine, speaking in a low, urgent voice. The table began to withdraw. Victor clawed at the straps holding his head. Felt them come free. He had to get up. He had to—

The current crashed into him again, so hard the room shattered into fragments—blood in his mouth, his heart losing rhythm, Porter, a pen light turning the world white, a stifled scream—then the pain erased everything.

∞

VICTOR woke on the exam table.

The lights on the MRI were dark, the opening threaded with scorch marks. He sat up, head spinning, as the world came back into focus. Porter lay several feet away, his body contorted, as if trapped in a spasm. Victor didn't need to feel for a pulse, or sense the man's empty nerves, to know that he was dead.

A memory, of another time, another lab, Angie's body, twisted in the same unnatural way.

Shit.

Victor got to his feet, surveying the room. The corpse. The damage.

Now that his senses had settled, he felt calm, clear-headed again. It was like the break after a storm. A stretch of peace before bad weather built again. It was only a matter of time—which was why every silent second mattered.

There was a syringe on the floor next to Porter's hand, still capped.

Victor slipped it into his pocket and went into the hall, where he'd left his coat. He drew out his cell as the text came in from Dominic.

1 minute, 32 seconds.

Victor took a steadying breath and looked around the empty offices.

He retraced his steps to the exam room, gathered up every scan and printout from Porter's tests. In the doctor's office, he cleared the appointment, the digital data, tore off the sheet on which the doctor had made his notes, and the one beneath it for safe measure, systematically erased every sign that he'd ever been inside the building.

Every sign aside from the dead body.

There was nothing to be done about that, short of setting fire to the place—an option he considered, and then set aside. Fires were temperamental things, unpredictable. Better to leave this looking as it did—a heart attack, a freak accident.

Victor slipped on his coat and left.

Back at the hotel suite, Sydney and Mitch were sprawled on the sofa, watching an old movie, Dol stretched at their feet. Mitch met Victor's gaze when he walked in, eyebrows raised in question, and Victor gave a small, almost imperceptible head shake.

Sydney rolled upright. "Where were you?"

"Stretching my legs," said Victor.

Syd frowned. Over the last few weeks, the look in her eyes had shifted from pure worry to something more skeptical. "You've been gone for hours."

"And I was trapped for years," countered Victor, pouring himself a drink. "It makes a body restless."

"I get restless too," said Sydney. "That's why Mitch came up with the card game." She turned to Mitch. "Why doesn't Victor have to play?"

Victor raised a brow and sipped his drink. "How does it work?"

Sydney took the deck up from the table. "If you draw a number card, you have to stay in and learn something, but if you draw a face card, you get to go out. Mostly just to parks or movies, but it's still better than being cooped up."

Victor cut a glance at Mitch, but the man only shrugged and rose, heading to the bathroom.

"You try it," said Syd, holding out the deck. Victor considered her a moment, then lifted his hand. But instead of drawing a card, he brushed the deck from Syd's palm, spilling cards across the floor.

"Hey," said Syd as Victor knelt and considered his options. "That's cheating."

"You never said I had to play fair." He plucked the king of spades from where it lay, upturned. "Here," he said, offering her the card. "Keep it up your sleeve."

Sydney considered the card for a long moment, and then palmed it right before Mitch returned. His eyes flicked between them. "What's going on here?"

"Nothing," said Syd without a second's hesitation. "Victor's just teasing me."

It was disconcerting how easily she lied.

Syd returned to the couch, Dol climbing up beside her, and Victor stepped out onto the balcony.

A few minutes later, the door slid open at his back, and Mitch joined him.

"Well?" asked Mitch. "What did Porter say?"

"He didn't have answers," said Victor.

"Then we find someone else," said Mitch.

Victor nodded. "Tell Syd we're leaving in the morning." Mitch slipped back inside, and Victor set his drink on the railing. He drew the syringe from his pocket, reading the label. Lorazepam. An anti-seizure drug. He had been hoping for a diagnosis, a cure, but until then, he would find a way to treat the symptoms.

∞

"I don't normally meet with patients after hours."

Victor sat across the table from the young doctor. She was slim, and dark, eyes keen behind her glasses. But no matter her interest, or suspicion, her practice was located in Capstone, a city with strong government ties, the kind of place where privacy was paramount, discretion mandatory. Where loose lips could end careers, even lives.

Victor slid the cash across the table. "Thank you for making an exception."

She took the money and considered the few lines he'd filled out on his intake. "How can I help you, Mr. . . . Lassiter?"

Victor was trying to focus through the rising sound in his skull, as she asked all the same questions, and he gave all the same answers. He laid out the symptoms—the noise, the pain, the convulsions, the blackouts—omitting what he could, lying where he had to. The doctor listened, pen scratching across her notepad as she thought. "It could be epilepsy, myasthenia gravis, dystonia—neurological disorders are hard to diagnose sometimes, when they present overlapping symptoms. I'll order some tests—"

"No," said Victor.

She looked up from her notes. "Without knowing what exactly—"

"I've had tests," he said. "They were . . . inconclusive. I'm here because I want to know what you would prescribe."

Dr. Clayton straightened in her chair. "I don't prescribe medications without a diagnosis, and I don't diagnose without compelling evidence. No offense, Mr. Lassiter, but your word is not sufficient."

Victor exhaled. He leaned forward. And as he did, he leaned on her, too. Not with his hands, but with his senses, a pressure just below pain. A subtle discomfort, the same kind that made strangers bend away, allowed Victor to pass unnoticed through a crowd. But Clayton couldn't escape so easily, and so the discomfort registered for what it was—a threat. A fight-or-flight trigger, simple and animalistic, predator to prey.

"There are plenty of dirty doctors in this city," said Victor. "But their willingness to prescribe is often inversely proportional to their skill as a physician. Which is why I'm here. With you."

Clayton swallowed. "The wrong diagnosis," she said steadily, "and the medication could do more harm than good."

"That is a risk," said Victor, "I'm willing to take."

The doctor let out a short, shaky breath. She shook her head, as if clearing her mind. "I'll prescribe you an anti-seizure medication and a beta blocker." Her pen scratched across the page. "For anything stronger," she said, tearing off the sheet, "you will have to admit yourself for observation."

Victor took the slip and rose. "Thank you, Doctor."

Two hours later, he tipped the pills into his palm and swallowed them dry.

Soon, he felt his heart slow, the buzzing quiet, and thought, perhaps, that he had found an answer. For two weeks, he felt better.

And then he died again.

VI

FOUR WEEKS AGO

HALLOWAY

VICTOR was late, and he knew it.

Linden had taken longer than expected—he'd had to wait for the garage to clear, wait for them to be alone. And then, of course, wait for the death he knew was coming, see it through so it didn't follow him back to the house where they'd been for the last nine days. It was a rental, another one of those short-stay places you could book for a day or a week or a month.

Sydney had chosen it, she said, because it looked like a *home*.

When Victor walked in, he was met by the smell of melted cheese and the crack of an explosion on the large TV. Sydney was perched on the arm of the couch, tossing Dol pieces of popcorn while Mitch stood at the kitchen counter, arranging candles on top of a chocolate cake.

The scene was so extraordinarily . . . normal.

The dog spotted him first, tail sliding back and forth across the hardwood floor.

Mitch met his gaze, forehead knotted in concern, but Victor waved him away.

Syd glanced over her shoulder. "Hey."

Five years, and in most ways Sydney Clarke looked the same. She was still short and slight, as round-faced and wide-eyed as she'd been the day they'd met on the side of the road. Most of the differences were superficial—she'd traded the rainbow leggings for black ones with little white stars, and her usual blond bob was constantly hidden by a collection of wigs, her hair changing as often as her mood. Tonight, it was a pale blue, the same color as her eyes.

But in other ways, Sydney had changed as much as any of them. The tone of her voice, her unflinching gaze, the way she rolled her eyes—an affectation she'd clearly taken on in an effort to stress her age, since it wasn't readily apparent. In body, she was still a child. In attitude, she was all teenager.

Now she took one look at Victor's empty hands and he could see the question in her eyes, the suspicion that he'd forgotten.

"Happy birthday, Sydney," he said.

It was a strange thing, the alignment of Syd's birthday with her arrival in Victor's life. Every year marked not only her age, but the time she'd been with him. With them.

"Ready for me to light the candles?" asked Mitch.

Victor shook his head. "Give me a few minutes to change," he said, slipping down the hall.

He closed the door behind him, left the lights off as he crossed the bedroom. The furnishings really didn't suit him—the blue and white cushions, the pastoral painting on one wall, the books on the shelf picked out for decoration instead of substance. The last, at least, he'd found a use for. An attractive history text sat open, a black felt-tip pen resting in the center. At this point, the left page had been entirely blacked out, the right down to the final line, as if Victor were searching for a word and hadn't found it yet.

He shrugged out of his coat and went into the bathroom, rolling up his sleeves. He turned the faucet on and splashed water on his face, the white noise of the tap matching the static already starting again inside his skull. These days the quiet was measured in minutes instead of days.

Victor ran a hand through his short blond hair and considered his reflection, blue eyes wolfish in his gaunt face.

He'd lost weight.

He had always been slim, but now when he lifted his chin, the light glanced off his brow and cheekbone, made shadows along his jaw, in the hollow of his throat.

A short row of pill bottles sat lined up along the back of the sink. He reached for the nearest one, and tipped a Valium into his palm.

Victor had never been keen on drugs.

Sure, the prospective escape held some appeal, but he could never get over the loss of *control*. The first time he'd purchased narcotics, back at Lockland, he wasn't even trying to get high. He was just trying to end his life, so he could come back *better*.

Irony of ironies, thought Victor, swallowing the pill dry.

VII

FOUR YEARS AGO

DRESDEN

VICTOR hadn't spent a lot of time in strip clubs.

He'd never understood their appeal—never been aroused by the half-naked bodies, their writhing oiled forms—but he hadn't come to the Glass Tower for the show.

He was looking for someone special.

As he scanned the hazy club, trying not to inhale the cloud of perfume and smoke and sweat, a manicured hand danced along his shoulder blade.

"Hello, honey," said a syrupy voice. Victor glanced sideways and saw dark eyes, bright red lips. "I bet we could put a smile on that face."

Victor doubted it. He had craved a lot of things—power, revenge, control—but sex was never one of them. Even with Angie . . . he'd *wanted* her, of course, wanted her attention, her devotion, even her love. He'd cared about her, would have found ways to please her—and perhaps found his own pleasure in that—but for him, it had never been about sex.

The dancer looked Victor up and down, misreading his disinterest for discretion, or perhaps assuming his proclivities went to less feminine places.

He brushed her fingers away. "I'm looking for Malcolm Jones." Self-styled entrepreneur, specializing in all things illicit. Weapons. Sex. Drugs.

The dancer sighed and pointed toward a red door at the back of the club. "Downstairs."

He made his way toward it, was nearly there when a small blonde crashed into him, releasing a flutter of apology in a high sweet lilt as he reached to steady her. Their eyes met, and something crossed her face, the briefest flutter of interest—he would have said recognition, but he was sure they'd never met. Victor pulled away, and so did she, slipping into the crowd as he reached the red door.

It swung shut behind him, swallowing the club from view. He flexed his hands as he followed a set of concrete steps down into the bowels of the building. The hall at the bottom was narrow, the walls painted black and the air thick with stale cigar smoke. Laughter spilled out of a room at the end, but Victor's way forward was blocked by a heavyset guy in a snug black shirt.

"Going somewhere?"

"Yes," said Victor.

The man surveyed him. "You look like a narc."

"So I've been told," said Victor, spreading his arms, inviting a search.

The man patted him down, then led him through.

Malcolm Jones was sitting behind a large desk in an expensive suit, a gleaming silver gun resting atop a stack of bills at his elbow. Three more men perched on various pieces of furniture; one watched the flat-screen mounted on the wall, another played on his phone, the third eyed the line of coke Jones was cutting on his desk.

None of them seemed overly concerned by Victor's arrival.

Only Jones bothered to look up. He wasn't young, but he had that hungry, almost wolfish look that came with people on the rise. "Who're you?"

"New customer," said Victor simply.

"How'd you hear of me?"

"Word spreads."

Jones preened at that, clearly flattered by the idea of his budding notoriety. He gestured at the empty chair across the desk. "What are you looking for?"

Victor lowered himself into the chair. "Drugs."

Jones gave him a once-over. "Huh, would have taken you for a weapons guy. Are we talking heroin? Coke?"

Victor shook his head. "Prescription."

"Ah, in that case . . ." Jones waved a hand, and one of his men rose and opened a locker, displaying an array of plastic pill bottles.

"We've got oxy, fentanyl, benzos, addy . . ." recited Jones as the other guy lined the bottles on the desk.

Victor considered his options, wondering where to start.

The episodes were multiplying, and nothing he did seemed to make a difference. He'd tried avoiding his power, on the theory that it was a kind of battery, one that charged with use. When that didn't work, Victor changed tactics, and tried using his power *more,* on the theory that perhaps it was a charge he had to *diffuse.* But that approach yielded the same results—again the buzz grew louder, again it became physical, again Victor died.

Victor surveyed the array of pills.

He could chart the electrical current's progress, but he couldn't seem to change it.

From a scientific perspective, it was damning.

From a psychological one, it was worse.

The pain itself he could hijack, to a point, but pain was only one facet of the nervous system. And only one aspect of most opiates. They were suppressants, designed not only to smother pain, but also sensation, heart rate, consciousness—if one kind didn't suffice, then he'd need a cocktail.

"I'll take them," he said.

"Which ones?"

"All of them."

Jones smiled coolly. "Slow down, stranger. There's a house limit of one bottle—I can't go giving you my whole supply. Next thing I know, it shows up on a corner at triple the price—"

"I'm not selling," said Victor.

"Then you don't need much," said Jones, his smile tightening. "Now, as for payment—"

"I said I'd *take* them." Victor leaned forward. "I never said anything about payment."

Jones laughed, a humorless, feral sound, taken up in a chorus by his men. "If you were planning to rob me, you could have at least brought a gun."

"Oh, I did," said Victor, holding out his hand. Slowly, as if performing a trick, he curled three of his fingers in, leaving his thumb up and his index extended.

"See?" he said, pointing the finger at Jones.

Jones no longer seemed amused. "You some kind of—?"

"Bang."

There was no gunshot—no earsplitting echo or spent cartridge or smoke—but Jones let out a guttural scream and fell to the floor as if hit.

The other three men went for their own guns, but their actions were slowed by shock, and before they could fire Victor leveled them all. No dial. No nuance. Just blunt force. That place beyond pain where nerves snapped, fuses blew.

The men crumpled to the floor like puppets with their strings cut, but Jones was still conscious. Still clutching his chest, searching frantically for a bullet wound, the wetness of blood, some physical damage to match what his nerves were telling him.

"The fuck . . . the fuck . . ." he muttered, eyes darting wildly.

Pain, Victor had learned, turned people into animals.

He gathered the pills, dumping bags and bottles into a black leather briefcase he found leaning against the desk. Jones shuddered on the floor before rallying, his attention latching on to the glint of metal on his desk. He started to lunge for it, but Victor's fingers twitched, and Jones sagged, unconscious, against the far wall.

Victor took up the gun Jones had been going for, weighed the weapon in his palm. He didn't have any special fondness for guns—they'd been rendered largely unnecessary, given his power. But in his current condition, it might be useful to have something... extraneous. Plus, it never hurt to have a visible deterrent.

Victor slipped the gun into his coat pocket and snapped the briefcase shut.

"A pleasure doing business with you," he said to the silent room as he turned and walked out.

AT THE SAME TIME...

June adjusted her ponytail and slipped through the velvet curtain into the private dance room. Harold Shelton was already inside, waiting, rubbing his pink hands on his thighs in anticipation.

"I've missed you, Jeannie."

Jeannie was home sick with food poisoning.

June was just borrowing her body.

"How *much* have you missed me?" she asked, trying to sound soft, breathy. The voice wasn't perfect, it never was. After all, a voice was nature *and* nurture, biology and culture. June could nail the pitch—that came with the body—but her real accent, with its light musical lilt, always snuck through. Not that Harold seemed to notice. He was too busy ogling Jeannie's tits through the blue-and-white cheerleading outfit.

It wasn't really June's preferred type, but it didn't have to be.

It just had to be his.

She did a slow circle around him, let her pink nails trail along his shoulder. When her fingers grazed his skin, she saw flashes of his life—not all of it, just the pieces that left a mark. She let them slide through her mind without sticking. She knew she'd never borrow his body, so she'd never need to know more.

Harold caught her wrist, pulling her into his lap.

"You know the rules, Harold," June said, easing herself free.

The rules of the club were simple: Look, but don't touch. Hands in your lap. On your knees. Under your ass. It didn't matter, so long as they weren't on the girl.

"You're such a fucking tease," he growled, annoyed, aroused. He tipped his head back, eyes glassy, breath sour. "What am I even paying for?"

June passed behind him, draped her arms around his shoulders. "You can't touch *me*," she cooed, leaning in until her lips brushed his ear. "But I can touch *you*."

He didn't see the wire in her hands, didn't notice until it wrapped around his throat.

Harold started fighting then, but the curtains were thick, and the music was loud, and the more people fought, the faster they ran out of air.

June had always liked the garrote. It was quick, efficient, tactile.

Harold wasted too much energy clawing at the wire instead of her face. Not that it would have made a difference.

"Nothing personal, Harold," June said as he stomped his feet and tried to twist free.

It was the truth—he wasn't on her list. This was just business.

He slumped forward, lifeless, a thin line of spittle hanging from his open lips.

June straightened, blew out a short breath, put away the wire. She studied her palms, which weren't *her* palms. They were marked with thin, deep lines where the wire had bit in. June couldn't feel it, but she knew that the real Jeannie would wake up with these welts, and the pain to go with them.

Sorry, Jeannie, she thought, stepping through the curtain, flicking it shut behind her. Harold was a big spender. He'd shelled out for a full hour of Jeannie's teen queen, which gave June a good fifty minutes to get as far from the body as possible.

She rubbed the welts from her hands as she started down the hall.

At least Jeannie's roommates were home—she'd alibi out. No one had seen June go into Harold's room, and no one had seen her leave, so all she had to do—

"Jeannie," called a voice, too close, behind her. "Aren't you on the clock?"

June swore under her breath, and turned around. And as she did, she *changed*—four years of collecting everyone she touched had given her an extensive wardrobe, and in a blink she shed Jeannie and picked out someone else, another blonde, one with the same shade, same build, but smaller tits and a round face, clad in a short blue dress.

It was a bloody work of art, that shift, and the bouncer blinked, confused, but June knew from experience—when people saw something they didn't understand, they couldn't hold on. *I saw* became *I think I saw* became *I couldn't have seen* became *I didn't see*. Eyes were fickle. Minds were weak.

"Only dancers and clients back here, ma'am."

"Not gunning for a peek," said June, letting her accent trip rich and full over her tongue. "Just looking for the ladies' room."

Max nodded at a door on the right. "Back out the way you came, and across the club."

"Cheers," she added with a wink.

June kept her pace even, casual, as she crossed the club. All she wanted now was a shower. Strip clubs were like that. The smell of lust and sweat, cheap drinks and dirty bills, so thick it coated your skin, followed you home. It was a trick of the mind—after all, June couldn't feel, couldn't smell, couldn't taste. A borrowed body was just that—borrowed.

She was halfway there when she knocked into a man, thin, blond, and dressed in all black. Not unusual, in a place like this, where businessmen leered alongside bachelors, but June reeled at the contact—when she'd brushed his arm, she'd seen . . . *nothing*. No details, no memories.

The man had barely registered her, was already moving away. He disappeared through a red door at the back of the club, and June forced herself to keep walking too, despite feeling like her world had shuddered to a stop.

What were the odds?

Slim, she knew—but not none. There'd been another, a few years ago, a young guy she'd passed on the street one summer night; knocked into, really—she'd had her head tipped back, he'd had his down. When they touched, she'd felt that same flush of cold, the same stretch of black where the memories should be. After months of taking on looks and forms with every touch, the absence of information had been startling, disconcerting. June hadn't known, then, what it meant—if the other person was broken, or if she was, if it was a feature or a glitch—not until she followed the guy and saw him run his hand along the hood of a car. Heard the sudden rumble of an engine starting under his touch, and realized he was *different*.

Not in the way *she* was different, but still, miles from *ordinary*.

She'd started looking for them, after that.

June, who'd never before been a fan of casual contact, unwanted touches, now found every excuse to brush fingers, kiss cheeks, searching for those elusive patches of darkness. She hadn't found another.

Until now.

June slipped behind a column, shedding the blond girl in favor of a man with a forgettable face. Up at the bar, she ordered herself a drink and waited for the stranger to resurface.

Ten minutes later, he did, carrying a black briefcase. He slipped out into the dark.

And June followed behind.

∞

THE streets weren't empty, but they also weren't crowded enough to hide a tail. Every time she dipped out of streetlight, she shifted form.

What would June do if the man in black noticed her?

What would she do if he didn't?

June didn't know *why* she was following the man, or what she planned to do when he stopped walking. Was it a gut feeling pulling her along, or just curiosity? She hadn't always been able to tell them apart. Before . . .

But June didn't like to think about before. Didn't want to, didn't need to. Dying might not have stuck, but her death itself had been real enough. No point in prying open that coffin.

June—that wasn't her real name either, of course. She'd buried that with the rest.

The only thing she'd kept was the accent. *Kept* was a strong word—the stubborn thing didn't want to go. A wisp of home in a foreign world. A memory, of green, and gray, of cliffs and ocean . . . She probably could have shed it, scrubbed it out along with everything else that made her *her*. But it was all she had left. The last thread.

Sentimental, she chided, quickening her step.

Eventually June stopped shifting, and simply followed in the stranger's wake.

It was strange, the subtle way other people veered around him, leaned out of his path.

They *saw* him, she could tell by the way they shifted, sidestepped. But they didn't really *notice*.

Like magnets, thought June. Everyone thought of magnets as having pull, attraction, but turn them around and they repelled. You could spend ages trying to force them together, and you'd get there, almost, but in the end they'd slide off.

She wondered if the man had that effect on the world around him, if it was part of his power.

Whatever it was, she didn't feel it.

But then again, she didn't feel anything.

Who are you? she wondered, annoyed by the man's opacity. She had been spoiled rotten by her power, by the easy knowing that came with it. Not that she saw everything—that would be a short road to long madness—but she saw enough. Names. Ages. Memories, too, but only the ones that really left a mark.

A person, distilled into so many bites.

It was disconcerting, now, to be deprived.

Ahead, the man stopped outside an apartment building. He stepped through the revolving door into the lobby, and June stood in the shadow of the building's eaves and watched him get into the elevator, watched the dial ascend to the ninth floor and then stop.

She chewed her lip, thinking.

It was late.

But it wasn't *that* late.

June turned through the wardrobe in her mind. Too late for a delivery, perhaps, but not a courier. She selected a young woman—more disarming, especially at night—in navy cycling gear, scooped up an undelivered envelope from the lobby, and pushed the call button on the elevator.

There were four doors on the ninth floor.

Four chances.

She put her ear to the first door and heard the dead silence of an empty apartment.

The same with the second.

At the third, she heard footsteps, and knocked, but when the door swung open she was greeted not by the man in black, but by a girl, a large dog at her side.

The girl was on the small side, with white-blond hair and ice blue eyes. The sight of her caught June off guard. She was twelve, maybe thirteen. Madeline's age. Madeline belonged to the Before— *before,* when June had had a family, parents, siblings, one older, three younger, the youngest, with those same strawberry curls—

"Can I help you?" asked the girl.

June realized she must have the wrong place. She shook her head and started to back away.

"Who is it?" asked a warm voice, a big guy with tattooed sleeves and a friendly smile.

"Delivery," said the girl. She was reaching for the package, her fingers nearly brushing June's, when *he* appeared.

"Sydney," said the man in black. "I told you not to answer the door."

The girl retreated into the room, the large dog trailing behind her, and the man stepped forward, his eyes, a colder, darker blue, flicking down to the package in June's hands.

"Wrong address," he said, closing the door in her face.

June stood in the hall, mind spinning.

She'd expected him to be alone.

People like them, they were supposed to be alone.

Were the others human, the big guy and the young girl? Or did they have powers too?

June came back the next day. Pressed her ear against the door and heard—nothing. She knelt before the lock, and a few seconds later the door swung open. The apartment was empty. No signs of the girl, or the dog, the big guy, or the stranger.

They were just—gone.

VIII

THREE YEARS AGO

CAPITAL CITY

IT was happening again. Again. Again.

Victor braced himself against the dresser, the pills from Malcolm Jones's supply arrayed before him, that ever-present hum turning to a high whine in his skull. He searched the labels again for something he hadn't tried—oxycodone, morphine, fentanyl—but he'd tried all of them. Every permutation, every combination, and they weren't working. None of them were working.

He stifled a frustrated growl and swept the open bottles from the counter. Pills rained down onto the floor as Victor surged out into the apartment. He had to get away before the charge reached its peak.

"Where are you going?" asked Sydney as Victor crossed the room.

"Out," he said tightly.

"But you just got back. And it's movie night. You said you'd watch with us."

Mitch put a hand on her arm. "I'm sure he won't be long."

Sydney looked between them, as if she could see the omissions, the lies, the space where truth had been carved out. "What's going on?"

Victor pulled his coat from the hook. "I just need some air." The charge was spilling out now, into the air around him, energy crackling through his limbs. Dol whimpered. Mitch winced. But Sydney didn't back down.

"It's raining," she protested.

"I won't melt."

But Sydney was already reaching for her own coat. "Fine," she said, "then I'll go with you."

"Sydney—"

But she made it to the door before him.

"Get out of my way," he said through clenched teeth.

"No," she shot back, stretching her small body across the wooden frame.

"*Move*," said Victor, a strange desperation creeping into his voice.

But Sydney held her ground. "Not until you tell me what's going on. I know you're hiding something. I know you're lying, and it's not fair, I deserve to—"

"*Move*," ordered Victor. And then, without thinking—there was no room for anything beyond the rising charge, the slipping seconds, the need to escape—Victor took hold of Sydney, and *pushed*, not against her nerves, but against her whole body. She stumbled sideways, as if hit, and Victor surged past her for the door.

He was almost there when the spasm hit.

Victor staggered, braced himself against the wall, a low groan escaping between clenched teeth.

Sydney was on her hands and knees nearby, but when he stumbled, all the anger drained out of her face, replaced by fear. "What is it? What's wrong?"

Victor bowed his head, struggling for breath. "Get her—out—"

Mitch was finally there, dragging Sydney back, away from Victor.

"*What's happening to him?*" she sobbed, fighting Mitch's grip.

Victor got the door open, and managed a single step before pain closed over him like a tide, and he fell.

The last thing he saw was Sydney, tearing free of Mitch's arms, Sydney, rushing toward him.

And then death erased it all.

∞

"SYDNEY?"

Victor dragged in a shallow breath.

"Sydney, can you hear me?"

It was Mitch's voice, the words low and pleading.

Victor sat up and saw the man kneeling on the floor, crouched over a small shape. Sydney. She was stretched on her back, her pale hair pooling around her head, her skin porcelain and her body still. Mitch shook her by the shoulder, put his ear to her chest.

And then Victor was up, the room tilting under his feet. His head felt heavy, his thoughts slow, the way they always did in the wake of an episode, and he turned his own dials up, sharpened his nerves to the point of pain. He needed it, to clear his mind.

"Move," he said, dropping to a knee beside her.

"Do something," demanded Mitch.

Sydney's skin was cold—but then, it was always cold. He searched for a pulse, and after several agonizing seconds of nothing, felt the faint flutter of her heart. Barely a beat. Her breath, when he checked, was just as slow.

Victor pressed a hand flat against her chest. He reached for her nerves and tried, as gently as possible, to turn the dial. Not far, just enough to stimulate a reaction.

"Wake up," he said.

Nothing happened.

He turned the dial up a fraction more.

Wake up.

Nothing. She was so cold, so still.

Victor gripped her shoulder.

"Sydney, *wake up*," he ordered, sending a current through her small form.

She gasped, eyes flying open, then rolled onto her side, coughing. Mitch rushed forward to soothe her, and Victor sagged backward, slumping against the door, his heart pounding in his chest.

But when Sydney managed to sit up, she looked past Mitch to Victor, her eyes wide, not with anger but sadness. He could read the question in her face. It was the same one crashing through his own head.

What have I done?

∞

VICTOR sat on the balcony and watched the snow fall, flecks of white against the dark.

He was freezing. He could have put on a coat, could have turned his nerves down, muted the cold, could have erased all sensation. Instead, he savored the frost, watched his breath plume against the night, clung to the brief period of silence.

The lights had come back on, but Victor couldn't bring himself to go inside, couldn't bear the look on Sydney's face. Or Mitch's.

He could leave.

Should leave.

Distance wouldn't save him, but it might protect them.

The door slid open at his back, and he heard Sydney's light steps as she padded out onto the balcony. She sank into the chair beside him, drawing her knees up to her chest. For a few minutes, neither spoke.

Once upon a time, Victor had promised Sydney that he wouldn't let anyone hurt her—that he would always hurt them first.

He'd broken that promise.

He studied his hands, recalling the moment *before*—when he'd forced Syd out of his way. He hadn't touched her nerves then, or at least he hadn't turned the dials. But he'd still *moved* her. Victor rose from his seat, thinking through the implications. He was halfway to the door when Sydney finally broke the silence.

"Does it hurt?" she asked.

"Not right now," he said, sidestepping the question.

"But when it happens," she persisted. "Does it hurt then?"

Victor exhaled, clouding the air. "Yes."

"How long does it hurt?" she asked. "How bad does it get? What does it feel like when you—"

"Sydney."

"I want to know," she said, voice catching. "I *need* to know."

"Why?"

"Because it's my fault. Because I did this to you." Victor started to shake his head, but she cut him off. "Tell me. Tell me the truth. You've been lying for all this time, the least you can do is tell me how it feels."

"It feels like dying."

Sydney's breath caught, as if hit. Victor sighed and stepped to the balcony's edge, the railing slick with ice. He ran his hand over the surface, cold pricking his fingers. "Did I ever tell you how I got my power?"

Syd shook her head, the blond bob swaying side to side. He knew he hadn't. He'd told her his last thoughts once, but nothing more. It wasn't a matter of trust or distrust so much as the simple fact that they'd both left their pasts behind, ones filled with a few things they wanted to remember, and many more things they didn't.

"Most EOs are the result of accidents," he said, studying the snow. "But Eli and I were different. We set out to find a way to effect the change. Incidentally, it's remarkably difficult to do. Dying with intent, reviving with control. Finding a way to end a life but keep it in arm's reach, and all without rendering the body unusable. On top of that, you need a method that strips enough control from the subject to make them afraid, because you need the chemical properties induced by fear and adrenaline to trigger a somatic change."

Victor craned his head and considered the sky.

"It wasn't my first try," he said quietly. "The night I died. I'd already tried once, and failed. An overdose, which, it turned out, provided too much control, and not enough fear. So I set out to try again. Eli had already succeeded, and I was determined to match him. I created a situation in which I couldn't take back control. One in which there was nothing *but* fear. And pain."

"How?" whispered Sydney.

Victor closed his eyes and saw Angie, one hand resting on the control panel.

"I convinced someone to torture me."

Syd drew a short breath behind him. Victor kept talking.

"I was strapped to a steel table, and hooked up to an electrical current. There was a dial, and someone to turn it, and the pain went up when the dial was turned, and I told them not to stop until my heart did." Victor pressed his palms against the icy rail. "People have an idea of pain," he said. "They think they know what it is, how it feels, but that's just an idea. It's a very different thing when it becomes concrete." He turned back toward her. "So when you ask me what the episodes feel like—they feel like dying all over again. Like someone turning up the dial inside me until I break."

Sydney's face was white. "I did this," she said under her breath, fingers gripping her knees. "I did this to you."

Victor went to Sydney's chair and knelt before it.

"Sydney, I am alive because of you," he said firmly. Tears spilled down Syd's cheeks. Victor reached out and touched her shoulder. "You saved me."

She met his eyes then, ice blue laced with red. "But I broke you."

"No," he started, then stopped. An idea flickered through his mind. The first spark of a thought, bright but brittle. He shielded its fragile heat, trying to coax it into something stronger, and as it kindled, he realized—

He'd been looking in the wrong place. Searching for ordinary solutions.

But Victor wasn't ordinary. What had happened to him wasn't ordinary.

An EO had broken his power.

He needed an EO to fix it.

IX

TWO YEARS AGO

SOUTH BROUGHTON

IT was amazing what passed for music.

Victor leaned against the bar as sound blared out from the stage, where a group of men slammed their hands against their instruments. The upside, he supposed, was the way they drowned out the rising sound in his own head. The downside was the ache forming in its place.

"Hey!" shouted the bartender. "Get you a drink?"

Victor twisted back toward the bar. Toward the man behind the counter.

Will Connelly was six-foot-three, with a square jaw, a shock of black hair, and all the markers of a potential EO.

Victor had done his homework, had instructed Mitch to rebuild a search matrix, the same one Eli, and then the police, had used to find EOs, the same one that had led Victor to Dominic.

It had taken two months to track down the first lead—a woman down south who could reverse age, but not injury—another three to find the second—a man who could take things apart and put them back together, sadly a skill which didn't really apply to living things.

Finding other EOs was hard enough.

Finding specific ones, with restorative abilities, was even harder.

Their latest lead was Will Connelly, who'd bailed from a hospital bed, sans discharge, a mere two days after his accident. The doctors had been stunned.

That suggested a healing ability.

The question was whether he could heal Victor.

So far, no one could.

"Well?" called Connelly over the music.

"Glen Ardoch," Victor called back, nodding at a bottle on the back wall. It was empty.

"Gotta grab some more," said Connelly, flagging another bartender before ducking out from under the bar. Victor waited a moment, then followed, trailing the other man down the hall. Connelly's hand was on the open storeroom door when Victor caught up.

"I've changed my order."

The bartender swung around, and Victor gave him a single forceful shove, tipping Connelly down the flight of stairs.

It wasn't a long flight, but there was a wall of metal kegs at the bottom and the bartender crashed against them with a noise that would have called attention, if not for the wailing of the band overhead.

Victor followed, taking the steps at a more leisurely pace as the man straightened, clutching his elbow. "You broke my fucking arm!"

"Well, then," said Victor, "I suggest you fix it."

Connelly's expression changed. "What? What are you ta—"

Victor flicked his fingers and the bartender staggered, biting back a scream.

There was no need to quiet him. The bass from the club overhead would have been loud enough to drown out a murder.

"Okay!" gasped Connelly. "Okay."

Victor's hold dropped away, and the bartender straightened. He took a few steadying breaths, and then his whole body shuddered, the motion so small and fast it seemed more a vibration than a shiver. As if he were *rewinding*. A fraction of a second, and his arm hung easily at his side, the pain gone from his face.

"Good," said Victor. "Now, fix *me*."

Connelly's face crumpled in confusion. "I can't."

Victor flexed, and the man staggered back into the crates and kegs. "I—*can't*—" he gasped. "Don't you think—if I could help other people—I would? Hell—I'd be a—fucking messiah. Not working—in this shithole bar."

It was a valid point.

"It only works—on me."

Fuck, thought Victor right before his phone rang. He dragged the cell out of his pocket and saw Dominic's name on the screen.

Dom, who only called Victor when there was trouble.

He answered. "What is it?"

"Bad news," said the ex-soldier.

In the storeroom, Connelly had grabbed a bottle off the shelf behind him and now lunged toward Victor. Or started to. But Victor raised a hand, and Connelly's whole body slammed to a stop as he caught the man's nerves, pinned them in place. He'd been practicing, since the night he moved Sydney. He'd learned that pain and motion were both facets of control. Hurting a body was simple; halting it was harder—but Victor was getting the hang of it.

"Go on," he said to Dom.

"Okay, so you know a lot of the guys who come out of the military, they go into private sector. Security. Task force. Muscle-for-hire kind of jobs. Some of it's aboveboard. Some of it's not. But there's always work for people in a certain field, if you're willing and able."

Connelly was still fighting Victor's hold, throwing all his weight against it as if they were arm-wrestling. As if this were a battle of muscle, not will.

"So I'm having drinks with an old army buddy," continued Dom, "well, he's drinking bourbon, I'm on club soda—"

"Summarize," urged Victor, forcing the bartender to his knees.

"Right, sorry. So he tells me about this new job posting. It's under the radar—no public listings, no paper ads or online posts, just word of mouth. No details. Nothing but a name. Letters, really. EON."

Victor frowned. "EON?"

Connelly tried to shout, but Victor clamped his jaws shut.

"Yeah. EON," said Dom. "As in ExtraOrdinary Observation and Neutralization."

Victor stilled. "It's a prison."

"Or something like it. They're looking for guards, but they're also training officers to hunt down people like us."

Victor turned the information over in his mind. "What else did your friend tell you?"

"Not much. But he gave me a card. Some cloak-and-dagger shit. Just those three letters on one side, a name and number on the back. Nothing else."

"Whose name?" asked Victor, even though he had a feeling he already knew the answer.

"Director Joseph Stell."

Stell. The name scraped against Victor's skin. The cop who'd first come for him at Lockland, on the heels of Angie's death; the reason he'd spent four years in a solitary cell, and another six in standard; the same man who'd tracked Eli to Merit a decade later, only to fall under Serena Clarke's spell. Stell was a dog with a bone—once he got his teeth in, he didn't let go. And now—this. An organization designed to hunt EOs.

"I thought you'd want to know," said Dominic.

"You were right." Victor hung up.

What a mess, he thought, shaking his head. Victor Vale was dead and buried in Merit Cemetery, but all it would take was a hunch—hell, bodies were dug up for a dozen reasons. And he'd left behind an empty coffin. The beginning of a trail. Not an obvious one, but enough to cause trouble. From there, how long would it take EON to catch on? To catch up?

"Let me *go*," growled Connelly through locked teeth.

"All right," said Victor, releasing his hold. The bartender staggered, unbalanced by the sudden freedom, and was halfway to his feet when Victor drew his gun and shot him in the head.

The music continued to rage overhead, unbroken, undisturbed.

"**FIVE** marshmallows," said Sydney, perched on the kitchen counter. Tonight her hair was a shock of purple.

"That's too many," said Mitch at the stove.

"Fine, three," said Syd.

"What about four?"

"I don't like even numbers—hey, Victor." Syd swung her legs absently. "Mitch is making hot chocolate."

"How domestic," he said, shrugging out of his coat. They didn't ask about his evening, or Connolly, but Victor could feel the tension in the air like a taut string. His silence on the subject was answer enough.

He caught Mitch's eye. "I need you to find out everything you can about EON."

"What's that?" asked Mitch.

"A problem." Victor relayed Dominic's intel, watching Sydney pale and Mitch's face shift from surprise to concern. When he was done, he turned toward his room. "Start packing."

"Where are we going?" asked Syd.

"Fulton. Capstone. Dresden. Capital City . . ."

Mitch frowned. "Those are all places we've already been."

"I know," said Victor. "We're going back. We need to clean up."

A shadow crossed Sydney's face. "You're going to kill them," she said. "All the people you've met with . . ."

"I don't have a choice," he said simply.

"Yes, you do," said Sydney, crossing her arms. "Why do you have to—"

"Some know my condition. Some know my power. But *all* of

them have seen my face. From here on out, we leave absolutely no trace, and that means before we go forward, we have to go back."

A trail of bodies, or a trail of witnesses—that was the choice they were faced with. Neither option was ideal, but at least corpses couldn't give statements. Victor's solution was logical, but Sydney wasn't having it.

"If you kill all the EOs you meet," she said, "how are you better than Eli?"

Victor's teeth clenched. "I take no pleasure in this, Sydney, but if EON finds them, they'll be one step closer to finding *us*. Do you want that to happen?"

"No, but—"

"Do you know what they'll do? First they'll kill Dol, and then they will take you, and me, and Mitch, and we will never see the light of day, let alone each other, *ever* again." Sydney's eyes widened, but Victor went on. "If you're lucky, they'll lock you in a cage. Alone. If you're not, they'll turn you into a science experiment—"

"Victor," warned Mitch, but he only stepped closer. Sydney stared up at him, fists clenched. He knelt so they were eye to eye.

"You think I'm acting like Eli? You think I'm playing God? Fine, you play, Sydney. You decide, right now, who should live. Us, or them."

Tears hovered on her lashes. She didn't look at him, kept her gaze focused on his shirtfront as her lips moved, short and soundless.

"What was that?" he asked.

This time, he heard it.

"Us."

X

FOUR WEEKS AGO

HALLOWAY

VICTOR braced himself against the sink, waiting for the drug to hit his system, wondered if the effects were, at this point, placebic. Less medicine and more a misplaced hope. For calm. For time. For control.

He pushed off the counter and returned to the bedroom, to the dresser, to the shallow stack of paper there, Jack Linden's face staring up from the top. Black streaks cut across the profile, erasing line after line after line until only two words remained. Five letters scattered inelegantly across the page.

FIXME

Victor stared at the words for a long moment, then crumpled the paper and flung it away.

They were running out of leads.

And he was running out of time.

3 minutes, 49 seconds.

"Victor!" called Syd impatiently.

He straightened.

"Coming," he called, drawing a shallow blue box from the top drawer.

The living room was dark.

Sydney knelt in front of the coffee table, where a small altar of presents waited beside the cake. Eighteen candles burned on top, their tips sending up colorful sparks. Mitch crossed his arms, looking pleased.

"Make a wish," he said.

Syd's eyes shifted from the cake to Mitch before landing on Victor. A shadow crossed her face, just before she blew the candles out.

EIGHTEEN candles—Sydney marveled at the number as she nudged them into even lines beside the half-eaten cake. Eighteen. Dol tried to lick a fleck of chocolate icing from the table, and Victor nudged the dog's face away as Mitch handed Syd her first present. She took the box, shook it with a mischievous grin, then tore the paper off and pulled out a red bomber jacket.

She had seen it in a shop window a few cities back, and stopped to admire it, admire how cool the lanky mannequin looked, the S curve of its body, hands on hips through the deep side pockets.

What Syd didn't say then was that she'd wanted the mannequin's shape as much as the clothes resting on it. On her, the jacket was too big—the sleeves a good six inches longer than her arms.

"I'm sorry," said Mitch. "It was the smallest size they had."

She managed a smile. "That's okay," she said. "I'll grow into it."

And she supposed she might. Eventually.

Mitch handed her the second box, a package with Merit on the return label. Dominic. She missed him—Victor was always on the phone with the ex-soldier, but none of them had actually *seen* him since they left Merit. It was the one city they never went back to.

Too many skeletons, she supposed.

Now, Sydney staggered at the weight of Dominic's present. Inside was a pair of steel-toed combat boots, each with a sole three inches thick. Syd dropped to the floor and laced them up. When she got to her feet, she made Mitch stand eye to eye with her so she could see how tall she was. She came to his sternum instead of his stomach, and he ruffled her wig playfully.

At last, Victor held out the shallow blue box.

"Don't shake it," he warned.

Syd knelt at the table and held her breath as she lifted the lid.

Inside, nested in velvet, lay the skeleton of a small, dead bird. No feathers, no skin, or muscle—only three dozen attenuated bones perfectly arranged in the narrow blue folds.

Mitch cringed at the sight of it, but Sydney rose, clutching the box to her like a secret.

"Thank you," she said with a smile. "It's perfect."

XI

FIVE YEARS AGO

MERIT

THE night Victor died, Sydney couldn't sleep.

Dominic had taken a handful of pills, washing them down with whiskey before collapsing on the couch, and it was only a matter of minutes before Mitch, bruised and bloody and a thousand miles away, sank into his own fitful doze.

But Syd sat up, with Dol at her feet, thinking of Victor's body in the morgue, of Serena's charred corpse in the Falcon Price lot, until finally she gave up on sleep entirely, tugged on her boots, and snuck outside.

It was just before dawn when Sydney reached the Falcon Price project. The darkest part of the night, Serena used to say. The time when monsters and ghosts came out.

The construction project was marked off with crime scene tape.

Sydney folded herself small and slipped behind the plywood fence, into the gravel lot. The police were gone, the noise and lights were gone, the chaos of the night reduced to numbered markers, and drying blood, and a white plastic tent.

Inside that tent, Serena's body. What was left of it. The fire had been hot—hot enough to reduce most of her sister to blackened skin and brittle bones. Syd knew the fire was out, but as she reached a hand into the charred remains, she still half expected the bones to burn her. But there was no heat, no warmth, no promise of life. Half of the bones had already crumbled, others threatened to fold under the barest touch, but here and there a few pieces retained their strength.

Sydney started digging.

She just wanted a token, something to remember her sister, a piece to hold on to. It wasn't until she was elbows-deep in the scorched heap that she realized what she was really doing.

Looking for a way to bring Serena back.

∞

SYDNEY started dying, but only in her dreams.

The nightmares began when they left Merit. Night after night, she'd close her eyes and find herself back on the frozen lake, the one that had cracked and broken and swallowed her and her sister up three years before.

In her dreams, Serena was a shadow on the far shore, arms crossed and waiting, watching, but Syd was never alone on the ice. Not at first. Dol stayed close, licking at the frozen ground, while Dom and Mitch and Victor formed a loose circle around her.

And in the distance, walking toward them across the lake, a man with broad shoulders and warm brown hair, an easy stride and a friendly smile.

Eli, who never aged, never changed, never died.

Eli, who made every hair on her neck stand on end in a way the cold never did.

"It's okay, kid," said Dom.

"We're here," said Mitch.

"I won't let him hurt you," said Victor.

They were all lying in the end.

Not because they meant to, but because they couldn't make it true.

The lake made a sound like branches breaking in the woods. The ice began to splinter beneath their feet.

"Get back!" she called, and she didn't know if she was talking to them or to Eli, but it didn't matter. Nobody listened.

Eli made his way across the lake, coming for them, for *her*. The ice stayed smooth and solid beneath him, but every time he took a step, someone else disappeared.

Step.

The lake shattered beneath Dominic.

Step.

Mitch sank like a stone.

Step.

Dol crashed and went under.

Step.

Victor plunged down.

Step.

One by one they drowned.

Step.

And then she was alone.

With *Eli*.

"Hello, Sydney," he said.

Sometimes he had a knife.

Sometimes he had a gun.

Sometimes he had a length of rope.

But Sydney's hands were always empty.

She wanted to fight back, wanted to hold her ground, wanted to face the monster, but her body always betrayed her. Her boots always turned toward the shore, slipping and skidding as she ran.

Sometimes she almost made it.

Sometimes she wasn't even close.

But no matter what she did, the dream always ended the same.

XII

FOUR YEARS AGO

DRESDEN

SYD sat up with a gasp.

She'd woken to the sound of cracking ice, the hiss and snap of a lake giving way. It took her a moment to realize the sounds hadn't followed her out of her dreams; they were coming from the kitchen.

The sound of cracking eggs.

The hiss and snap of bacon in a pan.

Sydney's parents had never made breakfast. There was always food—or at least, there was always money for food, in a jar by the sink—but there were no family meals—that would have required them to all be in the house at the same time—and unlike in the movies, no one was ever woken by the smell of breakfast, not on Christmas morning, not on birthdays, and certainly not on a random Tuesday.

Whenever Sydney woke to the sizzle of bacon or the pop of a toaster, she knew that Serena was home. Serena always made breakfast, a veritable banquet of food, way too much for them to eat.

"Hungry, sleepyhead?" Serena would always ask, pouring her a glass of juice.

And for a groggy moment, before the details of the room came into focus, Sydney almost leapt from the bed to ambush her sister in the kitchen.

Sydney's heart quickened. But then she saw the strange apartment walls, and the red metal tin on the unfamiliar nightstand, containing all that remained of Serena Clarke, and the reality came rushing back.

Dol whined softly from the edge of the bed, obviously torn between his loyalty to Syd and his canine love of food.

"Hungry, sleepyhead?" she asked softly, rubbing him between the ears. He gave a relieved huff and turned, nosing open the door. Sydney followed him out into the apartment. It was a rental, the eleventh one they'd stayed in, the fifth city. It was a nice place—they were always nice places. They'd been on the road—on the run—for nearly six months, and she still walked around holding her breath, half expecting Victor to send her away. After all, he never said Sydney could stay with them, after. He had simply never told her to leave, and she had never asked to go.

Mitch was in the kitchen, cooking breakfast.

"Hey, kid," he said. Mitch was the only one who got to call her that. "You want food?"

He was already dividing the eggs onto two plates, three for him and one for her (but she always got half the bacon).

She plucked a strip from her plate, split it with Dol, and looked around the rented apartment.

She wasn't homesick, exactly.

Sydney didn't miss her parents. She knew she should feel bad about that, but the fact of the matter was, she felt like she'd lost them way before she disappeared—her first memories were of packed suitcases and long-term sitters, her last were of two parent-shaped shadows leaving her behind in the hospital after the accident.

What she had now felt more like a family than her mother and father ever had.

"Where's Victor?"

"Oh . . ." Mitch had that look on his face, that carefully blank look that adults got when they were trying to convince you everything was fine. They always assumed that if they didn't *tell* you a thing, you wouldn't know it. But that wasn't true.

Serena used to say that she could tell when someone was lying, because all those unsaid things hung in the air, making it heavy, like the pressure before a storm.

Sydney might not know the full scope of Victor's lie, but the wrongness was still there, taking up space.

"He just stepped out for a walk," said Mitch. "I'm sure he'll be back soon."

Sydney knew Mitch was lying too.

He pushed his empty plate aside.

"Okay," he said, producing his deck of cards. "Draw."

It was a game they'd been playing since the first few days after Merit, when the need to keep a low profile clashed with the urge to go out, and Victor's absences meant Syd and Mitch spent a lot of time together (and the good-natured ex-con obviously had no idea what to do with a thirteen-year-old who could resurrect the dead).

"What would you be doing," he'd asked, "if you were . . ." He let the question trail off.

Sydney knew he was thinking *home* but she said, "Back in Brighton? I'd probably be in school."

"Did you like school?"

Sydney shrugged. "I liked learning."

Mitch brightened at that. "Me too. But I never got to stay in one place long. Foster care and all. So I didn't care much about *school* . . . but you don't need that to learn. I could teach you . . ."

"Really?"

Mitch colored a little. "Well, there's lots I don't know. But maybe we could learn together." That's when he drew the deck from his pocket. "How about this—hearts will be literature. Clubs is science. Diamonds is history. Spades is math. That should give us a good start."

"And face cards?" asked Syd.

Mitch flashed a conspiratorial smile. "Face cards, we go outside."

Now Sydney held her breath and pulled a card from the center, hoping for a king or queen.

She got a six of clubs.

"Better luck next time," said Mitch, pulling his laptop over. "Okay, let's see what kind of experiments we can do in this kitchen . . ."

They were halfway through creating a homemade lava lamp when the door swung open, and Victor walked in. He looked *tired,* his face tight, as if he were in pain. She felt the air go heavy on her shoulders.

"You hungry?" asked Mitch, but Victor waved him away and sank into a chair at the kitchen table. He took up his tablet and began absently swiping through. Mitch set a cup of black coffee at his elbow.

Sydney perched on the counter and studied Victor.

Whenever she'd resurrected an animal, or a person, she'd done it by visualizing a thread, something floating in the darkness. She pictured grabbing that thread and pulling it toward her, drawing them back into the light. But when it was done, she never really let go of the thread. Didn't know how, really. So she could feel it now when Victor was home, and when he was out pacing the city, could feel it still, no matter how far he went, as if his energy, his stress, vibrated up the invisible rope until the tremor reached her.

And so, even without the heavy air, the way Mitch looked at Victor, the way Victor didn't look at her, she *knew* that something was not right.

"What is it, Sydney?" he asked without looking up.

Tell me the truth, she thought. *Just tell me the truth.*

"Are you sure you're okay?" she asked.

Victor's cold blue eyes drifted up, meeting hers.

His mouth twitched into a smile, the way it did when he was lying. "Never better."

XIII

THREE YEARS AGO

CAPITAL CITY

SYDNEY wove around the base of the tree, sunlight dappling her skin.

She'd drawn a face card—the queen of diamonds—but the weather was so nice she would have played the spade Victor had slipped her just to get out of the apartment.

Victor.

Behind her eyes, Sydney saw him buckling against the door, saw him fighting back a scream as his body curled on the floor. There had been pain, too, a jolt of something straight through her chest, and then darkness, but that part didn't haunt her.

Victor haunted her. His pain haunted her. His dying haunted her.

Because it was Sydney's fault.

He had been counting on her, and she'd let him down.

She'd brought him back wrong.

Broken.

That was the secret. The lie.

"It feels like dying."

Sydney kept her eyes on the mossy ground as she paced. If anyone looked her way, they would probably assume she was searching for flowers, but it was late spring, the time when baby birds flung themselves out of the nest and hoped to fly. Not all of them made it. And Sydney was always searching for things to revive. Subjects to practice on.

Sydney already knew how to reach inside a body and pull it back to life. But what if the thing had been dead for a long time? What if the body wasn't all there? How much did there have to be, for her to find the thread? How little?

Dol snuffled in the grass nearby, and across the field Mitch leaned back against a slope, a battered paperback open on one knee, a pair of sunglasses perched on his nose.

They were in Capital City, as hilly as Fulton had been flat, a place with as many parks as skyscrapers.

She liked it here. Wished they could stay. Knew they wouldn't.

They were only here because Victor was searching for someone. Another EO. Someone who could fix what she'd broken.

Something cracked under Syd's foot.

She looked down and saw the crumpled body of a young finch. The bird had been there awhile, long enough for its small body to sink into the moss. Long enough for the feathers to fall away and a wing to come detached, the brittle bones shattering like an eggshell under her shoe.

Syd sank to her knees, crouching over the tiny corpse.

It was one thing, she'd learned, to breathe life back into a body. Another thing entirely to rebuild the body itself. You only got one chance—Sydney had learned that the hard way, threads unraveling, bones crumbling to ash under her touch—but the only way to get stronger was to practice. And Sydney wanted to get stronger—she *needed* to get stronger—so she curled her fingers gently over the bird's remains, and closed her eyes, and reached.

Cold rippled through her as she searched the darkness for a thread, a filament, a wisp of light. It was there somewhere, so faint she couldn't see it, not yet. She had to go by feel instead. Her lungs ached, but she kept reaching, knew she was almost, almost—

Sydney felt the bird twitch under her palm.

Flutter, like a pulse.

And then—

Sydney's eyes flew open, a faint plume of cold brushing her lips as the bird was rising on unsteady wings. Buffeting itself up into the branches of the tree.

Syd rocked back on her heels and let out a shaky breath.

"Well, *that* was quite a trick."

Her head snapped up, and for a second—just a second—she found herself staring at a ghost. White-blond hair, and ice blue eyes, a dazzling smile set into a heart-shaped face.

But it wasn't Serena.

Up close, the girl had higher cheeks than her sister, a broader chin, eyes that danced with a mischievous light. Dol's lip curled a little, flashing teeth, but when the stranger held out her hand, the dog sniffed it cautiously, and then calmed.

"Good boy," said the girl who wasn't Serena. There was a lilt in her voice, a kind of music. Her eyes flicked up to Sydney. "Did I scare you?"

"No," she managed, her throat constricting. "You just looked—like someone else."

The stranger flashed her a wistful grin. "Someone nice, I hope." She pointed up to the branches. "I saw what you did there, with the bird."

Sydney's heart quickened. "I didn't do anything."

The girl laughed, a light, airy sound. And then she crossed behind the trunk of the tree. When she reappeared on the other side, she was *someone else*. Only a second had passed, a step, but the blond girl was gone, and Sydney found herself staring into Mitch's familiar face.

"It's a big world, kiddo," he said. "You're not the only one with talents."

She knew it wasn't really him. Not just because the real Mitch was still reading across the field, but because of the accent that ran beneath his voice, even now.

The stranger took a step toward Sydney, and as she did, her body changed again. Mitch disappeared, replaced by a lanky young woman in a peasant skirt, her loose blond curls pulled up in a messy bun.

The girl looked down at herself. "This one's my favorite," she said, half to herself.

"How did you do that?" asked Syd.

The stranger raised a brow. "I didn't do anything," she said, echoing Syd's words. And then she broke into a smile. "See? Isn't it silly to lie when we both know the truth?"

Sydney swallowed. "You're an EO."

"EO?"

"ExtraOrdinary. That's what they call—us."

The girl mused. "ExtraOrdinary. I like that." She looked down, and chirped in delight. "Here," she said, retrieving a tiny bird's skull from the grass. "You've seen my trick. Show me yours again."

Sydney took the skull, which was no bigger than a ring. It was unbroken, unblemished—but not enough.

"I can't," she said, handing it back. "There's too much missing."

"Syd?" called Mitch.

The stranger drew a folded bookmark from her back pocket, and a pen from her curls. She scribbled something down the side, and held it out.

"In case you ever need a friend." She leaned in close. "Girls like us got to stick together," she added with a wink.

Mitch called Sydney's name again.

"Better go," said the stranger. "Wouldn't want the big guy to worry." She ran her fingers over Dol's muzzle. "You look after our girl," she told the dog.

"See ya," said Syd.

"You bet."

Mitch was waiting for her across the field. "Who were you talking to?" he asked.

Sydney shrugged. "Just some girl," she said, realizing she hadn't asked for a name. She glanced over her shoulder, and saw the stranger still leaning back against the tree, holding the little white skull up to the light.

That night, Sydney put the number in her phone.

The next, she sent the girl a text.

I forgot to tell you. My name is Sydney.

She held her breath and waited.

The reply came a few seconds later.

Nice to meet you, Sydney, it said.

I'm June.

XIV

FOUR WEEKS AGO

HALLOWAY

SYD was helping Mitch clear the cake when she felt the phone buzz in her back pocket.

She excused herself, slipped into her room and shut the door behind her before reading the text.

    June: Happy birthday, Syd xoxo

She felt herself smile.

    June: Get anything good?

Syd sent her a photo of the bomber jacket.

    Syd: Doesn't fit.
    June: Good thing vintage never goes out of style ;)

Sydney turned toward the closet mirror, studying her reflection. Eighteen.
Officially an adult, even if she didn't look it.
She considered the boots. The blue hair. The bomber jacket—it really was too big for her. How long before it fit? Ten years? Twenty?
Victor thought Sydney's aging—the lack of it—had something

to do with the way she'd died, the icy water that froze her limbs and stopped her pulse. All this time, and her vitals were still slow, her skin still cold to the touch. Everyone else was changing—Victor getting leaner and harder by the year, the lines around Mitch's eyes, Dol's muzzle edging white.

Only Sydney seemed to stay the same.

And Eli, she thought, a chill running through her. But he was gone. And she had to stop summoning him, stop inviting him into her head.

Syd sank onto the edge of the bed.

>**Syd**: Where are you?
>**June**: Just got to Merit.

Sydney's pulse quickened.

>**Syd**: Really? How long are you staying?
>**June**: On a job. Just passing through.
>**Syd**: I wish I could be there with you.
>**June**: You could be ;)

But they both knew it wasn't that simple.

Sydney wouldn't leave Victor, and as far as Victor was concerned Merit—and all of its skeletons—belonged in the past.

XV

TWO YEARS AGO

SOUTH BROUGHTON

THE dead mouse lay on Sydney's desk, curled atop a floral dish towel.

A cat had obviously gotten to it—there were bits and pieces missing, leaving the rodent more than half, but less than whole. It was late summer, and Syd had the window propped up to keep the smell from gathering.

Dol had his chin resting on the window frame, sniffing the air on the fire escape while she worked. More than once, she'd resurrected a small animal, only to have it race away from her fingers and out into the apartment, burying itself under a sofa or behind a cupboard. More than once, Mitch had been summoned to help extricate it. Victor had noticed her practicing, even encouraged it, but he had one rule: she couldn't keep any of the animals she brought back. They were to be set free. Or disposed of. (Dol, of course, was the sole exception.)

Down the hall, a door opened, closed, and the dog's ears perked. Victor was back.

Sydney held her breath and listened, hoping to glean good news from the tone of his voice, or Mitch's reaction. But within seconds she could tell—another dead end.

Her chest tightened, and she turned her attention back to the dead mouse, cupping her palms over the tiny furred corpse. Her backpack sat on the bed beside the desk, the small red tin resting on top.

Sydney's gaze flicked toward it, the action almost superstitious—like throwing salt over your shoulder, or knocking on wood—and then she closed her eyes, and reached. Past the body, to the darkness, searching for the thread. With every passing second, the cold climbed her fingers, spread past her wrists and up toward her elbows.

And then, at last, the thread brushing her fingers, a twitch against her palm.

Syd gasped, and blinked, and the mouse was whole, was alive, was scurrying out of her hands and across the desk.

She lunged and caught the small rodent, setting it on the fire escape and closing the window before it could follow her back in. She turned toward the hall, excited to tell Victor and Mitch about the feat, small as it was.

But halfway there, Syd slowed, stopped, held back by something in Mitch's voice.

". . . is it really necessary?"

"It's a calculation," answered Victor coldly. There was a pause. The sound of ice shifting in a glass. "You think I *enjoy* killing people?"

"No . . . I don't know . . . I think sometimes you make the easiest choice instead of the right one."

A low, derisive snort. "If you're still hung up on what happened with Serena . . ."

Sydney's breath caught on the name. A name no one had uttered in almost three years.

"There could have been another way," said Mitch.

"There wasn't," growled Victor, "and you know it, even if you want to pretend you don't."

Sydney pressed her hand over her mouth.

"Make me the villain of that night, Mitch. Wash your hands of any blame. But don't act like Serena Clarke was merely a victim or even a casualty of circumstance. She was an enemy, a weapon, and killing her wasn't just smart, or easy—it was right."

Victor's steps sounded on the hardwood as he came down the hall.

Syd scrambled back into her room. She went to the window and threw it open, stepping out onto the fire escape. She leaned her elbows on the metal rail, tried to pretend she was looking dreamily out at the city instead of making fists so tight her fingers ached.

But Victor didn't even slow down as he passed Sydney's door.

She sank to her knees when he was gone, bowing her head against the bars.

A memory washed over her, of that night. Of Serena's voice in her ear, telling her not to run, of the way Sydney's mind had gone smooth, her limbs soft under the order. Of the cold parking garage, and the gun against her head. Of the long pause, and then her sister's order—to go. To find somewhere safe. Some*where*, which had once been some*one*. Victor.

But Victor—

Some part of her had known.

Had to have known.

Sydney felt like she was going to scream. Instead, she left. Took the fire escape two stairs at a time, didn't even care about the way her steps rattled as she crashed down floor after floor.

She hit the street and kept going.

One block, three blocks, five—Sydney didn't know where she was going, only that she couldn't turn around. Couldn't look Victor in the eyes.

She drew her cell from her back pocket and dialed June. They'd been texting for almost a year, exchanging small notes, anecdotes about where they were, what they were doing, but Syd had never *called*.

The phone rang, and rang, and rang.

But no one answered.

Sydney's steps slowed, the initial wave of shock settling into something heavier. She looked around. She was on a narrow street, not an alley exactly, but not a main road, either. People said cities didn't sleep, but they did get quiet. And dark.

Turn around, said a voice in her head, but it sounded like Victor, so Sydney kept going.

Which was a mistake.

The thing about mistakes was that they weren't always big, or obvious. Sometimes they were simple. Small. The decision to keep walking. The turn left instead of right. Those few extra steps in the wrong direction.

Sydney was trying to call June again when she saw them—two men. One wearing a black leather jacket, the other with a kerchief slung around his throat.

She stopped walking, caught between turning around, which would mean putting her back to the men up ahead, or continuing forward, which would mean passing within arm's reach. They hadn't noticed her, at first, or at least they'd pretended not to, but now they looked at her and smiled.

The men didn't look dangerous, not like in the movies Syd watched with Mitch, but she knew that meant nothing—everyone who'd ever hurt her had *looked* safe. And the longer she stayed put, the more she felt the badness wafting off them like cheap cologne. Something she could smell and taste.

"Hey, little girl," said one, moving toward her. "You lost?"

"No," said Sydney. "And I'm not a little girl."

"Different time we're living in," said the second. "They grow up so fast."

Syd didn't know how they'd gotten so close to her, so quickly, but as she shuffled backward, turned to go, a hand caught her collar. The guy in the leather jacket wrenched her back against him, one arm wrapped around her shoulders. "Aw, now, don't be rude."

"Get off me," she snarled, but he was squeezing too hard, and she couldn't breathe, couldn't think. She felt something hard dig into her ribs, realized it was a gun. She twisted in his grip, trying to grab it.

"Careful," said the other one, closing in. "She's got spirit."

Syd tried to kick out at the other guy but he jumped back, wagging his finger. Her fingers skimmed the gun, but she couldn't quite get it.

The first man's breath was hot and sour on her cheek. "Come on, now, let's have some fun."

Syd slammed her head back into his nose—or tried, but her head only came to his chin. Still, she hit bone, heard the crack of a tooth, and she was free, stumbling to her hands and knees as the man reeled, the gun tumbling from his waistband. Syd lunged for it, fingers closing around the grip right before one of the men grabbed her ankle and *pulled*.

The street bit into her elbows and scraped her shin as she twisted around and raised the gun, barrel leveled at the man's heart. "Let *go*," she snarled.

"Oh shit," said the man in the kerchief, but the other one sneered at her, blood spilling from his mouth.

"That's an awfully big gun for such a little girl."

"Let *go*."

"You even know how to use it?"

"Yes." Sydney squeezed the trigger as she said it, bracing for the recoil, the bang.

But nothing happened.

The man laughed, a short barking sound, and knocked the gun from her hands. It went skidding away.

"Little bitch," he said, raising his boot as if she were a bug, something to crush. He brought it down hard. Or at least, he started to, but his leg seemed to lock up halfway, and then he toppled, a single horrifying sound leaking from his clenched teeth. An instant later, the second guy fell, limbs seizing, as Victor walked toward them, his collar up against the cold.

Relief washed over her, tangled with shock. "What are you doing here?"

The men on the ground writhed in muted agony, blood leaking from their noses and vessels breaking in their eyes.

Victor knelt to retrieve the discarded gun. "A little gratitude would be nice."

She rose on shaky legs, the anger catching up. "You *followed* me."

"Don't try for the moral high ground, Sydney. You snuck out."

"I chose to go. I'm not a captive."

"You're a *child*, and I promised to protect—"

"A promise you can't keep is just another *lie*," she snapped. She was sick of everyone lying.

Mitch had lied when he told her Victor was fine. Eli had lied when he said he wouldn't hurt her. Serena had lied when she said she'd never leave. And Victor had been lying every day since his return.

"I don't want you to save me," said Sydney. "I want to save myself."

Victor weighed the weapon in his hand. "All right," he said, offering her the gun. "The first step is to turn the safety off."

Sydney took the weapon, marveled at the weight in her hands. It was heavier than she expected. Lighter than she expected. Her thumb slid over the catch on the side.

"If you want," said Victor, turning back toward the mouth of the alley, "I'll teach you how to shoot."

Sydney wasn't ready for him to walk away.

"Victor," she called, gripping the gun. "Did you do it?"

Victor slowed to a stop. Turned. "Did I do what?"

Sydney held his gaze. "Did you kill Serena?"

Victor only sighed. The question didn't seem to take him by surprise, but he didn't answer it either. Sydney raised the gun, training it on his chest. "Did you *do* it?"

"What do you think?"

Sydney's grip tightened. "I need you to say it."

Victor moved toward her slowly, steadily. "I warned you when we met, I wasn't a good person."

"*Say it*," demanded Syd.

Victor came to a stop an arm's length away, halted only by the gun against his ribs. He looked down at her. "Yes. I killed Serena."

The words hurt, but the pain was dull. Not a knife wound, or a plunge into ice water, but the deep ache of a fear realized, a suspicion turned to truth.

"Why? Why did you do it?"

"She was unstable and unquantifiable, a danger to everyone in her path."

The way he talked about her, about everything, as if they were just factors in an equation.

But Serena wasn't a factor. A problem to be solved.

"She was my sister."

"She would have killed you."

"No," whispered Syd.

"If I hadn't killed her, the cops would still be under her control. Eli would never have been caught. He'd still be free."

Sydney shivered, the gun trembling in her grip. "Why did you burn her body?"

"I couldn't risk you bringing her back." Victor's hand drifted up to the gun. He wrapped his fingers loosely around the barrel, not tight enough to stop the action if she pulled the trigger, just enough to keep the weapon steady. "Is this what you want? Killing me won't bring her back either. Will you feel safer if I'm dead? Think hard, Sydney. We all have to live with our choices."

Sydney shuddered.

And then she let go of the gun.

Victor caught the weapon before it hit the ground. He ejected the clip, and then knelt so they were eye to eye.

"Look at me," he said coldly, catching Sydney's chin in his hand. "The next time you point a gun at someone, make sure you're ready to pull the trigger."

He straightened, set the weapon on a nearby crate, and walked away.

Sydney wrapped her arms around her ribs and sank to her knees on the pavement.

She didn't know how long she sat there before her phone finally rang. She drew the cell from her pocket with shaking hands and answered.

"Hey, kiddo," said June, sounding breathless. "Sorry, I was finishing a job. What's up?"

TEN minutes later, Sydney was sitting in a diner—the kind that stayed open all night—clutching a cup of black tea.

It had been June's idea.

The seat across from Syd was empty, but if she kept her eyes on her tea, and her ear to the cell phone, she could imagine the other girl sitting in the booth across from her. The sounds of another diner in another city—the bell of an order ready for pickup, a spoon stirring sugar in a cup—made a soft curtain of noise on the line.

"You said you were working," said Syd, making small talk. "What do you do?"

A pause on the line. "Do you really want to know?"

"Yeah."

"I kill people."

Sydney swallowed. "Bad people?"

"Sure, most of the time."

"Do you like your job?"

A soft sound, somewhere between an exhale and a laugh. "What would you think of me if I said yes?"

Syd looked up at the empty booth. "I'd think at least you were being honest."

"What happened tonight?" asked June. "Talk to me."

And Sydney did. The words just spilled out. She couldn't believe how easy it was to talk to June, how good it felt, amid so many secrets, to share some truth. She hadn't felt that ease with someone, not since Serena died. It was like taking a deep breath after being underwater.

Talking to June made her feel *normal*.

She told her about Victor, and Mitch. About her sister, about the day they drowned, the way they came back, her slowly, and Serena all at once. She told her about Serena's powers, and about Eli.

"Is he like us?" asked June.

"No," growled Sydney. She took a deep breath. "I mean, he's an EO. But he's not like us. He thinks we're wrong. That we shouldn't exist. So he started killing us. He killed dozens of people before Victor stopped him." Sydney's voice sank until it was barely a whisper. "My sister . . . she and Eli . . ."

But it wasn't all Serena's fault.

Her sister had been lost for a really long time when Eli found her. Sydney had been lost too, but Victor had been the one to find *her*.

It wasn't Serena's fault that Sydney got the hunter and she got the wolf.

"I know what happened to Serena," said June.

Sydney stiffened in her seat. "What?"

A sigh. "In order to take someone's face," said June, "I have to touch them. And when I do, I see things. Not everything—no room in my head for that much useless memory—just the bits that make them who they are, the ones that matter most. Loves, hates, important moments. Mitch—I touched his arm that day in the park, right before you and I met—and I saw him standing before a fire. There was a girl's body in the flames. But all I felt was his regret."

Sydney closed her eyes, swallowed hard. "Mitch didn't kill Serena," she said. "Victor did."

"Why would he do that?" asked June.

Sydney let out a shuddering breath. "My sister could control people. She had this hold on them. Could make them do anything she wanted, just by saying the words. She was strong, powerful. But . . . she was like Eli. She thought people like *us* were lost. Broken."

"Maybe she was right," said June.

"How can you—" started Sydney.

"Hear me out," pressed June. "Maybe we are broken. But we put ourselves back together. We *survived*. That's what makes us so powerful. And as for family—well, blood is always family, but family doesn't always have to be blood."

Sydney felt hollow, worn out. "What about you?" she asked. "Do you have a family?"

There was a long pause. "No," said June softly. "Not anymore."

"What happened to them? Did they die?"

"No," said June. "But I did." A long pause. "You see, they wouldn't recognize me."

"But you were *you* first. Can't you just . . . change back?"

"It's complicated. What I can do," she said slowly, "makes me invincible. But only as long as I'm someone else." June hesitated. "I buried someone. So did my family. There wasn't a grave, but I'm still gone. And it needs to stay that way. When I came back, I decided that no one would ever hurt me again. I gave up everything—everyone—in exchange for that."

Sydney frowned. "Was it worth it?"

A long silence.

And then June said, "Yes." The sound of a coffee mug shifting on a table. "But hey, like I said, not all family is blood, right? Sometimes we have to find a new one. Sometimes we get lucky, and they find *us*."

Sydney looked down into her tea. "I'm really glad we met."

"Me too."

Neither spoke for a few minutes, the ambient noise of their respective diners collapsing the distance. June hummed softly, and Syd wished she were really there, sitting across the table.

Sydney closed her eyes. "Hey, June?"

"Yeah, Syd?"

Her voice cracked. "I don't know what to do."

"You could leave."

She'd thought about it. She was so tired of moving, of living out of a backpack, of chasing down lead after lead, only to find dead ends. Sick of watching Victor suffer, of knowing it was her fault. But that was exactly why she couldn't go. Victor had killed Serena, yes, but Sydney was killing him. Over and over. She couldn't abandon him. She *wouldn't* abandon Mitch. They were her family. They were all that was left—they'd taken her in, given her hope.

"Syd?"

"I can't."

"Well, then," said June. Sydney heard coins drop on the table, June pushing back her seat. "I suggest you go home."

XVI

ONE YEAR AGO

EDGEFIELD

IT was too hot for Halloween.

They were in a college town somewhere down south, the air still sticky, the streets crowded with groups of teenagers heading to parties, and Sydney had decided to go out.

She stood at the bedroom mirror, adjusted the dark brown bob, put on the darkest lipstick she could find, traced black lines around both eyes. But the older she tried to look, the more ridiculous she felt. Syd tore the wig off and slumped back onto the bed.

She took up her phone, read the last few texts from June.

> **June**: So go out.
> **Syd**: I can't.
> **June**: Says who?
> **June**: You're 17.
> **June**: You can make your own decisions.
> **June**: They can't stop you.

Syd rolled to her feet, and began again.

She'd gone into a costume shop the day before with Mitch, found a generic anime schoolgirl getup. If looking older wouldn't work, maybe she could pass for someone *trying* to look young.

Syd combed her blond hair, pulled on the pleated skirt, and adjusted the bow at her throat. She slipped the gun—these days, she never went anywhere without it—into a tiny backpack, then marched out into the apartment.

Victor sat at the kitchen table, poring over profiles, Dol asleep at his feet. Mitch was on the couch, watching a college football game. He sat up when he saw her. "You dressed up."

"Yeah," she said, starting toward the door. "I'm going out."

Mitch crossed his arms. "Not alone, you're not." He was already pulling the deck of cards from his back pocket. Anger whipped through Sydney at the sight of them.

"This isn't a stupid game," she said. "It's my life."

"Sydney," said Mitch, a new firmness in his voice.

"Stop treating me like a child."

"Then stop acting like one," said Victor without looking up.

Mitch shook his head. "What's gotten into you?"

"Nothing," she snapped. "I'm just sick of being cooped up."

"Let her go," said Victor. "She's giving me a headache."

Mitch rounded on him. "You're not helping."

"She can take care of herself." His eyes met hers. "Isn't that right, Syd?" She bristled at the challenge in his voice. "Well," he sneered. "What are you waiting for?"

Sydney stormed out, slamming the door behind her. She made it down to the street before she stopped, folding onto the steps.

What's gotten into you?

She didn't know—but she knew that she couldn't stand another minute in that apartment. That cell. That imitation of a life. It wasn't just the heat, or the constant moving, or even having to watch Victor's life force wane like a candle. Sydney just wanted one night of feeling *normal*. Human.

A car flew past, a teen hanging out the window, smiling a rictus skeleton grin. Girls laughed as they stumbled by in too-short skirts and too-tall heels. Across the street, a group of guys in wolf masks threw their heads back and howled.

Sydney got to her feet and made her way to the corner, where a dozen flyers had been tacked to a telephone pole, advertising parties at clubs and frat houses. *Monsters Ball!* said one. *Scream Fest*, promised another, the letters dripping blood. *Heroes and Villains*, announced a third. Underneath, in parentheses, the disclaimer: *No Sidekicks.*

Sydney pulled the last flyer from the post and started walking.

∞

SHE could hear the music from the street.

The heavy bass poured through the open front door, where a guy in a cape was making out with a girl in a horned mask. The house beyond was filled with strobe lights, the staccato flashes paired to the music so the whole place looked like it was moving.

It was the kind of party her sister would have been at. The kind of crowd she would have had wrapped around her finger. That was the thing about Serena. By the time she got her powers, she was already used to being in control. Serena didn't bend to the world. She made the world bend to her.

But as Sydney climbed the steps, her resolve wavered. She hadn't been around this many people at once, not since she went to visit Serena at college. Right before everything went wrong.

Syd closed her eyes, could see her sister leaning in the doorway.

You're growing up.

Could feel the weight of Serena's arms around her.

I want you to meet Eli.

The cold of the soda in her hand.

You can trust him.

The crack of the gun sounding in the woods.

"Kawai'i."

Syd looked around and saw a dark-skinned girl in gladiator sandals perched on the front porch rail, long legs swinging as she smoked.

"Or is it chibi?" she went on, nodding at Syd's costume. "I can never remember..."

The girl offered up the cigarette, and Sydney reached to take it. She'd never smoked, but she'd seen Serena do it.

The trick is to hold the smoke in your mouth, like this.

The tip of the cigarette had glowed red, Serena had counted on her fingers one, two, three, and then exhaled a perfect plume of white. Now, Sydney did the same thing.

The smoke filled her mouth, hot and acrid. It tickled her nose, crept into her throat, and she quickly blew it out before she could start coughing.

Her head felt cloudy, but her nerves were settling.

She handed the cigarette back and stepped into the party.

The house was teeming with students. Dancing, shouting, moving, sprawling. Too many. Too much. She felt jostled by elbows, shoulders, capes, wings, caught up in the sea of bodies, motion.

Sydney stepped back, trying to get out of the waves, and collided with a man in a black domino mask. Her heart lurched. Eli. Her fingers flew toward her backpack—but it wasn't him. Of course it wasn't him. This boy was too short, too wide, his voice too high as he shuffled past her, calling out to a friend across the crowded room.

Sydney was just starting to relax when someone caught her wrist. She spun around to see a tall guy in a metal helmet and skin-tight spandex. "How did you get in here?" He raised her arm, and his voice, at the same time. "Who brought their kid sister?"

Sydney felt her face flush hot as heads turned.

"I'm not a *kid*," she snarled, pulling free.

"Yeah, sure, come on," he said, pushing her toward the front door.

What Sydney would have given, in that moment, for Victor's power instead of hers.

The college boy shoved her across the threshold. "Go trick-or-treat somewhere else."

Sydney stood on the front porch, face burning, as the party raged behind her and more guys and girls started up the path to the house.

Tears threatened to spill down her face. She fought them back.

"Hey, are you okay?" asked a guy in a cape, kneeling beside her. "You want to call someone—"

"Fuck off," said Sydney, marching down the steps, her face on fire.

She couldn't go home—not yet. And she couldn't bring herself to text June, either, so Sydney wandered the town alone for another hour, as the sticky heat finally cooled and the crowds in costumes thinned. She kept the backpack in her hand, the zipper parted and the gun in reach in case anyone tried anything.

No one did.

When she finally returned to the apartment, the lights were all off.

She slipped off her shoes, heard the soft sound of a body shifting on the couch, and turned, expecting to see Mitch.

But it was Victor, stretched out on the sofa, one arm across his eyes, his chest rising and falling in the slow, steady rhythm of sleep.

Dol lay on the floor beside him, awake, eyes shining in the dark, tail swishing softly at her arrival.

As Sydney padded across the apartment, the dog rose and followed in her wake, padding down the hall to her room and climbing up onto her bed without invitation. Syd eased the door shut and slumped back against it.

A few moments later she heard the soft scrape of furniture, the sound of Victor rising, the soft tread of his own steps as he passed her door, and closed his own.

He hadn't been asleep, she realized.

Victor had simply been waiting for Syd to come home.

XVII

FOUR WEEKS AGO

HALLOWAY

IT was late, but Sydney wasn't tired yet—too much sugar in her blood, too many thoughts in her head—and besides, she needed to see the birthday out as well as in.

It was tradition.

A memory, like a splinter—of Syd trying to stay awake as the minutes ticked toward midnight. Serena poking her in the ribs every time she started to doze.

Come on, Syd. You're almost there. It's bad luck to fall asleep. Get up and dance with me.

Sydney shook her head, trying to dislodge her sister's voice. She turned in a slow circle before the mirror, letting her blue hair fan around her face, and then tugged off the wig and undid the clips beneath. Her natural hair—a curtain of straight white-blond—came free, falling almost to her shoulders.

Syd caught her reflection again, but this time out of the corner of her eye.

Sometimes, if she squinted a little, she could almost, almost see someone else in the mirror.

Someone with sharper cheekbones, fuller lips, a mouth tugged into a sly grin. The ghost of her sister. An echo. But then the illusion would falter, and Sydney's eyes would come back into focus, and all she would see was a girl playing dress-up.

∞

SYDNEY shed the red bomber jacket and unlaced the steel-toed boots, turning her attention to Victor's gift. She took up the blue box and carried it to the room's small desk. Dol watched from the floor as she carefully lifted the box's lid, examining the contents. The bird's small skeleton was immaculate, intact. It looked like something out of a natural history museum—knowing Victor, it probably was.

Syd sat down, ran her fingers thoughtfully over the bird's wing, and wondered how old it was. The longer a thing had been dead, she'd learned, the harder it was to bring back. And the less of it remained, the more brittle its life was. So likely to crumble, or break, and when it did, it was gone forever. No second chances.

Nothing to grab hold of.

Sydney glanced at the red metal tin beside her bed. And then she took up a pair of tweezers and began removing bones, erasing the bird one piece at a time, until only a few fragments remained. The long bone at the top of one wing. A section of the spine. The heel of one foot.

She took a deep breath and closed her eyes, resting her hand on the partial skeleton.

And then, she reached.

At first she felt nothing beyond the bones under her palm. But she imagined herself reaching further, deeper, past the bird and the case and the desk, plunging her hand down into cold, empty space.

Her lungs began to ache. The chill spread through her fingers and up her arms, sharp and biting, and when she breathed out she could feel the plume of cold, like fog, on her lips. Light danced—far off and faint—behind her eyes, and her fingers brushed something, the barest hint of a thread. Syd pulled gently, gingerly. She kept her eyes closed, but she could feel the small skeleton beginning to rebuild, the ripple of muscle, of skin, the blush of feathers.

Almost—

But then she pulled just a *little* too hard.

The thread vanished.

The fragile light behind her eyes went out.

Sydney blinked, withdrew her hand, and saw the remains of the bird, its fragile skeleton now beyond repair. The bones—so carefully arranged in their velvet—were split and broken, the pile she'd set aside caving in, crumbling under their own weight.

She still wasn't strong enough.

Still wasn't ready.

When she moved to touch the bones, they fell apart, leaving only an ashy streak on the blue velvet lining, a pile of dust on her desk.

Ruined, thought Sydney, sweeping the remains into the trash.

XVIII

FOUR WEEKS AGO

MERIT CENTRAL HOSPITAL

I will ruin you.
I will ruin.
I will.
I—
Marcella opened her eyes.

She was greeted by sterile fluorescent lights, the antiseptic smell of scrubbed surfaces, and the papery thread count of hospital sheets. Marcella knew she shouldn't be here, shouldn't even be *alive*. But her pulse registered, a wavering green line on the machine beside her head, inexorable proof that she was. She drew a deep breath, and then cringed. Her lungs and throat felt raw, her skull pounding even through the high-grade painkillers being piped into her veins.

Marcella tested her fingers and toes, rolled her head gingerly side to side with calm precision and—she commended herself—startling composure. She had long ago learned to compartmentalize her feelings, shove the inconvenient and the unbecoming into the back of her mind like an old dress in a dark closet.

Her fingers crept along the sheets, and she tried to pull herself up, but at the slightest movement she was assaulted by her own body—her bruised and broken ribs, her burned and blistered skin. Marcella had also learned to embrace the various stings and aches and sears that went hand in hand with maintaining her appearance.

But this pain put those nips and tucks, those elected inconveniences, to shame.

This pain made a home in her skin, in her bones, moved like molten fire through her blood, her limbs. But instead of cringing away, Marcella focused in.

She once had a yoga instructor who compared the mind to a house. Marcella had rolled her eyes at the time, but now she imagined going room to room, switching off the lights. Here was fear, switch. Here was panic, switch. Here was confusion, switch.

Here was pain.

Here was anger.

Here was her husband, that cheating fuck.

Here was him slamming her head into the table.

Here was his arm sweeping the candles.

Here was her voice breaking, her lungs filling with smoke.

Here was his back as he walked away, and left her to die.

That light, she left on. She marveled at the way it grew brighter inside her head, at the warmth that came with it, rippling through her skin. Her fingers tightened on the bedrail. It went soft under her palm, the smooth metal rusting away, a red stain spreading along the steel. By the time she noticed, pulled away, a section the length of her forearm was already ruined, flaking onto the bed.

Marcella stared, uncomprehending.

She looked from her hand to the metal, and back, felt the heat still wicking off her skin. She clutched the thin hospital sheets instead, but they crumbled too, the fabric rotting away in the span of a breath, leaving only a patina of ash behind.

Marcella raised both hands now, not in surrender, but in fascination, the palms turned up toward her face, searching for an explanation, a fundamental change, and finding only her own ruined manicure, a familiar hand-shaped bruise going green around her wrist, a white hospital band with the wrong name printed on it: *Melinda Pierce.*

Marcella frowned. The other details were all correct—she

recognized her age, her date of birth—but it seemed someone had entered her into the system under a false name. Which meant they didn't want Marcus to know she was here. Or to know she was alive. A reasonable choice, she thought, considering the events of earlier that night. Or was it tomorrow? Time felt muddy.

The wounds felt fresh enough.

Without the sheets, she could see the bandages tracing their way up her legs, winding across her stomach, around her shoulder, the mirror image of a candelabra burned into her—

A police radio went off, the sharp static setting it apart from the dozens of other hospital sounds. Marcella's attention flicked to the door. It was closed, but through the glass insert she spotted a cop's uniform.

Slowly, Marcella managed to draw herself up from the bed, despite the various cables and cords connecting her to the medical bay. Her hand reached for the IV stand before she remembered the stretch of rusted steel, the crumbling sheet. She hesitated, but her palm felt cool again, and as her fingers closed around the plastic cord nothing terrible happened. Gingerly, Marcella disconnected the line and then, careful not to dislodge the heart monitor, she reached around and pulled the power cord instead.

The machines went quiet, their screens black.

Marcella's hospital gown hung loose, a mercy given the contact with her tender skin, but also a hindrance: she couldn't slip out wearing nothing but a sheet.

A sterile white wardrobe stood in the corner, and she went to it, irrationally hoping to find her clothes, her purse, her keys, but of course it was empty.

Beyond the door, she heard a gruff voice.

". . . still hasn't woken up . . . no, we've kept it off the news . . . I've already called WITSEC . . ."

Marcella sneered. WITSEC. She hadn't designed this life, built a future from nothing, just to spend it *hiding*. And she'd be damned if she disappeared before her husband. Marcella turned, surveying the room, but there was nothing but the one door, and a window looking out over Merit from at least six stories up.

One room, one door. One window.

And two walls.

Marcella picked the one opposite her bed, pressed her ear to the wall, and heard nothing—just the steady beep of more hospital equipment.

She brought her fingers to the plaster, barely touching.

Nothing happened.

Slowly, Marcella pressed her palm flat against the wall. Nothing. She glared at her hand, the nails cracked where her desperate fingers had dug into the silk-threaded carpet, clawed at the wood floor—

Her hand began to glow. Marcella watched the wall beneath her fingers warping, rotting, drywall slouching as if with damp, or gravity, or time, until a broad hole formed between the rooms, large enough to step through.

Marcella marveled, then, at her hand, at the damage it had done. So it wasn't a matter of force, but feeling.

That was fine.

Marcella had quite a lot of feelings.

She drew the power back into her chest, as if it were a breath. There it burned, less like a fuse than a pilot light. Steady and waiting.

Marcella stepped through the ruined wall, and into the next room.

The door to the room was ajar, and the woman in the bed—Alice Tolensky, according to the clipboard—was three inches shorter than Marcella and a good thirty pounds heavier.

Her clothes hung in the small, hospital-issued wardrobe.

Marcella wrinkled her nose as she considered the slip-on flats, the frills on the collar of the flower-printed blouse, the jeans with their elastic waist.

But beggars couldn't be choosers. Marcella was grateful for the room in the jeans when she had to pull them on. She stifled a breath as the denim grazed her bandages, then turned her attention back to the closet.

A knockoff leather purse slumped on the shelf. Marcella rifled through the contents and came up with a hundred dollars in cash and a pair of glasses.

She finished getting dressed, tugged her hair into a bun at the nape of her neck, slipped on the glasses, and stepped into the hall. The cop in front of her door was picking at a bandage on his hand. He didn't look up as Marcella turned and left.

A queue of taxis waited outside the hospital.

She climbed into the nearest one.

"Address?" rumbled the driver.

"The Heights." It was the first time she'd spoken, and her voice was raw from smoke, a fraction lower and edged with the luscious rasp that so many starlets craved. "On Grand."

The car pulled away, and Marcella leaned back against the leather seat.

She had always been good under pressure.

Other women could afford to panic, but being a mob wife required a certain level of poise. It meant staying calm. Or at least *feigning* calm.

At the moment, Marcella didn't feel like she was feigning anything. There was no fear, no doubt. Her head wasn't spinning. She didn't feel lost. If anything, this road she was on felt paved and straight, the end lit by a single, blinding light.

And beneath that light stood Marcus Andover Riggins.

2
REVELATION

I

FOURTEEN YEARS AGO

UNIVERSITY OF MERIT

EVERYONE was shitfaced.

Marcella sat on the kitchen counter, her heels knocking absently against the cabinets as she watched them stumble past, sloshing drinks and shouting to be heard. The house was filled with music, bodies, stale booze and cheap cologne, and all the other inane trappings of a college frat party. Her friends had convinced her to come, with the weak argument that it was just what students *did*, that there would be free beer and hot guys and it would be *fun*.

Those same girls were lost somewhere in the mass of bodies. Every now and then she thought she caught a glimpse of a familiar blond bob, a high brown ponytail. Then again, there were a dozen of them. Cookie-cutter college kids. More concerned with blending in than standing out.

Marcella Renee Morgan was *not* having fun.

She was nursing a beer in a glass bottle, and she was bored—bored by the music, and the boys who swaggered over every now and then to flirt, and then stormed away, sulking, when she turned them down. She was bored by being called beautiful, and then a bitch. Stunning, and then stuck up. A ten, and then a tease.

Marcella had always been pretty. The kind of pretty people couldn't ignore. Bright blue eyes and pitch-black hair, a heart-shaped face atop the lean, clean lines of a model. Her father told her she'd never have to work. Her mother said she'd have to work twice as hard. In a way, both of them were right.

Her body was the first thing people saw.

For most, it seemed to be the last thing, too.

"You're think you're better than me?" a drunken senior had slurred at her earlier.

Marcella had looked at him straight on, his eyes bleary, hers sharp, and said simply, "Yes."

"Bitch," he'd muttered, storming away. Predictable.

Marcella had promised her friends she'd stay for a drink. She tipped the bottle back, eager to finish the beer.

"I see you found the good stuff," said a deep voice, rich, with a faint southern lilt.

She glanced up and saw a guy leaning back against the kitchen island. Marcella didn't know what he was talking about, not until he nodded at the glass bottle in her hand with the plastic cup in his own. She gestured at the fridge. He crossed to it, retrieving two more bottles. He cracked them open against the counter's edge and offered one to her.

Marcella took it, considering him over the rim.

His eyes were dark blue, his hair sun-kissed, that warm shade between blond and brown. Most of the guys at the party hadn't shed their baby fat, high school still clinging to them like wet clothes, but his black shirt stretched tight over strong shoulders, and his jaw was sharp, a small cleft denting his chin.

"Marcus," he said by way of introduction. She knew who he was. She'd seen him on campus, but it was Alice who'd told her—Marcus Riggins was trouble. Not because he was gorgeous. Not because he was rich. Nothing so bland as all that. No, Marcus was trouble for one simple, delicious reason: his family was in the mob. Alice had said it like it was a bad thing, a deal breaker, but if anything, it only piqued her interest.

"Marcella," she said, uncrossing and recrossing her legs.

He smiled. "Marcus and Marcella," he said, lifting his drink. "We sound like a matching set."

Someone turned the music up, and his next words were lost under the bass.

"What did you say?" she called over the song, and he took the opportunity to close the gap between them. She shifted her legs to the side, and he stepped closer, smelling like apples and linen, clean and crisp, such a welcome change from the sticky, tacky grime of lazy, drunken bodies.

He rested his beer on the counter just beside her arm, the cold glass brushing her elbow and sending a small shiver through her. A slow smile crossed his face.

He leaned in close, as if telling her a secret. *"Follow me."*

He stepped back, taking the scent of linen and the blush of heat with him.

He didn't pull her off the counter, but she felt pulled, drawn in his wake as he turned away, slipped through the crowd. She followed him, through the party, up the stairs, down the hall to a bedroom door.

"Still with me?" he asked, glancing back.

The door swung open onto a room at odds with the rest of the frat house. The laundry was hampered, the desk clean, the bed made, the only clutter a neat stack of books on the comforter.

Marcella hovered in the doorway, waiting to see what he'd do next. If he would come to her, or make her come to him.

Instead, Marcus went to the window, slid up the glass, and stepped out onto a widow's walk. A fall breeze whispered through the room as Marcella followed, slipping off her heels.

Marcus offered his hand and helped her up and through. The city spiraled away beneath them, the darkened buildings a sky, the lights like stars. Merit always looked larger at night.

Marcus sipped his beer. "Better?"

Marcella smiled. "Better."

The music, obnoxiously loud downstairs, was now a muted pulse against her back.

Marcus leaned against the wooden rail. "You from here?"

"Not far," she said. "You?"

"Born and raised," he said. "What are you studying?"

"Business," she said shortly. Marcella hated small talk, but that was because so often it felt like a chore. Just noise, empty words meant to fill empty space. "Why did you bring me up here?"

"I didn't," he said, all mock innocence. "You followed me."

"You asked," she said, realizing he hadn't. There'd been no question in his voice, only a simple command.

"You were about to leave," said Marcus. "And I didn't want you to."

Marcella considered him. "Are you used to getting what you want?"

The edge of a smile. "I have a feeling we both are." He returned her long look. "Marcella the Business Major. What do you want to be?"

Marcella twirled her beer. "In charge."

Marcus laughed. A soft, breathy sound.

"You think I'm joking?"

"No," he said. "I don't."

"How do you know?"

"Because," he said, closing the narrow space between them, "we *are* a matching set." A breeze cut through, just crisp enough to make her shiver.

"We better go inside," said Marcus, pulling away.

He stepped back through the window, offering his hand. But this time he didn't lead.

"After you," he said, gesturing toward the bedroom door. It was still cracked open, music and laughter pouring up from the party below. But when Marcella reached the door, she hesitated, fingers coming to rest against the wood. She could picture Marcus standing a few feet behind her, hands in his pockets, waiting to see what she would do.

She pushed the door shut.

The lock caught with a soft click, and Marcus was there as if summoned, lips brushing the back of her neck. His hands slid, feather light, over her shoulders, against her waist. Heat flooded through her at the almost-touch.

"I won't break," she said, turning in time to catch Marcus's mouth with hers. He pressed into her, pushed her back against the wood. Her nails dug into his arms as he unbuttoned his shirt. His teeth scraped her shoulder as her own came off. They laid waste to the order of his room, shedding clothes, knocking over a chair, a lamp, sweeping the books from the bed as Marcus pressed her down into the sheets.

They fit together perfectly.

A matching set.

II

FOUR WEEKS AGO

DOWNTOWN MERIT

THE cab stopped in front of the Heights, a pale stone spire seated in the heart of the city. Marcella paid the driver in cash and climbed out, her limbs a dull roar of pain with every step.

When she had first discovered the secret apartment—on a goddamn bank statement—she'd assumed the worst, but Marcus had claimed the place was purely practical. A safe house. He'd even insisted on bringing her there, showing off his thorough work—her favorite designer labels in the closet, her brand of coffee in the cupboard, her shampoo in the shower.

And Marcella had actually believed him.

Found a way to make it *their* secret instead of his. Now and then she'd phone him up, insisting there was some emergency, and he'd somberly order her to meet him at the safe house, and he'd arrive to find her waiting, wearing nothing but a gold ribbon carefully wrapped and finished with a bow.

Now the image of the tawdry pink lipstick flared like pain behind Marcella's eyes.

What a fool.

The concierge rose from the front desk to greet her.

"Mrs. Riggins," said Ainsley, surprise lighting his face. He glanced quickly at her ill-fitting clothes, the bandages peeking out from collar and cuff, but the residents at the Heights paid for discretion as much as floor-to-ceiling windows (now Marcella wondered how many times Ainsley had employed that same discretion with her husband).

"Is . . . everything all right?" he ventured.

She flicked a wrist dismissively. "It's a long story." And then, after a moment, "Marcus isn't here, is he?"

"No, ma'am," he said solemnly.

"Good," said Marcella. "I'm afraid I've forgotten my keys."

Ainsley nodded briskly and rounded the desk to summon the elevator. When the doors opened, he followed her inside. As it rose, she rubbed her forehead, as if simply tired, and asked the date.

The concierge told her, and Marcella stiffened.

She'd been in the hospital for almost *two weeks*.

But that didn't matter, not now. What mattered was that it was a Friday night.

She knew exactly where Marcus would be.

The elevator stopped. Ainsley followed her out onto the fourteenth floor, unlocked the cream-colored door, and wished her a pleasant night.

Marcella waited until he was gone, then stepped inside and flicked on the lights.

"Honey, I'm home," she cooed to the empty apartment. She should have felt something—a pang of sorrow, or regret—but there was only the ache in her skin and the rising tide of anger beneath, and when she reached for one of the wineglasses on the counter, it warped under her touch and turned to sand. A thousand grains rained down between Marcella's glowing fingers, spilled onto the floor.

She stared down at her hand, the remains of the glass dusting her palm. The strange light was already sinking back beneath her skin, and when she reached for a fresh glass, it held under her touch.

A bottle of chardonnay sat chilling in the fridge, and Marcella poured herself a drink and flicked on the news—now eager to know what she'd missed—as she clicked the volume up and headed for the bedroom.

One of Marcus's shirts lay thrown across the bed . . . along with one of her own. The glass in her hand threatened to give, so Marcella set it aside. The doors to the walk-in closet were thrown wide, Marcus's dark suits lining one wall, while the rest was given over to a medley of couture dresses, blouses, heels.

Marcella glanced back at the clothes still twined in a lover's embrace atop the bed and felt her anger rising like steam. Fingers glowing, she ran her hand along her husband's side of the closet, and watched the garments fade and rot under her touch. Cotton, silk, and wool all withered and dropped from the hangers, crumbling by the time they hit the floor.

Hell hath no fury, she thought, dusting her palms.

Satisfied—no, not satisfied, nowhere *near* satisfied, but momentarily appeased—Marcella took up her drink and went into the luxury bathroom, where she set the glass on the rim of the marble sink and began to peel away the frumpy stolen clothes. She stripped until she was dressed in nothing but bandages. The sterile white wrappings weren't nearly as seductive as the gold ribbons, but they seemed to trace the same path across her leg, her stomach, her arms.

Marking her. *Mocking* her.

Marcella's hands twitched with the sudden urge to reach out and ruin something, anything. Instead she stood there and took in her reflection, every angle, every flaw, memorized it while she waited for the rage to pass—not vanish, no, simply retract, like a cat's claws. If this new power was temporary, a thing with limits, she didn't want to pass them. She needed her nails sharp.

The painkillers from the hospital were wearing off, and her head was ringing, so Marcella dug two Vicodin out of her emergency supply beneath the sink, washed them down with the last of the chardonnay, and went to get ready.

III

EIGHT YEARS AGO

UPTOWN

THE phone rang, and rang, and rang.

"Don't answer it," said Marcus, pacing. A dark tie hung loose, unknotted, around his neck.

"Darling," said Marcella, sitting on the edge of the bed. "You knew they'd call."

He'd been on edge for days, weeks, waiting for the phone to ring. They both knew who it would be: Antony Edward Hutch, one of the four heads of the Merit crime syndicate, and *Jack* Riggins's long-term benefactor.

Marcus had finally told her, of course, what his father did. How, for them, the word *family* wasn't just about blood—it was a profession. He'd told her in their senior year of college, looked like death when he said it, and Marcella had realized, halfway through the meal, that he was trying to break up with her.

"Is it like joining the clergy?" she'd asked, sipping her wine. "Did you take a vow of celibacy?"

"What? No . . ." he said, confused.

"Then why can't we face it together?"

Marcus shook his head. "I'm trying to protect you."

"Hasn't it occurred to you that I can protect myself?"

"This isn't like in the movies, Marcella. What my family does, it's brutal, and bloody. In this world, in *my* world, people get hurt. They die."

Marcella blinked. Set down her glass. Leaned in. "People die in *every* world, Marcus. I'm not going anywhere."

Two weeks later, he'd proposed.

Marcella adjusted the diamond on her finger as the phone stopped ringing.

A few seconds later, it started again.

"I'm not answering it."

"So don't."

"I don't have a choice," he snapped, running a hand through his sun-streaked hair.

Marcella rose to her feet and took his hand. "Huh," she said, holding it up between them. "I don't see any strings."

Marcus pulled free. "You don't know what it's like, having other people decide who you are, what you're going to be."

Marcella resisted the urge to roll her eyes. Of course she knew. People looked at her and assumed a whole lot. That a pretty face meant an empty head, that a girl like her was only after an easy life, that she would be satisfied with luxury, instead of power—as if you couldn't want both.

Her own mother had told her to aim high, that she should never sell herself cheap. (The correct saying, of course, was *short*. As in, don't sell yourself *short*.) But Marcella hadn't sold herself cheap *or* short. She'd chosen Marcus Riggins. And he was going to choose *this*.

The phone rang on, and on.

"Take the call."

"If I take the call," he said, "I take the job. If I take the job, I'm in. There's no getting back out."

Marcella caught him by the shoulder, interrupting the pendulum of his movement. He faltered, drew up short as she wrapped her fingers around his silk tie, and pulled him toward her. Something flashed in Marcus's eyes, anger, and fear, and violence, and Marcella knew that he could do this job, and do it well. Marcus wasn't weak, wasn't soft. He was simply stubborn. Which was why he needed her. Because where he saw a trap, she saw an opportunity.

"What do you want to be?" asked Marcella. The same question he'd asked her the night they met. One Marcus himself had never answered.

Now he looked at her, his eyes dark. "I want to be more."

"Then *be* more. That," she said, turning his face toward the phone, "is just a door. A way in." Her nails scraped against his cheek. "You want to be more, Marcus? Prove it. Pick up the phone and walk through the goddamn door."

The ringing stopped, and in the silence she could hear her quickening pulse, and his unsteady breath. The moment stretched taut, and then collapsed. They collided, Marcus kissing her, hard, and deep, one hand already sliding between her legs, the other dragging the nails from his cheek. He spun her around, bent her over the bed.

He was already hard.

She was already wet.

Marcella stifled a gasp of pleasure, *triumph,* as he pressed himself against her—into her—her fingers knotting in the sheets, her gaze drifting to the cell phone beside her on the bed.

And when it rang again, Marcus answered.

IV

FOUR WEEKS AGO

THE HEIGHTS

MARCELLA longed for a hot shower, but the first touch of water sent a searing pain over her tender skin, so instead she settled for a damp cloth, drawing lukewarm water from the bathroom sink.

The edges of her hair were singed beyond repair, so she took up the sharpest scissors she could find and started to cut. When she was done, her black waves ended just above her shoulders. A thick coil swept across her brow, hiding the fresh scar above her left temple and framing her face.

Her face, which had miraculously escaped the worst of the fight and the fire. She brushed mascara along her lashes and painted a fresh coat of red on her lips. Pain followed every gesture—each stretch and bend of tender skin a reminder in the shape of her husband's name—but through it all, Marcella's mind felt . . . quiet. Smooth. Silk ribbons, instead of knotted rope.

She returned to the closet, running her fingers lightly along the symphony of clothes that made up her wardrobe. A small, vindictive part of her wanted to choose something revealing, to put her injuries on display, but she knew better. Weakness was a thing best concealed. In the end she chose a pair of elegant black slacks, a silk blouse that wrapped around her sleek frame, and a pair of black stilettos, the heels as thin and chrome as switchblades.

She was just fastening the buckles on her second shoe when a newscaster's voice rose from the television in the other room.

"New developments in the case of the house fire that raged through the upscale Brighton development last week..."

She stepped out into the hall in time to see her own face on the screen.

"...resulting in the death of Marcella Renee Riggins..."

She'd been right, then. The police obviously wanted Marcus to believe she was dead. Which was probably the only reason she wasn't. Marcella took up the remote, turning up the volume as the camera cut to a shot of their house, the exterior charred and smoldering.

"Officials have yet to determine the cause of the fire, but it's believed to be an accident."

Marcella's grip tightened on the remote as the camera cut to a shot of Marcus running his hands through his hair, the picture of grief.

"Husband Marcus Riggins admitted to police that the two had quarreled earlier that night, and that his wife was prone to outbursts, but adamantly denied the suggestion that she'd set the fire herself, saying that she had never been violent or destructive—"

The remote crumbled in her hand, batteries liquefying as the plastic warped and melted.

Marcella let the mess fall from her fingers, and went to find her husband.

V

THREE YEARS AGO

DOWNTOWN MERIT

MARCELLA had always liked the National building. It was a feat of glass and steel, a thirty-story prism at the heart of the city. She'd coveted it, the way one might a diamond, and Tony Hutch owned the whole thing, from the marble lobby all the way to the rooftop gardens where he threw his parties.

They stepped through the front doors arm in arm, Marcus in a trim black suit, Marcella in a gold dress. She caught sight of a plainclothes cop lounging in the lobby, and shot him a toying wink. Half the Merit PD was in Hutch's pocket. The other half couldn't get close enough to do a damn thing.

The inside of the elevator was polished to a high shine, and as it rose, Marcella leaned against Marcus and considered their reflection. She loved the way they looked together. She loved his strong jaw and his rough hands, loved his steely blue eyes and the way he moaned her name. They were partners in crime. A perfect pair.

"Hello, handsome," she said, catching his eye.

He smiled. "Hello, gorgeous."

Yes, she loved her husband.

Probably more than she should.

The elevator doors opened onto a rooftop covered in lights, and music, and laughter. Hutch always knew how to throw a party.

Gauzy canopies and sofas piled with cushions, low gold-and-glass tables, servers slipping through the crowd with champagne flutes and canapés, but what drew Marcella's eye more than any of it was the city beyond. The view was incredible, the National high enough up that it seemed to look down on all of Merit.

Marcus led her through the bustling crowd.

As they moved, she felt the eyes of every man, and half the women, slide over her. Marcella's dress—made of a thousand pale gold scales—hugged her every curve and shimmered with each step. Her heels and nails were the same pale gold, as was the matching net of wire woven through her black hair, lacing tiny white-gold beads through the glossy updo. The only spots of color were her eyes, a vivid blue framed by black lashes, and her lips, which she'd painted crimson.

Marcus had told her to dress up.

"What's the point of having beautiful things," he'd said, "if you don't put them on display?"

Now he led her to the very center of the roof, to the marble star inlaid in the floor where the boss himself was holding court.

Antony Hutch.

He wasn't unattractive—lean and strong, with warm brown hair and a constant summer tan—but there was something about him that made Marcella's skin crawl.

"Tony, you've met my wife, Marcella."

Hutch's attention, when it landed on her, felt like a damp hand on bare flesh.

"Jesus, Marc," he said, "does she come with a warning label?"

"She does not," quipped Marcella.

But Hutch only smiled. "Seriously, though, how could I forget such a beauty?"

He stepped closer. "Is Marc here treating you well? You need anything, you just let me know."

"Why?" asked Marcella with a smirk. "Are you in the market for a wife?"

Hutch chuckled, and spread his arms. "Unfortunately, I like catching girls more than keeping them."

"That simply means," said Marcella, "you haven't found the right one."

Hutch laughed, and turned toward Marcus. "You got yourself a keeper."

Marcus looped his arms around her waist and kissed her temple. "Don't I know it?"

But his body was already twisting away from her, and soon Marcella found herself pushed to the outside of the circle as the group of men began to talk business.

"We're looking to expand our hold on the south side."

"Territory moves are always dangerous."

"Caprese's eyes are bigger than his stomach."

"You could squeeze him out more subtly," offered Marcella. "Pick up the blocks around him. It wouldn't be a direct attack—no grounds for retaliation—but the message is clear."

The conversation crumbled. The men went quiet.

After a pained moment, Marcus simply smiled. "My wife, the business major," he said blandly.

Marcella felt herself flush as the other men shared a knowing chuckle. Hutch looked at her, his own laugh slack, hollow. "Marcella, we must be boring you. I'm sure you'd be happier with the other wives."

Marcella's answer was already poised on her lips, but Marcus cut in first. "Go on, Marce," he said, kissing her cheek. "Let the men talk."

She wanted to grab his jaw, dig her nails in until they drew blood. Instead, she smiled. Arranged her face into a mask of serenity. Appearance was everything.

"Of course," she said. "I'll leave you boys to it."

She turned away, plucked a champagne flute from a passing server, held the glass so tight her fingers hurt. She felt their eyes follow her across the roof.

What's the point of having beautiful things, if you don't put them on display?

She hadn't realized, at the time, that Marcus had referred to her as a *thing*. The comment had slid off like a silk gown, pretty and weightless, but—

"Marcella!" called a woman in a familiar singsong voice. Her heels were pushing six inches, which was probably why she was sitting down, holding court in a dark red gown. It was the perfect color—Grace was blond, and fair, and the dress stood out like blood on skin.

"Have you been evicted?" asked Theresa, seated as well and sipping a large drink.

"God no," said Marcella, "they were boring me to tears."

"Too much shop talk," said Bethany, bangles clanging as she flicked her wrist. More beauty than brains in that one, thought Marcella, not for the first time.

"They may think they're kings," said Grace, "but we're the power behind the throne."

A tinkle of laughter sounded nearby.

There was a second group of women, clustered in another corner of the roof, in higher heels and shorter dresses. The girlfriends. The second and third wives. The side pieces. Newer models, Grace would say.

"How's Marcus?" asked Bethany. "I hope you're keeping him on a leash."

"Oh," she said, sipping her champagne, "he'd *never* cheat."

"What makes you so sure?" asked Theresa.

Marcella met Marcus's eyes across the roof.

"Because," she said, raising her glass, "he knows I'd kill him first."

∞

"DID you have a nice night?" Marcella asked later as the car pulled away from the party.

Marcus was all energy. "It went off without a hitch. Or a hutch."

He chuckled at his own joke. Marcella didn't. "He's taken a liking to me, I can tell. Said he'd call me in the morning. Something new. Something big." He pulled her close. "You were right."

"I'm always right," she said absently, looking out the window. "Let's stay in the city tonight."

"Good idea," said Marcus. He knocked on the partition, gave the driver the address of their place at the Heights, told him to hurry. And then he sat back, pressing against her. "They couldn't take their eyes off you. I don't blame them. Neither could I."

"Not here," she said, trying to force a little humor in her voice. "You'll ruin my dress."

"Fuck your dress," he breathed in her ear. "I want *you*."

But Marcella pushed him away.

"What's wrong?" he asked.

Marcella's gaze flicked toward him. "My wife, *the business major?*"

He rolled his eyes. "Marce."

"Let the men *talk?*"

"Oh, come on."

"You made a fool of me."

He made a sound too close to a laugh. "Don't you think you're overreacting?"

Marcella gritted her teeth. "You're very lucky I didn't *react* at the time."

Marcus soured. "This isn't a good look on you, Marce."

The car pulled up in front of the Heights, and Marcella resisted the urge to storm out. She flicked open the door and rose, smoothing the gold scales on her dress as she waited for Marcus to round the car.

"Good evening," said the concierge. "Nice night?"

"Flawless," said Marcella, stepping briskly into the elevator, Marcus in her wake. He waited until the doors were closed, then sighed, shook his head.

"You know what those guys are like," he muttered. "Old guard. Old money. Old values. You wanted this. You wanted me to do this."

"With *me*," she snapped. "I wanted us to do this, together." He tried to cut in, but she didn't let him. "I'm not a fucking coat, Marcus. You don't get to check me at the door."

The elevator stopped, and she strode out into the hall, heels clicking on the marble floor. She reached their door, but Marcus caught her hand and pinned her back against the wood. On a normal night, she would have thrilled at the swift display of strength, would have arched against him. But she wasn't in the mood.

Let the men talk.

"Marcella."

The laugh. The patronizing smiles.

"*Marcella*," said Marcus, drawing her face toward his. Her gaze toward his. And then she saw it—or maybe she just *wanted* to see it—there, beyond the flat, dark blue. A glimpse of the Marcus she'd met, young and hungry and utterly in love with her. The Marcus who wanted her, *needed* her.

His mouth hovered a breath from hers as he spoke. "Where I go, you go," he said. "We're in this together. Step for step."

Marcella wanted to believe him, needed to believe him, because she wasn't willing to let go, wasn't going to lose him, everything she'd built.

They never seem to realize.

We're the power behind the throne.

Marcella leaned forward and kissed him long, and slow, and deep.

"Show me," she said, leading him inside.

VI

FOUR WEEKS AGO

MERIT SUBURBS

MARCUS Andover Riggins had always been a man of routines.

An espresso in the morning, a bourbon before bed. Every Monday after breakfast, he got a massage, and every Wednesday at lunch, he swam laps, and every Friday night, rain or shine, from dusk until dawn, he played poker. Four or five members of Tony Hutch's crew all got together weekly at Sam McGuire's place, since Sam was single—or at least, he wasn't married. He had a rotation of sorts, a new girl every week, but none of them stuck.

Sam's was a nice place—they were *all* nice places—but he had a bad habit of leaving the back door unlocked instead of giving any of his short-term girls a key. Marcella had warned him a dozen times—someone could walk right in. But Sam would just smile, and say that no man would walk in on one of Tony Hutch's crew.

Perhaps, but Marcella Riggins was no man.

She let herself inside.

The back door gave onto the kitchen, where Marcella found a girl doubled over, ass in the air and head in the freezer, as she rummaged for ice. She wobbled in too-high heels, bangles clanging against the freezer, but the first thing Marcella noticed was the girl's dress. Dark blue silk, with a short rippling skirt—the same one that had hung for more than a year in Marcella's own closet at the Heights.

The girl straightened, and turned, her mouth forming a perfect pink circle.

Bethany.

Bethany, who had twice as many tits as thoughts.

Bethany, who asked about Marcus every time they met.

Bethany, who looked like a cheap knockoff of Marcella in those diamond earrings, that stolen dress, which wasn't stolen, of course, because the apartment in town had also been kept for *her.*

Bethany's eyes went wide. "Marcella?"

"Did you always know," she'd asked Marcus once, undoing the buttons on a blood-stained shirt, "that you had what it took to end a life?"

"Not until the gun was in my hand," he'd said. "I thought it would be hard, but in that moment, nothing was easier."

He was right.

But there was, it turned out, a crucial difference between destroying *things* and destroying *people.*

People *screamed.*

Or at least they tried. Bethany certainly would have, if Marcella hadn't already grabbed her by the throat, hadn't eroded through her vocal cords before anything more than a short, futile gasp could escape.

And even then, the men in the other room might have heard, if they hadn't been laughing so loudly.

It didn't take long.

One second Bethany's mouth was open in a perfect *O* of surprise and the next her plump skin had shriveled, her face twisting into a rictus grin that quickly pulled away to reveal the skull beneath, and then even that turned to ash, as all that was left of Bethany crumbled to the kitchen floor.

It was over so fast—there was hardly any time for Marcella to savor what she'd done, and no time to think about all the things she *should* be feeling, given the circumstances, or even to wonder at their peculiar absence.

It was just so *easy*.

As if everything had *wanted* to come apart.

There was probably some law about that.

Order giving way to chaos.

Marcella took up a dishcloth and wiped the dust from her fingers as another raucous laugh cut through the house. Then a familiar voice called out.

"Doll, where's that drink?"

Marcella followed the voice down the short hall that ran between the kitchen and the den where the men were playing.

"Where the fuck is my drink?" bellowed Marcus, chair scraping back. He was on his feet when she walked in.

"Hello, boys."

Marcus didn't have to feign surprise, since he'd expected her to be dead. His face drained of all color—what was the phrase, oh yes: as if he'd just seen a ghost. The other four men squinted through the haze of liquor and cigar smoke.

"Marce?" said her husband, voice laced with shock.

Oh, how she *longed* to kill him, but she wanted to use her bare hands, and there was a table between them, and Marcus was holding his ground, looking at her with a mixture of suspicion and worry, and Marcella knew what she had to do. She began to cry. It was easy—all she had to do was think of her life, the one she'd worked so hard for, going up in flames.

"I've been so worried," she said, breath hitching. "I woke up in a hospital, and you weren't there. The cops said there'd been a fire and I thought—I was afraid—they wouldn't tell me if you'd been hurt in it. They wouldn't tell me *anything*."

His expression flickered, suddenly uncertain. He took a step toward her. "I thought you were dead." A forced stammer, a mockery of emotion. "The cops wouldn't let me see your . . . I thought maybe you . . . what do you remember, baby?"

Still the pet names.

Marcella shook her head. "I remember making dinner. Everything after that is a blur."

She caught a glimpse of hope in his eyes—amazement, that he would get away with it, that he could have the best of both worlds: killing his wife *and* getting her back.

But instead of coming to her, he sank down into his chair. "By the time I got home," he said, "the fire trucks were there, the house was up in flames. They wouldn't let me in." Marcus slumped back, as if reliving the trauma. The grief. As if ten minutes earlier he hadn't been playing poker and waiting for his mistress—her one-time friend—to bring him his drink.

Marcella went to her husband, circled behind his chair, and wrapped her arms around his shoulders. "I'm just so glad . . ."

He took up her hand, pressed his lips against her wrist. "I'm all right, doll."

She nestled her face into his collar. Felt Marcus actually relax, muscles unwinding as he realized he was in the clear.

"Guys," said Marcus, "game's over."

The other men shuffled, about to rise.

"No," she whispered in her sweetest voice. "Stay. This won't take long."

Marcus tipped his head back, a furrow between his brows.

Marcella smiled. "You never were one to dwell on the past, Marcus. I loved that about you, the way things always just rolled off."

She lifted an empty glass from the table.

"To my husband," she said, right before the ruin rushed to her fingers in a blossom of red light. The glass dissolved, sand raining onto the felt poker table. A ripple of shock went through the table, and Marcus jerked forward, as if to rise, but Marcella had no intentions of letting go.

"We've had a good run," she whispered in his ear as the anger and hurt and hatred rose like heat.

She let it all out.

Her husband had told her a hundred stories about the way men died. No one ever held their tongue, not in the end. In the end, they begged and pleaded, sobbed and screamed.

Marcus was no exception.

It didn't last long—not out of some sudden mercy, Marcella simply lacked the control to draw it out. She *really* would have liked to savor it. Would have liked the chance to memorize his horrified face, but alas—that was the first thing to go.

She had to settle instead for the shock and terror on the faces of the other men.

Of course, that didn't last very long either.

Two of them—Sam, of course, and another man she didn't recognize—were scrambling to their feet.

Marcella sighed, her husband's remains collapsing as she knocked them aside and caught Sam's sleeve.

"Going so soon?" she asked, ruin surging to her fingers. He staggered, fell, his body breaking by the time it hit the floor. The other man drew a knife from a hidden fold of his coat, but when he lunged toward Marcella, she wrapped one glowing hand around the blade. It decayed and crumbled, ruin spreading in an instant from metal to hilt and then up the man's arm. He began to scream and pulled away, but the rot was already going through him like a wildfire, his body falling apart even as he tried to escape.

The last two men stayed seated at the card table, their hands up and their faces frozen. All Marcella's life, men had looked at her with lust, desire. But this was different.

This was *fear*.

And it felt good.

She took her husband's seat, settling in among his still-warm ashes. She used a kerchief to clear a streak of him from the poker table.

"Well?" said Marcella after a long moment. "Deal me in."

VII

FOUR WEEKS AGO

EASTERN MERIT

GROWING up, Dominic Rusher had never been a morning person.

But the army made him a get-the-fuck-up-when-you-hear-the-sound person, and anyway, sleep hadn't come easy since his accident, so Dom was on his feet by the third wail of the 4:30 a.m. alarm. He showered, wiped away the fog on the bathroom mirror, and found his reflection.

Five years had done a lot of good. Gone was the harrowed look of someone in constant pain, the gaunt features of a man trying and failing to self-medicate. In his place was a soldier, lean muscles winding over broad shoulders, tan arms strong and back straight, his hair cropped short on the sides, slicked back on top.

He'd gotten his shit together, too.

His medals were mounted on the wall, no longer thrown carelessly around the necks of empty liquor bottles. Next to them hung the X-rays. Each metal plate and bar, pin and screw, every way they'd put Dominic back together, glowing white against the backdrop of muscles and skin.

The place was clean.

And *Dom* was clean.

He hadn't had a drink or a dose since the night they dug up Victor—he wished he could say *since the night they met*, when Victor erased his pain, but the bastard had gone and *died*, left Dom high and dry and in a world of hurt. Those had been two dark nights, ones he didn't want to remember, but Dominic's control hadn't faltered since.

Even when Victor shorted out, and the pain came rushing back. Dom white-knuckled it, tried to treat the episodes as a reminder, the reprieves as a gift.

After all, it could be worse.

It *had* been worse.

Dom wolfed down a cup of too-hot coffee and a plate of too-runny eggs, slung on his jacket, grabbed his helmet from the door, and stepped out into the gray predawn.

His ride sat waiting in its usual spot—a simple black motorcycle, nothing fancy but the kind of thing he'd always wanted growing up and never been able to afford. Dom wiped the dew from the seat before swinging his leg over, kicked it into gear, and savored the low purr for a moment before setting off.

He rode through the empty streets as Merit began to wake around him. This early, most of the streetlights were in his favor, and Dom was out of the city in ten minutes. Merit tapered off to either side before giving way to empty fields. The sun rose at his back as the engine screamed beneath him and the wind buffeted his helmet, and for fifteen minutes he felt totally free.

He hit the turnoff and slowed, easing his bike down an unmarked road. Another five minutes, and Dom passed through an open gate, slowing as the building came into sight.

From the outside, it looked like nothing at all. A hospital, perhaps. Or a processing plant. A set of white blocks stacked together in a nondescript formation. The kind of place you'd drive by without a second glance, unless you knew what it was.

If you knew what it was, it became something far more ominous.

Dominic parked and dismounted, climbing the front steps. The doors parted onto a pristine white hall, sterile to the point of purity. An officer stood on either side, one manning an X-ray, the other a scanner.

"I've got parts," Dom reminded them, gesturing down his side.

The guy nodded, tapping away at the screen while Dominic set his phone, keys, jacket, and helmet in the tray. He stepped into the machine, waiting for the band of white light to scan up and then back down before reclaiming his possessions on the other side. He performed each task with an ease borne from habit. Amazing how things became normal, actions pressed into memory.

The locker room was the first door on the right. Dom set his jacket and helmet on a shelf and changed into a black uniform shirt, high-collared and long-sleeved. He washed his face, smoothed his hair, and patted his front pocket to make sure he had his access key.

Down the hall, and two floors up, he swiped himself into the control room and showed the senior officer the front of his key, where his face hung in holographic detail, right below the word *EON*.

"Dominic Rusher," he said with an easy smile, "reporting for duty."

VIII

FOUR WEEKS AGO

MERIT SUBURBS

STELL ducked under the yellow crime scene tape.

He didn't flash a badge—didn't need to. Everyone on the scene worked for EON. For him.

Agent Holtz was standing by the back door. "Sir," he said eagerly, his tone too bright for the early hour.

"Who called it in?" asked Stell.

"Good Samaritan called the cops. Cops called us."

"That obvious?"

"Oh yeah," said Holtz, holding open the door.

Agent Rios was already in the kitchen. Tall, tan, and keen-eyed, she'd been Stell's second-in-command for nearly four years. She was leaning against the counter, arms crossed, watching a tech photograph a pile of . . . something . . . on the tile floor. A large diamond glinted amid the mess.

"Same profile as the hospital?" asked Stell.

"Looks like it," said Rios. "Marcella Riggins. Age thirty-two. Spent the last thirteen days in a coma after her husband tried to burn down their house—with her inside. Can't really blame her for being mad."

"Mad is conceivable," said Stell. "Murder is a problem." He looked around. "How many dead?"

Rios straightened. "Four, we think. It's kind of hard to tell." She pointed at the kitchen floor. "One," she counted, then turned and led him down the hall to a room with a poker table, and a fairly grisly tableau. "Two," she said, nodding down at a ruined body on the floor. "Three," she pointed at a withered form only vaguely human. "And four," she said, gesturing to a pile of dust that coated the back of a chair and spilled onto the felt table. "Hell hath no fury..."

Stell counted the chairs. "Survivors?"

"If there were, they didn't go to the cops. The house belongs to Sam McGuire," said Rios. "Safe to assume he's here... somewhere."

Holtz whistled from the doorway. "You ever seen anything like this before?"

Stell considered. He had seen a lot since his first introduction to EOs a decade and a half before. Vale, with his ability to modulate pain; Cardale, with his ability to regenerate; Clarke, with her ability to control—and those were just the start. The tip of the iceberg. He'd since seen EOs who could bend time, move through walls, light themselves on fire, turn themselves to stone.

But this, Stell had to admit, was something new.

He ran his hand through the mess on the felt. "What is this? Ash?"

"As far as we can tell," said Rios, "it's Marcus Riggins. What's left of him. Or maybe this is. Or this."

"All right," said Stell, brushing the dust from his palms. "Compile the record. I want records of *everything*. Everything from the hospital. Everything from here. Shots and specs of every body, every room, every detail, even if you don't think it matters. It goes in the file."

Holtz raised his hand like a schoolboy. It was impossible to forget that he was new. "Who's the file for?"

"Our analyst," said Stell. But he knew how the agents and techs liked to talk. "You might have heard him called 'the hunting dog.'"

"Well," said Holtz, looking around. "Wouldn't it be easier to bring your dog to the scene, instead of trying to take the whole scene to the dog?"

"Perhaps," said Stell. "But his leash doesn't reach this far."

∞

THE lights in the EON cellblocks came on all at once.

Eli Ever opened his eyes, looking up at the cell's mirrored ceiling, and saw—himself. As always. Clear skin, brown hair, strong jaw; a copy of the boy he'd been at Lockland. A pre-med student at the top of his class, the peak of promise. As if the ice bath hadn't only stopped his heart, but had frozen time itself.

Fifteen years, and though his face and body remained unchanged, Eli had aged in other ways. His mind had sharpened, hardened. He'd shed some of his more youthful ideals. About himself. About God. But those were the kinds of changes that didn't show in the reflected glass.

Eli rose from the cot, stretched, and padded barefoot across the private cell that, for nearly five years, had marked the boundaries of his world. He went to the sink and splashed cold water on his face, then crossed to the low shelf that ran against one wall, folders stacked along its length. All of them were beige, ordinary, except for one—a thick black file at the end with a name printed on the front. *His* name. Eli never reached for that one—didn't need to—he'd memorized the contents. Instead, his fingers danced along the spines before coming to rest on one considerably thicker than the rest, unmarked, save for a simple black *X*.

One of his few open cases. A pet project of sorts.

The Hunter.

Eli sat at the table in the center of his cell and flipped back the cover, turned through the pages of the file, skimming past the reports of older killings to the most recent one.

The EO's name was Jack Linden. A mechanic three hundred miles west of Merit. He'd slipped through EON's algorithm, but not, apparently, the Hunter's notice. A crime scene photo showed the EO on his back, amid a sea of tools. He'd been gunned down at point-blank range. Eli ran a finger absently over the entry wound.

A pressure seal sounded nearby, and a few seconds later the far wall of Eli's cell turned clear, dissolving from solid white to fiberglass. A thickset man with salt-and-pepper hair stood on the other side, carrying another file, and, as always, a mug of coffee. The last fifteen years might not have touched Eli, but every single one had left its mark on Stell.

The man nodded at the beige folder in Eli's hands. "Any new theories?"

Eli let the file fall shut. "No," he said, setting it aside and rising from his chair. "What can I do for you, Director?"

"There's a new case," said Stell, setting the file and mug in the fiberglass cubby. "I want your thoughts."

Eli approached the barrier and collected both offerings.

"Marcella Riggins," he read aloud, returning to his seat and taking a long, slow sip of his drink.

Eli didn't *need* coffee, just as he didn't need to eat or sleep, but some habits were psychological. The steaming mug was a small piece of change in a static world. A concession, a prop, but one that allowed him to pretend, if only for a moment, that he was still human.

Eli set the coffee aside and began to turn through the file. It wasn't enough—it was never enough—but it was all they would give him. A stack of paper and Stell's power of observation. And so he flicked through page after page, skimming the evidence, the aftermath, before finally pausing on a photo of human remains, a diamond glinting in the ash. He set the file aside and met Stell's waiting gaze.

"All right," said Eli. "Shall we begin?"

IX

FIVE YEARS AGO

LOCATION UNCERTAIN

AFTER Eli killed Victor, it was all a blur.

First, the chaos. The red and blue lights, the sirens, the officers storming through the Falcon Price, and the horrible realization they weren't on *his* side.

Then came the cuffs, so tight they cut into Eli's wrists, and the black hood, swallowing the sight of Victor's corpse and the blood-slicked concrete, muffling the voices and the orders and the slammed doors, erasing *everything* but Eli's own breath, his pounding heart, his desperate words.

Burn the body. Burn the body. Burn the body.

Then came the cell—more like a concrete box than a room—and Eli slamming his fists against the door over and over until his fingers broke, and healed, broke, and healed, the only evidence the blood left smeared across the steel.

And then, in the end, there was the lab.

Hands forcing Eli down, cold steel on his back and straps cinched so tight they cut into skin, pale sterile walls and too-bright lights and the chemical smell of disinfectant.

In the center of it all, a man in white, his face swimming above Eli's. Dark eyes set deep behind black glasses. Hands drawing on plastic gloves.

"My name," said the man, "is Dr. Haverty."

He selected a scalpel as he spoke.

"Welcome to my lab."

Leaned in close.

"We are going to understand each other."

And then he began to cut. *Dissect*—that was the word for it when the subject was dead. *Vivisect*—that was the word when they were still alive. But when they couldn't die?

What was the word for that?

Eli's faith had faltered in that room.

He had found Hell in that room.

And the only sign of God was that, no matter what Haverty did, Eli continued to survive.

Whether he wanted to or not.

∞

TIME unraveled in Haverty's lab.

Eli thought he knew pain, but pain for him had become a bright and fleeting thing, an instant's discomfort. In the doctor's hands, it became a solid state.

"Your regeneration truly is remarkable," said the doctor, retrieving the scalpel with bloodstained gloves. "Shall we find its limit?"

You're not blessed, Victor had said. *You're a science experiment.*

Those words came back to Eli now.

And so did Victor.

Eli saw him in the lab, watched him circle the table at Haverty's back, slip in and out of Eli's line of sight as he studied the doctor's incisions.

"Maybe you're in Hell."

You don't believe in Hell, thought Eli.

The corner of Victor's mouth twitched. "But you do."

Every night, Eli would collapse onto his cot, shivering and sick from the hours pinned to the steel table.

And every morning, it would start again.

Eli's power had a single flaw—and ten years after Victor first discovered it, so did Haverty. Eli's body, for all its regeneration, couldn't reject foreign objects; if they were small enough, he healed around them. If they were large enough—a knife, a saw, a clamp, his body wouldn't heal at all.

The first time Dr. Haverty cut out Eli's heart, he thought he might *finally* die. The doctor held it up for him to see before cutting it free, and for a fraction of a second Eli's pulse faltered, failed, the equipment screamed. But by the time Haverty set the heart in its sterile tray, there was a new one already beating in Eli's open chest.

The doctor breathed a single word.

"Extraordinary."

THE worst part, thought Eli, was that Dr. Haverty liked to *talk*.

He kept up a casual stream of conversation as he sawed and sliced, drilled and broke. In particular, he was fascinated by Eli's scars, the brutal crosshatching on Eli's back. The only marks that would never fade.

"Tell me about them," he'd say, plunging a needle into Eli's spine.

"There are thirty-two," he'd say, drilling into Eli's bones.

"I counted," he'd say, cracking open Eli's chest.

"You can talk to me, Eli. I'm happy to listen."

But Eli couldn't talk, even if he wanted to.

It took all his effort not to scream.

X

TWENTY-FIVE YEARS AGO

THE FIRST HOME

ONCE upon a time, when the marks on his back were still fresh, Eli told himself that he was growing wings.

After all, his mother thought Eli was an angel, even if his father said he had the devil in him. Eli had never done anything to make the pastor think that, but the man claimed he could see the shadow in the boy's eyes. And whenever he caught a glimpse of it, he'd take Eli by the arm and lead him out to the private chapel that sat beside their clapboard house.

Eli used to love the little chapel—it had the prettiest picture window, all red and blue and green stained glass, facing east so it caught the morning light. The floor was made of stone—it was cold beneath Eli's bare feet, even in summer—and there in the center of the room was a metal cross, driven straight down into the foundation. Eli remembered thinking it seemed violent, the way the cross broke and split the floor, as if thrown from a horrible height.

The first time his father saw the shadow, he kept one hand on Eli's shoulder as they walked, the other clutching a coiled leather strap. Eli's mother watched them go, twisting a towel in her hands.

"John," she said, just once, but Eli's father didn't look back, didn't stop until they'd crossed the narrow lawn and the chapel door had fallen shut behind them.

Pastor Cardale told Eli to go to the cross and hold on to the horizontal bar, and at first Eli refused, sobbing, pleading, trying to apologize for whatever he'd done. But it didn't help. His father tied Eli's hands in place, and beat him worse for his defiance.

Eli had been nine years old.

Later that night, his mother treated the angry lash-marks on his back, and told him that he had to be strong. That God tested them, and so did Eli's father. Her sleeves inched up as she draped cool strips of cloth over her son's wounded shoulders, and Eli could just see the edges of old scars on the backs of her arms as she told him it would be okay, told him it would get better.

And for a little while, it always did.

Eli would do everything he could to be good, to be worthy. To avoid his angry father's gaze.

But the calm never lasted. Sooner or later, the pastor would glimpse the devil in his son again, and lead Eli back to the chapel. Sometimes the beatings were months apart. Sometimes days. Sometimes Eli thought he deserved it. Needed it, even. He would step up to the cross, and curl his fingers around the cold metal cross, and pray—not to God, not at first, but to his father. He prayed that the pastor would stop seeing whatever he saw, while he carved new feathers into the torn wings of Eli's back.

Eli learned not to scream, but his eyes would still blur with tears, the colors in the stained glass running together until all he saw was light. He held on to that, as much as to the steel cross beneath his fingers.

Eli didn't know how he was broken, but he wanted to be healed.

He wanted to be saved.

XI

FOUR YEARS AGO

EON——LABORATORY WING

STELL knocked his knuckles on the counter.

"I'm here to speak with one of your subjects," he said. "Eli Cardale."

"I'm sorry, sir, he's in testing."

Stell frowned. "Again?"

This was the third time he had come to see Eli, and the third time he'd been fed a line.

The first time, the excuse had been believable. The second, inconvenient. Now, it was obviously a lie. He hadn't pulled rank up until this point, but only because he didn't want the headache, or the reputation. EON was still a new venture, *his* venture—so new that the building around them wasn't even finished—but it was also his *responsibility*, and Stell knew in his gut that something was wrong. The unease pinched, like an ulcer.

"That's the same answer I was given last time."

The woman—Stell didn't know if she was a doctor, a scientist, or a secretary—pursed her lips. "This *is* a research lab, sir. Testing is a frequent component—"

"Then you won't mind interrupting the current session."

The woman's frown deepened. "With a patient such as Mr. Ever—"

"Cardale," corrected Stell. *Ever* had been a self-appointed moniker, aggrandizing and arrogant (if slightly prophetic). His real name was Eliot—Eli—Cardale.

"With a patient such as Mr. *Cardale*," she amended, "testing requires immense preparation. Ending an exam early would be a waste of EON resources."

"And this," said Stell, "is a waste of my time." He pinched the bridge of his nose. "I'll observe the session until it's finished."

A shadow crossed her face. "Perhaps if you'd rather wait here—" With that, Stell's unease turned to dread.

"Take me to him. *Now.*"

XII

TWENTY-THREE YEARS AGO

THE FIRST HOME

ELI sat on the porch steps and looked up at the sky.

It was a beautiful night, the strobe of red and blue lights painting the house, the lawn, the chapel. The ambulance and the coroner's van parked in the grass. One unnecessary, the other waiting.

He pressed a worn old Bible to his chest while the cops and medics moved around him as if in orbit, close but never touching.

"Kid's in shock," said an officer.

Eli didn't think that was true. He didn't feel shaken. Didn't feel anything but calm. Maybe that *was* shock. He kept waiting for it to wear off, for the steady hum in his head to give way to terror, to sadness. But it didn't.

"Can you blame him? Lost his mother a month ago. Now this."

Lost. That was a strange word. *Lost* suggested something misplaced, something that might be recovered. He hadn't lost his mother. After all, he'd been the one to find her. Lying in the tub. Floating in a white dress stained pink by the water, palms up as if in supplication, her forearms open from elbow to wrist. No, he hadn't lost her.

She'd left him.

Left Eli alone, trapped in a house with Pastor John Cardale.

A female medic brought a hand to Eli's shoulder, and he flinched, half from the surprise of contact, and half from the fact the latest welts were still fresh under his shirt. She said something. He wasn't listening. A few moments later, they wheeled out the body. The medic tried to block Eli's view, but there was nothing to see, only a black body bag. Death made clean. Neat. Sterile.

Eli closed his eyes and drew up the image of his father lying broken at the bottom of the stairs. A shallow red pool spreading around the pastor's head, like a halo, only in the dim basement the blood had looked black. His eyes wet, his mouth hinging open and closed.

What had his father been going down there to do?

Eli would never know. He opened his eyes and began to absently thumb the pages of the book.

"How old are you?" asked the medic.

Eli swallowed. "Twelve."

"Do you know your next of kin?"

He shook his head. There was an aunt somewhere. A cousin, maybe. But Eli had never met them. His world had been here. His father's church. Their congregation. There was a phone tree, he thought, a communication network used to spread the word when there was a celebration, a birth—or a death.

The woman slipped away from his side and spoke to two of the officers. Her voice was low, but Eli caught some of the words: "The boy has nothing."

But again, she was wrong.

Eli didn't have a mother, or a father, or a home, but he still had faith.

Not because of the scars on his back, or any of Pastor Cardale's less physical sermons. No, Eli had faith because of how it felt when he pushed his father down the basement stairs. When the pastor's head struck the basement floor at the bottom. When he finally stopped moving.

In that moment, Eli had felt *peace*. Like a small sliver of the world made right.

Something—someone—had guided Eli's hand. Given him the courage to place his palm flat against his father's back and push.

The pastor had fallen so fast, bounced like a ball down the old wooden steps before landing in a heap at the bottom.

Eli had followed slowly, taking each step with care as he drew his phone from his pocket. But he didn't dial, didn't push Call.

Instead, Eli sat down on the bottom step, safely away from the blood, and held the phone in his hands, and waited.

Waited until his father's chest stilled, until the pool of blood stopped spreading, and the pastor's eyes went empty, flat.

Eli remembered one of his father's sermons, then.

Those who don't believe in the soul have never seen one leave.

He was right, thought Eli, finally dialing 911.

There really was a difference.

"Don't worry," said the medic, returning to the front porch. "We're going to find somewhere for you to go." She knelt down in front of him, a gesture clearly meant to make him feel like they were equals. "I know it's scary," she said, even though it wasn't. "But I'm going to tell you something that helps me when I'm feeling overwhelmed. Every end is a new beginning." She straightened. "Come on, let's go."

Eli rose to his feet and followed her down the porch steps.

He was still waiting for the sense of calm to fade, but it didn't.

Not when they led him away from the house. Not when they perched him on the edge of the unused ambulance. Not when they drove him away. Eli looked back once, and only once, at the house, the chapel, and then he turned, facing forward.

Every end is a new beginning.

XIII

FOUR YEARS AGO

EON———LABORATORY WING

STELL entered the observation room just in time to see a man in a white lab coat crack open Cardale's chest. The patient was strapped to a steel table, and the surgeon was using some kind of saw, and a collection of clamps and metal pins, and Eli was not only still alive—he was *awake*.

A mask ran across the EO's nose and mouth, with a hose connected to a machine behind his head, but whatever it was feeding Eli, it didn't seem to be helping. The pain showed in every muscle, his whole body tensed against the restraints, the skin around his wrists and ankles white from pressure. A strap held Eli's head back against the steel table, denying him a view of his own dissection, though Stell doubted he needed to look to know what was happening. Beads of sweat ran down Eli's face and into his hair as the surgeon widened the cut in his chest.

Stell didn't know what he'd expected to find, but he hadn't expected *this*.

As the surgeon finished sawing through his patient's sternum and pinned the flesh back, Cardale groaned, the sound low and muffled by the mask. Blood poured out of his open chest, slicking the metal table, the lip of which was too shallow to contain the ceaseless flow. Ribbons of red spilled over the sides, dripping to the floor.

Stell felt sick.

"Remarkable, isn't he?"

He turned to find an average-looking man tugging off a pair of blood-slicked gloves. Behind round glasses, the doctor's deep-set eyes were bright, pupils dilated with the pleasure of discovery.

"What the hell do you think you're doing?" demanded Stell.

"Learning," said the doctor.

"You're torturing him."

"We're studying him."

"While he's *conscious*."

"Necessarily," said the doctor with a patient smile. "Mr. Cardale's regenerative abilities render any anesthesia useless."

"Then what's with the mask?"

"Ah," said the doctor, "one of my more genius moments, that. You see, we cannot *anesthetize* him, but that doesn't mean we can't dampen his functions a little. The mask is part of an oxygen deprivation system. It reduces the breathable air to twenty-five percent. It's taking all of his regenerative ability to stave off the damage done by starving the cells, which buys us a bit more time on the rest of the body before it heals."

Stell stared at Eli's chest as it struggled to rise and fall. From this angle, Stell could almost see his heart.

"We've never come across an EO like Mr. Cardale," continued the doctor. "His ability—if we find a way to harness it—could revolutionize medicine."

"EO abilities can't be harnessed," said Stell. "They aren't transferable."

"Yet," said the doctor. "But if we could understand—"

"Enough," said Stell, transfixed by the sight of Eli's ruined body. "Tell them to stop."

The doctor frowned. "If they take out the clamps, he'll heal, and we'll have to start all over again. I really must insist—"

"What's your name?"

"Haverty."

"Well, Dr. Haverty. I'm *Director* Stell. And I'm officially discontinuing this experiment. Make them stop, or lose your job."

The sick smile slid from Haverty's face. He pulled a microphone from the viewing room wall and clicked it on.

"Terminate the session," he ordered the surgeons still in the room.

The men and women hesitated.

"I said—terminate it," repeated Haverty curtly.

The surgeons began to methodically remove the various pins and clamps from Eli's open chest cavity. The moment they were gone, the tension in the EO's body began to recede. His back sank to the metal table, and his hands unclenched, the color returning to his limbs as his body put itself back together. Ribs cracked into place. Skin settled and fused. The lines of his face smoothed. And his breathing, while still labored (they left the mask on), began to even.

The only sign that something horrific had happened was the sheer quantity of blood left pooling on the table and floor.

"Are you happy now?" grumbled Dr. Haverty.

"I'm a long way from happy," said Stell, storming out of the observation room. "And you, Dr. Haverty—you're fired."

∞

"**PUT** your forehead against the wall and your hands through the gap."

Eli did as he was told, feeling for the break in the fiberglass. He couldn't see anything—his world had been a mottled black wall since the soldiers had thrown the hood over his head and dragged him from the concrete cell that morning. He knew, before they came, that something was wrong—no, not wrong, but certainly *different*. Haverty was a man of habit, and even though Eli didn't have a perfect sense of time, he had a tenuous enough hold to know their last session had ended too abruptly.

He found the gap in the fiberglass, a kind of narrow shelf, and rested his wrists on the lip. A hand jerked his hands farther into the gap, but a few moments later the cuffs came free.

"Take three steps back."

Eli retreated, expecting to meet another wall, but finding only space.

"Reach up and remove the hood."

Eli did, assaulted by the sudden brightness of the space. But unlike the sterile overheads of the operating theater, the light here was crisp, and clean, without being glaring. He was facing a floor-to-ceiling fiberglass wall, perforated by holes and interrupted only by the narrow cubby through which he'd placed his hands. On the other side stood three soldiers in head-to-toe riot gear, their faces hidden behind helmets. Two gripped batons—cattle prods, judging by the faint hum, the slight current of blue light. The third was coiling the discarded cuffs.

"What am I doing here?" asked Eli, but the soldiers didn't answer. They simply turned and left, steps echoing as they retreated. Somewhere a door opened, closed, pressurized, and as it did, the world beyond the fiberglass disappeared, the wall, transparent seconds before, becoming opaque.

Eli turned, taking in his new surroundings.

The cell was little more than a large cube, but after the months he'd spent strapped to various surfaces, sealed in a cell no bigger than a tomb, Eli was still grateful for the chance to *move*. He traced the perimeter of the cell, counted off the steps, took note of the features and their absences.

He noted four cameras set flush into the ceiling. There were no windows, no obvious door (he'd heard the fiberglass barrier retract into the floor, rise again behind him), only a cot, a table with one chair, one corner fitted with a toilet, sink, and shower. A wardrobe consisting solely of gray cotton lay folded on a floating shelf.

Victor's ghost ran a hand over the folded clothes.

"And so the angel trades Hell for Purgatory," mused the phantom.

Eli didn't know what this place was—only knew that he wasn't being strapped down, wasn't being cut open, and that was an improvement. He peeled off his clothes and stepped into the shower, luxuriated in the freedom of turning the water on and off, washed away the scents of rubbing alcohol and blood and disinfectant, expecting to see the water at his feet run thick with the grime of a year's torture. But Haverty had always been meticulous. They'd hosed Eli down every morning, and every night, so the only traces left behind were the scars that didn't show.

Eli lowered himself onto the cot, pressed his back into the wall, and waited.

XIV

TWENTY-THREE YEARS AGO

THE SECOND HOME

THE phone tree worked.

Eli arrived at the Russos' house that night with a backpack full of clothes, and the knowledge that his stay was temporary. A place for him to wait while the authorities tracked down a living relative, one willing to collect him.

Mrs. Russo met him at the door in a robe. It was late, and the Russo kids—there were five of them, ranging in age from six to fifteen—were already asleep. She took Eli's bag and led him inside. The house was warm and soft in a lived-in way, the surfaces scuffed, the edges worn smooth.

"Poor thing," she clucked under her breath as she led Eli into the kitchen. She gestured at the table for him to sit, and continued to murmur, more to herself than to him. The sound she made was so different from his own mother, whose whispered words had always been tinged with a hint of desperation. *My angel, my angel, you must be good, you must be light.*

Eli lowered himself into a rickety kitchen chair and stared down at his hands, still waiting for the shock to come, or go, whichever it was meant to. Mrs. Russo placed a steaming mug in front of him, and he curled his fingers around it. It was hot—uncomfortably so—but he didn't pull away. The pain was familiar, almost welcome.

What now? thought Eli.

Every end is a new beginning.

Mrs. Russo sat down across from him. She reached her hands out and wrapped them over his. Eli flinched back at the touch, tried to pull away, but her grip was firm.

"You must be hurting," she said, and he was—his hands were burning from the mug, but he knew she meant a deeper, heavier pain, and *that* he didn't feel. If anything, Eli felt lighter than he had in years.

"God never gives us more than we can bear," she continued.

Eli focused on the small gold cross that hung around her neck.

"But it's up to us to find the purpose in the pain."

The purpose in the pain.

"Come on," she said, patting his hand. "I'll make up the couch."

∞

ELI had never been a good sleeper.

He'd spent half of every night listening to his father move just beyond the door, like a wolf in the woods behind the house. A predator, circling too near. But the Russos' place was quiet, calm, and Eli lay awake, marveling at the way eight bodies under one roof could take up less space than two.

The quiet didn't last.

At some point Eli must have drifted off, because he started awake to raucous laughter and morning light and a pair of wide green eyes watching him from the edge of the couch. The youngest Russo girl perched there, staring at him with a mixture of interest and suspicion.

Four loud bodies came crashing suddenly into the room, a cacophony of limbs and noise. It was Saturday, and already the Russo children were running wild. Eli spent most of the time trying to stay out of their path, but it was hard in such a crowded house.

"Weirdo," said one of the boys, knocking into him on the stairs.

"How long is he staying?" asked another.

"Don't be un-Christian," warned Mr. Russo.

"Gives me the creeps," said the oldest boy.

"What's wrong with you?" demanded the youngest girl.

"Nothing," answered Eli, though he wasn't sure if that was true.

"Then act normal," she ordered, as if that were such a simple thing.

"What does normal look like?" he asked, at which point the girl made a small, exasperated sound and stormed away.

Eli waited for someone to come and get him, take him away—though he didn't know where they would take him—but the day passed, and darkness fell, and he was still there. That first night was the only one he spent alone. They put him in the boys' room after that, a spare mattress tucked in one corner. He lay there, listening to the other boys sleep with a mixture of annoyance and envy, his nerves too fine-tuned to let him rest among the various sounds of movement.

Eventually he got up and went downstairs, hoping to steal a few precious hours of stillness on the sofa.

Mr. and Mrs. Russo were in the kitchen, and Eli heard them talking.

"Something's not right with that boy."

Eli hovered in the hall, holding his breath.

"He's too quiet."

Mrs. Russo sighed. "He's been through a lot, Alan. He'll find his way."

Eli returned to the boys' room, climbed back into his bed. There, in the dark, the words repeated.

Quiet. Weirdo. Creep.

He'll find his way.

Act normal.

Eli didn't know what normal was, or even what it looked like. But he'd spent a lifetime studying his father's moods and his mother's silences, the way the air in the house changed like the sky before a storm. Now he watched the way the Russo boys roughhoused, noted the fine line between humor and aggression.

He studied the confidence with which the oldest—a boy of sixteen—moved among his younger siblings. He studied the guileless innocence the youngest played up, to get what he wanted. He studied the way their faces twisted into a pantomime of emotions like annoyance and disgust and anger. Most of all, he studied their joy. The way their eyes lit up when they were gleeful, the varying tones of their laughter, the dozen ways their smiles shone or softened depending on the exact nature of their delight.

Eli had never known there were so many kinds of happiness, let alone so many ways to express it.

But his study was cut short when, just two weeks into his stay with the Russos, Eli found himself uprooted again, deposited with another family in another house.

Act normal, the Russo girl had said.

And so Eli tried again. Started fresh. It wasn't a perfect imitation, not by far. But it was an improvement. The children at this new house still called him names, but the names had changed.

Timid, quiet, weirdo had been replaced by *strange, curious, intense.*

Soon came another family, and another chance.

Another opportunity to reinvent, to modify, to adjust aspects of that act.

Eli tested his theater on the families as if they were an audience, and used their feedback, the immediate, constant feedback, to tweak his performance.

Slowly *strange, curious, intense* had been refined, honed into *charming, focused, clever.*

Then something else changed.

Another car pulled up, and took him away, but this time it didn't drop him off with another of his father's flock.

This time, it took him to *family.*

∞

THE FIFTH HOME

Patrick Cardale did not believe in God.

He was John's estranged nephew, the son of a dead aunt that Eli had never met. Patrick was a professor at a local college, married to a painter named Lisa. They didn't have children. No one for Eli to mimic. No curtain of normalcy or noise for him to slip behind.

Eli sat on the sofa across from them. A captured audience. A solo act.

"How old are you?" asked Patrick. "Twelve?"

"Almost thirteen," said Eli. It had been more than six months since Pastor Cardale's accident.

"I'm sorry it took us so long," said Patrick, hands between his knees.

Lisa put a hand on his shoulder. "We'll be honest, it wasn't an easy decision."

Patrick shifted. "I knew you'd been raised a certain way. And I knew I couldn't give you that. John and I, we didn't see eye to eye."

"Neither did we," said Eli.

He realized he was making them uncomfortable, so he smiled. Not too wide, just enough to let Patrick know that he was okay.

"Come on," said Lisa, rising. "I'll show you to your room."

Eli rose to follow her.

"We can find you a church," she added, leading him down the hall. "If it's important to you."

But he didn't need a church. Not because he'd given up on God—but because church itself was the one place Eli had never felt Him. No, God had stood with Eli at the top of the cellar stairs. Given him each of those families to learn from. Led him here, to this house, and this couple, this new chance.

His room, when they got there, was comfortable and clean. A double bed, a closet, a desk. A pair of framed pictures hung on the wall over the desk, anatomical drawings, one of a hand, the other a diagram of a human heart. Eli stopped before them, studying the lines, startled by the intricacy, the elegance.

"You can take those down, if you don't like them," said Lisa. "Make the space yours. Put up posters or whatever boys your age do."

Eli glanced toward her. "How long am I staying?"

Lisa's eyes widened in surprise. Her face was an open book—that was the phrase people used. Eli had never really understood it until he looked at Lisa.

"As long as you want," she said. "This is your home now."

Eli didn't know what to say to that. He'd been living in increments of days, weeks, which wasn't really living, of course. Now, his future stretched before him, measured in months, years.

Eli smiled, and this time, it almost felt natural.

XV

FOUR YEARS AGO

EON

STELL sank into his office chair, and waited for the call.

His office, like the rest of EON, was composed of clean lines, spare and minimalist. Three thin screens drew a semicircle over his desk, and a vast grid on the wall live-streamed footage of each hall, access point, cell.

EON's cells were state-of-the-art fiberglass cubes, each floating in the middle of its own concrete hangar. The majority of the screens on the wall were still dark, positioned as they were in half-completed wings, or looking onto empty cells, but on the central screen, Eli paced the confines of his unit like a lion tracing the edges of its cage.

To think, none of this would have happened without Eliot Cardale.

Eli Ever.

Stell took up a black business card, turned it absently between his fingers. The word *EON*, ghosted in spot gloss, showed up only when it caught the light.

EON had been Stell's idea, yes, but it was at first a vague proposal, one motivated by his history with Vale and Cardale, by what he'd stopped, but also what he'd failed to. By the fact that ten years ago, Stell had put Victor in jail, and let Eli go free, and because of that choice—that failing to look beyond the obvious, to see through a single deceptive guise—thirty-nine people had died. It haunted him. Plagued him.

There had to be a way—to find EOs, to contain them. Maybe, one day, to use them. EOs were dangerous, yes, some catastrophically so, but what if, among the lost and the deranged, there were those who could be fixed, given purpose, made whole? What if death didn't change a person's nature, only amplified it?

By that logic, a wounded soldier might still want to serve.

That was the focus, the sharp point at the center of Stell's idea. A world where skilled EOs could help stop crimes instead of start them. And where the rest could be contained, kept from committing more atrocities.

A short, bright ring signaled the incoming call.

The curve of screens on Stell's desk lit up.

Stell brushed his fingers through the air, accepting the call, and seconds later a conference room appeared in front of him, five stern figures seated around a long wood desk.

The board of directors.

Three men and two women, all in dark suits—the standard uniform of government agencies and private ones alike. They looked like vague copies of each other. The same dark hair, the same narrow eyes, the same flat expressions.

"Director," said a man in charcoal, "do you care to explain why you removed a valuable test subject from the lab and fired one of our most prominent—not to mention valuable—scientists?"

"He was *dissecting* an EO."

The silence that followed wasn't loaded; on the contrary, it was empty. The members of the board stared at him as if he hadn't answered the question. As if they didn't see the problem.

"Last time I checked," said Stell, knitting his fingers, "I was the director of this institution. Are personnel changes above my pay grade?"

"Of course not, *Director*," said a woman in navy. "You have an intimate understanding of the needs and challenges on the ground. However—"

"EON may be your operation," cut in a man in black, "but we are its bank."

"And as its bank," said the man in charcoal, "we need to know our money is being well spent. In the interest of national security."

That last sentence, like an afterthought. As if the five wolves in dark suits weren't circling in search of profit.

"Haverty's methods may have been questionable," said the woman in navy, "but his research was promising. As for your EO, his ability made him uniquely qualified to undergo that research. Now you have deprived us of both scientist *and* subject."

"Let's discuss the EO," chimed in a new voice, a woman in black. "Eliot Cardale, alias Eli Ever. What have you done with him?"

"He's been relocated to a cell in the containment unit."

"To what end?"

"To *contain* him," said Stell. "Eli Cardale killed nearly forty people."

A man in gray sat forward. "They were almost all EOs, though, weren't they?"

"Is that supposed to make it better?"

The man waved the concern away. "I simply mean, your subject already has a proven skill."

"Killing EOs."

"Tracking them down."

"Isn't that the point of *your* organization?" asked the woman in navy. "To find and *contain* EOs before they can cause harm?"

"It is," said Stell through gritted teeth.

"Then," said the man in black, "I suggest you put him to use."

∞

THE lights went down, and came back up, and Eli was still alone.

A night passed, and no one came to collect him. No one dragged him from the cell. He wondered if this was what Victor's time in prison had felt like, after his arrest. The endless waiting. Entirely alone.

Eli leaned forward, elbows on his knees. He interlaced his fingers, but instead of praying, he stared over the tops of his knuckles at the farthest wall and listened, straining his senses for any clues. He was met only by the dampened silence of nested space.

"Just going to sit around and wait?" chided Victor, there again, haunting Eli. "How complacent."

Eli rose and went to the fiberglass divide, rapped his knuckles on the surface, then pressed his hands flat against it, testing the material.

"I assure you," said a familiar voice, "the cell is stronger than it looks."

The wall cleared, like a curtain dropping all at once from a window, and there, on the other side of the glass, stood Joseph Stell. The last time Eli had seen the cop was at the Falcon Price project, standing over Victor's dead body while a SWAT team dragged Eli away.

"Officer," he said.

"Actually, it's *Director* now."

"Congratulations," said Eli coolly. "Director of what?"

Stell held out his hands. "This place. Your new home. The department of ExtraOrdinary Observation and Neutralization." He stepped up to the glass. "I think you'll admit it's quite an upgrade from your previous circumstances."

"And as *director*, I assume you were responsible for those, too?"

Stell's expression darkened. "I wasn't adequately informed of the lab's methods. Had I been, it wouldn't have been allowed. As soon as I found out, you were extracted, and that branch of testing terminated. If it's any consolation, so was Haverty."

"Consolation . . ." echoed Eli, splaying his fingers across the fiberglass.

"I should warn you," said Stell, "if you try to strike any of these walls, a warning will go off, and the surface will electrify. Try a second time and, well, we both know it won't kill you, but it will hurt."

Eli's hand fell away. "How thorough."

"I underestimated you once, Mr. Cardale. I don't intend to do so again."

"I was never a danger to you, Director Stell. Wouldn't your energy and resources be better spent on EOs who represent a threat to the general public?"

Stell's mouth twitched into a grim smile. "You killed thirty-nine people. That we know of. You are a mass murderer."

The true number was closer to fifty, but Eli didn't say so. Instead, he turned, surveying his cell. "And what did I do to deserve such accommodation?"

Stell produced a simple manila folder and slid it through the slot in the fiberglass. Eli turned back and took it up, flicking through the pages. It was a profile, much like the ones the Merit PD had developed under Eli's instruction.

"You possess a unique and proven skill set," said Stell. "You are here to assist in the tracking and capture of other—"

Eli laughed, short and humorless. "If you wanted me to help you hunt EOs," he sneered, tossing the file onto the table, "you shouldn't have put me in a cell."

"Unlike you, we treat execution as a last resort."

"Half measures, then."

"*Humane* ones."

"Hypocrisy in action." Eli shook his head. "What you're doing, what *EON* is doing, is nothing but a pale version of my own work. So why am I the one in the cell?" Eli stepped as close as the fiberglass would allow. "Disagree with my methods, Stell. Doubt my motives. But you're a fool if you think what you're doing is different. The *only* difference between us is that you naively insist on preserving what I know should be destroyed. You want to pretend that capturing EOs is a mercy. To what end? So you can sleep easier without their blood on your hands? Or so that you can grow your collection of specimens and play God with their bodies? Because I played God once, Stell, and it did not end well." Eli rocked back on his heels. "I spent ten years trying to make amends for that, to undo the damage I wrought. Yes, I killed a great many EOs, but it wasn't out of cruelty or violence, or spite. I did it to protect people—living, innocent humans—from the monsters I'd found in the dark."

"Are you so sure they're *all* monsters?" challenged Stell.

"Yes," he said forcefully. There had been a time when Eli thought himself exempt from that label. Now he knew better. "EOs may look like humans, Stell, but they don't think or act like them."

Victor would have enumerated any number of symptoms— diminished sense of consequence, lack of remorse, self-absorption, amplification of demeanor and aspect—but Eli said only, "They have no soul." He shook his head. "You want to save EOs? Save them from themselves. Put them in the ground, where they belong. Unless that's your plan, I have no intention of helping."

In answer, Stell set another folder in the fiberglass slot between, this one black.

Eli cut a glance at the file. "Didn't you hear me?"

"This isn't another dossier," said Stell. "It's your other option."

Eli glimpsed his own name printed on the front of the file. He didn't reach for it, didn't need to—he knew what it was. What it meant.

"Take a day to think it over," said Stell. "I'll be back tomorrow for your answer."

He retreated, and the wall went solid again in his wake, turning the cell back into a tomb. Eli gritted his teeth. And then he swiped the black folder from the tray and carried it to the table where the thin manila file already waited.

Eli sank into a chair and flicked back the cover. On top was an X-ray, black and white, seemingly innocuous. He flipped past, and saw an MRI, the body lit up in red and blue and green. And then he turned the page again, and his throat constricted at the sight of the first photograph. A man's chest—*Eli's* chest—pried open by metal clamps to reveal ribs, lungs, a beating heart.

Every pre-med student did dissections. Eli had done a dozen his freshman year, peeled and pinned the skin of small animals out of the way to examine the organs beneath. The photos in the black folder reminded him of that. The only difference, of course, was that *Eli* had been alive.

The pain itself was gone, but the memory of it etched along his nerves, echoed through his bones.

Eli wanted to sweep the file from the table, tear it to shreds, but he knew he was being watched—he'd noted the cameras set into the ceiling, imagined Stell standing in some control room, a smug expression on his face. So Eli stayed seated, and turned through every page of the gruesome, graphic record, studying every photograph, every diagram, every scrawled note, every aspect of torture laid out in sterile detail, memorizing the black folder so that he would never have to look at it again.

You're not blessed, or divine, or burdened. You're a science experiment.

Maybe Victor was right.

Maybe Eli was just as broken, just as damned, as every other EO. It was true, he hadn't felt that presence the night he killed Victor. Hadn't felt anything like peace.

But that didn't absolve him of his task.

He still had a purpose. An obligation. To save others, even if he couldn't save himself.

XVI

TWENTY YEARS AGO

THE FIFTH HOME

ELI ran his fingers over the cover of the book.

It was massive, and heavy, and every single page detailed the marvels and miracles of the human body.

"I thought we should get you tickets to a game," said Patrick, "but Lisa insisted—"

"It's perfect," said Eli.

"See?" said Lisa, shouldering Patrick. "He wants to be a doctor. You've got to start young."

"From ministry to medicine," mused Patrick. "John must be rolling in his grave."

Eli laughed, an easy sound, practiced to perfection. The truth was, he didn't see the two avenues as separate. Eli had seen God the day he arrived, in the drawings on his wall; saw Him again now in the pages of this book, in the perfect fit of bones, the vast intricacies of the nervous system, the brain—the spark, like faith, that turned a body into a man.

Patrick shook his head. "What fifteen-year-old boy would rather have a book—"

"Would you rather I asked for a car?" asked Eli, flashing a crooked smile.

Patrick clapped him on the shoulder. These days, Eli didn't flinch.

His attention fell back to the anatomy textbook. Perhaps his interest wasn't strictly normal, but he could afford this small divergence.

At fifteen, the personality he'd crafted was nearly perfect. The day after he arrived, Patrick and Lisa had enrolled him in school, and Eli had realized the hard way that a six-month crash course in normalcy was a pale foundation of what he'd need to survive. But it was a big school, and Eli was a quick study, and soon *charming, focused, clever* had not only been cemented, they'd been joined by *handsome, friendly, athletic*. He ran track and field. He aced his classes. He had a winning smile and an easy laugh, and nobody knew about the scars on his back or the shadows in his past. Nobody knew that it was all an act, that none of it came naturally.

∞

LISA'S laughter rang through the house like bells.

Eli could hear it over the classical music in his earbuds as he did his chemistry homework. A few moments later, Patrick knocked on the doorframe, and Eli hit Pause.

"You guys off?"

"Yeah," said Patrick. "Show starts at seven, so we shouldn't be back late. Don't work too hard."

"Says the professor to the student."

"Hey, studies show that variation is good for retention."

"Come on!" called Lisa.

"I put money on the counter," said Patrick. "At least order a pizza. Steal a beer from the fridge."

"Will do," said Eli absently, already hitting Play.

Patrick said something else, but Eli didn't catch the words over the concerto. At nine, he finished his homework and ate leftovers at the kitchen counter. At ten, he went for a jog. At eleven, he went to bed.

And fifteen minutes later, his cell phone rang, a number he didn't recognize, a voice he didn't know.

"Is this Eliot Cardale?" said a man.

A stillness formed in Eli's chest. Not the kind he'd felt when he pushed his father down the stairs. No, this was colder, heavier. The weight of finding his mother floating in the tub. The exhaustion as he sank like a stone to the chapel floor.

"I'm afraid," continued the man, "there's been an accident."

∞

ELI wondered if *this* was shock. He sat on a flimsy plastic chair, a social worker at his side, the doctor straight ahead, an officer looming like a shadow. The cops had come to the house. Driven him to the hospital, even though there was nothing to see, or do. Dead on arrival. On *impact,* according to the doctor.

"I'm sorry, son," said the cop.

God never gives us more than we can bear.

Eli laced his fingers, bowed his head.

It's up to us to find the purpose in the pain.

"The driver didn't survive," continued the cop. "Toxicology's still out but we think he was drunk."

"How did they die?"

Eli realized, too late, that he'd asked the wrong question. A shadow crossed the doctor's face.

"I'm sorry," he said quickly. "I didn't—it's just—I'm going to be a surgeon, one day. I want to *save* lives. I just—I need to understand." He balled his hands into fists. "If you don't tell me, I'll lie awake, wondering. I think I would rather know."

The doctor sighed. "Patrick suffered a cervical fracture of C2 and C3," he said, touching the bones at the top of his own neck. "Lisa sustained a massive concussion, which resulted in an intracranial hemorrhage. In both cases, it would have been nearly instantaneous."

Eli was glad they hadn't suffered. "All right," he said. "Thank you."

"They didn't name a guardian," said the social worker. "Do you know if there's someone you can stay with? Until we get things sorted out?"

"Yes," he lied, digging out his phone. "I'll call a friend."

Eli rose and walked a little ways down the hall, but didn't bother dialing. There was no phone tree this time. And no point in pretending. Eli was popular, well liked, but he had always been careful to keep a measure of distance. Too close, and someone might see the seams in his facade, the subtle but constant effort of pretending. Better to be friendly, without being friends.

Eli returned to the social worker and the cop. The doctor had left. "I need to get some things from my place," he said. "Could you drop me off there?"

He let himself into the house, listened to the sound of the patrol car pulling away before he closed the door. He stood for several long seconds in the darkened hall.

And then turned and slammed his fist into the wall.

Pain flashed through Eli's hand, up his arm, and he hit the wall again and again until his knuckles split open, and blood dripped down his wrist, and he could breathe.

His legs folded under him, and Eli sank to the floor.

After everything, he was alone again.

God never gives us more than we can bear.

Eli told himself there was a plan, even if he couldn't see it. There was a purpose to the pain. He stared down at his bloody hand.

Stupid, he thought.

It would be hard to hide from the inevitable social workers, the school, the hundred eyes bound to latch on to every misstep, every crack in his persona.

Eli got up and went to the bathroom, rinsed the split knuckles under the sink and bandaged his hand with calm precision and steady fingers. He met his gaze in the mirror and forced the lines of his face back into their proper order.

And then Eli went to his room and began to pack.

NINETEEN YEARS AGO
THE SIXTH AND FINAL HOME

"Here we go."

Eli stood in the doorway, holding a box of books. The room was simple, empty save for a window, a narrow bed, and a desk.

"Bit sparse, I know," said the landlord, who insisted he call her Maggie. "But the windows are double glazed and the shower down the hall is hot." She gave him a measuring look. "Awfully young to be living on your own, aren't you?"

"I'm emancipated," explained Eli.

It had been the easiest route. He was nearly sixteen. Not many people wanted to take in a teenage boy, and Eli had no interest in becoming a ward of the state. His parents were dead. Patrick and Lisa were dead. The former had left him only scars, but the latter had left him some money—not much, but enough to cover living expenses so he could focus on finishing high school. Get into a good college.

"Thanks, Maggie," he said, crossing the threshold.

"All right, Eliot. You let me know if you need anything."

The wood floor creaked under her feet as she ambled off, creaked under his as he set the box on the desk and unpacked, arranging his schoolbooks in a neat stack.

"We are so sorry, Eliot," the principal had said.

"We have counselors," added the dean of students.

"Let us know how we can help," echoed his teachers.

"Please," Eli had begged them each in turn, "don't tell anyone."

Normal was such a fragile thing, so easily upset by even good intentions.

And so, under the guise of him wanting to grieve in peace, they kept his secret.

Eli unpacked the last two books—the battered Bible and the anatomy text. He set King James aside and sank into the chair, drawing the textbook closer.

It's up to us, he thought, *to find the purpose in the pain . . .*

Eli opened the heavy tome and paged through until he found the drawings of the head, and neck, the tracery of the brain, the delicate column of the spine.

Find the purpose.

He began to take notes.

XVII

FOUR YEARS AGO

EON

WHEN Stell returned the next day, Eli didn't look up.

He kept his head bowed over the file he was studying, had been studying for the better part of the night.

"I see you've decided to cooperate."

Eli gathered the papers back into a shallow stack. "I need a computer," he said.

"Absolutely not," said Stell.

Eli rose from the chair and carried the file to the fiberglass divide. "I spent *months* researching my targets. Confirming their abilities. Tracking their movements." He let the file fall from his fingers, paper sloughing to the floor. "You want me to do the same work from inside a concrete box, with nothing but basic information. This," he said, gesturing to the pages at his feet, "is not enough."

"It's what we have."

"Then you're not looking hard enough," snapped Eli. He turned his attention to a photo on the floor. "Tabitha Dahl," he said, scanning the paper. "Nineteen. College athlete, young, social, active, adventurer. Suffers a massive cardiac event due to an allergic reaction while hiking. Friend is able to resuscitate her. She makes it to a hospital. And then—she disappears. Parents file a missing persons report two weeks ago." Eli looked up. "Where would she go? How would she get there? Why is there nothing here about the friend she was with? How did she think and feel in the direct aftermath of her accident?"

"How are we supposed to obtain that kind of information?" asked Stell.

Eli threw up his hands. "She's nineteen. Start with social media. Hack the texts she sent to friends. Get into her life. Get into her head. An EO isn't just the product of their catalyst. They are the product of the person they were before. The circumstances, but also the psyche. I can help you find Tabitha Dahl. With the right insight, I can probably make a decent guess as to her power, but I can't do any of that with five pieces of paper."

A long silence followed. Eli waited patiently for Stell to break it. He did.

"I'll get you a computer," he said. "But access will be restricted, and the system will be twinned. I will see everything you search, as you search it. And the moment you go off-book, you will lose more than just your tech privileges. Are we clear?"

"I could do more than postulate," said Eli, kneeling to retrieve the papers. "If you let me out . . ."

"Mr. Cardale," said Stell. "I want to make something very clear. You can help us from inside this cell, or from inside a lab, but you will never, *ever* see the outside of this facility again."

Eli rose to his feet, but the director was already walking away.

XVIII

SEVENTEEN YEARS AGO

HAVERFORD COLLEGE

ELI made his way across campus, his collar up against the fall chill.

Haverford was a good school—not the best, but certainly the best he could afford, and close enough to commute from the boardinghouse. It was also massive, sporting a population that could rival most towns', and a campus so large that two months in, he was still discovering buildings.

Maybe that was why he hadn't seen the chapel sooner.

Or maybe, until now, the trees had simply hidden it, red and gold leaves obscuring the classic lines, the simple spire, the sloping white roof.

Eli's steps slowed at the sight of it. But he didn't turn around. The pull was subtle, but persistent, and he let himself be drawn to the steps.

He hadn't set foot inside a church in years, not since God became more . . . personal.

Now, as he stepped through the doors, the first thing he saw was the stained glass. Red and blue and green light dancing on the floor. And there, before the window, a stone cross. His palms began to tingle. Eli closed his eyes, willing back the memory of a deep voice, the whistle of the leather belt.

"Amazing, isn't it?" said an airy voice.

Eli blinked, and glanced sideways, and saw a girl. Slim and pretty, with wide brown eyes and honey blond hair.

"I've never been religious," continued the girl, "but I love the look of the buildings. You?"

"I'm not big on the buildings," he said with a wry smile, "but I've always been religious."

She pouted, shook her head. "Oh no, it will never work between us." The false sadness broke back into a smile. "Sorry, didn't mean to interrupt, you just looked sad."

"Did I?" Eli must have slipped, let the truth show through. But in an instant, he'd recovered, and turned the full force of his attention, and his practiced charm, on the girl. "Were you studying me instead of the building?"

Light danced in the girl's eyes. "I'm more than capable of admiring both." She held out her hand. "I'm Charlotte."

He smiled. "Eli." The bells rang once around them, and Eli held out his hand. "Have you had lunch?"

***

MAGGIE had appeared in the doorway of Eli's room the week before, a basket of laundry on her hip. "It's Friday night, Eliot."

"And?"

"And you're sitting in here doing calculus."

"Biology," he'd corrected.

Maggie had shaken her head. "All this work and no fun, for a boy your age, it's not normal."

That word. *Normal.* The center line of his calibration.

Eli had looked up from his homework. "What *should* I be doing?" he asked, one eyebrow raised to hide the earnestness of the question.

"Go to parties!" said Maggie. "Drink cheap beer! Make bad choices! Date pretty girls!"

He leaned back in his chair. "Do pretty girls count as bad choices, or are those two separate things?"

Maggie rolled her eyes and walked away, and Eli turned back to his paper, but he'd taken the words to heart. He'd gone to one or two frat parties, plastered on a lazy smile and sipped awful beer (which honestly felt like a bad choice).

But now, he had Charlotte.

A relationship, Eli had learned, was a universal shorthand for *normal*. A societal stamp of approval. Dating Charlotte Shelton in particular was more like a gold seal. She was old money, the breeding so deep she didn't even notice it lining her every seam.

She was cheerful, and pretty, and spoiled—she lived in the school dormitories, but only because she wanted an *authentic* college experience. Not that that desire for authenticity extended much beyond a single twin bed and a communal hall.

Charlotte came to Eli's boardinghouse once, and only once, and on her insistence. She knew he was an orphan (a word that seemed to generate in her an intense protective instinct), but the threadbare truth wasn't as romantic. He'd seen the pity masquerading as sympathy.

"I don't love you for your *stuff*," she'd insisted. "I have enough stuff for the both of us."

But after that, they didn't *share* a life—Charlotte just pulled Eli into hers.

And he let her.

It was easy.

It was simple.

She adored him.

And he enjoyed the attention.

Charlotte liked to say they were a perfect fit. Eli knew they weren't, but only he could see the jagged sides, the empty spaces.

"How do I look?" she asked as they climbed the steps to her parents' house—mansion—for Thanksgiving, sophomore year.

"Stunning," said Eli automatically, pairing the word with a wink.

Charlotte fixed his tie. She ran her fingers through his dark hair, and he let her, his own hand grazing the bottom of her chin, tipping her face up for a kiss.

"Don't be nervous," she whispered.

Eli wasn't.

The door swung open, and he turned, half expecting to see a butler, a grim old man in coattails, but instead he found an elegant, older version of Charlotte.

"You must be Eli!" said the woman brightly as a slim, stern man in a well-tailored suit appeared at her back.

"Thank you for having me," said Eli, holding out a pie.

"Of course," said Mrs. Shelton warmly. "When Charlotte said you didn't have plans, we insisted."

"Plus," said Mr. Shelton, shooting Charlotte a look, "it's about time we meet the boy our girl's been so taken with." They started down the hall, Charlotte and her mother arm in arm.

"Eli," said Mr. Shelton, putting a hand on his shoulder, "why don't I give you a tour while the ladies catch up."

It wasn't a question.

"Of course," said Eli, falling in step behind the man, who led him through a pair of doors into a private study. "This," he said, "is really the only room that matters."

He opened a cabinet and poured himself a drink.

"I can see why Charlotte likes you," he said, leaning back against his desk. "She's always had a weakness for charity cases. Especially handsome ones."

Eli stilled, his easy manner stiffening a fraction. "Sir, if you think I'm with Charlotte for her money or her station—"

"The truth doesn't matter, Mr. Cardale, only the optics. And they don't look good. I've done my homework on you. So much tragedy— you handle it with poise. While I admire how far you've come, the fact is, you're tracking mud into my home."

Eli's teeth clicked together. "We can't shape our past," he said. "Only our future."

Charlotte's father smiled. "Well put. And that's what I'm offering you. A bright future. Just not with my daughter. I've seen your grades. You're a smart young man, Eliot. Ambitious, too, Charlotte tells me. You want to be a doctor. Haverford is a decent college, but it's not the best. I know you got into other schools. Better schools. I assume you couldn't afford them."

Eli stared, amazed. He was being *bribed*.

Mr. Shelton pushed off the desk. "I know you care about my daughter. Hell, you might even think you love her . . ."

But Eli didn't.

If Mr. Shelton was better at reading people—or if Eli hadn't made himself so hard to read—he might have seen the simple truth. That Eli didn't need persuading. That Charlotte Shelton had always been, for him, a vehicle. A way to move through the world on an upward trajectory. What her father was now offering, *if* he was truly offering it, was a true chance for meaningful change, a great gain for a minor loss.

But what came next was a delicate maneuver.

"Mr. Shelton," started Eli, contorting his face with an aspect of tightly controlled defiance. "Your daughter and I—"

The man held up a hand. "Before you play the noble card, and insist you can't be bought, remember that you are both very young, and love is fickle, and whatever you have with Charlotte might feel real, but it won't last."

Eli exhaled, and looked down, as if ashamed. Let his features settle into a semblance of resignation. "What would you have me do, sir?"

"Tonight? Nothing. Enjoy your dinner. In a few days? Break things off. Pick one of those better schools. Chester, or Lockland. Transfer. The tuition won't be a problem."

"Boys!" called Mrs. Shelton from the kitchen. "Turkey's ready."

Mr. Shelton clapped Eli on the shoulder. "Come on," he said cheerfully. "I'm starving."

"Dad," warned Charlotte when they met her in the dining room. "Did you put him through the wringer?"

"Just a little." Mr. Shelton kissed his daughter on the cheek. "It's my duty to put the fear of God into whoever you bring home."

She turned her warm brown gaze on Eli. "I hope he wasn't being too rough on you."

Eli laughed softly and shook his head. "Not at all."

They took their seats, the table falling to easy conversation—so much spoken, so little said—as they passed platters and bowls.

And as Eli and Charlotte walked back to their car that night, she slipped her arm through his. "Everything okay?"

Eli glanced back at the front door, where Mr. Shelton stood watching. "Yes," he said, kissing her temple. "Everything's perfect."

XIX

TWO YEARS AGO

EON

ELI ran his fingers along the shelf where he kept the old case files. His own black folder sat like a stain at the edge of the row, a punctuation mark shifted to fit the growing sentence. Nineteen EOs tracked, hunted, captured, over a period of less than two years. Not bad, considering his limitations.

Eli had insisted on keeping the old folders, telling Stell that past work would inform future cases.

It was a partial truth—there were indeed patterns between EOs, shared traits, the same shadow cast over different faces. But the larger truth was simple: Eli found the markers satisfying. Not as satisfying as wrapping his hands around an EO's throat, feeling a pulse falter and still beneath his fingers. But an echo of that old calm still accompanied each closed case, the pleasant sense of things askew being set right.

There was another facet to the collection, a grim truth laid bare in the sheer number of folders.

"What have we done?" Eli muttered to himself.

But it was Victor who answered.

"What makes you think *we* did anything?"

He looked up and saw the thin blond ghost leaning back against the fiberglass wall.

"The number of EOs," said Eli, gesturing to the shelf, "it's skyrocketed over the last decade. What if we did something? What if we tore something in the fabric of the world? What if we set something in motion?"

Victor rolled his eyes. "We are not gods, Eli."

"But we *played* God."

"What if *God* played God?" Victor pushed off the wall. "What if EOs were part of His plan? What if these people, the ones you've spent your life slaughtering, were *supposed* to come back the way they did? What if you've been attempting to undo the very work of that higher power you worship?"

"Don't you ever wonder if it's our fault?"

Victor tipped his head. "Tell me, is it blasphemy, or simply arrogance, taking credit for God's work?"

Eli shook his head. "You've never understood."

Footsteps sounded nearby.

The wall went clear.

"Who are you talking to?" asked Stell.

"Myself," muttered Eli, waving Victor's ghost away like a wisp of smoke. "I've been thinking more about that electrokinetic teen . . ." He looked up. Stell was dressed for fieldwork, his broad frame cinched into a reinforced black suit.

"How did the extraction go?" asked Eli, managing to keep most of the disdain out of his voice. He'd spent two weeks researching the EO—Helen Andreas, forty-one, with the ability to disassemble and rebuild structures with a single touch. Eli had given EON's agents as much insight as he could, considering the confines of his situation.

"Not well," said Stell darkly. "Andreas was dead when we got there."

Eli frowned. EOs, despite their destructive tendencies, rarely veered toward suicide. Their sense of self-preservation was too strong. "Was it an accident?"

"Not likely," said Stell, holding a photo up to the fiberglass. In it, Andreas lay on the ground, blood pooling beneath her and a small dark circle burrowed into her forehead.

"Interesting," said Eli. "Any leads?"

"No . . ." Stell hesitated. There was something he wasn't saying. Eli waited him out. After a long moment, the man finally went on. "This wasn't an isolated incident. Two months ago, another suspected EO was found in the same way, in the basement of a club." Stell slid both pages through the slot. "Will Connelly. We were still monitoring him, since we didn't have enough data to construe the exact nature of his ability and assess his priority level, but we had suspected it was regenerative. Obviously not a power as efficient as your own, but something like it. At the time we assumed his death was a one-off, a run-in with the wrong people, someone to whom he owed a debt. Now . . ."

"Once is chance, twice, coincidence," said Eli. "Collect a third, and you have a pattern." He looked up from the paper. "The weapon?"

"Unregistered."

"Keep the ballistics on file anyway. If he—or she—is actively hunting EOs, it's only a matter of time before they strike again. In fact," continued Eli, "pull every killing that matches this style of execution over the last . . ."—Eli considered—"three years."

"Three? That's an oddly specific number."

And it was. Three years—that was how long Eli had been at EON. That was how long he'd been out of work. If there had been another hunter during his tenure, he would have known.

Which meant someone new had taken his place.

XX

SIXTEEN YEARS AGO

LOCKLAND UNIVERSITY

ELI arrived at Lockland nearly a week before the start of the spring semester.

He hadn't picked just *any* school—if Charlotte's father was picking up the tab, Eli intended to stretch the bill. Lockland was one of the best-ranked programs in the country. Now, he crossed the intimate campus, savoring the quiet stretches of lawn. It was a solid week before classes were due to start, and the place was luxuriously empty.

But his heart sank when he reached the dorms. He'd been hoping for a solo suite. Instead, he found a different setup: two desks, two beds, one window halfway between them. One of the beds was empty. On the other, a lean figure had stretched out, one arm behind his head, the other holding up a book.

At the sound of Eli's approach, the book fell away, revealing a slim face, wolfish blue eyes, and lank blond hair.

"You must be Eliot."

"Eli," he corrected, setting his backpack on the floor.

The other boy swung his legs off the bed and stood. He was an inch or two taller than Eli, but all angles, edges.

"Victor," he said, slipping his hands into his pockets. "Vale."

Eli cracked a smile. "Name like that, you should be a superhero."

Victor gestured down at himself. He was dressed in black jeans and a black polo. "Can you really see me in spandex?" The blue eyes flicked toward Eli's single suitcase, the box balanced on top. "You travel light."

Eli nodded at Victor's own side of the room. "You came early."

Victor shrugged. "Family is best in small doses."

Eli wasn't sure how to answer that, so he said nothing. The silence stretched between them, and then Victor cocked his head in a lupine way and said, "Are you hungry?"

∞

VICTOR speared another piece of broccoli.

"So, what are you studying?"

They were sitting in a large dining hall on campus, the restaurant stations along the wall each a capsule of a food culture.

"Pre-med," answered Eli.

"You too?" Victor stabbed a strip of beef. "And what brings you to the discipline?" His eyes flicked up and Eli felt . . . exposed. It was unsettling, the way that pale gaze bored into him. Not curious so much as cutting.

Eli looked down at his own food. "Same as most," he said. "I guess I felt a calling. You?"

"It seemed like an obvious fit," said Victor. "I've always been good at math and science, anything that can be distilled down into equations, cause and effect, absolutes."

Eli twirled pasta on his fork. "But medicine doesn't adhere to absolutes. Life isn't an equation. A person is more than the sum of their parts."

"Are they?" asked Victor. His expression was steady, his voice flat.

It was maddening—Eli was so used to disarming people, coaxing them into feeding him emotional cues, giving him something to play against.

But Victor showed no interest in playing.

"Of course," pressed Eli. "The parts themselves—muscle, organ, bone, blood—make a *body,* not a person. Without a divine spark, without a soul, they are only so much meat."

Victor clicked his tongue in disapproval. "You're religious, then."

"I believe in God," said Eli steadily.

"Well," said Victor, nudging away his plate. "You can live in the heavens. I'll take the earthly sphere."

A girl appeared, dropping into the seat beside Victor. "What have we here?" She mussed his fair hair with an ease clearly born of habit. Interesting. Victor didn't strike Eli as the type to welcome casual contact, but he didn't pull away, only favored her with a bored smile.

"Angie," said Victor, "meet Eli."

She flashed him a smile, and Eli felt like a mirror turned toward the sun, relieved to have a source of light he could reflect.

"We were just discussing God's place in medicine," said Victor. "Care to weigh in?"

"I'll pass." She plucked a piece of broccoli from his plate.

"It's rude to steal food."

"You never finish anything. Didn't your parents teach you to eat your vegetables?"

"No," said Victor blandly, "they told me to tap into my inner psyche and realize the truths of my potential. Vegetables never really came up."

Angie shot Eli a conspiratorial glance. "Victor's parents are self-help gurus."

"Victor's parents," said Victor, "are hacks."

Angie laughed, a small, affectionate sound. "You're such a weirdo sometimes."

"Only sometimes?" asked Victor. "I'll have to try harder." Those blue eyes flicked to Eli. "Normal is overrated."

Eli tensed—a small, inward clenching that didn't reach his face. *Normal is overrated.* Spoken like someone who didn't have to work so hard at it. Who hadn't needed *normal* to survive.

Victor cleared his throat. "Angie here is the brightest light in our engineering department."

She rolled her eyes. "Victor's too proud to fish for praise, but he's top of the pre-med class."

"But you haven't heard," said Victor soberly. "Eli here is going to give me a run for my money."

Angie eyed him with newfound interest. "Is that so?"

Eli smiled. "I'll do my best."

XXI

TWO YEARS AGO

EON

"YOU were right," said Stell.

Eli rose from his cot. "Don't sound so disappointed."

"We pulled the execution-style killings, then ran those deaths through our system to see if any of them had EO markers." Stell fed a piece of paper through the slot in the wall. "Meet Justin Gladwell."

Eli took it, staring down at the sparsely detailed profile, the mug shot of a man in his thirties with a two-day-old shadow. "Gunned down nearly a year ago. Abilities unknown. He wasn't even on our radar."

"They're outpacing you," said Eli, spreading the three profiles on his table. Justin Gladwell. Will Connelly. Helen Andreas. "Congratulations. You appear to have a new hunter."

"And you," said Stell, "appear to have a copycat."

Eli bristled a little. He didn't care for the idea of a surrogate. "No," he said, considering the series of corpses. "I would have tailored their deaths to suit. Would have made it look . . . organic. This person . . ."—he rapped his fingers on the table—"is preoccupied by something else."

"What do you mean?"

"I mean," said Eli, "that the killer clearly sees the executions as necessary, but I doubt it's their sole objective."

"We need to find this person as soon as possible," said Stell.

"You want me to hunt a hunter."

Stell raised a brow. "Is that going to be a problem?"

"On the contrary," said Eli. "I've been waiting for a challenge." He crossed his arms, studying the pictures. "One thing's almost certain."

"What's that?"

"Your hunter is an EO."

Stell stiffened. "How do you know?"

"Well, I don't *know*," said Eli. "I can only hypothesize. But what are the odds of an ordinary human successfully executing three distinct EOs without the slightest signs of resistance?" Eli held Gladwell's photograph up to the fiberglass. "A single, consistently positioned, point-blank headshot, in all three cases. A level of accuracy that means one of two things—either the shooter is an expert marksman, or the victims didn't put up a fight. Blood spray suggests they were conscious and upright when they were shot. Which means they simply stood there. Do you know many *ordinary* people who could convince or compel a person to go so willingly to their death?"

Eli didn't wait for an answer. He shook his head, studying the pictures, his thoughts turning. One week. Two months. Nine months.

"These killings are far apart," he mused. "Which suggests that either your hunter isn't very good at finding EOs, *or* they're not looking for *all* EOs."

"You think they're targeting specific people?"

"Or specific abilities," said Eli.

"Any ideas?"

Eli steepled his fingers.

Determining an EO's abilities postmortem was an impossible task. Abilities were hyperspecific, informed not only by the way in which the EO died, but also by their reason for wanting to live. He could speculate—but Eli hated speculating. It was dangerous, and inefficient. Educated guesswork was still guesswork, not a substitute for firsthand experience. Paper clues could only tell you so much—look at Sydney and Serena Clarke. The same near-death experience—a deep plunge in a frozen lake—resulting in two wildly disparate abilities. People were individual. Their psychology was specific. The trick, then, was to aim for vague shapes. Focus only on the outlines, the broadest conditions, and collect enough of those that he could find the pattern, the picture.

"Give me everything you can on these three," he said, sweeping his hand over the photos. "They may be dead, but that doesn't mean they don't still have secrets to tell."

Eli pointed at a box by Stell's feet. "What are those?"

Stell nudged it with his shoe. "These," he said, "are all the execution-style killings that fit the hunter's MO, but *not* the EO profile."

Humans. Of course. He hadn't considered that the hunter's scope might go beyond EOs. But that was because his own hadn't. What a careless assumption. "Can I see them?"

The box was too big for the fiberglass cubby, so Stell had to feed the papers through, a handful at a time. "What are you thinking?" Stell asked as Eli set the ream of paper on the table.

The dots floated in his mind, shifting as he tried to find the lines between them. "There's a pattern here," said Eli. "I haven't found it yet, but I will."

XXII

FIFTEEN YEARS AGO

LOCKLAND UNIVERSITY

"**TO** see a world in a grain of sand . . ."

Thunder rumbled in the distance, the clouds flushing blue. It was the start of senior year, and after unpacking, they'd gone up on the roof to watch the storm roll in.

". . . and Heaven in a wildflower," continued Eli.

He lifted his palm until it seemed to rest just beneath the lightning.

"Hold infinity in the palm of your hand . . ."

"Honestly, Eli," said Victor, perching on one of the folding chairs that scattered the makeshift patio, "spare me the scripture."

Eli's hand fell away. "It's not the Bible," he said testily. "It's Blake. Get some culture." He swept the bottle of scotch away from Victor. "And the point holds. There is no harm in seeing a creator behind the creation."

"There is when you purport to study *science*."

Eli shook his head. Victor didn't understand—would never understand—that it wasn't a matter of faith *or* science. The two were inextricable.

Eli took a cautious sip from the stolen bottle and sank into a second chair as the storm crept closer. It was their first night back, the first night in their new shared apartment. Victor had spent his summer avoiding his parents on some remote family vacation while getting a head start on organic chemistry. Eli had spent his at Lockland, interning under Professor Lyne. He cut a sideways glance at his friend, who was sitting forward, elbows on his knees, his attention seemingly transfixed on the distant lightning.

Initially, Victor had presented a dilemma. Eli Cardale's persona, so carefully constructed over the last decade, found little audience with his sober new roommate. There was no need for a steady smile, affability, the practiced ease. There was no point to them, not when Victor seemed so utterly disinterested. No, *disinterested* was the wrong word—Victor's attention was constant, acute—but the more charming Eli tried to be, the less Victor responded to it. In fact, he seemed *annoyed* by the effort. As if Victor knew it was just that. An effort. A show. Eli found himself culling the unnecessary trappings, trimming his persona down to the essentials.

And when he did that, Victor warmed.

Turned toward Eli like a face toward a mirror. Like to like. It frightened and thrilled Eli, to be seen, and to see himself reflected. Not *all* of himself—they were still so different—but there was something vital, a core of the same precious metal glinting through the rock.

Lightning flashed arterial lines of blue over the rooftop, and seconds later, the world around them shook with a concussive force. Eli felt the tremor through his bones. He loved storms—they made him feel small, a single stitch in a vast pattern, a drop of water in a downpour.

Moments later, the rain began to fall.

In seconds, the first drops became a downpour.

"Shit," muttered Victor, springing up from his seat.

He jogged toward the roof door.

Eli rose, but didn't follow. Within seconds he was soaked through.

"You coming?" shouted Victor over the rain.

"You go ahead," said Eli, the downpour erasing his voice. He tipped his head back and let himself be swallowed by the storm.

An hour later, Eli padded barefoot across the apartment, dripping rainwater in his wake.

Victor's door was closed, the lights out.

After reaching his room, Eli peeled off his soaked clothes and sank into his chair as the storm faded beyond the windows.

Two in the morning, classes starting the next day, but sleep still eluded him.

His cell phone sat on the desk, a handful of texts from Angie, but Eli wasn't in the mood for that, and anyhow, she was probably asleep by now. He ran a hand through his damp hair, slicking it back, and tapped his computer awake.

Something stuck with him, from the roof. The image of the lightning in his palm. Eli had spent the better part of the summer studying electromagnetism in the human body. The literal and metaphorical spark of life. Now, drifting in that exhausted early-hours space, the darkened room and the artificial light of the laptop keeping him conscious if not fully awake, his fingers slid over the keyboard, and he began to search.

For what, he wasn't exactly sure.

One screen, one page, one site, gave way to another, Eli's attention wandering between articles and essays and forums like a mind lost in a dream. But Eli wasn't lost. He was just trying to find the thread. He'd encountered a theory, some weeks before, on another insomniac night. Over the last month, it had grown roots, fed on his focus.

Eli still didn't know what made him click that first link. Victor would have blamed idle curiosity, or fatigue, but in Eli's trancelike state it felt eerily familiar. A hand resting over his own. A blessing. A push.

The theory Eli had discovered was this: that sudden, extreme trauma could lead to a cataclysmic, even permanent shift in physical nature and ability. That through life-or-death trauma, people could be rewired, remade.

It was pseudoscience at best.

But pseudoscience wasn't *automatically* wrong. It was simply a theory that hadn't been adequately proven. What if it could be? After all, people in duress did extraordinary things. Claimed feats of strength, moments of heightened ability. Was the leap so extreme? Could something happen in that life-or-death moment, that tunnel between darkness and light? Was it madness, to believe? Or arrogance, to not?

The page loaded, and Eli's heart quickened as he stared at the word across the top of the screen.

ExtraOrdinary.

XXIII

ONE AND A HALF YEARS AGO

EON

ELI knelt on the cell floor, a dozen pages spread before him. He'd narrowed the massive stack of killings to thirty. And then twenty. And now, at last, to six.

Malcolm Jones. Theodore Goslin. Ian Hausbender. Amy Tao. Alice Clayton. Ethan Barrymore.

Three drug dealers, two doctors, and a pharmacist.

He slipped the first three pages through the slot. "Run the ballistics in these against your executed EOs."

Stell turned through the papers. "There are a hundred gang and cartel killings in this pile. Why these three?"

"A magician doesn't reveal his secrets," said Eli blandly.

"And you're not a magician—you're a murderer."

Eli sighed. "How could I forget?" He nodded at the massive stack from which he'd culled the six names. "There are a hundred and seven gang and cartel killings in there, to be exact. Eighty-three of which we can rule out because they don't fit the clean point-blank execution model I requested. Of the remaining twenty-four, fourteen had records for specializing in illegal weapons, ten in pharmaceuticals. Given the fact that your target has used the same gun for each and every execution, I decided to assume this wasn't about acquiring weapons. We can narrow the list down even further because Jones's, Goslin's, and Hausbender's executions all involved other victims, which, in addition to furthering my theory that the man you're looking for is using a supernatural method of compulsion on his victims, negates the need for multiple samples from each scene, rendering three out of the original ten."

"You're sure it's a man?"

"I'm not *sure* of anything," said Eli, "but the odds favor a male killer. Female killers are rarer, and they tend to prefer more hands-on methods."

"And you think he's after drug dealers?" asked Stell.

Eli shook his head. "I think he's after *drugs*." He retrieved the other three profiles from the floor. "My theory is that your killer is either an addict, or very sick. Which brings me to these. Amy Tao, Alice Clayton, and Ethan Barrymore. The first two are doctors, the third is a pharmacist."

Stell paced beyond the fiberglass wall. "And the dead EOs? How do they factor in?"

"I stand by my theory that our hunter was—and probably still is—targeting specific abilities. Andreas's was destructive, but also restorative. Connelly's regenerative."

"Which supports your theory that he's sick."

There was, thought Eli, a grudging respect in Stell's voice.

"It's still only a theory," he demurred. "Let's start by confirming the ballistics."

∞

THE results came back two days later.

Alice Clayton and Malcolm Jones.

A doctor and a drug dealer, added to the tally of three dead EOs.

Eli's picture was growing. But it was still missing something.

He kept coming back to the gun.

Their hunter was methodical, precise—he had to know that varying the style of execution would have helped cover the trail. And yet he'd chosen to maintain a single technique. There were reasons people adhered to such a pattern—sometimes it was a signature, other times a matter of comfort, or precision, but in this case Eli had a feeling that the killer didn't want to get their hands dirty. Shooting was cold, efficient, and distant. But it was also clean. Sterile. It could be done at a distance, with no risk of biological data at the scene. The killer's choice of weapon, despite the drawbacks of pattern, suggested they cared more about maintaining their own anonymity than hiding the trail of bodies. Which in turn suggested that the killer's DNA was already in the system.

An EO who was known to authorities.

Eli's pulse quickened as pieces clicked together in the back of his mind.

It was madness. Irrational. Impulsive. But Eli felt again that gentle pressure at his back, guiding him forward as he booted the computer and started searching for strange or sudden deaths in the practicing medical field.

Eli spent the next forty-eight sleepless hours skimming every database and obit and news story. He knew he was making leaps instead of strides, but the ground was smooth and sloped beneath his feet. So instead of catching himself, Eli let gravity do the work.

And then, finally, he found an obituary for Dr. Adam Porter. A leading neurologist, discovered dead after hours at a private practice. It had been a heart attack, according to the coroner's report, but not at his desk, or on the way to his car, or safely at home. No, the body had been found on the hospital linoleum floor, next to a smoking MRI, its power blown.

A freak accident.

A massive current.

The patient records from that night were missing, a neat hole carved out in a busy schedule, but Eli could read the outline by the edges it left behind.

He knew the shape.

He'd seen it before.

Angie's body, twisted on the floor of the lab at Lockland, her back arched, mouth open, the last seconds of her life immortalized by pain.

A heart attack, they'd said.

A freak accident.

A massive current.

And at the center of both, an EO with the skill to hunt, the ability to manipulate his victim's bodies. Someone already in the system—because they were supposed to be dead.

"I killed you," muttered Eli.

Victor appeared again, as if summoned. Cold blue eyes and a cunning smirk. "You did."

"Then how?"

"Do you really need to ask?"

Eli clenched his teeth.

Sydney Clarke.

Serena had insisted on dispatching her little sister herself. Obviously her resolve had wavered. Sydney was still alive.

The girl who had a nasty habit of bringing people *back*. And of bringing EOs back wrong, too. Eli had seen it for himself when Sydney resurrected one of his prior kills, sent him back like a toy on the fritz, a note from Victor in hand.

I made a friend.

Now Eli got to his feet and looked up into the nearest camera. "Stell?" he asked, first quietly, and then louder.

A cool voice responded via the intercom. "The director is unavailable."

"When will he be back?" he demanded, but the voice didn't answer.

Eli bristled. He needed to see Stell, needed to look him in the eyes, ask him how he could be so stupid, ask him why he didn't burn the body.

He looked around for something to use, some way to get the director's attention.

But everything was bolted down. Except, of course, for him. He slammed his fist into the fiberglass wall.

There was a low tone as the walls began to charge.

"Inmate," ordered the disembodied voice. "Stand down."

Eli did not. He hit the fiberglass a second time. An alarm went off, and an instant later, a burst of electricity shot up Eli's arm and sent him staggering backward, his pulse losing rhythm for a single measure before it settled. He started toward the wall a third time, but before his fist connected, the lights cut out, and Eli was plunged into absolute black.

The sensory deprivation was so sudden, the darkness was so absolute, Eli felt like he was falling. He reached out to brace himself and stumbled, searched several seconds for the metal chair before sinking into it to wait.

Why didn't you burn the body?

Why didn't you . . .

But as Eli sat in the dark, playing the question over and over in his mind, he felt that invisible hand, the one that had been a guide for so long, now pulling him back. If Eli gave Victor over to Stell, over to EON, they would take him *alive*. Put him in a cell. No. Eli would not—could not—allow those half measures. Victor was too dangerous, he had to be put down, and Stell had already failed once.

Eli wouldn't entrust the task to him a second time.

The lights came up, the far wall went clear, and the director stormed into sight, dressed in a tailored black suit, his tie loose at the throat.

"What the hell?" demanded Stell. "You better have something groundbreaking after that stunt."

Eli faltered for only a second, then straightened, committed to his course.

"Actually," he said coldly. "I hit a *dead end*."

It wasn't a lie.

Suspicion flickered across Stell's face. "That's surprising, given how you've spent the last week. You seemed to be making strides."

Eli swore inwardly. He'd been so stunned by the discovery, so eager for the confrontation, and so startled by his own recanting, he hadn't considered the ramifications of changing his mind. The whiplash. A break in the pattern.

"Where did it fall apart?" pressed Stell.

"It hasn't," said Eli. "I just don't have any more leads."

"Then why the *fuck* did you call for me?" demanded the director.

Eli had made a mistake. He wasn't prone to making mistakes, except where Victor Vale was concerned. Victor had always possessed the unnerving ability to get under Eli's skin, interrupt his focus. And now Eli needed to disrupt Stell's own, find a way to redirect his attention, twist suspicion into . . . something easier. Anger—that was such a loud emotion.

"I guess," said Eli, infusing his voice with as much derision as he could muster, "I wanted to see what you would do. Now I know."

Stell looked at him, mouth open in surprise. And then, predictably, it crumpled into fury. "Do you *want* me to send you back to the lab?"

"That threat is beginning to feel stale."

Stell drew back, as if struck. "Is it?" he said darkly. "Allow me to refresh your memory."

Eli tensed as Stell raised his wristwatch to his mouth and spoke into a hidden comm, the words too low for him to hear.

"Wait," started Eli, his voice cut off by a metallic scrape overhead. Four small sprinklers emerged from the ceiling at the front of the cell. Icy water rained down, soaking Eli through in seconds.

He started to back up, but Stell's voice made him stop.

"Don't you dare retreat."

Eli held his ground. "Fine." He looked down at his hands, then up at Stell. "I won't melt."

"I know," said the director grimly.

Eli barely heard the hum over the sound of the water. He realized too late what was happening, managed just a step toward the fiberglass before the current hit him.

It was everywhere. Tearing up his legs, arcing through his chest, lighting every nerve. Eli buckled to his hands and knees as the electricity tore through him, conducted through the water. Enough volts to level a small beast, but Eli's own regeneration kept him conscious, caught in a suspended state of electrocution.

His jaw locked, a low, animal sound tearing between his teeth.

Stell turned and stormed away, his hand lifting in an almost dismissive motion. The wall went solid, white, and several terrible lurching seconds later, the current finally died. Eli collapsed to his side on the slick floor as the sprinklers slowed, and stopped.

He rolled onto his back, chest heaving.

And then, slowly, Eli got up, and crossed to the desk, sinking into the chair before the computer. Since the system was twinned with Stell's, the director would be able to pull up everything, be able to read the lines, if not the space between them.

Eli began to query other deaths, other causes, other leads. He couldn't bury the search that led him to Adam Porter, that missing link, but he could keep Stell from following the clean pattern of Eli's own thoughts. With every subsequent search, Eli frayed the thread, ventured down a course he'd earlier abandoned. Hopefully it would read as frustration with his own failure, a furious need to find the truth.

But as his fingers flew over the keyboard, creating a tangled web of false leads and dead ends, his own thoughts coalesced into a single, smooth train.

Eli would save Victor for himself.

XXIV

FOUR WEEKS AGO

EON

ELI had spent the better part of an hour listening to Stell talk about his new target. Marcella Renee Riggins, mob wife turned murderess. He flipped through the pages in the file as the director spoke, setting aside the newspaper clipping and the EON-issued backstory, focusing instead on the crime scene stills from the hospital—the bed with its rusted bar, its ruined sheets, and the much more striking hole in the hospital room wall.

"... nearly died in a fire, seems to be burning everything—and everyone—she can get her hands on—"

"She's not burning them," said Eli, skimming the photos.

"The piles of ash beg to differ."

Eli traced a finger along the hole in the wall, then flipped to the crime scene close-up of the debris on the kitchen floor.

He rose and pressed the photo against the fiberglass. "Do you see that? The edges of the diamond?"

Stell squinted. "It looks dirty. Which would make sense, considering it's sitting in a pile of human remains."

"It's not dirty," said Eli. "It's graphite."

"I don't follow."

Obviously. "Marcella isn't burning things. She's *eroding* them. If she'd been using heat, you might have been able to combat it with extreme cold. But with a corrosive ability like this, you're better off killing her."

Stell crossed his arms. "Is that the only advice you have to offer?"

"In this case, it's certainly the *best*," said Eli. He had seen power like Marcella's before. Raw, destructive, boundless. There was no place for power like that in this world. She would carve a swathe of chaos, until she was put down. "Do you know the half-life of carbon?"

"Off the top of my head?" asked Stell.

"It's nearly six thousand years. How long do you think it took her to kill the person wearing that diamond? How long do you think it will take her to penetrate whatever armor your men are wearing?"

"It won't be the first time our agents have gone up against someone with a touch-based ability."

"And assuming you capture her, do you even have a cell capable of containing someone with these powers?"

"Every power has its limits."

"Just listen—"

"I don't need to," cut in Stell. "Your philosophy is hardly a mystery at this point, Eli. If it were up to you, EON would never salvage anyone."

"It's in part *because* of me that you have salvaged the last twenty-two EOs. So listen when I tell you that someone this powerful belongs in the ground."

"You know the policy."

"I know you want to believe that all EOs are worth saving, but we aren't."

"We don't decide who lives and who dies," said Stell tersely. "We don't condemn EOs without confrontation."

"Now who's letting their ideals cloud their judgment?"

"Marcella will be offered the same opportunity as every other EO we engage—to come willingly. If she refuses, and the on-site team is unable to safely—"

"*Safely?*" snarled Eli. "This woman can reduce people to ash with a single touch. She can decay metal and stone. Do you value an EO's life above a human's? Because you are sending your agents on a suicide mission to sate your pride—"

"Stand down," said Stell.

Eli exhaled through clenched teeth. "If you don't kill her now, you'll wish you had."

Stell turned to go. "If you have no other suggestions—"

"Send me."

Stell glanced back, raising a thick brow. "What was that?"

"You want other options? Ones that won't get innocent humans killed?" Eli spread his arms. "Our abilities are complementary. She ruins. I regenerate. There's a cosmic elegance to it, don't you think?"

"And what if her power is faster?" asked Stell.

Eli's arms fell back to his sides. "Then I die," he said simply.

Once upon a time he had believed he survived because God willed it. That Eli was unbreakable because He had a purpose for him. These days, Eli didn't know what he believed, but he still hoped, fervently, desperately, that there was a reason for it.

Stell smiled grimly. "I appreciate the offer, Mr. Cardale. But I'm not letting you go that easily."

The wall went solid, swallowing the director from sight. Eli sighed, and crossed to his bed. He sank down onto his cot, elbows on his knees, fingers laced, head bowed. As if in prayer.

Eli hadn't expected Stell to say yes, of course.

But he had planted the seed. Had seen it take root behind Stell's eyes.

Now he simply had to wait for it to grow.

XXV

FOUR YEARS AGO

EON——LABORATORY WING

THOMAS Haverty was a man of vision.

So he wasn't at all surprised when Stell stripped him of his post at EON. Wasn't surprised when security escorted him from the lab, took his access card, his files, his crisp white coat. So many men of genius were stymied by short-sighted fools. Scientists condemned before they were lauded. Gods crucified before they were worshipped.

"This way, Mr. Haverty," said a soldier in a black suit.

"*Doctor*," he corrected as he stepped through the scanner, spread his arms, and let them search his clothes, his skin, his skeleton, all to make sure he hadn't stolen anything from the lab. As if Haverty would do something so obvious, so stupid.

They escorted him all the way to the parking lot, and proceeded to search his car, too, before returning his keys and signaling the security post to let him out. The gates slid closed behind him with grim finality.

Haverty drove the twenty-four miles back to the outer edge of Merit, to a small apartment on the southern side of the city. He let himself in, set the keys in their designated tray, peeled off his coat and shoes, and rolled up his sleeves.

A few stray flecks of Mr. Cardale's blood still stained the inside of his wrist, beyond the protection of his latex gloves. Haverty considered the dots for a moment, the strange pattern like a smattering of stars, a constellation waiting to be discovered.

He held his wrist out and went to his office. A windowless room, sterile and white and lined with refrigerated shelves of samples, vials of blood, small glass jars containing a dozen different drugs, folder after folder of hand-copied notes.

No, Haverty hadn't been foolish enough to steal from EON on his way out. Instead, he'd done it every day. Stolen his research one piece at a time. A single sample. A slide. An ampule. Each token small enough to be claimed an accident, if he'd been caught. A slip of the mind. Patience really was the highest virtue. And progress was a thing achieved one halting step at a time.

Every night—or morning—when he'd returned home, Haverty had taken up a notepad and reprinted word for word the notes he'd made in the sanctum of the EON compound.

Men ahead of their time were always, by definition, outside of it.

Haverty was no different. Stell couldn't see—EON couldn't see—but *he* knew that the ends would justify the means. He would show them. He would crack the ExtraOrdinary code, and change the face of science, and they would welcome him back. They would worship him.

He crossed the lab and drew a small glass slide from a top drawer, along with a scalpel, delicately scraping flecks of Eliot Cardale's brown-red blood onto the surface.

He had so much work to do.

XXVI

FOUR WEEKS AGO

SOUTHERN MERIT

NICK Folsetti sank onto the bench beside the block of lockers and began unwinding the tape from his hands. He ran his tongue along his inside cheek—he could still taste the tang of blood where his opponent had landed a punch.

The last of the tape came free, and Nick flexed, watching the skin on his knuckles tighten, harden to something like stone. It *wasn't* stone, of course, or anything else. It was more like all the softness went out of him. All the weakness erased. He flexed again, his fingers gaining a sudden flush of color as they softened back into flesh and bone.

Nick could only harden himself in pieces—hands, ribs, shins, jaw—and even then, it was a conscious thing.

But it was a hell of a thing.

He'd heard the whispers, of the soldiers who came looking for people like him. Had gone down the online rabbit hole, dug up everything he could on ExtraOrdinaries in those first few days before he realized that was probably a giant red flag and switched to incognito searches on public computers.

EON—that's what they were called. He kept picturing them like the people on TV shows, the ones who believed in ghosts or monsters or aliens. Nick had never been gullible, he didn't *really* think they existed, these hunters.

But then again, up until six months ago, when Nick, fresh out of the hospital, put his hand through a wall, and the *wall* was the only thing that broke, he hadn't believed in people like him either.

The bookie, Tavish, whistled from the doorway, a fresh toothpick between his teeth.

"For a guy your size, you sure can throw a punch." His chin bobbed toward the hall, the room, the ring. "Bigger stages than this, you know."

"You want me gone?" asked Nick.

"I didn't say that," said Tavish, shifting the toothpick in his mouth. "Just saying, you ever looking to go big, I could help you . . . for a cut."

"I'm not looking for more attention," said Nick. "Just cash."

"Suit yourself." The envelope arced through the air, landing on the bench beside him. It wasn't all that thick, but it was untraceable, and more than enough to get by until the next fight. Which was all Nick needed.

"See you in three nights," said Tavish, disappearing down the hall.

Nick thumbed through the cash, then tucked it in his coat and headed out.

The alley light above the door was on the fritz again, the alley a tangle of shadows, the kind that played tricks on your eyes this late at night.

Nick lit a cigarette, the red tip dancing before him in the dark.

There was a rager going on in one of the nearby warehouses, the heavy pulse of the club's bass blanketing the streets. Nick couldn't hear his own heart over the beat, let alone the footsteps coming up behind him.

Didn't know someone was there until the sudden flash of pain pierced his side. It caught him off guard, and for a second Nick thought he'd been shot, but when he looked down he saw, jutting between his ribs, a short metal dart. An empty vial.

He rounded, dizzy, expecting to see a cop, or a thug, or even an EON soldier, but there was only a single man, short and balding, wearing round glasses and a white lab coat.

That was the last thing Nick saw before his vision blurred, and his legs buckled, and everything went dark.

∞

NICK came to in a steel room—a shipping crate, or maybe a storage locker, he couldn't tell. His vision slid in and out of focus, his head pounding. Memory flickered back. The dart. The vial.

He tried to move, and felt the pull of restraints around his wrists and ankles, the rustle of plastic sheeting beneath his head.

Nick flexed, hardening his wrists, but it was no use. Solidity wasn't the same as strength. The bonds had just enough give. They didn't snap. He fought, then, thrashing against the table, until someone clicked their tongue.

"How quickly we devolve," said a voice behind his head. "People become animals the moment they are caged."

Nick twisted, craning until he caught the edge of a white coat.

"I apologize for the state of my lab," said the voice. "It's not ideal, I know, but science doesn't bow to aesthetics."

"Who the fuck *are* you?" demanded Nick, twisting desperately against the restraints.

The white coat approached the table, and became a man. Thin. Balding. With round glasses and deep-set eyes the color of slate.

"My name," said the man, adjusting latex gloves, "is Dr. Haverty."

Something glinted in his hand, thin and silver and sharp. A scalpel. "I promise, what's about to happen is in the interest of progress."

The man leaned in, bringing his blade to rest above Nick's left eye. The point came into perfect focus, close enough to brush his lashes, while the doctor slid into a blur of white beyond.

Nick gritted his teeth, and tried to retreat, out of the scalpel's path, but there was nowhere to go, so instead he forced all his focus into hardening his left eye. The scalpel came to rest against it with the plink of metal on ice.

The blur of the doctor's face parted into a smile. "Fascinating."

The scalpel vanished, and the doctor retreated from view. Nick heard the scrape and shuffle of tools, and then Haverty reappeared, holding a syringe, its contents a vivid, viscous blue.

"What do you want?" pleaded Nick as the needle disappeared from sight.

Seconds later, a pain pierced the base of his skull. Cold began to flood his limbs.

"What do I want?" echoed Haverty, as Nick shivered, shuddered, spasmed. "What all men of science want. To learn."

3
ASCENSION

I

THREE WEEKS AGO

EON

"**WHAT** about you, Rush?"

Dominic blinked. He was sitting at a table on the upper level of the canteen, Holtz on one side and Bara on the other. After getting Dom the job, Holtz had stayed close, helped him fit in at EON. A cheerful blond kid—Dom couldn't help but think of him that way, even though Holtz was a year older—with a mischievous smile and a perpetually good mood, they'd served together, two tours, before Dom stepped on an IED and found himself retired. It was nice to have a shared shift break, Bara's presence notwithstanding.

Rios sat alone one table over, the way she always did, a book open beside her food. Every time a soldier passed too close, she shot them a look, and they retreated.

"What *about* me?" asked Dom.

"If you were an EO," said Bara around a mouthful of sandwich, "what would your power be?"

It was an innocuous question—inevitable, even, given the environment. But Dom's mouth still went dry. "I—don't know."

"Oh, come on," pressed Bara. "You can't tell me you haven't thought of it."

"I'd want X-ray vision," said Holtz. "Or the ability to fly. Or the ability to transform my car into other cars whenever I get bored."

Rios looked up from her own table. "Your mind," she said, "truly is a marvel."

Holtz beamed, as if it were a compliment.

"But," she continued, "if you bothered to read the eval files, you'd know that an EO's power is tethered to the method of their NDE and the state of their mind at the time of incident. So tell me," she said, turning in her chair, "what kind of accident gets you the power to change the model of your car?"

Holtz made a comical frown, as if genuinely trying to puzzle it out, but Bara was clearly bored.

"What about you, Rios?" he shot back. "What would *your* power be?"

She returned to her book. "I'd settle for the ability to create quiet."

Holtz let out a nervous laugh.

Dominic let his eyes slide over the group.

He hadn't expected it to get easier—hadn't *wanted* it to get easier—but it had. That was the thing, it was amazing what you could get used to, how quickly the strange became mundane, the extraordinary normal. After leaving the army, he'd missed the camaraderie, the common ground. Hell, he'd missed the uniforms, the orders, the sense of routine.

What Dominic could never get used to were EON's *cells*. Or rather, the people kept inside them.

The complex's crisp white walls had become familiar—the obscure maze reduced to clean lines of rote muscle memory—but there would never be anything comfortable about the purpose of this place. If Dom ever found himself forgetting the building's true design, all he had to do was look at the surveillance footage, click through the images of three dozen holding cells.

Now and then, when Dom drew rounds, he had walk those cells, deliver meals, listen to the EOs beyond the fiberglass beg for him to let them out. Sometimes, when he drew eval, he had to sit across from them—the prisoners in their cells and Dominic in his camouflage as human—and ask them about their lives, their deaths, their memories, their minds. He had to pretend he didn't understand what they meant when they talked about those final moments, the desperate thoughts that followed them down into the dark, the ones that pulled them back out.

Across the table, Holtz and Bara were still tossing around hypothetical powers, and Rios had gone back to her book, but Dominic stared down at his food, his appetite suddenly gone.

II

TWO YEARS AGO

DOMINIC'S APARTMENT

HE turned the business card over in his hands, waiting for Victor to call him back.

The black ink caught the light, illuminating the three letters. *EON.*

Ten minutes later, the phone finally rang.

"Take the job."

Dominic froze. "You're not serious." But he could tell by the ensuing silence that Victor was. "These are the guys that hunt us. Capture us. Kill us. And you want me to *work for them?*"

"You have the background, the qualifications—"

"And if they peg me as an EO?"

A short, impatient sigh. "You have the ability to step outside of time, Dominic. If *you* can't avoid capture—"

"I can step out of time," said Dominic, "but I can't walk through walls. I can't open locks." Dom ran a hand through his hair. "With all due respect—"

"That saying usually precedes a no," said Victor coolly.

"What you're asking me to do—"

"I'm not asking."

Victor was a hundred miles away, but still Dominic flinched at the threat. He owed Victor everything, and they both knew it.

"All right."

Victor hung up, and Dom stared at the phone for a long time before he turned the card over, and dialed.

∞

A black van came for him at dawn.

Dominic had been waiting on the curb, watched as a man in street clothes climbed out and opened the back doors. Dom forced himself forward. His steps were slow, a body operating against drag.

He didn't want to do this. Every self-preserving nerve in his body was saying no. He didn't know what Victor was thinking, or how many steps ahead he was thinking it. In Dom's head, Victor went around acting like the world was one big game of chess. Tapping people and saying, "You're a pawn, you're a knight, you're a rook."

Dom chafed a little at the thought, but then, he'd learned not to ask questions in the army. To trust the orders as they came down, knowing that he couldn't see the whole scope. War needed both kinds of people—those who played the long game and those who played the short one.

Victor was the former.

Dominic was the latter.

That didn't make him a pawn.

It made him a good soldier.

He willed his body toward the van. But before he could climb in, the man held out a ziplock bag. "Phone, watch, anything that transmits data and isn't hardwired to your body."

Dominic had been careful—there were only a handful of numbers in his phone, and none of them named; Victor was *boss man*, Mitch was *big man*, Syd was *tiny terror*—but he still felt a nervous prickle as the bag disappeared and he was ushered into the van.

It wasn't empty.

Four other people—three men and one woman—were already sitting inside, their backs against the windowless metal walls. Dom took a seat as the doors slammed and the van pulled away. No one spoke, but he could tell the others were military—or ex-military—by the set of their shoulders, their close-cropped or tightly wound hair, the steady blankness in their faces. One had a prosthetic arm—an elaborate piece of biotech from the elbow down—and Dom watched the man's mechanical fingers tap absently on his leg.

There was one more pickup—a young black woman—and then the ground changed under the tires, the world outside drowned out by the engine as the van gained speed.

Dom had spent half his career in convoys like this, being transported from one base to another.

One of the men went to check his watch before remembering it had been confiscated. Dominic didn't mind—he could wait.

∞

TIME moved strangely for Dom.

Or at least, he moved strangely in time.

On paper he was only thirty-three, but he felt like he'd been alive for longer—and he guessed that, in a way, he had. Dom could step out of the flow of time, into the shadows, where the whole world became a painting in shades of gray, a dark between, a nowhere, where he was the only thing that moved.

Dom had never done the math, but he figured that he'd probably spent weeks—if not months—on the other side, the *out*side, his own timeline stretching out, losing shape.

Once, as an experiment, he had stepped into the shadows and stayed there, curious to know how long he could last out of time. It was like holding your breath, and at the same time it wasn't—there was oxygen in the space between, but there was also weight, pressure—a pressure that had nearly broken him before, when every step was pain. A pressure that now registered as drag, challenging, but by no means impermeable.

Since then, every morning and every night, Dominic spent time out of time. Sometimes he only moved around his apartment, and sometimes he went further afield, measuring the ground he could cover, instead of the seconds that passed.

∞

AS the transport van slowed, Dom's attention was pulled back to the metal bench, the darkened hull, the other waiting bodies.

A few minutes later, it finally came to a stop. The doors opened, and they were ushered out onto smooth asphalt. Dominic squinted, disoriented by the sudden morning light. They were standing in front of a building that had to be EON.

From the outside, it looked . . . innocuous. Bland, even. There was a perimeter wall, but no barbed wire, no obvious gunner posts.

The group reached the front doors, which parted with the hiss of an airlock. The lobby—if you could call it a lobby—was sleek and open, but between the front doors and that space was a security port. One by one, the six were called forward by name and instructed to empty their pockets and step into the scanner.

Klinberg. Matthews. Linfield.

Dominic's pulse quickened.

Bara. Plinetti.

Victor had said they couldn't hold him, but he didn't *know* that, not for sure. These people, their entire job was capturing people like him. Surely their technology had been adapted to that task. What if they'd found a way to measure the difference between a human and EOs? What if they could detect people like him?

"Rusher," said an officer, ushering Dominic forward. He let out a low breath and stepped into the scan.

An error sound—a ringing alarm—echoed through the lobby.

Dom staggered backward out of the scan, braced for the walls to open and black-clad soldiers to come pouring in. He was ready to step out of the world and into the shadows, ready to forfeit his identity, his anonymity, the whole fucking thing, and face Victor's wrath—but the officer only rolled his eyes. "You got parts?"

"What?" asked Dominic, dazed.

"Metal. In your body. You got to specify that kind of thing before you go in."

The soldier briskly typed in a new set of commands. "Okay. Now go."

Dom forced himself to step back in, praying the scan couldn't pick up his panic.

"Hold still."

He felt like he was being Xeroxed. A bright band of white light tracked up and then back down his body.

"Step out."

Dominic did, fighting to stop the tremor from showing in his limbs.

One of the other guys—Bara—clamped a hand on his shoulder. "Jeez, man, how tight are you wound?"

Dom managed a nervous chuckle. "Not much for loud noises," he said. "Blame an IED."

"Bad luck, man." The grip loosened. "But they put you back together well."

Dom nodded. "Well enough."

They were led to a room with no chairs, nowhere to sit, no signs of comfort at all. Just bare walls, empty floor. The door swung shut behind them. And locked.

"You think it's a test?" asked one of the women—Plinetti—after thirty minutes.

"If so, it's a shit one," said Matthews, stretching out on the floor. "It'll take more than a white box to fuck with me."

Dom rocked on his heels, shoulders tipping back against the wall.

"Could use some coffee," said Bara with a yawn.

The last guy—Klinberg—spoke up. "Hey," he said in a mock whisper. "You ever seen one?"

"One what?" asked the other woman. Linfield.

"You know. What they keep here."

What, he'd said. Not *who*. Dom resisted the urge to correct him as the door swung open and a female soldier walked in. She was tall and lean, with warm brown skin and short black hair. Most of the recruits sprang to their feet—attention was a hard habit to break—but the guy on the ground rose slowly, almost lazily.

"I'm Agent Rios," said the soldier, "and I'll be leading you through today's orientation." She strode the length of the room. "Some of you are wondering what we do here. EON is separated into Containment, Observation, and Neutralization. Containment teams are dedicated to the location, pursuit, and capture of EOs. Observation of those EOs is stationed here at the base."

Klinberg raised his hand. "Which team gets to kill them?"

Dominic's chest tightened, but Rios's expression didn't falter. "Neutralization is a last resort, and its teams are built from those who've proven themselves in other departments. Safe to say, Klinberg, *you* won't be killing EOs any time soon. If that's a deterrent for you, let me know so I can address the remaining five candidates without your distraction."

Klinberg had the sense to shut up.

"Before we begin," continued Rios, "you're about to sign a non-disclosure agreement. If you break it, you will not be arrested. You will not be sued." She smiled grimly. "You will simply *disappear*."

A tablet was passed around, and one by one they pressed their thumbs against the screen. Once it was back in Rios's hands, the soldier continued speaking. "Most of you have heard the term *EO*. And most of you are probably skeptical. But the fastest way to disabuse you of doubt is through a demonstration."

The doors opened at her back.

"Follow me."

∞

"KEEP your hands inside the ride," whispered Klinberg as they filed into the hall.

Remember this place, thought Dominic as he fell in line.

Remember everything. But it was a maze of white, sterile and uniform and disorienting. They passed through several sets of doors, each sealed, requiring a swipe from Agent Rios's key card.

"Hey," whispered Bara. "I heard they have that killer here. The one that offed, like, a hundred other EOs. You think it's true?"

Dom didn't answer. Was Eli really somewhere in this building? Agent Rios tapped a comm on her shoulder. "Cell Eight, status?"

"*Irritable,*" answered the person on the other end.

A grim smile crossed her lips. "Perfect."

She swiped them through a final door, and Dominic felt his heart lurch. They were in a hangar, empty except for a freestanding cell in the center of the room. It was a cube made of fiberglass, and trapped inside, like a firefly in a jar, was a woman.

She knelt in the middle of the floor, wearing a kind of jumpsuit, its fabric glossy, as if coated.

"Tabitha," said Agent Rios, her voice even.

"Let me out."

The recruits moved around the cube, as if she were a piece of art, or a specimen, something to be considered from every side.

Matthews even rapped his knuckles on the glass, as if he were at a zoo. "Don't feed the animals," he muttered under his breath.

Dominic felt sick.

The prisoner rose to her feet. "Let me *out.*"

"Ask nicely," said Rios.

The prisoner was beginning to glow, the light coming from beneath her skin, a deep red-orange like heated metal. "*Let me out!*" she screamed, her voice crackling.

And then, she *ignited.*

Flame licked up her skin, engulfing her from head to toe, her hair standing up in a plume of blue-white light, like the tip of a match.

Several of the recruits recoiled. One covered his mouth. Others stared in fascination. Surprise. Fear.

Dominic feigned shock, but the fear was real. It crept through his limbs, a warning, that old gut feeling that said *wrong wrong*

wrong—just like it had the second before Dom's foot hit the IED, the instant before his world changed forever. A fear that had less to do with the woman on fire, and more to do with the cell holding her, the heat that didn't even penetrate the foot-thick fiberglass.

Rios hit a switch on the wall, and sprinklers went off inside the cell, followed by the sizzle of a doused fire. The cube filled with steam, and when the water cut off and the white smoke cleared, the prisoner sat in a heap on the floor of the cell, soaking wet and heaving for breath.

"All right," said Rios, "show-and-tell's over." She turned toward the recruits. "Any questions?"

THE black van was waiting at the end of the day.

All the way back to the city, the other recruits chatted, making small talk, but Dom closed his eyes and focused on his breathing.

The "demonstration" had been followed by an interview, an explanation of training protocol, a psych eval, each procedure executed in a way so grounded, so ordinary, that they'd been clearly designed to make candidates forget the strangeness of EON's purpose.

But Dominic *couldn't* forget. He was still shaken from the sight of the woman on fire, and certain that he'd never get out with his secret intact, so he was surprised—and suspicious—when, at the end of it all, Rios told him to report back the next day for further training.

Dom closed his eyes as the van sped on. One by one it stopped and the others were deposited outside their homes. One by one, until he was the only one left, and as the van doors slammed shut on him, and him alone, Dom was gripped anew by panic. He was sure that he could feel freeway moving beneath the tires, sure that they were taking him back to EON, to his own fiberglass cube.

"Rusher."

Dominic looked up and realized that the van was idling, the back doors open, his apartment building visible beyond in the dusky light. The soldier handed Dom the ziplock bag containing his phone, and Dom got out, but as he climbed the steps and went inside, he couldn't shake the feeling he was being watched.

There, on the street, an unfamiliar car. He switched the TV on, returned to the window—it was still there, idling. Dom changed into workout clothes, took a deep breath, and slipped out of time.

The world went silent, and heavy, and gray, all the sound and movement leached out of the room. Dom made his way to the front door, fighting against the drag of frozen time.

Back when every step was pain, Dom couldn't bear to spend more than a few moments in this heavy, dark place. But after months of training, his limbs and lungs moved steadily—if not easily—against the resistance.

He descended the stairs, his steps soundless when earlier they had echoed. Through the front doors and onto the curb. Dom paused beside the unfamiliar car and bent to examine the figure in the driver's seat, a cell half raised to their ear. The man had the look of ex-mil, and the file on the seat beside him was printed with Dominic's name.

He looked back and up at his apartment, the glow of the TV a splash of light against the curtains. Then he turned and walked two blocks to the nearest subway. Halfway down the stairs, he stepped back out of the shadows and into the world, into light and color and time, and vanished into the evening commute.

∞

"**THEY'RE** watching my place," he said when Victor answered the phone.

He was jogging through a small park, his breath coming in short, even beats.

"I'd expect as much," said Victor, unfazed.

Dom slowed to a walk. "Why am I doing this?"

"Because ignorance is only bliss if you want to get caught."

With that, Victor hung up.

Dominic returned to EON the next day, via the black van, to find the initial group of six reduced to five. No Klinberg. By the third day, Matthews was gone too. Rios led them through exercises, drills, tests, and Dom did exactly as he was told. Tried to keep his head down and his expression blank. And still he expected to be cut.

Wanted to be cut.

He was heading back to the van on the third day when he was stopped by Rios.

"Director Stell would like a word."

Dominic stiffened. He'd never met the man, but he knew Stell's reputation. Knew he was the detective who sent Victor to prison back in college. The man who tracked Eli to Merit. And, of course, the man who'd started EON.

Run, said a voice in Dom's head.

He looked from Rios to the compound's entrance, the sliding doors hissing closed.

Run before they shut.

But if he did, that would be the end of it. His identity would be known, his cover blown. And then Dom would have to keep running. Always.

He forced himself to fall in line.

Rios led him to an office at the end of a long white hall. She knocked once, and opened the door.

Director Stell sat in a high-backed chair on the opposite side of a broad steel desk. He had black hair just starting to silver, his face reduced to angles as he stared down at a tablet.

"Mr. Rusher. Please sit down."

"Sir." Dominic sat.

The door closed behind him with a click.

"Something has been bothering me," said Stell without looking up. "You ever forget something, and you can't remember what it is? It's a vicious little mind game. Distracting, too. Like an itch you can't scratch." Stell set the tablet down, and Dominic saw his own face staring up from the screen. Not the photo taken in the security scan, or one pulled from hall surveillance. No, the photo was a few years old, from his time in the service. "It was your name," continued Stell. "I knew I'd heard it before, but I couldn't remember where." Stell turned the tablet and nudged it across the steel table. "Do you know what that is?"

Dominic scanned the screen. Beside his photo was a kind of profile, basic details—age, birthday, parents—along with facts about his life—address, schooling, etc.—but there was an error.

Dominic's middle name was listed here as Eliston.

His real middle name was Alexander.

"Have you heard of Eli Ever?" asked Stell.

Dom stilled, searching for the right answer, the right amount of knowledge. It had been public news—but how much of it, and which pieces? He'd only met Eli once, and only for an instant, the breath it took to step into the Falcon Price and pull Sydney—and her dog—out.

"The serial killer?" ventured Dom.

Stell nodded. "Eliot Cardale—known as Eli Ever in the press—was one of the most dangerous ExtraOrdinaries in existence. He killed nearly forty people, and briefly used the Merit police databases—and the police force, for that matter—to create a list of targets, profiles of those he suspected to be EOs. This," said Stell slowly, "is one of those profiles."

Once, when Dominic was overseas, he'd walked into a room and found a live bomb. Not like the IED he'd stepped on. No, he'd never had time to see that explosion coming. But the bomb in this room had been as big as a steel drum, and the whole place was booby-trapped around it. He remembered looking down, seeing the trigger wire, barely an inch in front of his left boot.

Dom had wanted nothing more than to run away, as far as possible, but he hadn't known where the other wires were, or even how he'd made it that far without triggering them. He'd had to pick his way out, one agonizing step at a time.

And here he was again, his footing precarious—one wrong move, and everything would blow.

"You're asking if I'm an EO."

Stell's gaze was steady, unflinching. "We have no way of knowing if every person Eli targeted was actually—"

Dominic slammed the tablet down on the table. "I gave my flesh and blood and bones to this country. I gave everything I had to this country. I *almost* died for this country. And I didn't get any special powers out of it. I wish I had—instead, I got a body full of scrap parts, and a lot of pain, but I'm still here, still doing what I can, because I want to keep people safe. Now, if you don't want to hire me, that's your choice. But have the balls to make up a better reason than this . . . *sir*."

Dominic sat back, breathless, hoping the outburst had been enough to convince the other man.

The silence stretched out. And then, at last, Stell nodded and said, "We'll be in touch."

Dismissed, Dom rose from his chair and left. He went into the men's room across the hall, and into the safety of a stall, before vomiting up everything in his stomach.

III

THREE WEEKS AGO

EON

BARA smacked his palm on the table and got up.

"Hate to eat and run," he said, "but I've got a mission."

"No way," said Holtz, "they cleared *you* for fieldwork?" He turned on Rios. "What gives? I've been petitioning for weeks to get on Containment."

Bara smoothed his uniform. "It's because I'm such an asset."

Rios snorted. "It's because you're totally useless here."

Bara put a hand to his heart, as if wounded, then shot back, "What about you?"

"What about me?"

"You don't do fieldwork."

She met his gaze, her gray eyes flat. "Someone has to make sure the monsters don't get out."

Dom was surprised. He'd been there for two years, and witnessed a handful of attempts—an EO managed to put a hole in one of the fiberglass walls, another tore free from restraints during a routine med check—but he'd never heard of an actual escape.

"Has an EO ever gotten out?"

Rios's mouth twitched at the corner. "People don't get out of EON, Rusher. Not once we put them here."

People. Rios was one of the only soldiers who referred to the EOs that way.

"Who're you hunting?" asked Holtz, who'd clearly resigned himself to living vicariously.

"Some crazy housewife," said Bara. "Burns holes in shit. Found her husband's secret apartment, at the Heights."

Holtz—who had had many girlfriends—shook his head. "Never underestimate an angry woman."

"Never underestimate a *woman*," amended Rios.

Bara shrugged. "Yeah, yeah. Place your bets. Poke your fun. But when she's rotting in a cell, you're all buying me drinks."

MEANWHILE, IN MERIT...

June closed her eyes and listened to the rain beat against her black umbrella.

She wished she were in a field somewhere, arms spread wide to catch the thunder, instead of standing on the curb outside the sleek urban high-rise.

She'd been waiting for nigh on ten minutes before someone finally came through the revolving doors, and just her luck, he was all paunch in an ill-fitting suit, complete with five-o'clock shadow and a comb-over.

June sighed. Beggars couldn't be choosers, she supposed. She started toward the building, brushing past the man at the corner. The barest touch—the kind that goes unnoticed amid the jostle and drip of a rainy day—and she had all she needed. He was on his way and she was on hers. She didn't bother changing, not until she reached the Heights' front doors.

An older man sat behind a concierge desk in the lobby. "Forget something, Mr. Gosterly?"

June made a short, gruff sound and muttered, "Always."

The elevator doors opened, and by the time they closed behind her, the reflection in the polished metal was hers again. Well, not *hers.* But the one she'd started with that morning. Peasant skirt and a leather jacket rolled to the elbows, a sly smile and hair that fell in loose brown curls. She'd picked it off the subway like a girl shopping the racks. It was one of her favorites.

As the elevator rose, she pulled out her cell and texted Syd.

For a long moment, nothing. And then three dots appeared beside the girl's name, to show that she was typing.

June watched, restless for an answer.

When it came to Sydney, she'd never been good at waiting.

IV

THREE YEARS AGO

CAPITAL CITY

IT had taken an entire year for June to find them again, and when she did, it was entirely by accident. Almost as if it were fate.

The trouble was, June didn't believe in fate. At least, she didn't *want* to believe in it, because fate meant everything happened for a reason, and there were too many things she wished never had. Besides, it was hard to believe in a higher power or a grand design when you killed people for a living.

But then fate—or luck, or whatever it was—went and handed her Sydney.

A year of looking for the man in black, with no luck, and then, fifteen hundred miles from Dresden, where they'd first crossed paths, June cut through a park on the way to a job and saw the blond girl again.

A year—but it was impossibly, undeniably her. She had been—and seemed to still be—at that age where changes happened overnight. Bodies grew inches, curves—but the girl looked the same. *Exactly* the same. Same blond bob and ice blue eyes, same narrow build, same giant black dog waiting like a shadow at her side.

June scanned the park—there was no sign of the man in black, but she glimpsed the other one sitting in the grass, tattoos wrapped around his forearms and a book open on his knee. She saw a flash of pink nearby, a forgotten Frisbee. She picked it up, spun it between her fingers, and then lobbed the plastic disc at the man's head.

It connected with a light crack, and June jogged up to him, a bouncy young brunette, all apologies and sunshine.

"It's all right," he said, rubbing the back of his head. "Takes more than a Frisbee to knock me over."

He offered it back, and when her fingers brushed his, his life flickered through her like a film reel. He was so open, so human. Mitch Turner. Forty-three. Foster homes and skinned knees and bloody knuckles in a street brawl. Computer screens and car tires screeching. Handcuffs and a prison cell and a cafeteria, a man with a makeshift knife, a muffled threat, and then—June saw a face she recognized.

And thanks to Mitch, she now had a name to go with it.

Victor Vale.

In Mitch's mind, the man was lean but not yet gaunt, washed out in prison grays instead of fitted blacks. A flick of his wrist, and another man who threatened collapsed with a scream.

That meeting, like a hinge in Mitch's mind—beyond that moment, his memories were all marked by Victor's blue eyes, his pale hair. Until they found *her*. Sydney, bloody and rain-soaked in a too-big coat. Sydney, who wasn't human. Sydney, who Mitch didn't know what to do with, how to handle. Sydney, and now a different kind of fear.

Loss.

And tucked into all of that, like a slip of paper in a book, a last memory. Another blond girl. A body buried by fire. A choice smothered by regret.

"Sorry," June heard herself say again, even as the man's memories flashed through her head. "My aim is just awful."

"Don't worry about it," said Mitch, radiating kindness, warmth.

He sat back in the grass with his book and smiled. June smiled back and said good-bye, her focus already turning to the girl under the tree.

Unknown Number: I forgot to tell you.
Unknown Number: My name is Sydney.

June cradled the cell phone in her palm. She already knew the girl's name, of course, but it was better, coming from her. June wanted things to happen naturally, even if they hadn't started that way.

Nice to meet you, Sydney, she wrote back. *I'm June.*

Good, she thought with a smile.

Now they could be proper friends.

V

THREE WEEKS AGO

THE HEIGHTS

THE elevator chimed as it reached the fourteenth floor. June stepped out into the hall and approached the cream-colored door. She half expected to find a spare key on the doorframe or under the mat, but there was nothing. No matter. Two thin bits of metal and a half minute later, she was in.

Marcella Riggins's apartment was pretty much what she expected: leather sofa, plush white rug, copper sconces, all money, no soul.

Still, there were a few surprising touches. The chunk of wood missing from the bedroom door, the rotted line like burned paper showing the path of destruction. The tiny, glittering pieces of glass on the counter and strewn across the floor. But the thing June inspected first was the record player. It was the kind rich people bought for decoration instead of function. But a small stack of albums leaned beside it, even if they too were just for show, and June flipped through until she found something upbeat, savoring the scratch of the needle.

Music poured into the apartment.

June closed her eyes and swayed a little.

The song reminded her of summer. Of laughter and champagne, the cold splash of pool water, of veranda curtains and strong hands and the scrape of the slate walk against her cheek and—

The song scratched to a stop as June removed the needle.

The past was the past.
Dead and buried.

She wandered through the bedroom, drew an absent hand across the clothes in the closet—half of which appeared to have fallen victim to Marcella's wrath. Her cell buzzed.

> **Syd**: I'm so bored.
> **Syd**: I wish I was there.

June wrote back.

> **June**: You could be.
> **Syd**: I can't.

The words were routine, at this point, even if they both knew the outcome wasn't really possible.

After all, June could be anyone, while Sydney, it seemed, could only be herself. Conspicuous in its constancy, Sydney's presence would negate June's own advantage. And, of course, there was the matter of the *others*—of Mitch, and more importantly, of Victor. June hadn't, at first, understood the nature of that relationship, or the degree of Sydney's attachment, until Sydney finally broke down and told her everything.

∞

It was last fall, and they were on one of their late-night calls, each of them perched on a rooftop, cities apart but under the same sky. Syd was tired—tired of living out of a backpack, tired of never settling down, tired of not getting to live a normal life.

June had wondered, of course, why they moved around so much—had spent a good long while assuming they were on the run. But there was more, she knew it, and she'd been waiting for Syd to confide in her.

That night, she was tired enough to tell the truth. "Victor's looking for someone who can help him."

"Help him how?"

"He's sick." A long pause. "I made him sick."

"How could *you* make him sick?"

"I thought I could save him. I tried. But it didn't work. Not the way it should have."

June hesitated then. She'd seen Sydney *save* small animals, knew what her intervention meant. "You *resurrected* Victor?"

The answer was barely a whisper. "Yes. I've brought people back before . . ." And then, still so softly, "But it's harder, when they're like us. You have to reach so much farther into the dark. I thought I grabbed hold of all the thread, but it was frayed, pieces everywhere, and I must have missed one, and now . . . his power isn't working right."

That last bit, like an opening in armor, a chance to ask the question that had plagued June since the day she brushed arms with the man in black. The mystery of his power—she'd glimpsed *something,* in Mitch's mind, the vague shape of it anyhow, had gleaned more from the big guy's fear, and from the careful way Sydney spoke, that Victor could do more than start cars or solve puzzles with his eyes closed.

"What *is* Victor's power?" she asked now, heard the girl swallow audibly.

"He hurts people."

A small shiver. "Sydney," June said slowly. "Has he ever hurt you?"

"No." And then, "Not on purpose."

Anger cut through June like a knife. Anger, and the grim determination to pry Sydney free from Victor's vise.

So far, she hadn't succeeded.

It didn't stop her from trying.

"If you ever want to leave . . ."

But June always knew the answer before it came.

June sighed. Sydney still blamed herself for Victor's situation, and until June could find a way to separate the girl from her shadow, Syd would say those same two words.

June put the phone away, turning her attention back to the task at hand, and the issue of Marcella Riggins. She plucked a framed photo from the dresser. No question, the woman was a stunner. Black hair, pale skin, long limbs. Pretty in the way that made nothing else about you matter. June had been that kind of pretty, once.

It was overrated.

June tossed the photo onto the bed and went to the window, intending to keep watch for Marcella.

Instead, she spotted a black van idling at the mouth of an alley.

That wouldn't do.

She donned the Mr. Gosterly costume a second time and went back downstairs. As she stepped through the revolving doors, she shed the aspect in favor of something even less form-fitting—a middle-aged man, haggard from too many nights spent sleeping rough. The homeless fellow staggered, as if drunk, and caught himself against the hood of the idling van. Then, without looking up, began to unbuckle his worn belt and relieve himself against the vehicle.

A door swung open, slammed closed.

"Hey!" shouted a voice, grabbing her borrowed body from behind.

June turned and stumbled forward into the soldier, as if losing his balance, and as she did, a switchblade slid out from her fingers with a neat little *snick*. She drove the blade up into the soldier's throat, then eased his body down against the alley wall.

One down.

How many more to go?

MEANWHILE, ACROSS TOWN . . .

Marcella sat on the patio of Le Soleil, sipping her latte as rain dripped from the awning and a hundred strangers passed beneath black umbrellas.

She couldn't shake the feeling she was being watched. She was, of course, used to being *noticed*, but this felt different. Intrusive. And yet there was no obvious source.

Despite her concern, Marcella wasn't in disguise—lying low had never been her style. But she'd conceded to a more subtle aesthetic, with her black hair in a simple high ponytail, her trademark stiletto pumps exchanged for more functional heeled black boots. Her nails, freshly painted gold, rapped against the side of her cup as she studied the subway station across the street. Marcella mapped out the station in her mind, envisioning the escalators that led down one level, and then two, terminating at the bank of storage lockers that ran along a white tile wall.

The locker in question was one of five they had, scattered across Merit. It had been Marcella's idea, to skim off the funds, in case a situation arose. Admittedly, she'd never envisioned a situation quite like *this*.

A siren wailed, and Marcella's fingers tensed on her coffee cup as the patrol car whipped around a nearby corner. But it surged past without stopping, and Marcella exhaled and brought the latte to her lips.

It was strange—in the days since her confrontation with Marcus, she'd been on edge, waiting for the cops to show up at any moment. She wasn't a fool. She knew they were the ones who'd kept her survival a secret. Knew her departure from the hospital was anything but subtle. And yet no one showed up, either to kill or to collect her.

She wondered what she would do when they did.

"Anything else?" asked the waiter.

Marcella smiled up at him from behind her sunglasses. "Just the check."

She paid and stood, flinching a little as she did—the burns were healing, but her skin was still tender and tight, aching with every motion. A useful reminder of Marcus's crime, and a shortcut to summoning this new power, if and when she needed it.

Marcella crossed the street and into the station.

She made her way to the lockers, found the number—the day they met—and spun the code Marcus had habitually used into the combination lock.

It didn't open.

She tried a second time, then sighed.

Her husband continued to disappoint her.

Marcella wrapped her fingers around the lock, and watched it rust away, the metal crumbling in her palm. The door swung open, and she pulled a stylish black-and-gold purse from the cubby. She drew the zipper back and examined the stacks of cash totaling fifty thousand.

It wasn't enough, of course, but it was a start.

For what? she asked herself.

The truth was, Marcella wasn't sure what to do next. Where to go. Who to become. Marcus had gone from being a foothold to a shackle, a hindrance.

Marcella took the purse and made her way back up to the street, and hailed a cab.

"Where to?" asked the driver as she slid into the backseat.

Marcella sat back and crossed her legs.

"The Heights."

The city slid past, innocuous enough, but when Marcella climbed out of the cab ten minutes later, she felt it again, that prickle like eyes against the back of her neck.

"Mrs. Riggins," said Ainsley, the Heights's concierge. His voice was steady, but his gaze lingered on her as she crossed the lobby, a careful tension in his face. He was standing too stiff, too still, working too hard at seeming calm.

Shit, thought Marcella, stepping smoothly into the elevator. As it rose, she unzipped the black-and-gold bag and reached past the money, fingers closing around the familiar grip of a handgun.

Marcella drew the weapon out, admiring the sleek chrome finish as she ejected the clip, checked the rounds, slid the safety off, each gesture performed with studied ease.

It was like wearing heels, she thought, racking the slide.

Just a matter of practice.

VI

TWO YEARS AGO

MERIT ARMORY

IT was her birthday, and they had the whole place to themselves.

Marcella could have picked a restaurant, a museum, a movie theater—any place she wanted—and Marcus would have found a way to make it hers for the night. He'd been surprised when she'd chosen the gun range.

She'd always wanted to learn how to shoot.

Her heels clicked across the linoleum, the bright fluorescents glaring down on case after case of weapons.

Marcus laid a dozen handguns on the counter, and Marcella ran her hands over the different models. They reminded her of tarot cards. When she was young Marcella had gone to a carnival, snuck into a little tent to learn her fortune. An old woman—the perfect image of a mythological or mythic crone—had spread the cards, and told her not to think, just to reach for the one that reached for her.

She had drawn the Queen of Pentacles.

The fortune teller told her it symbolized ambition.

"Power," said the woman, "belongs to those who *take* it."

Marcella's fingers closed around a sleek chrome Beretta.

"This one," she said with a smile.

Marcus took up a box of bullets and led her through into the shooting gallery.

He lifted a target—a full silhouette, head to toe, and marked by rings—and clipped it to the line. He hit a button, and the target skated away, five, ten, then fifteen meters before it stopped and hung suspended, waiting.

Marcus showed her how to load the magazine—it would take her months to manage without chipping a nail—and offered her the gun. It felt heavy in her hand. Lethal.

"What you're holding," he said, "is a weapon. It only has one purpose, and that's to kill."

Marcus turned Marcella to face the target, and wrapped himself around her like a coat, tracing the lines of her body with his own. His chest to her shoulders. His arms along her arms, hands shaping hers around the gun. She could feel his excitement pressing against her, but the gun range wasn't just a kinky setting for a birthday fuck. There would be time for that, later, but first, she wanted to learn.

She leaned her head back against her husband's shoulder. "Darling," she breathed. "A little space."

He retreated, and Marcella focused on the target, aimed, and fired.

The shot rang out across the concrete range. Her heart raced from the thrill. Her hands thrummed from the kickback.

On the paper target, a neat hole had been torn in the right shoulder.

"Not bad," said Marcus, "if you're shooting an amateur."

He took the gun from her hand. "The problem," he said, casually ejecting the magazine, "is that most professionals wear vests." He checked the rounds. "You shoot them in the chest, and you're dead." He slid the ammo back in with a swift, violent motion. His hands moved over the gun with the same short, efficient strokes he so often used on her. A confidence born out of practice.

Marcus swung the gun up, sighted for an instant, and then fired two quick shots. His hand barely moved, but the distance between the bullets could be measured in feet, not inches. The first struck the target in the leg. The second burrowed a neat hole between the cutout's eyes.

"Why bother with the first shot," she asked, "if you know you can make the second?"

Her husband smiled. "Because in my line of work, darling, the targets don't stand still. And most of the time, they're armed. Accuracy is much harder in the moment. The first shot throws the target off guard. The second is the kill."

Marcella pursed her lips. "Sounds messy."

"Death is messy."

She took back the gun, squared herself toward the target, and fired again. It tore the paper several inches to the right of the head.

"You missed," said Marcus, as if that wasn't obvious.

Marcella rolled her neck, exhaled, and then emptied the rest of the clip into the paper target. Some of the shots went wide, but a few punctured the paper head and chest, stomach, and groin.

"There," she said, setting the gun down. "I think he's dead."

A moment later, Marcus's mouth was on hers, their shuffling feet scattering the spent cartridges as he took her up against the back wall. The sex was brief, and rough, her nails leaving lines beneath his shirt, but Marcella's attention kept sliding past her husband to the ruined target, hanging like a shadow at his back.

Marcella didn't shoot any more that night. But she went back to the range alone, week after week, until her aim was perfect.

VII

THREE WEEKS AGO

THE HEIGHTS

THE elevator doors opened, and Marcella stepped out, one hand resting on the gun inside her bag. Out of the corner of her eye, she glimpsed a man walking casually toward her. He looked innocuous enough, dressed in a pullover and slacks, but black combat boots showed beneath the hems.

"Marcella Riggins?" he asked, continuing his slow advance.

She turned toward him. "Do I know you?"

"No, ma'am," he said with a smile. "But I was hoping we could talk."

"About what?" she asked.

His smile stiffened, set. "About what happened the other night."

"What happened . . ." she echoed, as if wracking her memory. "Do you mean when my husband tried to burn our house down around me? Or when I melted his face off with my bare hands?"

The man's expression stayed steady, even. His steps slowed, but didn't stop, each stride closing the gap between them.

"I think you should stay there . . ." Marcella drew the gun from her bag, not all the way, just enough to let him see the chrome polish along the back of the barrel.

"Come on, now," he said, lifting his hands as if she were a wild animal, something to be corralled. "You don't want to make a scene."

Marcella tipped her head. "What makes you think that?"

She swung the gun up and fired.

Her first shot took the man in the knee.

He gasped, buckled, and before he could even reach for the weapon holstered at his ankle, she fired a second shot into his head.

He collapsed, blood staining the runner.

She heard the steps behind her too late, and turned in time to see a dark figure, a soldier, armored head to toe in black tactical gear. Turned in time to see the arc of electricity leap from the end of a baton with a static hiss. Marcella's hand shot up and caught the weapon just as it skimmed her shoulder. Pain tore through her, sudden and bright, but Marcella tightened her grip, fingers flaring red. The strange light wrapped up over her wrist, a perfect mirror of the rot spreading through the instrument, then the hand holding it.

The attacker let go and staggered back with a yelp, clutching their arm, and Marcella slammed her heel into their chest, sending them to the floor. She knelt on top of them, fingers closing around the front of the soldier's helmet.

"Come on, darling," she said, "let me see your face."

The helmet warped, weakened, until she could tear the faceplate away.

A woman stared up at her, pain contorting the lines of her face.

Marcella tsked. "Not a good look," she said, wrapping her hand around the woman's exposed throat to stifle her scream as her body withered.

Then, the harsh metal sound of someone racking a round. Marcella looked up and saw a third soldier, his gun already leveled at her head. Her own weapon sat discarded several feet away—she'd dropped it when she went to catch the baton.

"Stand up," ordered the soldier.

Marcella considered him.

He was so focused on her, he didn't register the shape moving behind him, not until it reached out and wrapped an arm around his throat.

The shape—a man built like a heavyweight boxer—wrenched

the soldier back, and the gun went off, a steel dart grazing Marcella's cheek before burying itself in the wall behind her head.

The soldier didn't get a chance to fire again. The other man gripped the soldier's mask and wrenched it sideways, breaking his neck with an audible crack. When he let go, the soldier's body crumpled to the floor.

Marcella hadn't wasted any time. She was up again, the gun back in her hand and trained on the man who, for his part, seemed unfazed.

"Careful, now," he said, in a broad, musical voice. "Shoot me and you'll just kill a twenty-three-year-old from the suburbs who loves his ma."

"Who are you?" she demanded.

"Well, now, that's a little complicated."

And then, in front of Marcella's eyes, the man *changed*. Rippled, and was gone, replaced by a young woman with loose brown curls. "You can call me June." Marcella's eyes narrowed, and the woman smiled at her surprise. "Didn't think you were *that* special, did you?" She looked down at the three corpses, arms crossed. "You shouldn't leave these here for anyone to find." She knelt, and just like that, she was the boxer again, getting his hands under a pair of shoulders.

Marcella stared down in genuine surprise.

June looked up, impatient. "A little help?"

∞

MARCELLA pressed a hand towel to her cheek, her gun balanced on the edge of the sink. The thin line was still weeping blood. She checked her reflection in the bathroom mirror and hissed in annoyance.

The cut would heal, but they'd ruined a perfectly nice shirt.

"Who are you?" Marcella called over her shoulder to the living room, where the shapeshifter was patting down the soldiers' bodies.

"I told you," June called back in a lilting voice.

"No," said Marcella, "you really didn't."

She tossed the cloth aside and took up her gun, returning to the living room. The bodies lay side by side on the floor, the last—the one missing half its skull—staining her polished wood.

Death is messy.

"Don't be precious," said June, reading her face. "I doubt you'll want to hang about now anyway."

"Fucking cops," muttered Marcella.

"These aren't cops," said June. "They're trouble." She tore a small black patch from the shoulder of one uniform and held it up for Marcella to see. "Or more accurately, they're EON."

Marcella raised a brow. The patch itself was unmarked, save for a simple black *X* ghosted on the cloth. "Is that supposed to mean something to me?"

June rose to her feet. "It should," she said, stretching. "It stands for ExtraOrdinary Observation and Neutralization. ExtraOrdinary—EO—that's us. Which makes *them* the neutralizers." She nudged a body with the tip of her shoe. "Sharks that come swimming when you make a splash. You're lucky I found you, Ms. Riggins."

Marcella took up the half-ruined helmet. She upended it, shaking out the ash. "How *did* you find me?"

"Ah. Bethany."

Marcella scowled at the memory of her ex-friend. Her late husband's late mistress. *"Bethany."*

"Perky young thing, tits up to here."

"I know who she is."

"She liked to talk. A lot. About Marcus, and the place he'd put aside for her."

Marcella didn't realize she was gripping the helmet until it fell apart in her glowing hands. "And you?" she asked, dusting her palms. "Are you looking for my husband?"

"Oh, he's well dead. You made sure of that." June whistled. "That's quite a talent you have there."

"You don't know the half of it."

"I know you walked into a room with five men sitting round a table playing cards, and when you left, two were ash, one had a bullet in his head, and the other two are saying all kinds of strange things." June smiled conspiratorially. "Next time, you should probably just kill them all. No good having survivors running their mouths. See, Marcella," she added, stepping closer, "the problem is, one of those men, the ones you killed that night—he was mine."

"My condolences," said Marcella dryly.

June waved her hand. "Mine to *kill*. And in my line of work, it's poor form to take a bounty off another."

Marcella raised a brow. "You're a hit man?"

"Hey now, no need to be sexist. We come in all shapes. But yeah, sure. And the way I see it, you owe me a death."

Marcella crossed her arms. "Is that so."

"It is."

"Anyone in particular?"

"Matter of fact, I think you know him. Antony Hutch."

Marcella bristled at the name. A memory of the rooftop party, Hutch's wet, wandering gaze, his patronizing smile.

June was still talking. "He and I, we've got some unfinished business, of a personal nature. He's a hard man to catch on his ass. But see, I hear that he's looking for *you*."

Marcella wasn't surprised. After all, she had cut down his numbers. "You want me to kill Antony Hutch?"

June's expression darkened. "No. I just want you to get me close enough to say hello. And then, as far as I'm concerned, we're square. What do you say?"

"I could do that," said Marcella, tapping the gun against her leg. "Or I could just kill you."

"You could," countered June with a wry smile, "but it wouldn't be me you were killing."

Marcella's brow furrowed. "How's that?"

"Hard to explain," said June. "Easier to show you. This little dress-up game of mine, it's nothing. But you get me in a room with Tony Hutch, and you'll see what I can *really* do."

Marcella was intrigued. "Deal."

"Lovely," said June with a sudden, dazzling smile. She crossed to the window. "In the meantime, we should probably get out of here. Only a matter of time before they send more."

"I suppose you're right . . ." Marcella considered the bodies on her floor. "But it would be rude to go without leaving a note."

∞

"**FUCKING** hell," muttered Stell.

He'd already passed a scene in the lobby, where the concierge— an older man named Richard Ainsley—lay slumped forward in his chair, his throat slit.

The scene on the fourteenth floor told its own story.

Ash streaked across the hall runner, and a fine mist of blood spattered the floor and wall. Stell freed a dart from a neighbor's door. All the signs of a fight, but no bodies.

"Sir," called Holtz. "You should see this."

Stell stepped around the dark stains and through the open door into Marcella's apartment.

Two techs were securing the scene, bagging and recording everything they could, but as they stepped out of the way, Stell saw why Holtz had called him in.

If you don't kill her now, you'll wish you had.

Marcella Riggins hadn't tried to hide her work. On the contrary, she'd put it on display. The three agents' bodies—what was left of them—lay on the floor, their limbs arranged in a disturbing tableau.

A macabre version of *see no evil, hear no evil, speak no evil.*

The first soldier, missing a part of his skull, had his hands against his ears. The second, with a broken neck, had his own armored gloves over his eyes. And the third, little more than brittle bones inside a tactical suit, had no head at all.

Sitting like a centerpiece on the glass coffee table was a single ruined helmet.

How long do you think it will take her to penetrate whatever armor your men are wearing?

Stell examined the helmet and found a folded piece of paper tucked beneath.

Inside, in elegant, curving letters, there was a single line.

Stay out of my way.

Stell pinched the bridge of his nose. "Where were the rest of the agents?"

He'd assigned six to the mission. Six operatives for a single EO. It should have been enough. More than enough.

"We found one by the transport vehicle," said Holtz. "Two more in an alley." He didn't need to say that they were dead. The ensuing silence said enough.

"Cause of death?" asked Stell quietly.

"None of them were melted, if that's what you're asking. One broken neck. Two blades, to the throat and gut. Is it possible," ventured the young agent, "that Marcella wasn't acting alone?"

"Anything's possible," said Stell. But it did make sense. So far Marcella Riggins seemed to favor her bare hands or a gun, but four of the soldiers he'd sent had been killed in other, more varied ways.

Stell looked around. "Tell me this building has security."

"Closed circuit, in the public spaces," offered one of the techs. "Someone deleted the files, but they were clearly in a hurry. We should be able to pull footage from the lobby and hall."

"Good," said Stell. "Send it over as soon as you have it."

"What now?" asked Holtz.

Stell ground his teeth, and walked out.

VIII

THREE WEEKS AGO

EON

ELI turned through Marcella's file. Across the cell, Victor leaned, hands in his pockets, against the wall.

For so long, he'd thought Victor was haunting him—now that Eli knew that the man was *alive,* he knew the phantom was nothing but a figment of his own imagination. A touch of madness. He did his best to ignore it.

Footsteps sounded beyond the wall. Eli knew by the tread that it was Stell. And he knew, too, that the director of EON was angry.

The wall went clear, but Eli kept his head bowed over his work.

"I take it," he said dryly, "that the extraction was a resounding success."

"You know it wasn't."

"How many died?"

There was a long, weighted silence. "All of them."

"What a waste," muttered Eli, shutting the file in front of him. "All in the name of policy."

"No doubt you're feeling smug."

Eli rose from his chair. "Believe it or not, Director, I take no pleasure in the loss of innocent life." He plucked the latest photos from the cubby where Stell had set them. "I only hope you're ready to do the right thing."

Eli turned through the shots from the Heights. "She's not exactly subtle, is she?"

Stell only grunted.

Eli studied the rest of the photos and notes, reconstructing the fight in his mind.

He noticed two things fairly quickly. One—Marcella had a flair for the dramatic.

Two—she wasn't acting alone.

There was the obvious issue of timing, and the method of the killings, of course—but for Eli, the most damning evidence was subtler—a matter of gesture, aesthetic. The scene up on the fourteenth floor was grand, gruesome, theatrical; the killings near the transport van were simple, brutal, and efficient.

One was an exhibitionist.

The other was a trained killer.

Marcella was clearly the first, but then, who was the second? An ally? A colleague? Or simply someone with a vested interest?

"She's not alone," he mused aloud.

"You think so too," said Stell.

It was only a hypothesis, of course, but one soon confirmed by the arrival of security footage from the Heights. Eli had pulled the files up on his computer, while Stell did the same on his tablet, and together they watched in silence as Marcella executed the first two agents. Eli saw, with grim satisfaction, the appearance of the second figure, a large man who snapped the third agent's neck.

And then, as Eli watched, the man became a woman.

It happened between frames, the change so sudden it seemed like a glitch. But it wasn't a glitch at all. It was an *EO*.

A shapeshifter, by the looks of it. An insidious ability, one of the hardest kinds of EO to find.

"Son of a bitch," muttered Stell.

"I hope you're not going to insist on sparing this new one for the sake of policy."

"No," Stell answered grimly. "I think we've established that *neither* of them intends to cooperate. We'll have to plan accordingly."

"One or two, it makes no difference," said Eli. "They may not be human, but they're still mortal. Find them. Kill them. And be done with it."

"You make it sound simple."

Eli shrugged. It was, in theory. The task itself would be more challenging. It took all his restraint, but Eli did not suggest his own involvement a second time. That seed was too freshly planted, its roots too fragile. Besides, he knew what Stell's next course of action would be—he'd suggested it himself. A sniper at a safe distance, a clean-cut execution. If it went well, no more innocents would die. Of course, if it went well, there would be no need to let *him* out.

Eli tensed. That hand on his, the subtle pressure pushing him forward, pulling him back—for so long, he'd assumed it was God, but doubt was a slow, insidious force, wearing away at solid things. Eli still wanted, more than anything, to believe, knew that to demand proof, to ask for a sign, was not the same . . . but he needed something.

And so he told himself, if God willed it . . . if the mission failed . . . if it was meant to be—

And if it wasn't? If Eli was truly on his own?

No—he had seen his opportunity, and he had taken it. And now he had to wait.

Had to have faith.

"You know what you have to do," said Eli.

Stell nodded. "We have to find them again first."

"That shouldn't be hard," said Eli. "Marcella doesn't strike me as the type to run from a fight."

IX

THREE WEEKS AGO

DOWNTOWN

MARCELLA'S steel heels clicked across the lobby of the National building.

June followed a step behind, her steps muffled in her gladiator flats. She had taken on a new aspect—that's what she called them—this time, as a lanky girl with shoulder-length black hair and wide, dark eyes, spindly legs jutting from a pair of white shorts. She was barely sixteen by the looks of it, and when Marcella had asked, June had simply said, "I heard he likes them young."

"Can I help you?" asked the man behind the desk.

Marcella settled the sunglasses in her hair, blue eyes and long lashes on full display. "I certainly hope so," she said in a breathy voice.

She had long ago learned how to turn men into puppets.

It was simple, no special powers needed.

She smiled, and so did the man behind the desk.

She leaned in, and he leaned in to meet her.

"We're here to see Tony."

Marcella didn't have an appointment, but June was right: Hutch *had* been looking for her—he'd left a dozen voicemails on her cell since the card game. Half a minute later, they were on their way upstairs.

June slumped back against the elevator wall. She had gone suspiciously quiet, her mouth now pressed into a grim line. Her earlier humor had vanished, her gaze flicking nervously between the number pad on the wall, and her own reflection, and the gold trim on the ceiling.

The elevator chimed, and the doors slid open onto an elegantly appointed foyer, bookended by a pair of men in dark suits, their holsters visible beneath their tailored jackets. Beyond them, frosted glass doors led into the penthouse.

"Gentlemen," said Marcella, stepping forward.

Her outfit left little room for concealed weapons, but one of the suits still insisted on patting her down, his hands lingering on her hips and under her breasts. When the other guy reached to search June, she just sneered, and Marcella cleared her throat. "I'm pretty sure there are laws against that."

The suit huffed but stood down, clearly deciding it wasn't worth the fight. He tapped a code into a wall panel, and the frosted doors slid open. The space beyond looked more like a living room than an office. Broad white sofas and low glass coffee tables, decanters arranged along a sideboard.

Tony Hutch sat behind a glossy black desk, reading a paper, the city gleaming in the floor-to-ceiling windows at his back. Beyond the glass, a slate patio gave way to a shimmering blue pool, steam rising where the heated surface met the cool spring air.

Tony looked up from his paper and smiled.

They say people grow on you, and maybe that was true, because every time Marcella saw Tony, she felt the need to scrub him off her skin.

He rose and circled the desk, arms wide.

"Marcella, if beauty were a crime . . ." he said, reaching for her hand.

"Then I'd be running this city instead of you," she said dryly.

Tony laughed, even as his attention flicked sideways. "And who's this?"

"My niece, J—"

"Jessica," cut in June, holding out her hand, her accent smothered to a soft edge.

Tony took it, his eyes wandering over her. "Good looks clearly run in the family," he said, brushing his lips against her knuckles. With his head bent, he didn't see June's eyes narrow to slits. Marcella wondered, again, what June had meant by *personal business*.

The two suits were hovering by the glass doors, hands resting on their holsters, but Tony waved them away. "Stand down, boys." A wink. "I think I can handle things here."

Amazing, thought Marcella. Hutch had obviously seen her handiwork at the poker game, and still he treated her like a prop, a pretty but powerless bauble.

How many men would she have to turn to dust before one took her seriously?

The security retreated, and Tony turned toward the sideboard.

"Sit, sit," he said, gesturing at the two chairs in front of the desk. "Can I get you girls a drink?"

He didn't wait for an answer, just started scooping ice into crystal tumblers.

Marcella sank into a chair, but June wandered the suite, restless, examining the art. Marcella turned her attention to Tony. "Did you know about Bethany?"

Tony tutted. "Oh, that," he said, waving it away. "Look, I told Marc to get rid of her, but you know how men are. If dicks and hearts were in the same place—I mean, how many times have I tried to lure you away from your husband—but then, that's not why you're here."

"Why *am* I here, Tony?"

He returned to his chair. "You're here because you've got the sense to come when you're called. You're here to help me understand what the fuck is going on, because I've been hearing a lot of crazy shit, Marce, and all I know is three of my best guys are dead, and the other two seem to have the addled notion that it was *you* who killed them."

"Because it was."

Tony laughed, but there was no humor in it. "I'm not in the mood for games, Marce. I know you and Marcus had a spat—"

"A spat?" cut in Marcella. "He slammed my head against a table. He pinned my body beneath fifty pounds of iron, and set our house on fire with me inside it."

"And yet here you are, alive and well, while my top enforcer is a pile of dust on Sam McGuire's floor. So, you're gonna help me understand what really happened." He didn't bother to say *or else*, only sat back. "Look, I'm not an unreasonable man. You help me, and I'll help you."

Her mouth twitched. "How will you help me?"

"You were always too good for Marcus. I could give you the kind of life you deserve. The kind you're worth . . ."—that slimy smile—"if you ask nice."

Ask nice.

Play nice.

Marcella was so *fucking tired* of nice.

Across the room June let out a short, derisive laugh.

The smile slipped from Tony's face. "Something funny, kid?"

June turned toward them. "I asked you nice once, Tony," she said flatly. "It didn't make a bit of difference."

Tony's eyes narrowed. "Have we met before?"

June leaned her elbows on the back of the empty chair, and pouted. "Oh, Tony." This time, when she spoke, her accent was on full display, strong and sweet. "Don't you recognize me?"

The color drained from his face. "No . . ." Marcella didn't know if it was shock or a denial, but one hand went for the top drawer of his desk.

"Really?" June straightened, and as she did, the teen girl disappeared, replaced by a perfect replica of Tony Hutch himself. "What about now?"

Marcella watched as the Tony Hutch *behind* the desk drew a gun from the top drawer and fired three quick rounds into June's chest.

June looked down as the blood blossomed, sudden and bright across her shirt, but she didn't cry out, didn't fall, just smiled. Behind the desk, the *real* Hutch gasped and clutched his chest as three perfect holes appeared, blood spilling down his front.

"What was it you said to me?" asked June, leaning on the desk. "Ah, yes . . . Don't fight it, baby. You know you like it rough."

His lungs hitched once, twice, body shuddering to a stop.

As the man died, June seemingly lost hold of her powers.

The reflection of Tony fell away like clothes that no longer fit, and for an instant Marcella glimpsed someone *else*—a girl with auburn curls and hazel eyes and freckles like a band of stars across her nose—but it was only for an instant, and then June was back again, as the skinny dark-haired teen she'd worn into the office.

Marcella watched it all in amazement as the true potential of June's power settled over her.

The girl wasn't just a mirror, or a mimic.

She was a *living voodoo doll*.

Marcella broke into a grin just as the frosted doors were flung open and the two guards barreled in, weapons drawn.

June whipped around, no longer the teen girl, but a perfect mimic of the man who'd tried to frisk her. He raised his gun but faltered at the sight of himself, and in that instant of hesitation, June swept a letter opener from the desk and drove it down into her hand. Which was *his* hand.

The man gasped and dropped his gun as blood poured between his fingers. The second guard wavered—the shock of seeing Hutch dead, of seeing his partner suddenly in two places—and Marcella took the opportunity to grab Tony's gun from the desk and shoot the man in the head.

He dropped like a ball of lead. The other scrambled for his fallen weapon, but Marcella was there first, pinning his wounded hand to the floor with the heel of her shoe.

"You crazy bitch," he bleated as she bent down and wrapped her hand around his mouth.

"That's no way to talk to a lady," she said, digging her nails into his skin. It withered in her grip, flesh peeling back to reveal bone that thinned and cracked until the slightest pressure made it shatter.

Marcella straightened, dusting her palms. She swore softly. There was a crack in her manicure.

June whistled a low, appreciative sound. "Well, that was fun." She was perched on the sofa, legs swinging girlishly. She hopped down and started toward the glass doors, their surface now flecked with blood.

"Come on," she said, passing Tony's sideboard. "I need a *real* drink."

X

THREE WEEKS AGO

EAST MERIT

MARCELLA had been to her fair share of bars, but these days, most of them had glowing stained glass, leather booths—at the very least, a *menu*.

The Palisades had cracked windows, wooden stools, and a grimy chalkboard.

It wasn't that Marcella didn't know this world—the world of astringent well drinks and tabs paid in petty cash—but she'd left it behind on purpose. June, on the other hand, seemed right at home, elbows leaning on the sticky counter. She was herself again—not the girl Marcella had glimpsed so briefly in Hutch's office, or the one June had worn on their way in, but the one she had met at the Heights, with those loose brown waves, that long peasant skirt.

June ordered a double whiskey for herself and a martini for Marcella, which turned out to be straight vodka, ungarnished. Which, at the moment, she really didn't mind. She stood at the bar, sipping the drink.

"Fuck's sake, sit down," said June, swinging around in her seat. "And stop wrinkling your nose." The girl lifted her drink. "To a good day's work."

Marcella reluctantly perched on the stool, studying June over her glass.

She was brimming with questions. Two weeks ago, Marcella had been a beautiful, ambitious, but slightly bored housewife, with no idea that people like June, like *her*, existed. Now, she was a widow, one with the ability to ruin anything she touched, and she wasn't even the only one with powers.

"Can you be anyone?" she asked June.

"Anyone I touch," said the girl. "If they're alive. And if they're *human*."

"How does it work?"

"Dunno," said June. "How do you burn people alive?"

"I don't," said Marcella. "Burn them, that is. It's more like . . ."—she considered the drink in her hand—"ruining. Wood rots. Steel rusts. Glass returns to sand. People fall apart."

"What does it *feel* like?"

Like fire, thought Marcella, but that wasn't quite right. She remembered how it felt when Marcus crumbled in her arms. The simple, almost elegant way he came apart. There was something *raw* about her power. Something limitless. She said as much.

"Everything's got a limit," said June. "You should find yours."

The girl's gaze darkened, and Marcella remembered the space between bodies, the brief glimpse of that other shape. "Did you feel it?" she asked. "When he shot you?"

June raised a brow. "I don't feel anything."

"Must be nice."

June hummed thoughtfully, and then asked a very different kind of question. "Do you remember your last thoughts?"

And the strange thing was, Marcella did.

Marcella—who never remembered her own dreams, who rarely remembered a phone number or a catchphrase, who'd said a thousand angry things in the heat of passion and never recalled a single one of them—couldn't seem to forget. The words echoed inside her skull.

"*I will ruin you,*" she recited, softly. Almost reverently.

Now, somehow, she could.

It was as if she'd forged the power through her own formidable will, tempered it with pain and anger and the vicious desire to see her husband pay.

And so she had to wonder: what kind of life—what kind of *death*—made a power like June's? When Marcella asked, the girl went quiet, and in that quiet, Marcella felt the girl gaze into her own internal flame.

"My last thought?" June said at last. "That I would survive. And no one would *ever* be able to hurt me again."

Marcella raised her glass. "And now no one can. And on top of it, you can be anyone you want."

"Except myself." There was no self-pity in June's voice, only a wry humor. "Irony's a bitch."

"So is karma." Marcella twirled her glass. "You know my story," she said. "What's yours?"

"Private," said June shortly.

"Come on," she prompted.

June raised a brow. "Oh, sorry, if you thought this was a girls'-night-out kind of thing, where we get drunk and bond, I'll have to pass."

Marcella looked around. "Then what are we doing here?"

"Celebrating," said June, tossing back her drink and signaling for another before pulling a slip of rolled paper from her pocket. At first, Marcella thought it was a cigarette, but then, as June unfurled it, Marcella realized it was a *list*.

Four names in tight scrawl.

Three of them had already been crossed out.

And there, at the bottom—Antony Hutch.

As Marcella watched, June plucked a pen from the edge of the bar and struck the name out. "Well, that's done," she said, half to herself. And just like that, June was back, a manic light in her eyes as she spun in her seat, folded her arms on the bar. "What do *you* plan to do next?"

Marcella looked into her empty glass. "I think," she said slowly, "I'll take over the mob."

June snorted into her drink. "Brilliant."

But Marcella wasn't joking.

She had only settled for a place at her husband's side because no one would give her a seat at the table.

But she was done settling.

According to Marcus, power belonged to the man with the biggest gun. Marcella thought of the remains of Tony Hutch's body, staining his white carpet.

"How many of us do you think there are?"

"EOs?" June hesitated. "Who knows? More than you'd think. We don't exactly go around advertising."

"But you can find them."

The glass was halfway to June's mouth. Now it stopped. "What?"

"Your power," said Marcella. "You said when you touch someone, you can take their appearance, but only if they're human. Doesn't that mean you can tell when they're *not*?"

June's smile flickered, and returned twice as bright. "You're awfully sharp."

"So I've been told."

June stretched on her stool. "Sure, I can tell. Why? You looking to find more of us?"

"Maybe."

"Why?" June shot her a sideways glance. "Trying to eliminate the competition?"

"Hardly." She finished her drink and set the empty glass down, running a gold nail around the rim. "Men look at anyone with power and see only a threat, an obstacle in their path. They never have the sense to see power for what it really is."

"And what's that?" asked June.

"*Potential.*" Marcella tightened her fingers on the stem of her glass. "This ability of mine," she said as her hand glowed red, "is a weapon." As she spoke, the glass dissolved to sand, slipping through her fingers. "But why settle for one weapon when you can have an arsenal?"

"Because an arsenal stands out," said June.

Marcella's lips twitched. "Maybe it should. People with powers like ours, why should we hide? The life I had is gone. There's no getting it back. I'd rather make a new one. A better one. One where I don't have to pretend to be *weak* to survive."

June chewed her lip thoughtfully. And then, having answered what private question she'd been pondering, June sprang to her feet.

"Come on."

Marcella didn't know if it was the girl's sudden, infectious energy, or if she simply had nowhere else to go, but she stepped down from her stool.

"Where are we going?" asked Marcella.

June glanced back, a wicked light in her eyes.

"I'm in the mood for music."

∞

IF the Palisades had been a dump, the Marina was worse. An underground bunker, half bar and half seedy jazz club, and every surface sticky. Small round tables, trimmed by rickety chairs, half of them empty. A low stage along the back wall, bare but for a few instruments and a standing mic.

June slung herself into a vacant seat and gestured to the chair across from her.

"What are we doing here?" asked Marcella, eyeing the whole situation with suspicion.

"Darling," said June, with dramatic flair. "You must learn to blend in." As she said the words, she changed, shedding the bohemian brunette for an older black man in a faded button-down, sleeves rolled to the elbows.

Marcella stiffened. The lights were low, but not *that* low. She glanced around. "Not exactly subtle."

June chuckled, her voice smoky in the old man's throat. "I thought you were done with hiding." She flicked her hand dismissively at the half-empty club. "People can see an awful lot, and believe none of it." The old man rocked backward in his seat, the front legs coming off the floor as his face vanished into the club's deep shadow. When the chair tipped forward again, June was back to one of her usual selves, loose brown waves tumbling into her face. "Won't you sit?"

Marcella lowered herself into the wooden chair as June went on. "Truth be told, I didn't bring you for the music. Not directly. But if you're interested in other EOs, I might have a treasure for you."

She drew a phone from her pocket and scrolled through her texts, before turning the cell toward Marcella.

A single name stood out on the screen: *Jonathan Richard Royce.*

"Who is he?" she asked.

"A sax player," said June, "a decent one at that. Or he was, until he went and got addicted to heroin. Finds himself in debt to Jack Caprese."

Caprese, thought Marcella. That was a name she knew. Merit was carved up among four men: Hutch, Kolhoff, Mellis, and Caprese.

Hutch had the biggest portion, but Caprese had big eyes, and bigger teeth these days. And a bottomless appetite.

"He couldn't break the habit," continued June. "But he couldn't afford it, either. So Caprese's men go over to sort out the balance. Break a few fingers. Only Jonathan's wife is home too. She pulls a gun, and it all goes sideways. Wife dies. According to medical records, so does Royce. For a few minutes, anyway. But in the end, he pulls through. So Caprese sends more guys around, and those end up dead too. Now no one wants to take credit for a botched kill, and no one wants it getting out that they failed, but for all that they still need Royce in the ground. So they outsource."

"They called you."

June smiled. "Yeah, they called me. But I couldn't kill him."

Marcella raised a brow. "What, you had a change of heart?"

"Hardly," said June. "I mean I really *tried* to kill him. And I *couldn't*."

XI

THREE WEEKS AGO

MERIT CITY LIMITS

JONATHAN Royce owned one good suit, and it didn't even fit.

It had, once upon a time—when he was thirty pounds heavier—but now, it slumped and sagged, always on the verge of slipping off. Just like his wedding ring, staying on only because of a twice-broken knuckle. Jonathan had never been a large man, but these days he was all harsh angles, underslept and undernourished. It was ironic, really—Jonathan looked like an addict, even though he'd been clean since Claire's death.

Everyone he knew had dabbled—drugs and music went hand in hand, and the jazz scene was no exception.

But heroin was a hell of a high.

Not the roller coaster peaks of cocaine, or the mellow *que sera sera* of good weed, but a dreamy wave, a blissful way out of your own life, and your own head, a summer midnight swim in the ocean bare-assed kind of freedom—at first. Jonathan had seen the addiction coming, watched it roll in like a tide, but he was already wet, and he couldn't drag himself back to shore.

And just like a high tide, an undertow, it came and washed everything away.

Money. Joy. Safety. Sanity.

Every day, the tide a little higher. Every day, the water a little deeper. Every day, a little farther from shore. Easy to get swept away. All you gotta do is stop swimming.

Jonathan looped the tie around his neck, fumbling with the knot, his fingers aching.

It had been nearly a year, and the joints still hurt every day.

He wasn't even surprised, the night Caprese's men came to visit. He was already high. Claire was out with friends and Jonathan didn't have their money and he knew it and they knew it and there was the hammer and his hands—but then there she was walking in, there was Claire, screaming, there was Claire, pulling out a gun—where had she gotten that gun?—and then there was noise and pain and darkness.

Jonathan should have left Merit, after that.

Should have bailed the moment he came to in that hospital room with two broken hands and three bullet holes in his stomach and chest. But Claire's blood was still mingled with his on their kitchen floor, and he just couldn't bring himself to *go*. It just didn't make sense, that she was dead, that he was not—Claire didn't deserve it, didn't deserve this, to become a past tense, a footnote in someone else's story—and Jonathan had the strange but unshakable idea that he hadn't made it either. That he was a ghost, anchored to the place where it all happened, bound there until some grim business was done. So he stayed, and wore that one good suit he had to her funeral, dripped ash on it chain-smoking cigarettes in a cheap hotel room afterward, waiting for Caprese's men to find him and finish the job.

Funny thing, but until that night when Caprese's men showed up, Jonathan had never killed anyone before.

He thought it would be harder.

It *should* have been harder, should have been impossible, considering the number of men, the number of shots fired, but so much about that day was impossible. The blue-white shine, like a shield, knocking their bullets away. The cacophony of sound and violence, and when it was over, Jonathan, standing alone among the corpses.

Unscathed.

Untouched.

In his rare metaphysical moments, Jonathan thought it was Claire, looking out for him. But in his masochistic moments, of which there were far more, he knew it was punishment, the universe mocking him for what he'd failed to do.

The clock chimed seven, and Jonathan knotted his worn-out tie. He slid on the jacket, picked up his saxophone case, and headed to work.

His breath fogged before him as he walked, this part of Merit already dark, like it couldn't be bothered with streetlights. It was a half mile to the Marina, a patch of Merit they'd labeled Green Walk on the map, another bit of irony considering there was nothing but stone and asphalt in every direction.

The Ghost of Green Walk.

That was him. The man who couldn't die.

He was already—

"Hey," snarled a voice. "Give me your money."

Jonathan hadn't heard him coming, hadn't really been listening. But he felt the barrel jab into his back, a single nervous thrust, and he turned to find a kid, maybe sixteen, gripping the gun in both hands like it was a bat.

"Go home."

"You deaf or stupid?" growled the kid. "Don't you see this gun? I said, give me your fucking money."

"Or what?"

"Or I'll fucking shoot you."

Jonathan tipped his head back, looked at the sky. "So shoot."

Half the time, they didn't have the balls to fire. This one did. Not that it made any difference. The gun went off and the air glinted around Jonathan, like flint striking stone, that shine, like Claire's arms around him, telling him it wasn't his time, wasn't his turn. The bullet ricocheted, flung into the dark.

"The fuck?" said the kid.

"Quit while you're ahead," warned Jonathan, right before the kid emptied the magazine at Jonathan's head. Seven shots, and six of them rebounded uselessly into the dark, sparkling off bricks, asphalt, shattering a window. But the last bullet snapped back and hit the kid in the knee, and he went down screaming.

Jonathan sighed, and stepped over the writhing form, checking his watch.

He was late for work.

∞

THE Marina was half-empty.

It was always half-empty. Jonathan recognized most of the people who *did* show up, but something was different. He knew the moment he stepped in, like the air was full of snow. It was the two women near the back, the one like something out of a catalogue, red lips and glossy black hair, the other younger, with a mane of brown curls and a dangerous smile.

They watched him the whole set.

Maybe once upon a time, he'd drawn that kind of attention. But that was back when his hands could do better, back when he fit into the suit, back when his smile came easy, mostly because he was already high.

Jonathan was checked out—he made it through his set, hit the notes by habit instead of passion, and then went to the bar, carried on a wave of weak applause and a strong tide of self-loathing.

"Club soda," he said, sliding onto a stool. He could still feel eyes on him. Every now and then, Caprese sent someone around to try again, but it never took. Those two women didn't look like Caprese's usual killers, but maybe that was the point. He heard the neat click of the heels a second before the knockout appeared at his shoulder.

"Mr. Royce." Her voice was warm and sleek and laced with smoke.

The brunette hopped up on a stool. "Johnny boy," she said, and there was something about her accent, familiar, as if they'd met before, but he was sure he'd never seen her face.

"If Caprese sent you . . ." he muttered.

"Caprese," said the dark-haired woman, turning the name over in her mouth. "He's the one that killed your wife, right?"

Jonathan said nothing.

"And yet," she continued, "Jack Caprese is still alive. Flourishing, I've heard. While you're here in this shithole of a club, wasting away."

"Oy," chirped the other woman. "I like this place."

"Who are you?" asked Jonathan.

"June," said the brunette.

"Marcella," said the black-haired beauty. "But when it comes to people like us, the real question isn't who, is it? It's *what*."

The woman pressed a single gold nail against the bar and, as Jonathan watched, her finger glowed red, and the wood beneath began to warp and rot, wearing a hole straight through. The brunette—June—slid a coaster over the damage, only she wasn't the brunette anymore. She was Chris, the Palisades bartender, even though Chris was still on the other side of the counter, back turned while he polished a highball glass. By the time he turned back, so had she.

Jonathan's mouth went dry.

They had powers, like his shine. But the shine was a gift. The shine was a curse. The shine was *his*. There weren't supposed to be others with him, here in this hell.

"What do you want?" he asked, voice barely a whisper.

"That," said the beautiful woman, "is what I was just about to ask *you*."

Jonathan stared down into his club soda. He wanted his life back. But he had no life, not anymore. He wanted death, but he'd been deprived of that, too.

That night, after Caprese's men were all dead, and Jonathan wasn't, when the room was silent and dark and the world was empty, he had put the gun to his head and pulled the trigger, and that should have been the end of it, but it wasn't, because the shine was there again, like it or not, and that made him think of Claire, and how pissed she'd be, him throwing away a second shot. And thinking of Claire made him want to get high again, to float out to sea.

But the shine wouldn't let him.

Jonathan had told himself that he wouldn't try again.

He wouldn't let her down.

But it was like a whole new kind of drug, using that shine. A fearsome reminder that he was still alive.

June was frowning, as if she could read Jonathan's mind. But Marcella smiled.

"Why sit around sulking," she said, "when you could hurt the people who hurt you?"

But he *had* hurt them—he'd killed the men who killed Claire, and the ones who came for him, and everyone else Caprese sent. Every single one—except—

"Caprese," murmured Jonathan.

Was *that* why the shine wouldn't let him rest?

Why he couldn't get to Claire?

"I can help you get to him," said Marcella. She leaned in, close enough for him to smell her perfume. "I've heard a little about your talent, but I'd love to know more." She reached out and brought her fingers to rest against his arm. It was such a simple gesture, almost kind, right up until her palm flared red. The shine flashed along his skin, and she pulled back, considering her hand. "Hm," she said, as if she hadn't just tried to ruin him. "How do you do it?"

"I don't *do* anything," said Jonathan bitterly. "It just happens. Someone tries to hurt me—hell, I try to hurt myself—and it's there. Shielding me."

"Well, bully for you," said June, leaning back on the counter.

Marcella made a small, displeased hum. "I don't see how that helps me."

Jonathan stared into his glass. "I can share it."

Marcella's blue eyes narrowed. "What do you mean?"

Jonathan shook his head. This was how the shine mocked him. How he knew it wasn't a gift at all, but a curse, a shallow cut, not deep enough to kill, but more than enough to hurt. He'd just wanted to protect Claire, and he'd failed. Now, when he finally could, it was too late. She was already gone.

"Jonathan," pressed Marcella.

"I can shield someone else," he admitted, "so long as I can see them."

Marcella smiled. It was a dazzling smile, the kind that made you want to smile back, even when there was nothing to smile about.

"Well, in that case," she said, "let's talk about revenge."

XII

THREE WEEKS AGO

SOMEWHERE OUTSIDE OF BRENTHAVEN

VICTOR'S steps rustled in underbrush.

It was almost dusk, the sky sinking into violent shades around him as he picked his way through the woods. Now and then the silence was punctuated by distant gunfire as, across the reserve, hunters picked off their prey before the last of the light failed.

Victor was hunting too. He trailed a broad man in an orange vest, the shock of color picking him out from the surrounding mottle of green and gray. The trees were sparse, surrounded by fields to every side. A few miles south, a small cabin, the full extent of the man's footprint.

Despite his current attire, Ian Campbell had been a hard man to find.

He'd gone off the grid after his accident, a disappearance almost as complete as death.

Almost.

But in this day and age, it was impossible not to leave a mark.

It had taken Mitch months to track this particular EO down. But he'd done it. Because he knew, just as Victor knew, that they were running out of options. The stack of paper had dwindled down to a few spare sheets, and as the leads shrank, the length of Victor's deaths grew, the seconds ticking upward until they threatened to brush that lethal edge, the medically established threshold of no return.

A soft bleating sound alerted Victor to the likely object of Campbell's attention.

An injured deer lay in the brush, its side opened by a scattering of buckshot. As Victor slowed to watch from the shadow of a nearby tree, Campbell crouched over the injured deer, making gentle noises as he laid a hand on the animal's side.

And then, as Victor watched, the buckshot rose back up through muscle and skin, and rolled down the animal's sides into the grass.

Victor's breath caught.

He had become so accustomed to disappointment—to tracking EO after EO down, only to learn that their powers were incompatible, or worse, irrelevant—so he was caught off guard by the sight of Campbell's power. The realization that he'd finally found someone who could help.

The deer rose on unsteady legs, and then bounded away through the trees, unhurt.

Campbell watched it go. Victor watched Campbell.

"Is it a kindness," asked Victor, his voice breaking the stillness, "to loose prey back into the world, simply to be shot again?"

Campbell, to his credit, didn't jump. He straightened, brushing his palms against his jeans. "Can't do much about the hunters," he said. "But never could pass up a creature in pain."

Victor laughed, a humorless, hollow sound. "Then you should have no qualms about helping me."

Campbell's expression narrowed. "Animals are innocent," he said. "*People* are another matter. Most, I've found, don't deserve the help."

Victor bristled—it sounded like something Eli would say. His fingers twitched, the air beginning to hum, but Campbell surprised him by stepping forward instead of away.

"How are you hurt?" he asked.

Victor hesitated, unsure how to answer such a simple question with such a complicated answer. In the end, he said, "Mortally."

Campbell gave him a long, measured look.

"All right," he said. "I'll do what I can."

Victor's heart stuttered, not from an episode, but from hope. A thing so rare he'd forgotten what it felt like. He had been prepared to use force.

"There are limits," continued Campbell. "I can't stop nature. Can't change its course. I can't rewind death, but I *can* undo a violence."

"Then," said Victor, whose deaths had been shaped by blood and pain, "you are well suited to this."

Campbell held out his hand, and Victor, who had never been comfortable with contact, forced himself to still as the EO's hand came to rest on his shoulder.

Campbell closed his eyes, and Victor waited. Waited for humming in his skull to disappear, waited for the crackle in his nerves to ease and the ticking clock to finally stop—

But nothing happened.

After a long, empty second, Campbell's hand fell away, and Victor knew that he'd found another dead end. But he'd seen Campbell's power. It should have worked. It had to work.

"I'm sorry," said the man, shaking his head. "I can't help you."

"Why not?" snarled Victor.

For the first time, Campbell backed away. "When I said I could—I meant—I can heal a violence done by *someone else*. But whatever's happened to you, however you're hurt, you've done it to yourself."

Victor's anger sliced through him like a knife, sudden and deep. His hand clenched into a fist, and Campbell staggered back into the brush, a pained sob wrenching from his throat.

"Get up," demanded Victor. But he raised his hand as he said it, forcing Campbell upright. *"Fix me."*

"I can't!" gasped Campbell. "I told you, I can only heal the *innocent*. You're not a victim."

"Who are you to judge me?" growled Victor.

"No one," said Campbell. "The power judges for itself. I'm *sorry*, I—"

Victor shoved Campbell away with a snarl. Behind his eyes, he saw his death—not the most recent, or the one at Eli's hands, but the very first, the one in the lab at Lockland, the way he'd climbed onto the table, pressed his bare back against the cold steel, summoned death to him like a demon, a slave, an order.

In the woods, Campbell had struggled back to his feet.

Victor half expected the EO to run, but he didn't.

Darkness had swept in around them, but even in the lightless woods, Victor saw the genuine sadness in the other EO's eyes.

Victor briefly considered letting the man go. But if he'd found Campbell, it was only a matter of time before EON did too. Their reach seemed farther by the day.

"I'm sorry," said Campbell again.

"Me too," said Victor, drawing his gun.

The shots echoed through the woods.

The body collapsed, and Victor sighed, and slumped back against the nearest tree, the humming louder than ever in his head. He closed his eyes, suddenly, immeasurably tired.

If you kill all the EOs you meet, how are you better than Eli?

Whatever's happened to you, however you're hurt, you've done it to yourself.

His cell broke the silence. Victor dragged his eyes open and answered the call, rising to his feet. "Dominic." He heard the telltale sounds of a bar in the background. "You have news?"

"There's a new EO," said Dom. "A bold one. Name's Marcella Riggins."

"Is she a viable lead?" asked Victor as he started back the way he'd come.

"No," said Dom. "Her power is definitely of a destructive nature."

Victor sighed. "Then what is she to me?"

"I just thought you'd want to know. She's just drawing a lot of attention."

"Good," said Victor shortly. "Then EON can waste their time hunting her instead of me."

He knew, of course, thanks to Dominic, that they were already chasing him. Or rather, chasing *someone*. And he had a good idea who was leading the charge.

Victor had been disgusted, but not surprised, when he'd learned about the way Stell was using Eli Ever. Putting him back to work. Eli always did have a knack for finding his way to the center of a stage, and Stell had fallen for his charms before. Victor wondered if *that* was why EON hadn't gotten closer. Not because their pet had failed to see Victor's hand in the killings, but because he *had*.

It would be so like Eli, that self-righteous, self-absorbed need to handle things himself.

And every day the noose failed to tighten, Victor's suspicions grew.

As for Marcella Riggins, let her have the spotlight, as long as she could hold it. When it came to EOs, there was a kind of natural selection. Most had the sense to stay in the shadows, but when the need for attention outweighed a sense of self-preservation, the scales tended to balance themselves.

And people like Marcella never lasted long.

XIII

THREE WEEKS AGO

JUST OUTSIDE MERIT

RAIN slipped through the warehouse roof, the steady drip of water masking the clip of Marcella's heels against the concrete floor. The old cannery sat on the outskirts of town, a skeleton of pillars and steel beams and a rotting roof, one of the designated parcels of neutral ground in the city.

Their voices drifted through the bones of the building.

". . . in his own office . . ."

". . . it can't stand . . ."

". . . who's going to handle . . ."

". . . just one woman . . ."

". . . no way she's working alone . . ."

"What is it with men and places like this?" mused Marcella, her voice loud enough to carry as three heads came into sight. "I swear, you always pick the most morose places to gather."

The men turned toward her. Joe Kolhoff. Bob Mellis. Jack Caprese. She'd half expected to find them sitting at another round table, these self-proclaimed knights of Merit, but instead she found them huddled in the center of the dreary, leaking space.

Unbelievable, thought Marcella. Her husband reduced to ash, Tony dead at his desk, and yet they *still* didn't even bother to draw their guns. Neutral ground rules dictated that bosses didn't carry, but surely no one actually went into a meeting like this without at least *one* piece of artillery.

"Is it the ambiance?" Marcella wondered as she made her way toward them. "Or does like simply call to like? Defunct. Outdated. Obsolete. So many old buildings in this city," she said, nails trailing across a concrete pillar. "It's insane the money they waste on repairs and refurbishments. Sometimes it's better to just raze the whole thing and start fresh, don't you think?"

"The once-late Marcella Riggins," sneered Kolhoff. "You've got some nerve—"

"Oh, I like to think I've got a great deal of nerve, Joe."

"If you had a damn bit of *sense*," said Mellis, "you would have run."

"In these shoes?" she teased, glancing down at her steel heels. "And miss this lovely meeting?"

"You weren't invited," said Kolhoff.

"What can I say? My ears were burning."

"How did you find us?" demanded Caprese.

Marcella wandered between the pillars, nails skating over concrete. "My husband used to have a saying. *Knowledge may be power, but money buys both.*" Her hand fell away. "Turns out some of Hutch's men were more than willing to change sides, in exchange for a promotion."

"Bullshit," hissed Caprese. "Family doesn't turn."

Marcella rolled her eyes. "The amazing thing about these *families* of yours," she said, dragging her hand along another pillar, "is that they're only family to the ones on top. Head far enough down the tree, and you find a whole lot of people who don't really care who's in charge, as long as they're getting paid." She let her eyes wander to the warehouse wall, the lot beyond, where half a dozen black sedans idled. "I wonder how many of *your* men will jump at the chance to work for me, the moment you're gone."

Kolhoff bristled. Mellis drew a knife from his back pocket, flicking it lazily open. Caprese, finally, produced a gun. "I always thought you were a brazen bitch," he said, training the barrel on her, "but you're obviously a stupid one, too, coming here alone."

Marcella continued her path between the pillars, unconcerned by the weapons. "Who said I came alone?"

Jonathan's dress shoes tapped out a rhythm on the concrete as he came into sight. He moved as if in a trance, his dark eyes trained on Caprese as he walked straight toward him. The mob boss squeezed off a shot, and the bullet struck the air in front of Jonathan with a burst of blue-white light before ricocheting off, sparking on the concrete floor.

"What the fuck . . ." snarled Caprese, firing again and again as Jonathan closed the distance between them, bullets skating off before one finally bounced back, hitting Caprese squarely in the knee. He gasped, and buckled, clutching his leg.

Jonathan didn't say anything. He simply drew his own gun, aimed at the kneeling man's forehead, and fired.

Kolhoff and Mellis froze, their eyes wide as Caprese's body slumped, lifeless, to the cold ground.

Marcella clicked her tongue, pressing her hand flat against the final pillar. "If you had a damn bit of sense," she said, red light seeping from her palm, "you would have run."

The concrete beneath her hand gave way, and as it did, the other pillars began to shudder and lurch, each already weakened by her passing touch. The building let out a heavy groan as the columns crumbled and the roof bowed, buckled.

Mellis and Kolhoff were running now, but there was no point. June had already locked the doors. A massive chunk of stone came crashing down, Marcella in its path.

She watched it fall, fascinated, limbs fizzing with excitement and fear.

"Jonathan," she said, but he was already looking, and the air around her shimmered with blue-white light just before the rubble struck. Rocks shattered against the forcefield and slid off, raining harmlessly down around her.

Marcella remembered the first time she witnessed a demolition. The thing that struck her most, after that initial boom, was the quiet grace, the way the whole behemoth had sagged sleepily, sinking less like a mass of bricks and steel than a failed soufflé. It was, admittedly, a little less peaceful from this angle, and not nearly as quiet.

But Marcella savored it all the same.

Savored the men's screams, the warping metal and the broken rock and the way the whole world shook as the building fell down around them, burying Kolhoff, and Mellis, and Caprese. Three more men who'd stood in her way.

The wreckage carved a circle of destruction around Marcella, around Jonathan, leaving them unharmed, though barricaded. Contained. But there was nothing that could hold her now. Marcella brought her fingers to the nearest block of concrete and pressed, her whole hand flaring crimson, a violent light spreading like fire up her arm.

The concrete weakened, cracked, shattered, the obstacles laid to waste, the path made clear.

Marcella had yet to test the limit of her power. Or rather, had yet to *find* it. The destruction came so easily.

She strode out of the ruined building, Jonathan trailing like a shadow.

June was waiting at the edge of the rubble, eyes wide. "That wasn't exactly subtle."

Marcella only smiled. "Sometimes subtlety is overrated."

June gestured to the suited men spilling out of the waiting black sedans. "And what do we tell the cavalry?"

Marcella considered the men.

"Let's tell them," she said, "that the Merit mob is under new management."

MARCELLA collapsed onto the cream leather sofa, laughter bubbling across her lips. "You should have seen their faces, June..."

The city stretched beyond the floor-to-ceiling glass, glittering in the last shards of light.

Marcella had always wanted to live in the National.

Now that she was here, Hutch's penthouse felt like a temporary stop on the way to bigger, better things. But it was still a pretty one. Especially now that the blood had been scrubbed out. A few stubborn flecks remained, but Marcella didn't mind them. No, they were reminders of what she'd done. What she was capable of doing. Enemies reduced to stains under her feet.

As far as the standard personnel were concerned, Tony Hutch had gone on holiday, something he was prone to do.

He'd always been a man of many vices, used to his privacy.

Jonathan slipped like a ghost down the hall, but June lingered, perched on the edge of the sofa.

"You know," she said. "One body doesn't draw much notice. The trouble is when they start adding up. Mob boys don't exactly phone the feds every time someone bites it, but you're testing them. Do you not remember what I said, about EON?"

"All the more reason to stand out."

June crossed her arms. "How do you figure?"

Marcella curled a clump of black hair absently around one finger. "When people stay in the dark, it's easier to make them disappear." She sat up. "I just brought down an entire building. You can be anyone you want. And Jonathan can render us untouchable. We're not just impressive, we're invincible. We *should* stand out."

June shook her head. "If you want to survive—"

"But I don't want to *survive*," sneered Marcella. "I want to *thrive*. And I promise you, I'm just getting started."

The girl rolled her eyes. "What now? You're going to throw yourself a fucking party?"

A slow smile spread across Marcella's mouth. It wasn't such a bad idea.

"No," said June. "No, that was a joke—"

A gunshot went off from another room.

"Dammit," hissed Marcella, rising to her feet.

June followed, and together they found Jonathan standing in one of the bedrooms, the gun hanging limply from his fingers, a hole in the far wall where the bullet had ricocheted.

"What are you doing?" demanded Marcella.

"Didn't work," he murmured. "Thought it might. Now that Caprese's gone . . ."

"Sorry, Johnny," said June, "apparently you've still got work to do."

He sank onto the bed, head in his hands.

"Just wanted . . ." he said, gripping the gun in both hands, "to be with Claire . . ."

Marcella sighed, and pulled the weapon from his grip. His moroseness was killing her buzz.

"Come on," she said, turning on her heel, "we all clearly need a drink."

She didn't look back, but she heard Jonathan drag himself up from the bed and follow them into the main room.

June was in a restless mood, trading one aspect for another with every step. An old woman with a tattooed sleeve. A young black man in a tailored suit. A pretty twentysomething in a white minidress.

"You're making me dizzy," snapped Marcella.

June slumped onto the sofa, and took on a new aspect. She wasn't Marcella—couldn't be—but she was clearly meant to be close. Porcelain skin and black hair and legs for days. The face was too wide, the eyes green instead of blue. They followed Marcella to the sideboard lining the wall, with its collection of rare, expensive bourbons.

She set the gun on the crystal top and poured Jonathan a few fingers of something dark and strong. No ice.

"You missed quite a speech," said June. "Our girl's got big plans."

Marcella didn't rise to June's baiting. She handed the drink to

Jonathan. "That's right," she said. "And you're clearly meant to be a part of them." Marcella turned to June and offered her a glass. "What about you, June?"

She wasn't just asking about the drink, and they both knew it.

The other EO shook her head, but she was smiling, a playful, almost dangerous light in her eyes. "I've said my piece. Do as you please. After all, if EON comes calling, they won't catch *me*."

June took the drink, and Marcella held up her own. "A toast, to bigger, better—"

The window shattered behind them.

The bullet would have caught Marcella in the back, if Jonathan hadn't still been staring at her. Instead, it ricocheted in a burst of light, followed in quick succession by three more, shots whistling through the air.

One of them struck June. She stumbled, fell, her shape sloughing away as she did. For a second, barely a fraction of a second, Marcella saw the girl's true form again—the auburn hair, the band of freckles—and then that person was gone, replaced by a stranger, launching their body out of the line of fire.

"I told you—" started June.

"Not the time," snapped Marcella, as a decanter nearby exploded into glassy shards. "Keep your eyes on me," she ordered Jonathan. And then she turned, set down her glass of whiskey, and took up her gun.

The shots continued, a hail of fire that turned the air blue and white as Jonathan's forcefield reflected every shot. Marcella moved with a careful, calculated grace, forcing herself not to flinch amid the onslaught. It was exhilarating, knowing that her life wasn't, for the moment, in her own hands. Knowing that if Jonathan looked away, the shield would fall, and she'd be hit.

But sometimes, you had to have a little faith.

Marcella marched across the penthouse to the shattered floor-to-ceiling windows, the jagged rim of glass gaping open like a mouth. She touched the edge, and the remaining shards crumbled, crystals caught up and swept away by a gust of cold night air as Marcella stepped through the empty window, heels grinding on glass and sand and debris.

This, she thought, crossing the balcony, *is why you don't hide.*

This, she thought, lifting her own gun, *is why you let them see your strength.*

Marcella squinted through the flash and spark of Jonathan's shine, trying to find the flares of light that marked the sniper's rifle in the dark as she fired, again and again, emptying her clip into the night.

XIV

TWO WEEKS AGO

DOWNTOWN WHITTON

SYDNEY ran her fingers over the small bones.

Dol had found the bird in the gutter earlier that day, if it could be called a bird—it was a gnarled mess of sinew and feather, a single ruined wing. It was pitiful to start with, and worse still after Syd had pried it from the big dog's mouth, and now it lay sadly on a worn kitchen towel atop her borrowed bed. Dol watched, his chin resting on the comforter.

Somewhere beyond the doors, Mitch was making dinner, and humming an old song. They each had their own ways of coping with the stress, the fear, the hope. She turned her attention to the bird.

"What do you think?" she asked Dol.

The dog sighed, still sulking over the stolen prize. She scratched his ears—the closer he was, the stronger she could feel the threads that bound them, and the easier it was to remind her fingers what they were searching for.

Sydney took a deep breath, glanced at the red metal tin beside the bed, and then closed her eyes. She felt her way forward, let her hands come to rest on the sad remains, and reached.

It felt like a long fall.

It felt like emptiness and cold.

It felt like forever—and then Syd registered the faint blush of light, the twist and curl of a thread. No, not a thread. A dozen wisp-thin filaments, fragments scattered across the black stretch behind her eyes. They swam across her vision like fish, darting away from her touch, and Sydney's lungs began to ache, but she didn't give up. Slowly, painstakingly, she gathered the filaments, imagined fitting the fraying threads back together. Knotting them.

It took hours. Days. Years.

And only an instant.

As she tied the final knot, the thread glimmered, pulsed, became a flutter of feathers against her palm.

Sydney's eyes flew open as the bird moved beneath her fingers.

A sound escaped her throat, half laugh, half sob, a mixture of victory and shock, and then the sound was overtaken by the furious wing-beats and the squawk of a very surprised pigeon trying to escape the confines of her grip.

It pecked at her knuckles, and Sydney let go—a rookie mistake, as the bird took flight in the narrow room, searching for freedom, bouncing off the light fixture and the window, Dol bobbing his head as if trying to catch airborne apples.

Sydney lunged for the window and threw it open, and the bird escaped into the night in a flurry of gray feathers.

She stared after it, amazed.

She'd done it.

It was a bird, not a human, but Sydney had still taken only a few mangled bones and made the creature whole. Brought it back to life.

In seconds, she was across the room, prying the lid off the red metal tin. The last—the only—pieces of Serena Clarke lay nested inside, wrapped in a scrap of fabric. Sydney reached for them, heart racing—and stopped.

Her hand hovered over the remains.

What if it wasn't enough?

A bird wasn't a girl. If she tried, and failed, she'd never get another chance.

If she tried, and failed—but what else could she do? The rest of Serena was ash, scattered across a city hundreds of miles away.

Would it make a difference?

Sydney had never wondered if the *where* mattered as much as the *what*, but now, as she nestled the lid back on the tin, she thought, *Ghosts are tied to the place where they died.* She didn't believe in ghosts, but she had to believe in something—that thread of light, the closest thing she could find to a soul. If there was any of Serena left, beyond the bones in this box, it would be there.

Sydney would just have to wait.

XV

TWO WEEKS AGO

CAPSTONE

STELL'S plane had landed at dawn. He didn't know why a video conference wouldn't suffice, but the board had insisted on his presence, and short of outright defiance, Stell had had no choice but to go.

In his absence, he'd left Rios with strict instructions. No procedures were to be put into effect in his absence. No commands given or followed unless they came expressly from him.

The last thing Stell needed was a mutiny.

Now he stared across the nondescript conference table at five nondescript faces atop nondescript suits. Stell suspected that by the time he left the room, he wouldn't be able to pick any of them out of a lineup, let alone a crowd.

"First a failed EO capture," said the woman in black, "now a failed extermination."

"You've made quite a mess," added the man in gray.

"We've faced difficult EOs before," said Stell. "It's only a matter of time—"

"Only a matter of time," cut in the man in black, "before EON and its interests are both dragged into the spotlight."

"My team is doing everything we can," said Stell.

"That isn't strictly true," said the man in black. "We called you here because we believe your personal bias has prevented you from utilizing every asset at your disposal."

"Bias?" challenged Stell.

"We don't deny," added the woman in navy, "that you've been *integral* to the development of this organization—"

"*Development?* I *created* EON. I brought you the first intel, I explained the threat level—hell, I had to convince *several* of you of the very legitimacy of EOs."

The man in charcoal cleared his throat. "We are not questioning your contribution."

The man in gray leaned forward. "We know you have a strong personal attachment to the early ideals of this organization."

"Which is why," said in the woman in black, "you're not objectively qualified to judge its current needs."

"My subjectivity is an asset," said Stell. "You seem to think we're dealing with manufactured weaponry here. Only I seem to realize we're dealing with *people*."

"A case could be made," said the man in charcoal, "that they are *both*."

Stell shook his head. It always came back to this—to money, and power, and the board's desire for both. If the board had their way, they'd turn each and every captured EO into a weapon. Preferably single-use.

"Marcella Riggins makes a mockery of EON, and of you," said the woman in navy. "You claim you are doing everything you can, using every tool at your disposal, and yet you keep settling for low-range munitions when you have one perfectly suited to the task."

He understood then, with painful clarity.

Eli.

"At least *low-range* munitions have safety catches. Eli Cardale does not. I won't authorize him for use in the field."

The man in charcoal sat forward. "You yourself have advocated for this kind of utility."

"This is different," said Stell. "Eli isn't an ex-soldier. He's a mass murderer."

"One who has been cooperative for more than four years."

Stell shook his head. "You don't know him like I do."

"And so we return to the issue of objectivity," said the woman in navy.

"Insight isn't the same as bias," snapped Stell. "You think we have a mess on our hands right now. It's nothing compared to what would happen if we set him free."

"Who said anything about *free?*" asked the man in black. "There *are* countermeasures. According to our records, tracking devices were installed—"

"It's not just a matter of *losing* Eli," said Stell. "It's what he'll do before we find him again. He can't be controlled."

At this, the man in gray produced a briefcase. "With that in mind," he said, sliding it down the table, "a sturdier solution."

The clasps came open to reveal a smooth steel ring, nested on a bed of black. When Stell reached in, he discovered it was actually two rings, one pressed into the other. A seam ran along each circle, so that the fused collar could hinge open and closed.

"Haverty's methods were admittedly problematic," said the woman in black, "but in this case, they were also useful. His initial tests explored Cardale's general ability to heal. His second series explored the extent of that healing—and its limitations."

A small remote, flat as a credit card and half as wide, lay impressed in the fabric beneath the collar, a single button on the smooth dark surface.

"Haverty discovered a threshold. Anything smaller than, say, a pill, and Cardale's body could absorb it. Anything larger, and his body would physically reject the intrusion. However, if he was unable to reject the object, his body could not heal."

Stell thought of Eli, awake on the operating table, his chest pinned open as Haverty worked.

"We've had R and D on this project for months. Go ahead, try it."

Stell pressed the concave button, and the collar's inner ring collapsed, folding at the seam so that the band of metal transformed into a vicious spike.

"It's designed," explained the man in black, "to sever a human spinal column between the fourth and fifth vertebrae. In an ordinary person, such an injury would result in permanent paralysis. Due to Cardale's condition, the effects would obviously be temporary, but they should be just as effective."

"This is, of course, only an suggestion." The woman in navy shot him a thin smile.

"You are still EON's *director,* after all."

Stell returned the collar to the case, the board's logic warring with the lead weight in his stomach.

"But we would strongly advise you to handle this EO, and handle her swiftly. Using any and *every* means necessary."

∞

BACK IN MERIT

Stell's house key always stuck in the lock.

He knew he should get it fixed, but he didn't spend much time at home. Slept in his own bed one night in three. Ate most of his meals in EON's canteen. He wasn't sure what made him drive from the airport into the city instead of back toward EON, didn't even realize what he was doing until he was halfway there. But his head was still cluttered from the meeting with the board, and the two whiskeys on the plane had done nothing to clear it, and Stell realized he didn't want to step through those doors until he knew exactly what he planned to do.

About Marcella.

About Eli.

Stell shrugged out of his coat. Lit a cigarette, even before he set the steel briefcase on the kitchen table. Slid the clasps.

The smooth metal collar sat nested in its velvet groove.

You are not using your assets.

Was the board right?

Send me.

Stell lowered himself into a chair.

You will never see the outside of this cell.

Was he letting his past color his judgment?

Or was he just listening to his gut?

He rubbed his eyes. Took a long drag of the cigarette, filling his lungs with smoke. The collar glinted in its case, EON's solution—but not Stell's. Not yet.

His cell rang. Stell answered without looking at the screen.

"Hello?"

He'd expected Rios, or a member of the board, but the voice on the line was smooth, sultry.

"Joseph," it said with all the warmth of an old friend.

He frowned, stubbing out the cigarette. "Who is this?"

"You really have to ask?"

"Do I know you?"

"I should hope so. After all, your men have spent a great deal of time shooting at me."

Stell's fingers tightened imperceptibly on the phone.

Marcella Riggins.

"If I didn't know any better, I'd think you had something against me."

"How did you get this number?"

He could hear the smile in her voice. "I'm getting tired of killing your agents. Are you getting tired of burying them?" She didn't wait for him to answer. "Perhaps," she continued, "we could find a more sophisticated solution . . ."

"Most EOs only get one chance," said Stell. "I'm giving you two. Surrender now, and—"

A soft laugh. "Now, Joseph," she chided. "Why would I do a thing like that?"

"So you just called to gloat."

"Not at all."

"Then why?"

"I thought," she said airily, "perhaps we could get a drink."

That, at last, caught Stell off guard. "To what end?" he demanded. "So you can try to kill me?"

"That would be pointless. If I wanted you dead, you would be. You think this number is the only thing I know? I have to say, your choice of decor is tragically bland."

Stell's head snapped up.

"Of course," she went on, "you're really not home much, are you?"

Stell said nothing, but shifted so his back was to the wall, his eyes on the windows.

"Only a few photos," she went on, "—two sisters, I presume, by the way they look at you—"

"You've made your point," he said through clenched teeth.

"Well, in that case, I'll be at Canica Bar around seven. Don't make me drink alone."

Before he could answer, she hung up.

Stell slumped back against the wall, head spinning. He couldn't go. He *shouldn't* go. Marcella was a target, an enemy, someone to be dispatched, not negotiated with.

But he had to do something.

He looked from the steel briefcase to the cell phone in his hand.

Stell swore under his breath, and grabbed his coat.

XVI

TWO WEEKS AGO

DOWNTOWN MERIT

SOME women spent years planning their wedding.

Marcella had spent the last decade planning a hostile takeover.

Of course, she'd always assumed Marcus would be the face of it, but this was far more satisfying.

With the four heads of the Merit mob so cleanly dispatched, and the factions thrown into chaos—a chaos bolstered by rumor and eyewitness testimony—the bulk were already scrambling for solid ground. So many, so willing to serve.

There would be scuffles, of course, and Marcella was prepared for those, ready to subdue the ones who would invariably vie for control, ready to pay off the officials who might get in her way.

There was still the matter of EON, but Marcella had a play for that, too.

She put her back to the window, surveying the room, Jonathan polishing his saxophone in a chair, June perched on the spine of the sofa, playing on her phone. With Hutch's suite at the National ruined, they'd taken up residence in an uptown penthouse at First and White. One with windows made of reflective glass.

Fool me once, thought Marcella, as someone knocked.

Jonathan answered the door, stepping aside to reveal a trim man in a silk suit.

"Oliver!" Marcella smiled at the sight of him—smiled wider at the rack of clothes filling the foyer. Between the house fire and the incident at the Heights, Marcella was in dire need of a new wardrobe.

"Shit, Marce," said Oliver, "you've got some heavy security downstairs. Felt me up, down, and in between."

"Sorry," she said. "It's been a busy week."

"Excuse me for being a bit wary at the moment," said June. "But who the fuck is this?"

"This is Oliver," said Marcella cheerfully. "My personal shopper."

June burst into raucous laughter. "People are trying to kill you—kill *us*—and you've got time for a fucking wardrobe change?"

Oliver smirked. "Spoken like someone who doesn't understand the power of appearance."

"That so?" June hopped down from the back of the sofa. She moved toward Oliver, taking on and shedding a different appearance with every step. "Maybe you should explain it to me?"

Oliver went very still.

"And that," said Marcella dryly, "would be June."

His gaze shifted unsteadily back to her. "I, uh, heard . . . about Marcus. Hell, I heard about *you*. Lots of strange talk."

"Whatever you've heard," said June, "it's probably true."

Marcella gestured at Jonathan, standing in his worn-out suit. "Ollie, did you bring what I asked for?"

In reply, Oliver pulled a garment bag from the rack and unzipped it far enough to reveal a sharp black suit. Marcella plucked it from Oliver's hand.

"A gift," she said, offering the bag to Jonathan.

"Nothing for me?" inquired June.

"You already have a full closet," said Marcella. She turned toward the bedroom. "Come on. Let's see what you've brought."

By the time he started unzipping dress bags, Oliver had regained his usual color. "Gotta say, I was a little surprised to get your call," he said, adding hurriedly, "and glad, of course. You always were my favorite mannequin."

She plucked a few blouses from the rack as Oliver began to lay out dresses on the bed. For a moment the image overlaid with another in her mind, the garments left waiting atop tousled sheets.

Marcella let go of the blouse in her hand before she ruined it.

"You have outdone yourself," she said, eyes traveling over the array. A lace halter, trimmed in black leather. A crimson blazer with sharp shoulders and tapered wrists. A black gown with a dipping collar and a silk obi tie. A line of perfect, steel-heeled shoes.

She lifted one. The polish was so high, Marcella could almost see herself in the shine. Red lips and black hair painted themselves on the metal finish, her reflection warping, as if she were on fire.

Oliver turned his back while Marcella stripped and donned a short red dress that drew a clean line across her shoulder blades. She considered herself in the bedroom's full-length mirror, let her eyes travel appraisingly over the burns that traced along her left collarbone, the inside of her right forearm, the top of one pale thigh.

They were healing, the skin slipping from pink to silver.

"That one's stunning on you," said Oliver at Marcella's back. Her eyes slid past her own reflection just in time to see him draw a slim switchblade from his bag. Marcella didn't flinch.

"Zip me up?" she said lightly.

"Of course." Oliver started toward her, and Marcella waited until he was almost an arm's length away before turning suddenly. He slashed, and she caught the knife in her hand, her palm already glowing red. Before the weapon could so much as scratch her skin, it had crumbled.

"What a pity," she said, wrapping her other hand around Oliver's throat. "You had such good taste."

He managed the beginnings of a scream before the skin and muscle gave way to bone, and then ash, and then nothing.

"Christ," said June, appearing in the doorway. She took in the scene. "Well, that's what you get for having a personal shopper." She nodded at Oliver's remains. "Is there anyone who *doesn't* want to kill you?"

"Occupational hazard, it seems," said Marcella.

"So it seems," said June. "And how long do you think before our friends at EON try their luck again?"

Marcella turned back to the mirror, flicking a stray bit of ash from the hem of her dress. She met her reflection, and smiled.

"Let me worry about them."

XVII

TWO WEEKS AGO

CANICA BAR

A long chandelier rippled across the ceiling, spilling soft light over crystal and marble and clean linen.

Stell adjusted his tie, grateful he was still dressed from the meeting at Capstone.

"You have a reservation, sir?" asked the maître d'.

"I'm meeting someone," said Stell, cautiously. "I'm early but—"

"You can wait at the bar," said the maître d', nodding to a curve of glass and oak.

Stell ordered a whiskey several shelves higher than his usual brand and scanned the guests—some of the most powerful and prominent people in Merit. The district attorney. The mayor's wife. Corporate heads, and politicians, and more than one star athlete.

He saw *her* as soon as she arrived.

It was impossible *not* to see her, even in Canica's low light.

She was dressed in red—not exactly subtle, but nothing about her would have ever merited that word. Her black hair curled in loose waves around her face. Her lips were the same shade as the dress, her eyes a striking blue.

Stell had seen photos, of course.

None of them did Marcella Riggins justice.

Stell could sense other heads turning as she made her way to a table in the center of the restaurant. He took up his glass from the bar and followed.

When she saw him, a smile broke the sharp line of her red lips.

"Joseph," she said, wielding his first name like a weapon. "So glad you decided to come."

Her voice was warm, tinged with smoke.

"Ms. Riggins," said Stell, sinking into the chair opposite.

"Morgan," she corrected as a glass of red wine was laid at her elbow. "Given all that's happened, I no longer feel inclined to use my husband's name. But please, call me Marcella."

She spoke with an airy confidence, one gold nail toying with the rim of her glass, and Stell realized that it wasn't Marcella's *beauty* that had failed to translate in any of the photos he'd seen. It was something else.

Something he'd seen before.

In Victor Vale. In Eli Ever.

A rare kind of strength. A dangerous will.

Someone this powerful belongs in the ground.

Suddenly he understood Eli's stance, the stubborn resolve behind his declaration. Stell's hand drifted toward his holstered gun.

If you don't kill her, you'll wish you had.

His fingers brushed the safety.

But Marcella only laughed. "Come on, Joseph," she said. "I'm sure you've noticed, weapons don't really work on me."

Stell had seen the footage, of course—Marcella on the shattered balcony, the sniper's shots skating off the air around her. He'd also seen the image of the thin man in the dark suit. The one, he realized, who was now sitting several tables over, wearing sunglasses, despite the restaurant's low light. The set of the man's shoulders, the angle of his face, suggested he was staring directly at them.

Another EO, Stell wagered.

"Don't mind Jonathan," said Marcella. "It's not that I don't trust you, Joseph," she added congenially. "But, well, we're still getting to know each other."

A fresh whiskey appeared at Stell's elbow. He didn't remember finishing his first, but the glass was empty. He lifted the new tumbler, took a sip, and stopped, recognizing the taste.

It was a brand Stell kept in his apartment. One that he only poured when he had something in particular to celebrate.

Marcella smiled, knowingly. Her long legs uncrossed and recrossed, high heels glinting like knives at the edge of his sight.

"Tell me," she said, twirling the wineglass stem between her fingers. "Do you have the place surrounded?"

"No," said Stell. "Believe it or not, I'm not eager for anyone to know I'm sitting down with a terrorist."

Marcella pursed her lips. "It will take more than harsh words to wound me, Joseph."

The way she used his name, as if he were the wineglass between her fingers, something to be toyed with. "You wanted to meet," he said curtly. "Tell me why."

"EON," she said simply.

"What about it?"

"You seem to target us because of *what* we are, not *who*. That kind of indiscriminate attack is shortsighted, to say the least." Marcella leaned back in her seat. "Why make another enemy, when you could have an ally?"

"An ally," echoed Stell. "What could you possibly offer me?"

A slow, crimson smile. "What do you *want*? Less violence? Safer streets? Organized crime really has gotten out of hand lately."

Stell raised a brow. "You think you can change the course of the *mob*?"

Marcella's smile shone. "Haven't you heard? I *am* the mob now." She rapped her nails on the linen tablecloth. "No, you want to deal in kind, don't you? A more relevant currency? You want . . . EOs."

"You would hand over your own?"

"My own what?" Marcella scoffed. "Who are they to me?" Stell looked past her again to the man in the dark suit. Marcella read his expression. "I'm afraid June and Jonathan are not up for trade. They belong to me. But surely there are others, ones that have eluded your grasp?"

Stell hesitated. Of course, some EOs were harder to catch than others, but there was only one that had proved, so far, impossible.

"There is an EO," he said slowly, "one who seems to be targeting their own kind." He didn't elaborate, didn't share Eli's theory regarding their motivations. "So far they've killed seven other EOs."

Marcella's eyes widened in mock surprise. "Isn't that *your* job?"

"I don't approve of needless death," said Stell. "Regardless of whether the victim was human, or not."

"Ah, a man with morals."

"My *morals* are the only reason I agreed to this meeting. Because I'm tired of burying good soldiers—"

"And because you haven't figured out how to stop me," said Marcella. Stell swallowed, but she waved him away. "This is a last resort. Why else would you sit down with a terrorist?"

"Do you want a ceasefire, or not?" asked Stell tightly.

Marcella considered her wine. "This EO—am I to search in the dark, or will you give me a starting mark?"

Stell drew a notepad from his pocket and scribbled down a list. He tore the sheet off. "The last five cities where the killer struck," he explained, sliding the paper across the table.

Marcella slipped the sheet into her purse without reading it. "I'll see what I can do."

"You have two weeks," countered Stell.

It was long enough to produce results, but not long enough for Marcella to waste time. She was right—and she was wrong—this wasn't the last resort. Stell *did* have a way to stop her. But it wasn't the one he wanted. Two weeks would give him time to think, to plan, and if he couldn't find another option, then two weeks was how long he had to decide which was worse—letting Marcella walk free, or Eli.

"Two weeks," mused Marcella.

"That's how long this service buys you," said Stell. "If you succeed in producing the killer, then perhaps we can continue to find common ground. If you fail, then I'm afraid your value to EON will not merit your continued freedom."

"A man who knows what he wants," said Marcella with a feline smile.

"There is another term—you will stop drawing so much attention to yourself."

"*That's* going to be hard," she teased.

"Then stop drawing attention to your *power*," clarified Stell. "No more public demonstrations. No more grand displays. The last thing this city needs is a reason to fall apart."

"We certainly wouldn't want that," said Marcella coyly. "I'll find your target for you, Joseph. And in exchange, you will stay out of my business, and out of my way." She lifted her glass. "Do we have a deal?"

XVIII

TWO WEEKS AGO

EON

ELI studied the footage again, and again.

The mission at the National should have been simple.

But nothing about Marcella Riggins was proving simple.

"You should be celebrating," said Victor's ghost. "Isn't this what you wanted?"

Eli didn't answer. He focused on the footage from the scene, advanced the surveillance one frame at a time, watching as the glass shattered, the bullet—which should have taken Marcella in the back of the head—ricocheted, sparking off an invisible shield.

Eli paused the footage there, rapping his fingers thoughtfully on the table.

The odds of a single EO possessing more than one power were slim to none. No, it was far more likely, he surmised, that this particular skill belonged to the third, as yet unidentified EO, the one lurking like a shadow at the very back of the room.

Three EOs, working together—that itself was unusual. The vast majority were loners, isolated by either necessity or choice. Few looked for others, let alone found them.

"We did," observed Victor.

It was true. Both Eli and Victor had arrived at the same conclusion—that there was strength in numbers, potential in the complementary pairing of powers.

Now, apparently, so had Marcella.

Eli rolled the footage forward and watched her step through the hail of bullets onto the balcony. Watched as every single shot ricocheted. Watched as she raised her own gun in the general direction of the sniper.

There was something so brazen about the gesture . . .

EOs ran.

EOs hid.

Under pressure, an EO might fight back.

But they didn't do *this*.

Didn't *perform*.

Didn't use their powers with such obvious relish.

EOs were broken by definition, made reckless by the absence, the emptiness, the knowledge that their lives were over. It drove them to steal, to ruin, to self-destruct.

Marcella wasn't self-destructing.

She was preening. Baiting them. Daring them to try again, try harder.

She had taken out her husband—and that made sense, an act of revenge. Of closure. But then, she'd taken out his *competition*. That wasn't the mark of someone with nothing to lose. No, that was the mark of someone with something to *gain*. That was *ambition*. And ambition plus power was a very dangerous combination.

What would she do, if left unchecked?

The phantom in his head was right—he'd asked for a sign that he was needed, that this was right.

Marcella couldn't be allowed to continue in this manner.

And soon Stell would realize, if he hadn't already, that Eli was the only one who could put her down.

Footsteps sounded from beyond the fiberglass, and he looked up from the computer as Stell appeared on the other side of the wall.

"There you are," said Eli, rising to his feet. "I've gone through all the footage from the failed execution, and we're obviously going to need a much more tailored approach, especially considering there are . . ." Eli trailed off as Stell set a new case file in the tray.

"What's that?"

"We got a hit on a suspected EO two hours south of Merit."

Eli frowned. "And Marcella?"

"She isn't the only target we're tracking."

"But she's the most dangerous," said Eli. "And in the last three days she's collected two more. What are we going to do about—"

"*We* aren't going to do anything," said Stell shortly. "Your job is to analyze the files I give you. Or have you forgotten that you exist at the mercy of EON?"

Eli clenched his teeth. "There are three EOs working *together* in Merit, and you're just going to ignore them?"

"I'm not ignoring *anything*," countered Stell. "But we can't afford another failed op. Marcella and her partners need to be handled cautiously. You have two weeks to devise that *more tailored approach* you spoke of."

Eli drew up short. "Why two weeks?"

Stell hesitated at that. "Because," he said slowly, "that is how long I've given her to prove her worth as an asset."

Eli reeled. "You made a *deal*? With an *EO*?"

"The world is not black and white," said Stell. "Sometimes there are other options."

"Where were *mine*?" snapped Eli. "The lab or the cell—those are the only ones *I* was given."

"You killed forty people."

"And how many has she killed already? How many more lives will she destroy by the time you see fit to put her down?" Stell didn't answer. "How could you be so stupid?"

"You will remember your place," warned Stell.

"Why?" demanded Eli. "Tell me why you would make a deal with her."

But Eli knew. Of course he knew. *This* was how far Stell was willing to go to keep him in this cage, contained, controlled.

"What did you mean," he said through gritted teeth, "when you said her worth as an asset?"

Stell cleared his throat. "I've given her a mission. A chance to succeed where you have failed."

Eli stilled. No. The open file. The unsolved case. Victor.

"The hunter is *mine*," he growled.

"You've had two years," said Stell. "Perhaps it's time for fresh eyes."

Eli didn't realize he'd approached the fiberglass until he slammed his fist against it.

This time, the gesture wasn't calculated. It was pure rage, a moment of violent emotion turned to violent action. Pain flashed through him, and the wall hummed in warning, but Eli's hand was already falling away.

Stell's mouth twitched, a grim smile. "I'll leave you to your work."

Eli watched the director go until the wall went white, and then he turned and slumped back against it, sliding to the floor.

All of his patience, his subtle pressures. The ground beneath him shuddered, threatened to break. One misstep, and it would crumble, and he would lose Victor and Marcella both, and with them, justice, closure, and any hope of freedom. It might already be too late.

He studied the back of his hand, where a single smear of blood marred the knuckles.

"How many will die for the sake of his pride?" mused Victor.

Eli looked up and saw the phantom standing over him again.

He shook his head. "Stell would rather let the city burn than admit that we are on the same side."

Victor stared at the wall as if it were still a window. "He doesn't know how patient you are," he said. "Doesn't know you like I do."

Eli cleaned the blood from his hand.

"No," he said softly. "No one ever has."

XIX

TWO WEEKS AGO

FIRST AND WHITE

JUNE whistled softly as she rinsed the blood from her hands.

Marcella had swept out of the penthouse in her red dress, Jonathan trailing like a shadow at her heels. She didn't say where she was going, or when she'd be back, didn't ask June to come with, which was fine with her. Jonathan might be a lap dog, but June preferred to work alone.

Which, mind you, wasn't the same as *being* alone. Too much silence, too much space. But idle hands and all that—which is how June ended up wrists deep in someone else's blood.

She hadn't taken a new job in more than week. Hadn't needed to. Hutch had been the final name on her personal list, and Marcella had been working up a roster of *obstacles,* as she called them—men and women most likely to resist her rapid ascent—so whenever June got bored, she just went out and knocked a few off the list.

Marcella didn't seem to mind.

Some people were matches, a bit of light and no heat. And some were furnaces, all heat but little light. And then, once in a blue moon, there was a bonfire, something so hot and bright you couldn't stand too near without burning.

Marcella was a bonfire if ever June saw one.

Of course, even bonfires eventually went out, smothered by their own ashes. But in the meantime, June had to admire the other woman's ambition, and had to admit she was actually enjoying herself.

The only thing missing was Sydney's soft laugh, her bright smile . . .

June snapped the water off, dried her hands, met her gaze in the reflection.

No. Not hers. Not her hazel eyes. Not her red hair. Not her freckles.

But she'd found herself taking this aspect—brown waves, green eyes, sharp chin—more and more often. It felt strange, holding on to one face long enough for other people to remember it.

Was it worth it? Syd had asked her that night, when she confessed to giving up her face, her life, herself. And it was, it *was*, but that didn't stop June from craving the light of recognition in someone's eyes. The comfort of being seen, being known.

She could be anyone, these days, a million outfits at her disposal, but she tried not to get too attached to any one of them. After all, people died, and when they did, their shape vanished from her closet. (Sometimes she didn't even know they were gone until she went looking.)

Only one shape was guaranteed to be there, and it was the one she wouldn't wear.

June heard the door swing open, the signature click of Marcella's heels on the marble floor. June went to find her, and passed Jonathan on his way to the balcony, a cigarette between his teeth. Marcella shrugged out of a white trench coat.

"What have you been up to?" asked June, leaning against the wall.

"Making connections," said Marcella. She drew a folded piece of paper from her purse. "Since you have a knack for finding people—"

"I have a knack for *killing* people," corrected June. "Finding them is simply a prerequisite."

"Well, I have a job for you." Marcella held out the slip. "Did you know that there's someone out there killing EOs?"

"Yeah," said June, taking the folded slip. "It's called EON."

Marcella persisted. "I'm talking about an *EO*. Someone like us, *killing* people like us. Which I find rather vexing."

June unfolded the paper, her gaze flitting over the list.

Fulton.
Dresden.
South Broughton.
Brenthaven.
Halloway.

She stilled, recognition flitting like a pulse inside her chest. "What is this?"

"The locations," said Marcella, "of the EO's last five kills."

June didn't look at her phone, but she knew that if she did, if she opened her texts from Sydney, she'd see these same places listed, each in response to the question June always asked.

Where are you these days?

June wanted to know, because the world was big, wanted to know because Sydney was hers to protect. She read the list again.

So this was what Victor had been doing. Why the three of them were always on the move. But June doubted that he was purely an executioner. Doubted it was that simple.

We're looking for someone who can help.

Maybe that was true. Maybe Victor was being *thorough*. Covering his tracks afterward. It made sense, considering he was supposed to be dead.

"Let me get this straight," said June, pocketing the list, "there's an EO out there killing other EOs. And you want to find him."

"*EON* wants to find him," said Marcella. "And they want my help."

June let out a short, humorless laugh. "That's what you meant by *making connections*?"

"Indeed," said Marcella. "I told you I would handle them. But I had to give the boys something, and it was either you and Jonathan, or this." Marcella leaned on the marble counter. "They've given me two weeks to find this EO killer."

"And what happens then?"

"Oh," mused Marcella, tracing the veins in the stone, "I imagine that Director Stell will decide I'm more trouble than I'm worth."

"You don't seem worried," said June.

Marcella straightened. "He's underestimated what I can do with two weeks. In the meantime, I suppose we should find that EO."

June's mind was turning, but she kept her voice airy, light. "What are you going to do with him?"

"You know," said Marcella, "I haven't decided yet."

XX

A WEEK AND A HALF AGO

DOWNTOWN WHITTON

JUNE had texted Sydney on her way to the car, sat idling there until she saw the three small dots that signaled an incoming reply.

Syd: Whitton.

June put the location into her GPS, and shifted into gear as the map came up on the screen.

From there it was easy to find them.

How's the view? she'd asked. *Tell me what you see.*

Such a simple question, made routine by years of checking in, asking such small, seemingly innocuous questions as a way to condense the distance between them. June soon learned that Sydney and Victor and Mitch were staying in a nondescript apartment building, a ten-story stack of tan stone blocks on a street filled with the same, the only relief a small park on the corner, the bright flags on the hotel across the street.

June checked in to that same hotel the next day, and waited. Waited for proof that Victor was the EO killer, that he was the person Stell was looking for, the one Marcella promised to find.

She had been waiting for three days.

Victor came and went, a constant, restless force, carving slow circles through the small city, and June would follow at a distance, snapping photos with her phone. But so far, he'd yet to make a move. June was getting restless.

Still, it hadn't *all* been a waste of time. She'd gotten to see Syd—hadn't let the girl see her, of course, there would be time for that later—but once, she'd trailed Mitch and Sydney to a movie, sat right behind them, and let herself pretend they were there together, like a family.

It had been nice.

But mostly, June waited.

She hated waiting.

Right now, she was pacing on the curb outside the hotel, dressed as an old man, a cigarette hanging from her fingers.

She looked up, now and then, waiting for the balcony door five floors up and two over to slide open, waiting for Syd to emerge into the afternoon sun.

A few minutes later, she did.

That familiar blond bob caught the light as she stepped out onto the patio. June smiled—despite Sydney's complaints, she *was* growing up. The changes were subtle, sure, but June knew people well enough to read those subtleties, even if they had less to do with height and weight and more to do with posture, poise.

Syd had explained the problem of her aging, sometime around her sixteenth birthday. It was the cold—or, at least, that was Victor's theory—that the hypothermia she'd suffered had slowed *everything* about her. Syd had complained that, at the rate things seemed to be going, her teens would take forever. But then June had pointed out that so would her twenties, and in her own experience, those were the best years, anyway. Syd had gotten quiet then, silence stretching across cities.

"And by the time I'm thirty," she'd said, "everyone I know will be dead. Except for Eli."

Eli. The way Sydney said that name, as if she was afraid that speaking it too loud would somehow summon him.

"What about you?" she'd asked June with sudden curiosity. "Do you age?"

June had hesitated. She'd glimpsed the shape that hung in the back of her wardrobe, the one she never took out. It hung so perfectly still, beneath its film of disuse, but there was no denying.

"I do."

Now, June watched as Sydney sank into a patio chair, head bowed over her phone even as she put her feet up on that giant black dog, who didn't seem to mind at all.

A few seconds later, June's cell gave a soft ping.

>   **Syd**: Are you still in Merit?

She tipped her head up to savor the warm blue sky, and then lied.

>   **June**: Yeah. It's raining. I hope the weather's nicer there.

The front door across the street swung open, and a wraith of a man stepped out, shielding his eyes from the sun. It had been three years since June had seen Victor Vale. He didn't look well. His face was a rock worn with deep hollows. And the way he moved—as if he were a length of cord, strung so tight that any force might snap it.

He hurts people, Sydney had said.

But June had been watching for days, and aside from the way strangers bent out of his path, she hadn't seen him use his power once. He didn't look that strong.

He's sick. It's my fault.

Victor started down the block. June stubbed out her cigarette and followed, merging with a small group of pedestrians as it passed. With each intersection, strangers peeled away, but others joined, and all the while June kept Victor in her sights. He moved like a ghost through the city, slipping out of its bright heart and into seedier parts, before arriving in a district known as the Brickworks.

Four warehouses, squat brick buildings like pillars, or compass points, framed the blocks that made up the Brickworks, and between them, a network of bars, betting shops, strip clubs, and darker fare.

You didn't need a line or a fence to find the place where good neighborhoods gave way to bad ones. June had lived in enough of both to know by feel. The shift from new steel to old stone. Double-glazed windows to spidering glass. The polish worn off, and never repainted. Curbs glittering with the remains of the last broken bottle.

The Brickworks didn't even pretend to be respectable.

Few places could exude that much trouble in the middle of the day, and given the sheer number of illicit businesses, June guessed the local police were getting a cut to look the other way. By the time she stepped across the proverbial tracks, she'd shifted into an old biker, all gristle and bone and tattooed sleeves.

It wasn't the first time Victor's wanderings had led him—and by extension June—to this corner of the city. He was obviously looking for someone. But the tangle of buildings and the broad daylight made it hard to follow too closely. June fell back, and when Victor's pale head vanished through a door at the back of a bar, she changed tactics, returned to the street and circled until she found a half-rusted ladder hanging from a structurally unstable fire escape.

June hauled herself up onto the nearest warehouse roof, boots skimming the tar as, somewhere nearby, a door crashed open. She crossed the roof in time to see a man go crashing backward into a stack of empty crates, muttering curses.

Victor came into view a few seconds later. The man on the ground got up and started toward Victor, only to buckle, as if he'd been struck.

Victor's cool voice wafted up like smoke.

"I will ask you one more time . . ."

The man said something, the words low and unintelligible from June's position on the roof. But Victor clearly heard him. With a single, upward flick of his hand, the man was forced up to his feet, and Victor shot him in the head.

The silencer muffled the violence of the gun's retort, but not its impact. Blood sprayed across the bricks, and the man fell lifeless to the ground. A second later, something seemed to fall in Victor, too. His poise, so tightly held, began to fray, and he swayed a little on his feet before slumping back against the opposite wall. He ran a hand through his light hair, and let his head tip back against the brick as he looked up.

June lunged backward, breath held, waiting for some sign that he'd seen her. But Victor's gaze had been miles away. She heard his footsteps, slow and even, and by the time she chanced another look over the rooftop edge, he had disappeared around the corner.

∞

JUNE found him again, at the edge of the Brickworks, followed half a block behind as she dialed Marcella's number.

She hesitated before she hit Call, not because she had any lingering doubts, but simply because the words would carry weight, consequence, and not just for Victor. Putting him in EON's path meant endangering Sydney, too.

But June would be there. She'd keep her girl safe.

The phone rang once, and then Marcella answered. "Well?"

June studied the man in black. "His name is Victor Vale."

"That was fast," said Marcella. "And you're sure he's the one they're looking for?"

"Positive," said June.

"And his power?"

"Pain," said June.

She could hear Marcella's smile. "*Interesting.* Is he alone?"

"Yes," said June. "As far as I can tell."

The words came out effortlessly. Lying was a skill made easy by habit.

Besides, Sydney was *hers*, and June didn't know if she wanted to share. If she could get the girl to Merit, maybe. If Marcella succeeded, if the time came when EOs didn't have to hide, or run. June knew Sydney was tired of running. In the meantime, there was no need for Marcella to know about the girl. Not yet.

"I'll stay here," continued June. "Keep an eye on things. Wouldn't want Victor to slip away." She frankly didn't care if EON got their hands on Victor, but she wasn't about to let Sydney fall into the same trap. "Unless you need me," she added.

"No," said Marcella. "We'll survive a little longer without your sparkling wit."

"You know you miss me," said June. "Has Merit built a statue in your honor yet?"

Marcella only laughed. "Not yet," she said, "but they will."

And June honestly couldn't tell if she was joking.

∞

AS June followed Victor home, she toyed with the idea of killing him then and there.

She knew she *shouldn't*, but the idea was tempting. It would certainly make things simpler. And she was pretty sure she could manage the kill—the pain wasn't an issue, but that physical control of his would likely make things difficult. Still, June did love a challenge. She turned the idea over like a butterfly knife as she walked. After all, Marcella planned to hand Victor over to EON. Wouldn't it be a mercy, to cut him down instead? It was a boon, of course, that in killing Victor, Sydney would be free—free of her guilt and her attachment.

June was still mulling it over when, halfway down the block, Victor stumbled.

His step changed, lost its smooth stride. She saw him lurch to a stop, and then start again, his steps faster, more urgent.

June quickened her pace, but as Victor reached the intersection, the light changed, and there was a jostle of bodies, a taxi pulled too far forward, honking horns and hurrying shapes, and in that second, June lost him.

She swore, doubling back.

She hadn't been that far behind.

Where could he have gone?

He wasn't on the main road, which meant he'd slipped down a side street. June checked one, and then another, and she was at the mouth of the third when she caught sight of him, his back to her, doubled over and clutching at the wall. She started toward him, shifting into a middle-aged woman with mousy brown hair, innocuous, forgettable, and was just about to call out, ask if he was all right, when Victor collapsed.

As he did, the air around him rippled, and a second later, something slammed into June with all the force of a truck. If a truck were made of current instead of steel.

June was thrown backward, her latest shape sloughing away by the time she hit the pavement. Had she been anyone else, the force would have killed her.

As it was, she *felt* it. Not the blast itself, but the back of her head where it hit the ground. Pain cut a shallow line across her scalp, and June sat up, rubbing her head. Her fingers came away dotted with red, and her breath caught, not at the sight of the blood, but the arm, familiar pale skin dotted with freckles.

She was herself. Vulnerable. Exposed.

"Fuck." June staggered to her feet, swapping out the body—*her* body—for another, shuddering with relief as the pain was erased along with every other trace of her true form.

And then she remembered Victor.

He was slumped, motionless, against the alley wall. His head lolled against his chest.

He's sick, Sydney had said. *I made him sick.*

But the body on the ground wasn't just sick. It was *dead*. No pulse, no color, no signs of life.

Amazing—after all the time June had spent persuading herself *not* to kill him, he'd gone and died anyway.

At least, she *thought* he was dead. He certainly *looked* dead.

Cautiously, June moved toward the body.

She crouched, and touched his shoulder, and as she did, something leapt through her fingers, flickered through her mind. Memories. Not all of them, not even a handful, only one. A lab. A redhead. A current. A scream. It moved through her like static shock, a single glimpse, brief, and impossible, bright, and then gone.

June recoiled, shaking out her hand, and then she drew her gun and brought the barrel to rest against the man's forehead. Whether or not he was really dead, she could make it stick. He'd made it so easy. Maybe fate was shining on June after all.

She thumbed off the safety, let her finger come to rest against the trigger.

And then stopped.

June could think of a dozen reasons to make sure Victor was dead, and only one to stay her hand.

Sydney.

This was the one thing Sydney would never forgive, if she found out. Besides, June didn't want to steal the girl this way. Wanted to win her, fair and square. She'd told Sydney once that people should choose their family, and she'd meant it.

June wanted Sydney to *choose* her.

So she lowered the gun. Was just sliding the weapon back into her coat when suddenly, impossibly, Victor *moved*.

June nearly jumped out of her skin.

Few things caught her by surprise these days, but the sight of Victor Vale, shuddering back to life, was enough to give her a fright. His fingers twitched, a small current running visibly over his skin, and then his chest inflated as he drew a deep breath, and opened his eyes, and looked up.

"Oh, Christ," said June, one hand to her racing heart. "I thought you were dead!"

For a moment, Victor stared at her with the blank gaze of the very drunk, or the hopelessly lost. And then, quick as a spark, the light went on behind his eyes.

If he was surprised to find himself sitting on the ground, it didn't show.

He started to say something, and then stopped, and drew a small black object from between his teeth. A mouth guard. June realized that whatever had happened just now, it wasn't the first time.

Victor was looking at June now, his gaze cold and clear.

"Do I know you?" he asked, and there was no thickness in his voice, no disorientation, only study.

"Don't think so," said June, talking as fast as she could think, relieved she'd shifted into another disarming body, the black-haired girl she'd used in Hutch's office. "I was just walking past and saw you lying on the ground. Should I call an ambulance?"

"No," said Victor quietly, rising to his feet.

"No offense, sir, but you didn't look too well a moment ago."

"I have a condition."

Bullshit, thought June. Seizures were a condition. What she'd seen just now was death.

"I'm fine now," he insisted.

That bit seemed true. Whatever had come over Victor, it was already gone. The man who stood before her now was the picture of control. He turned, heading back toward the street.

June had a clear shot at the back of his head, but she also had the strange certainty that if she went for her gun now, she'd never get the shot off.

The air was humming with power, and none of it was hers. So June's hand stayed at her side as she watched Victor go, swearing inwardly.

She should have killed him when she had the chance.

XXI

ONE WEEK AGO

DOWNTOWN WHITTON

SYDNEY Clarke was getting stronger.

She'd resurrected three more birds since the first, each feat performed using fewer and fewer pieces.

She was just setting her latest victory free when she heard the front door close.

Victor was home.

She hadn't told him yet, about the successes—she knew he'd be proud, wanted to see that pride turned toward her—but she didn't want to jinx them, didn't want him to look at her and glimpse the motive behind her progress, the reason for her intensity.

Victor was too good at seeing through things.

Sydney shut the window and started toward the bedroom door, but halfway there, she felt her steps slow, something catch in her throat.

The two voices beyond were muffled, but distinct.

Victor's, low and steady. "He was incompatible."

Mitch's halting reply. "That was the last one."

Something pitched inside Sydney's chest.

The last one.

She pressed a hand against her sternum, as if trying to stop its fall. She realized what it was as it slipped between her fingers. Hope.

"I see." That was all Victor said.

As if it were a mild setback and not a death knell.

Sydney's head came to rest against the bedroom door, her most recent victory forgotten. She waited until the space beyond was quiet. And then she stepped out into the hall.

The door to Victor's room was closed, and Mitch was a dark shape out on the patio, his head bowed, his elbows resting on the rail.

In the kitchen, a piece of paper sat crumpled on top of the trash. Sydney drew it out, smoothed it on the counter.

It was Victor's last EO profile.

His last lead.

The page had been reduced to a wall of black lines, interrupted only by five letters, scattered across the page.

FIXME.

Sydney held her breath. Behind her eyes, the surface of a lake cracked under Victor's feet.

XXII

ONE WEEK AGO

DOWNTOWN MERIT

BY the end of the first week, Stell knew he'd made a terrible mistake.

He knew it when he saw the sinkhole on Broadway. Knew it when he was called to the collapsed building on Ninth. And he certainly knew it when he stepped into the ballroom at the Continental.

He moved through the vast space, a hazard mask cinched over his nose and mouth. The ballroom was high-ceilinged and ornate, a popular place for business execs and powerful families alike to throw parties. Stell assumed that was what had been happening the night before. After all, the tables were still laid out, the gossamer and ribbons still drew ghostly lines through the air.

Only the *people* were missing.

No, not missing. A fine patina of ash covered every surface. It was all that was left of the forty-one guests in the Continental's evening register.

Needless to say, the scene had tripped the Merit PD's *strange shit* alarm.

Stell had seen enough—he retreated into the hall, pulling the mask from his face as he dialed.

Two rings later, Marcella's smooth voice answered. "Hello, Joseph."

"Do you want to tell me," hissed Stell, "what I'm looking at right now?"

"I couldn't say."

"Then I'll tell *you*," he snapped. "I'm standing outside a ballroom at the Continental. It looks like a fucking snowstorm in there."

"How peculiar."

"What part of lying low did you *not* understand?"

"Well," she said coyly, "I didn't sign my name in the ashes."

He pinched the bridge of his nose. "You are making it very hard to look the other way."

"Crime *has* gone down, as promised."

"No," said Stell, "it's simply been *consolidated*." He lowered his voice as he paced the hall. "Tell me you have something to show me, besides this gross display. Preferably something related to the subject of our mutual interest."

Marcella sighed. "You really do take the fun out of things. I thought we could have lunch to celebrate, but since you're obviously busy, I'll go ahead and tell you now. I found your EO killer."

Stell stiffened. "Is he with you now?"

"No," said Marcella. "But don't worry. A deal's a deal. And I still have a week."

"Marcella—"

"I'm sending you a photo. To whet your appetite."

XXIII

ONE WEEK AGO

EON

SHE really was clever, thought Eli.

He lay, stretched out on the cot, staring up at his reflection in the mirror ceiling as he turned the problem like a coin between his fingers.

Through some combination of strategy and luck, Marcella had managed to flank herself with two compatible powers. He lined them up in his mind.

The ruiner. The shapeshifter. The forcefield.

Up close. Long distance. And everything between. Together, their powers were nearly impregnable. But find a way to separate them, and Marcella would die just like anyone else.

Footsteps sounded beyond the glass, and a second later, the far wall went clear, revealing a very red-faced Stell. "Did you know?"

Eli blinked and sat up. "I'm not omniscient, Director. You'll have to be more specific."

Stell slammed a piece of paper against the barrier. A printout. A photograph. Eli swung his legs off the cot and approached the glass. Stilled when he saw the face in the photo. There he was, the narrow face, hawkish in profile, chin grazing the collar of his trench coat. Not a good photo, not a *clear* photo, but Eli would recognize him anywhere.

Victor Vale.

"Two years," said Stell. "That's how long you've had to track him down, and Marcella delivers this in less than two weeks. You buried it. You *knew*."

But Eli realized, staring at the photo, that he hadn't known, not really. He'd wanted to be right, wanted to be sure, but there had always been that fissure, a line of doubt. Now, it sealed, smoothed, solid enough to bear the weight of the truth.

"I guess you didn't burn the body."

"God *dammit*, Eli," snarled Stell. He shook his head. "How is this possible?"

"Victor's always been terrible at staying dead."

"*How?*" demanded Stell.

"Serena's little sister had the inconvenient ability to resurrect the dead."

"Sydney Clarke? You listed her among your kills."

"Technically," said Eli, "Serena was supposed to take care of her. Obviously she got cold feet."

One more thing he'd have to handle himself.

Eli dragged his gaze away from the photo. "What are you going to do about him?"

"I'm going to find him. You two can each have a cell to rot in."

"Oh, great," said Eli dryly. "We can be neighbors."

"This isn't a fucking joke," snapped Stell. "All your talk of cooperation, I knew it was a ruse. I *knew* you couldn't be trusted."

"In the name of *God*," scoffed Eli. "How many excuses will you find to vindicate your own stubbornness?"

"He's been out there, killing humans and EOs, and you *knew*."

"I *suspected*—"

"And you didn't say anything."

"You didn't burn the body!" roared Eli. "I put him down, and *you* let him get back up. Victor Vale's continued existence, and the deaths he's since accrued—those are *your* failures, not mine. Yes, I kept my suspicions from you, because I hoped I was *wrong*, hoped that you hadn't been so foolish, hadn't failed so catastrophically. And if you had, well, then I knew my warnings would fall on deaf ears. You want Victor? Fine. I'll help you take him *again*."

He went to the low shelf, drew the hunter's folder from the row of case files.

"Unless you'd rather let Marcella lead you through her hoops instead."

He dropped the folder in the open tray.

"I'm sure once she figures out Victor's value, she'll make you pay every cent."

Stell said nothing, his face a poor imitation of a stone wall as he slowly reached for the file. But Eli, of course, could still see every crack.

"My advisement," he said, "is on the last page."

Stell skimmed the instructions in silence, and then looked up. "You think this will work?"

"It's how *I'd* catch him," said Eli, truthfully.

Stell turned to go, but Eli called him back.

"Look me in the eye," said Eli, "and tell me that when you find Victor, you will kill him once and for all."

Stell met his gaze. "I'll do as I see fit."

Eli flashed a feral grin. "Of course you will," he said.

And so will I.

XXIV

TWO DAYS AGO

DOWNTOWN WHITTON

SYDNEY was back on the ice.

It stretched in every direction. She couldn't see the banks, couldn't see anything but the frozen stretch of lake ahead, behind, the plume of her own breath.

"Hello?" she called.

Her voice echoed across the lake.

The ice crackled just behind her and she spun around, expecting to see Eli.

But there was no one there.

And then, from somewhere in the distance, a sound.

Not the cracking of the lake. A short, sharp tone.

Sydney sat up.

She didn't remember falling asleep, but she was curled on the sofa, Dol at her feet and thin morning light seeping in the windows.

The sharp tone sounded again, and Syd looked around for her phone before she realized that the sound was coming from Mitch's computer. The laptop sat open on the table a few feet away, pinging like a beacon.

Sydney tapped the computer awake.

Mitch's black lock screen came up, and she typed in the password—*benedición*. The screen gave way to a matrix of code, way beyond the basics he'd been teaching her. But Syd's attention went to the corner of the screen, where a small icon bounced up and down.

Results (1).

Sydney clicked the icon, and a new window popped up.

Her breath caught. She recognized the page's format from the paper she'd found crumpled in the trash. It was a profile. A distinguished man, dark-skinned with a trim white beard, staring out at her from a professional photo.

Ellis Dumont. Fifty-seven. A surgeon who'd been in an accident the year before. He hadn't abandoned his old life; maybe that was why he hadn't shown up in the system. Not enough markers. But this—this was the important part. Ever since he'd returned to work, his patients' recovery rate had skyrocketed. There were links to news articles, pieces praising this man with a near prescient ability to discover what was wrong.

She scrolled down the page until she found Dumont's current location.

Merit Central Hospital.

Sydney surged to her feet and hurried down the hall. The soft hush of the shower spilled from Mitch's room. Victor's door was ajar, the space beyond dark. She could just make out the lines of his body on the bed, his back to her.

The first and only time she'd ever woken him, it had been from a nightmare, and he'd lit her up like a Christmas tree. The pain had echoed in her nerves for hours.

She knew it probably wouldn't happen again, but it was still hard to force herself forward. In the end, it was a wasted fear.

"I'm not asleep," said Victor softly.

He sat up and turned to face Sydney, his eyes narrowing.

"What is it?"

Sydney's heart was racing. "There's something you should see."

She sat, perched on the edge of the sofa, as Victor read the profile, his expression carefully blank. She wished she could read his mind. Hell, she wished she could read his face.

Mitch appeared in the doorway, large towel draped over his bare shoulders. "What's going on?"

"Get your things," said Victor, rising to his feet.

"We're going to Merit."

XXV

TWO DAYS AGO

FIRST AND WHITE

MARCELLA leaned back in her chair and admired the view.

The city spilled away beyond her floor-to-ceiling windows, rolled out like a carpet beneath her feet.

Once upon a time she'd stood on the rooftop of a college frat and thought she could see all of Merit. But it had only been a few small blocks, the rest swallowed up by higher buildings. *This* was a real view. *This* was her city.

She turned back toward the desk, where the cards sat waiting.

They'd arrived in a lovely silk box—one hundred crisp white invitations, the front of each embossed with an elegant gold *M*.

She drew one from the box and flicked it open.

The words were printed in curling black, the edges embossed with gold.

*Marcella Morgan and her associates
request your presence at the exclusive reveal
of Merit's most extraordinary venture.
The future of the city starts now.*

*The Old Courthouse.
This Friday, the 23rd. 6 p.m.
Invitation admits 2.*

Marcella smiled, turning the card between her fingers.

What now? June had asked. *You're going to throw yourself a fucking party?*

Marcella knew the girl had meant it as a joke, but Stell had tipped his hand, the night they met, and let a face card show.

No more grand displays. The last thing this city needs . . .

But, of course, Stell hadn't really been talking about the city. He meant *EON*. Yes, a little publicity would be bad for their business.

And so, that was exactly what Marcella planned to give them.

She was done playing by other people's rules. Done hiding. If you lived in the dark, you died in the dark. But stand in the light, and it was that much harder to make you disappear.

And Marcella Renee Morgan wasn't going anywhere.

XXVI

TWO DAYS AGO

ON THE ROAD

MITCHELL Turner had a bad feeling.

He got them, now and then, the way other people got migraines or déjà vu.

Sometimes it was dull, abstract, a sense of wrongness that crept in like night, slow but inevitable. Other times it was sudden and sharp, like a pain in his side. Mitch didn't know where the feelings came from, but he knew to listen when they did.

Bad feelings were warnings, when you had bad luck.

And all Mitch's life, he'd had bad luck.

Bad luck made sure he was the one who got caught.

Bad luck landed him in jail.

Bad luck crossed his path with Victor's—though he didn't see it at the time.

It was like a rubber band. Mitch could only get so far away before the invisible hand slipped and he went crashing back into trouble. Other people were always surprised when bad things happened. When good things stopped. Not him. When Mitch had one of those feelings, he listened.

Watched his step.

Kept one eye on the breakable things in his life.

He glanced in the rearview mirror and saw Sydney, curled up in her red bomber jacket, booted feet draped over Dol. She was wearing a pink wig, the synthetic strands falling over her eyes. Mitch shot a surreptitious glance at the passenger's seat and saw Victor staring out the window, his face unreadable as ever.

Merit rose in the distance ahead of them.

"Everything that goes around, comes around," said Victor. His cool blue gaze cut sideways. "You should keep driving."

Mitch frowned in confusion.

"If this doesn't work," added Victor softly. "Even if it does. Take Syd and—"

"We're not leaving," said Sydney, bolt upright in the backseat.

Victor sighed. "I should have," he murmured.

The bad feeling nipped like a shadow at Mitch's heels. How long had it been following him? Days? Weeks? Months? Had it been there since the night at Falcon Price, when he set fire to Serena's body? Or was it simply the fact that when it came to Mitch's luck, it was only a matter of time before it ran out?

"How far?" asked Sydney in the backseat.

Mitch's throat felt dry when he answered.

"We're almost there."

∞

FUCK.

June had overslept, woken with the sun full up and in her eyes. This is why she preferred killing to stalking—you could do it on your own schedule.

She lurched out of bed, stumbled to the window, studied the apartments across the street. There was no sign of Syd on the balcony. No glimpse of Victor or Mitch in the rooms beyond. For days, they'd passed like shadows through the apartment, lounged on furniture, taken the dog for walks.

Now, the curtains were pulled back, and the place looked barren.

June swore, and got dressed.

She crossed the road, caught the door just as someone was coming out. They didn't even look twice—and why should they? She was just a kid, thirteen, gangly, innocent. June loped up the stairs, shifting again before she reached the fifth-floor landing, ready to pass herself off as a college kid, canvassing for politicians.

She knocked on their door, but no one answered.

June pressed her ear to the wood, swore again at the wall of silence, then produced a few narrow picks and let herself in.

The door swung open.

The apartment was empty.

A horrible déjà vu—of another city, another abandoned place, a full year of useless searching—but June steadied herself. Sydney was no longer a stranger. They knew each other. Trusted each other. June returned to her hotel room and fetched her phone from the bedside table, sighing with relief.

Sydney had already texted.

> **Syd**: You'll never guess where we're going.

June knew the answer before she even read Sydney's next message. *Merit.*

Five minutes later, June was on the road, driving a solid twenty over the speed limit as she barreled toward Merit in their wake. She called Marcella on the way.

"He's on the move," she said, catching herself before she said *they*. "And headed to Merit."

"Well," said Marcella, "I wonder what gave him that idea."

"It wasn't you?"

"No," she said, sounding a little put out. "But this is better. See that he gets here safely. We'll welcome him with open arms."

June frowned as she wove around a semi. "I thought you were trading him to EON."

"I never said that," replied Marcella pointedly. "I told you I hadn't decided yet. And I haven't. You know I like to know my options, and I have to admit that Stell's reaction to the news of Victor Vale has piqued my interest. I've done a little homework, and this Vale is quite an interesting case. He could turn out to be an asset. Or perhaps not. But I certainly don't plan on handing him over to EON until I've had a chance to meet him."

Never one to waste a weapon, thought June.

"Who knows," mused Marcella. "Maybe he'll prove pliable."

Victor struck June as many things—*pliable* wasn't one of them. If anything, he seemed to be rather intransigent, cold smoke to Marcella's fire. But opposites attracted for a reason. Would it be such a bad thing? June had always assumed she'd have to pry Sydney from Victor's grasp, but maybe she wouldn't have to. Maybe he would join them, three EOs becoming five. That was a nice number, wasn't it? Five. Almost a family.

Marcella was still talking.

"I want you to make contact," she was saying. "Arrange a meeting with our new friend. I'll send you the details. Oh, and June?"

"Yeah?"

"Somebody convinced Victor to come to Merit, and it wasn't me."

"My money's on EON."

"That would probably be a good bet. Obviously, we can't let them get to Victor first. So do try not to lose him."

June swore again, and gunned the engine.

4
JUDGMENT DAY

I

THE DAY BEFORE

MERIT

THE Kingsley was a blade of a building, thrust up through the city's skyline.

But Victor hadn't chosen the place for the modern aesthetics. No, the selling point had been its underground parking, which mitigated the problems of exposure—a tattooed man with a shaved head, a giant black dog, and a short blond child would always stand out, even in a city like Merit—and the closed-circuit security, which Mitch would have hacked by the time they unpacked, and—much to Sydney's apparent delight—a rooftop garden.

Mitch set their bags down inside the door.

"Don't get comfortable," said Victor. "We're not staying long."

Mitch and Sydney shouldn't have come at all, but Victor had long given up trying to dissuade them. Attachment was a vexing thing, as pernicious as weeds.

He should have left, before it ever took root.

"I'll be back," he said, turning toward the door.

Sydney caught his arm. "Be careful," she said.

What a nuisance, Victor told himself, even as he rested his hand on her head.

"Careful is a calculated risk," he said. "And I'm very good at making those."

Victor pulled away, forcing Syd to let go, and left without looking back.

He took the elevator to the street and stepped out, alone, into the afternoon sun, checking his watch. It was just after three. According to Mitch, the doctor's shift at Merit Central ended at five. Victor would be there to meet him.

Ellis Dumont.

A more spiritual person might have seen the EO's sudden appearance as a sign of divine intervention, but Victor had never put much stock in fate, and even less in faith. Dumont's presence in the matrix was convenient to the point of suspicion, his location in Merit its own red flag.

No, Dumont was either a gift or a trap.

Victor was inclined to think the latter.

But he couldn't afford to stake his life on it.

His latest episode had crossed the four-minute threshold. He'd come back, but Victor knew he was playing a dangerous game. The odds were terrible, the stakes monumental.

It was Russian roulette, except that a bullet would be a cleaner end.

He had considered that, a quick, clean death. Not a suicide, of course—a reset. But that would introduce another factor, another risk. If he died again—truly died—would Sydney be able to bring him back? And if she did, how much of his power would be left? How much of *him*?

Four blocks later, Victor turned the corner and stepped through the sliding glass doors into a gym. He would have preferred to meet in a bar, but Dominic Rusher was five years sober, and in a moment of distraction Victor had agreed to meet him here instead.

He'd always hated gyms.

He'd avoided sports in school, avoided the weight yard in prison, preferring to hone his strength in other ways. He *had* enjoyed swimming, once. The soothing repetition, the measured breath, the way physical mass had no bearing on skill.

Now, as he strode past the hulking, sweating masses lifting

weights, he had a vivid memory of watching football players trying to swim, attacking the pool as if they could muscle it out of the way. The current worked against them. They sank like stones. Spluttered for air. Bested by something as simple and natural as water.

Dominic was waiting for him in the locker room.

At first glance, Victor hardly recognized the ex-soldier. If the last five years had whittled Victor down, they'd had the opposite effect on Dom. The change was startling—apparently, as startling as Victor's own transformation.

Dominic's eyes widened. "Victor. You look . . ."

"Yeah, like shit, I know." He tipped his shoulder against the steel lockers. "How's the job?"

Dom scratched his head. "Well enough, all things considered. But remember that EO I told you about? The one making a scene?"

"Marcella." Victor hadn't meant to hold on to that name, but something about it, about her, had stuck in his mind. "How long did she last?"

Dom shook his head. "They haven't caught her yet."

"Really?" Victor had to admit, he was impressed.

"But the thing is," said Dom, "they don't seem to be *trying*. And she's not exactly keeping the lowest profile. She killed six of our agents, clipped a sniper—hell, every day she does something new. But orders are to hold." He lowered his voice. "There's something going on. I just don't know what. Above my pay grade, obviously."

"And Eli?" prompted Victor.

"Still in his vault." Dom shot him a nervous look. "For now."

Victor's eyes narrowed. "What do you mean?"

"It's just a rumor," said Dom, "but apparently some of the higher-ups think he should be playing a more *active* role."

"They wouldn't do something that stupid."

But then, people did stupid things all the time. And Eli could charm almost anyone.

"Anything else?" he asked.

Dominic hesitated, rubbing at his neck. "It's getting worse."

"I've noticed," said Victor dryly.

"Yesterday Holtz found me heaving my guts out in a closet. And last week I broke into a cold sweat in the middle of a training seminar. I've claimed hangover, PTSD, anything I can think of, but I'm running out of lies."

And I'm running out of lives, thought Victor, pushing off the lockers.

"Good luck," called Dom as he left.

But Victor didn't need luck.

He needed a doctor.

∞

SYDNEY stepped out into the sun on the rooftop garden of the Kingsley building.

It was a blue sky day, but the air was still cold. It made her think of the lake, her thirteenth birthday, the skin of ice over the melted water. Her fingers tightened on her cell. The text had come in while she was unpacking, three short words that made her nervous.

>   **June**: Call me. Now.

Sydney called.

It rang, and rang, and when June finally answered, all Syd heard was music, too loud and fraying at the edges. June's lilting voice broke through, telling her to hold on, and a second later the music dropped away, replaced by the low hum of an engine.

"Sydney," said June, her voice high and clear. "Just the girl I need."

"Hey," said Syd. "We just got to Merit. What's going on? Are you here?"

"On my way back," said June. "Had a bit of work outside the city. Look," she went on, "I need you to do something for me."

There was a tension in June's voice, an urgency Syd had never heard before.

"What is it?" she asked.

A short exhale, like static on the line. "I need you to tell me where Victor is."

The words fell like a rock in Sydney's stomach. "What?"

"Listen to me," pressed the other girl. "He's in trouble. There are some really dangerous people in Merit, and they know he's here, and they're looking for him. I want to keep him safe, I do—and I *can*—but I need your help."

Safe. Syd's mind tripped over the word. If Victor was in trouble—but *why* was he in trouble, and how did June know? Who was looking for him? EON?

She started to ask, but June cut her off.

June, who'd never even raised her voice.

"Do you trust me or not?"

She did. She wanted to. But—

"Where is he, Sydney?"

She swallowed. "Merit Central Hospital."

II

THE DAY BEFORE

MERIT CENTRAL HOSPITAL

IT was seventeen minutes past five.

Victor leaned back against Dumont's gray sedan in the hospital parking garage and scrolled through Dom's texts as he waited for the doctor. The buzzing in his skull seemed to ratchet up as he skimmed the most recent times.

3 minutes, 49 seconds.
3 minutes, 52 seconds.
3 minutes, 56 seconds.
4 minutes, 04 seconds.

The stairwell door clattered open across the garage.

Victor glanced up and saw Dumont, dark skin, gray hair, head bowed over his tablet as he headed toward his car. Toward Victor.

Victor didn't move, simply waited for the doctor to come to him.

"Dr. Dumont?"

The man looked up, brows furrowing. Victor thought he saw something cross the doctor's face. Not surprise, exactly, but fear. "Can I help you?"

Victor studied him, fingers flexing. "I certainly hope so."

Dumont looked around the parking garage. "I'm off work," he said, "but you can make an appointment—"

Victor didn't have time for this—he took hold of the doctor's nerves, and twisted. Dumont buckled with a shocked cry. He clutched his chest, sweat breaking out along his brow.

Having made his point, Victor let go.

Dumont sagged back against his car. "You're—an EO."

"Just like you," said Victor.

"I don't—hurt people," said Dumont.

"No? Then how does *your* power work?"

Dumont let out a shaky breath. "I can see—how people are broken. I can—see how—to put them back together."

Relief swept through Victor. Finally, a promising lead.

"Good," he said, stepping toward the doctor. "Show me."

Dumont shook his head. Victor was about take hold of the doctor's nerves again when the stairwell door swung open and a small huddle of nurses stepped out, talking animatedly. A car beeped nearby. Victor shifted to block their view.

"Not here," muttered Dumont.

"Then where?" asked Victor.

The doctor nodded at the hospital. "My office is on the seventh—"

"No," said Victor. Too many eyes. Too many doors.

Dumont rubbed his forehead. "The fifth floor is under renovation. It should be empty. That's the best I can do."

Victor hesitated, but the humming in his head was spreading to his limbs. He was running out of time.

"Fine," he said, "lead the way."

MEANWHILE, ACROSS TOWN . . .

Sydney tried to call Victor, but it went straight to voicemail every time.

What did June mean when she said he was in trouble?

They'd been careful. They were always careful.

Do you trust me or not?

In that moment, Sydney had. She hoped she hadn't made a mistake.

Footsteps sounded behind her. Sydney's hand went automatically to the gun she now kept tucked in her coat, thumb already resting against the safety.

But then she recognized the heavy tread, and turned to see Mitch striding toward her across the rooftop garden.

"There you are," he said cheerfully.

She let go of the gun. "Hey," she said. "Just admiring the view." She tried to keep her voice light, but her head was still spinning, and she was afraid it would show on her face, so she turned her back on Mitch. "It's weird, isn't it? How cities change. Buildings go up, and come down, and it looks the same—and different."

"Like you," said Mitch, ruffling her pink wig. The gesture was light, easy, but there was a strain in his voice, and the silence, when it fell, was heavy. Syd's mind was on Victor, but she knew Mitch's was on her sister.

They'd never talked about what really happened to Serena. It had been too soon, and then too late. The wound had healed, as best as it could.

But now that they were back in Merit, the finished Falcon Price building glinting in the distance, the air was thick with everything they'd never said.

"Hey, Syd," started Mitch, but she cut him off.

"Do you ever wish you were an EO?"

Mitch's brow crinkled, caught off guard by the question. He didn't answer right away. He'd always been careful like that, sorting out his words before he said them.

"I remember when I first met Victor," he said at last. "These guys inside were giving me a hard time, and he just . . ." Mitch slid his hand through the air. "He made it look so easy. I guess to him it probably was. But watching it made me feel . . . small."

Syd laughed. "You're the biggest guy I know."

He flashed her a smile, but it was sad at the edges. "Sometimes it feels like I'm in a fight, and all I've got are my hands, and the other guy has a knife. But that guy with the knife, eventually he's going to face someone with a gun. And the one with the gun is going to go up against someone with a bomb. The truth is, Syd, there will always be somebody stronger than you. That's just the way the world works." He looked up at the shining skyscraper. "It doesn't matter if you're a human versus a human or a human versus an EO or an EO versus an EO. You do what you can. You fight, and you win, until you don't."

Sydney swallowed, and turned her attention back to the skyline. "Any word from Victor?" she asked, trying to keep her voice light.

Mitch shook his head. "Not yet. But don't worry." His hand came to rest on her shoulder. "He can take care of himself."

MERIT CENTRAL HOSPITAL

Their steps echoed on the stairs.

"What exactly happens at the apex of these episodes?" asked Dumont.

"Nerve impairment. Muscular seizure." Victor ticked off the symptoms. "Atrial fibrillation. Cardiac arrest. Death."

Dumont glanced back. *"Death?"*

Victor nodded.

"Do you know how many times you've died? Are we talking about three to four recurrences or a dozen—"

"One hundred and thirty-two."

The doctor's face went slack. "That's . . . not possible."

Victor considered him dryly. "I assure you, I've kept track."

"But the sheer strain on your body." Dumont shook his head. "You shouldn't be alive."

"That is both the cause and the crux of our problem, isn't it?"

"Have you experienced cognitive impairment?"

Victor hesitated. "There's a brief period of disorientation immediately after. And it's getting longer."

"It's a miracle you're still forming sentences."

Miracle. Victor had always hated that word.

They reached the fifth floor, and Dumont pushed open a set of doors. He hit a switch and the lights came on, one shuddering wave at a time, illuminating a broad floor that was indeed in the process of being torn apart and put back together. Plastic sheeting hung in makeshift curtains, equipment covered in white tarps, and for an instant Victor imagined himself back in the half-built Falcon Price building, voices bouncing off concrete.

"There are some exam rooms this way," said Dumont, but Victor refused to move.

"This is far enough."

They were standing in the middle of the tangled space. Victor would have preferred a clean line of sight to the exits, but the tarping made that impossible.

Dumont set his things down and shrugged out of his coat.

"How long have you been an EO?" asked Victor.

"Two years," said the doctor.

Two years. And he'd only just shown up in their search matrix.

"Go ahead and sit down," said Dumont, gesturing to a chair. Victor continued to stand.

"Tell me something, Doctor. When you were dying, what were your final thoughts?"

"My final thoughts?" echoed Dumont, considering. "I thought about my family . . . how much I'd miss them . . . how I didn't want to leave . . ." He stumbled over the answer, as if he couldn't remember. Perhaps he was simply nervous, but as he stammered, Victor was reminded of an actor forgetting their lines.

"And you said your power is to diagnose a person's ailments?"

It didn't fit.

An EO's near-death experience was colored so strongly by their last moments, their will to survive, but also their dire, most desperate wishes. Dumont's final moments, final thoughts, should have shaped his power, and yet—

The doctor managed a nervous smile. "I thought I was meant to be diagnosing *you*."

Victor parroted the smile. "Yes, of course. Go ahead."

But Dumont hesitated, patting his shirt pocket.

"Is something wrong?" asked Victor, fingers drifting toward his holstered gun.

"I don't have my glasses." Dumont turned away. "I must have left them downstairs. I'll just go and—"

But Victor was already behind him.

He couldn't afford to use his power—pain generated noise, and noise drew attention—so Victor settled for pressing the gun against the base of the doctor's spine and wrapping his free hand over the doctor's mouth. "The trouble with conventional weapons," he said in the doctor's ear, "is that the damage they do is so permanent. If you make a sound, you will never walk again. Do you understand?"

Dumont nodded once.

"You're not an EO, are you?"

A short sideways flick. *No.*

"Are they waiting for your signal?"

The doctor shook his head and tried to speak, his words muffled against Victor's palm. Victor drew his hand away, and the doctor repeated himself.

"They're already here."

As if on cue, Victor heard doors swing open, the shuffle of steps.

"I'm sorry," continued Dumont. "They have people at my house. Watching my family. They said if I—"

Victor cut him off. "Your motives are irrelevant. The only thing I need to know is how to get out." He slid the gun's safety off. "Exits. Tell me."

"There's a service elevator—the others won't stop here—and two internal stairs."

And of course, there was the way they'd come in, the most direct route—and the one with the least amount of cover.

Boots shuffled across the linoleum nearby, the harsh overhead lights casting shadows on the plastic sheeting. Victor needed to be able to see his targets. But he didn't need to be able to see them *clearly*.

He reached for the nearest shadow and it buckled with a cry as the pretense of surprise shattered, and shots rang out, and the fifth floor plunged into chaos.

∞

VICTOR'S hand twitched, and two more soldiers went down screaming, before they cut the lights. A second later he heard the telltale sound of a metal clasp, the hiss of air, and then the canisters came rolling across the ground, filling the air with smoke.

"Hold your breath," he ordered, dragging Dumont back against the wall as scopes traced red lines through the billowing white. The smoke burned Victor's eyes, clawing at his senses, and through it all the crackle of energy was spreading through his limbs—warning.

Not yet, he thought. *Not yet.*

The service elevator groaned open, and Victor had time to see the barrel of a gun, the first traces of black armor, combat boots. He twisted sideways, releasing his hostage as he ducked out of the soldiers' line of fire.

Dumont threw up his hands as Victor reached the stairwell.

"Don't shoot!" called the doctor, coughing as the smoke hit his lungs.

The soldiers pushed past him as Victor surged into the stairwell and started down.

More footsteps rose up from below, but Victor had the high ground now. By the time the first soldier saw him, Victor already had their nerves in his grasp. He twisted the dial all the way up, and they fell, like puppets without strings.

Victor rounded their bodies and continued down. He was nearly to the third-floor landing when the first spasm hit.

For a second, he thought he'd been shot.

Then he realized, with horror, that he was out of time. The current arced through him, lighting his nerves, and he bowed his head, steadying himself against the rail before forcing his body onward.

He made it to the first floor, and opened the door just in time to see a soldier heading straight for him, weapon raised. Before Victor could summon the strength or the focus to bring the soldier down, someone else had done it for him.

A silencer swung into view, followed by three muted thumps as the gun fired point-blank into the side of the soldier's head. It wasn't enough to pierce the helmet, but it caught him off guard, and half a second later the shooter—a female doctor—stepped into sight. She stepped right into the soldier's arms, and then—almost elegantly—drove a blade up under his helmet.

The soldier dropped like a stone, and the female doctor turned on Victor.

"Don't just stand there," she hissed, her voice strangely familiar. Footsteps sounded overhead and below. *"Find another way out."*

Victor had questions, but there was no time to ask.

He turned and continued down the stairs toward the hospital sublevels. Burst through a set of doors into an empty hall, the sign at the end marked MORGUE in small, mocking letters. But beyond that—an exit sign. Halfway there, the next spasm hit, and Victor stumbled, one shoulder slamming hard into the concrete wall. His knee buckled, and he went down.

He tried to force himself back up as the doors swung open behind him.

"Stay down!" ordered a soldier as Victor collapsed to the floor.

"We've got him," said one voice.

"He's down," said another.

He couldn't get up, couldn't get away. But Victor still had one weapon. The current climbed higher, the dial turned up, and he held on as long as possible, clutching to life one fractured, agonizing second at a time until the boots came into sight.

And then, Victor let go.

Let the pain crash over him in a final wave, washing everything away.

∞

VICTOR came to in the dark.

His vision slid in and out for a second before finally coming into focus. He was lying on a gurney, the ceiling much lower than it should be. Victor tested his limbs, expecting to find them restrained, but there was nothing on his wrists or ankles. He tried to sit up, and pain closed tightly around his chest. Two of his ribs felt broken, but he could still breathe.

"I started CPR," said a voice. "But I was worried it would do more damage than good."

Victor turned his head and saw the figure in the dark.

Dumont.

The doctor was sitting on a bench a couple feet away, half hidden by shadow.

Victor looked around, and realized he was lying in the back of an ambulance.

The seconds before his episode came back in fragments, broken frames, but they didn't explain how he'd gotten from the basement floor to here.

"I found you," explained the doctor, unprompted, "outside the morgue. Well, I found the soldiers first."

"You didn't turn me over to EON," observed Victor. "Why?"

Dumont examined his hands. "You could have killed me up on the fifth floor. You didn't."

It hadn't been an act of mercy. There had simply been no point.

"And the soldiers?" asked Victor.

"They were already dead."

"So was I."

Dumont nodded. "Medicine is full of calculated risks and split-second decisions. I made one."

"You could have walked away."

"I may not be ExtraOrdinary," said Dumont, "but I *am* a doctor. And I took an oath."

A siren tore through the air nearby, and Victor tensed, but it was only another ambulance, pulling out of the bay. The bay . . .

"We're still at the hospital?" asked Victor.

"Obviously," said Dumont. "I said I'd help you live, not help you *escape*. Frankly, I was beginning to doubt your odds of doing either."

Victor frowned, feeling his pockets for his phone. "How long was I gone?"

"Nearly four and a half minutes."

Victor swore under his breath. No wonder the doctor hadn't driven away.

"I should run some tests," continued Dumont, producing a penlight, "make sure your cognitive function hasn't been—"

"That won't be necessary," said Victor. There was nothing Dumont could do for him now—nothing that would make a difference. And while four and a half minutes was far too long to be dead, it wasn't long enough for EON's enforcement team to clear out. They would still be on-site. How long until more joined them?

Victor nodded at the front of the ambulance. "I assume you can drive?"

Dumont hesitated. "I can, but . . ."

"Get behind the wheel."

Dumont didn't move.

Victor wasn't in the mood to torture him, so he resorted to logic instead. "You said they had eyes on your family. If you go back in there now, they'll know you helped me escape."

Dumont frowned. "And how does driving you away make me less complicit?"

"You're not an accomplice," said Victor, producing a pair of cable-ties from a toolbox. "You're a hostage. I can tie you to the steering wheel now, or later. It's up to you."

The doctor silently climbed behind the wheel. Victor took the passenger's seat. He flipped the sirens on.

"Where am I going?" asked Dumont.

Victor turned the question over. "There's a bus station on the southern edge of the city. Drive."

Dumont hit the gas, and the ambulance peeled out of the bay. After a few blocks, Victor killed the sirens and the lights. He sat back in the seat, flexing his fingers. He could feel the doctor cutting glances at him.

"Eyes on the road," said Victor.

Ten minutes later, the bus depot came into sight, and Victor pointed to an empty stretch of sidewalk.

"There," he said.

As Dumont started guiding the ambulance off the road, Victor reached over, took the wheel, and jerked it, forcing the vehicle up onto the curb.

"Don't forget," he said, "you're in distress." Before Dumont could protest, Victor zip-tied his hands to the wheel. "Do you have a phone on you?" Dumont nodded at his pocket.

Victor drew the cell from the doctor's coat and threw it out the window.

"There," he said, climbing out of the ambulance.

Now he had a head start.

III

THE DAY BEFORE

EON

STELL stood before the bay of screens, arms crossed, watching it all fall apart. Radio chatter crackled from the speaker on the desk.

"No sign of target."

"Soldiers down."

"Seal the perimeter."

What a goddamned catastrophe, thought Stell, sinking down into his chair.

Eli's trap had succeeded, but his own agents had failed. Three of them were dead—two bleeding from their ears and noses on a sublevel, one knifed in the throat on the first floor—the rest had been fucking useless.

Whether Victor had seen past the bait to the hook, or simply wriggled free, one thing was clear—he hadn't done it alone.

Several of Stell's agents had been shot at by a male orderly, a receptionist, and a female doctor—but Stell had a feeling they were all the same person. One of his men had shot back, caught the doctor in the shoulder. At that same moment, halfway across the hospital, a doctor matching her *exact* description had collapsed, bleeding, in the middle of scrubbing in for surgery.

The shapeshifter—*Marcella's* shapeshifter—had been there.

And she'd helped Victor escape.

Stell took up his phone and dialed.

"Joseph," said that smooth voice.

"Where is Victor Vale?" demanded Stell through gritted teeth.

"You were cheating."

"This isn't a game. You agreed to deliver him. Instead, you are the reason he's still free. When do you intend to uphold your end of the deal?"

Marcella sighed. "Men are always so impatient. Perhaps it comes from a lifetime of being given what you want, when you want it. Sometimes, Joseph, you just have to wait."

"When?"

"Tomorrow," said Marcella. "Before the party."

Stell's chest tightened. "What party?"

"Didn't you get my invitation?" A stack of mail sat forgotten on the edge of Stell's desk. He began rifling through it. "I considered holding on to him until after . . ."

Stell found the card, crisp and white, with a gold *M* embossed on the front. It was unstamped. Someone had delivered it by hand. Stell broke the seal.

"It would certainly keep you out of my way," Marcella was saying, "but then again, I wouldn't want you to miss the show . . ."

Marcella Morgan and her associates . . .

Stell read the invitation once, and then again—he couldn't believe what he was looking at. He didn't *want* to believe it.

. . . Merit's most extraordinary venture.

"This is the opposite of lying low," he growled.

"What can I say? I've never been understated."

"We had a deal."

"We did," said Marcella. "For two weeks. Beyond that, we both knew it wouldn't last. But I have appreciated the ceasefire. It gave me time to print my invitations."

"Marcella—"

But she'd already hung up.

Stell swept a mug from his table. It shattered, dark drops of coffee painting the floor.

In seconds, Rios was there.

"Sir?" she asked, surveying the broken cup, the papers displaced in his search for the card, the crisp white invitation crumpled in his hand.

Stell slumped back in his chair, Eli's voice playing in his head.

You made a deal?

Someone this powerful belongs in the ground.

Send me.

Stell's gaze went to the slim silver briefcase the board had given him, the collar nested inside.

Agent Rios was still standing there, silent, waiting.

Stell rose to his feet. "Prepare a transport team for tomorrow."

Rios raised a brow. "For which prisoner?"

"Cardale."

∞

STELL found Eli sitting on the edge of his cot, fingers laced and head bowed, as if he were praying.

Or simply waiting.

At the sound of Stell's approach, his head drifted up. "Director. Has my trap yielded any results?"

Stell hesitated. "Not yet," he lied. There was no reason for Eli to know about Vale's escape, and a dozen reasons to keep him in the dark. Especially considering what he was about to do. "Have you been considering the problem of Marcella?"

Eli rose. "My assessment hasn't changed."

"I'm not asking for your sentence," said Stell, "I'm asking for your method. How would you dispatch her?"

"How would *I*?"

"You *do* still believe you are the best equipped for the task."

A ghost of a smile. "I do."

"Let me be very clear," said Stell. "I don't trust you."

"You don't have to," said Eli.

Stell shook his head. What was he thinking? "We still don't know if you can even defeat Marcella."

Eli smiled grimly. "Haverty spent a year trying to find the limits of my regeneration. He never succeeded."

"Her power isn't the only problem," said Stell. "After all, Marcella is not acting alone."

"Neither am I," pressed Eli, gesturing at the cell, at EON. "The hard part isn't killing three EOs, Director. It's collecting them in one place, and then separating them so they can't work together. Do that, and your agents can take care of the other two EOs while I see to Marcella. I assure you, under the right conditions, defeating them is more than possible."

Conditions.

Stell slid Marcella's invitation through the fiberglass slot. "Will this work?"

Eli took the card, his eyes dancing across the words.

"Yes," he said, "I think it will."

IV

THE NIGHT BEFORE

MERIT

VICTOR needed a drink.

He spotted a bleak stretch of low buildings, bland, forgettable, a bar sandwiched between them, and started across the street, digging his cell from his pocket.

Mitch answered on the second ring.

"We were getting worried. What happened with Dumont?"

"It was a trap," said Victor flatly. "He was only human."

Mitch swore. "EON?"

"Indeed," said Victor. "I got away, but I won't risk leading them back to the Kingsley."

"Is that him?" called Syd in the background. "What happened?"

"Should we leave?" asked Mitch.

Yes, thought Victor. But they couldn't. Not now. The movement would only draw EON's further attention. They'd set their trap at the hospital, lain in wait. They'd gotten Victor to come to them, which meant they hadn't been able to find him. But that didn't mean they *wouldn't*. Did they already know about Sydney? What would happen if they found her instead?

"Stay in the apartment," he said. "Don't answer the door. Don't let anyone in. Call me if you notice anything or anyone outside."

"What about you?" asked Mitch.

But Victor didn't have an answer to that question yet, so instead he hung up and stepped into the bar. It was a dive, poorly lit and more than half-empty. He ordered a whiskey and settled into a booth along the back wall where he could keep an eye on the bar's only door and the handful of patrons while he waited.

Victor had pocketed a battered paperback from the center console of the ambulance—now he dug it out, along with a black felt pen, and let the broken spine fall open under his hand.

Old habits. The pen cut a steady path, blacking out the first line, and then the second. He felt his pulse slow with each erasure, each measure of text reduced to a solid black streak. The first word was always the hardest to find. Now and then, he searched for a specific one, and then erased the text around it, but most of the time, though Victor was loath to admit it, even to himself, the practice felt less like a physical act than a metaphysical one.

He let the pen skate across the page, waiting for a word to stop its path. He cut through *pride, fall, change,* before finally coming to a stop at the word *find*. His pen skipped over a solo *a* two lines later, then continued down the page until it found *way*.

Victor was running out of time, and out of leads, but he wasn't giving up.

Sydney, Mitch, Dominic—they all behaved as though surrender were a risk, an option. But it wasn't. Some fractional part of Victor wished he could stop trying, stop fighting, but it simply wasn't in him. That same stubborn will to survive, the very trait that first made him into an EO, now prevented him from acquiescing. From admitting defeat.

Whatever's happened to you, however you're hurt, you've done it to yourself.

That's what Campbell had said. And the EO was right. Victor had always been the master of his fate. He had climbed onto that steel table. He had coerced Angie into flipping the switch. He had goaded Eli into killing him five years before, knowing Sydney would bring him back.

Every action had been his own design, every step his own making. If there was a way out of this, he would find it.

If there wasn't, he would make one himself.

The bar's only door swung open, and a few moments later Victor heard a voice, the words lost in the crowd, but the accent unmistakable.

He looked up.

There was a small, brunette woman with fox-sharp features leaning across the bar. He'd never seen the person before, but Victor knew it was her—the woman from the strip club. The concerned Samaritan from the alley, too. And of course, most recently, the doctor who'd helped him escape EON. It wasn't just the accent that Victor recognized. It was the look in the woman's eyes—*behind* her eyes, really—as she glanced toward him, the mischievous smile that lit her face. If it *was* her face.

They were an EO—that much was obvious.

He watched as the shapeshifter took up their drink and headed toward him.

"Is this seat taken?" Again, that lilting voice.

"That depends," said Victor. "The Glass Tower—was that the first time we met?"

A wry smile cut across the vulpine face. "It was."

"But not the last."

"No," said the EO, sinking into the chair across from him. "Not the last."

Victor curled his fingers around his glass. "Who are you?"

"Think of me as a kind of guardian angel. You can call me June."

"Is that your real name?"

"Ah," said June wistfully, "*real* is a murky thing, for someone like me."

The woman sat forward, and as she did, she changed. There was no hinge, no transition—the brunette girl dissolved, replaced by strawberry curls and dark blue eyes in a heart-shaped face.

"Do you like it?" asked June, as if she were asking his opinion of a new dress, not a distorted reflection of the only girl Victor had ever loved. "It's the best I can do, considering the real one is dead."

"Change," said Victor tersely.

"Aw," June sulked. "But I picked her just for you."

"*Change*," he ordered.

The blue-eyed gaze leveled on him, a challenge, a dare. Victor rose to meet it. His fingers twitched as he took hold of her nerves, turned the dial in her chest—but if the woman felt any pain, it didn't register on her face. Her power—somehow it was shielding her.

"Sorry," said June with a wan smile. "You can't hurt *me*."

A faint emphasis on the last word.

Victor leaned forward. "I don't need to."

He splayed his hand across the worn wood table, pinning her body to the chair.

A faint crease formed between June's eyes, the only hint of struggle as she fought his hold.

"There are so many nerves in a human body," said Victor. "Pain is only one of the possible signals. A single instrument in a symphony."

A smirk fought its way onto the girl's mouth. "But how long do you think you can hold me? An hour? A day? Until your next death? I wonder, which one of us will give up first?"

They were at an impasse.

Victor let go.

June exhaled, rolling her neck. As she did, the girl with the strawberry curls fell away, replaced by the brunette she'd been wearing before. "There. All better?"

"Why have you been following me?" asked Victor.

"I have a vested interest," said June. "And I'm not the only one. There's an EO in this city who would very much like to meet you. Perhaps you've heard of her."

Marcella Riggins.

The EO currently treating Merit like her own personal playground. The one who, against all odds, had yet to burn out.

"I see," said Victor slowly. "So you're just the messenger."

A flicker of annoyance crossed June's face. "Hardly."

"And why," he asked, "would I want to meet with Marcella?"

June shrugged. "Curiosity? The fact you've got nothing to lose? Or maybe—you'll do it for Sydney's sake."

Victor's expression darkened. "Is that supposed to be a threat?"

"No," said June, and for once there was no mischief, no malice, in her voice. Her expression was open, honest. She hadn't changed faces, but the difference was just as striking. "I do care what happens to that girl."

"You don't even know her."

"Everyone's got secrets, Victor. Even our darling Syd. How do you think I found you today at Merit Central? She looks out for you, and you should be doing the same for her. I know you're sick. I've seen you die. And we both know Sydney's got a long life ahead. What happens when you're not around to protect her?" The earnestness dissolved, replaced once more by that wry twist of the lips, that sly glint of light behind the eyes. "She's a powerful girl, our Syd. She'll need allies when you're gone, and we both know you already killed her first choice."

Victor looked down into his drink. "Is that what Marcella is, then? An ally?"

"Marcella," said June pointedly, "is *powerful*."

"What exactly *is* her power?"

"Come see for yourself."

June swiped the battered paperback and pen.

"Tomorrow," she said, scribbling the details on the inside cover. "And just so you know," she added, rising. "When Marcella makes an offer, she only does it once." She nudged the book back toward him.

"Don't waste it."

V

THE NIGHT BEFORE

FIRST AND WHITE

JUNE hummed softly as the elevator rose.

When she reached the top floor, she found two men in dark suits standing outside the penthouse door. They were new, and one had the poor sense to try to stop her as she passed.

"Where do you think you're going?"

June looked down at the hand on her shoulder. When she looked back up at the man, she was *him,* down to the last hairy knuckle and acne scar.

"I go where I please," she said, her accent coming through in his deep voice.

The security pulled back as if burned.

"I'm . . . I'm sorry," he said, genuine fear flashing across his face. That—that was a pleasant change. She'd gotten surprise, shock, even awe once or twice, but never such a simple thing as *fear.* They hadn't known *who* she was, but they knew *what.* An EO. And it clearly scared the shit out of them.

Maybe Marcella was right. Maybe EOs shouldn't be the ones hiding.

"Not to worry," said June, cheerfully, shifting back into the brunette. "Honest mistake."

They scrambled to open the door, and she stepped into the penthouse, marveling a little at the strange comfort of *returning.*

We really need a dog, she thought. *Something to greet you when you get home.*

She reached the open living room, where Jonathan sat slumped on a leather sofa, palms pressed against his eyes.

"Johnny boy, why so glum?" Her steps slowed at the sight of a large red-brown stain on the floor. "Well, that's new."

"Yeah," said Jonathan, looking up, "she's been busy."

"I can see that. And where is our fearless leader tonight?" Jonathan didn't answer, didn't need to. Marcella's voice streamed from her office.

"Why would I want flowers?"

"They're lilies," said a man's voice. "I thought they'd make an elegant centerpiece."

"*I'm* the elegant centerpiece."

"Without something to soften the space, I'm afraid it will look awfully *austere*."

"This is the beginning of a new age," snapped Marcella, "not a fucking sweet sixteen. Get rid of them."

The man hesitated. ". . . If you're sure . . ."

June heard the telltale click of heels on marble. "Well, perhaps you do know best . . ." There was a shuffle, a gasp, and June stepped through the door just in time to see the man crumble in Marcella's grip.

"Oh, I've missed this," said June pleasantly as what was left of the man fell to the floor. She considered the ruined heap, adorned only by a few tattered bits of silk and a silver cufflink. Marcella was burning hotter, faster, and—as far as June could tell—she still had yet to find her limit.

Marcella leaned back against her desk and took up a cloth, wiping her hands. "I've always hated having to repeat myself." She glanced up. "Shouldn't you be watching over our new arrival?"

"I've had enough babysitting for one day," said June. "I delivered your message."

"*And?*"

"He's a tough one to predict, but I think he'll come."

"I certainly hope so," said Marcella. "I *am* glad you made it back in time."

"For what?" asked June.

Marcella handed her a card.

June took it up, turned it over, eyes flitting over the paper. She shook her head, baffled and amused. "Jesus, Marcella, anyone ever told you that you're batshit crazy?"

Marcella pursed her lips. "Several times," she said. "It's an insult men love to aim at ambitious women. But aren't you forgetting, June—this was *your* idea."

"It was a joke and you know it." June flicked the card away. "How many people did you send that to?"

Marcella ticked them off on her fingers. "The mayor, the chief of police, the district attorney, the director of EON." She waved her hand. "And a few hundred of the most powerful—well, *formerly* most powerful—people in this fine city."

June shook her head in disbelief. "Drawing this kind of attention is a *very bad idea*. You're putting a target on our backs."

"There's already one there. Haven't you noticed? They're going to come for us, one way or another, June, and if we stay hidden, no one will ever know we were there. So let them see us. Let them see what we can do." Marcella smiled, that radiant, seductive smile. "Admit it, June. There's a part of you that wants to stand in that light. No more running. No more hiding."

Marcella didn't understand that June would *always* be hiding. But the woman was right about one thing.

People had tried to bend June. Tried to break her. Tried to make her feel small.

Perhaps it was time for them to understand how small *they* were. June could never be herself, not the self she was before, but she could be someone. She could be seen.

And when EON came calling, well, they wouldn't catch *her*.

Which left only one question, really.

Who was she going to wear?

VI

THE LAST MORNING

MERIT

SYDNEY crashed to her hands and knees on the ice.

She tried to get away, but Eli grabbed the collar of her coat, dragging her backward.

"Come now, Sydney," he said. "Let's finish what we started."

She sat up, gasping for air.

Syd didn't remember falling asleep. She'd spent most of the night tossing and turning, restless. It wasn't the Kingsley—she'd spent five years getting used to strange new places. It was Victor—or rather, his absence.

The apartment felt wrong, too empty without him.

He had a way of taking up space, and even when he started to move like a ghost, coming and going, he never *stayed* gone. There was always that thread connecting him to Sydney, and whenever he was out late, she'd lie in bed and feel it spool away beneath her hand, and then draw tight when he returned.

But Victor hadn't come back last night.

Dumont had been a trap, and Victor had almost been caught in it. He'd gotten away, and wouldn't come back until it was safe. He'd gotten away—and Sydney knew he'd had help. She checked her phone again, saw the notes from last night.

Syd: thank you

June: of course ;)

Syd got up and wandered out of her room, found Mitch at the table twisting a pair of wires and fitting them into a small black box. Sydney was always amazed that such big hands could do such precise work.

"What's that?" she asked.

Mitch smiled. "Just a precaution," he said, holding up the device. She realized she'd seen it before, or something like it, spotted them in the corners of doorways wherever she and Mitch and Victor played house.

"Have you heard from him?"

Mitch nodded. "This morning," he said. "And as soon as he gets back, we're leaving."

Sydney's chest tightened. She couldn't leave Merit. Not yet. Not before she tried—

She ducked back into her room and got dressed, pulled on the boots and the bomber jacket, and then went to the dresser, where she'd hidden the small red tin. She tucked the box deep in her pocket and started out into the apartment and toward the front door.

"Come on, Dol," she called.

The dog drew up his lazy head.

"Syd," said Mitch. "We need to stay inside."

"And he needs a walk," protested Sydney.

Dol, for his part, didn't seem excited.

"I took him out earlier on the rooftop," said Mitch. "The building's gardener won't be happy, but it'll have to do. I'm sorry, kiddo. I don't like being cooped up either, but it isn't safe—"

Sydney shook her head. "If EON knew where we were, they would have already come for us."

Mitch sighed. "Maybe. But I'm not willing to take the chance."

There was a steadiness to his words, a stern resolve. Sydney chewed her lip, considering. Mitch had never *prevented* her from leaving before, not physically. She wondered if he would.

She didn't want to make him do that. She sighed, shrugging out of her coat.

"Fine."

Mitch relaxed, visibly relieved. "All right. I'll start lunch. You hungry?"

Syd smiled. "Always," she said. "I'm going to take a shower first."

Mitch was already in the kitchen, turning on the stove, as she slipped down the hall, tugging the coat back on. She went straight past the bathroom and into Mitch's bedroom, sliding the window open as Dol padded into the room behind her.

"Stay," she whispered.

The dog opened his mouth, as if to bark, but his tongue simply lolled.

"Good boy," she said, swinging her leg over the sill. "Keep Mitch safe."

Syd was about to climb down the fire escape, but then she hesitated, digging out the playing card she always kept with her—the one Victor had plucked from the fallen deck so long ago, and then slipped like a secret into her palm.

The king of spades.

It was battered now, edges worn from five years of back pockets, a rough crease along the middle.

In their game, a face card meant freedom.

Syd told herself she wasn't breaking the rules—and if she was, well, she wasn't the only one.

She dropped the card on the floor, and tugged the window shut behind her.

VII

THE LAST MORNING

DOWNTOWN MERIT

VICTOR stood on the street, the stolen paperback open in his hand.

He'd lingered in the bar until just after midnight before checking into a nearby motel, the kind that clearly wasn't eager to draw police attention. After a few restless hours on creaking springs, he'd gotten up again, and walked the thirty-four blocks through the waking heart of Merit to the address June had scribbled inside the battered front cover.

119 Alexander Place. 12 p.m.

It was, of all things, an art gallery. Large glass windows looked out onto the curb, revealing glimpses of the paintings inside. It was almost noon, and Victor hadn't decided yet if he was going in.

He weighed the options in his mind, along with June's words.

It could simply be another kind of trap. Or it could be an opportunity. But in the end, it was sheer curiosity that propelled him forward. For the EO who had managed to evade EON's net. For the woman who had held her ground instead of running.

Victor crossed the street, climbed the three short steps, and stepped into the White Hall Gallery.

It was larger than it looked from the street—a series of broad, blank rooms, linked together by archways. Abstract paintings dotted the walls, blotches of color against the white. In his black attire, Victor felt like an ink spill. Ideal for slipping through crowds on the street, but far more conspicuous in such a stark environment. So he didn't bother trying to blend in, didn't pretend to admire the art, simply set off to find Marcella.

A handful of men and women stood scattered through the rooms, but none of them were real patrons. Victor glimpsed holsters beneath fitted suits, fingers resting on the open mouths of handbags. Hired guns, he thought, wondering if June was hidden among them. He didn't spot anyone with her tells.

But he did find Marcella.

She was in the largest gallery, facing away from him, her black hair pulled up, a silk blouse dipping low between her shoulder blades. Still, he knew it was her. Not because he'd seen a photograph, but because of the way she stood, with all the casual grace of a predator. Victor was used to being the strongest person in the room, and it was both familiar and unsettling to see that confidence on someone else.

They weren't alone in the room.

A thin man in a black suit leaned against the wall between two paintings. His dark hair was slicked back, his eyes hidden behind a pair of sunglasses. The white walls made the gallery unnaturally bright, but not bright enough to merit shades—meaning they served an alternate purpose.

"I've never understood art," mused Marcella, loud enough for Victor to know she was addressing him. "I've been to a hundred galleries, stared at a thousand paintings, waiting to feel inspired or awestruck or enamored—but the only thing I ever really felt was *bored*."

As Victor watched, she reached out and pressed one gold nail to the surface of the painting. Under Marcella's touch, the canvas rotted, and crumbled, pieces drifting to the floor.

"Don't worry," she said, turning on one metal heel. "I own the building, and everything in it." She raised a brow. "Except for you, of course." She gave him a cursory look. "Do you like art, Mr. Vale? My husband did. He always had a fondness for beautiful things." Marcella lifted her chin. "Do you think I'm beautiful?"

Victor considered her—the willowy limbs, the red lips, the blue eyes framed by thick black lashes. He glanced from her, to the ruins of the painting on the gallery floor, and back. "I think you're powerful."

Marcella smiled, clearly pleased with the answer.

Victor sensed a ghost of movement at his back, and glanced over his shoulder to see another man enter the room, one with a goatee and a mischievous smile.

"I believe you've already met June," said Marcella. "In one form or another."

The man winked, that telltale light in his eyes.

"And this is Jonathan," said Marcella, flicking her fingers in the direction of the thin man against the wall.

Jonathan didn't answer, beyond the slight nod of his head.

"So," said Victor, "instead of art, you're collecting EOs."

Marcella's red lips split into a smile. "Do you know what I wanted to be when I grew up?"

"President?"

Her smile widened. "Powerful." Her steel heels clicked against the marble as she came toward him. "When you think about it, it's really all anyone ever wants. Once upon a time, power was determined by lineage—the age of blood. Then it was determined by money—the age of gold. But I think it's time for a new age, Victor. The age of power itself."

"Let me guess," said Victor. "I'm either with you or against you."

Marcella tsked. "Such black-and-white thinking. I swear, men are so busy looking for enemies, they rarely remember to make friends." She shook her head. "Why can't we work together?"

"I work alone."

Marcella raised a knowing brow. "Now, we both know that's not true."

Victor's eyes narrowed, but he said nothing. Marcella seemed more than happy to hold the stage.

"Money in the right hands can get all kinds of things. Knowledge. Insight. Eli Ever's files from his time with the Merit PD, perhaps. He and Serena Clarke made quite a pair, but I think you got the better deal with her little sister, Sydney."

Victor kept his poise, but across the room June stiffened, the color draining from her face. "Marcella—"

But the woman held up a hand, gold nails catching the light.

"I've heard about your own talents," she continued. "I'd like to see them for myself."

"You want me to audition?"

Her lips twitched. "Call it what you like. I've shown you mine. And Jonathan's. And June's, for that matter. I think it's only fair . . ."

Victor needed no further prompting. He flexed his hand toward the thin man in the suit, expecting him to buckle immediately—and was surprised when instead, the air in front of him flashed blue and white with an almost electric crackle. And beyond that, nothing happened. Strange. Victor could *feel* the other man's nerves, just as present as before he'd tried to impact them. But in that exact instant, it had been like a short-circuit, almost like lightning trying to strike something grounded.

A forcefield.

Marcella smiled. "Oh, sorry. I should have said, Jonathan's off-limits." She looked around. "A little help?"

She hardly raised her voice, but the room began to fill. The six men and women Victor had passed earlier came spilling in.

Marcella smiled.

"I have a reward," she said, "for whoever brings this man to his knees."

For a moment, no one moved.

And then, everyone did.

A brick of a man lunged toward him, and Victor took hold of nerves, and twisted violently. The man buckled, screaming, as Victor leveled the two approaching in his wake, then turned toward a woman as she drew a blade.

A conductor's flick of Victor's fingers, and she collapsed too.

The fifth went down on his side, curling in against the pain, while the sixth tried to reach for his gun—Victor forced his hand flat to the marble and continued turning the dials up until all six writhed and spasmed on the floor.

He held Marcella's gaze, waiting for her to say *enough*, order him to stop. Waiting for any sign of her discomfort. But Marcella only watched the scene unfold, her blue eyes bright, unflinching.

Up until then, she had reminded Victor of Serena, expecting the world to bend to her will. But in that moment, she reminded him of *Eli*. That zealous light in her eyes, the coiled energy, the conviction.

Victor had seen enough.

He turned his power on Marcella. Not a subtle impression, either, but a sudden, blunt-force blow, strong enough to fry nerves and level a body. She should have collapsed on the spot, buckled like dead weight to the cold marble. Instead, Marcella took a single surprised breath and then Jonathan's head flicked imperceptibly toward her. As soon as it did, the air crackled, the space around Marcella filling with the same blue-white flare that had shielded Jonathan moments before.

Victor realized his error. Marcella was more like Eli than he'd guessed. Her uncanny self-assurance was an arrogance born from invincibility. Albeit a borrowed one.

Victor dropped his hold on the rest of the room, and left them gasping on the floor.

Marcella pursed her lips as the shield flickered out. "That wasn't very sporting."

"Forgive me," answered Victor dryly. "I guess I got carried away." He looked down at the men and women on the floor. "I take it I failed your test."

"Oh, I wouldn't say that. Your performance was . . . illuminating."

Marcella produced a crisp white envelope.

June took the card and delivered it to Victor.

"What's this?" he asked.

"An invitation."

They stood there for a second, neither willing to put their back to the other.

At last Marcella broke into a smile. "You can see yourself out," she said. "But I do hope we meet again."

Victor wanted nothing less, but he had a feeling they would.

∞

"**WELL**," said Marcella, watching Victor go. "That was enlightening."

June hadn't said a word since Marcella mentioned Sydney, hadn't trusted herself to speak. Now she cleared her throat.

"Do you still think he might be useful?"

"Undoubtedly," said Marcella, taking out her phone.

"Should I follow him?"

"No need." Marcella punched in a number. "I've seen enough." Someone answered, and Marcella said, "He's staying at the Kingsley, on Fifteenth. But right now, he's moving west on Alexander. Happy hunting, Joseph."

June's stomach dropped.

How did Marcella already know where they were staying? Where *Sydney* was staying?

She gave June a bland look. "You didn't think you were the only one keeping an eye on things, did you?"

June swallowed. "Do what you want with Victor, but Sydney isn't part of this."

"Maybe she wouldn't have been," said Marcella, pointedly, "if you'd told me the truth about the girl's power instead of keeping her to yourself." She flicked her fingers dismissively toward the door. "But go ahead. See if you can get to her before they do."

VIII

THE LAST MORNING

THE KINGSLEY

"**SYDNEY!**" called Mitch, flipping the grilled cheese in the pan.

She didn't answer.

That bad feeling, the one he'd had on the way to Merit, began to crystalize from a general dread into something specific. Like the vague first signs of an illness that suddenly sharpened into the flu.

"Sydney!" he called again, shifting the pan off the stove so lunch wouldn't burn. He started toward the bathroom, slowing when he noticed the door was open. As was the door to Syd's room.

And the one to his own.

Mitch glimpsed a black tail swishing absently just inside the door, and found Dol sprawled on his bedroom floor, facing the window and chewing on a scrap of paper.

Mitch knelt down and pried the paper from the dog's lolling mouth, stilling at the sight of the crown, the sideways profile. It was a face card.

The king of spades.

Mitch was on his feet, already dialing Sydney's cell. It rang, and rang, and rang, but no one answered. He swore, and was just about to chuck the phone onto the bed when it went off in his hand.

Mitch answered, praying it was Syd.

"Pack up," ordered Victor. "We're leaving."

Mitch made an uneasy sound.

"What is it?" demanded Victor.

"Sydney," said Mitch. "She's not here."

A short exhale. "Where?"

"I don't know. I was making lunch and—"

Victor cut him off. "Just find her."

∞

SYDNEY stood on the curb, looking up.

Five years ago, the Falcon Price had been a construction project, rebar and concrete surrounded by a plywood fence. Now, it rose high above her, a gleaming tower of glass and steel. All the evidence of the crimes committed that night hidden beneath fresh cement, drywall, plaster.

She didn't know what she'd expected to find. What she'd expected to *feel*. A ghost? A remnant of her sister? But now that Sydney was here, she could only see Serena rolling her eyes at that idea.

Syd knelt, reaching into her bag for the secret she'd carried so long. She eased the lid off the red metal tin, folded back the strip of cloth. For the first time in five years, Sydney let her fingers skim the soot-covered shards of bone. The finger joint. The piece of rib. The knot of a hipbone. All that was left of Serena Clarke. All that was left—besides whatever was left here.

Sydney laid the bones out on top of their cloth wrapping, arranged them just so, leaving a fraction of space for the missing, drawing imaginary lines where the other bones should be.

She took a deep, shuddering breath, and was about to bring her hands to the remains when her phone rang, the high sound cutting through the quiet. How stupid. She should have shut it off. If she had already gotten started, if her hands and her mind had been reaching past the bones when that noise happened, Sydney could have lost the thread, could have fumbled her only chance. Ruined everything.

She dug the phone from her pocket and saw Mitch's name flash across the screen. Sydney switched the cell off, and turned her attention back to her sister's bones.

IX

THE LAST AFTERNOON

EON

"**WHAT** do you mean, *transport protocol?*"

Dominic had been in the locker room, buttoning up his uniform shirt, when Holtz burst in, face bright. He'd finally been tapped for field duty. Or rather, for transport.

"They're letting Stell's hunting dog out," he said.

Dom's chest tightened. "What?"

"Eli Cardale. They're letting him out of his cage—to go after that crazy mob wife, the one who killed Bara."

Dom was on his feet. "They can't."

"Well, they are," said Holtz.

"When?"

"Right now. Orders came in from the director. He was gonna handle it himself, but there's some big op going down in the city—another EO—and Stell just blew through like a storm. Before he left, he told us to initiate the extraction . . ."

But Dom was still stuck on the words before. "Another EO?"

"Yeah," said Holtz, pulling a suit of matte black armor from the wall. "That mystery guy, the one who's been killing off other EOs."

Dom's mouth had gone dry.

"What are the odds?" mused Holtz. "So much excitement in one day."

Holtz finished strapping in and turned to go, but Dominic caught his arm. "Wait."

The other soldier frowned down at the place where Dom's fingers dug into his sleeve. But what could Dom say? What could he do? He couldn't stop the missions—all he could do was warn Victor. Dom forced himself to let go.

"Just be careful," he said. "Don't go ending up like Bara."

Holtz flashed that cheerful, dogged smile, and was gone.

Dominic counted to ten, then twenty, waiting until Holtz's steps had receded, until he was left with only the thud of his heart. Then he walked out of the locker room, turned right, and headed for Stell's office—and the only phone inside the building.

He kept his gait even, his steps casual—but with every forward stride, Dom knew he was going further down a one-way road. He stopped outside the director's door. Last chance to turn around.

Dom pushed open the door, and stepped inside.

∞

VICTOR knew he was being followed.

He sensed the weight of their steps, felt their attention like a drag. At first he assumed it was June, or one of Marcella's human guards, but as their steps quickened, and the sound of one person became two, Victor began to suspect another source. He'd been heading directly back to the Kingsley. Now, he veered left, cutting through a crowded stretch of downtown Merit's restaurants and cafés.

His phone buzzed in his pocket.

He didn't recognize the number, but answered without slowing his step.

"They're on to you," said Dominic, his voice low, urgent.

"Yeah," said Victor, "thanks for the heads-up."

"It gets worse," said Dom. "They're letting Eli out."

The words were a knife, driven so precisely between Victor's ribs.

"To catch me?"

"No," said Dom. "I think it's actually meant to catch *Marcella*."

Victor swore under his breath. "You can't let that happen."

"How am I supposed to stop it?"

"Figure it out," said Victor, hanging up.

He could feel them lapping at his heels. Hear the sound of car doors swinging closed.

Victor crossed the street and stepped into a nearby park, a sprawling network of running paths, vendor carts, open lawns, packed tight with people in the midday sun. He didn't look back. He hadn't been able to pick his pursuers out of the crowd, not yet. Population was working in their favor, but it could also work in his.

Victor picked up his pace, allowing a hint of urgency to creep into his stride.

Catch up, he thought.

He heard a set of steps quickening, clearly expecting him to break into a run. Instead, Victor turned on his heel.

He doubled back on the crowded path, and started walking again in the opposite direction, forcing his pursuer to either stop and retreat, or maintain the illusion by continuing toward him.

Nobody stopped.

No one retreated.

Usually people bent away from Victor, their attention veering like water around a stone. But now, in the tangle of joggers and walkers and ambling groups, one man was still looking straight at him.

The man was young and dressed in civilian clothes, but he had the gait of a soldier, and the moment their eyes met, a ripple of tension crossed the younger man's face. He drew a gun, but as he swung the weapon up, Victor flicked his own fingers, a single, vicious pull of an invisible thread, and the man fell to his knees on the path, the gun skidding out of his hand. Victor kept walking as the crowd turned, half in worry at the man's scream and half in horror at the sight of the weapon on the park's pavement.

Chaos erupted, and in that chaos Victor cut left, onto a different path, aiming for the street side of the park. Halfway there, a second figure rushed toward him, a woman with cropped dark hair.

She didn't draw a weapon, but she had one hand to her ear and her lips were moving.

A group of cyclists whipped around the corner and Victor cut across the path just before they passed, a sudden, whooshing barricade that bought him just enough time to step between two carts and out of the park.

Victor moved swiftly, cutting across traffic and down a side street, seconds before an unmarked van skidded around the corner at the other end. It drove straight at him. He reached for the man behind the wheel, turning the dial up until the driver lost control and the van veered, slamming into a hydrant. Victor heard more footsteps, the hiss of radio static. He ducked into the nearest subway stop, swept past the turnstile and down the stairs, taking them two at a time toward the train pulling into the station below.

He made his way to the very end of the platform, but instead of boarding the train, he slipped past the pedestrian barricade and into the mouth of the tunnel, pressing his body against the wall as the bells chimed and the subway doors hissed shut.

A man reached the platform just in time to watch the train slide by.

Victor lingered in the tunnel, watching the man scan the cars, hands on his hips, his black hair edging to gray.

Stell.

Even after five years, Victor recognized him immediately. He watched as the former detective turned around, finally, and stormed back up the stairs.

Victor knew he should try again to get to the Kingsley—but first, he needed to have a word with the director of EON.

The next train pulled in, and Victor slipped into the press of bodies following in Stell's wake.

X

THE LAST AFTERNOON

EON

DOM stared at Stell's bank of computer screens.

Figure it out.

His mind spun like tires in mud, searching for purchase, his attention flicking from the desk to the door to the grid of camera footage on the far wall. There, upper right, three soldiers in full gear moved down a white hall. In another window, the familiar shape of Eli Cardale sat waiting.

Fuck.

Dom turned toward the trio of screens on Stell's desk. He didn't know the first thing about hacking into computers.

But he knew someone who did.

Mitch answered on the second ring. "Who is this?"

"Mitch, it's Dominic."

A shuffle of movement. "This isn't a good time."

Footsteps sounded in the hall beyond Stell's office. Dom pressed the cell to his chest and held his breath. When they were gone, he raised the phone, talking quickly. "Sorry, but I'm working on Victor's orders."

"Aren't we all."

"I need to hack a computer."

The metal sound of a zipper sliding. "What kind?"

"The kind at EON."

The line went quiet, and Dom assumed Mitch was thinking, but then he heard a laptop click open, a booting sound. "What kind of encryption?"

"No idea." He tapped the computer away. "It's just a password screen."

Mitch made a sound like a muffled laugh. "Governments. Okay. Do exactly what I tell you . . ."

He started speaking a foreign language—that's what it sounded like, anyway—but Dom did as he was told, and three agonizing minutes later, a green ACCESS GRANTED appeared on the screen, and he was in.

Dom hung up, brought up the grid of folders, each one marked by a cell number. Every other computer in EON had a folder like this one. And every other folder started with *Cell 1*.

But Stell's computer had another option—*Cell 0*.

Dom opened the drive and Eli Ever—Eliot Cardale—appeared onscreen, sitting at a table in the center of his cell, turning through a black folder. As Dom keyed in the codes, his vision sharpened, his focus narrowing the way it had when he was in the field. Time seemed to slow. Everything fell away except the screen, the commands, and the blur of his fingers across the keyboard.

A second window appeared with the cell block controls, scanning past lighting and temperature to security, emergency, lockdown.

Dominic couldn't prevent EON from letting Eli out. But he could slow them down. He was just about to key in the codes Mitch had given him, send the whole cell into lockdown, when someone cleared their throat behind him.

Dom spun around, and saw Agent Rios standing there, looking unimpressed. He didn't have time to wonder where she'd come from, didn't even have time to step *out* of time—into the safety of the shadows—before Rios slammed a cattle prod into his chest and Dom's world went white.

ELI was getting restless.

He scanned the images in the black folder one last time as he waited for Stell.

The director had made the plan very clear—Eli would be escorted from the facility under guard and, upon completion of the mission, returned to his cell. If he disobeyed in any way, at any point, he would be returned to the lab instead, where he would spend the rest of his existence being dissected.

That was *Stell's* plan.

Eli had his own.

Steps sounded beyond the wall, and he set his file aside and rose, expecting as usual to see Stell. Instead, when the wall went clear, he saw a fleet of EON soldiers dressed in black, their faces hidden behind sleek, close-fitting masks. Even with the visors up, only their eyes were visible. One pair green, one blue, one brown.

"All this fuss," muttered Green Eyes, sizing him up. "Doesn't look all that dangerous to me."

"Oh," said Eli, crossing the cell, "there are EOs out there *far* more dangerous than I am."

"But how many people have *they* killed?" asked Blue Eyes. "I'm guessing it's less than you."

Eli shrugged. "That depends."

"On what?" asked Brown Eyes—a woman, judging by her voice.

"Whether you consider EOs people," said Eli.

"Enough," said Blue Eyes, stepping toward the barrier. "Let's get going."

Eli held his ground. "Where is Director Stell?"

"Busy."

Eli doubted Stell would hand over such a delicate task—unless it was truly urgent.

Or personal.

Could Stell have already found Victor?

Ships in the night, thought Eli grimly. But he couldn't afford to worry about Victor Vale right now.

"Inmate," ordered Blue Eyes. "Approach the divide and put your hands through the slot."

Eli did, felt the heavy metal cuffs close around his wrists.

"Now turn around, place your back to the slot, and kneel."

Eli hesitated. That wasn't protocol. Cautiously, he did as he was told, expecting a dark hood to come down over his head. Instead, cold metal slid around his throat. Eli tensed, resisted the urge to pull away as the steel closed around his throat.

"The hunting dog gets a collar," said Blue Eyes.

Eli stood, running his fingers along the band of metal. "What is this?"

Brown Eyes held up a slim remote. "Didn't think we'd let you out without a leash . . ."

She pressed a button, and a single high note, like a warning tone, sounded in Eli's ears before pain pierced the back of his neck. Eli's vision went white, his body folding beneath him.

"And down he goes," said Blue Eyes as he hit the cell floor.

Eli couldn't move, couldn't feel anything below the shard of metal driven between his vertebrae.

"Come on, Samson," said Green Eyes, "we're on a schedule."

The tone sounded again, and the steel spike withdrew. Eli gasped, chest lurching as his spine healed and sensation flooded back into his limbs. He pushed himself to his hands and knees, and then up to his feet. A small pool of blood on the cell floor was the only sign of what they'd done.

Brown Eyes waved the remote. "You try to escape, you try to attack us—hell, you piss us off—I'll put you down."

Eli studied the slim remote in the soldier's hand, and wondered if it was the only one.

"Why would I do that?" he said. "We're on the same side."

"Yeah, sure," said Green Eyes, thrusting a hood through the slot. "Put it on."

Eli was led, blind and bound, through doorways and down halls, a soldier gripping each arm. He felt the ground shift beneath him from concrete to linoleum, and then to asphalt. The air changed, a breeze grazing his skin, and he wished the hood were off, wished he could see the sky, breathe in fresh air. But there would be time for that. A few feet more, and then their progress halted. Eli was turned around, maneuvered until his back came up against the metal side of a van.

Doors swung open, and he was half dragged into the back of the van, forced a little too roughly onto a steel bench against one wall. A strap went around his legs, another around his chest. His handcuffs were locked to the bench seat between his knees. The soldiers climbed in, and the doors were thrown shut, and the van's engine revved as it pulled away from EON.

Eli smiled beneath the hood.

He was cuffed and collared—but he was one step closer to free.

XI

THE LAST AFTERNOON

THE FALCON PRICE

A couple years ago, Mitch had taught Sydney about magnets.

They'd spent a whole day testing their effects, the attraction and repulsion. Syd had always thought of magnetic force as a pull, but she'd been shocked to discover the strength of their push. Even a small flat disc could exert so much force against another.

She felt that same repulsion now, as her fingers hovered over her sister's bones.

Sydney tried to will her hands down as something inside her heart pushed back.

Why couldn't she do it?

Sydney had to bring Serena back.

She was her *sister*.

Family isn't always blood.

June had said that—June, who'd never betrayed Sydney. June, who'd protected Victor. But she wasn't *Serena*.

And if EON was chasing them now, Serena could help. Serena could do anything. Could make *other people* do anything.

It was a terrifying power to start with—but how bad would it be if Serena came back *wrong*? What would that power look like when it was fractured, broken?

For so long, Sydney had assumed she was afraid of failing. Afraid that she'd slip, lose the threads, and with that, her only chance at reviving Serena.

But the longer she stared at her sister's bones, the more Sydney realized—she was just as scared of succeeding.

Why had she waited so long? Was it really because she thought it had to happen *here*? That the connection would be strongest back where it had first been broken?

Or—was it because it gave her an excuse to wait?

Because Sydney was afraid to see her sister again.

Because Sydney wasn't ready to face Serena.

Because Sydney wasn't sure she *should* bring her sister back, even if she could.

Tears blurred her vision.

She realized, suddenly, that in all her nightmares, Serena had never once saved her. She was there, on the banks of the frozen river, waiting, watching as Eli stalked Syd across the ice. As he wrestled her to the frozen ground. As he wrapped his hands around Syd's throat.

Serena hadn't pulled the trigger on Sydney that night.

But she hadn't stopped Eli from shooting her either.

Sydney missed her sister.

But she missed the version of Serena who had loved and protected Sydney, made her younger sister feel safe, and seen. And that Serena had died in ice, not fire.

Sydney's fingers finally came to rest against Serena's bones. But she didn't reach beyond them, didn't search for the lingering thread. She simply folded them up inside the strip of cloth, and put them back in the red metal tin.

Her legs were shaking as she pushed herself up to her feet.

Syd shoved the container deep into her pocket, heard the scrape of metal on metal as the tin came to rest against the gun. In her other pocket, her fingers found her cell phone. She dug it out as she left the Falcon Price lot and headed back toward the Kingsley, watched it restart in her palm. Her boots dragged to a stop.

There were so many missed calls.
A handful from Victor.
Then a dozen from Mitch.
And text after text after text from June.
Sydney took off running.

SHE tried to call Mitch, but it went straight to voicemail.
Tried to call Victor, but no one answered.
At last, June picked up. "Sydney."
"What's going on?" she asked.
"Where are you?" demanded June, sounding breathless.
"I had all these missed calls," said Syd, slowing to a walk, "and I can't get ahold of anyone, and I—"
"Where *are* you?" repeated June.
"On my way to the Kingsley."
"No," said June. "You can't go back there."
"I have to."
"It's too late."
Too late. What did she mean?
"Just stay where you are and I'll come to you. Sydney, listen to me—"
"I'm sorry," said Syd, right before she hung up. It had taken her twenty-five minutes to walk to the Falcon Price. She made it home in ten. The Kingsley finally came into sight, down the block and across the street. Syd slammed to a stop as she noticed the two black vans idling on the corner, one near the entrance, the other at the mouth of the parking garage. They were unmarked, but there was something ominous about the tinted glass, the windowless sides.
Arms wrapped around her shoulders.
A hand closed over her mouth.
Sydney twisted, tried to scream, but a familiar voice sounded in her ear.

"Don't fight, it's me."

The arms let go, and Syd turned to see June, or at least a version of her, one with loose brown curls and sharp green eyes. Sydney sagged in relief, but June's attention twitched, drawn to something over Syd's shoulder.

"Come on," said June, gripping her hand.

Syd resisted. "I can't just leave them."

"You can't save them like this. What are you going to do? Storm in there? Think. If you go in there now, you'll just get yourself caught by EON, and what good will you be to anyone then?"

June was right, and Syd hated that she was. Hated that her power wasn't enough to protect them.

"We need a plan," said June. "So we'll think of one. I promise." She squeezed Sydney's hand. "Come on."

This time, Syd let herself be pulled away.

∞

IT was beginning to rain as Victor followed Stell through the streets of downtown Merit.

He plucked a black umbrella from a corner stand without paying, and vanished beneath it, one bloom of darkness among dozens. Half a block ahead, the detective stopped beside a black van and a sedan, and convened with a cluster of soldiers in sodden street clothes, their manner and posture nullifying any meaningful disguise.

Victor lingered nearby, folding himself into the huddle at the bus stop. He watched Stell rake a hand through his salt-and-pepper hair, the picture of frustration. Watched him gesture at the soldiers, who got back into their vehicles, while Stell himself set off on foot.

Victor fell in step behind him.

Stell walked for ten, fifteen minutes more before swiping into a residential building. Victor caught the front door just as the elevator closed. He watched it ascend one floor, then two, before stopping. Victor took the stairs instead and arrived just as Stell was unlocking the front door, watched the man stiffen as he registered the other man's presence, realized that he wasn't alone.

Stell turned, drawing his service weapon before he saw Victor, and froze.

Victor smiled. "Hello, Detective."

Stell's hand was steady on the gun. "It's been a while."

"I'm surprised it took you so long."

"In my defense," said Stell, "I assumed you were dead."

"You know what they say about assuming," said Victor dryly. "We EOs are hard to keep down." He nodded at the weapon. "Speaking of down."

Stell shook his head, grip tightening on the gun. "I can't do that."

Victor flexed his hand. "Are you sure?" He splayed his fingers, and shock crossed Stell's face like lightning as his own hand opened, let the gun fall to the floor.

"You're not the only one who's traded up," said Victor, moving toward the detective. The air caught audibly in Stell's throat as he tried to back away, and couldn't.

"Pain is specific, but relatively simple," continued Victor. "Now, animating a body, articulating it—that requires precision, the firing of certain nerves, the pulling of specific strings. Like a marionette."

"What do you want?" hissed Stell.

I want to stop dying, thought Victor.

But Stell couldn't help with that.

"I want you to keep Eli in his goddamn cage."

Surprise crossed the detective's face. "That isn't your call."

"How could you be so stupid?" growled Victor.

"I do what I have to," said Stell, "and I certainly don't answer to—"

Victor's hand clenched into a fist, and Stell doubled over in pain. He caught himself against the wall, gave a sharp whistle through gritted teeth, and a second later every other door in the hall swung open, soldiers streaming in, weapons raised.

"I want him alive," ordered Stell.

Careless, Victor chided himself. The cop had baited his own trap, and he had stepped inside.

"You've always preferred being predator to prey," observed Stell.

Victor's teeth clicked together. "Did Eli teach you that?"

"Give me a little credit," said Stell. "You guys aren't the only ones who can spot a pattern."

"What happens now?" asked Victor, trying to sense the number of bodies surrounding him. How much power would he have to use to level the ones he couldn't *see*?

"Now," said Stell, "you come with us. This doesn't have to get violent," he continued. "Get on your knees and—"

Victor didn't wait for him to finish. He reached out with everything he had. Two bodies hit the floor behind him, another buckling at the edge of his sight.

Then Stell shot Victor in the chest.

He staggered, his hand going to his ribs. But there was no blood, only a red dart, buried deep. A vial, already empty. Whatever it held, it was strong—Victor wrenched the dart out, but his limbs were already going numb.

He cranked the dial up on his own nerves, clung to the pain to regain focus.

Victor brought two more soldiers to their knees before another shot pierced his side. A third took him in the leg, and he felt himself slip. He tried to brace himself against the wall, but his legs were already folding, his vision flickered, then dimmed. He saw the soldiers swarming in, and then—

Nothing.

XII

THE LAST AFTERNOON

ACROSS TOWN

THREE blocks from the Kingsley, June was making instant cocoa while Sydney perched on the edge of the nondescript hotel bed. Outside, it had started to rain. Syd tried Victor's phone again, but it was off now, just like Mitch's. She'd even tried Dominic's number, but there was no answer there, either.

June had told her everything—EON's task force, their mission to catch Victor and Sydney, the simple fact that June had to choose quickly, knowing she only had time to reach one. She'd been so worried—and by the time she got to the Kingsley, the EON soldiers were already there.

Which meant that Mitch—

June seemed to read Syd's mind.

"The big guy can take care of himself," she said, carrying over two mugs, "and if he can't, what difference would *you* have made? No offense, Syd, but your power wouldn't protect him—it would only get you caught, and Mitch wouldn't have wanted that." She paused. "Drink up, you're shivering."

Sydney wrapped her fingers around the hot mug. June sank into a nearby chair. It was so weird, seeing her again. Syd had had the other girl's voice in her ear for more than three years, the words on her phone, but she'd only seen June's face once before, and of course, it wasn't really hers. It wasn't even the one she was wearing now.

Sydney took a long, scalding sip, cringing not at the heat but the sugar—June had made it way too sweet.

"What do you really look like?" she asked, blowing on the steam.

June winked. "Sorry, kiddo, a girl's gotta have some secrets."

Syd looked down at the cocoa and shook her head. "What am I going to do now?"

"*We*," said June, "are going to think of something. We'll get through this, you and me. We just have to lie low until it's over, and then—"

"Until *what* is over?" demanded Syd. "I can't just stay here when Victor and Mitch are in trouble."

June leaned forward, resting a hand on Syd's boot. "They're not the only ones who can protect you."

"It's not about protection," said Syd, pulling away. "They're my *family*."

June stiffened, but Sydney was already on her feet, abandoning the half-empty mug beside the bed.

June could have grabbed her, but she didn't. She simply watched her go.

Sydney was almost to the door, reaching for the handle, when it seemed to drift out of reach. The floor had tilted, too. And suddenly, it was all Syd could do to keep from falling over.

She squeezed her eyes shut, but that only made things worse.

When Sydney opened them again, June was there, reaching out to steady her. "It's okay," she said, her accent soft, melodic. "It's okay."

But it wasn't.

Syd tried to ask what was going on, but her tongue felt leaden, and when she tried to pull away, she stumbled, head spinning.

"You'll understand," June was saying. "When this is all over, you will . . ."

Sydney's vision blurred, and June's arms closed around her as she fell.

THE road jostled under Eli's feet as the transport made its way toward Merit.

Five minutes into the drive, the hood had come off, trading the dark, woven interior of the fabric for the dark, windowless interior of the van itself. Not a vast improvement, but certainly a step.

The brown-eyed soldier sat on the bench to Eli's right. The other two sat across from him. They rode in silence, Eli attempting to track the distance with one part of his mind, while the rest traced over the details of the plan he'd been given, pondered the problem of Marcella and her chosen compatriots.

He felt Brown Eyes staring at him.

"Something on your mind?" asked Eli.

"I'm trying to figure out how a guy like you kills thirty-nine people."

Eli raised a brow. "You can't kill what's already dead. You can only dispose of it."

"Does that apply to you, too?"

Eli considered. For so long, Eli had thought himself the exception, not the rule. Now he knew better. And yet Eli had been given this specific power. A memory flashed through his mind—kneeling on the floor, slicing open his wrists over and over and over to see how many times it would take before God let him die.

I would bury myself if I could.

"Must be nice," said Green Eyes. "To be unkillable."

A second memory—of lying on that lab table, his heart in Haverty's hands.

Eli said nothing.

A few minutes later, the van came to a stop on a busy street—Eli could hear the noise even before the back door swung open and Stell himself climbed in. "Briggs," he said, nodding at the woman. "Samson. Holtz. Any trouble here?"

"No sir," they said in unison.

"Where have you been?" demanded Eli.

"Believe it or not," said Stell, "you weren't the highest priority."

He'd meant it as a jab, but Eli saw only its truth, written in the lines of the director's face.

Victor.

The van drove on for a few more blocks before pulling into an alley, where the three soldiers climbed out—but not Stell. He turned his attention to Eli. "They are going ahead to secure the room. In a minute, you and I are going to leave this van and go inside. You make a scene, and that collar will be only the *first* of your problems."

Eli held out his cuffed wrists. "If you want to keep a low profile, these should probably come off."

Stell leaned forward, but simply tossed a coat over Eli's outstretched hands, hiding them from view. Eli sighed, and followed the director out of the van. He looked up at the stretch of blue sky, and breathed in fresh air for the first time in five years.

Stell brought a hand to Eli's shoulder, kept it there as they wove through the cars in front of the hotel.

"Remember your instructions," warned Stell as they stepped through the doors and crossed the lobby to the bank of elevators.

The soldiers were waiting on the fifth floor.

Two in the hall, one still clearing the room.

They'd taken off their helmets in an effort to blend in, revealing three young, good-looking soldiers. A woman in her early thirties, compact and strong and stoic. A young man, handsome and blond, thirty at most, who looked like he would have won Most Likable while in school. A second man, wide-jawed and smug, who reminded Eli of the frat boys he'd hated in college, the kind who would crush a beer can on their heads as if the feat were something to be proud of.

Once inside, Stell finally removed Eli's handcuffs.

He rubbed his wrists—they weren't stiff, or sore, but it was a hard habit to shake, that urge, and the small gestures that made people ordinary. Human. Eli surveyed the room. It was an elegant hotel suite, with a large bed and two tall windows. A garment bag hung on the back of the bathroom door, another had been cast onto the bed. A chair sat beneath one of the large windows, a low desk beneath the other, its surface adorned with a pad of paper and a pen.

Eli started toward it.

"Stay away from the windows, inmate."

Eli ignored him, resting his hand on the desk. "We're here *because* of this window." His fingers closed around the pen. "This view."

He leaned across the desk and looked out at the Old Courthouse across the street.

What a perfect choice, thought Eli. After all, a courthouse was a place of judgment. Justice.

He straightened, slipping the pen up his sleeve, and started for the bathroom.

"Where do you think you're going?" demanded Green Eyes.

"To take a shower," said Eli. "I need to be presentable."

The soldiers looked to Stell, who stared at Eli for a long moment before nodding. "Sweep it," he ordered.

Eli waited while the soldiers secured the bathroom, making sure there was no way out, removing anything that might be even vaguely construed as a weapon. As if Eli himself weren't the weapon of choice today.

When the soldiers were satisfied, he unhooked the garment bag from the bathroom door and stepped inside. He was pulling it shut when one of the soldiers caught the door. "Leave it open."

"Suit yourself," said Eli.

He left a foot of clearance, for modesty. Hung up the borrowed suit, and turned on the shower.

With his back to the open door, Eli freed the stolen pen from the cuff of his EON-issued jacket and held it between his teeth as he stripped off the clothes, let them pool around his feet.

He stepped into the shower, the frosted glass door falling shut behind him. He ran his fingers over the surface of the steel collar, searching for a weakness, a groove or clasp. But he found none. Eli hissed in annoyance.

The collar, then, would have to wait.

He removed the stolen pen from his mouth, and under the static of the water's spray, snapped it in two.

It was hardly ideal, but it was the closest thing to a knife he was likely to get.

Eli closed his eyes, and summoned the pages from the black folder. He'd studied them thoroughly, memorized the photos and scans that had accompanied each of Haverty's experiments.

The record had been gruesome but revealing.

The first time Eli had noticed the shadow on an image of his forearm, he'd taken it for a swatch, just one of those markers used to signal direction on an X-ray. But then it showed up again on an MRI. A small metal rectangle, the faint impression of a grid.

And he knew exactly what it was.

Eli found the same mark on a scan of his lower spine. At his left hip. The base of his skull. Between his ribs. Disgust had welled like blood as Eli realized—every time Haverty had cut or pried or pinned him open, the doctor had left a tracking device behind. Each one small enough so that Eli's body, instead of rejecting the objects, simply healed around them.

It was time they came out.

Eli brought his makeshift scalpel to his forearm and pressed down. The skin split, blood rising instantly along the jagged edge, and an old voice in his head noted that the heat and moisture would act as anticoagulants, before he reminded that voice that his healing power rendered the fact irrelevant.

He clenched his teeth as he drove the plastic deeper.

Haverty had never bothered with shallow wounds. When he opened Eli up, he did it down to bone. The static of the spray would have provided a buffer, but Eli didn't make a sound.

Still, as his fingers slipped and slid, and blood ran down the drain, Eli felt a tremor of residual panic pass through him. The only kind of mark left by Haverty's work. Invisible, but insidious.

At last, the tracker came free, a sliver of dark metal clutched between stained fingers. Eli set it in the soap dish with a shaky breath.

One down.
Four to go.

∞

THE KINGSLEY

Mitch rolled over, and spit a mouthful of blood onto the hardwood floor.

One eye was swelling shut, and he couldn't breathe through his broken nose, but he was alive. He could move. He could think.

For now, that would have to be enough.

The apartment was empty. The soldiers were gone.

They'd left Mitch behind.

Human.

That one word—a judgment, a sentence—had saved his life. The EON soldiers lacked either the time or the energy to deal with someone so tangential to their pursuit.

Mitch forced himself to his hands and knees with a groan. He had a muddled memory of movement, grasping at consciousness as the soldiers spoke.

We've got him.

It took a long time for the words to sink into Mitch's bruised skull.

Victor.

He got, haltingly, to his feet and looked around, taking in the trashed apartment, the bloodstained floor, the dog lying on the floor nearby.

"Sorry, boy," he murmured, wishing he could do more for Dol. But only Sydney could have helped him now, and Mitch had no idea where she was. He stood there, amid the carnage, torn between the need to wait for her and the need to go find Victor, and for a second the two forces seemed to pull him physically, painfully apart.

But Mitch couldn't do both, and he knew it, so he asked himself, what would Victor do? What would Syd? And when the answers were the same, he knew.

Mitch had to leave.

The question was where to *go*.

The soldiers had taken his laptop, and he had crushed his primary cell, but Mitch crouched—which turned out to hurt just as much as standing up—and felt under the lip of the sofa, dislodging the small black box and the burner smartphone that it was feeding into.

His *butler*.

In the old black-and-white movies he'd always loved, a good butler was neither seen nor heard, not until they were needed. And yet they were always there, tucked innocently into the background, and always seemed to know the comings and goings of the house.

The concept behind Mitch's device was the same.

He booted the phone and watched as the data from the soldiers' electronic tracking streamed in. Calls. Texts. Locations.

Three phones. And they were all in one place.

Got you.

All his life, people had underestimated Mitch. They took one look at his size, his bulk, his tattooed arms and shaved head, and made a snap judgment: slow, stupid, useless.

EON had underestimated him too.

Mitch looked around, found the playing card Sydney had left behind. He scribbled a quick instruction on the back, and rested the playing card on the dog's motionless side.

"Sorry, boy," he said again.

And then Mitch grabbed his coat, and his keys, and went to save Victor.

XIII

THE LAST AFTERNOON

EON

VICTOR opened his eyes, and saw only himself staring back.

His lean limbs, sallow skin, black clothes, reflected in the polished ceiling. He was lying on a narrow cot against the wall of a square space, quickly discernible as some type of cell.

Panic slid like a needle beneath Victor's skin. Four years he'd spent in a place like this—no, not quite like this, not as clever, not as advanced—but just as empty. He had been buried alive in that solitary confinement cell, and every day Victor had sworn that once he got out he would *never* let himself be trapped again.

He brought a hand to his chest and felt the bruise between his ribs where the first dart had gone in, scraping bone. He sat up, paused for a moment to let the lingering nausea pass, then stood. There was no clock in here, no way to tell how long he'd been unconscious, aside from the constant hum of his power, its strength and volume growing with each passing minute.

Victor looked around, and resisted the urge to call out, unnerved by the idea that no one would answer, that the only response he'd be greeted by was his own echo. Instead, he studied the surroundings. The walls, which he'd originally taken for rock, were actually plastic, or maybe fiberglass. He could feel a subtle charge coursing through it—a deterrent, no doubt, against escape.

He looked up, scanning the ceiling for cameras, and was interrupted by a familiar voice filling the cell.

"Mr. Vale," said Stell. "We've come a long way, only to find ourselves back where we started. The difference, of course, is that this time, you won't be getting out."

"I wouldn't be so sure of that," said Victor, forcing his voice to hold its edge. "But I have to admit, this isn't exactly sporting."

"That's because this isn't a game. You're a murderer, and an escaped convict, and this is a prison."

"What happened to my trial?"

"You forfeited it."

"And Eli?"

"He serves another purpose."

"He's playing you," sneered Victor. "And by the time you figure out how, it will be too late."

Stell didn't rise to the bait, leaving Victor in silence. He was running out of patience, and out of time. He looked up at the cameras. He may be in a cage, but Victor *had* prepared for the possibility. He had left himself a key.

The question was—where was Dominic Rusher?

∞

DOM tugged at the steel standard-issue handcuffs, but they were bolted to the table.

Three years, and his only fear had been waking up in an EON cell. Instead, he'd woken up in an interrogation room.

He was sitting in a metal chair, cuffed to a steel table, and he was alone, the only door clearly locked, the control panel on the wall marked by a solid red line.

Panic flickered through him, and Dom had to remind himself that they didn't *know* he was an EO.

Not yet.

And he needed to keep it that way as long as possible.

Dom was truly trapped—he could slip out of time, but it wouldn't do a damn bit of good, because even without time, he would still be *chained to a fucking table*. And he'd be even more screwed because the moment he crossed *back* into reality, the slip would show, the gap between where he'd been and where he was. Maybe it would just look like a stutter, a shutter, a glitch. But there were no glitches in a place like EON, and everyone watching him on camera would know what it meant. What he was.

So Dom waited, counting time in his head, wondering where Eli was now, hoping Victor, at least, had gotten away.

Finally, the keypad turned from red to green.

The door unsealed, and two soldiers came in.

Dom had been hoping for a friendly face, but instead he got Rios again, joined by a hard-edged, brutish soldier named Hancock. Dom's attention hung on the sliver of shrinking freedom as the door behind Rios swung shut, and the codes went red again.

Shit.

Rios crossed to the table and set down a file. Dom's file. He scanned the tops of the pages, searching for paperclips, staples, anything he might be able to use.

"Agent Rusher," said Rios. "You want to tell us what you were doing in the director's office?"

Dom had put his short time awake to good use. He was ready for this line of questioning. "I was trying to stop a murderer from escaping."

Rios raised a brow. "How do you figure that?"

Dom sat forward. "Do you know about Eli Ever? Or Eliot Cardale, or whatever name he wants to go by? Do you know what he did?"

"I've read his file," she said. "And I've read yours."

"Then you know I was one of his targets. I still don't know why—but I should be dead. Would have been, too, if Eli had gotten to me. So when I heard that Stell planned to have him transported off-site,

I couldn't let that happen, couldn't have that maniac loose in Merit again."

"That wasn't your call, soldier."

"So fire me," said Dom.

"That's not *my* call," said Rios. "You'll be held here until the director returns to make a decision."

Rios was shuffling the file as she spoke, and Dom caught sight of a metal staple just before Hancock's comm went off. The low static muffled the words, but one of them leapt out.

Vale.

Dom tried to hide the recognition on his face as Hancock lifted the comm to his ear.

Vale . . . awake . . .

"In the meantime," continued Rios. "I suggest—"

"How did you get into Stell's office?" asked Dom, changing directions. She looked up, a shadow crossing her face. Dom pressed on. "There's only one door, and I was facing it. But you showed up *behind* me."

Rios's eyes narrowed. "Hancock," she said. "Go call Stell. Ask him what he wants us to do next."

Dominic really did want to hear Rios's explanation, but not as much as he needed to get out. He waited as Hancock swiped his keycard, waited as the line turned green and the door clicked open.

"Now, Agent Rusher," she continued, "let's disc—"

He didn't give her a chance to finish. Dominic took a deep breath, like a swimmer before a dive, and jerked backward, the world parting around him as he slipped out of time, and into the shadows.

The room hung in perfect stillness, a painting in shades of gray—Rios, frozen, her face unreadable. Hancock, halfway through the door. Dominic, still handcuffed to the table.

He rose, pulling the stapled pages toward him, and got to work prying the bit of metal loose. He worked the sliver free, then straightened it out, and began fitting the slim bar between the teeth of the handcuff and the locking mechanism. It took several tries, the weight of the shadows like wet wool draped across his limbs, and a red welt rising on Dominic's wrist from the constant applied pressure, but finally the lock came loose. He pried the handcuff open, repeated the same grueling process with the other side, and was free.

Dom fastened the cuffs back around Rios's wrists, then ducked under Hancock's frozen arm into the hall. The air dragged around him like an ocean tide as he approached the nearest control room. There was only one other soldier there, a female agent named Linfield, sitting in front of a console, and frozen mid-stretch. Dominic freed the cattle prod from her holster and brought it to the base of her neck before stepping back into the flow of time.

A flash of blue-white light, the crackle of current, and Linfield slumped forward. Dom pushed her chair aside and started searching, hands flying across the keyboard.

He didn't have long. Every second Dom stood in the real world was a second exposed, a second he could be caught, captured, a second alarms were going up, and soldiers were invariably crashing toward him. And yet, despite it all, the world narrowed as he typed, his heart racing, but the pulse strong, steady. He'd always been good under pressure.

Dom didn't have time to figure out which cell Victor was being kept in, so he chose the fastest option.

He opened them all.

∞

ONE minute Victor had been pacing the confines of his silent, empty cell, and the next the world was plunged into motion and sound. An alarm, high and bright, wailed as the farthest wall of the cell dropped away, the solid pane of fiberglass retracting into the floor.

Lights flashed white overhead, but instead of going into lockdown, the facility seemed to be *opening*. Coming apart. To every side, Victor heard the metal crank of seals breaking, doors unlocking.

About time.

He stepped out of the cell, only to find himself in a second, larger chamber, this one cast in concrete instead of plastic. It was roughly the size of a small airplane hangar—he circled until he found a door. It swung open under Victor's touch and gave way onto a white hall.

He made it three steps before whatever Dominic had managed to cause was suddenly reversed.

Doors slammed, locks sealed, alarms cut off and then started again, the lights no longer white but a deep arterial red, like a twisted game of Simon Says.

But Victor didn't stop moving.

Not when a hail of distant gunfire echoed in a nearby hall, not when boots sounded on slick linoleum, not when plumes of white gas began to pour through the overhead vents.

A barrier slammed across the hall in front of him and so Victor doubled back, holding his breath as he swung around a corner, found himself face to face with two EON soldiers, helmeted and armed.

He lunged for their nerves as their weapons flew up, but Victor was too late—their fingers reached the triggers an instant before his power could reach *them*.

The shots rang out, a burst of gunfire, and Victor lunged sideways, but the hall was narrow, and there was no escape.

A bullet—not a tranquilizer this time, but slim, piercing steel—grazed his side right before his power knocked the hands on the guns off course. But Victor's own hold faltered too, and in that stolen second the guns adjusted, retrained on his head, his heart.

The soldiers fired, the hall filling with the sharp retorts, and Victor braced for the impact.

It never came.

Instead, an arm wrapped around his shoulders, Dominic's body twisting in front of Victor like a shield as he pulled them both back into the dark.

The world went suddenly, perfectly, still.

They were standing in the same place, in the same hallway, but all the violence and urgency had been sucked out of the space, replaced by silence and calm. The advancing soldiers hovered, frozen in time, the bullets carving lines of motion as they hung suspended in the air.

Victor dragged in a few steadying breaths, but when he tried to speak, nothing came out. The shadows were a void, swallowing not only color and light, but also sound.

Dominic's face was a grim mask a foot from Victor's own as the soldier's hand tightened on his sleeve, and he tipped his head in a wordless command.

Follow me.

XIV

THE LAST EVENING

FIRST AND WHITE

ONCE again, Marcella had chosen to wear gold.

She'd come a long way since that pivotal night on the National's roof, shedding not only her husband but the scalloped decadence of that first dress, trading it for the polished sheen of white-gold silk. It molded to her body like liquid metal, rising up around her throat and plunging down between her shoulder blades, pooling in the small of her back.

To my beautiful wife.

In a certain light, the milky fabric seemed a second skin, the soft shimmer brushed onto bare flesh, turning her to gold.

What's the point of having beautiful things if you don't put them on display?

Marcella tucked a coil of black hair behind one ear, admiring the liquid way the gold earring fell from the lobe. A bracelet circled one wrist. Her nails, painted to match.

If beauty were a crime.

A net of white-gold beads, like a band of stars, over her hair.

Does she come with a warning label?

Her heels, thin as blades and just as sharp.

My wife, the business major.

The only drops of color the steady blue of her eyes and the vivid, vicious red of her lips.

You don't want to make a scene.
Her hand drifted to the mirror.
I always thought you were a brazen bitch.

The glass silvered under Marcella's touch, burning black in spots as if it were film, erosion spreading until it swallowed the gold dress and the blue eyes and the red lips set in a perfect smile.

Jonathan was leaning against the wall, fidgeting with his gun, ejecting and reinserting the magazine the way Marcus used to punch the end of his pen when he was restless.

Click, click. Click, click. Click, click.

"Stop that," she ordered, turning toward him. "How do I look?"

Jonathan gave her a long, considering stare. "Dangerous."

Marcella smiled. "Come zip me up."

He slid the gun back into its holster. "Your dress has no zipper."

She gestured at the heels. He came forward, and knelt, and she lifted one foot onto his waiting knee.

"No matter what happens tonight," she said, tipping up his chin. "Keep your eyes on me."

∞

SYDNEY woke up in an empty bathtub.

She was curled on her side, wrapped in a large comforter in the deep white basin, and for a second she had no idea where she was. And then, haltingly, she remembered.

The Kingsley. June. The hotel, and the cup of too-sweet chocolate.

Sydney got to her feet, head pounding from whatever June had put in the drink—and grateful she hadn't drunk more of it. She stumbled out of the tub and tried the bathroom door, but the handle only turned a couple inches.

Syd knocked, and then pounded. Threw her shoulder into the door and felt the resistance, not of a lock, but an object forced against the other side. Syd turned, surveying the small, windowless room, and saw the note sitting on the sink.

> *I'll explain everything when this is over.*
> *Just trust me.*
> *-J*

She felt herself tremble, not with fear, but anger. *Trust?* June had *drugged* her. Locked her in a hotel bathroom. She'd thought that June was different, that she saw Sydney as a friend, a sister, an equal. But for all that talk of trust, of independence, of letting Sydney make her own choices, June had still done *this*.

Syd had to get out of here.

Had to find Victor, and save Mitch.

She felt for her phone, only to remember she'd left it on the coffee table. But as she dug her hands into her bomber jacket, she felt the small metal tin with Serena's bones in one pocket, and the cool steel of the gun in the other. June obviously hadn't thought to frisk her. After everything, she'd treated Sydney like a naive child.

Syd drew out the gun, fingers flexing on the grip as she aimed at the doorknob, then reconsidered, shifted the barrel toward the hinges on the other side.

The shot echoed, deafening, against the tile and marble, hard surfaces reflecting it back at an earsplitting level.

Sydney fired twice more, then threw her weight into the door again, felt the hinges break, the wood swing free.

And she was out.

XV

THE LAST EVENING

EON

THE white halls stretched in a strange tableau.

Soldiers kneeling at corners, and frozen mid-stride in halls. A woman on fire, the flames licking at the soldiers trying to approach. A man on his knees on the ground, arms being wrenched behind him. Clouds of gas lit by the red strobe of the emergency lights.

And weaving through the scenes, Victor and Dom, making their way out of EON. It was slow, agonizingly slow, the air dragging like water at their arms and legs, and Victor holding Dom's sleeve like a blind man—and in some ways, he was blind, blind to the path through the maze.

And then Dominic dropped.

There was no warning. Not even a stumble.

He simply sank to the floor.

Victor knelt too—it was that or let go—but as Dom's back came to rest against the wall, Victor saw the front of his uniform, black on black, but shining wet.

The bullets had torn tidy, coin-sized holes.

The shootout in the hall. In that brief instant, when Dom had surged out of the shadows and before he'd pulled them back—

"You fool," muttered Victor, soundlessly.

He pressed his hand against the wound, felt the shirt soaked through with blood. How Dominic had stayed on his feet so long, Victor didn't know.

Dom shuddered, as if cold, so Victor severed his nerves, and said, "Get up."

But Dominic couldn't hear him.

"Get up," he mouthed again.

This time Dominic tried, rose a couple of inches, only to slip back to the floor. His mouth moved, the words lost, but Victor understood.

Sorry.

"Sorry," said the ex-soldier—and Victor realized that he could hear Dominic's voice this time. The shadows were crumbling around them, color and life sweeping in through the cracks. Victor tensed, tightened his hold on Dominic's arm. But it wasn't *his* grip that was slipping.

It was Dom's.

"Hold on," ordered Victor, but Dom's head lolled to the side, and the colorless, soundless space between time collapsed back into chaos and noise, gas and gunfire.

Blood slicked Victor's palms, streaked the floor, stretched behind them in a vivid breadcrumb trail, shockingly red against the sterile white surfaces.

Victor started to draw Dominic to his feet, but the ex-soldier was dead weight now, his skin gray, waxy, his eyes open, but unseeing. Victor let go, easing the body back against the wall as soldiers barreled around the corner.

This time Victor moved first.

No hesitation, no calculation, just blunt and brutal force.

He dropped them like stones in deep water.

Victor stepped over their limp bodies.

The facility's front doors came into sight, one long, empty hall standing between him and freedom.

And then a soldier stepped through the wall in front of him.

There was no sliding door, no hidden hall. She came straight out of the wall, as if it were an open door. She stood before him, unmasked, dark eyes sharp and a cattle prod hanging from one hand.

An *EO,* working for EON.

Victor didn't have time to be surprised.

The soldier lunged for him, blue light crackling across the top of the baton. Victor leapt backward, reaching for her nerves, but before he could get a grip on them, she cut sideways, vanished again through the wall.

An instant later, she was behind him.

Victor spun, catching her wrist just before the electric baton found bare skin.

"You're troublesome," he said, the words swallowed up by the wailing alarms.

He wrenched her nerves, and the soldier gasped in pain, but didn't crumple.

Instead, she slammed her boot into Victor's wounded side.

He went down hard on the white floor, and she was on top of him—or would have been, if his hand hadn't shot out at the last second, dragging her body to a stop.

The soldier fought his hold, even as he forced her hand to turn the cattle prod back on herself. Her eyes narrowed in concentration as her will warred with his, but Eli was loose, and Sydney was lost, and those two things made Victor immovable.

He flexed one hand, drove it toward his chest, and in a mirror motion, the soldier drove the cattle prod into her own.

Blue light, the crackle of energy, and the EO collapsed, unconscious.

Victor rose, swept around her body to the wide glass doors. But they didn't open.

There was no escape.

∞

MITCH didn't know what to do.

His car idled a hundred feet beyond the high metal gates of the EON complex as the rain turned from a drizzle to a downpour.

He sat behind the wheel, now jury-rigging the butler's small black box to hack the gate's frequency instead of tracking signals. That would get him closer to the building, but it still didn't answer the problem of how he was going to get in, or rather, how he was going to get Victor *out*. Or even where to start looking for him.

There was a guard in a security booth inside the gate, and who knew how many officers inside the building, and it would take a hell of a lot more than a smartphone and a hacking fob to crack the security around a place like EON. Which meant, if Mitch was getting in, he'd have to use force.

He was still wracking his brain for the best of several bad plans when the rain eased a little, enough for Mitch to make out the building's front doors—and the distinctive figure standing just beyond them.

Victor.

Mitch hit the button on the black box, and the gates to EON began to slide open. He gunned the engine and shifted into drive, tires skidding in the rain before lurching forward through the gate, and straight toward EON.

Victor leapt out of the way just before Mitch crashed his car through the front doors. The glass, reinforced as it was, didn't shatter, but it did buckle, bow, and as Mitch reversed the car, Victor was able to pry the doors open and slip through.

He threw himself into the front seat.

Mitch's foot was already on the gas.

The guard from the security tower was running toward them, but Victor flicked his hand, as if the soldier were only a bug, a nuisance, and the other man collapsed.

Mitch's car, its front end a mess of crumpled metal, barreled through the open gate and drove away.

He checked the rearview mirror—nobody was behind them, not yet. He glanced sideways at Victor.

"That's a lot of blood."

"Most of it is Dominic's," replied Victor grimly.

Confusion washed over Mitch. He didn't want to ask. Didn't really need to. The only answer that mattered was in Victor's eyes as they avoided his.

"Where's Sydney?" he asked.

"I don't know."

"You drop me off," said Victor, "and you find her, and then you get the hell out of this city."

"Drop you off where?"

Victor pulled the invitation from his back pocket. It was crumpled, and bloodstained, but the gold lettering on the front was clear.

"The Old Courthouse."

XVI

THE LAST EVENING

DOWNTOWN MERIT

THE rain was finally easing by the time Marcella stepped outside.

Three cars sat idling on the curb ahead, one elegant black town car flanked by two SUVs. The security detail swept around them, four men in crisp black suits, raised umbrellas masking them from sight.

Marcella wasn't taking any chances.

Stell would be getting desperate, and desperate men did reckless things.

They reached the sedan, and Jonathan held open her door. When he wasn't wallowing, he could be quite a gentleman.

Marcella slid into the backseat, and noticed she wasn't alone. A man sat across from her, tan and elegant in a pale gray suit. He was staring out the window, and sulking profoundly.

"Well?" asked Marcella. "Did you get to her in time?"

The man nodded, and spoke in that familiar lilt. "It was a near thing," said June, "but I did."

"Good," said Marcella briskly. "You'll bring her to me, of course, when this is done."

June's borrowed eyes flicked sideways, but when she spoke, her voice was steady. "Of course."

Jonathan climbed in on the other side. Marcella had no trouble seeing June behind her many faces—but Jonathan jumped a little at the sight of a stranger.

"Johnny boy," cooed June. "Rest easy, now, the prodigal EO has returned to the fold."

Marcella considered June. "Is that what you're wearing?"

The man's mouth tugged into a wry smile. "Am I too pretty?" And just like that, he vanished, smooth, high cheekbones replaced by a bag lady with a hooked nose. "Is this better?"

Marcella rolled her eyes, glad to see June restored to her usual humor.

"Surely," she said, "there's a happy medium."

June gave a dramatic sigh and dissolved into a middle-aged man with a groomed mustache and an attractive, if mildly forgettable face. "Better?"

"Much," said Marcella.

June gave her a sweeping look. "You look like Snow White killed the queen and stole the mirror."

Marcella flashed a cool smile. "I'll take that as a compliment."

June settled back in her seat. "You would."

∞

ELI smoothed his hair back and buttoned his shirt.

He'd dumped the fragments of the broken pen into the toilet tank. The tracking devices he slipped into the pocket of his suit jacket.

It felt good to be back in real-world clothes, even if they were on the formal side. He'd donned a hundred different costumes in the service of his work. All he was missing was a weapon—a knife, a length of wire. But he could make do with his bare hands. He'd certainly done it before.

Eli was just knotting the borrowed tie when he heard the commotion beyond the bathroom door, the radio chatter mixing with Stell's gruff voice. Eli undid the knot and started again, working slowly as he listened.

"No . . . God dammit . . . who was it? No . . . we continue as planned . . ."

Eli waited until it was obvious there was nothing more to glean, then emerged, taking in the scene. Stell's cheeks were ruddy. He had never had much of a poker face. And only one man could cause so much consternation.

Victor.

"Everything okay?" asked Eli.

"Just focus on the task," ordered Stell, pulling on his own suit jacket and running a hand through salt-and-pepper hair. *More salt by the day,* thought Eli. Some people really *weren't* suited for this line of work.

He wasn't the only one who'd gotten dressed.

The woman now wore a silk black jumpsuit, the kind that belonged on a catwalk, not a field agent.

The young blond was still in his uniform, but the square-jawed soldier wore a black jacket over a crisp white shirt open at the throat.

Eli hummed thoughtfully. "The invitation only admits two."

In answer, Stell produced a second card.

"A replica?" wondered Eli aloud. If it was a copy, it was flawless.

"No," said Stell. "It's the one Marcella sent to the district attorney. Lucky for us, he's out of town." He handed the spare invitation to the female soldier. "Holtz," he said, nodding at the blond, "will stay outside."

"Always the short straw," muttered the soldier.

Stell checked his watch.

"It's time."

∞

THE black van was gone when Sydney got back to the Kingsley.

She found the apartment door broken, ajar, and she drew her gun, clutching it in both hands as she stepped through.

The first thing Syd saw was blood. Fat drops of it, leading down the hall, then a small pool on the hardwood floor smeared by the edge of a handprint.

And the body.

Dol.

Syd scrambled to the dog's side, sinking to her knees beside his still form. She knocked the playing card from atop his chest, ran her fingers through his fur. Closed her eyes, and reached, felt the thread of the dog's life dancing away, dodging her grip. Every time, it was harder. Every time, she had to reach deeper. As Sydney worked, a terrible aching cold wound through her, and she felt her lungs seize, her breath trip, and then at last she caught the thread, dragged Dol back to life. Again.

The dog's chest heaved, and Syd sank back, gasping for air.

Her attention drifted to the king of spades, now overturned, a note in Mitch's tight script on the back.

Went to find Victor.

Syd got to her feet, and so did Dol, shaking off his death as if it were rain. He pressed himself against her side as if to ask, *What now?*

Syd looked around. She didn't have a phone.

Didn't have a clue where anyone had gone.

But she did have *something*—the invisible tether that ran between her and the things she brought back.

Sydney didn't know if it would be enough, but she had to try. She closed her eyes and reached for another thread. Felt it go taut against her fingers.

"Come on," she said to Dol, stepping around the blood.

When they reached the street, Syd paused, closing her eyes again. Felt her world tip ever so slightly to the left. As if to say, *This way.*

She started walking.

∞

"DRIVE faster," said Victor, trying to ignore the buzzing in his skull, those first warnings of a building charge.

It would wait. It had to wait.

"Why?" demanded Mitch, even as he sped toward Merit. "Why are we going toward this mess instead of away?"

Victor found a roll of paper towels in the backseat and pressed them to the shallow wound along his ribs. "Eli will be there."

"All the more reason to go the other way. You two can circle each other forever, but there's only one way it ends, Victor, and it's not in your favor."

"Thanks for the confidence," said Victor, dryly.

Mitch shook his head. "You and your vengeance . . ."

But it wasn't vengeance.

Whatever's happened to you, however you're hurt, you've done it to yourself.

Campbell had been right.

Victor had to take responsibility. For himself. And for the monster he'd helped to create. Eli.

"You're going in like that?" Mitch was asking.

Victor turned the card over in his hand. "I have an invitation."

But he looked down at himself. Mitch had a point.

He'd lost his favorite trench coat, somewhere between the confrontation in Stell's hallway and waking up in the cell. A thin slice ran along his black T-shirt. He'd done his best to rinse the blood from his hands with a bottle of water, but it was still under his nails.

He had no weapons, and no plan.

Only the knowledge—the *certainty*—that Eli would run, the first chance he got.

And Victor would be there to stop him.

XVII

THE LAST NIGHT

THE OLD COURTHOUSE

ELI stepped through the doors into the grand foyer, wicking rain from his hair.

The venue was already brimming with people, men and women in evening attire. The toast of Merit, it seemed, all in one place. The two soldiers had already entered, several people ahead, and had immediately dissolved into the crowd.

Eli and Stell advanced, and were stopped by a pair of security guards with handheld metal detectors.

"Law enforcement," said Stell brusquely, displaying his sidearm.

"Sorry, sir," said the guard. "This is a weapons-free event."

The irony, thought Eli, spreading his arms as the baton drifted over him. Not so much as a beep. Stell reluctantly surrendered his gun. They passed a coat check station, and Eli shrugged out of his jacket and handed it to the clerk, watching the tracking devices drift away. That still left the problem of the collar, but between stepping out of the shower and into the suit, Eli had come up with a plan.

They stepped into the courthouse's grand atrium, a circular chamber surrounded by pillars and topped by a dome. Eli craned his head, admiring the building. It was a showpiece of classic architecture. High-ceilinged and hollow, equal parts elegant and austere.

Wrought-iron sconces bloomed like metal bouquets on each of the pillars. Broad silver dishes—an echo of the scales in Justice's hand—sat atop polished marble tables that seemed to rise straight out of the floor. A viewing balcony ran along the base of the dome, looking down on the atrium below, and in the atrium's center, on a marble stand, a bronze statue of Justice herself rose toward the ceiling, nearly two stories tall.

There was no sign of Marcella, not yet, but that didn't surprise Eli. She would make an entrance, that much he could predict. Jonathan, he guessed, wouldn't be far from her side, but June would be impossible to spot, at least until she made a move.

Eli spotted the two EON soldiers, carving their slow security sweeps through the thickening crowd.

The hall echoed with laughter, the light low, the air dancing with champagne flutes and jewelry and bodies clustering close. Bystanders. Moving pieces. Distractions.

Stell was at his shoulder.

"When the time comes," said Eli, "will you be able to get the bystanders out?"

"I'll do my best," said Stell. "Getting their attention might be difficult."

Eli scanned the space, thinking. The windows were high and narrow, useless, the crowd thick . . . but that could work in their favor. Panic was contagious. Like dominos, all you had to do was fell the first one.

"I'll be right back."

Stell caught his shoulder. "Where are you going?"

"To get you a gun." Eli nodded at Marcella's security, all dressed in trim black suits. "Haven't you noticed? The guests may not be allowed to carry, but her men certainly are."

Stell didn't let go.

"At some point," said Eli calmly, "you have to let out my leash."

The director stared at him for a long, hard moment, and then his hand finally fell away. Eli turned and slipped through the crowd, trailing one of the security guards as they split off down a hall toward the bathroom. Eli followed him in, watched the guard vanish into a stall, waited for another man at the sink to finish washing up and leave. Eli slid the bolt in the man's wake, and approached the stall door.

It swung open, and Eli slammed his shoe into the guard's chest, sent him reeling back into the wall. Eli caught him by the tie before he could fall, drew the guard's holstered gun, and pressed it tight to his chest to muffle the shots.

Eli eased the body back onto the seat.

It had been a long time since he killed a human. But forgiveness would have to wait.

He returned to Stell's side, and presented the director with the stolen gun, low and easy, as if it were a handshake among friends. Stell looked at him with bald surprise. They both knew that Eli was the one holding the weapon, Eli the one with his finger near the trigger. But he spun the weapon in his hand, offering Stell the grip instead of the barrel.

After a pause, Stell took the gun, and Eli turned and plucked a champagne flute from a passing tray. He might as well enjoy the party.

∞

"LAST call for second thoughts," murmured June. "Or second call for last ones."

Rain drummed on the roof of the town car as it pulled up outside the Old Courthouse.

"Don't be somber," said Marcella. "It's a party."

"It's madness," countered June.

Marcella's lips twitched. "Good thing there's method in it."

It was a gamble, of course. A risk. An ambitious play.

But she used to tell Marcus, the world wasn't made for the faint of heart.

Nothing ventured, nothing gained.

And if Marcella's plan went up in flames, well, she'd take the whole damn city with her.

As she stepped out of the car, the broad umbrellas appeared again, ushering her to the waiting bronze doors of the Old Courthouse.

From inside, Marcella could hear the clink of ice and crystal glasses, the murmur and melody of an eager crowd. She brought her hand to the polished metal, splayed her fingers across the surface, gold nails gleaming, as June and Jonathan took their places behind her.

Marcella smiled.

"Showtime."

MITCH'S car screeched to a stop in front of the Old Courthouse.

Pain lanced through Victor's side as he got out, but he didn't dare turn it down, not with the episode building in his bones.

"Victor—" started Mitch.

He glanced back. "Remember what I said. Find Syd, and leave."

Victor climbed the short stone steps, pushed open the bronze doors, his free hand wrapped as casually as possible across his ribs. He handed his invitation to the suit at security, who hesitated at the blood flecking the cream paper.

He looked at Victor, who stared coldly back, leaning on the man's nerves as he did until the discomfort registered on his face.

The security waved him through.

Victor headed for the atrium, doubling back at the sight of the coat check. His eyes trailed over the jackets and shawls that had already been checked in, landing on a black wool trench on the left, with a high collar and black leather trim.

Victor flagged the clerk. "I lost my ticket," he said, "but I'm here to claim my coat." He nodded at the trench.

The kid—and he really was just a kid—wavered. "I . . . I'm sorry . . . I can't return a coat without a valid claim—"

Victor forced the kid's mouth shut, watched his eyes widen in surprise, confusion, horror as he pinned him still. "I can break your bones without lifting a finger," he said smoothly. "Would you like me to show you?"

The kid's nostrils flared in panic as he shook his head.

Victor released his hold, and the clerk stumbled back, gasping, fingers trembling as he pulled the trench from the rack.

He shrugged on the coat. He felt in the pockets and found a twenty. "Thanks," he said, tucking the cash into the short glass jar.

The atrium was crowded, full of bodies and noise. Victor made a slow circle of the chamber, hugging the outer edge as he wove between guests, scanning the crowd.

And then, across the hall, through the crowd, a familiar face.

One that hadn't changed in fifteen years.

Eli.

For a moment, the gala seemed to fade into the background, the details and sounds retreating until only the singular man stood in sharp detail.

Victor didn't realize his feet had begun to move until a hand pulled him back, dragged him sideways behind the nearest marble pillar. Victor was already reaching for the assailant's nerves when he saw the familiar tattoos spiraling up the man's broad arm.

"I told you to drive," said Victor, but then he noticed a sly gleam in Mitch's eyes, the strange set of his mouth, that familiar lilt present beneath Mitch's casual hello.

June.

"Get off me," ordered Victor.

June didn't let go. "You have to stop her."

"I'm not here for Marcella."

"You should be," said June. "She's got her sights on Sydney."

"Because of *you*."

"No," protested June. "I never told her. But she knows, and now she wants her. And from what I've seen, Marcella—"

As if on cue, the crowd parted, and a golden figure ascended the stone dais in the center of the room.

Victor pulled free of June, looking to where Eli had been, but the man was gone. *Shit.* He scanned the crowd, searching the sea of dark suits until he caught movement. Most of the men and women were standing still, their attention transfixed on Marcella's ascent. Eli slid through them like a shark, his own focus just as clear.

Victor mirrored Eli's progress, the two of them cutting matching lines toward the dais, and the statue, and the woman in gold.

And then, at last, Eli noticed him.

Those cold, dark eyes slid past Marcella and landed on Victor. Surprise flickered across Eli's face, and then sank away, replaced by a grim smile as the barrel of a gun came up against the base of Victor's spine, and Stell's gruff voice sounded in his ear.

"That's far enough, Mr. Vale."

∞

MARCELLA had spent her life on display.

But tonight, she finally felt *seen.*

Every pair of eyes was focused on her as she took the dais, every pair curious and bright and waiting for the reveal, because they knew there was more. More than beauty, more than charm. Whether they knew it or not, they'd come to see power.

When Marcella spoke, her voice carried, buoyed by the marble hall and the stillness of the crowd, their faces upturned, like flowers hungry for the light.

"I'm so glad," she said, "that you could join me tonight."

As she spoke, Marcella made a slow circle around the dais, savoring her hold on the gathered audience, the most powerful people in Merit—or so they *thought.*

"I know the invitation was a touch enigmatic, but I promise you, the best things are worth the wait, and what I have to offer you is better shown than told . . ."

∞

JUNE took the stairs two at a time.

She'd shed Mitch's bulky frame for a slimmer one, and with the added quickness to her steps, she loped up to the balcony that overlooked the atrium with its sea of people. At their center, Marcella was making a slow circle around the base of the statue.

June found Jonathan tucked in a shadow, watching the show. He rested his elbows on the wrought-iron rail, all his focus on Marcella's luminous form.

"Some of you have money," Marcella's voice rang out, "and some of you have influence. Some of you were born with power, and others built it from nothing. But you are all here because you are impressive. You are lawyers, journalists, executives, law enforcement. You lead this city. You shape it. You protect it."

"Do you see that man?" said June, pointing to the pale blond head moving through the crowd.

"Victor Vale," said Jonathan blandly.

"Yeah."

If Victor wouldn't help her willingly, June would force his hand. He was a creature of self-preservation.

They all were.

"If he gets too close to Marcella," she said, "shoot him."

Jonathan drew his handgun from the holster under his suit jacket, his eyes never drifting from Marcella.

"Don't kill him," added June. "Not unless you have to. She doesn't want him dead."

Jonathan shrugged. His complacence had always annoyed her, but for once June was glad he didn't ask questions.

"Thanks, Johnny boy," she said, slipping back down the stairs.

∞

"STELL." Victor gritted his teeth as, across the gallery, Eli continued his slow, methodical approach to the dais, where Marcella still held court.

"You understand the importance of power," she was saying. "What you don't yet understand is that *those* ideas of power are outdated."

Stell dug the gun into Victor's back. "I'm not letting you get in the way."

"Is that so?" Victor scanned the crowd.

"That is why I'm here," continued Marcella. "To open your eyes."

Eli was almost to the dais as her hand drifted up, coming to rest on the statue's bronze robes. "To show you what real power—"

Victor chose a man at random, and twisted his nerves.

A scream split the air, and for an instant Marcella's voice was washed out, the crowd's interest diverted. In that same instant, Victor rounded, slamming his elbow back into the side of Stell's head.

Stell's gun went off, but Victor was already out of the bullet's path, moving determinedly toward the platform, and Marcella, and Eli. At the sound of the firearm discharging, the tense crowd had shattered into panic. The guests surged away, a wave of bodies frantically pushing toward the exit. Only Victor and Eli still moved inward, toward the center of the room and the golden figure on her stand.

Victor was almost there when another gunshot went off, the ground sparking as the bullet struck the marble a foot away. He looked up and saw Jonathan up on the balcony, recognized the EO's intent just in time to see him line up a second shot.

The bullet tore through Victor's shoulder, the pain hot and white, blood welling instantly.

He swore, reaching for Jonathan's nerves before the man could fire a third time.

Victor caught them, turned the dial, as he had in the art gallery, and just like in the art gallery, the blue-white light of Jonathan's forcefield flared up, instantly shielding him. Victor felt his hold slipping, but this time he didn't let go.

Every object had a shatter point, a limitation to its tensile strength.

Apply enough force, and it *would* break.

XVIII

THE LAST NIGHT

THE OLD COURTHOUSE

FOR five years, Victor Vale had lived in Eli's head. First as a ghost, then as a phantom. But both, Eli realized now, had been critically flawed, a version of his rival that had been trapped in amber, unchanging—like him. The *real* Victor showed every one of the last five years, and then some, worn thin. He looked sick—just as Eli had suspected. No matter.

He would make things right.

But first—Marcella.

She was stepping down from the statue, her face contorted not with fear but with fury as she headed straight for Eli. "Are *you* behind this interruption?"

"Apologies," he said, "I was just so eager to meet you."

"You'll regret that," Marcella sneered, stepping within range.

Eli reached to grab her, but that blue-white light flashed up between them, forcing his hand away. Rebuffing him, but not *her*. Marcella stepped into the circle of his arms, and brought her fingers to his cheek.

"You really should have run with the rest of them," she said, hand flaring red.

Pain lashed across Eli's face, a wave of agony as his skin dissolved, exposing teeth, jaw. But even as the rot spread, he could feel it reversing, the muscle and skin healing. The amusement melted from Marcella's eyes and mouth, replaced by surprise, shock.

"Why would I run?" said Eli, his cheek knitting back together. "I'm here to kill you."

Marcella pulled back, suddenly uncertain.

He had missed that—the expression on their faces before they died. The way the scales trembled and shook before they fell into balance. As if the EO knew—that they were wrong, that their lives—what they took for lives—were stolen. That it was time to let go.

A gunshot went off nearby, and then another, and seconds later the air above flared blue and white, crackling with energy. Victor stood, head craned, and when Eli followed his gaze, he saw Jonathan at the heart of the storm. Victor spread his hands, and the air surged, the EO above swallowed from sight.

The surprise on Marcella's face cracked, showed fear.

Eli had a theory. He decided to test it.

With Jonathan preoccupied, Eli reached out and wrapped a hand around Marcella's throat.

There was no light around her this time, no forcefield shock, only soft white skin under his fingers.

Marcella's hands flew up, digging into Eli's arms, the sleeves of his suit quickly crumbling. The skin beneath peeled back, then healed, then peeled away again.

But Eli didn't let go.

Across the gallery, Stell and his soldiers were trying to clear the panicked crowd, while on the other side of the statue Victor continued to unleash his own power on Jonathan, as if the other EO were only a circuit, something to overload and interrupt.

To think that, in a way, the two of them were working together again. Like old times—or like they could have been, perhaps.

It was almost poetic, thought Eli, just before he saw an EON soldier appear behind Victor.

"No!" shouted Eli.

But either no one heard him, or they didn't care. The soldier reached Victor and wrapped an arm around his throat, hauling him backward and breaking his focus.

The blue-white light of Jonathan's forcefield vanished, and then reappeared an instant later, this time protectively thrown around Marcella.

There was a noise—like thunder—a violent crack—and then Eli was thrown backward. Pain tore through his back as he struck the nearest pillar, hitting several feet off the ground. But Eli didn't fall. He looked down and saw one of the sconce's metal limbs jutting from his chest.

Eli gritted his teeth as he struggled to push himself forward, pry his body off the iron bar.

Marcella started toward him, rubbing her throat.

"You must be Eli Ever," she said hoarsely. "The great EO executioner. I have to admit," she said, putting her hand against his stomach, "I'm underwhelmed."

Marcella pushed Eli back down the bar, iron scraping his insides as his back hit the pillar.

He let out a snarl.

"You don't seem to be healing," said Marcella, holding up a stained palm. "Still planning to kill me?"

"Yes," hissed Eli, blood leaking between his teeth.

Marcella clicked her tongue.

"Men."

She dug her nails into his injured stomach. Pain flared through Eli as layers of skin and muscle peeled away, and organs shriveled, and he began to die.

∞

ELI'S strangled scream cut through the marble hall as Victor was forced to the floor.

"Can't hurt what you can't see," said the EON soldier at his back, which wasn't strictly true. Especially when they were foolish enough to have put their arm around his throat.

The soldier cried out, as if his arm had been broken. No doubt it felt that way. As soon as the limb slackened around Victor's throat, he swung up to his feet and turned on the soldier, felling the man with the short flick of a now-expert hand.

The soldier slumped, unconscious, to the marble, and Victor turned his attention back to Eli, pinned against a metal fixture, a few feet off the ground.

Shots echoed through the courthouse. Stell seemed to have figured out that Jonathan's particular ability required a line of sight, and was now emptying his own gun at the EO up on the balcony above. Blue-white light flared, but then Stell's gun clicked, the magazine already empty, and Jonathan retaliated, unleashing a hail of his own bullets, forcing both Victor and Stell to dive behind adjacent pillars.

Victor was genuinely torn.

If he took down Jonathan, Eli might be able to kill Marcella.

If he didn't, Marcella might actually kill Eli—a death Victor longed for.

And one he still wanted for himself.

In the end, Victor's decision was made for him, not by Eli, or Marcella, but by June.

June—who appeared before him, once again wearing Mitch, and put a gun to the big man's head. "I asked nicely, but you didn't listen."

June brought her finger to the trigger.

"Kill Marcella," she ordered, "or lose him."

Everything about June, from the steady hand, to the even gaze, told Victor that she would shoot Mitch, simply to make a point, let alone get what she wanted.

"When this is over," said Victor, "you and I are going to have words."

And with that, he rounded the pillar, already reaching for

Jonathan's nerves. The shield flared up anew, blue and white and defiant, and sweat beaded on Victor's skin. He'd never unloaded this much charge into one person, and his own nerves crackled and hummed from the sheer effort, threatening to short out once and for all.

But at last, the forcefield began to splinter.

∞

ELI'S vision swam as Marcella's hand clawed deeper.

But he still saw the burst of light on the balcony behind her.

Eli's lips moved, as if in pleading, and when Marcella leaned closer, he slammed his head into hers as hard as he could. Without Jonathan's protection, the blow landed, and Marcella staggered back, holding her cheek. She spun, and saw Jonathan's own cracking shield. She started across the room toward Victor, leaving Eli pinned to the pillar.

The wrought-iron bar still jutted from his front, though Marcella had half ruined it—along with his stomach. Eli slammed his fist down into the rusted metal, and it crumbled away.

He got his foot up against the pillar behind him and pushed himself off the lower remains of the bar, dropping to the floor. Eli's stomach was a ruin of blood and gore, but without the wrought iron driven through it, the wound was already healing. Organs closing, tissue knitting back into clean, smooth flesh.

A deafening crack cut through the courthouse as Jonathan's forcefield finally shattered. The EO toppled forward over the banister and fell, hitting the floor below with the dull thud of dead weight on stone.

Victor swayed and then sank to one knee, gasping from the effort. He didn't see Marcella moving toward him, her stride quickening as her hands began to glow.

Eli reached her first, wrapping his arms around her shoulders, pinning her back against him.

"Honestly," she snarled, "take a hint."

Her power flared, fast, and hot, and Eli's world went white with pain as she pitted her strength against his.

Back in the lab, Haverty had measured Eli's rate of recovery, the speed with which he healed, had marveled at the way it never slowed, like a battery that couldn't run down. But none of Haverty's tests had strained Eli's body the way that Marcella's power did now.

She tipped her head back against his shoulder. "Are you having fun yet?"

The air itself rippled with the strength of her will.

Marcella's power was no longer coming from her hands alone. It radiated around them both, warping the nearest table, sending hairline cracks across the thinning marble at their feet. It ate away his suit and her dress, melting, ruining, erasing everything, until they stood in a shallow pool of ash atop the weakening floor, Eli's arms—caught in a constant transformation from skin, to muscle, to bone, and back—pressed against Marcella's bare chest.

"If you're counting on my modesty," said Eli. "You should know, I have very little left."

Eli pressed himself against her, head bowed in a strange, almost loving embrace as at last the steel collar around his throat rusted, fell away.

Eli smiled through the agony, his final chains gone.

The ground beneath them was wearing visibly now. Eli tightened his grip, his body screaming in protest. "I've killed fifty EOs," he hissed, "and you're nowhere near the strongest."

Marcella's power wicked through the air. The bronze statue a dozen feet away began to rust, crumble. The pillars swayed, unsteady, and the whole building trembled, brittle, the marble beneath their feet wearing away, the same way Eli's body did, layer by layer.

The marble thinned like melting ice beneath them, first translucent, then transparent.

"It appears," said Marcella, "that we are evenly matched."

"No," said Eli as the floor splintered, cracked. "*You* can still die."

Eli slammed his foot down into the fragile marble, and it shattered beneath them.

∞

VICTOR was halfway to his feet, one hand clutching his wounded shoulder, when the floor gave way. He staggered backward, boots searching for solid ground as the force of the crash rippled through the building.

Only once he was beyond the wave of destruction did Victor see the full scope of what had happened.

It was like a blast turned inward, an implosion.

One second Eli and Marcella were tangled together, engulfed in light at the center of the atrium, and the next they were gone, plunging like meteors through the marble floor. The force of the collapse set off a chain reaction. The walls shook. The pillars toppled. The glass dome cracked and shattered.

The hole was vast, a drop of twenty, maybe thirty feet onto solid stone floor.

There was no sign of June, but Victor saw Stell nearby, unconscious, one foot pinned beneath a broken pillar.

The building stopped shaking. Victor stepped to the edge of the hole and looked down. Marcella lay stretched at the bottom of the chasm, her limbs draped over broken stone, her black hair loose and her head tilted at a wrong angle.

Rubble shifted, and Eli staggered to his feet beside her, naked and bloody, his broken bones knitting themselves back together as he rose. He looked down at Marcella's body, and crossed himself, and then he craned his head and looked up through the broken floor.

His eyes met Victor's, and for a second neither man moved.

Run, thought Victor, and he could see the response in Eli's coiled frame.

Chase me.

A rock came free near Eli's bare foot, skittering down the pile of rubble, and both surged into motion.

Eli spun, climbing over the wreckage, as Victor turned, searching for another way down. The nearest stairs had collapsed, the elevator was unresponsive. He finally found a stairwell, and took the steps two and three and four at a time, lunging down to the lower level, to the wreckage and the remains of Marcella Morgan.

But by the time Victor got there, Eli was already gone.

XIX

THE LAST NIGHT

THE OLD COURTHOUSE

THE building was a ruin, the tangle of stone still shifting and settling, as Eli climbed out of the wreckage. Dust and glass rained down around him as he pried open a door, found a back stairwell intact, and climbed. The door at the top opened onto a parking garage. Sirens wailed nearby as he strode, naked, across the concrete toward the side street.

It had been hard to walk away from Victor.

There would be time for him again. But first, Eli needed to put distance between himself and the courthouse—and EON's reach.

"Excuse me, sir," called a security guard, approaching, "you can't—"

Eli slammed his fist into the man's jaw.

The guard dropped like a stone, and Eli stripped him, tugging on the stolen uniform as he stepped around the arm of the parking barrier and out into the alley.

It had been five years since Eli's arrest, longer still since the last time he needed to disappear. Amazing how quickly the mind went down old paths. Eli felt calm, in control, his thoughts ticking off with soothing linearity.

Now, he just needed to—

Pain lanced his side.

Eli winced, and looked down to see a dart jutting between his ribs. He pulled the dart free and held it up to the light, squinting at the dregs of an electric blue liquid in the vial. A strange shiver ran through him. A tightness in his chest.

Footsteps sounded behind him, slow and steady, and Eli turned around, only to find a ghost.

A monster.

A devil in a white lab coat, deep-set eyes peering out from behind round glasses.

Dr. Haverty.

Eli's mouth went dry. He flashed back to steel tables slick with blood, felt hands inside his open chest, but despite the bile rising in his throat, Eli forced himself to hold his ground.

"All our time together," he said, tossing the dart away, "and you really thought something like that would work?"

Haverty cocked his head, glasses shining. "Let's find out."

The doctor swung the gun up, and fired a second dart into Eli's chest.

Eli looked down, expecting to see the neon liquid, but the contents of this vial were clear. He plucked out the dart.

"I don't sleep," he said, tossing it away, "but I still dream. And I've so often dreamed of killing you."

He started toward Haverty, but halfway there his front knee buckled. Folded, as if it had gone to sleep. The world rocked sideways, and Eli collapsed to his hands and knees in the street, limbs suddenly sluggish, head spinning.

This wasn't right.

None of this was right.

He was on his back now, Dr. Haverty kneeling beside him, measuring his pulse. Eli tried to pull free, but his body didn't listen.

And then, for the first time in thirteen years, Eli Ever passed out.

VICTOR surged out up the stairs and out into the parking garage, the steel door crashing behind him. His shoulder was still bleeding, leaving a veritable breadcrumb trail on the concrete. On top of that, the humming had spread to his limbs, the tone pitching to a whine inside his head. He was running out of time.

He scanned the garage—would Eli take a car, or set off on foot? There were no empty spaces, not here on the street level, and the odds of Eli wasting precious seconds on higher floors was slim.

On foot, then.

He started toward the exit, and saw the security guard slumped on the ground, his body propped up against the booth. He'd been stripped to shorts and socks. Victor stepped past him and out onto the side street.

There were too many alleys, too many ways for Eli to go, and every time Victor chose wrong, it would only increase Eli's lead.

Something shimmered on the ground nearby, and Victor knelt to retrieve it. A tranquilizer dart.

He looked up, and noted a pair of security cameras mounted high overhead.

He felt in the pockets of the stolen coat, and was relieved to find a cell phone. He dialed Mitch's number, hoping for once the man hadn't obeyed his orders.

It rang two times, three, and then Mitch picked up. "The courthouse is coming down! What the hell's going on?"

"Where are you?" asked Victor.

A moment's hesitation. "About two blocks away."

He was relieved to hear it.

"I still haven't gotten ahold of Syd."

"Well, since you're still here," said Victor, looking up at the security cameras, "I need you to hack something."

∞

STELL ground his teeth as Holtz and Briggs helped pry his leg free from the wreckage.

He'd broken something, he knew, but he'd gotten lucky. Samson's body was buried somewhere at the bottom of the wreckage, swallowed up along with more than half of the courthouse floor. The rest of the building didn't look very stable.

"Another ambulance is on its way," said Briggs over the noise of the approaching sirens.

Holtz had kept the crowds at bay, done everything he could to minimize civilian exposure during the incident. But now emergency crews were rapidly arriving, and the crowd outside was too curious, too used to getting their way, demanding answers, explanations, casualty reports.

Stell's mind spun, but he only had a few minutes to contain the scene here.

Marcella Morgan's body lay draped atop the broken marble far below, a testament to her own destructive power.

Heaped at the farthest edge of the ruined floor was the second EO—Jonathan—one hand hanging like a rag doll over the chasm's edge.

There was no sign of June.

Or Victor.

Or Eli.

"Pull up the trackers."

"I already did," said Briggs, grimly.

She offered Stell Eli's coat in one hand. In the other, she held out five small tracking devices.

Stell's stomach dropped.

"It gets worse," said Holtz, producing the rusted remains of Eli's collar, broken, useless.

Stell swept the shards from Holtz's hand, and they rained down onto the ruined floor.

"Call in everyone we have," he ordered. "And find Cardale."

XX

THE LAST NIGHT

LOCATION UNCERTAIN

THE first thing Eli noticed was the smell.

The antiseptic odor of a lab, but beneath that, something sickly sweet. Like rot. Or chloroform. His other senses caught up, registered a too-bright light. Dull steel. His head was cotton, his thoughts syrup. Eli didn't remember what it felt like to be drunk—it had been so long since anything affected him—but he thought it must have been more pleasant. This—the dry-mouthed, head-pounding longing to retch—was not.

He tried to sit up.

Couldn't.

He was lying on a plastic sheet on top of a crate, his wrists zip-tied to the wood slats beneath. A strap ran across his mouth, holding his head down against the crate. Eli's fingers felt for something, anything, found only plastic.

"Not as fancy as my old lab, I know," said Haverty, swimming into focus. "But it will have to do. Needs must, and all." The doctor dipped out of Eli's sight, but never stopped talking. "I still have friends in EON, you know, and when they told me you were being released, well—I don't know if you believe in fate, Mr. Cardale"—he heard tools being shifted on a metal tray—"but surely you can see the poetry in our reunion. You are, after all, the reason for my breakthrough. It's only right that you're now going to be my first *true* test subject."

Haverty reappeared, holding a syringe in Eli's line of sight. That same electric blue liquid danced inside.

"This," he said, "is, as you might have guessed, a power suppressant."

Haverty brought the blade to Eli's chest and pressed down. The skin parted, blood welled, but as Haverty withdrew the knife, Eli *kept bleeding*. The pain continued too, a dull throb, until *slowly*, Eli felt the wound drag itself back together.

"Ah, I see," mused Haverty. "I erred on the side of a low dose, to start. I gave the last subject too much too fast and he just kind of . . . came apart. But, see, that's why you're the perfect candidate for this kind of trial." Haverty took up the syringe. "You always have been." He plunged the needle into Eli's neck.

It hurt, like cold water racing through his veins.

But the strangest thing wasn't the sensation of pain. It was the spark of memory—a bathtub filled with cracking ice. Pale fingers, trailing through the frigid water. Music on the radio.

Victor Vale, leaning against the sink.

You ready?

"Now," said Haverty, dragging Eli back to the present. "Let us try again."

XXI

THE LAST NIGHT

WAREHOUSE DISTRICT

VICTOR paused outside the bland gray building. It was a storage facility. A two-story grid of climate-controlled, room-sized lockers where people abandoned furniture or art or boxes of old clothes. This was as far as Mitch's camera work had gotten Victor. But it was far enough.

There had been another man, according to Mitch. Glasses and a white coat. Eli, dragged behind him, unconscious.

Those words made no sense. The night of Eli's transformation, Victor had watched as Eli tried to drink himself into oblivion. But the liquor didn't even touch him.

After his death, nothing could.

Victor made his way through the ground-floor grid, scanning the roll-up doors for one without a lock. His shoulder had stopped bleeding, but it still ached—he didn't dampen the pain, needed every sense firing, especially with the charge building in his limbs, threatening to spill over.

Victor heard a male voice—one he didn't recognize—coming from a storage container on his left. He knelt, fingers curling around the base of the steel door as the voice carried on in a casual, conversational way. He inched the door up one foot, two, holding his breath as he braced for an inevitable rattle or clank. But the voice beyond didn't stop talking, didn't even seem to notice.

Victor ducked under the rolling door, and straightened.

Instantly he was hit by a stench, slightly noxious, and far too sweet. Chemical. But he soon forgot the smell as he registered the scene before him.

A tray of hospital-grade tools, a man in a white coat, his back to Victor and his gloves slick with blood as he leaned over a makeshift table. And there, strapped to the surface, Eli.

Blood spilled down his sides from a dozen shallow wounds.

He wasn't *healing*.

Victor cleared his throat.

The doctor didn't jump, didn't seem at all surprised by Victor's arrival.

He simply set the scalpel down and turned, revealing a thin face, deep-set eyes behind round glasses.

"You must be Mr. Vale."

"And who the hell are you?"

"My name," said the man, "is Dr. Haverty. Come in, take a—" Victor's hand closed into a fist. The doctor should have buckled, dropped to the floor screaming. He should have at least staggered, gasped in pain. But he didn't do any of those things. The doctor simply smiled. ". . . seat," he finished.

Victor didn't understand. Was the man another type of EO, someone whose own powers rendered him untouchable? But no—Victor had been able to feel June's nerves, even if he'd had no effect on them. This was different. When he reached for the doctor's body, Victor felt—nothing. He couldn't sense the man's nerves. And suddenly, Victor realized he couldn't sense his own, either.

Even the building episode, the terrible energy ready to spill over moments before, was now gone.

His body felt . . . like a body.

Dull weight. Clumsy muscle. Nothing more.

"That would be the gas," explained the doctor. "Remarkable, isn't it? It's not technically a gas, of course, just a compressed airborne version of the power-suppressant serum I'm currently testing on Mr. Cardale."

Victor registered motion over the doctor's shoulder, but he kept his focus on Haverty. Had the doctor himself turned around, he would have noticed Eli's fingers reaching out, feeling for the edge of the table—would have seen them find the scalpel Haverty had so foolishly set down. But Haverty's attention hung on Victor, and so he failed to notice Eli slipping free.

"I've read your file," the doctor continued. "Heard all about your fascinating power. I'd love to witness it myself, but as you can see, I'm in the middle of another—"

Haverty turned to gesture then, finally, at Eli on the table, but Eli was no longer there. He was on his feet now, scalpel flashing in the fluorescent light.

Eli struck, the knife parting the air—and the doctor's throat.

Haverty staggered back, clutching at his neck, but Eli had always had a deft hand. The scalpel bit swift and deep, severing jugular and windpipe, and the doctor sank to his knees, mouth opening and closing like a fish as blood pooled on the concrete beneath him.

"He never stopped talking," said Eli curtly.

Victor was very aware of the knife in Eli's hands, the absence of any weapon in his own. His eyes went to the tray of tools, more scalpels, a bone saw, a clamp.

Eli put a shoe up on Haverty's back and pushed the doctor's body over.

"That man can burn in hell." His dark eyes drifted up. "Victor." A pause. "You were supposed to stay dead."

"It didn't take."

A grim smile crossed Eli's face. "I have to say, you don't look well." His fingers tightened on the scalpel. "But don't worry, I'll put you out of your—"

Victor lunged for the tray of instruments, but Eli knocked it sideways.

Tools scattered across the floor, but before Victor could reach any of them Eli caught him around the middle, and they went down hard, Eli's scalpel driving down toward Victor's injured shoulder. He knocked Eli's arm off course at the last instant and the blade scraped against concrete, drawing sparks.

With Eli unable to heal and Victor unable to hurt—they were finally on equal ground.

Which wasn't *equal* at all.

Eli was still built like a twenty-two-year-old quarterback.

Victor was a gaunt thirty-five, and dying.

In the blink of an eye, Eli had forced his elbow up against Victor's throat, and Victor had to throw all his strength into keeping one arm from stabbing him and the other from crushing his windpipe.

"It always comes down to this, doesn't it?" said Eli. "To us. To what we did—"

Victor drove a knee up into Eli's wounded stomach, and Eli reeled, rolling sideways. Victor staggered to his feet, shoes slipping in Haverty's blood. He caught up one of the fallen instruments, a long thin knife, as Eli lunged at him again. Victor dodged back half a step, and kicked out Eli's knee. His scalpel-holding hand hit the ground for balance and Victor brought his boot down, pinning hand and blade both to the floor as he swung his own knife toward Eli's chest.

But Eli got his arm up just in time, and the knife sank into his wrist, blade driving deep, and through. Victor let out a guttural scream, but when he tried to pull free, Eli caught his hand in a vise grip, and twisted. Victor lost his balance and went down, Eli on top of him, the blade now in his grip. He brought it down, and Victor threw his hands up and caught Eli's wrists, the blood-slicked knife suspended between them.

Eli loomed over him, leaning his weight on the blade. Victor's arms trembled from the effort, but little by little, he lost ground until the tip of the knife parted the skin of his throat.

EVERY end may be a new beginning, but every beginning had to end.

Eli Ever understood that, leaning over his old friend.

Victor Vale, weary, bleeding, broken, *belonged* in the ground.

It was a mercy to put him there.

"My time will come," he said, as the knifepoint sliced Victor's skin. "But yours is now. And this time," he said, "I'll make sure you—"

A sound tore through the steel room, sudden and deafening.

Eli's grip faltered as pain, molten hot, tore through his back—through skin and muscle and something deeper.

Victor still lay beneath him, gasping, but alive, and Eli went to finish what he'd started, but the knife hung from his fingers. He couldn't feel it. Couldn't feel anything but the pain in his chest.

He looked down, and saw a broad red stain blossoming across his skin.

His breath hitched, copper filling his mouth, and then he was back on the floor of a darkened apartment at Lockland, sitting in a pool of blood, carving lines into his arms and asking God to tell him why, to take the power when he didn't need it anymore.

Now, as he looked up from the hole in his chest, he saw the girl, her white-blond hair and ice blue eyes, so familiar, beyond the barrel of the gun.

Serena?

But then Eli was falling—

He never hit the ground.

XXII

THE LAST NIGHT

SAFE

SYDNEY stood at the mouth of the storage locker, still gripping the gun.

Dol whined behind her, pacing nervously, but Sydney kept the weapon trained on Eli, waiting for him to get back up, to turn on her, to shake his head at her weapon, her futile attempt to stop him.

Eli didn't rise.

But Victor did. He struggled to his feet, one hand to the shallow wound at his throat as he said, "He's dead."

The words seemed wrong, impossible. Victor didn't seem to believe them, and neither could Sydney.

Eli was—*forever*. An immortal ghost, a monster who would follow Sydney through every nightmare, every year, plaguing her until there was no one left to hide behind, nowhere left to run.

Eli Ever wouldn't die.

Couldn't die.

But there he was on the ground—lifeless. She fired two more shots into his back, just to be sure. And then Victor was there, guiding the gun from her white-knuckled grip, repeating himself in a slow, steady voice.

"He's dead."

Sydney dragged her eyes away from Eli's body, and studied

Victor. The ribbon of blood running from his throat. The hole in his shoulder. The arm he'd wrapped around his ribs.

"You're hurt."

"I am," said Victor. "But I'm alive."

Car doors slammed nearby, and Victor tensed. "EON," he muttered, putting himself in front of Sydney as footsteps pounded down the hall. But Dol only watched, and waited, and when the door rose the rest of the way, it wasn't soldiers, but Mitch.

He paled as he took in the storage locker, the makeshift operating table, the bodies on the floor, Victor's injuries, and the gun in Sydney's hand. "EON's not far behind me," he said. "We have to go. Now."

Sydney started forward, but Victor didn't follow. She pulled on his arm, felt instantly guilty when she saw the pain cross his face, and realized how much of the blood in here must be his.

"Can you walk?" she pleaded.

"You go ahead," he said tightly.

"No," said Sydney. "We're not splitting up."

Victor turned and, cringing, knelt in front of her.

"There's something I have to do." Sydney was already shaking her head, but Victor reached out and put a hand on her cheek, the gesture so strange, so gentle, it stopped her cold.

"Syd," he said, "look at me."

She met his eyes. Those eyes that after everything still felt like family, like safety, like home.

"I have to do this. But I'll meet you as soon as I'm done."

"Where?"

"Where I first found you."

The location was burned into Syd's memory. The stretch of interstate outside the city.

The sign that read MERIT—23 MILES.

"I'll meet you at midnight."

"Do you promise?"

Victor held her gaze. "I promise."

Sydney knew he was lying.

She always knew when he was lying.

And she also knew she couldn't stop him. Wouldn't stop him. So she nodded, and followed Mitch out.

∞

VICTOR didn't have much time.

He waited until Mitch and Syd were out of sight, and then returned to the storage unit. He fought to focus as he dragged his aching limbs across the room, stepping around Eli's body.

It was like a magnet, constantly drawing his eye, but Victor forced himself not to stop and look at it. Not to think about what it meant, that Eli Cardale was really, truly dead. The way the knowledge knocked Victor off-balance. A counterweight finally removed.

An opposite but equal force erased.

Instead, Victor turned his attention to Haverty's tools, and got to work.

EXODUS

I

AFTER

STELL'S APARTMENT

VICTOR ran his fingers over the surface of his phone.

11:45 p.m.

Fifteen minutes until midnight, and he was not on his way out of town.

Victor settled back into the worn armchair, tuning the dials of his own nerves, to test their strength. Haverty's serum had worn off a few hours before—it had been like a limb returning to feeling, nerves initially pins-and-needles sharp before finally settling back under control.

But as Victor's power returned, so had the humming in his head, the crackle of static. The beginnings of another episode. But only the beginnings. That was the strange thing—before stepping into the storage locker, his limbs had been buzzing, the current minutes from overtaking him. When Haverty's serum suppressed his power, it had suppressed the episode, too. Reset something, deep inside Victor's nervous system.

He drew a vial from his coat pocket—one of six that he'd collected from Haverty's storage locker. Its contents were an electric blue, even in the darkness of the empty apartment.

The liquid represented an extreme solution, but it also represented progress.

He'd have to be mindful—each time Victor used the serum, he

would be trading a death for a window of vulnerability, a period without powers—but he was already making notes—plans, really.

Perhaps, with the right dosage, he could find a balance. And *perhaps* was more than Victor had had to work with in a very long time.

His phone lit up—he had switched it to silent, but it still flashed brightly, a familiar number on the screen.

Sydney.

Victor didn't answer.

He watched the screen until it gave way again to darkness, then slipped the phone in his pocket as footsteps sounded beyond the door. A few seconds later, the rattle of a key in the lock, and Stell limped into view, one foot encased in a medical boot. He tossed his keys into a bowl, didn't bother turning on the lights, just hobbled to the kitchen and poured himself a drink.

The director of EON had the liquor halfway to his lips when he finally realized he wasn't alone.

He set the drink back down.

"Victor."

To his credit, Stell didn't hesitate, simply drew a gun and aimed it at Victor's head. Or at least, he meant to. But Victor stilled the man's hand.

Stell grimaced, fighting the invisible weight around his fingers. But it was a battle of wills, and Victor's would always be stronger.

Victor lifted his own hand, turning it, and like a puppet, so did Stell, until his gun was resting against his own head.

"It doesn't have to end like this," said Stell.

"Twice you locked me in a cage," said Victor. "I don't intend to let it happen a third time."

"And what will killing me do?" snapped Stell. "It won't stop the rise of EON. The initiative is bigger than me, and growing every day."

"I know," said Victor, guiding Stell's finger to the trigger.

"God dammit, *listen*. If you kill me, you will make yourself EON's number-one enemy, their primary target. They will never stop hunting you."

Victor smiled grimly.

"I know."

He closed his hand into a fist.

The gunshot split the room, and Victor's hand fell back to his side as Stell's body toppled to the floor.

Victor took a deep breath, steadying himself.

And then he pulled a slip of paper from his pocket. A page from the battered paperback, the lines blacked out except for five words.

Catch me if you can.

Victor left the door open behind him.

As he stepped out into the dark, he drew his phone from his pocket.

It was buzzing again, Sydney's name a streak of white against the black backdrop. Victor switched the phone off, and let it slip from his fingers into the nearest trash can.

And then he turned his collar up, and walked away.

II

AFTER

OUTSIDE MERIT

SYDNEY pressed the phone to her ear, listened as the ringing gave way to silence, the automated voicemail, the long beep.

It was fifteen minutes after midnight, and there was no sign of Victor. The car idled in the darkness just beyond the sign—MERIT—23 MILES—Mitch tense in the driver's seat, and Dol leaning out the back window.

Sydney paced the grassy shoulder and tried to call Victor one last time.

It went straight to voicemail.

Sydney hung up, and found herself about to text June—before she remembered that she no longer had her own phone. Which meant that Sydney didn't have June's number anymore. And even if she did . . .

Syd shoved the burner phone back in her pocket. She heard the car door open, Mitch's heavy steps in the grass as he approached.

"Hey, kid," he said. His voice was so gentle, as if afraid of telling her the truth. But Syd already knew—Victor was gone. She stared at the distant skyline of Merit, shoved her hands in her coat, felt her sister's bones in one pocket, the gun in the other.

"It's time to go," she said, returning to the car.

Mitch turned on the engine, pulled back onto the highway. The road stretched ahead, flat and even and endless, almost like the surface of a frozen lake at night.

Sydney resisted the urge to look back again.

Victor might be gone, but there was still that thread, tangling their lives. It had led Sydney to him once before, and it would lead her there again.

No matter how long or far she had to look.

Sooner or later, she would find him.

If Sydney had anything, it was time.

III

AFTER

EON

HOLTZ shivered, not at the sight of the corpse on the steel table, but from the cold.

The storage room was fucking freezing.

"Not so tough now," muttered Briggs, her breath a cloud of fog.

And it was true.

Lying there, under the cold white light, Eliot Cardale looked . . . young. All his age had been contained in those eyes, flat as a shark's. But now they were closed, and Cardale looked less like a serial-killing EO and more like Holtz's kid brother.

Holtz had always wondered at the gap between body and corpse, the place where a person stopped being a he or a she or a they, and instead became an *it*. Eliot Cardale still looked like a person, despite the shockingly pale skin, the still-glistening bullet wounds—small, dark circles with serrated edges.

Nobody knew how Haverty had been able to render Eli human—or at least mortal. Just like they didn't know who had shot the EO, or who had killed the ex-EON scientist—though everyone seemed to assume it was Victor Vale.

"Holtz," snapped Briggs. "I'm freezing my ass off, and you're making moony eyes at a corpse."

"Sorry," said Holtz, his breath pluming. "Just thinking."

"Well, stop *thinking*," she said, "and help me load this thing."

Together, they maneuvered Cardale's corpse into cold storage, which was basically just a permanent stretch of deep drawers in the basement of the EON complex, dedicated to indefinitely housing the remains of deceased EOs.

"One down," she said, scribbling notes on her clipboard, "one to go."

Holtz's eyes flicked to the other body that waited, patiently, on its own steel plank.

Rusher.

Holtz had avoided looking at his old friend as long as possible. Not just because of the gunshot wounds that stood out in livid marks against the old scars, but because he couldn't believe his eyes—Dominic had survived so much. They'd served together for four years, and worked here, side by side, for another three.

And all that time, Holtz had never known what Rusher was.

Rios was always telling them not to make assumptions, that EOs weren't ducks—they didn't have to walk like one and talk like one and smell like one to *be* one.

But still.

"It's crazy, isn't it?" he murmured. "Makes you wonder how many are out there. And *here*. If I was an EO, you better believe this is the last place I'd be."

Briggs wasn't listening.

He couldn't blame her.

EON was in a state of emergency. They'd gotten the place back under lockdown pretty quickly, but they'd still lost four EOs in the process, a third of the soldiers were in medical—five had died. The gala mission had been a total disaster, EON's first unkillable EO was dead, possibly from the efforts of their own ex-employee, and the director hadn't even bothered to come to work today.

Holtz needed a drink.

Briggs sealed the doors to cold storage and they climbed back to the main levels.

Holtz swiped through security and stepped outside, grateful that his shift was finally over.

His car sat waiting on the employee side of the lot. It was a sleek yellow speedster, the kind that took on an animal grace—it didn't just drive. It prowled and growled and rumbled and purred, and the other EON soldiers loved to give him shit for it, but Holtz hadn't craved many things since he'd gotten out of the army—just fast cars and pretty girls—and he was only willing to pay for one of them.

He climbed behind the wheel, engine revving pleasantly as he jacked up the heat, still trying to shake off the chill of cold storage, the lingering shock of the last twenty-four hours. As he pulled through the gate, Holtz cranked up the radio, trying to drown out the sound of the gravel drive. He shook his head—EON, he assumed, could surely afford to have paved their private road, but apparently they didn't want to encourage any traffic. So if you were a civilian, hitting gravel in this area was a sign you'd gone the wrong way.

Though some people didn't get the message—like this asshole, Holtz thought, looking down the road.

A car had parked on the shoulder, a low, black coupe, its taillights glaring and its hood raised.

Holtz slowed, wondering if he should call it in, but then he saw the girl. She'd had her head bent over the engine, but as he drew up beside her car, she straightened, scrubbing at her forehead.

Blond hair. Red lips. Tight-fitting jeans.

Holtz rolled down the window. "This is private property," he said. "I'm afraid you can't stop here."

"I didn't want to," she said, "the stupid thing just up and *died*."

Holtz caught the edge of an accent, a melodic lilt. God, he loved accents.

"And of course," the girl went on, kicking a tire, "I don't know shite about cars."

Holtz eyed the low black beast. "That's quite a car for someone who doesn't know shite."

She smiled at that, a dazzling, dimpled smile. "What can I

say?" she said in that musical voice. "I have a weakness for nice things." She pulled her hair up off her neck. "Think you can help?"

Holtz didn't know shite—*shit*—about cars either, but he wasn't about to admit it. He got out and rolled up his sleeves, approaching the engine. It reminded him of the fake bombs he'd had to defuse in basic training.

He toggled and poked and made low humming sounds as the girl stood at his shoulder, smelling of summer and sunshine. And then, miraculously, his fingers brushed over a hose and Holtz realized it had simply come free. He reconnected it.

"Try starting it now," he said, and a second later, the coupe's engine rumbled to life. The girl let out a joyful sound.

Holtz shut the hood, feeling triumphant.

"My hero," she said with mock sincerity but genuine affection. She dug through her wallet. "Here, let me pay you . . ."

"You don't have to do that," he said.

"You bailed me out," she said. "There has to be something I can do."

Holtz hesitated. She was out of his league, but—fuck it.

"You could let me buy you a drink."

He braced himself for the inevitable rejection, wasn't surprised when the girl shook her head. "No," she said, "that won't do. But I'll buy *you* one."

Holtz grinned like an idiot.

He would have gone with her right then, left the black coupe on the side of the private road and driven her anywhere she wanted, but she apologized—she was running crazy late, thanks to the breakdown—and asked if he would take a rain check.

Tomorrow night?

He agreed.

She held out her hand, palm up. "Got a phone?"

He offered up his cell, flushing slightly when her fingers lingered on his, their touch feather light, but electric. She added her name and number to his contacts and passed it back.

"Tomorrow, then?" she asked, turning toward her car.

"Tomorrow, then . . ." Holtz looked down at the entry in his phone. "April."

She glanced back at him through thick lashes, and winked, and Holtz climbed into his yellow speedster and drove away, still watching April, haloed in the rearview mirror. He kept waiting for her to disappear, but she didn't. Life was strange and wonderful sometimes.

And tomorrow, he had a date.

∞

JUNE watched the yellow car shrink into the distance.

Idiot, she thought, starting up the road, this time on foot.

By the time she reached the gates of EON, she looked for all intents and purposes like Benjamin Holtz, Observation and Containment, age twenty-seven. Loved his little brother and hated his stepdad and still had nightmares about the things he'd seen overseas.

"What's this?" asked the security guard, rising from the booth.

"Stupid car broke down," she muttered, doing her best to imitate Holtz's northeastern accent.

"Ha!" said the security guard. "That's what you get for choosing style over substance."

"Yeah, yeah," said June.

"What you need is a good midlevel sedan—"

"Just let me in so I can grab a van and some cables and get my shit back on the road."

The gates parted, and June stepped through. Easy as pie. She crossed the lot on foot and whistled at the sight of the front doors. It looked like someone had driven a car into them. Inside, a soldier looked up from some kind of scanning station.

"Back so soon?" he asked, rising to his feet.

"Left my wallet somewhere."

"Won't get far without that."

"You're telling me."

Small talk was an art form, one of those things that made people's eyes gloss over. Go silent, and they might start wondering why. But keep them talking about nothing at all, and they wouldn't even blink.

"You know the drill," said the soldier.

June did not. This fell soundly in the realm of minutiae, something that rarely conveyed with a touch. Making a guess, she stepped into the scanner, and waited.

"Come on, Holtz," said the soldier. "Don't be a pain in my ass. Arms up."

She rolled her eyes, but spread her arms. It was like standing inside a copier, a beam of white light that moved from head to toe, followed by a short chime.

"All clear," said the soldier.

June saluted him, a casual flick of her fingers as she started down the hall. She needed to find a computer. It should have been easy, a building as fancy as this one, but every hallway looked alike. Identical, even. And every identical hallway was studded with even more identical doors, almost none of them marked, and the farther into the maze June went, the farther she'd have to walk out. So she settled instead for simplicity, pointing herself toward the nearest door. Halfway there, it swung open. A female soldier stepped out, took one look at Holtz, and rolled her eyes.

"Forget something?"

"Always," said June. She didn't pick up her pace, but her fingers caught the door just before it closed. June slipped inside, and found a small room with four computer consoles. Only one of them was occupied.

"Finally," the soldier said, "I've had to piss for an hour . . ."

He started to swivel toward June, but she was already there, one arm hooking around his throat. She pinned him against the chair, cutting off his ability to speak, to shout for help. His back arched as he fought her hold, throwing punches made clumsy by shock and the sudden lack of oxygen. But Benjamin Holtz was no weakling, and June had killed her fair share of men. The soldier did manage to get a pen and jam it back into June's thigh, but of course, it wasn't her thigh.

Sorry, Ben, she thought, tightening her hold.

Soon enough, the soldier stopped fighting. He went limp, and she let go, rolling his chair out of the way so she could get to his computer. June hummed as her fingers slid over the keyboard.

She had to hand it to EON. They had a very user-friendly system, and half a minute later she'd found the file she needed. It had been labeled ALIAS: JUNE. She skimmed through, curious to see what they'd found—which wasn't much. But still enough to merit the trip.

"Good-bye," she whispered, erasing the file—and herself—from the system.

June went out the way she'd come in.

Retraced her steps down the hall, past security and the gates, back to the waiting black coupe. June opened the car door, and by the time she climbed behind the wheel, she was herself again.

Not the leggy brunette, or the thin teen, or any of the dozen faces she'd recently worn, but a spritely girl, with strawberry curls and a splash of freckles across her high cheeks.

June let herself sit in that body for a moment, breathe with her own lungs, see with her own eyes. Just to remember what it felt like. And then she reached out and started the engine, sliding into something safer. The kind of person you wouldn't look twice at. The kind who gets lost in the crowd.

June glanced in the rearview mirror, checked her new face, and drove away.

Read the *New York Times* bestselling

Shades of Magic

Series

"Addictive and immersive."
—*Entertainment Weekly*
(Grade A) on *A Gathering of Shadows*

"Compulsively readable."
—*NPR*
on *A Darker Shade of Magic*

"Feels like a priceless object, brought from another, better world of fantasy books."
—*io9*
on *A Darker Shade of Magic*

TOR DARKER-SHADE.COM

THE SHADES OF MAGIC SERIES COLLECTOR'S EDITION BOXED SET!

With revamped covers, reading ribbons, and fan art, the collector's edition boxed set also features exciting bonus material!

TOR   DARKER-SHADE.COM

Praise for *Vicious*

"As epic and gripping as any classic comic . . . Will resonate with superhero fans as well as readers who have never heard of Charles Xavier or Victor von Doom."
—*Publishers Weekly* (starred review)

"Dark and intricate and daring . . . I loved it."
—Dan Wells, *New York Times* bestselling author of *I Don't Want to Kill You*

"A brilliant exploration of the superhero mythos and a riveting revenge thriller."
—*The Guardian* (UK)

"A fun, morally flexible revenge tale . . . *Vicious* methodically ratchets up the tension as Victor and Eli circle each other for the inevitable kill."
—Daniel H. Wilson, *New York Times* bestselling author of *Robopocalypse*

"Supremely plotted and incredibly well-written."
—*The Independent* (UK)

"Schwab's artful chronology-bending plotting rivals that of any Iain Banks novel, and her writing is a sly, cynical treat. *Vicious* is a grungy spin on timeworn tropes."
—*Financial Times* (UK)

"Stark, cynical novel . . . Urgent, insightful prose. Vicious? Yes, that certainly applies. We'd also add dangerous and surprising."
—*SFX*

"Schwab was able to bring that same combination of modern mythmaking and over-the-top storytelling together into a superb novel."
—*SFFWorld*

Praise for V. E. Schwab

"Desperate gambits, magical battles, and meaningful sacrifice make this a thrilling read."
—*Kirkus Reviews* (starred review) on *A Conjuring of Light*

"Flawless prose . . . The bittersweet conclusion is a fitting one for a fantastic, emotionally rich series that redefines epic."
—*Publishers Weekly* (starred review) on *A Conjuring of Light*

"One of the most inventive fantasy trilogies out there."
—*Bustle* on *A Conjuring of Light*

"Adventure beckons, and Schwab's smart, exhilarating story doesn't let go until the very end. And, not even then."
—*Shelf Awareness* on *A Conjuring of Light*

"Addictive and immersive, this series is a must-read."
—*Entertainment Weekly* (Grade A) on *A Gathering of Shadows*

"The book is still filled with incident and emotion, with difficulty and heartbreak and anger. And it frankly feels subversive."
—NPR on *A Gathering of Shadows*

"[This has] all the hallmarks of a classic work of fantasy. Its plot is gripping. Its characters are memorable. [Its setting] is otherworldly yet believable. Schwab has given us a gem of a tale. . . . This is a book to treasure."
—Deborah Harkness, *New York Times* bestselling author of the All Souls trilogy, on *A Darker Shade of Magic*

"Feels like a priceless object, brought from another, better world of fantasy books."
—*io9* on *A Darker Shade of Magic*

"Full of magic, intrigue, adventure, deception, a bit of piracy . . . This will engage both adult and young adult fantasy readers alike."

—*Booklist* on *A Darker Shade of Magic*

"Schwab (*Vicious*) creates an ingenious set of nesting alternate Londons in this imaginative, well-crafted fantasy. Confident prose and marvelous touches—a chameleon coat, a scarlet river of magic, a piratical antiheroine—bring exuberant life to an exhilarating adventure among the worlds."

—*Publishers Weekly* (starred review) on *A Darker Shade of Magic*

TOR BOOKS BY V. E. SCHWAB

Vicious
Vengeful

A Darker Shade of Magic
A Gathering of Shadows
A Conjuring of Light

VICIOUS

V. E. SCHWAB

TOR

A TOM DOHERTY ASSOCIATES BOOK
NEW YORK

This is a work of fiction. All of the characters, organizations, and events portrayed in this novel are either products of the author's imagination or are used fictitiously.

VICIOUS

Copyright © 2013 by Victoria Schwab

All rights reserved.

Edited by Miriam Weinberg

A Tor Book
Published by Tom Doherty Associates
175 Fifth Avenue
New York, NY 10010

www.tor-forge.com

Tor® is a registered trademark of Macmillan Publishing Group, LLC.

The Library of Congress has cataloged the hardcover edition as follows:

Schwab, Victoria.
   Vicious / V. E. Schwab.—1st ed.
     p. cm.
   "A Tom Doherty Associates Book."
   ISBN 978-0-7653-3534-0 (hardcover)
   ISBN 978-1-4668-2217-7 (ebook)
   1. Great powers—Fiction. 2. Ambition—Fiction. 3. Heroes—Fiction. I. Title.
   PS3619.C4848 V53 2013
   813'.6—dc23

                                                                2013023963

ISBN 978-1-250-18350-7 (second trade paperback edition)
ISBN 978-1-250-16026-3 (second hardcover edition)
ISBN 978-1-250-30048-5 (signed edition)

Our books may be purchased in bulk for promotional, educational, or business use. Please contact your local bookseller or the Macmillan Corporate and Premium Sales Department at 1-800-221-7945, extension 5442, or by email at MacmillanSpecialMarkets@macmillan.com.

First Edition: September 2013
First Trade Paperback Edition: January 2015
Second Edition: May 2018

Printed in the United States of America

0   9

To Miriam and Holly, for proving time and again that they are ExtraOrdinary

Life—the way it really is—is a battle not between Bad and Good, but between Bad and Worse.
—Joseph Brodsky

1

WATER, BLOOD, AND THICKER THINGS

I

LAST NIGHT
MERIT CEMETERY

VICTOR readjusted the shovels on his shoulder and stepped gingerly over an old, half-sunken grave. His trench billowed faintly, brushing the tops of tombstones as he made his way through Merit Cemetery, humming as he went. The sound carried like wind through the dark. It made Sydney shiver in her too big coat and her rainbow leggings and her winter boots as she trudged along behind him. The two looked like ghosts as they wove through the graveyard, both blond and fair enough to pass for siblings, or perhaps father and daughter. They were neither, but the resemblance certainly came in handy since Victor couldn't very well tell people he'd picked up the girl on the side of a rain-soaked road a few days before. He'd just broken out of jail. She'd just been shot. A crossing of fates, or so it seemed. In fact, Sydney was the only reason Victor was beginning to believe in fate at all.

He stopped humming, rested his shoe lightly on a tombstone, and scanned the dark. Not with his eyes so much as with his skin, or rather with the thing that crept beneath it, tangled in his pulse. He might have stopped humming, but the sensation never did, keeping on with a faint electrical buzz that only he could hear and feel and read. A buzz that told him when someone was near.

Sydney watched him frown slightly.

"Are we alone?" she asked.

Victor blinked, and the frown was gone, replaced by the even calm he always wore. His shoe slid from the gravestone. "Just us and the dead."

They made their way into the heart of the cemetery, the shovels tapping softly on Victor's shoulder as they went. Sydney kicked a loose rock that had broken off from one of the older graves. She could see that there were letters, parts of words, etched into one side. She wanted to know what they said, but the rock had already tumbled into the weeds, and Victor was still moving briskly between the graves. She ran to catch up, nearly tripping several times over the frozen ground before she reached him. He'd come to a stop, and was staring down at a grave. It was fresh, the earth turned over and a temporary marker driven into the soil until a stone one could be cut.

Sydney made a noise, a small groan of discomfort that had nothing to do with the biting cold. Victor glanced back and offered her the edge of a smile.

"Buck up, Syd," he said casually. "It'll be fun."

Truth be told, Victor didn't care for graveyards, either. He didn't like dead people, mostly because he had no effect on them. Sydney, conversely, didn't like dead people because she had such a marked effect on them. She kept her arms crossed tightly over her chest, one gloved thumb rubbing the spot on her upper arm where she'd been shot. It was becoming a tic.

Victor turned and sunk one of the spades into the earth. He then tossed the other one to Sydney, who unfolded her arms just in time to catch it. The shovel was almost as tall as she was. A few days shy of her thirteenth birthday, and even for twelve and eleven twelfths, Sydney Clarke was small. She had always been on the short side, but it certainly didn't help that she had barely grown an inch since the day she'd died.

Now she hefted the shovel, grimacing at the weight.

"You've got to be kidding me," she said.

"The faster we dig, the faster we get to go home."

Home wasn't home so much as a hotel room stocked only with Sydney's stolen clothes, Mitch's chocolate milk, and Victor's files, but that wasn't the point. At this moment, home would have been any place that *wasn't* Merit Cemetery. Sydney eyed the grave, tightening her fingers on the wooden grip. Victor had already begun to dig.

"What if...," she said, swallowing, "...what if the other people accidentally wake up?"

"They won't," cooed Victor. "Just focus on *this* grave. Besides..." He looked up from his work. "Since when are *you* afraid of bodies?"

"I'm not," she snapped back, too fast and with all the force of someone used to being the younger sibling. Which she was. Just not *Victor's*.

"Look at it this way," he teased, dumping a pile of dirt onto the grass. "If you do wake them up, they can't go anywhere. Now dig."

Sydney leaned forward, her short blond hair falling into her eyes, and began to dig. The two worked in the dark, only Victor's occasional humming and the thud of the shovels filling the air.

Thud.

Thud.

Thud.

II

TEN YEARS AGO
LOCKLAND UNIVERSITY

VICTOR drew a steady, straight, black line through the word *marvel*.

The paper they'd printed the text on was thick enough to keep the ink from bleeding through, so long as he didn't press down too hard. He stopped to reread the altered page, and winced as one of the metal flourishes on Lockland University's wrought-iron fence dug into his back. The school prided itself on its country-club-meets-Gothic-manor ambience, but the ornate railing that encircled Lockland, though *striving* to evoke both the university's exclusive nature and its old-world aesthetic, succeeded only in being pretentious and suffocating. It reminded Victor of an elegant cage.

He shifted his weight and repositioned the book on his knee, wondering at the sheer size of it as he twirled the Sharpie over his knuckles. It was a self-help book, the latest in a series of five, by the world-renowned Drs. Vale. The very same Vales who were currently on an international tour. The very same Vales who had budgeted just enough time in their busy schedules—even back before they were best-selling "empowerment gurus"—to produce Victor.

He thumbed back through the pages until he found the beginning of his most recent undertaking and began to read. For the first time he wasn't effacing a Vale book simply for pleasure. No, this was for credit. Victor couldn't help but smile. He took an immense pride in paring down his parents' works, stripping the expansive chapters on empowerment down to simple, disturbingly effective messages. He'd been blacking them out for more than a decade now, since he was ten, a painstaking but satisfying affair, but until last week he'd never been able to count it for anything as useful as school credit. Last week, when he'd accidentally left his latest project in the art studios over lunch—Lockland University had a mandatory art credit, even for budding doctors and scientists—he'd come back to his teacher poring over it. He'd expected a reprimand, some lecture on the cultural cost of defacing literature, or maybe the material cost of paper. Instead, the teacher had taken the literary destruction as art. He'd practically supplied the explanation, filled in any blanks using terms such as *expression, identity, found art, reshaping.*

Victor had only nodded, and offered a perfect word to the end of the teacher's list—*rewriting*—and just like that, his senior art thesis had been determined.

The marker hissed as he drew another line, blotting out several sentences in the middle of the page. His knee was going numb from the weight of the tome. If *he* were in need of self-help, he would search for a thin, simple book, one whose shape mimicked its promise. But maybe some people needed more. Maybe some people scanned the shelves for the heftiest one, assuming that more pages meant more emotional or psychological aid. He skimmed the words and smiled as he found another section to ink out.

By the time the first bell rang, signaling the end of Victor's art elective, he'd turned his parents' lectures on how to start the day into:

Be lost. Give up. give In. in the end It would be better to surrender before you begin. be lost. Be lost And then you will not care if you are ever found.

He'd had to strike through entire paragraphs to make the sentence perfect after he accidentally marked out *ever* and had to go on until he found another instance of the word. But it was worth it. The pages of black that stretched between *if you are* and *ever* and *found* gave the words just the right sense of abandonment.

Victor heard someone coming, but didn't look up. He flipped through to the back of the book, where he'd been working on a separate exercise. The Sharpie cut through another paragraph, line by line, the sound as slow and even as breathing. He'd marveled, once, that his parents' books were in fact self-help, simply not in the way they'd intended. He found their destruction incredibly soothing, a kind of meditation.

"Vandalizing school property again?"

Victor looked up to find Eli standing over him. The library-plastic cover crinkled beneath his fingertips as he tipped the book up to show Eli the spine, where VALE was printed in bold capital letters. He wasn't about to pay $25.99 when Lockland's library had such a suspiciously extensive collection of Vale-doctrine self-help. Eli took the book from him and skimmed.

"Perhaps . . . it is . . . in . . . our . . . best interest to . . . to surrender . . . to give up . . . rather than waste . . . words."

Victor shrugged. He wasn't done yet.

"You have an extra *to*, before *surrender*," said Eli, tossing the book back.

Victor caught it and frowned, tracing his finger through the makeshift sentence until he found his mistake, and efficiently blotted out the word.

"You've got too much time, Vic."

"You must make time for that which matters," he recited, "for that which defines you: your passion, your progress, your pen. Take it up, and write your own story."

Eli looked at him for a long moment, brow crinkling. "That's awful."

"It's from the introduction," said Victor. "Don't worry, I blacked it out." He flipped back through the pages, a web of thin letters and fat black lines, until he reached the front. "They totally murdered Emerson."

Eli shrugged. "All I know is that book is a sniffer's dream," he said. He was right, the four Sharpies Victor had gone through in converting the book to art had given it an incredibly strong odor, one which Victor found at once entrancing and revolting. He got enough of a high from the destruction itself, but he supposed the smell was an unexpected addition to the project's complexity, or so the art teacher would spin it. Eli leaned back against the rail. His rich brown hair caught the too bright sun, bringing out reds and even threads of gold. Victor's hair was a pale blond. When the sunlight hit him, it didn't bring out any colors, but only accentuated the *lack* of color, making him look more like an old-fashioned photo than a flesh-and-blood student.

Eli was still staring down at the book in Victor's hands.

"Doesn't the Sharpie ruin whatever's on the other side?"

"You'd think," said Victor. "But they use this freakishly heavy paper. Like they want the weight of what they're saying to sink in."

Eli's laugh was drowned by the second bell, ringing out across the emptying quad. The bells weren't buzzers, of course—Lockland was too civilized—but they *were* loud, and almost ominous, a single deep church bell from the spiritual center that sat in the middle of campus. Eli cursed and helped Victor to his feet, already turning toward the huddle of science buildings, faced in rich red brick to make them seem less sterile. Victor took his time. They still had a minute before the final bell sounded, and even if they were late, the teachers would never mark them down. All Eli had to do was smile. All Victor had to do was lie. Both proved frighteningly effective.

∞

VICTOR sat in the back of his Comprehensive Science Seminar—a course designed to reintegrate students of various scientific disciplines for their senior theses—learning about research methods. Or at least being *told* about research methods. Distressed by the fact that the class relied on laptops, and since striking through words on a screen hardly gave him the same satisfaction, Victor had taken to watching the other students sleep, doodle, stress out, listen, and pass digital notes. Unsurprisingly, they failed to hold his interest for long, and soon his gaze drifted past them, and past the windows, and past the lawn. Past everything.

His attention was finally dragged back to the lecture when Eli's hand went up. Victor hadn't caught the question, but he watched his roommate smile his perfect all-American-political-candidate smile before he answered. Eliot—Eli—Cardale had started out as a predicament. Victor had been none too happy to find the lanky, brown-haired boy standing in the doorway of his dorm a month into sophomore year. His first roommate had experienced a change of heart in the first week (through no fault of Victor's, of course) and had promptly dropped out. Due either to a shortage of students or perhaps a filing error made possible by fellow sophomore Max Hall's penchant for any Lockland-specific hacking challenge, the student hadn't been replaced. Victor's painfully small double was converted into a much more adequate single room. Until the start of October when Eliot Cardale—who, Victor had immediately decided, smiled too much—appeared with a suitcase in the hall outside.

Victor had initially wondered what it would take to recover his bedroom for a second time in a semester, but before he put any plans into motion, an odd thing happened. Eli began to . . . grow on him. He was precocious, and frighteningly charming, the kind of guy who got away with everything, thanks to good genes and quick wits. He was born for the sports teams and the clubs, but he surprised everyone, especially Victor, by showing no inclination whatsoever to join either. This small defiance of social norm earned him several notches in Victor's estimation, and made him instantly more interesting.

But what fascinated Victor *most* was the fact that something about Eli was decidedly *wrong*. He was like one of those pictures full of small errors, the kind you could only pick out by searching the image from every angle, and even then, a few always slipped by. On the surface, Eli seemed perfectly normal, but now and then Victor would catch a crack, a sideways glance, a moment when his roommate's face and his words, his look and his meaning, would not line up. Those fleeting slices fascinated Victor. It was like watching two people, one hiding in the other's skin. And their skin was always too dry, on the verge of cracking and showing the color of the thing beneath.

"Very astute, Mr. Cardale."

Victor had missed the question *and* the answer. He looked up as Professor Lyne turned his attention to the rest of his seniors, and clapped his hands once, with finality.

"All right. It's time to declare your thesis."

The class, composed mostly of pre-med students, a handful of aspiring physicists, and even an engineer—not Angie, though, she'd been assigned a different section—gave a collective groan, on principle.

"Now, now," said the professor, cutting off the protest. "You knew what you were getting into when you signed up."

"We didn't," observed Max. "It's a mandatory course." The remark earned him a ripple of encouragement from the class.

"My sincerest apologies then. But now that you're here, and seeing as there's no time like the present—"

"Next week would be better," called out Toby Powell, a broad-shouldered surfer, pre-med, and the son of some governor. Max had only earned a murmur, but this time the other students laughed at a level proportionate to Toby's popularity.

"Enough," said Professor Lyne. The class quieted. "Now, Lockland encourages a certain level of . . . industriousness where theses are concerned, and offers a proportionate amount of freedom, but a word of warning from *me*. I've taught this thesis seminar for seven years. You will do yourselves no favors by making a safe selection and flying under the radar; *however,* an ambitious thesis will win no points on the grounds of ambitiousness alone. Your grade is contingent upon execution. Find a topic close enough to your area of interest to be productive without selecting one you already consider yourselves expert on." He offered Toby a withering smile. "Start us off, Mr. Powell."

Toby ran his fingers through his hair, stalling. The professor's disclaimer had clearly shaken his confidence in whatever topic he'd been about to declare. He made a few noncommittal sounds while scrolling through his notes.

"Um . . . T helper 17 cells and immunology." He was careful not to let his voice wander up at the end into a question. Professor Lyne let him hang for a moment, and everyone waited to see if he would give Toby "the look"—the slight lift of his chin and the tilt of his head that he had become famous for; a look that said, *perhaps you'd like to try again*—but finally he honored him with a small nod.

His gaze pivoted. "Mr. Hall?"

Max opened his mouth when Lyne cut in with, "No tech. Science yes, tech no. So choose wisely." Max's mouth snapped shut a moment as he considered.

"Electrical efficacy in sustainable energy," he said after a pause.

"Hardware over software. Admirable choice, Mr. Hall."

Professor Lyne continued around the room.

Inheritance patterns, equilibriums, and radiation were all approved, while effects of alcohol/cigarettes/illegal substances, the chemical properties of methamphetamines, and the body's response to sex all earned "the look." One by one the topics were accepted or retooled.

"Next," ordered Professor Lyne, his sense of humor ebbing.

"Chemical pyrotechnics."

A long pause. The topic had come from Janine Ellis, whose eyebrows hadn't fully recovered from her last round of research. Professor Lyne gave a sigh, accompanied by "the look," but Janine only smiled and there wasn't much Lyne could say. Ellis was one of the youngest students in the room and had, in her freshman year, discovered a new and vibrant shade of blue that firework companies across the world now used. If she was willing to risk her eyebrows, that was her own business.

"And you, Mr. Vale?"

Victor looked at his professor, narrowing down his options. He'd never been strong in physics, and while chemistry was fun, his real passion lay in biology—anatomy and neuroscience. He'd like a topic with the potential for experimentation, but he'd also like to keep his eyebrows. And while he wanted to hold his rank in the department, offers from med schools, graduate programs, and research labs had been coming in the mail for weeks (and under the table for months). He and Eli had been decorating their entry hall with the letters. Not the offers, no, but the letters that preceded them, all praise and charm, batting lashes and handwritten postscripts. Neither one of them needed to move worlds with their papers. Victor glanced over at Eli, wondering what he would choose.

Professor Lyne cleared his throat.

"Adrenal inducers," said Victor on a lark.

"Mr. Vale, I've already turned down a proposal involving intercourse—"

"No," Victor said, shaking his head. "Adrenaline and its physical and emotional inducers and consequences. Biochemical thresholds. Fight or flight. That kind of thing."

He watched Professor Lyne's face, waiting for a sign, and Lyne eventually nodded.

"Don't make me regret it," he said.

And then he turned to Eli, the last person to answer. "Mr. Cardale."

Eli smiled calmly. "EOs."

The whole class, which had devolved more and more into muffled conversation as students declared their topics, now stopped. The background chatter and the sound of typing and the fidgeting in chairs went still as Professor Lyne considered Eli with a new look, one that hung between surprise and confusion, tempered only by the understanding that Eliot Cardale was consistently top of the class, top of the entire pre-medical department, even—well, alternating with Victor for first and second spot, anyway.

Fifteen pairs of eyes flicked between Eli and Professor Lyne as the moment of silence lasted and became uncomfortable. Eli wasn't the kind of student to propose something as a joke, or a test. But he couldn't possibly be serious.

"I'm afraid you'll have to expand," said Lyne slowly.

Eli's smile didn't falter. "An argument for the theoretical feasibility of the existence of ExtraOrdinary people, deriving from laws of biology, chemistry, and psychology."

Professor Lyne's head tilted and his chin tipped, but when he opened his mouth, all he said was, "Be careful, Mr. Cardale. As I warned, no points will be given for ambition alone. I'll trust you not to make a mockery of my class."

"Is that a yes, then?" asked Eli.

The first bell rang.

One person's chair scraped back an inch, but no one stood up.

"Fine," said Professor Lyne.

Eli's smile widened.

Fine? thought Victor. And, reading the looks of every other student in the room, he could see everything from curiosity to surprise to envy echoed in their faces. It was a joke. It had to be. But Professor Lyne only straightened, and resumed his usual composure.

"Go forth, students," he said. "Create change."

The room erupted into movement. Chairs were dragged, tables knocked askew, bags hoisted, and the class emptied in a wave into the hall, taking Victor with it. He looked around the corridor for Eli and saw that he was still in the room, talking quietly, animatedly, with Professor Lyne. For a moment the steady calm was gone and his eyes were bright with energy, glinting with hunger. But by the time he broke away and joined Victor in the hall, it was gone, hidden behind a casual smile.

"What the hell was that?" Victor demanded. "I know the thesis doesn't matter much at this point, but still—was that some kind of joke?"

Eli shrugged, and before the matter could be pressed, his phone broke out into electro-rock in his pocket. Victor sagged against the wall as Eli dug it out.

"Hey, Angie. Yeah, we're on our way." He hung up without even waiting for a response.

"We've been summoned." Eli slung his arm around Victor's shoulders. "My fair damsel is hungry. I dare not keep her waiting."

III

LAST NIGHT
MERIT CEMETERY

SYDNEY'S arms were beginning to ache from lifting the shovel, but for the first time in a year, she wasn't cold. Her cheeks burned, and she was sweating through her coat, and she felt alive.

As far as she was concerned, that was the *only* good thing about digging up a corpse.

"Couldn't we do something else?" she asked, leaning on the shovel.

She knew Victor's answer, could feel his patience thinning, but she still had to ask because asking was talking, and talking was the only thing distracting her from the fact that she was standing over a body, and digging her way toward it instead of away from it.

"The message has to be sent," said Victor. He didn't stop digging.

"Well then, maybe we could send a *different* message," she said under her breath.

"It has to be done, Syd," he said, finally looking up. "So try to think of something pleasant."

She sighed, and started digging again. A few scoops of dirt later, she stopped. She was almost afraid to ask.

"What are *you* thinking of, Victor?"

He flashed a small, dangerous smile. "I'm thinking about what a lovely night it is."

They both knew it was a lie, but Sydney decided she'd rather not know the truth.

∞

VICTOR wasn't thinking of the weather.

He hardly felt the cold through his coat. He was too busy trying to picture what Eli's face would look like when he received their message. Trying to picture the shock, the anger, and threaded through it all, the fear. Fear because it could only mean one thing.

Victor was out. Victor was free.

And Victor was coming for Eli—just as he'd promised he would.

He sunk the shovel into the cold earth with a satisfying thud.

IV

TEN YEARS AGO
LOCKLAND UNIVERSITY

"**YOU'RE** seriously not going to tell me what that was about?" asked Victor as he followed Eli through the massive double doors and into the Lockland International Dining Suite, more commonly known as LIDS.

Eli didn't answer as he scanned the eating hall for Angie.

The whole place resembled a theme park, in Victor's opinion, all the mundane trappings of a cafeteria hidden beneath plastic and plaster facades that were out of scale and out of place beside each other. Circling a quad-sized stretch of tables, eleven eatery options each boasted different menus in different fonts with different decor. By the doors was a bistro, complete with a low little gate erected for a waiting line. Next to it Italian music played, several pizza ovens gaping behind the counter. Across the way the Thai, Chinese, and sushi places sat in paper-lantern colors, bright and primary and inviting. Joining these were a burger joint, a carving station, a comfort food kitchen, a salad bar, a smoothie shop, and a basic café.

Angie Knight was sitting near the Italian eatery, twirling pasta on her fork, her coppery curls wandering into her eyes as she read a book pinned beneath her tray. A small prickle ran through Victor when he spotted her, the voyeuristic thrill of seeing someone before they see you, of being able to simply watch. But the moment ended when Eli saw her, too, and caught her gaze without a word. They were like magnets, thought Victor, each with their own pull. They showed it every day in class, and around campus, people always drifting *toward* them. Even Victor felt the draw. And then when they got close enough to each other . . . well. Angie's arms were around Eli's neck in an instant, her perfect lips against his.

Victor looked away, giving them a moment of privacy, which was absurd considering their public display of affection was very . . . public. A female professor looked up from a folded paper several tables over, one eyebrow quirking before she turned the page with a loud crack. Eventually, Eli and Angie managed to pry themselves apart and she acknowledged Victor with a hug, a gesture that was simple but genuine, all the warmth, but none of the heat.

And that was okay. He was not in love with Angie Knight. She didn't belong to him. Even though he met her first, even though *he'd* been a magnet for her once, and she'd wandered toward him in LIDS that first week of school freshman year, and they'd had smoothies because it was still ungodly hot out even in September, and her face was red from track and his was red from her. Even though she hadn't even *met* Eli until sophomore year when *Victor* brought his new roommate to sit with him at dinner because it seemed like good karma.

Fucking karma, he thought as Angie pulled away and floated back to her seat.

Eli grabbed soup and Victor bought Chinese, and the three sat in the growing noise of the eating hall and ate and made mindless conversation, even though Victor desperately wanted to find out what the hell Eli was thinking picking *EOs* as a thesis. But Victor knew better than to interrogate him in front of Angie. Angie Knight was a *force*. A force with long legs and the most severe case of curiosity that Victor had ever encountered. She was only twenty, had been coveted by the top schools since she could drive, had been given a dozen business cards followed by a dozen offers and just as many follow-ups, both subtle and not-so-subtle bribes, and here she was at Lockland. She'd recently accepted an offer from an engineering firm, and upon graduation would be the youngest—and, Victor wagered, the brightest—employee of their company. She wouldn't even be able to drink yet.

Besides, judging by the looks the other students had given Eli when he made his thesis selection, word would reach her soon enough.

Finally, after a lunch dotted with pauses and occasional warning glances from Eli, the bell rang and Angie left for her next class. She wasn't even supposed to *have* a next class, but she'd taken on an extra elective. Eli and Victor sat and watched her cloud of red hair bob away with all the glee of someone off to eat cake, not explore forensic chemistry or mechanical efficacy or whatever she'd picked up as a pet project this time.

Or rather, Eli watched her go, and Victor watched Eli watch her, something twisting in his stomach. It wasn't just that Eli stole Angie from Victor—that was bad enough—but somehow Angie had stolen Eli from him, too. The more interesting Eli, anyway. Not the one with perfect teeth and an easy laugh, but the one beneath that was glittering and sharp, like broken glass. It was in those jagged pieces that Victor saw something he recognized. Something dangerous, and hungry. But when Eli was with Angie, it never showed. He was a model boyfriend, caring, attentive, and *dull*, and Victor found himself studying his friend in Angie's wake, searching for signs of life.

Several quiet minutes passed as the eating halls thinned and emptied, and then Victor lost patience and kicked Eli under the wood table. His eyes drifted lazily up from his food.

"Yes?"

"Why EOs?"

Eli's face slowly, slowly, began to open, and Victor felt his chest loosen with relief as Eli's darker self peeked through.

"Do you believe in them?" asked Eli, drawing patterns in what was left of his soup.

Victor hesitated, chewing on a piece of lemon chicken. *EO. ExtraOrdinary.* He had heard of them, the way people hear about any phenomena, from believer sites and the occasional late-night exposé where "experts" analyze grainy footage of a man lifting a car or a woman engulfed in fire without burning. Hearing *about* EOs and believing *in* EOs were very different things, and he couldn't tell by Eli's tone which camp he fell into. He couldn't tell which camp Eli wanted *him* to fall into, either, which made answering infinitely harder.

"Well," prompted Eli. "Do you believe?"

"I don't know," Victor said truthfully, "if it's a matter of believing . . ."

"Everything starts with belief," countered Eli. "With faith."

Victor cringed. It was a kink in his understanding of Eli, the latter's reliance on religion. Victor did his best to overlook it, but it was a constant snag in their dialogues. Eli must have sensed he was losing him.

"With wonder, then," he amended. "Do you ever *wonder?*"

Victor wondered about lots of things. He wondered about himself (whether he was broken, or special, or better, or worse) and about other people (whether they were all really as stupid as they seemed). He wondered about Angie—what would happen if he told her how he felt, what it would be like if she chose him. He wondered about life, and people, and science, and magic, and God, and whether he believed in any of them.

"I do," he said slowly.

"Well, when you wonder something," said Eli, "doesn't that mean part of you *wants* to believe in it? I think we want to prove things, in life, more than we want to disprove them. We *want* to believe."

"And you want to believe in superheroes." Victor's voice was carefully devoid of judgment, but he couldn't smother the smile that crept across his mouth. He hoped Eli wouldn't take offense, would only see it as good humor—levity, not mockery—but he didn't. His face snapped shut.

"Fine, yeah, it's stupid, right? You caught me. I didn't give a shit about the thesis. I just wanted to see if Lyne would let me get away with it," he said, flashing a rather hollow smile and pushing up from the table. "That's all."

"Wait," said Victor. "It's not all."

"That's *all*."

Eli turned, dumped his tray, and walked out before Victor could say more.

VICTOR always kept a Sharpie in his back pocket.

As he wandered the aisles of the library searching for books to kick-start his own thesis, his fingers itched to take it out. His failed conversation with Eli had set him on edge, and he longed to find his quiet, his peace, his personal Zen, in the slow obliteration of someone else's words. He managed to make his way to the medical section without incident, adding a book on the human nervous system to one he'd already picked up on psychology. After finding a few smaller texts on adrenal glands and human impulse, he checked out, careful to keep his fingertips—permanently stained from his art projects—hidden in his pockets or under the lip of the counter while the librarian looked over the books. There had been a few complaints during his time at Lockland about books being "vandalized," if not outright "ruined." The librarian looked at him over the stack as if his crimes were written on his face instead of his fingers, before finally scanning in the books and handing them back.

Back in the university-issued apartment he shared with Eli, Victor unpacked his bag. He knelt in his bedroom and slid the marked-up self-help book onto a low shelf beside two others he'd checked out and altered, silently pleased that no return calls had been placed on any of them yet. The books on adrenaline he left on his desk. He heard the front door open and shut and wandered into the living room a few minutes later to find Eli flopping down onto the couch. He'd set a stack of books and stapled printouts on the university-issued wooden coffee table, but when he saw Victor come in, he reached instead for a magazine and began to flip through it, feigning boredom. The books on the table were on everything from brain function under stress to human will, anatomy, psychosomatic responses . . . but the printouts were different. Victor picked up one of them and sank into a chair to read it. Eli frowned faintly as he did it, but didn't stop him. The printouts were captures from Web sites, message boards, forums. They would never been seen as admissible sources.

"Tell me the truth," said Victor, tossing the pages back onto the table between them.

"About what?" asked Eli absently. Victor stared, blue eyes unblinking, until Eli finally set the magazine aside, sat up, and pivoted, setting his feet firmly on the ground so he could mirror Victor's position. "Because I think they might be real," he said. *"Might,"* he emphasized. "But I'm willing to consider the possibility."

Victor was surprised at the sincerity in his friend's voice.

"Go on," he said, offering his best *trust me* face.

Eli ran his fingers over the stack of books. "Try to look at it like this. In comic books there are two ways a hero is made. Nature and nurture. You have Superman, who was born the way he was, and Spider-Man, who was made that way. You with me?"

"I am."

"If you do even a basic Web search for EOs"—here he gestured at the printouts—"you find the same divide. Some people claiming that EOs are born ExtraOrdinary, and others suggesting everything from radioactive goo and poisonous insects to random chance. Let's say you manage to find an EO, so you've got the proof they *do* exist, the question becomes how. Are they born? Or are they *made*?"

Victor watched the way that Eli's eyes took on a sheen when he spoke of EOs, and the change in his tone—lower, more urgent—matched with the nervously shifting muscles in his face as he tried to hide his excitement. The zeal peeked through at the corners of his mouth, the fascination around his eyes, the energy in his jaw. Victor watched his friend, mesmerized by the transformation. He himself could mimic most emotions and pass them off as his, but mimicking only went so far, and he knew he could never match this . . . *fervor*. He didn't even try. Instead he kept calm, listened, his eyes attentive and reverent so that Eli wouldn't be discouraged, wouldn't retreat.

The last thing Victor wanted him to do was retreat. It had taken nearly two years of friendship to crack through the charming, candy shell and find the thing Victor had always known lurked within. And now, slouching around a coffee table stacked with low-res screen shots of sites run by grown men in their parents' basements, it was as if Eliot Cardale had found God. Even better, as if he had found God and wanted to keep it a secret but couldn't. It shone through his skin like light.

"So," said Victor slowly, "let's assume EOs do exist. You're going to figure out *how*."

Eli flashed him the kind of smile a cult leader would covet. "That's the idea."

V

LAST NIGHT
MERIT CEMETERY

THUD.

Thud.

Thud.

"How long were you in prison?" asked Sydney, trying to fill the quiet. The sound of digging, when combined with Victor's absent humming, wasn't helping her nerves.

"Too long," answered Victor.

Thud.

Thud.

Her fingers hurt dully from gripping the shovel. "And that's where you met Mitch?"

Mitch—Mitchell Turner—was the massive man waiting for them back in the hotel room. Not because he didn't like graveyards, he told them emphatically. No, it was just that *someone* had to stay behind with Dol, and besides, there was work to do. Lots of work. It had nothing to do with the bodies.

Sydney smiled when she thought of him scrounging for excuses. It made her feel a fraction better to think of Mitch, who was roughly the size of the car—and could probably lift one with ease—being squeamish about death.

"We were cellmates," he said. "There are a lot of very bad people in jail, Syd, and only a few decent ones. Mitch was one of them."

Thud.

Thud.

"Are you one of the bad ones?" asked Sydney. Her watery blue eyes stared straight at him, unblinking. She wasn't sure if the answer mattered, really, but she felt like she should know.

"Some would say so," he said.

Thud.

She kept staring. "I don't think you're a bad person, Victor."

Victor kept digging. "It's all a matter of perspective."

Thud.

"About the prison. Did they . . . did they let you out?" she asked quietly.

Thud.

Victor left the shovel planted in the ground, and looked up at her. And then he smiled, which she noticed he seemed to do a lot before he lied, and said, "Of course."

VI

A WEEK AGO
WRIGHTON PENITENTIARY

PRISON was less important than what it afforded Victor. Namely, time.

Five years in isolation gave him time to think.

Four years in integration (thanks to budget cuts and the lack of evidence that Vale was in any way abnormal) gave him time to practice. And 463 inmates to practice on.

And the last seven months had given him time to plan this moment.

"Did you know," said Victor, skimming a book from the prison library on anatomy (he thought it particularly foolish to endow inmates with a detailed sense of the positions of vital organs, but there you go), "that when you take away a person's fear of pain, you take away their fear of death? You make them, in their own eyes, immortal. Which of course they're not, but what's the saying? We are all immortal until proven otherwise?"

"Something like that," said Mitch, who was a bit preoccupied.

Mitch was Victor's cellmate at Wrighton Federal Penitentiary. Victor was fond of Mitch, in part because Mitch was thoroughly unconcerned with prison politics, and in part because he was *clever*. People didn't seem to catch on because of the man's size, but Victor saw the talent, and put it to good use. For instance, Mitch was presently trying to short out a security camera with a gum wrapper, a cigarette, and a small piece of wire Victor had secured for him three days before.

"Got it," said Mitch a few moments later, when Victor was thumbing through the chapter on the nervous system. He set the book aside, and flexed his fingers as the guard came down the aisle.

"Shall we?" he asked as the air began to hum.

Mitch took a long look around their cell, and nodded. "After you."

VII

TWO DAYS AGO
ON THE ROAD

THE rain hit the car in waves. There was so much of it that the wiper blades did nothing to clear it away, only managed to move it around on the windows, but neither Mitch nor Victor complained. After all, the car was stolen. And obviously stolen *well*; they'd been driving it without incident for almost a week, ever since they swiped it from a rest stop a few miles from the prison.

The car passed a sign that pronounced MERIT—23 MILES.

Mitch drove and Victor stared out past the downpour at the world as it flew by. It felt so fast. Everything felt fast after being in a cell for ten years. Everything felt free. For the first few days they had driven aimlessly, the need to move outweighing the need for a destination. Victor hadn't known where they were driving. He hadn't decided yet where to start the search. Ten years was long enough to plan the details of the prison break down to the minutiae. Within an hour he had new clothes, within a day he had money, but a week out and he still didn't have a place to start looking for Eli.

Until that morning.

He'd picked up *The National Mark,* a nationwide paper, from a gas station, flipping absently through, and fate had smiled at him. Or at least, *someone* had smiled. Smiled straight up from a photo printed to the right of a news article titled:

CIVILIAN HERO SAVES BANK

The bank was located in Merit, a sprawling metropolis halfway between Wrighton's barbed-wire walls and Lockland's wrought-iron fences. He and Mitch had been heading there for no other reason than the fact that it was somewhere to go. A city full of people Victor could question, persuade, coerce. And a city that was already showing promise, he thought, lifting the folded paper.

He had bought the copy of *The National Mark,* but taken only that page, slipping it into his folder almost reverently. It was a start.

Now Victor closed his eyes, and tipped his head back against the seat while Mitch drove.

Where are you, Eli? he wondered.

Where are you where are you where are you where are you?

The question echoed in his head. He'd wondered it every day for a decade. Some days absently, and others with such an intense need to know that it hurt. It actually *hurt,* and for Victor, that was something. His body settled back into the seat as the world sped by. They hadn't taken the freeway—most escaped convicts knew better than that—but the speed limit on the two-lane highway was more than satisfactory. Anything was better than standing still.

Sometime later, the car hit a small pothole, and the bump jarred Victor from his reverie. He blinked, and turned his head to watch the trees that bordered the road zip past. He rolled down the window halfway to feel that speed, ignoring Mitch's protests about the rain splashing into the car. He didn't care about the water or the seats. He needed to *feel* it. It was dusk, and in the last dregs of the day Victor caught sight of a shape moving down the side of the road. It was small, head bowed and clutching at itself as it trudged down the narrow shoulder of the highway. Victor's car passed it before he frowned and spoke up.

"Mitch, go back."

"For what?"

Victor turned his attention to the massive man behind the wheel. "Don't make me ask again."

Mitch didn't. He threw the car into reverse, the tires slipping on the wet pavement. They passed the figure again, but this time going backward. Mitch shifted the car again into drive, and crawled up alongside the shape. Victor rolled down his window the rest of the way, the rain pressing in.

"You all right?" he asked over the rain.

The figure didn't respond. Victor felt something prickle at the edge of his senses, humming. Pain. It wasn't his.

"Stop the car," he said, and this time Mitch put the vehicle promptly—a little *too* promptly—into park. Victor got out, zipped his coat up to his throat, and began to walk alongside the stranger. He was a good two heads taller.

"You're hurt," he said to the bundle of wet clothes. It wasn't the arms crossed tightly over the form's chest that gave it away, or the dark stain on one sleeve, darker even than the rain, or the way the figure pulled back sharply when he reached out a hand. Victor smelled pain the way a wolf smelled blood. Tuned to it.

"Stop," he said, and this time the person's steps dragged to a halt. The rain fell, steady and cold, around them. "Get in the car."

The figure looked up at him then, and the wet hood of the coat fell back onto a pair of narrow shoulders. Water blue eyes, fierce behind smudged black liner, stared up at him from a young face. Victor knew pain too well to be fooled by the defiant look, the set jaw around which wet blond hair curled and stuck. She couldn't be more than twelve, thirteen maybe.

"Come on," he pressed, gesturing to the car that had stopped beside them.

The girl just stared at him.

"What's going to happen to you?" he asked. "Couldn't be worse than what already has."

When she made no motion toward the car, he sighed and pointed at her arm.

"Let me look at that." He reached out, letting his fingers graze her jacket. The air around his hand crackled the way it always did, and the girl let out a barely audible breath of relief. She rubbed at her sleeve.

"Hey, stop that," he warned, knocking her hand away from the wound. "I didn't fix it."

Her eyes danced between his hand and her sleeve, and back again.

"I'm cold," she said.

"I'm Victor," he said, and she offered him a small, exhausted flicker of a smile. "Now what do you say we get out of the rain?"

VIII

LAST NIGHT
MERIT CEMETERY

"**YOU'RE** not a bad person," repeated Sydney, flinging dirt onto the moonlit grass. "But Eli is."

"Yes. Eli is."

"But he didn't go to prison."

"No."

"Do you think he'll get the message?" she asked, pointing at the grave.

"I'm pretty sure," said Victor. "And if he doesn't, your sister will."

Sydney's stomach twisted at the thought of Serena. In her mind, her big sister was two different people, two images overlapping in a way that blurred both, and made her feel dizzy, ill.

There was the Serena from before the lake. The Serena who'd knelt on the floor in front of her the day she left for college—they both knew she was abandoning Sydney to the toxic, empty house—and who used her thumb to wipe tears from Sydney's cheek, saying over and over, *I'm not gone, I'm not gone.*

And then there was the Serena from after the lake. The Serena whose eyes were cold and whose smile was hollow, and who made things happen with only words. The one who lured Sydney into a field with a body, cooing at her to show her trick, and then looking sad when she did. The one who turned her back when her boyfriend raised his gun.

"I don't want to see Serena," said Sydney.
"I know," said Victor. "But I want to see Eli."
"Why?" she asked. "You can't kill him."
"That may be." His fingers curled around the shovel. "But half the fun is trying."

IX

TEN YEARS AGO
LOCKLAND UNIVERSITY

WHEN Eli picked up Victor from the airport a few days before the start of spring semester, he was wearing the kind of smile that made Victor nervous. Eli had as many different smiles as ice cream shops had flavors, and this one said he had a secret. Victor didn't want to care, but he did. And since he couldn't seem to keep himself from caring, he was determined to at least keep himself from showing it.

Eli had spent the whole break on campus doing research for his thesis. Angie had complained because he was supposed to go away with her; Angie, as Victor predicted, was not a fan of Eli's thesis, neither the subject matter nor the percent of his time it was occupying. Eli claimed the holiday research stint was a token to placate Professor Lyne, to prove he was taking the thesis seriously, but Victor didn't like it because it meant that Eli had a head start. Victor didn't like it because he had, of course, petitioned to stay over break, too, applied for the same exemptions, and had been denied. It had taken all his control to hide the anger, the desire to pen over Eli's life, and rewrite it into his. Somehow he managed only a shrug and a smile, and Eli promised to keep him in the loop if he made any headway in their—Eli had said *their*, not *his*, and that had helped placate him—area of interest. Victor had heard nothing all during break; then a few days before he was scheduled to fly back to campus, Eli called to say he'd found something, but refused to tell his friend what it was until the two were back on campus.

Victor had wanted to book an earlier flight (he couldn't wait to escape the company of his parents, who had first insisted on a Christmas together, and then on reminding him daily of the sacrifice they were making, since holidays were their most popular tour slots) but he didn't want to seem too eager, so he waited out the days, working furiously on his own adrenal research, which felt remedial by comparison, a simple issue of cause and effect, with too much documented data to make for much of a challenge. It was regurgitation. Competently organized and elegantly worded, yes, but dotted by hypotheses that felt, to Victor, uninspired, dull. Lyne had called the outline solid, had said that Victor was off to a running start. But Victor didn't want to run while Eli was busy trying to fly.

And so, by the time he climbed into the passenger seat of Eli's car, his fingers were rapping on his knees from the excitement. He stretched in an effort to still them, but as soon as they hit his legs again, they resumed their restless motion. He'd spent most of the flight storing up indifference so that when he saw Eli, the first words out of his mouth wouldn't be *tell me,* but now that they were together, his composure was failing.

"Well?" he asked, trying unsuccessfully to sound bored. "What did you find?"

Eli tightened his grip on the steering wheel as he drove toward Lockland.

"Trauma."

"What about it?"

"It was the only commonality I could find in all the cases of EOs that are even close to well-documented. Anyway, bodies react in strange ways under stress. Adrenaline and all that, *as you know.*

I figured that trauma could cause the body to chemically alter." He began to speak faster. "But the problem is, *trauma* is such a vague word, right? It's a whole blanket, really, and I needed to isolate a thread. Millions of people are traumatized daily. Emotionally, physically, what-have-you. If even a fraction of them became ExtraOrdinary, they would compose a measurable percentage of the human population. And if that were the case EOs would be more than a thing in quotation marks, more than a hypothesis; they'd be an actuality. I knew there had to be something more specific."

"A genre of trauma? Like car accidents?" asked Victor.

"Yes, exactly, except there weren't indicators of any common trauma. No obvious formula. No parameters. Not at first."

Eli let his words hang in the car. Victor turned the radio from low to off. Eli was practically bouncing in his seat.

"But?" prompted Victor, cringing at his own obvious interest.

"But I started digging," said Eli, "and the few case studies I could dig up—unofficial ones, of course, and this shit was a pain to find—the people in them weren't just traumatized, Vic. They *died*. I didn't see it at first because nine times out of ten when a person doesn't stay dead, it isn't even recorded as an NDE. Hell, half the time people don't realize they've *had* an NDE."

"NDE?"

Eli glanced over at Victor. "Near death experience. What if an EO isn't a product of just any trauma? What if their bodies are reacting to the greatest physical and psychological trauma possible? Death. Think about it, the kind of transformation we're talking about wouldn't be possible with a physiological reaction alone, or a psychological reaction alone. It would require a huge influx of adrenaline, of fear, awareness. We talk about the power of will, we talk about mind over matter, but it's not one over the other, it's both at once. The mind and the body both respond to imminent death, and in those cases where both are strong enough—and both would *have* to be strong, I'm talking about genetic predisposition and will to survive—I think you might have a recipe for an EO."

Victor's mind whirred as he listened to Eli's theory.

He flexed his fingers against his pant legs.

It made sense.

It made sense and it was simple and elegant and Victor hated that, especially because *he* should have seen it first, should have been able to hypothesize. Adrenaline was *his* research topic. The only difference was that he'd been studying temporary flux, and Eli had gone so far as to suggest a permanent shift. Anger flared through him, but anger was unproductive so he twisted it into pragmatism while he searched for a flaw.

"Say something, Vic."

Victor frowned, and kept his voice carefully devoid of Eli's enthusiasm.

"You've got two knowns, Eli, but no idea how many unknowns. Even if you can definitively say that an NDE and a strong will to survive are necessary components, think of how many other factors there could be. Hell, the subject might need a dozen other items on their ExtraOrdinary checklist. And the two components you do have are too vague. The term *genetic predisposition* alone comprises hundreds of traits, any or all of which could be crucial. Does the subject need naturally elevated chemical levels, or volatile glands? Does their present physical condition matter, or only their body's innate reactions to change? As for the mental state, Eli, how could you possibly calculate the psychological factors? What constitutes a strong will? It's a philosophical can of worms. And then there's the entire element of chance."

"I'm not discounting any of those," said Eli, deflating a little as he guided the car into their parking lot. "This is an additive theory, not a deductive one. Can't we celebrate the fact that I've potentially made a key discovery? EOs require NDEs. I'd say that's pretty fucking cool."

"But it's not enough," said Victor.

"Isn't it?" snapped Eli. "It's a start. That's something. Every theory needs a place to start, Vic. The NDE hypothesis—this cocktail of mental and physical reactions to trauma—it holds water."

Something small and dangerous was taking shape in Victor as Eli spoke. An idea. A way to twist Eli's discovery into *his*, or at least, into *theirs*.

"And it's a *thesis*," Eli went on. "I'm trying to find a scientific explanation for the EO phenomena. It's not like I'm actually trying to *create* one."

Victor's mouth twitched, and then it twisted into a smile.

"Why not?"

∞

"BECAUSE it's suicide," said Eli in between mouthfuls of sandwich.

They were sitting in LIDS, which was still fairly empty before the start of the spring semester. Only the Italian eatery, the comfort food kitchen, and the café were open.

"Well, yes, necessarily," Victor said, sipping a coffee. "But if it worked . . ."

"I can't believe you're actually suggesting this," said Eli. But there was something in his voice, woven through the surprise. Curiosity. Energy. That fervor Victor had sensed before.

"Let's say you're right," pressed Victor, "and it's a simple equation: a near death experience, with an emphasis on the *near*, plus a certain level of physical stamina, and a strong will—"

"But you're the one who said it's *not* simple, that there have to be more factors."

"Oh, I'm sure there are," said Victor. But he had Eli's attention. He liked having his attention. "Who knows how many factors? But I'm willing to admit that the body is capable of incredible things in life-threatening situations. That's what *my* thesis has been about, remember? And maybe you're right. Maybe the body is even capable of a fundamental chemical shift. Adrenaline has given people seemingly superhuman abilities in times of dire need. Glimpses of power. Perhaps there's a way to make the change a lasting one."

"This is mad—"

"You don't believe that. Not entirely. It's your thesis after all," said Victor. His mouth quirked as he stared down into his coffee. "Incidentally, you'd get an A on that."

Eli's eyes narrowed. "My thesis was meant to be theoretical—"

"Oh really?" said Victor with a goading smile. "What happened to believing?"

Eli frowned. He opened his mouth to answer, but was cut off by a pair of slender arms around his neck.

"What has my boys looking so stern?" Victor looked up to see Angie's rust-colored curls, her freckles, her smile. "Sad the holidays are over?"

"Hardly," said Victor.

"Hey Angie," said Eli, and Victor watched the light fold in behind his eyes even as he pulled her in for one of those movie-star kisses. Victor swore inwardly. He had worked so hard to bring it out, and Angie was undoing all of Eli's focus with a kiss. He pushed up from the table, annoyed.

"Where you going?" asked Angie.

"Long day," he said. "I just got back, still have to unpack . . ."

His voice trailed off. Angie was no longer paying attention. She had her fingers tangled in Eli's hair, her lips against his. Just like that, he'd lost them both.

Victor turned, and left.

X

TWO DAYS AGO
THE ESQUIRE HOTEL

VICTOR held the hotel door open while Mitch carried Sydney—wounded and soaking wet—inside. Mitch was massive, head shaved, almost every inch of exposed skin inked, and about as broad as the girl was tall. She could have walked, but Mitch had decided that carrying her would be easier than trying to get her arm up around his shoulders. He had also carried two suitcases, which he dropped by the door.

"This'll do, I think," he said, looking cheerfully around the luxurious suite.

Victor set down another, much smaller case, peeled his wet coat off, and hung it up, rolling his sleeves as he directed Mitch to put the girl in the bathroom. Sydney craned her head as she was carried through the room. The Esquire Hotel, located in downtown Merit, was bare in a way that made her wonder if they'd thrown pieces of furniture out, and she found herself looking down to see if there were indents where chair legs or couch feet had once been. But the floor throughout was wood, or something manufactured to look like it, and the bathroom was stone and tile. Mitch set her in the shower—a large, doorless marble space—and disappeared.

She shivered, feeling nothing but a dull, pervasive cold, and Victor appeared several minutes later, carrying an armful of miscellaneous clothing.

"One of these should fit you," he said, dropping the pile on the counter beside the sink. He stood outside the bathroom door while she pulled her own wet clothes off and examined the pile, wondering where these new clothes had come from. It looked as though they'd raided the contents of a laundry room, but the things were dry and warm and so she didn't complain.

"Sydney," she called at last, her voice muffled by the shirt caught halfway over her head and the door between them. "That's my name."

"Pleasure," said Victor from the hall.

"How did you do that?" she called out as she searched through the shirts.

"Do what?" he asked.

"Make the pain stop."

"It's a . . . gift."

"A gift," mumbled Sydney bitterly.

"Have you ever met someone with a gift before?" he asked through the door.

Sydney let the question hang, the ensuing silence punctuated only by the sound of clothes being ruffled, tugged on, discarded. When she finally spoke again, all she said was, "You can come in now."

Victor did, and found her in sweatpants that were too big and a spaghetti strap top that was too long, but both would do for now. He told her to sit very still on the counter while he examined her arm. When he cleaned away the last traces of blood, he frowned.

"What's wrong?" she asked.

"You've been shot," he said.

"Obviously."

"Were you playing with a gun or something?"

"No."

"When did this happen?" he asked, fingers pressed to her wrist.

"Yesterday."

He kept his eyes on her arm. "Are you going to tell me what's going on?"

"What do you mean?" she asked hollowly.

"Well, Sydney, you have a bullet in your arm, your pulse is several beats too slow for someone your age, and your temperature feels about five degrees too cold."

Sydney tensed, but said nothing.

"Are you hurt anywhere else?" he asked.

Sydney shrugged. "I don't know."

"I'm going to give the pain back, a little," he said. "To see if you have any other injuries."

She gave a small, tight nod. His grip tightened a fraction on her arm, and the dull, pervasive cold warmed to an ache, pinching into sharp pain at different points on her body. She gasped for breath, but bore with it as she told him the places where the pain was worst. She watched him as he worked, his touch impossibly light, as if he was afraid of breaking her. Everything about him was light—his skin, his hair, his eyes, his hands as they danced through the air above her skin, touching her only when absolutely necessary.

"Well," said Victor, once he'd bandaged her up and taken back what was left of the pain. "Aside from the bullet wound, and a twisted ankle, you seem to be in decent shape."

"Aside from that," said Sydney drily.

"It's all relative," said Victor. "You're alive."

"I am."

"Are you going to tell me what happened to you?" he asked.

"Are you a doctor?" she countered.

"I was supposed to be one. A long time ago."

"What happened?"

Victor sighed and leaned back against the towel rack. "I'll trade you. An answer for an answer."

She hesitated, but finally nodded.

"How old are you?" he asked.

"Thirteen," she lied because she hated being twelve. "How old are you?"

"Thirty-two. What happened to you?"

"Someone tried to kill me."

"I can see that. But why would someone try to do that?"

She shook her head. "It's not your turn. Why couldn't you become a doctor?"

"I went to jail," he said. "Why would someone try to kill you?"

She scratched her shin with her heel, which meant she was about to lie, but Victor didn't know her well enough to know that yet. "No idea."

Sydney almost asked about jail, but changed her mind at the last moment. "Why did you pick me up?"

"I have a weakness for strays," he said. And then Victor surprised her by asking, "Do you have a gift, Sydney?"

After a long moment, she shook her head.

Victor looked down, and she saw something cross his face, like a shadow, and for the first time since the car pulled up beside her, she felt afraid. Not an all-consuming fear, but a low and steady panic spreading over her skin.

But then Victor looked up, and the shadow was gone. "You should get some rest, Sydney," he said. "Take the room down the hall."

He turned, and was gone before she could say thank you.

∞

VICTOR made his way into the suite's kitchen, separated from the rest of the main room by only a marble counter, and poured a drink from the stash of liquor he and Mitch had been assembling since departing Wrighton, and which Mitch had brought up from the car. The girl was lying and he knew it, but he resisted the urge to resort to his usual methods. She was a kid, and clearly scared. And she'd been hurt enough already.

Victor let Mitch take the other bedroom. The man would never fit on the couch, and Victor didn't sleep much anyway. If he did happen to get tired, he certainly didn't mind the plush sofa. That had been his least favorite thing about prison. Not the people, or the food, or even the fact that it was *prison*.

It was the damned cot.

Victor took up his drink and wandered the wooden laminate floor of the hotel suite. It was remarkably realistic, but gave no squeak, and he could feel the concrete beneath. His legs had spent long enough standing on concrete to know.

An entire wall of the living room was made of floor-to-ceiling windows, a set of balcony doors embedded in the center. He opened them, and stepped out onto a shallow landing seven stories up. The air was crisp and he relished it as he rested his elbows on the frozen metal rail, clutching his drink, even though the ice made the glass cold enough to hurt his fingers. Not that he felt it.

Victor stared out at Merit. Even at this hour, the city was alive, a thrumming, humming place filled with people he could sense without even stretching. But at that moment, surrounded by the cold, metallic city air and the millions of living, breathing, *feeling* bodies, he wasn't thinking about any of them. His eyes hovered on the buildings, but his mind wandered past them all.

XI

TEN YEARS AGO
LOCKLAND UNIVERSITY

"WELL?" asked Victor later that night. He'd had a drink. A couple drinks. They kept a stocked beer shelf in the kitchen for gatherings, and a supply of hard liquor in the drawer under the bathroom sink for the very bad days or the very good ones.

"There's no way," said Eli. He saw the tumbler in Victor's hand, and headed to the bathroom to pour himself one, too.

"That's not strictly true," said Victor.

"There's no way to create enough control," clarified Eli as he took a long sip. "No way to ensure survival, let alone any form of abilities. Near death experiences are still near *death*. It's too great a risk."

"But if it worked . . ."

"But if it didn't . . ."

"We could create control, Eli."

"Not enough."

"You asked me if I ever wanted to believe in something. I do. I want to believe in this. I want to believe that there's *more*." Victor sloshed a touch of whiskey over the edge of his glass. "That we could *be* more. Hell, we could be heroes."

"We could be dead," said Eli.

"That's a risk everyone takes by living."

Eli ran his fingers through his hair. He was rattled, unsure. Victor liked seeing him that way. "It's just a *theory*."

"Nothing you ever do, Eli, is meant to be theoretical. I see it in you." Victor was very proud of verbalizing the observation in one try, considering his level of inebriation. Nevertheless, he needed to stop talking. He didn't like people to know how closely he watched, matched, mimicked them. "I see it," he finished quietly.

"I think you've had enough."

Victor looked down at the amber liquid.

The moments that define lives aren't always obvious. They don't always scream *LEDGE*, and nine times out of ten there's no rope to duck under, no line to cross, no blood pact, no official letter on fancy paper. They aren't always protracted, heavy with meaning. Between one sip and the next, Victor made the biggest mistake of his life, and it was made of nothing more than one line. Three small words.

"I'll go first."

He'd thought about it in the car on the way back from the airport, when he asked *why not?* He'd thought about it as they ate lunch, and then as he walked around campus, finishing his coffee, thought about it all the way back to the residence halls and the upperclassmen's apartments beyond them. Somewhere between the third and fourth tumbler, the question mark had become a period. There wasn't a choice. Not really. This was the only way to be more than a spectator to Eli's great feats. To be a participant. A contributor.

"What do you have on you?" he asked.

"What do you mean?"

Victor quirked a pale eyebrow, unamused. Eli didn't do drugs, but he always had them, the fast way on Lockland's campus—and Victor wagered any campus—to make cash, or a few new friends. Eli seemed to see, then, where Victor was going.

"No."

Victor had already vanished back into the bathroom, and emerged with the bottle of whiskey, which was still very full.

"What do you have?" he asked again.

"No."

Victor sighed, crossed to the coffee table and swiped a piece of scrap paper, scribbling out a note. *See the books on the bottom shelf.*

"There," he said, handing it to Eli, who frowned. Vic shrugged, took another swig.

"I worked hard on those books," he explained, steadying himself on the arm of the couch. "They're poetry. And they're a better suicide note than anything I'd be able to come up with right now."

"No," said Eli again. But the word was distant and dull, and the light in his eyes was growing. "This isn't going to work." Even as he said it, he was walking toward his room, toward the side table where Victor knew he kept the pills.

Victor pushed off the couch, and followed.

∞

HALF an hour later, lying on the bed with an empty bottle of Jack and an empty bottle of painkillers side by side on the nearest table, Victor began to wonder if he'd made a mistake.

His heart jackhammered, forcing blood too fast through the veins. His vision swam and he closed his eyes. A mistake. He sat up suddenly, certain he'd vomit, but hands pushed him back to the bed and held him there.

"No go," said Eli, easing up only when Victor swallowed and focused on the ceiling tiles.

"Remember what we talked about," Eli was saying. Saying something about fighting back. About will.

Victor wasn't listening, couldn't hear much over his pulse, and how could his heart pound any harder? He was no longer wondering whether or not he'd made a mistake. He was certain. Certain that in twenty-two years of life, this was the worst plan he had ever come up with. This was the wrong *method,* the fading, rational part of Victor said, the part that had been studying adrenaline and pain and fear. He shouldn't have washed the amphetamines down with whiskey, shouldn't have done *anything* to dull the nerves and senses, to ease the process, but he'd been nervous . . . afraid. Now he was going numb, and that scared him more than pain because it meant he might just . . . fade.

Fade right into death without noticing.

This was wrong wrong wrong . . . but that voice was drifting off, replaced by a spreading, sinking—

It could work.

He forced the thought through the dulling panic. It could work, and if it *did* work, he wanted the chance to hold the power, the evidence, the proof. He wanted to *be* the proof. Without it, this was Eli's monster, and he was merely the wall off which Eli bounced his ideas. With it, he *was* the monster, essential, inextricable from Eli's theories. He tried counting tiles, but he couldn't keep track. Even though his heart was straining, his thoughts seeped in like syrup, new ones pouring through before the old had left. Numbers began to overlap, to blur. Everything began to blur. His fingertips felt numb in a worrying way. Not cold exactly, but as if his body were beginning to draw its energy in, to shut down, starting with the smallest parts. The nausea faded, too, at least. Only the rushing pulse warned him that his body was failing.

"How are you feeling?" asked Eli, leaning forward in a chair he'd pulled up to the bed. He hadn't had a drink, but his eyes were shining, dancing with light. He didn't look worried. He didn't seem afraid. Then again, he wasn't the one about to die.

Victor's mouth felt wrong. He had to focus too hard to form the words.

"Not great," he managed.

They'd settled for a good old-fashioned overdose for several reasons. If it failed, it would be the easiest to explain. Also, Eli could wait to call it in until they'd entered a crisis zone. Reaching the hospital too early meant it wouldn't be a near death experience, just a very unpleasant one.

The numbness was eating its way through Victor's body. Up his limbs, through his head.

His heart skipped, then slammed forward in a disconcerting way.

Eli was talking again, low and urgent.

Each time Victor blinked it got harder to open his eyes again. And then, for a moment, fear crackled through him. Fear of dying. Fear of Eli. Fear of everything that could happen. Fear of nothing happening. It was so sudden and so strong.

But soon the numbness ate that, too.

His heart skipped again and there was a space where pain should have been, but he'd had too much to drink to feel it. He closed his eyes to focus on fighting back but all the darkness did was eat him up. He could hear Eli speaking, and it must have been important because he was raising his voice in a way he never did, but Victor was sinking, straight through his skin and the bed and the floor, right down into black.

XII

TWO DAYS AGO
THE ESQUIRE HOTEL

VICTOR heard something break, and looked down to find he'd clutched his drink too tightly, and shattered the glass. He was gripping shards, ribbons of red running down over his fingers. He opened his fist, and the broken glass tumbled over the banister into the hotel restaurant's shrubbery seven stories below. He looked down at the fragments still embedded in his palm.

He didn't feel them.

Victor went inside and stood at the sink, picking the largest shards of glass out of his skin, watching the fragments glitter in the stainless steel basin. He felt clumsy, numb, unable to get the smaller pieces out, so he closed his eyes, took a low breath, and began to let the pain back in. Soon his hand burned, his palm painted with a dull ache that helped him determine where the lingering glass was embedded. He finished extricating the pieces, and stood staring at his bloodied palm, shallow waves of pain rippling up his wrist.

ExtraOrdinary.

The word that started—ruined, changed—everything.

He frowned, turning up his nerves the way one would a dial. The pain sharpened, spread to a pins-and-needles prickle radiating out from his palm, down his fingers and up his wrist. He turned the dial up again and winced as the pins-and-needles became a blanket of pain across his body, not dull but sharp as knives. Victor's hands began to shake but he continued, twisting the dial in his mind until he was burning, breaking, shattering.

His knees buckled, and he caught himself on the counter with a bloody hand. The pain switched off like a blown fuse, leaving Victor dark. He steadied himself. He was still bleeding, and he knew he should get the medical kit they'd brought up from the car for Sydney; not for the first time, Victor wished he could trade abilities with Eli.

But first he wiped the blood from the counter, and poured himself another drink.

XIII

TEN YEARS AGO
LOCKLAND MEDICAL CENTER

OUT of nothing came pain.

Not the pain Victor would later learn to know and hold and use, but the simple, too-human pain of a poorly executed overdose.

Pain and dark, which became pain and color, and then pain and glaring hospital lights.

Eli was sitting in a chair by Victor's bed, just as he had been in the apartment. Only now there were no bottles, no pills. Just beeping machines and thin sheets and the worst headache Victor Vale had ever experienced, including the summer he decided to raid his parents' special collections while they were on a European tour. Eli's head was down, his fingers clasped loosely the way they were when he prayed. Victor wondered if that's what he was doing now, praying, and wished he would stop.

"You didn't wait long enough," he whispered when he was sure Eli wasn't busy with God.

Eli looked up. "You stopped breathing. You almost flatlined."

"But I didn't."

"I'm sorry," said Eli, rubbing his eyes. "I couldn't . . ."

Victor sagged back into the bed. He supposed he should be thankful. Erring too early was better than erring too late. Still. He dug his fingernail under one of the sensors on his chest. If it *had* worked, would he feel different? Would the machines go crazy? Would the fluorescent lights shatter? Would the bed catch fire?

"How do you feel?" asked Eli.

"Like ass, Cardale," snapped Victor, and Eli winced, more from the use of that last name than the tone. Three drinks in, high on the wave of discovery, before the pills kicked in, they'd decided that when they were done, Eli would go by Ever instead of Cardale, because it sounded cooler, and in the comics heroes had important, often alliterative names. So what if neither one of them had been able to think of any examples? In that moment, it seemed to matter. For once Victor had the natural advantage, and even though it was the smallest, most inconsequential kind of thing, the way a name fell from the tongue, he liked having something Eli didn't. Something Eli wanted. And maybe Eli didn't *really* care, maybe he was just trying to keep Victor conscious, but he still looked stung when Victor called him *Cardale,* and right now that was enough.

"I've been thinking," started Eli, leaning forward. There was a barely contained energy to his limbs. He twisted his hands. His legs bounced a little in his chair. Victor tried to focus on what Eli was saying with his mouth, not his body. "Next time, I think—"

He stopped when a woman in the doorway cleared her throat. She wasn't a doctor—no coat—but a small nametag over her heart identified her as something worse.

"Victor? My name is Melanie Pierce. I'm the resident psychologist here at Lockland Medical."

Eli's back was to her, and his eyes narrowed on Victor, warning. He waved at Eli dismissively, both to tell him to get out and to confirm that he wouldn't say anything. They'd come this far. Eli rose and mumbled something about going to call Angie. He closed the door behind him.

"Victor." Ms. Pierce said his name in that slow, cooing way, running a hand over her mousy brown hair. It was big in that middle-aged, Southern way. Her accent was unplaceable but her tone was clearly patronizing. "The staff here told me that your emergency contacts couldn't be reached."

What he thought was *thank god*. What he said was, "My parents, right? They're on tour."

"Well, in these circumstances, it's important for you to know that—"

"I didn't try to kill myself." Partial lie.

An indulgent twitch of her lips.

"I just partied a little too hard." Total lie.

A lean of her head. Her hair never moved.

"Lockland's pretty high stress. I needed a break." Truth.

Ms. Pierce sighed. "I believe you," she said. Lie. "But when we release you—"

"When is when?"

She pursed her lips. "We are obligated to keep you here for seventy-two hours."

"I have class."

"You need time."

"I need to go to class."

"It's not up for discussion."

"I wasn't trying to kill myself."

Her voice had tightened into something less friendly, more honest, impatient, normal.

"Then why don't you tell me what you *were* doing."

"Making a mistake," said Victor.

"We all make mistakes," she said, and he felt ill. He didn't know if it was an aftereffect of the overdose, or just her prepackaged therapy. His head fell back against the pillow. He closed his eyes but she kept talking. "*When* we release you, I'm going to recommend that you meet with Lockland's counselor."

Victor groaned. Counselor Peter Mark. A man with two first names, no sense of humor, and a sweat gland issue.

"That's really not necessary," he mumbled. Between his parents, he'd had enough involuntary therapy to last several lifetimes.

Ms. Pierce's patronizing look returned. "I feel it is."

"If I agree to it, will you release me now?"

"If you don't agree to it, Lockland will not welcome you back. You'll be here for seventy-two hours, and during that time you'll be meeting with me."

He spent the next several hours planning how to kill someone else—Ms. Pierce, specifically—instead of himself. Maybe, if he told her, she'd see that as progress, but he doubted it.

XIV

TWO DAYS AGO
THE ESQUIRE HOTEL

THE drink dangled precariously from Victor's freshly bandaged hand as he paced. No matter how many times he made it from one wall of the hotel room to the other and back, the restlessness refused to ebb. Instead, it seemed to charge him, a mental static crackling in his head as he moved. The urge to scream or thrash or pitch his new drink against the wall came on suddenly, and he closed his eyes, and forced his legs to do the one thing they didn't want to do: stop.

Victor stood perfectly still, trying to swallow the energy and chaos and electricity and find in its place *stillness*.

In prison, he'd had moments like this, this same shade of panic peaking like a wave before crashing over him. *End this,* the darkness had hissed, tempted. How many days had he resisted the urge to reach out, not with his hands but with this *thing* inside him, and ruin everything? Everyone?

But he couldn't afford to. Not then, not now. The only way he'd even made it out of isolation was by convincing the staff, beyond a shadow of a doubt, that he was normal, powerless, no threat, or at least no more of a threat than the other 463 inmates. But in those cell-locked moments of darkness, the urge to break everyone around him became crippling. Break them all, and just walk out.

Now, just as then, he folded in, doing his best to forget he even had a power to wield against others, a whim as sharp as glass. Now, just as then, he ordered his body and mind to still, to calm. And now, just as then, when he closed his eyes and searched for silence, a word rose up to meet him, a reminder of why he couldn't afford to break, a challenge, a name.

Eli.

XV

TEN YEARS AGO
LOCKLAND MEDICAL CENTER

ELI slumped into the hospital chair beside Victor's bed, dropping a backpack to the laminate floor beside him. Victor himself had just finished his last session with the resident psych, Ms. Pierce, in which they had explored his relationship with his parents, of whom Ms. Pierce was—unsurprisingly—a fan. Pierce left the session with the promise of a signed book and the sense that they'd made serious progress. Victor left the session with a headache and a note to meet with Lockland's counselor a minimum of three times. He'd negotiated his seventy-two-hour sentence down to forty in exchange for that signed book. Now he was waging battle with the hospital bracelet, unable to pry it off. Eli leaned forward, produced a pocket knife, and snapped the strange paper-plastic-hybrid material. Victor rubbed his wrist and stood, then winced. Nearly dying, it turned out, had not been pleasant. Everything hurt in a dull, constant way.

"Ready to get out of here?" asked Eli, shouldering his backpack.

"God yes," said Victor. "What's in the bag?"

Eli smiled. "I've been thinking," he said as they wound through the sterile halls, "about my turn."

Victor's chest tightened. "Hmm?"

"This was indeed a learning experience," said Eli. Victor muttered something unkind, but Eli continued. "Booze was a bad idea.

As were painkillers. Pain and fear are inextricable from panic, and panic aids in the production of adrenaline and other fight or flight chemicals. As you know."

Victor's brow creased. Yeah, as he knew. Not that his drunken self had cared.

"There are only a certain number of situations," continued Eli as they passed through a pair of automatic glass doors and into the cold day, "where we can introduce both enough panic and enough control. The two are in most cases mutually exclusive. Or at least, they don't have much overlap. The more control, the less need to panic, etc. etc."

"But what's in the bag?"

They reached the car, and Eli tossed the item in question into the backseat.

"Everything we need." Eli's smile spread. "Well. Everything but the ice."

∞

IN fact, "everything we need" amounted to a dozen epinephrine pens, more commonly known as EpiPens, and twice as many one-use warming pads, the kind hunters keep in their boots and football fans in their gloves during winter games. Eli grabbed three of the pens and lined them up on the kitchen table beside the stack of warmers, and then stepped back, casting one sweeping motion over it as if offering Victor a feast. Half a dozen bags of ice leaned against the sink, small rivers of cold condensation wetting the floor. They'd stopped for it on the way home.

"You swiped this?" asked Victor, lifting a pen.

"Borrowed in the name of science," countered Eli as he took up a hand warmer and turned it over to examine the removable plastic coating on the back that served as an activation mechanism. "I've been shadowing at Lockland Med since freshman year. They didn't even blink."

Victor's head was pounding again.

"Tonight?" he asked, not for the first time since Eli had explained his plan.

"Tonight," confirmed Eli, plucking the pen from Victor's grip. "I considered dissolving the epinephrine directly into saline and having you administer it intravenously, since that would give a more reliable distribution, but it's slower than the EpiPens, and dependent on better circulation. Besides, given the nature of the setup, I thought we'd be better off with a more user-friendly option."

Victor considered the supplies. The EpiPen would be the easy part, the compressions more difficult and more damaging. Victor had CPR training, and an intuitive understanding of the body, but it was still a risk. Neither pre-med clusters nor innate skill could truly prepare a student for what they were trying to do. Killing something was easy. Bringing it back to life took more than measurement and medicine. It was like cooking, not baking. Baking took a sense of order. Cooking took a flair, a little art, a little luck. This kind of cooking took a *lot* of luck.

Eli took up two more EpiPens, and arranged the three in his palm. Victor's gaze wandered from the pens to the warmers to the ice. Such simple tools. Could it be that easy?

Eli said something. Victor dragged his attention back.

"What?" he asked.

"It's getting late," Eli said again, gesturing beyond the bags of ice to the window behind the sink, where light was bleeding rapidly out of the sky. "Better get set up."

VICTOR ran his fingers through the ice water, and recoiled. Beside him, Eli slit the last bag open, watching it rupture and spill ice into the tub. With the first few bags, the ice had crackled and broken and half dissolved, but soon the water in the bath was cold enough to keep the cubes from melting. Victor retreated to the sink and leaned against it, the three EpiPens brushing his hand.

They'd talked through the order of operations several times by now. Victor's fingers trembled faintly. He gripped the lip of the counter to still them as Eli tugged off his jeans, his sweater, and finally his shirt, exposing a series of faded scars that hatched his back. They were old, worn to little more than shadows, and Victor had seen them before, but never asked. Now, as he faced the very real possibility that this would be the last conversation he'd ever have with his friend, curiosity got the better of him. He tried to shape the question, but it wasn't necessary, because Eli answered without prompting.

"My father did it, when I was a kid," he said softly. Victor held his breath. In more than two years, Eli had never once mentioned his parents. "He was a minister." There was a far-off quality to his voice, and Victor couldn't help but notice the *was*. Past tense. "I don't think I've ever told you that."

Victor didn't know what to say, so he said the most useless word in the world. "Sorry."

Eli turned away, and shrugged his shoulders, the scars on his back warping with the gesture. "It all worked out."

He stepped up to the tub, his knees resting against the porcelain front as he looked down at the shimmering surface. Victor watched him watch the bath, and felt a strange mixture of interest and concern.

"Are you scared?" he asked.

"Terrified," said Eli. "Weren't you?"

Victor could vaguely remember a flicker of fear, a matchstick's worth, fluttering before being gutted by the effects of the pills and the whiskey. He shrugged.

"You want a drink?" he asked. Eli shook his head.

"Alcohol warms the blood, Vale," he said, eyes still fixed on the icy water. "That's not exactly what I'm going for here."

Victor wondered if Eli would actually be able to do it, or if the cold would crack his mask of ease and charm, shatter it to reveal the normal boy beneath. The bath had handles somewhere beneath the icy surface, and they'd done a walk-through before dinner—neither had been terribly hungry—Eli climbing into the then-dry tub, curling his fingers around the handles, tucking his toes under a lip at the foot of the bath. Victor had suggested cord, something to bind Eli to the tub, but Eli had refused. Victor wasn't sure if it had been bravado or a concern for the state of the body should this fail.

"Any day now," said Victor, trying to diffuse the tension. When Eli didn't move, didn't humor him with even a hollow smile, Victor reached over to the toilet, where his laptop rested on the closed lid. He opened a music program and clicked play, flooding the small tiled room with the heavy base of a rock song.

"You better turn that shit down when you're searching for a pulse," said Eli.

And then he closed his eyes. His lips were moving faintly, and even though his hands hung at his sides, Victor knew he was praying. It perplexed him, how someone about to play God could pray to Him, but it clearly didn't bother his friend.

When Eli's eyes floated open, Victor asked, "What did you say to Him?"

Eli lifted one bare foot to the rim of the bath, gazing down at the contents. "I put my life into His hands."

"Well," said Victor, earnestly, "let's hope He gives it back."

Eli nodded, and took a short breath—Victor imagined he could hear the faintest waver in it—before he climbed into the tub.

∞

VICTOR perched on the tub, clutching a drink as he stared down at Eliot Cardale's corpse.

Eli hadn't screamed. Pain had been written across every one of the forty-three muscles Victor's anatomy class taught him twined together in the human face, but the worst Eli had done was let a small groan escape between clenched teeth when his body first broke the surface of the icy water. Victor had only brushed his fingers through, and the cold had been enough to elicit a spark of pain up his entire arm. He wanted to hate Eli for his composure, had almost hoped—*almost hoped*—that it would be too much for him to bear. That he would break, give up, and Victor would help him out of the tub, and offer him a drink, and the two would sit and talk about their failed trials, and later, when it was a safe distance behind them, they would laugh about how they'd suffered for the sake of science.

Victor took another sip of his drink. Eli was a very unhealthy shade of whitish-blue.

It hadn't taken as long as he'd expected. Eli had gone quiet several minutes ago. Victor had shut the music off, the heavy beat echoing in his head until he realized it was his heart. When he'd ventured a hand down into the ice bath to search for Eli's own pulse—fighting back a gasp at the biting cold—there had been none. He'd chosen to wait a few more minutes, though, which is why he'd poured the drink. If Eli did manage to come back from this, he wouldn't be able to accuse Victor of rushing.

When it became evident that the body in the bath wouldn't somehow revive on its own, Victor set the drink aside, and got to work. Dragging Eli from the tub was the hardest part, since he was several inches taller than Victor, stiff, and submerged in a basin of ice water. After several attempts and a good deal of quiet cursing (Victor was naturally quiet, but even more so under pressure, which gave his peers the distinct impression he knew what he was doing, even when he didn't), he tumbled back to the tiles, Eli's body hitting the floor beside him with the sickening thud of dead weight. Victor shivered. He bypassed the EpiPens for the stack of blankets and warmers, remembering Eli's instructions, and quickly toweled the body off. He then activated the warmers and placed them at the vital points: head, back of the neck, wrists, groin. This was the part of the plan that required luck and art. Victor had to decide at what point the body was warm enough to begin compressions. Too soon meant too cold and too cold meant the epinephrine would put too much stress on the heart and organs. Too late meant too long and too long meant a much greater chance of Eli being too dead to fix.

Victor snapped the bathroom's heat lamp on, despite the fact that he was sweating, and grabbed the three pens from the counter—three was the limit, and he knew that if there was no cardiac response by the third pen, it was too late—and set them on the tiles beside him. He rearranged them, returned them to their straight lines, the small behavior giving him a sense of control while he waited. Every few moments, he checked Eli's temperature, not with a thermometer, but against his own skin. They had realized during their walk-through that they didn't own a thermometer, and Eli, in a rare display of impatience, had insisted on Victor using his judgment. It could have been a death knell, but Eli's faith in Victor revolved around the fact that everyone at Lockland believed him to have an affinity for medicine, an effortless, nearly preternatural understanding of the human body (in truth, it was far from effortless, but Victor did have a knack for guessing). The body was a machine, only necessary pieces, every component at every level, from muscle and bone down to chemical and cell, operating on action and reaction. To Victor it just *made sense.*

When Eli felt warm enough, he began compressions. The flesh beneath his hands was coming up to temperature, making the body feel less like a Popsicle and more like a cadaver. He cringed as the ribs cracked beneath his tangled hands, but didn't stop. He knew that if the ribs didn't separate from the sternum, he wasn't pushing hard or far enough to hit the heart. After several sets, he paused to grab the first pen, and jabbed it down into Eli's leg.

One count, two count, three count.

No response.

He started pumping again, trying not to the think about the breaking ribs and the fact that Eli still looked thoroughly, undeniably dead. Victor's arms burned and he resisted the urge to cast sideways glances at his cell phone, which had tumbled from his pocket in the struggle to extricate Eli from the tub. He closed his eyes, continued counting and pressing his intertwined fists up and down and up and down and up and down over Eli's heart.

It wasn't working.

Victor took up the second pen, and plunged it into Eli's thigh.

One count, two count, three count.

Still nothing.

For the first time, panic filled Victor's mouth like bile. He swallowed, and resumed compressions. The only sounds in the room were his whispered counts and his pulse—*his* pulse, not Eli's—and the odd sound of his hands trying desperately to restart his best friend's heart.

Trying. And failing.

Victor began to lose hope. He was running out of chances, out of pens. There was only one left. His hand slid from Eli's chest, shaking as his fingers curled around it. He raised the pen, and stopped. Beneath him, sprawled on the tiles, was the lifeless body of Eli Cardale. Eli, who showed up in the hallway sophomore year with a suitcase and a smile. Eli, who believed in God and had a monster inside just like Victor, but knew how to hide it better. Eli, who got away with everything, who had slipped into his life and stolen the girl and the top rank and the stupid holiday research grant. Eli, who, despite it all, meant something to Victor.

He swallowed, and drove the pen into his dead friend's chest.

One count, two count, three count.

Nothing.

And then, somewhere between Victor giving up and reaching for his phone, Eli gasped.

XVI

TWO DAYS AGO
THE ESQUIRE HOTEL

VICTOR heard the tread of barefoot steps behind him as Mitch came into the room. He saw the hulking figure in the reflective sheen of the windowpane, felt him the way he felt everyone, as if they were all under water, himself included, and every movement made ripples.

"You're wandering," said Mitch, meeting Victor's gaze in the glass.

It was a small, familiar phrase, one Mitch had often used when he'd found Victor staring off between the bars, squinting faintly, as if trying to see through the walls to something in the distance. Something important.

Now Victor blinked, eyes sliding from the window and Mitch's ghostly reflection to the fake wood floor. He listened to Mitch's footsteps recede into the kitchen, the soft sound of the fridge opening, a carton being taken out. Chocolate milk. It was all Mitch wanted to drink now that he was out, since they didn't have any at Wrighton. Victor had quirked a brow, but let the man have his whims. Prison left a hunger in you, a craving. The exact nature of the want depended on the person.

Victor wanted something, too.

He wanted to watch Eli bleed.

Mitch leaned his elbows on the counter, and drank his milk in silence. Victor thought his cellmate after getting out might have a plan of his own, people he'd want to see, but he had only looked at Victor over the hood of the stolen car and asked, "Where next?" If Mitch did have a past, he was clearly still running from it, and in the meantime, Victor was more than willing to give him something to run *to*. He liked making people useful.

His gaze eventually wandered past Mitch's reflection to the Merit night, the ice in his nearly empty drink clinking as the glass shifted in his grip. The two had been in each other's company for a long time. They knew when the other wanted to talk, and when they wanted to think. The only problem was that more often than not, Victor wanted to think, and more often than not, Mitch wanted to talk. Victor could feel Mitch beginning to fidget under the weight of the quiet.

"Quite a view," he said, tipping his glass toward the windows.

"Yeah," said Mitch. "Been a long time since I've seen a view that grand. Next place we go, I hope it has windows like this."

Victor nodded again, absently, brought his forehead to rest against the cool glass. He couldn't afford to think of *next*, or *after*. He'd spent far too long thinking of *now*. Waiting for *now*. The only *next*s in his world were the short, quick ones standing between him and Eli. And they were falling away so fast.

Mitch yawned. "You sure you're okay, Vic?" he asked, returning the carton to the fridge.

"Dandy. Night."

"Night," said Mitch, wandering back to his room.

Victor watched Mitch go in the glass, before two pale smudges—his own eyes, ghosted against the darkened buildings—brought him back. Victor turned away from the wall of windows, and finished his drink.

A folder sat on a side table beside the leather couch, a handful of papers escaping from within. A face gazed steadily out from a picture, the right eye and cheek obscured by the folder's front, and Victor set the empty glass on the table and flicked the cover back to reveal the rest of the face. It was the page from the copy of *The National Mark* he'd bought that morning.

CIVILIAN HERO SAVES BANK

Below ran the article on the young, precocious man who had been in the right place at the right time and had risked his life to stop an armed robber at a local branch.

Smith & Lauder Bank, a landmark in the northern financial sector of Merit, was the site of a foiled robbery yesterday when a civilian hero put himself between a masked assailant and the money. The civilian, who wishes to remain nameless, told authorities that he noticed the man behaving suspiciously several blocks from the bank, and that a bad feeling was all that led him to follow. Before he reached the bank, the man pulled on a mask, and by the time the civilian caught up, the robber had already plunged inside. In a fearless display, the civilian went in after him. According to the customers and employees trapped inside, the robber at first appeared unarmed, but then proceeded to fire an undetermined weapon up at the stained-glass ceiling, shattering it and raining shards down on the captured populace. He then took aim at the bank vault, but was derailed by the arrival of the civilian. The bank manager reports that the robber took aim at the civilian when he tried to intercede, and then chaos erupted. Shots were fired, and in the mayhem the customers and employees managed to escape the building. By the time the police reached the scene, it was over. The robber, later identified as a troubled man named Barry Lynch, had been killed in the firefight, but the civilian was uninjured. It was a bad day with a happy ending, a remarkable display of courage by a citizen of Merit, and there is no doubt the city is thankful to have such a hero on her streets.

Victor had blacked out most of the article in his usual fashion, and what was left, was this:

a

site

a civilian hero

nameless,

a bad feeling

fearless

unarmed

and in the mayhem

████████████████████████████ uninjured. It was █
████████████████ a remarkable display ████████
██
████████████████████████

It had calmed something in Victor, the blotting out of the words, but the revised state of the article didn't change the fact that several things about it were clearly amiss. First, the robber himself. Barry Lynch. Victor had had Mitch go scrounging, and from what little they could dig up, Barry had several EO markers. Not only had he suffered an NDE, but he'd racked up a string of arrests in the months following, each for theft with an unidentified weapon. The cops never found it on his person, so he was let go; Victor had to wonder if Barry *was* the weapon.

Even more concerning—and more intriguing—than a potential EO was the photograph of the civilian hero. He had asked to remain nameless, but nameless and anonymous are not the same, especially where papers are concerned, and there, below the article, was a picture. A grainy photo of a young man turning away from the scene and the cameras, but not before casting a last, almost cocky, glance back at the press.

The smile on the man's face was unmistakable, young and proud, the same smile he used to flash Victor. The *exact* same smile.

Because Eliot Cardale hadn't aged a day.

XVII

TEN YEARS AGO
LOCKLAND UNIVERSITY

ELI took several gulping breaths, cradling his chest. His eyes struggled open, fought to focus. He took in the room around him, the view from the blanketed floor, before leveling his unsteady gaze on Victor.

"Hey," he said shakily.

"Hey," said Victor, fear and panic still scribbled over him. "How do you feel?"

Eli closed his eyes, rolled his head from side to side. "I . . . I don't know . . . I'm fine . . . I think."

Fine? Victor had cracked his ribs, broken at least half by the feel of it, and Eli felt *fine*? Victor had felt like death. Worse than. Like every fiber of his being had been plucked or torqued or twisted or cramped. Then again, Victor hadn't *died,* right? Not the way he was certain Eli had. He'd sat and watched, made sure Eliot Cardale was nothing but a corpsicle. Maybe it was shock. Or the three shots of epinephrine. That's what it had to be. But even with shock and a nowhere near healthy dose of adrenaline . . . *fine?*

"Fine?" he asked aloud.

Eli shrugged.

"Can you . . ." Victor wasn't sure how to finish the question. If their absurd theory had worked and Eli had somehow acquired an ability by simply dying and coming back, would he even know it? Eli seemed to know the question's end.

"I mean, I'm not starting fires with my mind, or making earthquakes or whatever. But I'm not dead." There was, Victor could hear, a faint waver of relief in his voice.

As the two sat in a pile of damp blankets on the water-streaked bathroom floor, the whole experiment seemed *idiotic*. How could they have risked so much? Eli took another long, low breath, and got to his feet. Victor rushed to catch his arm, but Eli shook him off.

"I said I'm fine." He left the bathroom, eyes carefully avoiding the tub, and vanished into his room in search of clothes. Victor plunged his hand down through the icy water one last time and pulled the plug. By the time he'd cleaned up, Eli had reappeared in the hall, fully dressed. Victor found him examining himself in a wall mirror, frowning faintly.

Eli's balance faltered, and he put a hand on the wall to steady himself.

"I think I need . . . ," he started.

Victor assumed the line would end with "a doctor" but instead Eli met his eyes in the mirror, and smiled—not his best—and said, "A drink."

Victor managed to pull his own mouth into something like a smile, then, too.

"That I can do."

∞

ELI insisted on going out.

Victor thought they could just as easily get wasted in the comfort of their apartment, but since Eli had experienced the more recent of their two traumas and seemed rather intent on being in public, perhaps wanting to live it up, Victor indulged him. Now the two were on the far side of drunk—or at least, Victor was; Eli seemed remarkably lucid considering the sheer quantity of alcohol he'd consumed—swaying and sauntering down the road that ran so conveniently from the local bar back to their apartment building, eliminating the need for a vehicle.

Despite a festive air, both had done their best to avoid the subject of what had happened, and how lucky Eli—and really both of them—had been. Neither seemed eager to talk about it, and in the absence of any ExtraOrdinary symptoms—other than feeling extraordinarily *lucky*—neither had reason to gloat as much as thank their stars. Which they did freely, tipping imaginary but brimming glasses skyward as they stumbled home. They poured invisible liquor on the concrete as a gift to earth or God or fate or whatever force had let them have their fun and live to know it had been nothing more than that.

Victor felt warm despite the flurries of snow, alive, and even welcomed the last dregs of pain from his own unpleasant proximity to death. Eli beamed dazedly at the night sky, and then he stepped off the sidewalk. Or tried to. But his heel caught the edge, and he stumbled, landing on his hands and knees among a patch of dirty snow, and tire tracks, and broken glass. He hissed, recoiled, and Victor saw blood, a smear of red against the dingy, snow-dusted street. Eli proceeded to sit on the lip of the curb, tilting his palm toward the nearest streetlamp to get a better look at the gash there, glittering with the remains of someone's abandoned beer bottle.

"Ouch," said Victor, leaning over him to examine the cut and nearly losing his balance. He caught himself on the streetlamp as Eli cursed softly and pulled the largest shard out.

"Think I'll need stitches?"

He held his bloody hand up for Victor to inspect, as if the latter's vision and judgment were any better than his own right now. Victor squinted, and was about to reply with as much authority as he could muster, when something happened.

The cut on Eli's palm began to *close*.

The world, which had been swaying in Victor's vision, came to an abrupt stop. Stray flakes hung in the air, and their breath hovered in clouds over their lips. There was no movement except that of Eli's flesh healing.

And Eli must have felt it, because he lowered his hand into his lap, and the two gazed down as the gash that had run from pinkie to thumb knitted itself back together. In moments, the bleeding had stopped—the blood already lost now drying on his skin—and the wound was nothing more than a wrinkle, a faint scar, and then not even that.

The cut was just . . . gone.

Hours passed in blinks as the two let it sink in, what that meant, what they had done. It was extraordinary.

It was ExtraOrdinary.

Eli rubbed his thumb over the fresh skin of his palm, but Victor was the first to speak, and when he did, it was with an eloquence and composure perfectly befitting the situation.

"Holy shit."

∞

VICTOR stared up at the place where the lip of their apartment building's roof met the cloudy night. Every time he closed his eyes he felt like he was falling over, getting closer and closer to the brick, so he tried to keep them open, focusing on that strange seam overhead.

"Are you coming?" asked Eli.

He was holding the door open, practically bouncing in his eagerness to get inside and find something else that could physically wound him. Zeal burned in his eyes. And while Victor didn't exactly *blame* him, he had no desire to sit around and watch Eli stab himself all night. He'd watched him try all the way home, leaving a dotted red trail in the snow from the blood that escaped before the wounds could heal. He'd seen the ability. Eli was an EO, in the (regenerating) flesh. Victor had felt something when Eli had come back to life seemingly EO-free: relief. With Eli's new abilities being thrust into his wavering line of vision all the way home, Victor's relief had dissolved into a ripple of panic. He would be relegated to sidekick, note-taker, the brick wall to bounce ideas off of.

No.

"Vic, you coming or not?"

Curiosity and jealousy ate at Victor in equal parts, and the only way he knew to stifle both, to quell the urge to wound Eli himself—or at least to try—was to walk away.

He shook his head, then stopped abruptly when the world continued swinging side to side.

"Go on," he said, mustering a smile that came nowhere near his eyes. "Go play with some sharp objects. I need to take a walk." He descended the stairs, and nearly fell twice in three steps.

"Are you fit to walk, Vale?"

Victor waved him on inside. "I'm not driving. Just going to get some air."

And with that, he took off into the dark, with two goals on his mind.

The first was simple: to put as much distance as he could between himself and Eli before he did something he'd regret.

The second was trickier, and his body hurt to even think of it, but he had no choice.

He had to plan his next attempt at death.

XVIII

TWO DAYS AGO
THE ESQUIRE HOTEL

I want to believe that there's more. That we could be more. Hell, we could be heroes.

Victor's chest tightened when he looked at Eli's unchanging face in the newspaper photograph. It was disconcerting; all he had of Eli was a mental picture, a decade old, and yet it lined up perfectly, like duplicate slides, with the one on the page. It was the same face in every technical way . . . and yet it wasn't. The years had worn on Victor in more obvious ways, hardening him, but they hadn't left Eli untouched. He didn't appear a day older, but the arrogant smile he'd often flashed in college had given way to something crueler. Like that mask he'd worn for so long had finally fallen off, and this was what lurked behind it.

And Victor, who was so good at picking things apart, at understanding how they worked, how *he* worked, looked at the photo, and felt . . . conflicted. Hate was too simple a word. He and Eli were *bonded*, by blood and death and science. They were alike, more so now than ever. And he had missed Eli. He wanted to see him. And he wanted to see him *suffer*. He wanted to see the look in Eli's eyes when he lit them up with pain. He wanted his attention.

Eli was like a thorn beneath Victor's skin, and it hurt. He could turn off every nerve in his body, but Victor couldn't do a damned thing about the twinge he felt when he thought of Cardale. The worst part of going numb was that it took away everything but this, the smothering need to hurt, to break, to kill, pouring over him like a thick blanket of syrup until he panicked and brought the physical sensations back.

Now that he was so close, the thorn seemed to burrow deeper. What was Eli doing here in Merit? Ten years was a long time. A decade could shape a man, change everything about him. It had changed Victor. What about Eli? Who had *he* become?

He fidgeted under the sudden urge to burn the photo, to shred it, as if damaging the paper could somehow cause damage to Eli, too, which of course it couldn't. Nothing could. So he sat down, and set the page aside, beyond arm's reach so he wouldn't be tempted to ruin it.

The paper called Eli a *hero*.

The word made Victor laugh. Not just because it was absurd, but because it posed a question. If Eli really was a hero, and Victor meant to stop him, did that make *him* a villain?

He took a long sip of his drink, tipped his head back against the couch, and decided he could live with that.

XIX

TEN YEARS AGO
LOCKLAND UNIVERSITY

WHEN Victor got home from his labs the next day, he found Eli sitting at the kitchen table, carving up his skin. He was dressed in the same sweatpants and shirt Victor had found him in the night before when he had finally come home from his walk, several degrees closer to sober, and with the beginnings of a plan. Now Victor grabbed a candy bar and hung his bag on the back of a wooden kitchen chair before sinking into it. He peeled away the wrapper and tried to ignore the way his appetite fizzled as he watched Eli work.

"Shouldn't you be shadowing at the hospital today?" asked Victor.

"It's not even a conscious process," murmured Eli reverently as he drew the blade up his arm, the wound healing in the knife's wake, a blossom of appearing and disappearing red, like a sick magic trick. "I can't stop the tissue from repairing."

"Poor you," teased Victor coolly. "Now if you don't mind . . ." He held up the candy bar.

Eli paused midcut. "Squeamish?"

Victor shrugged. "Just easily distracted," he said. "You look awful. Have you slept? Eaten?"

Eli blinked, and set the knife aside. "I've been thinking."

"The body doesn't survive on thoughts."

"I've been thinking about this ability. Regeneration." His eyes glittered as he spoke. "Why of all the potential powers I ended up with this one. Maybe it's not random. Maybe there's some correlation between a person's character and their resulting ability. Maybe it's a reflection of their psyche. I'm trying to understand how this"—he held up a blood-stained, but uninjured hand—"is a reflection of me. Why He would give me—"

"*He?*" asked Victor incredulously. He wasn't in the mood for God. Not this morning. "According to your thesis," he said, "an influx of adrenaline and a desire to survive gave you that talent. Not God. This isn't divinity, Eli. It's science and chance."

"Maybe to a point, but when I climbed into that water, I put myself in His hands—"

"No," snapped Victor. "You put yourself in *mine*."

Eli fell silent, but began to rap his fingers on the table. After several moments he said, "What I need is a gun."

Victor had taken another bite of chocolate, and nearly choked. "And why's that?"

"To truly test the speed of regeneration. Obviously."

"Obviously." Victor finished his snack as Eli pushed up from the table to pour himself some water. "Look, I've been thinking, too."

"About what?" asked Eli, leaning back against the counter.

"About my turn."

Eli's brow crinkled. "You had it."

"About my *next* turn," Victor said. "I want to try again tonight."

Eli considered Victor, head cocked. "I don't think that's a good idea."

"Why not?"

Eli hesitated. "I can still see the line from your hospital bracelet," he said at last. "At least wait till you're feeling better."

"Actually, I'm feeling fine. Better than. I feel wonderful. I feel like roses and sunshine and glitter."

Victor Vale did not feel like glitter. His muscles ached, his veins still felt strangely starved of air, and he couldn't shake the headache that had trailed him since he'd opened his eyes beneath the fluorescent white of the hospital lights.

"Give yourself time to recover, okay?" said Eli. "And then we'll talk about trying again."

There was nothing overtly wrong with the words, but Victor didn't like the way he said them, the same calm, cautious tone people use when they want to let someone down slowly, smoothing a "no" into a "not right now." Something was wrong. And Eli's attention was already drifting back toward his knives. Away from Victor.

He clenched his teeth against the curse on his tongue. And then he shrugged carefully.

"Fine," he said, swinging his bag back onto his shoulder. "Maybe you're right," he added with a yawn and a lazy smile. Eli smiled back, and Victor turned toward the hall and his room.

He swiped an epinephrine pen on the way, and closed the door behind him.

∞

VICTOR hated loud music almost as much as he hated crowds of drunk people. The party had both, and was made more insufferable by Victor's own sobriety. No booze. Not this time. He wanted—needed—everything to be sharp, especially if he was going to do this alone. Eli was still, presumably, at the apartment, carving up his skin while he assumed Victor was in his room, sulking or studying or both. What Victor had actually been doing was climbing out his window.

He'd felt fifteen again, a kid sneaking out to a party on a school night while his parents sat in the living room and laughed at something mindless on the TV. Or at least, Victor imagined this was what it would have been like had he needed to sneak out. Had anyone ever been home to catch him at it.

Victor moved through the party largely unnoticed, but not unwelcome. He earned a few second glances, but those were mostly because he rarely made an appearance at these kinds of events. He was an outsider by choice, a good enough mimic to charm his way into social circles when he wanted, but more often than not he preferred to stand apart and watch, and most of the school seemed content to let him.

But here he was, winding his way through bodies and music and sticky floors, the epinephrine pen tucked into the inside pocket of his coat, a small Post-it affixed to it that read *Use Me*. Now, as he found himself surrounded by lights and noise and bodies, Victor felt as if he'd wandered into another world. Is this what normal seniors did? Drank and danced with bodies interlocking like puzzle pieces to music loud enough to drown out thoughts? Angie had taken him to a few parties freshman year, but those had been different. He couldn't remember anything about the music or the beer, only her. Victor blinked the memory away. Sweat coated his palms as he took a plastic cup, and dumped the contents into a withering house plant. Holding something helped.

At one point he found himself on the balcony, looking down at the frozen lake that ran behind the frats. The sight made him shiver. He knew for optimum results he should mimic Eli, recreate the successful scenario, but Victor couldn't—wouldn't—do that. He had to find his own method.

He pushed off the banister, and retreated back into the house. As he continued on a circuit through the rooms, his eyes flicked around, appraising. He was amazed at how myriad the options for a suicide were, and yet how limited the options for one with any certitude of survival.

But Victor was certain of one thing: he wasn't leaving here without his turn. He wouldn't go back to the apartment and watch Eli joyfully saw at his skin, marvel at this strange new immortality he hadn't even tried *that* hard to find. Victor wouldn't stand there and coo and take notes for him.

Victor Vale was not a fucking sidekick.

By his third lap around the house, he'd scored what he considered to be enough cocaine to induce cardiac arrest (he wasn't sure, having never engaged in that kind of activity). He'd had to buy from three separate students, since each only had a few hits on them.

On his fourth lap around the house, while working up the nerve to *use* the cocaine, he heard it. The front door opened—he couldn't hear that over the music, but from his place on the stairs, he felt the sudden burst of cold—and then a girl squealed and said, "Eli! You made it!"

Victor swore softly, and retreated up the stairs. He heard his own name as he wound through the bodies. He broke through and reached the second-floor landing, then found an unoccupied bedroom with its own bathroom at the back. Halfway through the room, he stopped. A bookcase lined one wall, and there in the center, his own last name leapt out at him in capital letters.

He pulled the massive self-help book from the wall, and opened the window. The sixth book in a series of nine on emotional action and reaction hit the thin coat of snow below with a satisfying thud. Victor shut the window and continued into the bathroom.

On the sink he set his things in order.

First, his phone. He punched in a text to Eli but didn't hit Send, and set the device to one side. Second, the adrenaline shot. He'd be up to temperature, so hopefully a single direct injection would suffice. It would be hell on the body, but so would everything else he was about to do. He set the needle beside the phone. Third, the coke. He made a neat pile, and began to separate it into lines with a hotel card he found in his back pocket, a relic from the winter trip his parents had dragged him on. Despite an upbringing that would have driven most kids to drugs, Victor had never been much inclined to do them, but he had a good idea of the steps, thanks to a healthy diet of crime dramas. Once the cocaine was in its lines—seven of them—he pulled a dollar from his wallet and rolled it into a narrow straw. As seen on TV.

He looked in the mirror.

"You want to live," he told his reflection.

His reflection looked unconvinced.

"You need to live through this," he said. "You need to."

And then he took a breath and bent over the first line.

The arm came out of nowhere, wrapped around his throat, and slammed him back into the wall opposite the vanity. Victor caught his balance and straightened in time to see Eli run his hand through several hundred dollars' worth of coke, brushing it all into the sink.

"What the fuck?" Victor hissed, lunging for it. He wasn't fast enough. Eli's coke-dusted palm shoved him back again, pinned him to the wall, leaving a white print on the front of his black shirt.

"What the fuck?" parroted Eli with shocking calm. "What the *fuck*?"

"You weren't supposed to be here."

"*You* come to a party, people notice. Ellis texted me when you showed up. And then Max texts and tells me you're buying out the coke. I'm not an idiot. What were you thinking?" His free hand grabbed the cell on the sink. He read the text. He made a sound like a laugh, but his fingers tightened around Victor's collar as his other hand pitched the phone into the shower, where it broke into several pieces on impact.

"What if I hadn't heard my phone?" He let go of him. "What then?"

"Then I'd be dead," said Victor with feigned calm. His eyes drifted to the EpiPen. Eli's attention followed. Before Victor could move, Eli grabbed the pen and drove it down into his own leg. A small gasp escaped his gritted teeth as the contents flooded his system, jarring his lungs and heart, but in moments he recovered.

"I'm only trying to protect you," Eli said, casting the used cartridge aside.

"My hero," growled Victor under his breath. "Now fuck off."

Eli considered him. "I'm not leaving you here alone."

Victor stared past him to the sink, the edge still dusted with cocaine.

"I'll meet you downstairs," he said, gesturing to his shirt, the sink, the phone. "I have to clean up."

Eli didn't move.

Victor's cool eyes tracked up to meet his. "I've got nothing else on me." And then, a ghost of a smile. "Frisk me if you want."

Eli gave a cough of a laugh, but then his face sobered. "This isn't the way to do it, Vic."

"How do you know? Just because the ice worked doesn't mean something else won't—"

"I don't mean the method. I mean *alone*." He brought his coke-free hand to rest on Victor's shoulder. "You can't do this alone. So promise me you won't."

Victor held his gaze. "I won't."

Eli walked past him, into the bedroom.

"Five minutes," he called as he left.

Victor listened to the party flood in as Eli opened the door, then cut out again when he slammed it behind him. Victor stepped up to the sink, and ran his hand along the surface. It came away white. His fingers curled into a fist, and hit the mirror. It cracked—one, long, perfect line down the middle—but didn't shatter. Victor's knuckles throbbed, and he ran them under the sink, reaching blindly for a towel as he wiped at the lingering powder. His fingers came across something, and a sudden shock of pain went up his hand. He recoiled, and turned to see a socket on the wall, a clumsy Post-it taped beside it that said *Bad outlet do not touch seriously.*

Someone had gone in with a red pen and added punctuation.

Victor frowned, his fingers tingling from the small jolt.

And then the moment froze. The air in his lungs, the water in the sink, the flurries just beyond the window in the other room. All of it froze, the way it had in the street last night with Eli, only it wasn't Eli's hand this time but Victor's, burning faintly from the shock.

He had an idea. Retrieving the three pieces of his cell from the shower floor and fitting them back together, he typed in the message. Victor had promised he wouldn't do it alone. And he wouldn't. But he didn't need Eli's help either.

Save me, he texted, along with the address of the frat.

And then he hit Send.

XX

TWO DAYS AGO
THE ESQUIRE HOTEL

DOWN the hall and behind a door, Sydney Clarke lay curled in a nest of sheets. She'd listened to the sounds of Victor's steps in the other room, slow and soft and even as dripping water. She'd heard the glass break, heard the sound of the tap running, and then again, the steps, drip drip drip. She'd heard Mitch, his heavy tread, the muffled conversation, only tones reaching her through the walls. She'd heard Mitch's retreat down the hall. And then, quiet. The *drip drip drip* of Victor's pacing replaced by an odd stillness.

Sydney didn't trust stillness. She had come to believe that it was a bad thing. A wrong, unnatural, dead thing. She sat up in the strange bed in the strange hotel, her watery blue eyes unfocused on the door, stretching to hear through the wood and silence beyond. When still nothing greeted her, she slid from the bed in her too-large stolen sweats, and padded barefoot from her room and into the hotel suite's spacious living room.

Victor's bandaged hand was now draped over the arm of a couch facing the windows, a shallow glass dangling loosely from his fingers, only a sip's worth of liquid left inside, and most of it melted ice. Sydney tiptoed around the couch to face him.

He was asleep.

He didn't look peaceful, but his breathing was low, even.

Sydney perched on a chair and considered the man who had

saved her . . . no, she had saved herself . . . but found her, taken her in. She wondered who he was, and if she should be afraid of him. She didn't feel afraid, but Sydney knew not to trust fear, and certainly not to trust the absence of it. She hadn't been afraid of her sister, Serena, or even her sister's new boyfriend (at least not afraid *enough*) and look where that had gotten her.

Shot.

So she sat on the balls of her feet atop the leather chair and watched Victor sleep, as if the frown lines that lingered even now would rearrange and tell her all his secrets.

XXI

TEN YEARS AGO
LOCKLAND UNIVERSITY

DURING their freshman year, before Eli had ever set foot on campus, Angie had been drawn to Victor. In some ways they were opposites—Angie didn't seem to take anything seriously, and Victor didn't seem to take anything lightly—but in more ways they were alike; both young, dangerously smart, and lacking in patience when it came to the usual college crowd and their juvenile reaction to the sudden freedoms from parental restraint. Because of their shared sentiments, Victor and Angie both found themselves in constant need of an out, a reliable escape from situations they'd rather not be in, people they'd rather not be with.

And so, sitting in the comfort food kitchen in LIDS one day, they devised a fairly rudimentary code.

Save me.

The code was understood to be used sparingly, but always respected. Save first, ask questions later. When texted, along with an address, it meant that one desperately needed the other to bail them out, be it from a party or a study session or a bad date. Victor himself never had the luxury of a *date* with Angie, bad or otherwise, unless you counted the food they sometimes grabbed after bailing each other out—which Victor did. Nights spent in the same burger joint off campus, splitting shakes. He preferred chocolate but she always wanted some awful concoction, all swirled flavors and toppings, and in the end he didn't really care because he'd never remember what it tasted like anyway, only how the cold of it made Angie's lips redder, and the way their noses almost touched whenever they tried to drink at the same time, and how from that close up he could see the flecks of green in her eyes. He'd pick at his fries and tell her about the idiots in his study session. She would laugh, and spoon out the last of her shake, and recount how awkward her date had been. Victor would roll his eyes as she ran through the particular offenses, and think of how he would have done things differently, and of how thankful he was that someone—anyone—had pushed Angie Knight into wanting to be saved.

And by him.

Save me.

It had been a year and a half since Victor had thought to use that code. The last time had been before Eli—and certainly before Eli and Angie became a fused entity—but she still came to save him.

She pulled up in the frat's parking lot in her hatchback, right to the spot where Victor was waiting after half climbing and half falling from the same window through which he'd thrown his parents' book. And for a moment, one very small moment, after he climbed into the car and before he explained, it had been like freshman year again, just the two of them escaping a bad night, and he wanted so badly to let her drive to their old burger joint. They would slump into a booth, and he would tell her that parties hadn't gotten any better, and she would laugh, and somehow it would make everything okay.

But then she asked where Eli was, and the moment passed. Victor closed his eyes, and asked her to drive him to the engineering labs.

"They're closed," she said even as she guided the car in that direction.

"You have a swipe card."

"What's this about?"

Victor surprised himself by telling her the truth. She knew about Eli's thesis, but he told her about the most recent discovery, about the role of NDEs. He told her about his own desire to test the theory. He told her about his plan. The only thing he didn't tell her was that Eli had already successfully done it. That he held on to for a moment. And to her credit, Angie listened. She drove, knuckles whitening on the wheel, lips pressed into a line, and let Victor talk. He finished as she was pulling into the parking lot of the engineering labs, and she didn't say anything until she'd parked, and shut the engine off, and shifted in her seat to face him.

"Have you lost your mind?" she asked.

Victor managed a tight smile. "I don't think so."

"Let me get this straight," she said. The short red hair framed her face, frizzing in the winter weather. "You think that if you die, and manage to come back, you'll turn into what, one of the X-Men?"

Victor laughed. His throat was dry. "I was hoping for Magneto." The attempt at levity failed, the look between shock and horror and annoyance still firmly scrawled across Angie's face. "Look," he said, sobering, "I know it sounds crazy—"

"Of course it does. Because it *is* crazy. I'm not going to help you off yourself."

"I don't want to die."

"You just told me you did."

"Well, I don't want to stay dead."

She rubbed her eyes, rested her forehead for a moment on the steering wheel, and let out a groan.

"I need you, Angie. If you don't help me—"
"Don't you *dare* spin it that way—"
"—I'll just end up trying by myself again—"
"Again?"
"—and doing something stupid I *won't* recover from."
"We can get you help."
"I'm not suicidal."
"No, you're delusional."

Victor tipped his head back against the seat. His pocket buzzed. Eli. He ignored it, knowing it would be a matter of moments before Eli contacted Angie instead. He didn't have much time. Certainly not enough to convince her to help him.

"Why can't you just . . . ," mumbled Angie into the steering wheel, ". . . I don't know, OD? Something peaceful?"

"The pain's important," explained Victor, inwardly wincing. She wasn't so upset at what he was doing, then. Only that he was involving her. "Pain and fear," he added. "They're both factors. Hell, Eli killed himself in an ice bath."

"*What?*"

A grim, triumphant smile itched on his lips as he played the card. Victor had known that Eli wouldn't have told Angie yet. He was counting on it. The betrayal showed in her eyes. She got out, slammed the door, and sunk back against it. Victor followed, rounding the car. He drew tracks in the snow as he went. Through the partially tinted glass he could see her phone on the driver's seat. A red light flashed on its front. Victor turned his attention toward Angie.

"When did he do it?" she asked.
"Last night."

She looked at the film of snow on the concrete between them.

"But I came by this morning, Vic. He looked fine."

"Exactly. Because it worked. It *will* work."

She groaned. "This is crazy. You're crazy."

"You know that's not true."

"Why would he . . ."

"He didn't tell you anything?" prodded Victor, shivering in his thin jacket.

"He's been weird lately," she mumbled. Then her attention narrowed. "What you're asking me to do . . . it's crazy. It's *torture*."

"Angie . . ."

She looked up, eyes blazing. "I don't even believe you. What if it goes wrong?"

"It won't."

"What if it *does*?"

His phone buzzed angrily in his pocket.

"It can't," he said as calmly as he could. "I took a pill."

Her eyebrows knitted.

"Eli and I," he began to explain, "we isolated some of the adrenal compounds that kick in during life-or-death situations. We fabricated them. Essentially the pill acts like a trigger. A jump start."

It was all a lie, but he could see that its feigned existence impacted Angie. Science, even completely fictional science, held sway. Angie swore, and tucked her hands into her jacket pockets.

"Fuck, it's cold," she muttered, turning toward the building's front doors. The engineering lab itself was a problem, Victor knew. Security cameras. If something did go wrong, there would be footage.

"Where's Eli now?" she asked as she swiped her access card. "If you're in this together, why are you here with me?"

"He's busy relishing his new status as a god," said Victor bitterly, following her through the key-coded entry, scanning the ceiling for the red light of recording equipment. "Look, all you have to do is use the electricity to turn me off. Then turn me back on. The pill will do the rest."

"I study currents and the effects on devices, Victor, not people."

"A body is a machine," he said quietly. She led the way into one of the electrical engineering labs and flicked a switch. Half the lights turned on. Equipment was stacked along one wall, a variety of machines, some that looked medical, others technical. The room was full of tables, long and thin but large enough to rest a body on. He could feel Angie waver beside him.

"We'd have to plan it out," she said. "Give me a couple weeks, and maybe I could modify some of the equipment in here for—"

"No," said Victor, crossing to the machines. "It has to be tonight."

She looked aghast, but before she could protest, he took the lie he'd started, and ran with it.

"That pill I told you about . . . I already took it. It's like a switch, whether on or off depends on what state the body's in." He met her gaze, held it, and sent up a silent prayer that she didn't know half as much about hypothetical adrenal compounds as she did about circuits. "If I don't do this soon, Angie"—he winced for good measure—"the compound will kill me."

She paled.

He held his breath.

His phone vibrated again.

"How long?" she asked at last.

He took a step toward her, letting one of his legs nearly buckle under some imaginary strain. He caught himself on the edge of a table with a grimace, and found her gaze as the buzzing in his pocket stopped.

"Minutes."

"THIS is mad," whispered Angie over and over as she helped bind Victor's legs to the table. He worried that even now, with the machines around them humming to life and her busy winding the rubber strap around his ankles, she might back out, so he doubled up in fake pain, curled in on himself.

"Victor," she said urgently. "Victor, are you okay?" There was pain and panic in her voice and he had to fight the urge to stop, to soothe her, and promise it would be okay.

Instead he nodded, and said through gritted teeth, "Hurry."

She rushed to finish the knots, showed him the rubber-coated bars on the table where he could put his hands. Her halo of red hair had always looked electrified, but tonight it rose around her cheeks. Victor thought it made her look haunting. Beautiful. The first day they met, she'd looked like this. It had been hot for September; her face was flushed, and her hair had a life of its own. He'd looked up from his textbook and saw her, standing at the entrance to LIDS, clutching a folder to her front as her eyes wandered over the room in an appraising way—lost but unconcerned. And then they landed on Victor at his table with his book, and her face lit up. Not full-wattage light, but a steady glow as she crossed the room, and slid without preamble into the seat across from him. They didn't even talk, that first day. Just passed the same hour in the same space. Angie had later referred to the two of them as concordant frequencies.

"Victor." Her voice saying his name drew him back to the cold table in the lab.

"I want you to know," she said as she began to fix sensors to his chest, "that I will never, ever forgive you for this."

He shivered under her touch. "I know."

His coat and shirt were cast off on a chair, the contents of his pockets set on top. Amid the keys and a wallet and a pre-med lab badge, sat his phone, the ringer turned off. It blinked angrily at him, flashing first blue and then red and then blue again, and so on, signaling it had both voice mail and texts waiting.

Victor smiled grimly. *Too late, Eli. It's my turn.*

Angie was standing by a machine chewing the nails off one of her hands. The other rested on a set of dials. The machine itself was whirring and whining and blinking. A language Victor didn't know, which scared him.

Her eyes caught on something, and she took hold of it, crossing back to him. It was a strip of rubber.

"You know what to do," said Victor, surprised by the calm in his voice. Everything beneath his skin was trembling. "Start at the low setting, and go up."

"Turn off, turn on," she whispered, before holding the rubber above his mouth. "Bite down on this."

Victor took a last deep breath, and forced his mouth to open. The strap was between his teeth, his fingers testing their grip on the small table bars. He could do this. Eli held himself under. Victor could, too.

Angie was back at the machine. Their eyes met, and for an instant everything else vanished—the lab and the humming machines and the existence of EO and Eli and the years since Victor and Angie had shared a milkshake—and he was just happy to have her looking at him. Seeing him.

And then she closed her eyes, and turned the dial a single click, and the only thing Victor could think of was the pain.

VICTOR fell back against the table in a cold sweat.

He couldn't breathe.

He gasped, expecting a pause, a moment to recover. Expecting Angie to change her mind, to stop, to give up.

But Angie turned the dial up.

The need to be sick was overcome by the need to scream and he bit into the rubber strap until he thought his teeth would crack but a moan still escaped, and he thought Angie must have heard, and she'd turn the machine off now, but the dial went up again.

And again.

And again.

Victor thought he would black out but before he could, the dial turned up and the spasm of pain brought him back to his body and the table and the room and he couldn't escape.

The pain kept him there.

The pain tied him down as it shot through every nerve in every limb.

He tried to spit out the strap but he couldn't open his mouth. His jaw was locked.

The dial went up.

Every time Victor thought the dial couldn't go any further, the pain couldn't get any worse, and then it did and it did and it did, and Victor could hear himself screaming even though the strap was still between his teeth and he could feel every nerve in his body breaking and he wanted it to stop. He wanted it to *stop*.

He begged Angie but the words were cut short by the strap and the dial turning up again and the sound in the air like cracking ice and shredding paper and static.

The darkness blinked around him and he wanted it because it meant the pain would stop but he didn't want to die and he was afraid that the darkness was death and so he pulled violently back from it.

He felt himself crying.

The dial went up.

His hands ached where they gripped the table bars, cramped in place.

The dial went up.

He wished for the first time in his life that he believed in God.

The dial went up.

He felt his heart skip a beat, felt it grind and then double.

The dial went up.

He heard a machine warn, then alarm.

The dial went up.

And everything stopped.

XXII

TWO DAYS AGO
THE ESQUIRE HOTEL

SYDNEY watched the lines in Victor's face deepen. He must be dreaming.

It was late. The night beyond the floor-to-ceiling glass was dark—or as dark as it could be, in a city like this—and she stood and stretched, and was about to go back to bed when she saw the piece of paper, and everything in her went cold.

The newspaper article sat open beside Victor on the couch. The heavy bars of black on the page were the first thing that caught her attention, but the photo beneath was what held it. Sydney's chest tightened, sudden and sharp, and she couldn't breathe. It felt like she was drowning, *again*—Serena calling from the patio, a picnic basket hooked on the elbow of her winter coat, telling Syd to hurry up, or the ice would be all melted, which it was, underneath that brittle shell of frost and snow—but when she squeezed her eyes shut, it wasn't the half-frozen water of the lake that folded over her, but the memory of the field a year later, the stretch of frozen grass and the body and her sister's encouragement and then the sound of the gunshot, echoing in her ears.

Two different days, two different deaths, overlapping, swirling together. She blinked both memories away, but the photo was still there, staring up at her, and she couldn't tear her gaze away, and before she knew what she was doing, her hand was reaching out, stretching past Victor, toward the paper and the smiling man on its front.

It all happened fast.

Sydney's fingers curled around the newspaper page but as she lifted it, her forearm grazed Victor's knee and before she could shift her weight or pull back he shot forward, eyes open but empty, hand vising around Sydney's small wrist. Without warning, pain tore up her arm and through her small body, crashing over her in a wave. It was worse than drowning, worse than being shot, worse than anything she had ever felt. It was like every one of her nerves was shattering, and Sydney did the only thing she could.

She screamed.

XXIII

TEN YEARS AGO
LOCKLAND UNIVERSITY

THE pain had followed him up again, and Victor came to, screaming.

Angie was fumbling with his hands, trying to coax them free of the bars. He shot forward, clutching his head. Why was the electricity still running? The pain was a wave, a wall, wracking his muscles, his heart. His skin was tearing with it, and Angie was talking but Victor couldn't hear anything through the agony. He curled in on himself and stifled another scream.

Why wouldn't the pain stop? WHY WOULDN'T IT STOP?

And then, as sudden as a flipped switch, the pain was gone, and Victor was left feeling . . . nothing. The machines were off, the lights sprinkled across their fronts all dead. Angie was still talking, her hands running over skin, unbuckling the ankle straps, but Victor didn't hear her as he stared down at his hands and wondered at the sudden hollowness, as if the electricity had gutted his nerves and left only shells.

Empty.

Where did it go? he wondered. *Will it come back?*

In the sudden absence of pain, he found himself trying to remember how it felt, to drum up the sensation, a shadow of it, and as he did the switch clicked again, and the energy was there, crackling like static through the room. He heard the crinkle of the air, and then he heard a scream. He wondered for an instant if it was coming from him, but the pain was beyond Victor now, outside of him, humming over his skin without touching it.

He felt slow, dazed, as he tried to process the situation. Nothing hurt, so who was screaming? And then the body crumpled to the lab floor beside his table, and the space between his thoughts collapsed, and he snapped back to his senses.

Angie. *No.* He jumped down from the table to find her writhing on the floor, still screaming in pain, and he thought *stop!* but the electrical buzzing in the room continued to grow around him. *Stop.* She clutched her chest.

Victor tried to help her up but Angie cried out even louder when he touched her and he stumbled back, confusion and panic pouring through him. *The buzzing,* he thought. He had to turn it down. He closed his eyes and tried to imagine it as a dial, tried to imagine turning some invisible device. He tried to feel calm. Numb. He was surprised by how easily it came to him in the midst of chaos, the calm. And then he realized how horribly quiet the room had gone. Victor opened his eyes, and saw Angie sprawled on the floor, head back, eyes open, red hair a cloud around her face. The humming in the air had faded to a tingle, and then to nothing, but it was still too late.

Angie Knight was dead.

XXIV

TWO DAYS AGO
THE ESQUIRE HOTEL

THE hotel room was pain and noise and chaos.

Victor came to, dazed, trapped between the school lab and the hotel room, Angie's scream in his head and Sydney's in his ears. Sydney? But the girl was nowhere to be seen, and he was being pinned back against the couch by Mitch, whose whole body was shaking visibly from the effort, but unbudging as the room hummed around them.

"Turn it off," growled Mitch under his breath, and Victor woke fully. His eyes narrowed, the humming died, and everything in Mitch slackened, all signs of pain gone. He let go of Victor's shoulders, and slumped back onto a chair.

Victor took a low, steadying breath, and ran his hand slowly over his face and through his hair, before his attention settled on Mitch.

"Are you all right?" he asked.

Mitch looked tired, unamused, but safe. It wasn't the first time he'd had to intervene. Victor knew that when he had bad dreams, other people always suffered.

"I'm swell," Mitch said, "but not too sure about her." He pointed to a nearby shape in too large sweats, and Victor's gaze swiveled to Sydney, who sat on the floor, dazed. He'd shut down their nerves the moment he realized what was happening, or at least dulled them as much as he was safely able, so he knew she was physically all right. But she did look shaken. A pang of guilt, something foreign after a decade in jail, nudged his ribs.

"Sorry," he said quietly. He reached out to help her up, but thought better. Instead he stood, and made his way toward the hall bathroom.

"Mitch," he called back. "See she gets to bed."

And with that he closed the door behind him.

XXV

TEN YEARS AGO
LOCKLAND UNIVERSITY

VICTOR didn't revive Angie. He didn't try. He knew he should, or should want to, but the last thing he needed was more evidence of himself at the crime scene. He swallowed hard, cringing both at his ability to be so rational at a moment like this, and at the thought of the term. Crime. Scene. Besides, he could *feel* that she was dead. No charge. No energy.

So he did the only thing he could think to do. He called Eli.

"Where the *hell* are you, Vale?" A car door slammed in the background. "You think this shit is funny—"

"Angie's dead."

Victor hadn't been sure whether or not he would say that, but the words had formed and spilled out before he could catch them. He'd expected them to hurt his throat, to lodge in his chest, but they flowed out unrestricted. He knew he should be panicking, but he felt numb, and the numbness made him calm. Was it shock, he wondered, this steadiness that came to him now, that had been so easy to summon with Angie dying at his feet? Or was it something else? He listened to the silence on the other end of the phone until Eli broke it.

"How?" growled Eli.

"It was an accident," said Victor, maneuvering his cell so he could pull his shirt back on. He'd had to step around Angie's body to reach it. He didn't look at her.

"What did you do?"

"She was helping me with a test. I had an idea and it worked and—"

"What do you mean it worked?" Eli's tone went cold.

"I mean . . . I mean it worked this time." He let it sink in. Eli clearly understood, because he stayed quiet. He was listening. Victor had his attention, and he liked that. But he was surprised that Eli seemed more interested in his experiment than in Angie. Angie, who had always kept his monsters back. Angie, who was always getting in the way. No, she had been more than a distraction to both of them, hadn't she? Victor looked down at the body then, expecting to feel some shade of the guilt that had washed over him when he'd lied to her before, but there was nothing. He wondered if Eli had felt this strange detachment, too, when he woke up on the bathroom floor. Like everything was real, but nothing mattered.

"Tell me what happened," pressed Eli, losing patience.

Victor gazed around the room at the table, the straps, the machines that had once hummed but now appeared to have burned out, fuses blown. The whole place was dark.

"Where are you?" he snapped when Victor didn't answer.

"The labs," he said. "We were—" The pain came out of nowhere. His pulse quickened, the air thrummed, and a breath later Victor doubled over. It crackled over him, through him, lit up his skin and his bones and every inch of muscle in between.

"You were *what*?" demanded Eli.

Victor clutched at the table, biting back a scream. The pain was horrific, as if every muscle in his body had cramped. As if he were being electrocuted all over again. *Stop*, he thought. *Stop*, he begged. And then he finally pictured the pain as a switch, and snapped it off, and it was gone.

His pulse dropped, the air thinned, and he felt *nothing*. Victor was left gasping, dazed. He'd dropped the phone to the linoleum. He reached down a shaking hand and lifted the cell back to his ear.

Eli was practically shouting. "Look," he was saying, "just stay there. I don't know what you've done, but stay there. You hear me? Don't move."

And Victor might have actually stayed put, if he hadn't heard the double-click.

The landline in their apartment had been provided by the university. It made a faint double-click when it was lifted from its spot on the wall. Now, as Eli spoke to him on his cell and instructed him to stay put, and as Victor tried to get his coat on, he could just make out that small double-click in the background. He frowned. A double-click, followed by three tonal taps: 9-1-1.

"Don't move," Eli said again. "I'll be right there."

Victor nodded carefully, forgetting how easy it was to lie when he didn't have to look Eli in the face.

"Okay," he said, "I'll be here." He hung up.

Victor finished pulling on his coat, and cast a last glance at the room. This was a mess. Aside from the body, the scene didn't scream murder, but the contorted shape of Angie's corpse showed it wasn't exactly natural, either. He took a sanitary wipe from a box in the corner and cleaned the bars on the table, resisting the urge to wipe down every object in the room. Then it *would* look like a crime. He knew he was written on this lab, somewhere, despite how careful he'd been. He knew he was probably on the security footage, too. But he was out of time.

Victor Vale left the lab, and then he ran.

AS he made his way toward the apartment—he needed to speak to Eli in person, needed to make him understand—he marveled at how good he felt physically. High from the chase, and from the kill, but free from pain. Then, at the edge of a streetlight, he looked down and saw his hand was bleeding. He must have caught it on something. But he didn't feel it. And not just in the adrenaline-blots-out-minor-injuries way. He didn't feel it at *all*. He tried to summon that strange humming air, tried to lower his own pain threshold a fraction, just to see how he was *really* faring, and ended up doubled over, bracing himself against a light post.

Not so good, then.

He definitely felt like he'd died. Again. His hands ached from gripping the handles on the table, and he wondered if any bones were broken. Every muscle in the rest of his body groaned, and his head hurt so much he thought he might be sick. When the sidewalk began to tip, he threw the switch back. Pain blinked out. He gave himself a moment to breathe, to regain himself, and straightened in the pool of light. He felt *nothing*. And right now, nothing felt amazing. Nothing felt heavenly. He tipped his head back, and laughed. Not one of those maniacal laughs. Not even a loud laugh.

A cough of a laugh, an amazed exhale.

But even if it had been louder, no one would have heard it, not over the sirens.

The two squad cars screeched to a stop in front of him, and Victor hardly had time to process their arrival before he was thrown to the concrete, cuffed, and a black hood thrust over his head. He felt himself being shoved into the backseat of the cop car.

The hood was an interesting touch, but Victor supremely

disliked the sensation of being blindfolded. The car would turn, and his weight would shift, and without any visual cues or physical discomfort to orient himself, he'd nearly topple over. They seemed to be taking the turns purposefully fast.

Victor realized that he could react. Fight back without having to touch them. Without even having to *see* them. But he restrained himself.

It seemed unnecessarily dangerous to hurt the cops while they were driving. Just because he could turn his own pain off didn't mean he wouldn't die if they wrecked the vehicle, so he focused his attention on staying calm. Which was, again, too easy, given all that had happened. The calm troubled him; the fact that the physical absence of pain could elicit such a mental absence of panic was at once unnerving and rather fascinating. If he weren't currently in the back of a cop car, he would have wanted to make a thesis note.

The car turned hard, slamming him against the door, and Victor swore, not out of pain so much as habit. The cuffs dug into his wrists and when he felt something warm and wet run down his fingers, he decided to lower his threshold. Feeling nothing could lead to injury, and he wasn't Eli. He couldn't heal. He tried to feel. Just a little and—

Victor gasped and tipped his head against the seat. Hot pain tore through his wrists where the metal dug in, and magnified, his threshold plummeting. He clenched his jaw and tried to find balance. Tried to find normal. Sensation was nuanced. Not on and off, but an entire spectrum, a dial with hundreds of notches, not a switch. He closed his eyes despite the darkness of the hood, and found a place between numb and normal. His wrists ached dully, something closer to stiffness than sharp pain.

This was going to take some getting used to.

Finally the car stopped, the door opened, and a pair of hands guided him out.

"Can you take the hood off?" he asked the darkness. "Don't you have to read me rights? Did I miss that part?"

The person guiding him nudged him to the right and his shoulder clipped a wall. Campus police, maybe? He heard a door open, and felt a slight change in the sounds of the space. This new room had almost no furniture and smooth walls, he could tell by the echo. A chair screeched back, someone pushed Victor down into it, uncuffed one of his hands and recuffed them both to a place on a metal table. Footsteps faded, and were gone.

A door closed.

The room was silent.

A door opened. Footsteps drew closer. And then at last the hood came off. The room was very, very bright, and a man sat down across from him, broad-shouldered, black-haired, and unamused. Victor looked around at the interrogation room, which was smaller than he imagined, and a bit shabbier. It was also locked from the outside. Any stunt in here would be an utter waste.

"Mr. Vale, my name is Detective Stell."

"I thought those hoods were only used for spies and terrorists and bad action movies," said Victor, referring to the pile of black fabric now sitting between them. "Is it even legal?"

"Our officers are trained to use their judgment in order to protect themselves," said Detective Stell.

"Is my eyesight a threat?"

Stell sighed. "Do you know what an EO is, Mr. Vale?"

He felt his pulse tick up at the word, the air buzzing faintly around him, but swallowed, willed himself to find his calm. He nodded slightly. "I've heard of them."

"And do you know what happens when someone shouts EO?"

Victor shook his head. "Every time someone makes a 911 call and uses that word, I have to get up out of bed, and come all the way down to the station to check things out. Doesn't matter if the call-in's a prank by some kids, or the ravings of a homeless man. I have to take it seriously."

Victor furrowed his brow. "Sorry someone wasted your time, sir."

Stell rubbed his eyes. "Did they, Mr. Vale?"

Victor gave a tight laugh. "You can't be serious. Someone told you I was an EO"—he already knew who, of course—"and you actually believe them? What the hell kind of ExtraOrdinary am I supposed to be?" Victor stood but the cuffs were locked firmly to the table.

"Sit down, Mr. Vale." Stell pretended to examine his papers. "The student who called in the report, a Mr. Cardale, also said that you confessed to the murder of student Angela Knight." His eyes flicked up. "Now, even if I want to overlook this EO business, and I'm not saying I do, I take a body pretty damn seriously. And that's what we've got on our hands over at Lockland's engineering school. So, is any of this true?"

Victor sat and took a few long, deep breaths. Then he shook his head. "Eli's been drinking."

"Is that so?" Stell sounded unconvinced.

Victor watched a drop of blood fall from the cuffs to the table. He was careful to keep his eyes on the one, two, three drops as he spoke. "I was at the labs when Angie died." He knew the security cameras would show as much. "I needed to get away from a party, and she came and picked me up. I didn't want to go home, and she said she had work to do . . . it's thesis time and all . . . so I went with her to the engineering school. I left the room for a couple minutes, just to get a drink, and when I came back . . . I saw her on the floor and called Eli—"

"You didn't call 911."

"I was upset. Distraught."

"You don't seem distraught."

"No, now I'm pissed off. And in shock. And cuffed to a table." Victor raised his voice, because now seemed like an appropriate time to do so. "Look, Eli was drunk. Maybe he still is. He told me it was my fault. I kept trying to explain that it had been a heart attack, or a malfunction in the equipment—Angie was always messing around with voltage—but he wouldn't listen. He said he'd call the police. So I left. Made my way home to *talk* to him. And that's where I was heading when the cops showed up." He looked up at the detective, and gestured to their current situation. "As for this EO stuff, I'm as confused as you are. Eli's been working too hard. His thesis is on EOs, did he tell you that? He's obsessed with them. Paranoid. Doesn't sleep, doesn't eat, just works on his theories."

"No," said Stell across the table, making a note. "Mr. Cardale neglected to mention that." He finished writing, and tossed the pen aside.

"This is insane," said Victor. "I'm not a murderer, and I'm not an EO. I'm a pre-med student." At least the last one was true.

Stell looked at his watch. "We'll keep you overnight in a holding cell," he explained. "Meanwhile, I'll send someone over to see Mr. Cardale, test his blood alcohol level, and get his full statement. If, in the morning, we have proof that Mr. Cardale's testimony is compromised, and no evidence ties you to the death of Angela Knight, we'll let you go. You'll still be a suspect, understand? That's the best I can do right now. Sound good?"

No. It didn't sound good at all. But Victor would make do. The hood stayed off as an officer led him to the cell, and on the way he made careful note of the number of cops and the number of doors and the time it took to reach the holding area. Victor had always been a problem-solver. His problems had certainly been growing bigger, but the rules still held. The steps to solving a problem, from elementary math to breaking out of a police station, remained the same. A simple matter of understanding the problem, and selecting the best solution. Victor was now in a cell. The cell was small and square and came complete with bars and a man who was twice his age and smelled like piss and tobacco. A guard sat at the end of a hallway reading a paper.

The most obvious solution was to kill the cellmate, call the guard over, and kill the guard. The alternative was to wait until morning, and hope that Eli failed a breathalyzer, that the security cameras were limited to the entryways, and that he'd left no material evidence in the lab to link him to the death.

Picking the best solution really depended on your definition of *best*. Victor examined the man slumped against the cot, and got to work.

∞

HE took the long way home.

The first touches of dawn warmed the sky as he walked, rubbing the dried blood from his wrists. At least, he consoled himself, he hadn't killed anyone. Victor was, in fact, quite proud of his restraint. He thought, for a moment, that the chain-smoking cellmate might be dead, but he was still breathing, the last time Victor had checked. Admittedly, he hadn't wanted to get too close. As he made his way home, he felt a trickle of wet on his face and touched the place below his nose. It came away red. Victor wiped his face on his sleeve, and made a mental note to be more careful. He'd pushed himself a lot in one night, especially considering he'd died first.

Sleep. Sleep would help. But it would have to wait.

Because first, he had to deal with Eli.

XXVI

TWO DAYS AGO
THE ESQUIRE HOTEL

VICTOR stood in the bathroom and waited for the hotel to quiet around him. Beyond the door he heard Mitch lead Sydney back to bed, muttering an apology on his behalf. They should never have picked her up, but he couldn't shake the feeling that she would come in handy. She had secrets, and he planned to learn them. Still, he really hadn't meant to hurt her. He prided himself on control, but for all his efforts, he hadn't found a way to fully manage his power during sleep. Which is why he didn't sleep, or at least, not much.

He ran cold water over his hands and face, waiting for the faint electrical buzz to stop. When it didn't, he turned it inward, wincing as the humming vanished from the air around him and reappeared in his bones, his muscles. He clutched the granite counter as his body grounded the current, and several long moments later, the shudder passed, leaving Victor tired, but stable again.

He met his gaze in the mirror and began to unbutton his shirt, exposing the scars from the bullets of Eli's gun one by one. He ran his fingers over them, touching the three spots where he'd been shot the way a man might cross himself. One tucked under his ribs, one above his heart, and one that had actually hit him in the back, but at close enough range that it passed right through. He'd memorized their position so that when he did see Eli, he could repay the gesture. Hell, if the bullets lodged, there was a chance Eli would heal around them. It gave Victor a modicum of pleasure to think of that.

Perhaps the wounds would have earned him some respect in prison, but by the time he'd integrated, they were long faded. Besides, Victor had found other ways of asserting himself at Wrighton, from the subtle discomfort inmates felt when they displeased him to the instant agony he used more sparingly, the kind of pain that left them gasping at his feet. But he didn't only *cause* pain; Victor also took it away. He'd learned to gift painlessness, to trade it. Amazed by the lengths men would go to avoid any form of suffering, Victor had become a dealer in a drug only he could provide. Jail had, in some ways, been pleasant.

But even there Eli had haunted him, tarnished his enjoyment by clinging to his thoughts, whispering in his head, ruining his peace. And after ten years of waiting, it was Victor's turn, to get into Eli's head and do some ruining.

He rebuttoned his shirt, and the scars vanished again, from view but not from memory.

XXVII

TEN YEARS AGO
LOCKLAND UNIVERSITY

VICTOR hoisted himself up onto his windowsill, thankful that he'd left it cracked, and that they lived on the first floor and thus he was only forced to contend with the five steps' worth of height leading from the street up to the building's entrance. He paused on the sill, straddling it as morning light seeped into everything around him, and listened for sounds within the apartment. The place was quiet, but Victor knew Eli was home. He could *feel* him.

His heart fluttered gently with the thrill of what would happen next, but that was all it was, a flutter. No pounding panic. This new calm was becoming unsettling. Victor struggled to assess it. The absence of pain led to an absence of fear, and the absence of fear led to a disregard for consequence. He knew it was a bad idea to break out of the cell, just as he knew what he was about to do was a bad idea. A worse idea. He could track his thoughts better now, marveled at the way they circled round to solutions that bypassed caution and favored the immediate, the violent, the rash, the way a crippled man favors his good leg. Victor's mind had always been drawn to those solutions, but he had been impeded by an understanding of right and wrong, or at least what he knew others saw as right and wrong. But now, this . . . this was simple. Elegant.

He paused long enough to smooth his hair in the mirror, distressed by how grungy death and half a night in a cell had made him look. Then he met his own eyes—the new calm had made them a fraction paler—and his reflection smiled. It was a cold smile, a slightly foreign one, bordering on arrogant, but Victor didn't mind. He rather liked that smile. It looked like something Eli would wear.

Victor stepped out of his room and made his way gingerly down the hall to the kitchen. On the table were a set of knives and a notebook, half a page filled with Eli's tight script and dotted with blood. As for Eli himself, Victor could see him on the living room couch, head bowed forward in thought, or maybe prayer. Victor paused a moment to watch him. It seemed odd that Eli couldn't sense Victor's presence the way Victor sensed his. That was the problem with an inward ability like healing. Self-absorbed to the last, he thought as he took up a large knife and dragged its tip along the table, eliciting a high scratch.

Eli spun up from the couch in a fluid motion. "Vic."

"I'm disappointed," said Victor.

"What are you doing here?"

"You turned me in."

"You killed Angie." The words snagged slightly in Eli's throat. Victor was surprised by the emotion in his friend's voice.

"Did you love her?" he asked. "Or are you just mad I took something back?"

"She was a *person,* Victor, not a thing, and you murdered her."

"It was an accident," he said. "And it's your fault, really. If you had just helped me . . ."

Eli ran his hands over his face. "How could you do this?"

"How could *you?*" asked Victor, lifting the knife fully from the table as he spoke. "You called the cops and you accused me of being an EO. I didn't rat *you* out, you know. I could have." He scratched his head with the tip of the knife. "Why would you tell them something so silly? Did you know they have special people who come in if there's an EO suspected? Some guy named Stell. Did you know that?"

"You've lost it." Eli sidestepped, keeping his back to the wall. "Put the knife down. It's not like you can hurt me."

Victor smiled at the challenge. A quick step forward, and Eli tried to step back on instinct but met the wall and Victor met him.

The knife slid in. It was easier than he imagined. Like a vanishing act, one moment the metal glinted and the next it was gone, buried in Eli's stomach to the hilt.

"You know what I figured out?" Victor leaned into him as he spoke. "Watching you in the street that night, picking the glass from your hand? You can't heal yourself until I take the knife out." He twisted it, and Eli groaned. His feet went out from under him and he began to slide down the wall, but Victor hoisted him up by the handle.

"I'm not even using my new trick yet," he said. "It's not as flashy as yours, but it's rather effective. Want to see it?"

Victor didn't wait for a response. The air buzzed around him. He didn't worry about a dial. Up. That's all he cared about. Up. Eli screamed, and the sound made Victor feel good. Not in a sun-is-out-and-life-is-wonderful way, of course, but in a punishing way. A controlling way. Eli had betrayed him. Eli deserved a little pain. He would heal. When this was over, he wouldn't even have a scar. The least Victor could do was try to make an impression. Victor let go of the knife handle and watched Eli's body collapse to the floor.

"A note for your thesis," he said as his friend lay there, gasping. "You thought our powers were somehow a reflection of our nature. God playing with mirrors, but you're wrong. It's not about God.

It's about us. The way we think. The thought that's strong enough to keep us alive. To bring us back. You want to know how I know?" He turned his attention to the table, looking for something new and sharp. "Because all I could think about when I was dying was the pain." He cranked the dial up in his mind, and let the room fill with Eli's screams. "And how badly I wanted to make it stop."

Victor turned the dial down again, and heard Eli's screams fade as he reached the table. He was looking over the various blades when the room exploded with noise. A very sudden, very loud noise. Drywall crumbled a foot away, and Victor turned back to find Eli clutching his stomach with one hand and a gun with the other. The knife was on the floor in a satisfying amount of blood, and Victor wondered with a scientific curiosity how long it would take Eli's body to regenerate itself. Then the second shot rang out, much closer to Victor's head, and he frowned.

"Do you even know how to use that?" he asked, thumbing a long, thin knife. Eli's hands were shaking visibly around the gun's grip.

"Angie is dead—," said Eli.

"Yes, I know—"

"...but so are you." It wasn't a threat. "I don't know who you are, but you're not Victor. You're something that's crawled into his skin. A devil wearing him."

"Ouch," said Victor, and for some reason, the word made him laugh. He couldn't stop laughing. Eli looked disgusted, and it made Victor want to stab him again. He felt behind him for the nearest knife, and watched Eli's fingers tighten on the gun.

"You're something else," he said. "Victor died."

"*We* died, Eli. And we both came back."

"No, no, I don't think so. Not entirely. Something's wrong, missing, gone. Can't you feel it? I can," said Eli, and he actually sounded *scared*. Victor was disappointed. He'd hoped that maybe Eli felt it, too, this calm, but apparently he felt something else entirely.

"Maybe you're right," said Victor. He was willing to admit that he felt different. "But if I'm missing something, then so are you. Life is about compromises. Or did you think because you put yourself in God's hands that He would make you all you were and more?"

"He did," growled Eli, pulling the trigger.

This time he didn't miss. Victor felt the impact, and looked down at the hole in his shirt, glad he'd bothered to turn his pain off. He touched the spot and his fingers came away red. Distantly, he knew this was a bad place to be shot.

Victor sighed, looking up. "That's a little self-righteous, don't you think?"

Eli took a step closer. The wound in his stomach had already healed, and the color was back in his face. Victor knew he needed to keep talking.

"Admit it," he said, "you feel different, too. Death takes something with it. What did it take from you?"

Eli lifted the gun again. "My fear."

Victor managed a dark smile. Eli's hands were shaking, and his jaw was clenched. "I still see fear."

"I'm not afraid," said Eli. "I'm just sorry."

He fired again. The force nudged Victor back a step. His fingers closed around the nearest knife and he swung, digging it into Eli's outstretched arm. The gun clattered to the floor, and Eli lunged back to avoid another blow.

Victor meant to follow it up, but his vision blurred. Just for a moment. He blinked, desperate to refocus.

"You may be able to turn the pain off," said Eli, "but you can't stop the blood loss."

Victor took a step forward but the room leaned. He braced himself against the table. There was a lot of blood on the floor. He wasn't sure how much of it was his. When he looked up again, Eli was there. And then Victor was on the ground. He pushed himself to his hands and knees but couldn't seem to force his body farther up. An arm buckled beneath his weight. His eyes unfocused again.

Eli was talking, but he couldn't quite make out the words. And then he heard the gun scraping across the floor as it was lifted, cocked. Something hit him in the back, like a soft punch, and his body stopped listening. Darkness crept in at the edges of his sight, the kind he'd wanted so badly when the pain on the table had been too much.

A thick darkness.

He began to sink into it as he heard Eli moving around the room, talking into his phone, something about medical attention. He was twisting his voice to sound panicked, but his face, even the blur that was his expression, was calm, composed. Victor saw Eli's shoes walk away before everything faded.

XXVIII

TWO DAYS AGO
THE ESQUIRE HOTEL

MITCH led Sydney back to her room, and closed the door behind her. She stood in the dark for several minutes, dazed by the echo of pain, and the photo in the newspaper, and Victor's pale eyes, dead before he came back to himself. She shivered. It had been a long two days. She'd spent the night before under an overpass, tucked into the place where two concrete corners met, trying to stay dry. Winter had dissolved into a cold, wet spring. It had started raining the day before she'd been shot, and hadn't stopped since.

She tucked her fingers into the cuff of the stolen sweatshirt. Her skin still felt strange. Her whole arm had been on fire, the gunshot wound a blazing center in a web of pain, and then the power had been cut. That was the only way Sydney could think of it, like the thing connecting her to the pain had been severed, leaving in its place a pins-and-needles numbness. Sydney rubbed at her skin, waiting for the feeling to come back. She didn't like numbness. It reminded her of cold, and Sydney hated being cold.

She pressed her ear to the door and listened for signs of Victor, but the bathroom door stayed firmly shut, and finally, as the prickle left her skin, she crawled back to the too-big bed in the strange hotel, curled in on herself, and tried to find sleep. At first it wouldn't come, and in a weak moment she wished Serena were there. Her sister would perch on the edge of the bed, and stroke her hair, claiming the gesture made thoughts quieter. Sydney would close her eyes and let everything hush, first her mind and then the world as her sister's touch dragged her down into sleep. But Sydney caught herself, twined her fingers in the hotel sheets, and remembered that Serena—the one who would have done those things—was gone. The thought was like cold water, sending Sydney's heart into rapid fire all over again, so she decided not to think of Serena at all, and instead tried a counting trick one of her sitters had taught her. Not counting up, or counting down, just counting one-two-one-two as she breathed in and breathed out. One-two. Soft and steady, like a heartbeat, until finally the hotel room sank away, and she slept.

And when she did, she dreamed of water.

XXIX

LAST YEAR
BRIGHTON COMMONS

SYDNEY Clarke died on a cool March day.

It was just before lunch, and it was all Serena's fault.

The Clarke sisters looked identical, despite the fact that Serena was seven years older, and seven inches taller. The resemblance stemmed partly from genes and partly from Sydney's adoration of her big sister. She dressed like Serena, acted like Serena, and was, in almost every way, a miniature version of her sister. A shadow, distorted by age instead of sun. They had the same blue eyes and the same blond hair, but Serena made Sydney cut hers short so people wouldn't stare. The resemblance was that uncanny.

As much as they looked like each other, they bore little resemblance to their parents—not that they were often around to provide comparison. Serena used to tell Sydney that those people weren't their parents at all, that the girls had washed ashore in a small blue boat from some faraway place, or been found in the first-class compartment on a train, or been smuggled in by spies. If Sydney questioned the story, Serena would simply insist that her sister had been too young to remember. Sydney was still fairly sure they were just fantasies, but never *entirely* sure; Serena was very good at telling tales. She had always been convincing (that was the word her sister liked to use for *lying*).

It had been Serena's idea to walk out on the frozen lake and have a picnic. They used to have them every year, right around New Year's when the lake in the center of Brighton Commons was nothing but a block of ice, but with Serena off at college they hadn't had the chance. So it was a long weekend in March, toward the end of Serena's spring break, and a few days shy of Sydney's twelfth birthday, when they finally got to pack their lunch and head out onto the ice. Serena wore the picnic blanket as a cape and regaled her little sister with the latest tale of how the two had come to be called Clarkes. It involved pirates, or superheroes, Sydney wasn't paying attention; she was too busy taking mental pictures of her sister, shots she'd cling to when Serena left again. They reached what Serena deemed to be a good bit of lake, and she tugged the blanket from her shoulders, spread it out on the ice, and began to unload the eclectic assortment of food she'd found in the pantry.

Now, the problem with March (as opposed to January or February) was that even though it was still quite cold, the depth of the ice was waning, uneven. Small patches of warmth during the days caused the frozen lake by their house to begin to melt. You wouldn't even notice the change, unless it broke beneath you.

Which it did.

The cracks were small and silent beneath a film of snow as the two arranged their picnic, and by the time the sound of splitting ice had grown loud enough for them to hear, it was too late. Serena had just started another story when the ice gave way, plunging both into the dark, half-frozen water.

The cold forced all the air from Sydney's lungs, and even though Serena had taught her how to swim, her legs got tangled in the blanket as it sank, dragging her down with it. The icy water bit at her skin, her eyes. She clawed toward the surface and Serena's kicking legs but it was no use. She kept sinking, and kept reaching, and all she could think as she sank farther and farther away from her sister was *come back come back come back*. And then the world began to freeze around her, and there was so much cold, and that began to vanish, too, leaving only darkness.

Sydney later learned that Serena *had* come back, that she had pulled her up through the freezing water and onto the unfreezing lake before collapsing beside her.

Someone had seen the bodies on the ice.

By the time the rescue crew got out to them, Serena was barely breathing, her heart stubbornly dragging itself through every beat—and then it stopped—and Sydney was the cool blue-white of marble, just as still. Both girls were dead at the scene, but because they were also technically frozen, they couldn't officially be declared, and the paramedics dragged the Clarke sisters to the hospital to warm them up.

What followed was a miracle. The sisters came back. Their pulses started, and they took a breath, and then another—that's all living is, really—and they woke up, and they sat up, and they spoke, and they were, in every discernable way, alive.

There was only one problem.

Sydney wouldn't warm up. She felt fine, more or less, but her pulse was too slow, and her temperature too low—she overheard two doctors say that with her stats, she should be in a coma—and they deemed her too fragile to leave the hospital.

Serena was another matter entirely. Sydney thought she was acting strange, even moodier than usual, but no one else—not the doctors and nurses, not the therapists, not even their parents, who had cut a trip short when they heard about the accident—seemed to notice the change. Serena complained of headaches, so they gave her painkillers. She complained of the hospital, so they let her go. Just like that. Sydney had heard them talking about her sister's condition, but when she walked up and said she wanted to leave, they stepped aside and let her pass. Serena had always gotten her way, but never like this. Never without a fight.

"You're going? Just like that?" Sydney was sitting in her bed. Serena was standing in the doorway in street clothes. She had a box in her hands.

"I'm missing school. And I hate hospitals, Syd," she said. "You know that."

Of course Sydney knew. She hated hospitals, too. "But I don't understand. They're just letting you go?"

"Seems so."

"Then tell them to let me go, too."

Serena stood beside the hospital bed, and ran her hand over Sydney's hair. "You need to stay a little longer."

The fight bled out of Sydney, and she found herself nodding, even as tears slid down her cheeks. Serena brushed them away with her thumb, and said, "I'm not gone." It reminded Sydney of sinking beneath the surface, of wanting her sister so badly to *come back*.

"Do you remember," she asked her big sister, "what you were thinking in the lake? When the ice broke?"

Serena's brow crinkled. "You mean, besides *fuck, it's cold*?" Sydney almost smiled. Serena didn't. Her hand slid from Sydney's face. "I just remember thinking *no*. No, not like this." She set the box she'd been holding on the side table. "Happy birthday, Syd."

And then Serena left. And Sydney didn't. She asked to leave, and they refused. She pleaded and begged and promised she was fine, and they refused. It was her birthday, and she didn't want to spend it alone in a place like this. She couldn't spend it here. But they still said no.

Her parents both worked. They had to go.

A week, they promised her. Stay a week.

Sydney didn't have much choice. She stayed.

SYDNEY hated evenings at the hospital.

The whole floor was too quiet, too settled. It was the only time the heavy panic set in, panic that she would never leave, never get to go home. She would be forgotten here, wearing the same pale clothes as everyone else, blending in with the patients and the nurses and the walls, and her family would be outside in the world and she would bleed away like a memory, like a colorful shirt washed too many times. As if Serena knew exactly what she'd need, the box by Sydney's bed contained a purple scarf. It was brighter than anything in her small suitcase.

She clung to the strip of color, wrapped the scarf around her neck despite the fact that she wasn't very cold (well, she was, according to the doctors, but she didn't *feel* very cold), and began to walk. She paced the hospital wing, relishing the moments when the nurses' eyes flicked her way. They saw her, and they didn't stop her, and that made Sydney feel like Serena, around whom the seas kept parting. When Sydney had walked the entire floor three times, she took the stairs to the next one. It was a different shade of beige. The change was so subtle that visitors would never notice, but Sydney had been staring at the walls on her own floor enough to pick out their paint chip on one of those walls with ten thousand colors, two hundred kinds of white.

People were sicker on this floor. Sydney could smell it even before she heard the coughing or saw the stretcher being wheeled from a room, bare but for a large sheet. It smelled like stronger disinfectants here. Someone in a room down the hall shouted, and the nurse wheeling the stretcher paused, left it in the hall, and hurried into the patient's room. Sydney followed to see what the fuss was about.

A man in the room at the end of the hall was unhappy, but she couldn't understand why. Sydney stood in the hall and tried to catch a glimpse, but a curtain was drawn in the room, bisecting it and shielding the shouting man from view, and the stretcher was blocking her way. She leaned on the gurney, just a little, and shivered.

The sheet she was touching had been put there to cover something. The something was a body. And when she brushed against it, the body twitched. Sydney jumped back, and covered her mouth to keep from shouting. Pressed against the beige wall she looked from the nurses in the patient's room to the body under the sheet on the stretcher. It twitched a second time. Sydney wrapped the tails of her purple scarf around her hands. She felt frozen all over again but in a different way. It wasn't icy water. It was fear.

"What are you doing here?" asked a nurse in an unflattering shade of beige-green. Sydney had no idea what to say, so she simply pointed. The nurse took her wrist and began to lead her down the hall.

"No," said Syd, finally. *"Look."*

The nurse sighed and glanced back at the sheet, which twitched again.

The nurse screamed.

SYDNEY was assigned therapy.

The doctors said it was to help her cope with the trauma of seeing a dead body (even though she didn't actually see it) and Sydney would have protested, but after her unsupervised trip to the next floor up she found herself confined to her room, and there wasn't any other way for her to spend her time, so she agreed. She refrained, however, from mentioning the fact that she had touched the body a moment before it came back to life.

They called the person's recovery a miracle.

Sydney laughed, mostly because that's what they had called *her* recovery.

She wondered if someone had accidentally touched her, too.

∞

AFTER a week, Sydney's body temperature still hadn't come back up, but she seemed otherwise stable, and the doctors finally agreed to release her the next day. That night, Sydney snuck out of her hospital room and went down to the morgue, to find out for sure if what had happened in that hall was truly a miracle, a happy accident, a fluke, or if she somehow had something to do with it.

Half an hour later she hurried out of the morgue, thoroughly disgusted and spotted with stale blood, but with her hypothesis confirmed.

Sydney Clarke could raise the dead.

XXX

YESTERDAY
THE ESQUIRE HOTEL

SYDNEY woke up the next morning in the too-large bed in the strange hotel, for a moment unsure of where, when, or how she was. But as she blinked away sleep, the details trickled back, the rain and the car and the two peculiar men, both of whom she could hear talking beyond the door.

Mitch's brusque tone and Victor's lower, smoother one, seemed to seep through the walls of her room. She sat up, stiff and hungry, and adjusted the oversized sweatpants on her hips before wandering out in search of food.

The two men were standing in the kitchen. Mitch was pouring coffee and talking to Victor, who was absently crossing out lines in a magazine. Mitch looked up as she walked in.

"How's your arm?" asked Victor, still blacking out words.

There was no pain, only a stiff feeling. She supposed she had him to thank for that.

"It's fine," she said. Victor set his pen aside and rolled a bag of bagels across the counter toward her. In the corner of the kitchen sat several bags of groceries. He nodded at them.

"Don't know what you eat, so . . ."

"I'm not a puppy," she said, fighting back a smile. She took a bagel and rolled the bag back across the counter, where it butted up against Victor's magazine. She watched him black out the lines of text, and remembered the article from last night, and the photo that went with it, the one she'd been reaching for when Victor woke. Her eyes drifted back to the couch. It wasn't there anymore.

"What's wrong?"

The question brought her back. Victor had his elbows on the counter, fingers loosely intertwined.

"There was a paper over there last night, with a picture on it. Where is it?"

Victor frowned, but slid the newspaper page out from under the magazine, and held it up for her to see. "This?"

Sydney felt a shiver, somewhere down deep.

"Why do you have a picture of him?" she asked, pointing at the grainy shot of the civilian beside the block of mostly blacked-out text.

Victor rounded the counter in slow, measured steps, and held the article up between them, inches from her face.

"Do you know him?" he asked, eyes alight. Sydney nodded. "How?"

Sydney swallowed. "He's the one who shot me."

Victor leaned down until his face was very close to hers. "Tell me what happened."

XXXI

LAST YEAR
BRIGHTON COMMONS

SYDNEY told Serena about the incident in the morgue, and Serena laughed.

It wasn't a happy laugh, though, or a light laugh. Sydney didn't even think it was an oh-dear-my-sister-has-brain-damage-or-delusions-from-drowning laugh. There was something stuck in the laugh, and it made Sydney nervous.

Serena then told Sydney, in very calm, quiet words (which should have struck Sydney as odd right then and there because Serena had never been terribly calm or quiet) not to tell *anyone else* about the morgue, or the body in the hall, or anything even remotely related to resurrecting dead people, and to Sydney's own amazement, she didn't. From that moment, she felt no desire to share the strange news with anyone but Serena, and Serena seemed to want nothing to do with it.

So Sydney did the only thing she could. She went back to middle school, and tried not to touch anything dead. She made it to the end of the school year. She made it through the summer . . . even though Serena had somehow convinced the faculty to let her do a trip to Amsterdam for credit, and didn't come home, and when Sydney heard this she was so mad she almost wanted to tell or show someone what she could do, just to spite her sister. But she didn't. Serena always seemed to call, just before Sydney lost her temper. They would talk about nothing, just filling up space with how-are-yous and how-are-the-folks and how-are-classes and Sydney would cling to the sound of her sister's voice even though the words were empty. And then, as she felt the conversation ending, she'd ask Serena to come home, and Serena would say *no, not this time,* and Sydney would feel lost, alone, until her sister would say *I'm not gone, I'm not gone,* and Sydney would somehow believe her.

But even though she believed those words with a simple, unshakeable faith, it didn't mean they made her happy. Sydney's slow-beating heart began to sink over the fall, and then Christmas came and Serena didn't, and for some reason her parents—who'd always been adamant about one thing, and that was spending Christmas together, as if one well-represented holiday could make up for the other 364 days—didn't seem to mind. They hardly even noticed. But Sydney noticed, and it made her feel like cracking glass.

So it's no surprise that when Serena finally called and invited her to come visit, Sydney broke.

∞

"COME stay with me," said Serena. "It'll be fun!"

Serena had avoided her little sister for nearly a year. Sydney had kept her hair short, out of some vague sense of deference, or perhaps just nostalgia, but she was *not* happy. Not with her big sister, and not with the deviant flutter in her own chest at her sister's offer. She hated herself for still idolizing Serena.

"I'm in school," she said.

"Come for spring break," pressed Serena. "You can come up and stay through your birthday. Mom and Dad don't know how to celebrate anyway. I always planned everything. And you know I give you the best gifts."

Sydney shivered, remembering how the last birthday had gone. As if reading her mind, Serena said, "It's warmer here in Merit. We'll sit outside, relax. It will be good for you."

Serena's voice was too sweet. Sydney should have known. Forever and ever after Sydney would know, but not then. Not when it mattered.

"Okay," said Sydney at last, trying to hide her excitement. "I'd like that."

"Great!" Serena sounded so happy. Sydney could hear the smile in her voice. It made her smile, too. "I want you to meet someone while you're here," added Serena, in an afterthought kind of way.

"Who?" asked Sydney.

"Just a friend."

XXXII

A FEW DAYS AGO
UNIVERSITY OF MERIT

SERENA threw her arms around her little sister.

"Look at you!" she said, dragging her sister inside. "You're growing up."

Sydney had barely grown at all, actually. Less than an inch in the year since the accident. It wasn't just her height, either. Sydney's nails, her hair, everything about her crept forward. Slowly. Like melting ice.

When Serena teasingly mentioned her still-short hair, Sydney pretended the look had simply grown on her, implied that it had nothing to do with Serena anymore. Still, she wrapped her arms around her sister, and when her sister hugged back, Sydney felt as if broken threads, hundreds and hundreds of them, were stitching the two back together. Something in her started to thaw. Until a male voice cleared its throat.

"Oh, Sydney," said her sister, pulling away, "I want you to meet Eli."

She smiled when she said his name. A boy, college-aged, was sitting in a chair in Serena's apartment—one of the ones usually reserved for upperclassmen—and he stood up at the mention of his name, and stepped forward. He was handsome, with broad shoulders and a firm handshake and eyes that were brown but alive in that glittering, almost drunk sort of way. Sydney had a hard time looking away from him.

"Hi, Eli," she said.

"I've heard a lot about you," he said.

Sydney didn't say anything, because Serena had never mentioned Eli until the phone call, and then she'd only called him *a friend*. Judging by the way they looked at each other, that wasn't the whole truth.

"Come on," said Serena. "Put your stuff away and then we can all get to know each other."

When Sydney hesitated, Serena pulled the duffel from her sister's shoulder and walked away, leaving her alone with Eli for a moment. Sydney wondered why she felt like a sheep in a wolf's den. There was something dangerous about Eli, about the calm way he smiled and the lazy way he moved. He leaned on the arm of the chair he'd been sitting in.

"So," he said. "You're in eighth grade?"

Sydney nodded. "And you're a sophomore?" she asked. "Like Serena?"

Eli laughed soundlessly. "I'm a senior, actually."

"How long have you been dating my sister?"

Eli's smile flickered. "You like to ask questions."

Sydney frowned. "That's not an answer."

Serena came back into the room holding a soda for Sydney. "You two getting along?" And just like that the smile was back on Eli's face, broad enough that Sydney wondered how long until his cheeks would start to hurt. Sydney took the drink and Serena went to Eli and leaned against him, as if declaring allegiance. Sydney sipped the soda and watched as he kissed her sister's hair, his hand curling around her shoulder.

"So," said Serena, examining her little sister, "Eli wants to see your trick."

Sydney nearly choked on the soda. "I . . . I don't—"

"Come on, Syd," pressed Serena. "You can trust him."

She felt like Alice in Wonderland. Like the soda must have had a little *drink me* tag and now the room was shrinking, or she was growing, or either way there wasn't enough space. Enough air. Or had it been the cake that made Alice grow? She didn't know . . .

She took a step back.

"What's the matter, sis? You were pretty eager to show *me*."

"You told me not to . . ."

Serena's brow furrowed. "Well, now I'm telling you to do it." She pushed off Eli and came up to Sydney, wrapping her in a hug. "Don't worry, Syd," she whispered in her ear. "He's just like us."

"*Us?*" Sydney whispered back.

"Didn't I tell you?" cooed Serena. "I have a trick, too."

Sydney pulled away. "What? When? What is it?" She wondered if that had been the thing stuck in Serena's laugh the night she told her about raising the dead. A secret. But why didn't her sister tell her? Why wait until now?

"Uh-uh," Serena said, wagging her finger. "Trade you. You show us yours, and we'll show you ours."

For a very long moment, Sydney didn't know whether to run, or feel elated that she wasn't alone. That she and Serena . . . and Eli . . . had something to share. Serena took Sydney's face between her hands.

"You show us yours," she said again, smooth and slow.

Sydney found herself taking a deep breath, and nodding.

"Okay," she said. "But we have to find a body."

ELI held open the front passenger door. "After you."

"Where are we going?" asked Sydney as she climbed in.

"On a road trip," said Serena. She got behind the wheel and Eli took the backseat, directly behind Sydney. She didn't like that, either; didn't like that he could see her but she couldn't see him. Serena asked absently about Brighton Commons as the university buildings beyond the car gave way to smaller, sparser structures.

"Why wouldn't you come home?" asked Sydney under her breath. "I missed you. I needed you and you promised you weren't gone but—"

"Don't dwell," said Serena. "What matters is that I'm here now, and you're here, too."

The structures gave way to fields.

"And we're going to have a ball," said Eli from the backseat. Sydney shivered. "Isn't that right, Serena?"

Sydney glanced at her sister, and was surprised to see a shadow cross Serena's face as she met Eli's gaze in the rearview mirror.

"That's right," she said at last.

The road got narrower, rougher.

When the car finally stopped, they were at the seam between a forest and a field. Eli got out first, and led the way out into the field, the grass coming up to his knees. Eventually he stopped and looked down.

"Here we are."

Sydney followed his gaze, and felt her stomach lurch.

There, tucked amid the grass, was a corpse.

"Dead bodies aren't that easy to come by," explained Eli lightly. "You have to go to a morgue, or a cemetery, or make one yourself."

"Please don't tell me you . . ."

Eli laughed. "Don't be silly, Syd."

"Eli shadows over at the hospital," explained Serena. "He stole a cadaver from the morgue."

Sydney swallowed. The corpse was dressed. Weren't cadavers supposed to be naked?

"But what is the body doing out here?" she asked. "Why didn't we just go to the morgue?"

"*Sydney,*" said Eli. She really didn't like the way he kept using her name. Like they were close. "There are *people* in a morgue. And not all of them are dead."

"Yeah, well, we didn't have to drive half an hour away," she shot back. "Aren't there any fields, or abandoned lots, near the college? Why are we all the way—"

"Sydney," Serena's voice cut through the chill March air. "Stop whining."

And she did. The complaint died in her throat. She rubbed at her eyes, and her hand came away with black smudges from the makeup she'd put on in the cab as it wove its way toward the University of Merit. She'd wanted to impress Serena by looking grown up. But right now, she didn't feel grown up. Right now, she wanted nothing more than to curl into a ball, or to crawl out of her own skin. Instead she stood very still and looked down at the corpse of a middle-aged man and thought of the last time she'd been with a body (she didn't count the dead hamster in school because no one even knew it had died and it was small and furry and didn't have human eyes). The memory of the morgue, of the cold, dead skin against her fingertips. The chill like taking a large gulp of ice water, so large that the shiver ran down to her toes. It had been harder to make them dead again. She'd panicked. The woman in the morgue had tried to get up off the table. She hadn't thought about what to do next so she'd grabbed the closest weapon she could find—a knife, part of an autopsy kit—and driven it down into the woman's chest. She had lurched, then slumped back to the metal slab. Apparently raising the dead didn't mean they couldn't be killed again.

"Well?" said Eli, gesturing at the body like he was offering Sydney a gift, and she wasn't being very grateful.

She looked to her sister for answers, for help, but somewhere between the car and the body, Serena had changed. She seemed tense, her forehead crinkling in a way that she'd always tried to avoid because she said she didn't want wrinkles. And she wouldn't meet her sister's eyes. Sydney turned back to the body, and knelt gingerly beside it.

She didn't see what she did as raising the dead, not really. They weren't zombies, as far as she could tell—she didn't have prolonged exposure to her subjects, aside from the hamster, and she wasn't sure how a zombie hamster's behavior would differ from that of a normal one—and it didn't matter what they'd died of. The man under the sheet in the hospital hall had apparently suffered a heart attack. The woman in the morgue had already had her organs removed. But when Sydney touched them, they didn't just come back, they *revived*. They were okay. Alive. Human. And, as she found out in the morgue, as susceptible to mortality as they'd been before, just not the form that killed them. It perplexed Sydney, until she remembered the day on the frozen lake when the ice water had swallowed her up and she'd reached for Serena's leg and been a fraction too late, too slow, to catch it—*come back, come back*—and how badly she'd wanted a second chance.

That's what Sydney was giving these people. A second chance.

Her fingers hovered over the dead man's chest for a moment as she wondered if he *deserved* a second chance, then chided herself.

Who was she to judge or decide or grant or deny? Simply because she could, did that mean she should?

"Any day now," said Eli.

Sydney swallowed and forced herself to lower her fingers onto the dead man's skin. At first, nothing happened, and panic swept over her at the thought of finally having a chance to show Serena, and failing to do it. But the panic fell away when, moments later, the ice-water chill flooded through her veins, and the man beneath her shuddered. His eyes flew open and he sat up, all so fast that Sydney went stumbling backward to the grass. The once-dead man looked around, confused and angry, before his eyes locked on Eli, and his whole face contorted with rage.

"What the hell is—"

The gunshot rang in Sydney's ears. The man fell back into the grass, a small red tunnel between his eyes. Dead again. Eli lowered his gun.

"Impressive, Sydney," he said. "That's quite a unique gift." The humor, along with that horrible false cheer and fake smile, was gone, wiped away. In a way, Eli wasn't quite as frightening, because she'd always been able to see the monster in his eyes. Now it had finally stopped hiding. But the gun, and the way he held it, made him scary enough.

Sydney got to her feet. She really wished he would put the weapon down. Serena had retreated several feet, and was toeing a patch of frozen wild grass.

"Um, thank you?" said Sydney, her voice wavering. Her feet slid backward through the grass without her meaning to. "Are you going to show me your trick now?"

He almost laughed. "I'm afraid mine lacks the showmanship." And then he raised the gun, and leveled it at her.

In that moment, Sydney felt no surprise, no shock. It was the first thing Eli had done that seemed *right* to her. Genuine. Fitting. She wasn't afraid to die, she didn't think. After all, she'd done it once. But that didn't mean she was ready. Sadness and confusion coiled in her, not toward him, but toward her sister.

"Serena?" she asked quietly, as if maybe she didn't notice her new boyfriend was pointing a gun at her little sister. But Serena had turned away, arms crossed tightly over her chest.

"I want you to know," said Eli, fingers flexing on the gun, "that it is my grim task to do this. I have no choice."

"Yes, you do," whispered Sydney.

"Your power is wrong, and it makes you a danger to—"

"I'm not the one holding a gun."

"No," said Eli, "but your weapon is worse. Your power is *unnatural*. Do you understand, Sydney? It goes against nature. Against God. And this," he said, taking aim, "this is for the greater good."

"Wait!" said Serena, suddenly turning back. "Maybe we don't have to—"

Too late.

It happened fast.

Shock and pain hit Sydney in one loud blast.

Serena's voice had stolen her a moment, a fraction of a moment, and as soon as she saw Eli's fingers tighten on the trigger Sydney had cut to the side, lunging for a branch as the gun fired. She had the broad stick in her grip and swung into Eli before she even felt the blood running down her arm. The branch knocked the gun to the ground and Sydney spun, and ran for her life. She reached the edge of the forest before the shots started again. As she tumbled through the trees, she thought she heard her sister calling her name, but this time she knew better than to look back.

XXXIII

YESTERDAY
THE ESQUIRE HOTEL

VICTOR stood very, very still, as he listened to Sydney's story.

"Is that everything?" he asked when she was done, even though he could tell it wasn't, that by the time the account left Sydney's lips, it had bites taken out. He had watched her pause to filter out the specific nature of her power every time she opened her mouth. In the end she'd only conceded that she *had* an ability, and that her sister's new boyfriend, Eli, had demanded a demonstration, and then tried to execute her for it—*execute,* that was the word she used—but that was all. *Executing EOs,* Victor's mind spun. What was Eli playing at? Had there been others? There had to have been. The stunt in the bank with Barry Lynch, how did that tie in? Had he contrived a scene to kill the man in broad daylight?

A hero? Victor now scoffed at the word. That's what the paper had been so eager to call Eli. And for a moment, Victor had believed the headline. He had been willing to play the villain when he thought Eli was *actually* a hero; now that the truth of his old friend was proving itself to be much darker, Victor would relish the role as opposition, adversary, foe.

"That's all," lied Sydney, and Victor didn't get mad. He didn't feel the need to hurt her, to pry the final truths loose—he couldn't blame her for hesitating; after all, the last time she revealed her powers to someone, she'd nearly died for it—because even if she wasn't telling him everything, she'd told him something vital. Eli wasn't just close. He was *here*. In Merit. Or at least, he had been a day and a half before. Victor propped his elbows on the counter and took in the small girl whose path had crossed his own.

He had never believed in fate, in destiny. Those things lurked too close to divinity for Victor's taste, higher powers and the dispensation of agency. No, he chose to see the world in terms of probability, acknowledging the role of chance while taking control wherever it was possible. But even he had to admit that if there was a Fate, it was smiling on him. The newspaper, the girl, the city. If he'd possessed even a fraction of Eli's religious zeal, he might think God was pointing him on a path, a mission. He wasn't willing to go that far, to buy in, but he still appreciated the show of support.

"Sydney . . ." He tried to suppress his excitement, forcing a calm he didn't feel into his voice. "Your sister's college, what is it called?"

"It's U of Merit. On the other side of the city. It's huge."

"And the school apartment, the one your sister was staying in. Do you remember how to get there?"

Sydney hesitated, picking at the bagel still in her lap.

Victor gripped the counter. "This is important."

When Sydney didn't move, Victor took her by the arm, curling his fingers over the place she'd been shot. He'd taken away the pain, but he wanted her to remember, both what Eli had done, and what *he* could do. She froze beneath his touch as with his free hand, he tugged the collar of his shirt down so she could see the first of the three scars made by Eli's gun.

"That's two of us he's tried to kill." He let go of her arm and his shirt collar. "We got lucky. How many other EOs haven't? And if we don't stop him, how many other EOs *won't*?"

Sydney's blue eyes were wide, unblinking.

"Do you remember where your sister lives?"

For the first time, Mitch spoke up. "We won't let Eli hurt you again," he said over his glass of chocolate milk. "Just so you know."

Victor had opened Mitch's laptop, and pulled up a campus map. He turned the screen toward her.

"Do you remember?"

After a long moment, Sydney nodded. "I know the way."

∞

SYDNEY couldn't stop shaking.

It had nothing to do with the cold March morning and everything to do with fear. She sat in the front seat and navigated. Mitch drove. Victor sat in the back and fiddled with something sharp. It looked to Sydney, who'd glanced back once or twice, like a fancy knife that could be flicked open or closed. She turned forward and hugged her knees as the streets went by. The same streets that slid past the taxicab window a few days before as it took her to Serena. The same streets that slid past the window of Serena's car as she drove them to the field.

"Turn right," said Sydney, making a concerted effort to stop her teeth from chattering. Her fingers wandered to the spot on her arm where the bullet had passed through. She closed her eyes but saw her sister, felt her arms around her, the soda can cold in her hand and Eli's eyes on her when Serena said *Show us*. The field and the body and the gunshot and the woods and—

She decided to keep her eyes open.

"Turn right again," she said. In the backseat, Victor opened and closed the knife. Sydney remembered hating it when Eli sat behind her, the weight of his eyes on the back of her seat, on her. She didn't mind it now with Victor there.

"Here," she said. The car slowed, and stopped along the curb. Sydney looked out the window at the apartment buildings that hugged the eastern edge of campus. Everything looked the same, and that felt wrong, like the world should have registered the events of the last few days, should have changed the way *she* had changed. Cool air blew against her face and Sydney blinked and realized Victor was holding the car door open for her. Mitch was standing on the path to the apartment, kicking a loose piece of concrete.

"Coming?" asked Victor.

She couldn't will her feet to move.

"Sydney, look at me." He rested his hands on the car roof and leaned in. "No one is going to hurt you. Do you know why?" She shook her head, and Victor smiled. "Because I'll hurt them first."

He held the door open wide for her. "Now get out."

And Sydney did.

∞

THEY made an odd picture, knocking on the door to 3A: Mitch, towering and tattooed; Victor in head-to-toe black—less like a thief and more like a Parisian, groomed and elegant—and Sydney, sandwiched between them, in blue leggings and a large red coat. These clothes had appeared this morning, and still felt dryer-warm. They even fit a little better. She particularly liked the coat.

After several rounds of polite knocking, Mitch removed a set of picks from his coat pocket, and was busy saying something about how easy these school locks were in a way that made Sydney wonder more about his preprison life, when the door swung open.

A girl in pink and green pajamas looked at them, and her expression confirmed the oddness of the trio's collective appearance.

The girl, however, was not Serena. Sydney's heart fell.

"You selling cookies?" she asked. Mitch laughed.

"Do you know Serena Clarke?" asked Victor.

"Yeah, sure thing," said the girl. "She gave me the apartment, like, yesterday. Said she didn't need it anymore, and my roommate was driving me *up the wall* so Serena told me to take this one until the end of the year. I'm about to graduate anyway, thank *God*, I'm so done with this fucking school."

Sydney cleared her throat. "Do you know where she went?"

"Probably with that boyfriend of hers. He's a hottie, but kind of a dick, to be honest. He's one of those time-suck guys that always wants to be with her—"

"Do you know where *he* lives?" asked Victor.

The girl in the pink and green pajamas shook her head and shrugged. "Nope. Ever since they started dating last fall she's been so weird. I've hardly seen her. And we used to be tight! Like movies-and-chocolate-on-menstrual-time tight. And then he showed up and *bam*, it's Eli this and Eli that—"

Sydney and Victor both tensed at the name.

"No idea then," he cut in, "where we might find them?"

She shrugged again. "Merit's a big city, but I saw Serena in class yesterday—that's when she gave me the keys—so she can't have gone far." Her eyes flicked between them, and seemed to land on Sydney. "You look so much like her. You her little sister? Shelly?"

Sydney opened her mouth but Victor was already turning her away.

"We're just friends," he said, guiding her down the path. Mitch followed.

"Well, if you see them," called the girl, "thank Serena for the apartment. Oh, and tell Eli he sucks."

"Will do," called Victor as the three made their way back to the car.

※

"**THIS** is hopeless," whispered Sydney, sliding onto the couch.

"Hey now," said Mitch. "A week ago, Eli could have been anywhere in the world. Now, because of you, we have him narrowed down to a city."

"If he's still here," said Sydney.

Victor paced the line of the couch. "He's here." The thorn dug deep beneath his skin. So close. How badly he wanted to walk out into the streets and shout his old friend's name until he came out. It would be so easy. Fast, efficient . . . and foolish. He needed a way to lure him out without leaving the shadows himself. He was catching up to Eli, but he wanted to be a step ahead before he turned to face him. He had to find a way to make Eli come to *him*.

"What now?" asked Mitch.

Victor looked up. "Sydney wasn't the first target. I'm willing to bet she won't be the last. Can you make me a search matrix?"

Mitch cracked his massive knuckles. "What kind?"

"I want a way to find potential EOs. See if there are others he's gotten to. And if there are any he hasn't found yet."

"Worried for their safety?" asked Mitch. Victor had been thinking more about using them as bait, but he didn't say it, not in front of Sydney.

"Limit the search to the last year, keep it in-state, and look for flags," he said, trying to summon Eli's thesis work. He'd prattled on about markers once or twice, in the spaces between other topics. "Search police reports, work evaluations, school and medical records. Search for any sign of near death experience—it will probably be classified under trauma—psychological instability in the aftermath, odd behavior, leave of absence, discrepancies in records made by shrinks, uncertainty in records made by cops..." He began to pace again. "And while you're at it, get Serena Clarke's school records, her class schedule. If Eli's tied himself to her in some way, then it might be easier to find her than him."

"Aren't all those records classified?" asked Sydney.

Mitch beamed and flicked open his laptop, settling in at the counter.

"Mitchell," said Victor. "Tell Sydney what you were in prison for."

"Hacking," he said cheerfully.

Sydney laughed. "Seriously? I had you pegged as more of a beat-someone-to-death-with-their-own-arm type."

"I've always been big," said Mitch. "That's not my fault." He cracked his knuckles again. His hands were larger than the keyboard.

"And the tattoos?"

"It's best to look the part."

"Victor doesn't look the part."

"Depends on what part you're going for. He cleans up well."

Victor wasn't listening. He was still pacing.

Eli was close. Eli was in this city. Or had been. What on earth could Sydney's sister do, that he had found her so valuable? If Eli was executing EOs, why had he spared Serena? Victor was glad he had, though. She had given him a reason to stay in Merit, and he needed Eli tethered. Mitch's large fingers were a blur across the keyboard. Window after window unfolded on his sleek black screen. Victor couldn't stop pacing. He knew the search would take time, but the air was humming, and he couldn't will his feet to stop, couldn't force himself to find stillness, to find peace, not now when Eli was finally in reach. He needed freedom.

He needed air.

XXXIV

YESTERDAY
DOWNTOWN MERIT

SYDNEY followed him into the street.

Victor hadn't heard her, not for a block, but when he finally glanced back and saw her there, her expression turned cautious, almost scared, as if she'd been caught breaking a rule. She shivered and he gestured to a nearby coffee shop. "Care for a drink?"

"Do you really think we'll find Eli?" she asked several minutes later as they made their way down the sidewalk, gripping coffee and cocoa respectively.

"Yes," said Victor.

But he did not elaborate. After several long moments of Sydney's fidgeting beside him, it was clear that she wanted to keep talking.

"What about your parents?" he asked. "Won't they notice you missing?"

"I was supposed to stay with Serena all week," she said, blowing on her drink. "And besides, they travel." She glanced over at him, then trained her gaze on the to-go cup. "When I was in the hospital last year, they just left me there. They had *work*. They always have work. They travel forty weeks a year. I had a watcher, but they let her go because she *broke a vase*. They made time to replace the vase, because apparently it was a focal piece in the house, but they were too busy to find a new watcher, so they said I didn't need one. Staying alone would be good practice for life." The words spilled out, and she sounded breathless by the end. Victor said nothing, only let her settle, and a few moments later, she added, calmer, "I don't think my parents are an issue right now."

Victor knew far too well about those kinds of parents, so he let the matter fall. Or at least, he tried to. But as they rounded the corner, a bookstore came into view, and there in the front window, a massive poster announced the newest Vale book, on sale this summer.

Victor cringed. He hadn't spoken to his own parents in nearly eight years. Apparently having a convicted offspring—at least one that didn't show any inclinations toward being rehabilitated, especially not with the "Vale system"—wasn't great for book sales. Victor had pointed out that it wasn't that *bad* for book sales, either, that they might be able to capitalize on that niche—morbid curiosity buyers—but his parents hadn't been impressed. Victor wasn't terribly distraught about the falling-out, but he'd also been spared their window displays for nearly a decade. To their credit, they sent a set of books to his cell in isolation, which he'd cherished, rationing the destruction to make it last as long as possible. When he finally integrated he found that the penitentiary library had, not surprisingly, stocked a complete set of Vale self-help books, and he'd corrected those in his trademark fashion until Wrighton caught on and denied him access.

Now Victor wandered into the store, Sydney close behind, and bought a copy of the newest book, entitled *Set Yourself Free,* and subtitled *From the Prison of Your Discontent*. It felt like a pretty obvious jab. Victor also bought a handful of black Sharpies from the turnstile by the checkout counter, and asked Sydney if she wanted anything, but she simply shook her head and clutched her to-go cup of cocoa. Back out front, Victor considered the storefront window, but he feared the Sharpies weren't big enough and besides, he didn't intend to get picked up for vandalism of all things, so he was forced to leave the window untouched. It was a shame, he thought, as they walked on. There had been an excerpt, blown up large and pasted on the window, and in a passage studded with overwrought gems—his favorite being "out of the ruins of our self-made jails . . ."—he had seen the perfect opportunity to spell out a simple but effective "We . . . ruin . . . all . . . we touch."

He and Sydney continued on their stroll. He didn't explain the book, and she didn't ask. The fresh air felt good, the coffee infinitely better than even bribery and pain could get him in prison. Sydney blew absently on her hot chocolate, small fingers curled around it for warmth.

"Why did he try to kill me?" she asked quietly.

"I don't know yet."

"After I showed him my power, and he was about to kill me, he called it a grim task. He told me he didn't have a choice. Why would he want to kill EOs? He said he was one, too."

"He is an ExtraOrdinary, yes."

"What's his power?"

"Self-righteousness," Victor said. But when Sydney looked confused, he added, "He heals. It's a reflexive ability. In his eyes, I think that makes it somehow pure. Divine. He can't technically use his power to hurt others."

"No," said Sydney, "he uses guns for that."

Victor chuckled. "As for why he seems to think it's his personal duty to dispose of us"—he straightened—"I suspect it has something to do with me."

"Why?" she whispered.

"It's a long story," said Victor, sounding tired. "And not a pleasant one. It's been a decade since I had a chance to philosophize with our mutual friend, but if I had to guess, I'd say Eli believes he's somehow protecting people from us. He once accused me of being a devil wearing Victor's skin."

"He called me unnatural," said Sydney softly. "Said my power went against nature. Against God."

"Charming, isn't he?"

It was after lunch and the people had almost all slunk back into their offices, leaving the streets strangely bare. Victor seemed to be leading them farther and farther away from the crowds, onto narrower streets. Quieter streets.

"Sydney," he said some time later, "you don't have to tell me your power if you don't want, but I need you to understand something. I'm going to do everything I can to beat Eli, but he's not an easy opponent. His power alone makes him nearly invincible, and he may be crazy, but he's cunning. Every advantage he has makes it harder for me to win. The fact that he knows your power, and the fact that I *don't*, puts me at a disadvantage. Do you understand?"

Sydney's steps had slowed, and she nodded, but said nothing. It took all of Victor's patience not to force her hand, but a moment later, that patience was rewarded. The two of them passed an alley, and heard a low whine. Sydney broke away and turned back, and when Victor followed, he saw what she had seen.

A large black shape stretched on the damp concrete, panting. It was a dog. Victor knelt just long enough to run a finger down its back, and the whining faded. Now the only sounds it made were shuddering breaths. At least it wouldn't be in pain. He stood again, frowning the way he did whenever he was thinking. The dog looked mangled, as if it had been hit by a car and staggered the few feet into the alley before crumpling.

Sydney crouched down by the dog, stroking its short black fur.

"After Eli shot me," she said in a soft, cooing voice, as if speaking to the dying dog instead of Victor, "I swore I'd never use my power again. Not in front of anyone." She swallowed hard, and looked up at Victor. "Kill it."

Victor arched an eyebrow. "With what, Syd?"

She gave him a long, hard look.

"Please kill the dog, Victor," she said again.

He looked around. The alley was empty. He sighed and pulled a handgun from its place against his back. Digging in his pocket he retrieved a silencer, and screwed it on, glancing over it at the wheezing dog.

"Scoot back," he said, and Sydney did. Victor took aim, and pulled the trigger once, a clean shot. The dog stopped moving, and Victor turned away, already dismantling his gun. When Sydney didn't follow, he glanced back to find her crouching over the dog again, running her hands back and forth along its bloody coat and its crushed ribs in small, soothing motions. And then, as he watched, she went still. Her breath hovered in a cloud in front of her lips, and her face tightened in pain.

"Sydney—," he started, but the rest of the sentence died in his throat as the dog's tail *moved*. One slight swoosh across the dirty pavement. And then again, right before the body tensed. The bones cracked back into place, the chest inflated, the rib cage reformed, and the legs stretched. And then, the beast sat up. Sydney backed away as the dog pushed itself to its four feet, and looked at them, tail wagging tentatively. The dog was . . . huge. And very much alive.

Victor watched, speechless. Up until now he'd had factors, thoughts, ideas about how to find Eli. But as he watched the dog blink and yawn and breathe, a plan began to take shape. Sydney looked cautiously his way, and he smiled.

"Now *that*," he said, "is a gift."

She petted the dog between the ears, both of which stood roughly eye level with her.

"Can we keep him?"

VICTOR tossed his coat onto the couch as Sydney and the dog wandered in behind him.

"It's time to send a message," he announced, dropping the Vale self-help book he'd bought onto the counter with a flourish and a thud. "To Eli Ever."

"Where the hell did that dog come from?" asked Mitch.

"I get to keep him," said Sydney.

"Is that blood?"

"I shot him," said Victor, searching through his papers.

"Why would you do that?" asked Mitch, closing the laptop.

"Because he was dying."

"Then why isn't he dead?"

"Because Sydney brought him back."

Mitch turned to consider the small blond girl in the middle of their hotel living room. "Excuse me?"

Her eyes went to the floor. "Victor named him Dol," she said.

"It's a measurement of pain," explained Victor.

"Well, that's morbidly appropriate," said Mitch. "Can we get back to the part where Sydney *resurrected him*? And what do you mean you're going to send Eli a message?"

Victor found what he was looking for, and turned his attention to the hotel's floor-to-ceiling windows and the sun beyond them, trying to gauge the amount of light that stood between him and full night.

"When you want to get someone's attention," he said, "you wave, or you call out, or you send up a flare. These things are dependent on proximity and intensity. Too far away, or too quiet, and there's no guarantee the person will see or hear you. I didn't have a bright enough flare before, a way to guarantee his attention short of making a scene myself, which would have worked, but I'd have lost the advantage. Now, thanks to Sydney, I know the perfect method and message." He held up the news article and with it, the notes Mitch had made for him on Barry Lynch, the supposed criminal from the foiled bank robbery. "And we're going to need shovels."

XXXV

LAST NIGHT
MERIT CEMETERY

THUD.

Thud.

Thud.

The shovel hit wood, and stuck.

Victor and Sydney cleared the last of the dirt away, and tossed the shovels up onto the grass rim around the grave. Victor knelt and pulled the coffin lid back. The body within was fresh, well preserved, a man in his thirties with dark, slicked-back hair, a narrow nose, and close-set eyes.

"Hello, Barry," said Victor to the corpse.

Sydney couldn't take her eyes from the body. He looked slightly . . . deader . . . than she would have liked, and she wondered what color his eyes would be when they opened.

There was a moment of silence, almost reverent, before Victor's hand came down on her shoulder.

"Well?" he said, pointing to the body. "Do your thing."

∞

THE corpse shuddered, opened its eyes, and sat up. Or at least, it tried to.

"Hello, Barry," said Victor.

"What . . . the . . . hell . . . ?" said Barry, finding the lower two thirds of his body pinned beneath the bottom half of the coffin lid, which was presently being held shut by Victor's boot.

"Are you acquainted with Eli Cardale? Or maybe he goes by Ever now."

Barry was clearly still grasping the exact details of his situation. His eyes snapped from the coffin to the wall of dirt to the night sky, to the man with blond hair interrogating him and the girl sitting at the grave opening, swinging her small legs in their bright blue leggings. Sydney looked down, and was surprised and a bit disappointed to find that Barry's eyes were an ordinary brown. She'd hoped they would be green.

"Fucking Ever," Barry growled, banging his fist against the coffin. He flickered in and out of sight a little each time, like a shorting projection. The air made faint whooshing noises, like far-off explosions every time he did. "He said it was a tryout! Like, for a Hero League or some shit—"

"He wanted you to rob a bank to prove you were a hero?" Skepticism dripped from Victor's voice. "And then what?"

"What the fuck does it look like, ass hat?" Barry gestured down at his body. "*He killed me!* The bastard walks right up in the middle of a demonstration *he* told me to do, and he shoots me."

So Victor was right. It had been a setup. Eli had staged a killing as a rescue. He had to admit, it was one way to get away with murder.

"I mean, I'm dead, right? This isn't some shit prank?"

"You *were* dead," said Victor. "Now, thanks to my friend, Sydney, you're a bit less dead."

Barry was spluttering curses and crackling like a sparkler. "What did you do?" He spat at Sydney. "You broke me." Sydney frowned as he continued to short out, lighting up the grave in a strange, camera-flash kind of way. She had never resurrected an

EO before. She wasn't sure if all the pieces would—*could*—come back. "You broke my power, you little—"

"We have a job for you," cut in Victor.

"Fuck off, does it look like I want a *job*? I want to get out of this fucking coffin."

"I think you want to take this job."

"Blow me. You're Victor Vale, right? Ever told me about you when he was trying to recruit me."

"It's nice that he remembers," said Victor, his patience wearing thin.

"Yeah, think you're high and mighty, causing pain and shit? Well I'm not afraid of you." He flickered in and out again. "Got that? Let me out and I'll show *you* pain."

Sydney watched Victor's hand tighten into a fist, and felt the air hum around her, but Barry didn't seem to feel anything. Something was wrong. She'd gone through the motions, given him a second chance, but he hadn't come back the way the ordinary humans had, not all the way. The air stopped humming, and the man in the coffin cackled.

"Hah, see? Your little bitch messed up, didn't she? I don't feel a thing! You can't hurt me!"

At that, Victor straightened.

"Oh, sure I can," he said pleasantly. "I can shut the lid. Put the dirt back. Walk away. Hey," he called up to Sydney, who was still swinging her legs over the side of the grave. "How long would it take for an undead to become dead again?"

Sydney wanted to explain to Victor that the people she resurrected weren't *undead*, they were *alive*, and, as far as she could tell, they were perfectly mortal—well, aside from this little nerve issue—but she knew where he was going with this and what he wanted to hear, so she looked down at Barry Lynch, and shrugged dramatically. "I've never seen an undead go dead again on their own. So I'm guessing forever."

"That's a long time," said Victor. Barry's cursing and his taunts had died away. "Why don't we let you think on it? Come back in a few days?" Sydney tossed Victor his shovel, and a spray of dirt tumbled down on the coffin lid like rain.

"Okay, wait, wait, wait, wait," begged Barry, trying to claw his way out of the coffin and finding his feet trapped. Victor had nailed his pants to the wooden floorboards before they got started. It had been Sydney's idea, actually, just to be safe. Now Barry panicked and flickered and began to whimper, and Victor rested the spade under the man's chin and smiled.

"So you'll take the job?"

XXXVI

LAST NIGHT
THE ESQUIRE HOTEL

"**WHAT** happened back there, Sydney?"

Victor was still knocking dirt off his boots as they climbed the stairs to the hotel room—he didn't like elevators—with Sydney taking the steps two at a time beside him.

"Why didn't Barry come back the way he should?"

Sydney chewed her lip. "I don't know," she said, winded from the climb. "I've been trying to figure it out. Maybe . . . maybe it's because EOs have already had their second chance?"

"Did it feel different?" pressed Victor. "When you tried to resurrect him?"

She wrapped her arms around herself, and nodded. "It didn't feel right. Normally, it's like there's this thread, something to grab onto, but with him, it was hard to reach, and it kept slipping. I didn't get a good hold."

Victor was quiet until they reached the seventh floor.

"If you had to try again . . ." but his question faded as they reached their room. There were voices beyond the door, low and urgent. Victor slid the gun from his back as he turned the key and the door swung open on the hotel suite, only the back of Mitch's tattooed head peering over the couch in front of a TV. The voices continued on the screen in black-and-white. Victor sighed, shoulders loosening, and put the gun away. He should have known it was nothing, should have felt the absence of new bodies. He chalked up the slipup to distraction as Sydney bobbed past him into the apartment and the people on the screen argued on in dapper suits and hushed voices. Mitch had a thing for classics. Victor had arranged on numerous occasions to have the TV in the prison commons, which was usually programmed to sports or old sitcoms, set to show old black-and-whites instead. He appreciated Mitch's incongruities. They made him interesting.

Sydney tugged off her shoes by the door and went to scrub the grave dirt and the lingering feel of the dead from beneath her fingernails. The giant black dog looked up from the floor beside the couch as she passed, tail thumping. Somewhere after reviving the dog and before leaving to revive Barry, Victor had cleaned the lingering blood and grime off Dol's fur, and the beast almost looked normal as it got to its feet and followed Sydney lazily from the room.

"Hey, Vic," called Mitch, waving without looking away from the tuxedoed men on the screen. The laptop sat beside him, and hooked up to it was a small, very new printer that hadn't been there when they left.

"I don't keep you around to warm the couch, Mitch," said Victor as he crossed into the kitchen.

"You find Barry?"

"I did." Victor poured himself a glass of water and slumped against the counter, watching the bubbles flee to the top of the glass.

"He agree to deliver your message?"

"He did."

"So where is he? I know you didn't actually let him *go*?"

"Of course not." Victor smiled. "I put him back for the night."

"That's cold."

Victor shrugged, and took a sip. "I'll let him out in the morning to run his errand. And what have you been up to?" he said, tipping the glass toward him. "I hate to interrupt *Casablanca* for business but..."

Mitch stood and stretched. "You ready for the world's biggest case of good news–bad news?"

"Go on."

"The search matrix is still sifting." He held out a folder. "But here's what we've got so far. Each one's got enough markers to make them EO candidates." Victor took it, and began to spread the pages out on the counter. There were eight in total.

"That's the good news," said Mitch.

Victor stared down at the profiles. Each page had a block of text, lines of stolen information—names and ages and brief medical summaries following brief lines on their respective accidents or traumas, psych notes, police reports, antipsychotic and painkiller prescriptions. Information distilled, messy lives made neat. Beside the text on each profile was a picture. A man in his late fifties. A pretty girl with black hair. A teenage boy. All of the photos were candids, the subjects' eyes looking at or around the camera, but never directly at the photographer. And all of the photos had been *x*-ed out with a thick black Sharpie.

"What's with the *x*'s?" asked Victor.

"That's the bad news. They're all dead."

Victor looked up sharply. "All of them?"

Mitch looked sadly, almost reverently, at the papers. "Looks like your hunch about Eli was right. These are just the Merit area, like you asked. When I started getting hits, I opened a new search, and expanded the parameters to cover the last ten years and most of the country. I didn't print those results—too many—but there's definitely a pattern."

Victor's gaze drifted back down to the files, and stuck. He couldn't tear his eyes from the thick black x's on the photos. Perhaps he should feel responsible for unleashing a monster on the world, for the bodies that monster left in his wake—after all, he made Eli what he was, he urged him to test his theory, he brought him back from the dead, he took away Angie—but as he stared down into the faces of the dead, all he felt was a kind of quiet joy, a vindication. He'd been right about Eli *all along*. Eli could preach all he liked about Victor being a devil in stolen skin, but the proof of Eli's own evil was spread across the counter, on display.

"This guy is doing damage," said Mitch as he lifted another, much, much smaller stack from beside the printer, and set them on the counter, faceup. "But here's a positive postscript for you." Three pictures gazed, glanced, or stared up at Victor, unaware. A fourth was in the process of printing itself out with a soft buzzing sound. When the machine spit it out, Mitch paused the movie and delivered the sheet to the counter. None of the photos were crossed out.

"They're still alive?"

Mitch nodded. "For now."

Sydney reappeared just then in sweats and a T-shirt, trailed by Dol. Victor wondered absently if things brought back by the girl felt a connection to her, or if Dol simply possessed the usual unconditional affection inherent in most canines, and appreciated the fact that he was tall enough to look Sydney in the eyes. She patted his head absently and grabbed a soda from the fridge, climbing onto one of the counter stools, clutching the can in both her hands.

Victor was stacking the dead and set them aside. There was no need for Sydney to look at them right now.

"You okay?" he asked.

She nodded. "I always feel strange after. Cold."

"Wouldn't you rather have a hot drink, then?" asked Mitch.

"No. I like holding this. I like knowing at least I'm warmer than the can."

Mitch shrugged. Sydney leaned forward to look at the four profiles while the program plodded on in the background.

"They're all EOs?" she whispered.

"Not necessarily," said Victor, "but if we're lucky, one or two."

Victor's eyes skimmed the collage of private information that ran beside the photos. Three of the potentials were young, but one was older. Sydney reached over and took up one of the profiles. It was a girl named Beth Kirk, and she had bright-blue hair.

"How do we know which one he'll go after first? Where do we start?"

"Matrix can only do so much," said Mitch. "We'll have to guess. Pick one and hope we get there before Eli."

Victor shrugged. "No need. They're irrelevant now." He didn't care about the blue-haired girl, or any of them for that matter. He was more interested in what the dead proved about Eli than what the living offered *him*. He'd meant them only as bait anyway, to be dug up and used as lures, but Sydney herself—her gift, and the message they'd made with it—had rendered these EOs extraneous to his plans.

Sydney looked appalled by his answer. "But we have to warn them."

Victor plucked Beth Kirk's profile from her grip, and set it face-down on the counter.

"Would you rather I warn them," he asked gently, "or save them?" He watched the anger slide from her face. "It's a waste, going after the victims instead of the killer. And when Eli gets our message, we won't even need to hunt him down."

"Why's that?" she asked.

Victor's mouth quirked up. "Because he'll be hunting *us*."

2

An ExtraOrdinary Day

I

THIS MORNING
TERNIS COLLEGE

ELI Ever sat in the back of the history seminar, tracing the wood grain of the desk and waiting for the lecture to end. The class was being taught in an auditorium at Ternis College, an exclusive private school half an hour or so outside Merit city limits. Three rows in front of him, and two spaces to the left, sat a girl with blue hair named Beth. It wasn't such a strange thing, the hair, but Eli happened to know that Beth only started dying it that color after it had all gone white. The white was the product of trauma, a trauma that had nearly killed her. Technically it *had*, in fact. For four and a half minutes.

Yet here Beth was, alive and attentively taking notes on the Revolutionary War or the Spanish American War or World War II—Eli wasn't even sure what the name of the course was, let alone which conflict the professor was currently teaching—while the blue strands fell around her face, and trailed across her paper.

Eli couldn't stand history. He figured it probably hadn't changed that much in the ten years since he'd taken it, just another one of Lockland University's many prerequisites, meant to round every student into a smooth little ball of knowledge. He stared at the ceiling, then at the spaces between the professor's half-cursive, half-print notes, then back at the blue hair, then at the clock. Class was nearly over. His pulse quickened as he pulled the slim dossier out of his satchel, the one Serena had put together for him. It explained, in painstaking detail, the blue-haired girl's history, her accident—tragic, really, the sole survivor of a nasty crash—and her subsequent recovery. He brushed his fingertips over the photo of Beth, wondering where it had come from. He rather liked that hair.

The clock ticked on, and Eli slid the dossier back into his bag, and pushed a pair of thick-framed glasses up his nose—they were plain glass, not prescription, but he'd noticed the trend around the Ternis College campus and followed suit. Looking the part agewise was never a problem, of course, but styles changed, almost too fast for him to keep track. Beth could choose to stand out if she wanted, but Eli did everything in his power to blend in.

The professor finished his lecture a few blessed minutes early, and wished them all a good weekend. Chairs scraped. Bags were hoisted. Eli rose and followed the blue hair out of the auditorium and down the hall, carried on a wave of students. When they reached the outer door, he held it open for her. She thanked him, tucked a cobalt strand behind her ear, and headed across the campus.

Eli followed.

As he walked, he felt for the place in his jacket where his gun would be, a product of habit, but the pocket was empty. The dossier had told him enough to make him wary of anything that might succumb to magnetism, so he'd left the weapon in his glove box. He'd have to do this the old-fashioned way, which was fine. He didn't often let himself indulge, but he couldn't deny that there was something simple and satisfying about using his hands.

Ternis was a small school, one of those cozy private affairs made up of mismatched buildings and an abundance of tree-lined paths. Beth and he were both on one of the larger paths that bisected the campus, and there were enough students around to keep Eli's pursuit from seeming at all conspicuous. He crossed the campus at a safe distance, enjoying the morning, taking in the crisp spring air, the beauty of the late afternoon sky and the first green leaves. One of them pulled loose from a tree and landed on the girl's blue hair, and Eli admired the way it made both colors seem brighter as he slipped his gloves on.

When they were almost to the parking lot, Eli began to pick up his pace, closing the gap between them until he was within arm's reach.

"Hey!" he called behind her, feigning breathlessness.

The girl slowed, and turned to look at him, but kept walking. Soon he was beside her.

"It's Beth, right?"

"Yeah," she said. "You're in Phillips's history section with me."

Only for the past two classes, but he'd been sure to catch her eye both times.

"Sure am," said Eli, flashing his best college-kid grin. "I'm Nicholas." Eli had always liked the name. Nicholas and Frederick and Peter, those were the ones he found himself using the most. They were important names, the kind held by rulers, conquerors, kings. He and Beth passed through the parking lot, row after row of cars, the school shrinking in the distance behind them.

"Sorry, can I ask you a favor?" asked Eli.

"What's up?" Beth tucked a stray lock of hair behind her ear.

"I don't know where my head was during class," he said, "but I missed the assignment. Did you write it down?"

"Sure," she said as they reached her car.

"Thanks," he said, biting his lip. "I guess there were better things to look at than the board."

She giggled shyly as she set the bag on the hood and unzipped it, digging around inside.

"Anything's better than the board," she said, pulling out her notebook.

Beth had just turned to face him with the notes when his hand closed around her throat, and he slammed her back into the side of the car. She gasped, and he tightened his grip. She dropped the notebook and clawed at his face, raking the black-rimmed glasses off, carving deep scratches across his skin. He felt blood trickle over his cheek but didn't bother wiping it away. The car behind her began to shake, the metal trying to bend, but she was too new to her power and the car was too heavy, and she was running out of air and fight.

There had been a time when he spoke to the EOs, tried to impart to them the logic, the necessity, of his actions, tried to make them understand before they died, that they were already dead, already ash, held together by something dark but feeble. But they didn't listen, and in the end, his actions conveyed what his words had failed to. He'd made an exception for Serena's little sister, and look where that had gotten him. No, words were wasted on them all.

So Eli pinned the girl against the car, and waited patiently until the struggle slowed, and weakened, and stopped. He stood very, very still, and relished the ensuing moment of quiet. It always came to him, right here, when the light—he'd say the *life,* but that wasn't right, it wasn't life, only something *posing* as life—went out of their eyes. A moment of peace, a measure of balance being restored to the world. The unnatural made natural.

Then the moment passed, and he peeled his gloved fingers away from the girl's throat and watched her body slide down the warped metal of the car door and onto the concrete, blue hair falling across her face. Eli crossed himself as the angry red scratches on his cheek knitted and healed, leaving only smooth, clear skin beneath the drying blood. He knelt to retrieve his prop glasses from the ground beside the body. His cell rang as he straightened them on his nose, and he fished the phone from his coat.

"The Hero Line," he answered smoothly. "How can I assist you?"

∞

ELI had expected Serena's slow laugh—the Hero bit was an inside joke—but the voice on the other end was gravelly and most certainly male.

"Mr. Ever?" asked the man.

"Who is this?"

"This is Officer Dane with the Merit PD. We got a call of a robbery in progress at Tidings Well Bank, at Fifth and Harbor."

Eli frowned. "I have my own job, Officer. Don't tell me the cops want me to do theirs, too. And how did you get this number? It's not how we agreed to communicate."

"The girl. She gave it to me." Something exploded in the background, showering the line with static.

"It better be urgent."

"It is," said Officer Dane. "The robber is an EO."

Eli rubbed his forehead. "Don't you have special tactics? Surely they teach you those somewhere. I can't exactly walk in and—"

"The fact he's an EO isn't the problem, Mr. Ever."

"Then do tell me," said Eli through gritted teeth. "What is?"

"He's been identified as Barry Lynch. You . . . that is, he's . . . he's supposed to be dead."

A long pause.

"I'm on my way," said Eli. "Is that all?"

"Not quite. He's making a scene. Shouting for you specifically. Should we shoot him?"

Eli closed his eyes as he reached his car. "No. Don't kill him until I get there." Eli hung up.

He opened the door and climbed in, hitting speed dial. A girl's voice answered, but he cut her off.

"We have a problem. Barry's back."

"I'm watching it on the news. I thought you—"

"Yes, I killed him, Serena. He was very dead."

"Then how—"

"How is he robbing a bank at Fifth and Harbor?" Eli snapped, gunning the car. "How is he suddenly *not* dead? That's a good question. Who could possibly have resurrected Lynch?"

There was a long quiet on the other end of the phone, before Serena answered. "You told me you killed her."

Eli gripped the wheel. "I thought I did." He had hoped, anyway.

"The way you killed Barry?"

"I may have been more certain about Lynch than I was about Sydney. Barry was definitely, undeniably dead."

"You told me you followed her. You told me you finished—"

"We'll talk about this later," he said. "I have to go kill Barry Lynch. Again."

∞

SERENA let the phone slip through her fingers. It landed on the bed with a soft thud as she turned back to the hotel television, where the robbery coverage continued. Even though the action was happening within the bank, and the cameras were stuck on the street behind a thick border of yellow tape, the scene was causing quite a stir. After all, it had been in all the papers, the robbery last week at Smith & Lauder. The civilian hero had come out of the firefight unscathed. The robber had come out in a body bag.

No surprise that the public was disconcerted, then, to find the robber alive and well enough to rob another bank. His name ran in ticker-tape fashion along the bottom of the screen, the bold-lettered scrawl announcing *Barry Lynch Alive Barry Lynch Alive Barry Lynch Alive* . . .

And that meant Sydney was alive. Serena had no doubt that the strange and disquieting feat had somehow been her sister's work.

She took a sip of too-hot coffee, and winced faintly when it burned her throat, but didn't stop. She clung to the fact that inanimate objects weren't subject to her power. They didn't have minds or feelings. She couldn't will the coffee *not* to burn her, couldn't will knives *not* to cut her. The people holding the things were hers, but not the things themselves. She took another sip, eyes wandering back to the television where a photo of the previously deceased EO now filled the right half of the screen.

But why had Sydney done it?

Eli had promised Serena that her sister was dead. She'd warned him not to lie, and he'd looked her in the eyes and told her that he'd shot Sydney. And that hadn't been a lie exactly, had it? She'd been standing right there when he pulled the trigger. Her jaw clenched. Eli was getting better at fighting back, finding little loopholes in her power. Redirections, omissions, evasions, delays. Not that she didn't appreciate the small defiance—she did—but the thought of Sydney, alive and hurt and in the city, made it hard to breathe.

It was never supposed to go like this.

Serena closed her eyes, and the field and the body and her sister's frightened face filled her vision. Sydney had done her best to look brave that day, but she couldn't hide the fear, not from Serena, who knew every line on her sister's face, who'd perched on the edge of her sister's bed so many nights, smoothing those lines one by one with her thumb in the dark. Serena should never have turned back, never called her sister's name. It had been a reflex, an echo of life before. She'd reminded herself over and over that the girl in the field wasn't her sister, not really. Serena knew the girl who looked like Sydney *wasn't* Sydney, the same way she knew that *she* wasn't Serena. But it didn't seem to matter the moment right before Eli pulled the trigger; Sydney had looked small and frightened and so very *alive* and Serena had forgotten that she wasn't.

Her eyes drifted open, only to settle on the still-streaming headline—*Barry Lynch Alive Barry Lynch Alive Barry Lynch Alive*—before she snapped the TV off.

Eli said it best. He called EOs *shadows*, shaped like the people who made them but gray inside. Serena felt it. From the moment she woke up in the hospital, she felt as if something colorful and bright and *vital* was missing. Eli went on to say it was her soul; he claimed *he* was different and Serena let him think that because the only other option was to tell him otherwise, and then he'd believe it.

But what if he was right? The thought of having lost her soul made Serena sad in a distant way. And the thought of poor small Syd all hollowed out made her ache, and made it easier to believe Eli when he said it was mercy, returning EOs to the earth. It had been harder when Sydney was standing in her doorway, flushed from the cold and blue eyes bright, like the light was still in them. Serena had faltered, tripped over the *what-ifs* whispering in her head as they trudged into the field.

Sydney's sin, Eli claimed, was double. Not only was she an EO, unnatural and wrong, but she also possessed the power to corrupt others, to poison them by filling their bodies with something that looked like life, but wasn't. Maybe that was what Serena had seen in Sydney's eyes, a false light she'd mistaken for her sister's life. Her soul.

Maybe.

Whatever it was that made her pause, the fact was that Serena had faltered, and now her sister—the shadow in her shape—was alive, and apparently here in the city. Serena pulled on her coat, and went to look for Sydney.

II

THIS MORNING
THE ESQUIRE HOTEL

VICTOR savored the scalding water of the hotel shower as he rinsed the last of the grave dirt from his skin. Barry Lynch had been surprisingly receptive when he revisited the cemetery this morning. Victor had gone back just before dawn, scooped out the foot of dirt he'd put back on top of Lynch, to make the grave look empty if anyone chanced to walk by, and pried the lid off to find Barry's terrified eyes staring up at him. Pain and fear are inextricable—a lesson that went back to Victor's studies at Lockland—but pain has multiple forms. Victor might not be able to physically hurt Barry Lynch, but that didn't mean he couldn't make him suffer. Barry, for his part, seemed to get the message. Victor had smiled, and helped the once-dead man out of his coffin—even though he hated the way the man's strangely nerveless skin felt against his own—and as he passed him the note and sent him on his way, Victor felt confident that Lynch would follow through. But just to be certain, he'd told him one last thing. He'd taken several steps back, and then turned toward Barry, and said it as an afterthought.

"The girl, Sydney, the one who brought you back. She can change her mind at any point. Snap her fingers, and drop you like a stone. Or rather, like a corpse. Do you want to see?" he asked, digging the phone from his pocket. He began to dial. "It's really quite a clever trick."

Barry had paled, and shaken his head, and Victor had sent him on his way.

"Hey, Vale!" Mitch's voice reached him through the bathroom walls. "Get out here."

He snapped the shower water off.

"Victor!"

Mitch was still shouting his name when he stepped into the hall a minute later, toweling off his hair. Sun was streaming in through the tall windows, and he winced at the brightness. Late morning, at least. His message should be well on its way.

"What is it?" asked Victor, at first worried, but then he saw Mitch's face, the broad, open smile. Whatever the man had done, he was proud of it. Sydney appeared, with Dol close behind, his tail wagging lazily.

"Come see this." Mitch gestured to the profiles spread out on the kitchen counter. Victor sighed. There were more than a dozen now—and most of them dead-ends, he was sure. They couldn't seem to get the search matrix exact enough. He'd spent the previous evening, and most of the night, looking over the pages, wondering how Eli did it, if he followed every lead, or if he knew something Victor didn't, saw something Victor hadn't. Now before his eyes, Mitch began turning papers facedown, eliminating profile after profile from the mix until only three were left. One was the blue-haired girl, and the second an older man he'd studied last night, but the third was new, it must have been freshly printed.

"This," said Mitch, "this is Eli's current list of targets."

Victor's cool eyes flicked up. He began to shift his weight from foot to foot. His fingers tapped out a beat. "How did you figure that out?"

"It's a great story. Stand still and I'll tell you."

Victor forced himself to stop moving. "Go on," he said, scanning the names and faces.

"So, I'm seeing this pattern," said Mitch. "I keep ending up in police files. *Merit* police files. So I think, what if the cops are already working on their own database, right? Maybe we could compare it with ours. You mentioned, way back when, that one cop knowing about EOs. Or someone with the cops. And then I think, hey, maybe I can just borrow *their* data, instead of going through all the hassle—I mean it's nothing beyond my reach, but it takes time—but what if they've done some of the work for me? So I start browsing in Merit PD's 'Persons of Interest' database. And something catches my eye. I used to love those puzzles growing up where they ask you to spot the difference. I rocked that shit. Anyway—"

"They're flagged," said Victor, eyes skimming the profiles.

Mitch's posture fell. "Man, you always ruin a punch line. But yeah . . . and I made it easy for you to see," he said as he pouted. "I turned the pages down. Easy to see a pattern when it's all that's in front of you . . ."

"What do you mean, flagged?" asked Sydney, standing on her tiptoes to see the pages.

"Look," Victor said, gesturing to the profiles. "What do all these people have in common?"

Syd squinted at the paper, but shook her head.

"The middle names," said Victor.

Sydney read them aloud. "Elise, Elington, Elissa . . . They all have 'Eli' in them."

"Exactly," said Mitch. "They've been flagged. Specifically for our friend, Eli. Which means—"

"He's working with the cops," said Victor. "Here in Merit."

Sydney stared down at the photo of the girl with the blue hair. "How can you be sure?" she asked. "What if it's a coincidence?"

Mitch looked smug. "Because I did my homework. I cross-checked the theory by pulling up some of their old profiles, 'Persons of Interest' now deceased, all of which had conveniently found their way into the digital trash bin. Which is its own red flag, by the way, but I found matches to Eli's killings over the last four months." He dropped the dead EO folder on the table. "Including your man Barry Lynch. The one you just spent the night digging up."

Victor had started to pace.

"It gets better," said Mitch. "The flagged profiles were created by one of two cops." He tapped the top right corner of a page. "Officer Frederick Dane. Or Detective Mark Stell."

Victor's chest tightened. Stell. What were the odds? The man who'd had Victor arrested ten years ago, the one who'd been on EO duty at the Lockland precinct, and the one who, when Victor recovered from his multiple gunshot wounds, personally escorted him to the isolation wing of Wrighton Penitentiary. Stell's involvement, along with Eli's testimony, was the reason Victor spent five years in solitary confinement (he wasn't declared an EO on the records, of course, only an extreme danger to himself and others, and it had taken him half a decade of deliberately not hurting anyone—at least not in a conscious or appreciable way—to get himself integrated).

"You listening?" asked Mitch.

Victor nodded absently. "The men flagging the profiles, they are, or have been, in direct contact with Eli."

"Exactly."

Victor toasted the air with his water, his thoughts miles away. "Bravo, Mitch." He turned to Sydney. "You hungry?"

But Sydney didn't seem to be listening. She had taken up the folder with the dead EOs, and was flipping through, almost absently, when she stopped. Victor looked over her shoulder and saw what she saw. Short blond hair and water blue eyes stared up at her beside a cleanly printed name: Sydney Elinor Clarke.

"My middle name is Marion," she said quietly. "And he thinks I'm dead."

Victor stooped over and swiped the page. He folded the paper and tucked it inside his shirt pocket with a wink.

"Not for long," he said, tapping his watch. "Not for long."

III

THIS MORNING
TIDINGS WELL BANK

ELI parked a block and a half from the yellow tape of the crime scene barrier, and repositioned the prop glasses on his nose before getting out. He could see, as he wound his way behind the eyes of the crowd of morbid spectators and the gathering photographers, to the back of the bank, and the crime was no longer in progress. People lingered, lights flashed, but the relative quiet—sirenless, gunless, shoutless—told him enough.

He stiffened when he saw Detective Stell, even though Serena promised it was safe. Still, the detective had come to Merit a few months before to investigate a string of killings in the area—Eli's handiwork, of course—and even Serena's assurances couldn't entirely wipe away Eli's doubt regarding the detective's loyalty. Stell, who now had salt-and-pepper hair and a permanent crease between his eyes, met him behind the building, and lifted the tape so he could pass. Eli pushed the prop glasses up his nose a second time. They were a fraction too big.

"How Clark Kent of you," said Stell drily. Eli was not in the mood.

"Where is he?"

"Dead." The detective led the way into the bank.

"I told you I wanted him alive."

"Didn't have a choice. He started firing, or whatever you want to call it. Couldn't aim worth a damn. Like that power of his was on the fritz. Didn't stop him from making a mess, though."

"Civilians?"

"No, he ordered those all out." They reached a black sheet cast over a vaguely human shape. Stell nudged it with his boot. "Media wants to know why a madman who's supposed to be dead enters a bank with a weapon, but doesn't try to rob it, and doesn't take any prisoners. All he does is kick everyone out, and fire at the air and scream and scream for someone named Eli Ever."

"You should have never let that story run last week."

"Can't stop the press from using their eyes, Eli. You're the one who wanted to make a scene."

Eli didn't like the man's tone, had never liked it, never trusted the thread of combativeness that ran through it.

"I needed a demonstration," Eli growled. He didn't want to admit that there was more to it than that, that he'd *wanted* an audience. It had been Serena's idea, he was sure, before it became his.

"A demonstration is one thing," said Stell. "But did you need a spectacle?"

"It covered up the murder," said Eli as he threw back the black sheet. "How was I supposed to know he wouldn't stay dead?" Barry Lynch's brown eyes gazed up at him, shallow and dead. He could hear the whispers from the other cops milling around, hushed voices wondering who he was, what he was doing there. He tried to look official as he stared down at the dead man.

"You dragged me out here for nothing," he said under his breath. "Now that he's dead."

"Forgive me, but he was dead before, remember? And besides," added Stell, "this time he left a note."

Stell handed Eli a plastic bag. Inside was a crumpled piece of paper. He withdrew the paper and unfolded it gingerly.

It was a stick-figure drawing. Two people holding hands. A thin man in black and a girl, half his height with short hair, and wide eyes. The stick-girl's head was cocked slightly, and a small red spot marked her arm. Three similar spots, no bigger than periods, dotted the stick-man's chest. The stick-man's mouth was nothing more than a faint grim line.

Beneath the drawing ran a single sentence: *I made a friend.*

Victor.

"You okay?"

Eli blinked, felt the cop's hand on his arm. He slid free, folded the paper, and put it in his pocket before anyone could see or say otherwise.

"Get rid of the body," he said to Stell. "Burn it this time."

Eli went back the way he'd come. He didn't stop, not until he was safely in his car. In the relative privacy of the side street in Merit, he pressed his hand against the drawing in his pocket, and a phantom pain started in his stomach.

Victor lifted the knife from the table. "You called the cops and you accused me of being an EO. I didn't rat you out, you know. I could have. Why would you tell them something so silly? Did you know they have special people that come in if there's an EO suspected? Some guy named Stell. Did you know that?"

"You've lost it." *Eli sidestepped.* "Put the knife down. It's not like you can hurt me."

Victor smiled then. He looked like someone else. Eli tried to step back, but the wall came up behind him. The knife buried itself in his stomach. He felt the tip scratch at the skin of his back. The pain had been sharp, persistent, dragging itself out instead of flashing forward and dissolving.

"You know what I figured out?" *Victor growled.* "Watching you in the street that night, picking the glass from your hand? You can't *heal yourself until I take the knife out."* He twisted it, and pain exploded behind Eli's eyes, a dozen colors. He groaned and began to slide down the wall, but Victor hoisted him up by the handle.

"I'm not even using my gift yet," Victor said. "It's not as flashy as yours, but it's rather effective. Want to see it?"

Eli swallowed hard, and dialed Serena as he put the car in gear and headed for the hotel. He didn't wait for her to speak.

"We have a problem."

IV

TEN YEARS AGO
LOCKLAND UNIVERSITY

ELI Ever sat on the steps of his apartment in the cold morning and ran his fingers through his hair before realizing they were covered in blood. Caution tape surrounded him in streamers of yellow, too bright against the dull winter dawn. Red and blue lights dotted the icy ground and every time he looked at them, he ended up spending minutes trying to blink the colors away.

"If you could tell us one more time . . . ," said a young cop.

Eli touched his stomach, the echo of pain still there even though the skin had healed. He rubbed his hands together and watched blood flake off into the sidewalk snow. He wove a distress he wasn't sure he felt back into his voice as he recounted everything from Victor's panicked call the night before, confessing to Angie's murder, to his sudden appearance in their living room, gun in hand. Eli left out the knives, having scrubbed and returned them to their drawers before the police arrived. It was odd, the way his brain had made space around the weedy panic, helping his hands and legs do what needed to be done even as a fading voice in the back of his mind screamed and his best friend lay shot full of holes on their living room floor. Something in Eli had gone missing—fear, that's what he'd told Victor—right down the drain with the icy bath water.

"So you wrested the gun from Mr. Vale." Wrested had been Eli's word, not the officer's.

"I taught a self-defense seminar last summer," he lied. "It's not that hard."

And then he pushed himself shakily to his feet. He was covered in blood, arms curled carefully around his ribs to hide the knife hole in his shirt. Two other officers had already questioned him about it. He'd told them he got lucky. He didn't know how the weapon could have missed him. But it did. Obviously. Look, hole in shirt, no hole in Eli. Fortunately the cops had been too interested in Victor's bleeding out on the hardwood floor to care much about Eli's magic trick. *One lucky man,* they muttered, and he wasn't sure if they'd been talking about him, or Victor, who had managed to avoid dying, for now.

"And then you shot him three times."

"I was distraught. He'd just killed my girlfriend." Eli wondered if he was in shock, if that was the thing keeping Angie's death from sinking in the way the knife had. He wanted to care, he wanted to care *so badly,* but there was this gap between what he felt and what he wanted to feel, a space where something important had been carved out. And it was growing. He'd told Victor the thing he lost was his fear but that wasn't quite true because he was still scared. He was scared of that rift.

"And then?" prompted the cop.

Eli rubbed his eyes. "And then he came after me. I panicked. I didn't know what to do. I tried not to kill him." He swallowed, wishing he had a glass of water. "Look, do you think I could go clean up?" he asked, gesturing to his ruined clothes. "I need to go see Angie . . . her body." The officer called past the yellow tape, and was given the all-clear. The ambulance was long gone. All that was left was a mess. The officer held up the tape to let him pass.

A trail of red wound through the living room. Eli stopped and stared at it. The fight replayed behind his eyes as relentlessly as the police lights, and he forced himself to veer toward the bathroom. When he caught sight of himself in the bank of mirrors, he stifled a laugh. One of those ill, halfway-to-tears laughs. Blood stained his shirt. His pants. His face. His hair. Eli did his best to wash it off, scrubbing his arms OR-style in the sink. His favorite shirt, a bold red one that Victor always said made him look like a ripe tomato, was ruined.

Victor. Victor was wrong. About everything.

"If I'm missing something, then so are you. Life is about compromises. Or did you think because you put yourself in God's hands that He would make you all you were and more?"

"He did," said Eli aloud to the sink. He did. He would. He had to. Whatever this gap was, it was there for a reason, there to make him stronger. He had to believe that.

Eli washed his face, cupped water over his hair until the red ran out of it. He pulled on fresh clothes, and was just about to duck back under the yellow tape across his front door when he caught the end of the young officer's remark to another cop.

"Yeah, Detective Stell's on his way."

Eli paused, and stepped backward into the apartment.

"Did you know they have special people that come in if there's an EO suspected? Some guy named Stell. I bet you didn't know that."

Eli turned, made a line for the back door, only to find his path blocked by a very large cop.

"Everything all right, sir?" asked the cop. Eli gave a slow nod.

"Door's taped," he said. "Just trying to get out of everyone's way."

The large cop nodded, and stepped aside. Eli was through the back door and into the small communal courtyard by the time the large officer reached the younger one. He didn't look guilty, he told himself. Not yet.

Victor was the guilty one. The Victor that he knew was dead, replaced by something cold and vicious. A twisted, violent version of himself. Victor had never been good, or sweet—he'd always had a sharp edge; Eli had been drawn to the metallic glint of it—but he'd never been this. A murderer. A monster. After all, he'd *killed Angie*. How? How had it happened? With pain? Was that possible? The medical part of his mind tried to break it down. A heart attack? Would the pain cause a short-circuit, like electricity? Would the body shut down? Would the functions freeze? He dug his nails into his palms. This was *Angie*. Not a science experiment. A person. The one who'd made him feel better, saner, kept him afloat when his mind began to sink. Was that it, then? Was Angie the missing thing? Wouldn't it be lovely to make the gap another person instead of a part of himself? But no, that wasn't it. Angie had helped, she'd always helped, but he'd felt the hole before she died, felt it even before *he* died. The feeling—the *lack* of it—had only ever come in glimpses, like a cloud passing overhead. But from the moment he woke up on the bathroom floor, the shadow had settled over him, a sign that something was wrong.

Not wrong, he forced himself to think. *Different.*

Eli got to his car, thankful he'd parked two blocks away (less chance of getting a ticket there), and threw it into gear. He drove past the engineering labs, slowing only enough to see the yellow tape there, too—marking out Victor's path of destruction—and the huddle of emergency vehicles. He kept going. He needed to get to the pre-med buildings as fast as possible. He needed to find Professor Lyne.

∞

ELI strode through the automatic doors and into the lobby of the three clustered buildings reserved for the medical sciences, an empty backpack slung on one shoulder. The lobby of the center lab had been painted an awful pale yellow. He wasn't sure why they insisted on painting labs such sickly shades—maybe to prepare the pre-med students for the equally sad palettes of most of the hospitals they aspired to work in, or perhaps on some misguided notion that pale meant clean—but the color made the place seem lifeless, now more than ever. Eli kept his head down as he made his way up two flights of stairs, until he reached the office where he'd spent most of his free time since the start of winter break. Professor Lyne's nameplate hung on the door, letters gleaming. Eli tried the handle. It was locked. He searched his pockets for something to use on the lock, and came up with a paper clip. If it worked on television, it could work here. He knelt before the handle.

Before Victor had come back to campus, Eli had taken his discovery to Professor Lyne, who had gone from skeptical to intrigued as his theories gained weight. Eli had enjoyed getting the professor's attention back in the fall, but it was nothing compared to the relish he felt earning Lyne's respect. His research, now *their* research, had taken on a new focus under the professor's guidance, reinterpreting the hypothetical qualities of existing EOs—the NDEs and their physical and psychological aftermath—into a potential system for *locating* them. A kind of search matrix. At least, that had been the charted course of study until Victor showed up and suggested that they could potentially *make* an EO instead. Eli had never shared this idea with Professor Lyne. He hadn't had the chance. After Victor's failed attempt, Eli had become too preoccupied with his own trial, and then after his success—and it *was* a success, missing pieces aside—he hadn't wanted to share. He'd been watching Lyne's interest sharpen from curiosity into fascination in a way that Eli knew well. Certainly well enough to distrust it.

Now he was glad he'd kept the new direction to himself. In less than a week, Eli's research had ended Angie's life, ruined Victor's (if he lived), and changed his own. Even though the dark turn in the thesis and the ensuing destruction had both been Victor's fault, his actions had also revealed the grim truth of their discoveries, and where they would inevitably lead. And now Eli knew exactly what he had to do.

"Can I help you?"

Eli looked up from his lock-picking, which wasn't going well, to find a janitor leaning on a broom, eyes flicking from Eli to his straightened paper clip. He forced a casual laugh and stood up.

"I hope so. God, I'm such an idiot. I left a folder in Lyne's office. He's my adviser. I need it for my thesis." He was talking too fast, the way actors did on TV when they wanted the audience to pick up on the fact they were lying. His hands were slick. He paused, forcing himself to breathe. "Have you seen him, by the way?" Inhale, exhale. "I can wait around a little while." Inhale, exhale. "Be the first rest I've had in weeks." He stopped and waited to see if the janitor would buy the story.

After a long moment, the man pulled a set of keys from his pocket and unlocked the door.

"I haven't seen him yet, but he should be in soon. And in the future," he offered as he turned away, "it takes two paper clips."

Eli smiled with genuine relief, waved his thanks, and went inside, urging the door closed with a click. He let out a low sigh, and got to work.

There are times when the marvels of scientific advancement expedite our processes, making our lives easier. Modern technology provides machines that can think three or five or seven steps ahead of the human mind, machines that offer elegant solutions, a selection of contingency plans, Bs and Cs and Ds in case A isn't to your liking.

And then there are times when a screwdriver and a bit of elbow grease are all that's necessary to get the job done. Eli admitted that it wasn't terribly creative, or aesthetically pleasing, but it was efficient. Their research was stored in two places. The first was a blue folder in the third drawer of the wall cabinet, which Eli removed and slid into his backpack. The second was on the computer.

He dismantled Professor Lyne's computer the simplest, most fail-safe way he knew how: by physically removing the hard drive and crushing it underfoot, then putting the remnants into his backpack alongside the folder with the intent of tossing the whole bag into some crematorium or wood-chipper for good measure. He'd have to hope Professor Lyne didn't think to store a copy of the research anywhere else.

Eli zipped the bag closed, and did his best to position the computer so that at first glance it didn't appear to be missing a hard drive at all. He had just shouldered the backpack and returned to the hall, and was in the process of trying to relock Lyne's office door when he heard a cough and turned to find the professor himself barring his path, coffee in one hand, briefcase in the other. They considered each other, Eli's hand still resting on the doorknob.

"Good morning, Mr. Cardale."

"I'm withdrawing my thesis," said Eli without preamble.

Lyne's brow crinkled. "But you'll fail."

Eli shifted the bag and pushed past him. "I don't care."

"Eli," said Professor Lyne, following. "What's this about? What's going on?"

They were alone in the hall. Eli spoke, but didn't slow his pace. "It has to stop," he said under his breath. "Right now. It was a mistake."

"But we're just getting started," said Professor Lyne. Eli shoved the door to the stairwell open and stepped onto the landing, Lyne trailing behind him. "The discoveries you've made," said Lyne, "the ones *we'll* make . . . they'll change the world."

Eli turned on him. "Not for the better," he said. "We can't pursue this. Where does it lead? We make it possible to find EOs, and then what? They get taken, examined, dissected, explained, and someone decides to stop studying and start creating." His stomach twisted. It would happen, just like that, wouldn't it? He was proof. Wooed by the prospect, the potential, the chance to prove something instead of disprove.

Do you ever wonder?

"Would that be so bad?" asked Lyne. "To create something ExtraOrdinary?"

"They aren't ExtraOrdinary," snapped Eli. "They're *wrong*."

Eli blamed himself. Victor was right, he'd played God, even as he asked for His help. And God in His mercy and might had saved Eli's life, but destroyed everything that touched it. "I won't give anyone the tools to make more of them. All these roads lean to ruin."

"Don't be dramatic."

"It's over. I'm done." Eli's grip tightened on the bag. Lyne's eyes narrowed.

"I'm not," said Lyne, his hand coming to rest on Eli's shoulder, fingers curling around the backpack strap. "We have an obligation to science, Mr. Cardale. The research must continue. And discoveries of this magnitude must be shared. Stop being so selfish."

Lyne gave a sharp tug on the bag, but Eli stood his ground, and before he knew what was happening, the two men were fighting over the backpack. Eli shoved Lyne off him and up against the railing, and somewhere in the struggle, Lyne's elbow met Eli's lip hard, splitting it. Eli wiped the blood away and ripped the bag from Lyne's grip, tossing it to the side only to realize that Lyne had stopped fighting for it. The professor stood, eyes wide, and Eli felt before he saw in Lyne's eyes what was happening. The skin of his lip knit cleanly back together.

"You . . ." Eli saw Lyne's expression shift from shock to glee. "You did it. You're one of them." He could already see the experiments, the papers, the press, the obsession. "You're an—"

Lyne didn't get a chance to finish, because at that moment, Eli gave him a sharp shove backward, down the stairs. The word was drawn out into a short cry, then cut off sharply by the first of several thuds as Lyne's body tumbled down the steps. He hit the bottom with a crack.

Eli stared down at the body, willing himself to feel horrified. He didn't. There it was again, that gap between what he knew he should feel and what he did, mocking him as he looked down at Lyne. Eli wasn't sure if he'd meant to push the professor down the stairs, or if he'd only meant to push him away, but the damage was done now.

"It was Victor's idea, putting the theory to the test," he found himself saying as he descended the steps. "The method took some tweaking, but it worked. That's why I know this has to stop." Lyne twitched. His mouth opened, made a sound between a groan and a gasp. "Because it works. And because it's wrong." Eli stopped at the base of the stairs beside his teacher. "I died begging for the strength to survive, and it was granted. But it's a trade, Professor, with God or the devil, and I've paid for my gift with the lives of my friends. Every EO has sold a part of themselves they can never have back. Don't you see?" He knelt beside Lyne, whose fingers twitched. "I can't let anyone else sin so heinously against nature."

Eli knew what he had to do, felt it with a strange and comforting certainty. He brought one hand almost gently under Lyne's jaw, the other cradling his chin. "This research dies with us."

With that, he twisted sharply.

"Well," said Eli softly. "With *you*."

Lyne's eyes emptied and Eli set his head gently back against the ground, sliding his fingers free as he stood. There was a moment of such perfect quiet, the kind he used to feel in church, a sliver of peace that felt so . . . right. It was the first time he'd felt like himself, like *more* than himself, since he'd come back to life.

Eli crossed himself.

Then he made his way back up the stairs, pausing a moment to consider the body, bent, neck broken in a way that looked believable considering the fall. The coffee had tumbled with the professor, and left a trail down the steps, the shattered cup beside his shattered body. Eli had been careful not to step in the liquid. He wiped his hands on his jeans, and retrieved the backpack from the landing, but couldn't bring himself to leave. Instead he stood there, waiting, waiting for the sense of horror, the nausea, the guilt, to come up to meet him. But it never came. There was only quiet.

And then a bell rang through the building, taking the quiet with it, and Eli was left with only a body and the sudden urge to *run*.

∞

ELI crossed the parking lot as his mind spun over what to do next. The peace he'd felt in the stairwell had been replaced by a prickling energy and the voice in his head that whispered *go*. It wasn't guilt, or even panic, more like self-preservation. He reached his car, and slid the key into the door, and that's when he heard the steps behind him.

"Mr. Cardale."

Go growled the thing in his head, so clear and so tempting, but something else held him in place. He turned the key in the car door, locking it with a small click.

"Can I help you?" he asked, turning toward the man. He was broad-shouldered and tall, with black hair.

"My name is Detective Stell. Were you coming or going?"

Eli pulled the key from the door. "Coming. I thought I should tell Professor Lyne. About Victor, that is. They were close."

"I'll walk with you."

Eli nodded, and took a step from the car before frowning. "I'll leave my bag here," he said, unlocking the door and tossing the backpack—folders and hard drive and all—into the backseat. "I don't feel up to class today."

"I'm sorry for your loss," said Detective Stell automatically.

Eli counted the steps back to the pre-med labs. He got to thirty-four before he heard the sirens, and looked up sharply. Beside him, Stell swore and picked up his pace.

They'd found Lyne's body, then.

Run run run, hissed the thing in Eli's head. It sang in the same tone and speed as the sirens.

And he did run, but not away. His feet carried him toward the building's entrance, and through, following the emergency response team as it made its way to the base of the stairs. When Eli saw the body, he made a strangled sound. Stell pulled him away, and Eli let his legs go out beneath him, knees hitting the cold floor with a crack. He winced even as the bruises bloomed and faded under his pant legs.

"Come on, son," Stell was saying, pulling him back. But Eli's gaze was leveled on the scene. Everything was playing out as it should, as it *needed* to, the loose threads being snipped. Until he saw the janitor, leaning against the wall, watching, frowning in the way people frown when they're puzzling out a riddle.

Shit, thought Eli, but he must have said it aloud, because Stell tugged him to his feet and said, "Shit indeed. Let's go." There were too many deaths too fast. He knew he'd be a suspect. Had to be. *Run,* said the thing in his head, urgent, and then pleading, plucking his muscles and nerves. But he couldn't. If he ran now, they'd follow.

So he didn't run. In fact, he played the part of victim pretty well. Devastated, angry, traumatized, and above all, cooperative.

When Detective Stell pointed out that everyone around him was either dead or close to it, Eli did his best to look heartbroken. He explained Victor's jealousy, both over his girlfriend, and over his rank in the class. Victor had always been a step behind. He must have snapped. People do.

When Detective Stell asked Eli about his thesis, he explained that it had been his, until Victor usurped it, went behind his back and started working with Lyne. And then he leaned in, and told Stell that Victor hadn't been himself the past few days, that something was different, wrong, and that if he survived—he was still in ICU—they should all be very careful.

Eli's thesis was waived, in light of the trauma. *Trauma.* The word haunted him through his police questioning and his academic meetings all the way to the school-sanctioned single apartment they'd moved him into. *Trauma.* The word that had helped him crack the code, helped him pinpoint the origins of EOs. *Trauma* became a kind of hall pass. If only they knew how much *trauma* he had sustained. They didn't.

He stood in the new apartment with the lights off, and let his backpack—they'd never searched the car for it—fall to the floor beside him. It was the first time he'd been alone—truly alone—

since he'd left the party in search of Victor. And for a moment, the gap between what he should feel and what he felt snapped shut. Tears began to stream down Eli's face as he sank to his knees on the hardwood floor.

"Why is this happening?" he whispered to the empty room. He wasn't sure if he meant the sudden and ferocious sadness or Lyne's murder or Angie's death or Victor's change or the fact that he was still here in the middle of all of it, unscathed.

Unscathed. That was exactly what it was. He had wanted strength, begged for it as the ice water leached the heat and life from his body, but he'd been given *this*. Resilience. Invincibility. But why?

EOs are wrong, and I am an EO, so I must be wrong. It was the simplest of equations, but it wasn't right. Somehow, *it wasn't right.* He knew in his heart with a strange and simple certainty that EOs *were* wrong. That they shouldn't exist. But he felt with equal certainty that *he* wasn't wrong, not in the same way. Different, yes, undeniably different, but not wrong. He thought back to what he'd said in the stairwell. The words had spilled out on their own.

But it's a trade, Professor, with God or the devil . . .

Could that be the difference? He'd seen a demon wearing his best friend's skin, but Eli didn't feel like there was any evil in *himself.* If anything, he felt hands, strong and steady, guiding him when he pulled the trigger, when he snapped Lyne's neck, when he didn't run from Stell. Those moments of peace, of certainty, they felt like faith.

But he needed a sign. God had seemed, in the past few days, like a match-light next to the sun of Eli's discoveries, but now he felt like a boy again, needing sanction, approval. He pulled a pocketknife from his jeans, and clicked it open.

"Would You take it back?" he asked the dark apartment. "If I were no longer of Your making, You would take this power back, wouldn't You?" Tears glistened in his eyes. "Wouldn't You?"

He cut deep, carving a line from elbow to wrist, wincing as blood welled and spilled instantly, dripping to the floor. "You'd let me die." He switched hands and carved a matching line down his other arm, but before he'd reached his wrist, the wounds were closing, leaving only smooth skin, and a small pool of blood.

"Wouldn't You?" He cut deeper, through to bone, over and over, until the floor was red. Until he'd given his life to God a hundred times, and a hundred times had it given back. Until the fear and the doubt had all been bled out of him. And then he set the knife aside with shaking hands. Eli dipped his fingertips in the slick of red, crossed himself, and got back to his feet.

V

AROUND NOON
THE ESQUIRE HOTEL

ELI parked on the street.

He hadn't trusted hotel garages since an incident with an earth-shaking EO three years earlier. It had taken him two full hours to heal, and that was only after he managed to dig himself out of the rubble. Besides, the check-ins and checkouts, tickets and tolls and barricades . . . garages made quick exits impossible. So Eli parked, crossed the road, and passed through the hotel's elegant entry, a stone and light marquee announcing Merit's pride, THE ESQUIRE. It had been Serena's choice, and he hadn't been in the mood to defy her. They'd only been there a couple days, since the *mishap* with Sydney. He'd really hoped the girl would bleed to death in the woods, that maybe one or two of the bullets he'd fired after her would find skin instead of wood and air. But the drawing in his pocket—and the dead-undead-dead-again Barry Lynch suggested otherwise.

"Afternoon, Mr. Hill."

It took Eli a moment to remember that *he* was Mr. Hill, and then he smiled, and nodded at the woman behind the front desk. Serena was better than a fake ID. He hadn't had to present *any* ID, in fact, when they checked in. Or a credit card. She did come in handy. He didn't like being so dependent on someone else, but he managed to twist it in his mind, to assure himself that while

Serena made things easier, smoother, she was sparing him effort that he was more than capable of exerting, if necessary. In this way, she wasn't essential, only terribly convenient.

Halfway to the elevator, Eli passed a man. He made a quick mental profile of the stranger, half out of habit and half out of a gut feeling of wrongness, a kind of sixth sense acquired over a decade of studying people as if they were all spot-the-difference pictures. The hotel was expensive, sleek, the majority of its clientele in suits. This man was wearing something that might pass for a suit, but he was massive, tattoos peeking out from his pushed-up sleeves and collar. He was reading something as he walked, and never looked up, and the woman behind the desk didn't seem concerned, so Eli shelved the man's face somewhere in mental reach, and went upstairs.

He took the elevator to the ninth floor and let himself in. The suite was pleasant yet sparse, with an open kitchen, floor-to-ceiling windows, and a balcony-aided view over Merit. But no Serena. Eli tossed his satchel onto the couch and sat down at the desk in the corner where a laptop sat on top of a daily paper. He woke the device and, as the Merit Police database loaded, pulled the folded drawing from his pocket and set it on the desk, smoothing its corners. The database gave a small chirp, and he entered through the digital back door Officer Dane and Detective Stell had set up for him.

He then scrolled through the folders until he found the file he was looking for. Beth Kirk stared at him, blue hair framing her face. He stared back at her for a moment, and then dragged the profile into the trash.

VI

TEN YEARS AGO
LOCKLAND UNIVERSITY

ELI was sitting in the school-sanctioned single apartment, eating Chinese takeout from LIDS, when the report came on the news. Dale Sykes, a custodian at Lockland University, had been involved in a fatal hit-and-run accident while walking home from work the night before. Eli speared another piece of broccoli. He hadn't meant to do it. That is to say, he hadn't set out in his car with the *intent* to kill the janitor. But he *had* unearthed Sykes's rotation schedule, and he *had* gotten in his car at the same time that Sykes clocked out of his once-a-week night shift, and he *had* seen him crossing the road, and he *had* sped up. But it was a series of circumstances lined up in such a way that any one of them could so easily have shifted in a matter of seconds and spared the man's life. It was the only way Eli could think of to give the janitor a chance, or rather, to give God a chance to intervene. Sykes wasn't an EO, no, but he was a loose end, and as Eli's car drove over him with a *thud-thud,* and that moment of quiet filled Eli's chest, he knew he'd done the right thing.

Now he sat slumped in a chair at the kitchen table while the story played out on-screen, and looked over his Chinese food at two stacks of paper. The first was made up of his own thesis notes, specifically early case studies—Web site stills, testimonies, and the like. The second stack held the contents of Lyne's blue folder. Eli's theory on the causation of EOness was there, but Lyne had added his own notes on the circumstances and factors used to identify a potential EO. To near death experiences the professor had added a term Eli had heard him use before, Post-Traumatic Death Disorder, or the psychological instabilities resulting from the NDE, and another one that must be new, Rebirth Principle, or the patients' desire either to escape the life they had before, or to redefine themselves based on their ability.

Eli had crinkled his nose at the second one. He didn't like recognizing himself in these notes. He had a good reason for reading them, though. Because what he'd felt when he drove over Dale Sykes was the same thing he felt when he tried to end Victor's life. Purpose. And he was beginning to figure out what that purpose was.

EOs were an affront to nature, to God; that he knew. They were unnatural and they were strong, but Eli would always be stronger. His power was a shield against theirs, impenetrable. He could do what ordinary people couldn't. He could stop them.

But he had to find them first. Which is why he was combing through the research, pairing Lyne's methods with the case studies, hoping one of them would give him a place to start.

Victor had always been better at these kinds of puzzles. He could take one look and see the connective threads, no matter how thin. But Eli persisted, scouring his files as the news in the background came and went and came again, and finally he found it. A lead. From a newspaper article Eli had saved on a whim. A man's family had been killed in a freak accident, crushed to death. It had happened only a few months after he himself had nearly died in a building collapse. Only his first name—Wallace—was given, and the paper, which came from a city about an hour away, called him a local. Eli stared at the name for several minutes before digging up a screenshot of an online forum, one of those sites where 99.5 percent of the people are hacks looking for a little attention. But Eli had been thorough, and printed it off anyway. He'd even found a list of members who belonged to the site. One of them, a Wallace47, had only posted once on a buried thread. It was dated last year, between his own accident and that of his family's. All it said was *No one is safe near me.*

It wasn't much, but it was a start. And as he tossed his takeout container in the trash and snapped the television off, Eli wanted to go, to run, not away, but *toward* something. He had a goal. A mission.

But he knew he had to wait. He counted down the days until graduation, all the while feeling the attention of the professors, the counselors, and the cops on him like the sun in summer. At first it was glaring, but eventually, as the months wore on, it lessened until, by the time he took his exams, most even forgot to look concerned when he entered the room. When the year finally ended, he packed casually, did a last, lazy pass through his place, and locked the door. He slid the key into a school-sanctioned white envelope and dropped it off in the mailbox outside residential services.

And then, and only then, when the campus of Lockland had vanished in the distance, Eli shrugged off the name Cardale in favor of Ever, and went out to seek his purpose.

∞

ELI didn't enjoy killing.

He did quite like the moment after. The glorious quiet that

filled the air as his broken bones healed and his torn skin closed, and he knew that God approved.

But the killing itself was messier than he anticipated.

And he didn't like the term. *Killing.* What about *removal*? *Removal* was a better word. It made the targets sound less like humans, which they weren't really . . . semantics. Regardless, it was messy. The profusion of violence on television had led Eli to believe that killing was clean. The small cough of a gun. The quick jab of a knife. A moment of shock.

The camera cuts away and life goes on.

Easy.

And to be fair, Lyne's death *had* been easy. So had Sykes's, really, since the car had done the work. But as Eli peeled a blood-soaked pair of latex gloves from his hands, he found himself wishing the camera would cut to a more pleasant moment.

Wallace had put up a fight. Late fifties, but ox-strong. He'd even bent one of Eli's favorite knives before snapping it right in two.

Eli leaned against the brick wall and waited for his ribs to notch back into place before hauling the body toward the nearest pile of trash. The night was warm and he checked himself for blood before leaving the alley, the quiet already fading, leaving a strange sadness in its wake.

He felt lost again. Purposeless. Even with his lead, it had taken him three weeks to find the EO. It was a slow, clumsy pursuit. He'd wanted to be sure. He'd needed proof. After all, what if he guessed wrong? Eli had no desire to rack up a body count of humans. Lyne and Sykes had been exceptions, victims of circumstance, their deaths unfortunate, but necessary. And, if Eli was being honest with himself, sloppy. He knew he could do better. Wallace had been an improvement. As with any pursuit, there was a learning curve, but he firmly believed in the old saying.

Practice makes perfect.

VII

AROUND NOON
THE ESQUIRE HOTEL

VICTOR and Sydney sat in the hotel room, eating cold pizza and looking over the profiles Mitch had set out for them. Mitch himself had gone to run an errand, and even though Victor's eyes tracked over the profile of a middle-aged man named Zachary Flinch, his mind was far more on the cell phone—ready and within reach on the counter beside him—and on the name Stell, than his papers. His fingers tapped out a quiet beat on his leg. On the opposite side of his phone sat the profile of a younger man named Dominic Rusher.

Sydney sat perched on a nearby stool, finishing her second slice of pizza. Victor saw her steal a glance at Eli's newspaper photo, tucked beneath the corner of the third profile, which belonged to the blue-haired Beth Kirk. He watched as she reached out and drew the article free, staring down at it with her wide, blue eyes.

"Don't worry, Syd," said Victor. "I'll make him hurt."

For a moment she was quiet, her face a mask. And then it cracked. "When he came after me," she said, "he told me it was for *the greater good*." She spat the last three words. "He said I was unnatural. That I went against God. That was the reason he gave for trying to kill me. I didn't think it was a very good reason." She swallowed. "But it was enough for my sister to hand me over."

Victor frowned. The issue of Sydney's sister, Serena, still bothered him. Why hadn't Eli killed her yet? He seemed hell-bent on killing everyone else.

"I'm sure it's complicated," he said, looking up from the profile in his hands. "What can your sister do?"

Sydney hesitated. "I don't know. She never showed me. She was supposed to, but then her boyfriend kind of shot me. Why?"

"Because," he said, "Eli's keeping her around. There must be a reason. She must be valuable to him."

Sydney looked down, and shrugged.

"But," added Victor, "if it were based on value alone, he would have kept you around. His loss is my gain."

A ghost of a smile crossed Sydney's mouth. She tossed her pizza crust to the black mass on the floor. Dol perked and caught it before it hit the ground. He then hoisted himself to his feet, and made his way around the counter to Victor, eyeing his crust expectantly. Victor fed it to him, and gave the dog's ears—which came to his stomach, even sitting on the stool—a short scratch. He looked from the beast to Sydney. He really was collecting strays.

Victor's cell rang.

He dropped the paper and lifted the phone, all in one motion. "Yes?"

"Got him," said Mitch.

"Dane or Stell?"

"Dane. And I even found us a room."

"Where?" asked Victor, pulling on his coat.

"Look out your window."

Victor strode up to the floor-to-ceiling panes, and took in the view. Across the road, and two buildings down, was the skeleton of a high-rise. Wooden construction walls encircled the scaffolding, a banner that read FALCON PRICE was plastered on the front, but there were no workers. The project had either been paused, or abandoned.

"Perfect," said Victor. "I'm on my way."

He hung up, and saw Sydney already off her stool and clutching her own red coat, waiting. He couldn't help but think she had the same expression as Dol, expectant, hopeful.

"No, Sydney," he said. "I need you to stay here."

"Why?" she asked.

"Because you don't think I'm a bad person," he said. "And I don't want to prove you wrong."

∞

VICTOR wound his way through the plastic sheeting that cordoned off the unfinished spaces of the high-rise's ground floor, his steps echoing off concrete and steel. The fine coat of dust on the more exposed outer rooms of the building suggested a recently abandoned project, but the quality of the materials and the prime location made him think it wouldn't stay abandoned for very long. Buildings in transition were perfect places for meetings like this.

A few veils of tarp later, he found Mitch and a man in a foldout chair. Mitch looked bored. The man in the chair looked indignant and, under that, terrified. Victor could practically feel the fear, a fainter version of the radarlike ripple caused by pain. The man was lean, with short dark hair, and a sharp jaw. His hands were bound behind his back with duct tape, and he was still in his uniform, the collar darkened in places by blood. The blood came from his cheek, or his nose, or perhaps both, Victor couldn't quite tell. A few drops had dripped onto the badge over his heart.

"I have to admit," said Victor, "I was hoping for Stell."

"You said either one would do. Stell was out. I caught this one on a smoke break," said Mitch.

Victor smiled beatifically as he turned his attention to the man in the chair. "Smoking's bad for you, Officer Dane."

Officer Dane said something, but the duct tape over his mouth made it unintelligible.

"You don't know me," continued Victor. He put his boot on the side of the foldout chair, and tipped it. Officer Dane tumbled out, hitting the floor with a crack and a muffled yelp, and Victor caught the chair before it fell, turned it in one lithe motion, and sat down. "I'm a friend of a friend. And I'd greatly appreciate your help." He sat forward, resting his elbows on his knees. "I want you to tell me your access codes to the police database."

Officer Dane frowned. So did Mitch.

"Vic," he said, hunching over so Dane wouldn't hear. "What do you need that for? I hacked you in."

Victor didn't seem to care if the officer overheard. "You gave me eyes, and I'm grateful. But I want to make a post, and in order to do that, I need a recognized ID." It was time to send another message, and Victor wanted every detail perfect. The flagged profiles had author tags, and as Mitch himself had pointed out, all of them belonged to one of two people: Stell or Dane.

"Besides," said Victor, sliding to his feet, "this way's more fun."

The air in the room began to hum, the exposed skeleton of the building reflecting back the energy until the whole space buzzed.

"You should wait outside," he said to Mitch.

Victor had perfected his art, could pick a person out of a crowd and drop them like a stone, but he still didn't like bystanders. Just in case. Now and then he got a touch too zealous, and the pain spilled over, leaked into others. Mitch knew him well enough, and didn't ask questions, just tugged a veil of plastic tarp aside, and left.

Victor watched him go, flexing his fingers as if he needed them supple. He felt a faint pang of guilt at involving Mitch in this at all. It's not as though hacking was the only reason the man had ended up in such a high security prison, but still. Abducting an officer was a serious offense. Not as serious as the crimes Victor himself was about to commit, of course, but given Mitch's record, it wouldn't look good. He'd considered dismissing his friend as soon as they were on the free side of the Wrighton Penitentiary fence, but the simple fact was that Victor didn't possess superhuman strength, and someone would have to help him dispose of bodies. That, and he'd grown rather accustomed to Mitch's presence. He sighed, and turned his attention to the officer, who was trying to speak. Victor crouched, his knee digging down into the man's chest as he peeled the duct tape back.

"You don't know what you're doing," growled Officer Dane. "You'll fry for this."

Victor smiled quietly. "Not with your help."

"Why should I help you?"

Victor returned the tape to his mouth, and stood.

"Oh, you shouldn't." The hum in the air sharpened, and Officer Dane's body spasmed, his scream muffled by the tape. "But you will."

VIII

THIS AFTERNOON
THE ESQUIRE HOTEL

ELI was still staring down at the gridded screen of the police database when he heard the door open behind him. He tapped the screen, closing the profile of a suspected EO named Dominic Rusher just as a pair of slim arms wrapped around his shoulders, and a pair of lips grazed his ear.

"Where have you been?" he asked.

"Looking for Sydney."

He tensed. "And?"

"No luck yet, but I've put the word out. At least we'll have a few more pairs of eyes. How was the bank?"

"I don't trust Stell," said Eli for the hundredth time.

Serena sighed. "How was Barry Lynch?"

"Dead again by the time I got there." He lifted the childlike drawing from the desk, handed it blindly back to her. "But he left this."

He felt the drawing plucked from his fingers, and a moment later, Serena said, "I didn't know Victor was so thin."

"This isn't a time for joking," snapped Eli.

Serena spun his chair to face her. Her eyes were cold as ice. "You're right," she said. "You told me you killed Sydney."

"I thought I did."

Serena leaned down, and slid the prop glasses from Eli's face.

He'd forgotten he was still wearing them. She tucked them into her hair like a makeshift headband, and kissed him, not on the lips, but between the eyes, the place that wrinkled whenever he resisted her.

"Did you really?" she breathed against him.

He forced his skin to smooth beneath her kiss. It was easier to think when she wasn't looking in his eyes.

"I did."

He sighed inwardly with relief as he said it. Two small words—half truth at most—and nothing more. It was hard, and it left him drained, but there was no doubt, he was getting better at holding back.

She pulled away enough to hold him with her cold blue eyes. He could see the devil in them, silver-tongued and cunning, and Eli thought, not for the first time, that he should have killed her when he had the chance.

IX

LAST FALL
UNIVERSITY OF MERIT

THE music was loud enough to shake the pictures on the walls. An angel and a wizard made out on the stairs. Two naughty cats tugged a vampire between them, a guy with yellow contacts howled, and someone spilled a Solo cup of cheap beer near Eli's feet.

He snagged the horns from a devil by the front door, and set them on top of his head. He'd seen the girl walk in, flanked by a Barbie and a Catholic schoolgirl flaunting numerous uniform infractions, but *she* was in jeans and a polo, blond hair loose, falling over her shoulders. He'd lost sight of her for only a moment, and now her friends were there, weaving through the crowd with interlocking fingers held over their heads, but she was gone. She should have stood out, the lack of costume conspicuous at a Halloween party, but she was nowhere to be found.

He swept through the house, avoiding the attempts of several pretty undergrads to delay him. It was flattering, and after all, he looked the part—he'd looked the part for ten years—but he was here on business. And then, after several unsuccessful tours of the first floor, *she* found *him*. A hand pulled him onto the stairs, into the shadows.

"Hi there," whispered the girl. All the music, and the shouting, and somehow he could still hear her.

"Hi," he breathed against her.

Her fingers intertwined with his as she led him up the stairs, away from the deafening party, and into a bedroom that wasn't hers, judging by the way she glanced around before stepping through. *College girls*, thought Eli cheerfully. You had to love them. He pulled the door shut behind him and the world in the room became blissfully quiet, the music dulled into a kind of thrum. The lights were off and they left them off, the only illumination pouring in through the window in the form of moonlight and street lamps.

"A Halloween party and no costume?" teased Eli.

The girl pulled a magnifying glass from her back pocket.

"Sherlock," she explained. Her movements were slow, almost sleepy. Her eyes were the color of water in winter and he didn't know what her power was. He hadn't studied her long enough, hadn't waited for a demonstration, or rather, had been studying and waiting for weeks, but hadn't been able to catch sight of the ability, whatever it was, so he'd decided to get a bit closer. It broke his rules and he knew it, and yet here he was.

"And you are?" she asked. Eli realized he was too tall for her to see. He bowed his head and pointed to the horns balanced on top. They were red and sequined, and glittered in the darkened room.

"Mephistopheles," he said. She laughed. She was an English major. He knew that much. And it was fitting, he thought. One devil to lure another.

"Original," she said with a bored smile. Serena Clarke. That was the name in his notes. She was beautiful in the most careless way. The little makeup she wore looked like an afterthought, and Eli had a hard time breaking her gaze. He was used to pretty girls, but Serena was different, *more*. When she pulled him in for a kiss, he nearly forgot the chloroform in his back pocket. Her hands slid down his spine to his jeans and he peeled them away just before her fingers skimmed the bottle and the folded cloth. He guided her hands up the wall and over her head, pinning them there as they kissed. She tasted like cold water.

He'd meant to push her out the window.

Instead he let her push him back onto a stranger's bed. The chloroform dug into his hip, but when he looked away from her she guided his eyes and his attention back with only a finger and a smile and a whispered command. A thrill ran through him. One he hadn't felt in years. Longing.

"Kiss me," she said, and he did. Eli couldn't, for the life of him, *not* kiss her, and as his lips found hers, she pinned his hands above him playfully, her blond hair tickling his face.

"Who are you?" she asked. Eli had decided that tonight his name would be Gill, but when he opened his mouth what came out was, "Eli Ever."

What the hell?

"How alliterative," said Serena. "What brings you to the party?"

"I came to find you." The words came out before Eli even noticed he was talking. He stiffened under her, and somewhere in his mind, he knew that this was bad, knew he needed to get up. But when he went to free himself, the girl cooed, "Don't go, lie still," and his body betrayed him, relaxing beneath her fingers even as his heart hammered in his chest.

"You stand out," she said. "I've seen you before. Last week."

Actually, Eli had been following her for *two* weeks, hoping to catch a glimpse of her ability. No such luck. Until now. He willed his body to move, but it wanted to lie beneath her. *He* wanted to lie beneath her.

"Are you following me?" She said it almost playfully, but Eli answered, "Yes."

"Why?" she asked, letting go of his hands, but still straddling him.

Eli managed to push himself onto his elbows. He fought the answer down like bile. *Don't say to kill you. Don't say to kill you. Don't say to kill you.* He felt the words claw their way up his throat.

"To kill you."

The girl frowned decidedly, but didn't move. "Why?"

The answer poured out. "You're an EO," he said. "You have an ability that goes against nature, and it's dangerous. *You're dangerous.*"

Her mouth quirked. "Says the boy trying to kill me."

"I don't expect you to understand—"

"I do, but you're not going to kill me tonight, Eli." She said it so casually. He must have frowned, because she added, "Don't look so disappointed. You can always try again tomorrow."

The room was dark and the party thudded on beyond the walls. The girl leaned forward and plucked the red sequined horns from his dark hair, nestling them in her own blond waves. She was lovely, and he struggled to think straight, to remember why she had to die.

And then she said, "You're right, you know."

"About what?" asked Eli. His thoughts felt slow.

"I'm dangerous. I shouldn't exist. But what gives you the right to kill me?"

"Because I can."

"Bad answer," she said, running her fingers along his jaw. And then she let her body slip down on top of his, jean to jean and hip to hip and skin to skin.

"Kiss me again," she ordered. And he did.

∞

SERENA Clarke spent half her time wishing she were dead, and the other half telling everyone around her what to do, and wishing *someone* wouldn't do it.

She'd asked to leave the hospital, and the sea of staff had practically parted to let her pass before her IV was even out. It had been pleasant, at first, getting her way so easily, if not a little foreign. Serena had always been strong, always ready to fight for something she wanted. But suddenly there was no need, because the fight had gone out of everyone else. The world went limp around her, a complacent glaze filling the eyes of anyone she met and spoke to. The lack of opposition, of tension, became maddening. Her parents simply nodded when she said she wanted to go back to school. Her teachers ceased to be a challenge. Her friends bent and bent and bent to every whim. Boys lost their fire, gave her anything she wanted, and anything she didn't want, but was bored enough to ask for.

Where before Serena's world had bowed beneath the strength of her will, now it simply bowed. She didn't have to argue, she didn't have to try.

She felt like a ghost.

And worst of all, Serena hated to admit how easy and addictive it was, getting her way, even when it made her miserable. Every time she got tired of trying to make people fight her, she would slink back into the comfort of control. She couldn't turn it off. Even when she didn't order, even when she only suggested, only asked, they did it.

She felt like a god.

She dreamed of people who could fight back. Of wills strong enough to resist her.

And then one night, she got mad—truly mad—at the boy she was seeing, at the stupid, glazed look in his eyes that she knew too well, and when he refused to fight her, refused to deny her, because for some infuriating reason she couldn't order him to do *that*, his desire to bend superseding any attempt at violence, she told him to go jump off a bridge.

And he did.

Serena remembered sitting cross-legged on her bed and listening to the news, her friends huddled on the comforter around her—but not touching; there seemed to be a thin wall separating them from her, fear, or maybe awe—and it was then she realized that she wasn't a ghost, or a god.

She was a monster.

∞

ELI examined the small blue card the girl had slipped in his pocket the night before. On one side she'd written the name of a café off the main library—the Light Post, it was called—along with a time, *2 p.m.* On the other side, she'd written *Scheherazade*—she'd even spelled it correctly. Eli knew the reference, of course. *Arabian Nights.* The woman who told the sultan stories and never finished at night, lest he kill her. Instead she drew the stories over until the next day.

As he made his way through U of Merit's campus, he felt hungover for the first time in a decade, his head heavy and his thoughts slow. It had taken him most of the morning to drag fully free of the girl's compulsion, to think of her as a target. Only a target.

He slipped the card back into his pocket. He knew Serena wouldn't show up. She'd be a fool to come anywhere near him after last night. After he'd admitted his intentions. And yet there she was, sitting on the patio of the Light Post wearing sunglasses and a dark blue sweater, her blond hair wisping around her face.

"Do you have a death wish?" Eli asked, standing beside the table.

She shrugged. "I've done it once. The novelty must be wearing off." She gestured to the empty chair across from her. Eli weighed his options, but he couldn't exactly kill her in the middle of campus, so he sat down.

"Serena," she said, sliding the sunglasses on top of her head. In the daylight, her eyes were even lighter. "But you already know my name." She sipped her coffee. Eli said nothing. "Why do you want to kill me?" she asked. "And don't say because you can."

The moment Eli's thoughts formed they were sliding across his tongue. He frowned as the words spilled out. "EOs are unnatural."

"You said that already."

"My best friend became one, and I saw the change. Like a devil had climbed into his skin. He killed my girlfriend, and then he tried to kill me." He bit into his tongue and managed to stem the flow of words. Was it her eyes, or her voice that was compelling him?

"So you go around blaming every other EO you can find," said Serena. "Punishing them in his place?"

"You don't understand," he said. "I'm trying to *protect* people."

She smiled behind her coffee. It wasn't a happy smile. "Which people?"

"The normal ones."

Serena scoffed.

"The natural ones," pressed Eli. "ExtraOrdinaries shouldn't exist. They haven't just been given a second chance, they've been given a weapon and no manual. No rules. Their very existence is criminal. They aren't whole."

The thin smile fell from Serena's red lips. "What do you mean?"

"I mean that when a person revives as an EO, not all of them comes back. Things are missing." Even Eli, blessed as he was, knew that he was missing pieces. "Important things like empathy and balance and fear and consequence. Those things that might temper their abilities, they're missing. Tell me I'm wrong. Tell me you feel all those things the way you did before."

Serena leaned forward, setting her coffee on a stack of books. She didn't contradict him. Instead, she said, "And what is your ability, Eli Ever?"

"What makes you think I have one?" He spat the words out as quickly as he could, filling the need to speak. It was such a small victory, countering like that, but he knew she registered it. And then her smile sharpened.

"Tell me your power," she said.

This time he answered. "I heal."

She laughed, loud enough that one or two students glanced over from tables across the patio. "No wonder you have a wicked sense of entitlement."

"What do you mean?"

"Well, your gift doesn't impact anyone else. It's reflexive. So in your mind *you're* not a threat. But the rest of us are." Serena tapped the stack of books, and Eli could make out psychology titles mingled in with the English books. "Am I close?"

Eli wasn't sure he liked Serena very much. He wanted to tell her about his covenant, but instead he asked, "How did you know I'm an EO?"

"Everything about you," she said, sliding her sunglasses back on, "is chock full of self-loathing. I'm not judging. I know the feeling." Her watch gave a small beep, and she dragged herself to her feet. Even that simple motion was lovely and fluid, like water. "You know, maybe I should let you kill me. Because you're right. Even though we come back, something stays dead. Lost. We forget something of who we were. It's scary and wonderful and monstrous."

She looked so sad in that moment, ringed with afternoon light, and Eli had to resist the urge to go to her. Something fluttered in him. She reminded him of Angie, or rather, how *he* had felt around Angie before everything had changed. Before *he* had changed. Ten years of staring across the chasm at the things he'd lost, and now, looking at this girl, it was like the chasm was shrinking, the gap pulling closed until his fingers could almost—*almost*—skim the other side. He wanted to be close to her, wanted to make her happy, wanted to reach across the rift and remember—he bit down again until he tasted blood to clear his mind. He knew the feelings weren't his, not entirely, not naturally. There was no going back. He was the way he was for a reason. A purpose. And this girl, this monster, had a dangerous, complicated gift. It wasn't a simple compulsion. It was an attraction. A want to please. A need to please. They were her feelings filtering through him, not his own.

"We're all monsters," she said, taking up her books. "But so are you."

Eli was only half listening, but still the words began to trickle through him, and he pushed them violently away before they could settle in his mind. He got to his feet, but she was already turning away.

"You can't kill me today," she called back. "I'm late for class."

⦿

ELI sat on a bench outside the psychology building, his head tipped back. It was a beautiful day, cloudy but not gray, cold but not bitter, and the breeze that tugged at his collar and wove through his hair kept him alert. His mind was clear again, now that Serena was gone, and he knew he had a problem. He needed to kill the girl without seeing her, without hearing her. If she were unconscious, he mused, then he might be able to—

"Aren't you picturesque." The voice was cool and warm at once. Serena clutched her books to her chest and looked down at him. "What were you thinking about?" she asked.

"Killing you," he said. It was almost freeing, not being able to lie.

Serena shook her head slowly and sighed. "Walk me to my next class."

He stood.

"Tell me," she said, weaving her arm through his. "At the party last night, how were you going to kill me?"

Eli watched the clouds. "Drug you and push you out the window."

"That's cold," she said.

Eli shrugged. "But believable. Kids get drunk at parties. After discretion, their balance is the next thing to go. They fall. Sometimes out of windows."

"So," she said, leaning against him. Her hair tickled his cheek. "Do you have a cape?"

"Are you mocking me?"

"More of a mask type, then."

"What are you getting at?" he asked as they reached her next building.

"You're the hero . . . ," she said, finding his eyes, ". . . of your own story, anyway." She started up the steps. "Will I see you again? Do you have me penciled in for a redo sometime this week? I just want to know, so I can bring my mace. Put up a fight at least, for realism's sake."

Serena was the strangest girl Eli had ever met. He told her so. She smiled, and went inside.

∞

SERENA'S eyes brightened when she saw him again the next day.

Eli was waiting on the building steps in the late afternoon with a cup of coffee in each hand. The dusk smelled like dead leaves and far-off fires; his breath escaped in small clouds as he held one of the coffees out to her, and she took it and slipped her arm through his again.

"My hero," she said, and Eli smiled at the inside joke. In nearly ten years he hadn't let anyone close. Certainly not an EO. Yet here he was, walking through the twilight with one. And he liked it. He tried to remind himself that the sensation was false, projected, tried to convince himself that this was research, that he was only trying to understand her gift, and how best to eliminate her, even as her let her guide him down the steps and away from the campus.

"So you protect the innocent world from the big bad EOs," she said as they made their way, arm in arm. "How do you find them?"

"I have a system." As they walked, he explained to her his method. The careful narrowing down of targets based on Lyne's three steps. The periods of observation.

"Sounds tedious," she said.

"It is."

"And then when you find them, you just kill them?" Her steps slowed. "No questions? No trial? No assessment of whether they're a danger or a threat?"

"I used to talk to them. Not anymore."

"What gives you the right to play judge and jury and executioner?"

"God." He hadn't wanted to say the word, hadn't wanted to

give this strange girl the power of knowing his beliefs, of twisting and bending them to her own.

She pursed her lips, the word hanging in the air between them, but she didn't mock him.

"How do you kill them?" she asked eventually.

"It depends on their ability," he said. "Default is a gun, but if there's a concern regarding metal, or explosives, or the setup, I have to find another method. Like with you. You're young and you'd probably be missed, which would be messy, and that therefore ruled out a crime. I needed to make it look like an accident."

They turned onto a side street lined with small apartment buildings and houses.

"What's the strangest way you've ever killed someone?"

Eli thought about it. "Bear trap."

Serena cringed. "No details necessary."

A few minutes passed in silence as they walked.

"How long have you been doing this?" asked Serena.

"Ten years."

"No way," she said, squinting at him. "How old are you?"

Eli smiled. "How old do I look?"

They reached her apartment and stopped.

"Twenty. Maybe twenty-one."

"Well, I guess I'm technically thirty-two. But I've looked this way for ten years."

"Part of that whole healing thing?"

Eli nodded. "Regeneration."

"Show me," said Serena.

"How?" asked Eli.

Her eyes glittered. "Do you have a weapon on you?"

Eli hesitated a moment, then withdrew a Glock from his coat.

"Give it to me," said Serena. Eli handed it over, but he had the self-possession to frown as he did it. Serena stepped away from him and took aim.

"Wait," said Eli. He looked around. "Maybe not out here, in the street? Let's go inside."

Serena considered him for a long moment, then smiled, and led him in.

X

THIS AFTERNOON
THE ESQUIRE HOTEL

"**VICTOR** sent you a message," said Serena, brushing her fingers over Sydney's stick figure in the drawing. There was a fleck of brownish red on the corner of the paper, and she wondered whose blood it was. "Are you going to send one back?"

She watched as the answer climbed up Eli's throat. "I don't know how," he said under his breath.

"He's here in the city," she said.

"So are millions of other people, Serena," growled Eli.

"And they're all on your side," she said. "Or they can be." She took Eli's hand, drew him up from the chair. Her hands slid around his back, pulled him close until his forehead rested against hers. "Let me help you."

She watched his jaw clench. Eli couldn't resist her, not really, but he was *trying*. She could see the strain in his eyes, in the space between his brows, as he fought the compulsion. Every time she asked a question. Every time she gave a small order. There was a pause, as if Eli were trying to reprocess the command, twist it until it was his. As if he could take back his will. He couldn't, but she loved to see him try. It gave her something to hold on to. She took it in, savored his resistance. And then, for his sake, she forced him to bend.

"Eli," she said, her voice, even and unmovable. "Let me help you."

"How?" he asked.

Her fingers slipped into his front pocket, and drew out his phone. "Call Detective Stell. Tell him we need a meeting with the Merit PD. *All* of them." Victor wasn't the only one in the city. Sydney was here, too. Find one, and they would find the other—the drawing told them as much. Eli stared down at his phone.

"It's too public," he said, fingers punching in the numbers even as he struggled to think. "It makes *us* too public. I haven't made it this long by standing in spotlights."

"It's the only way to flush them out. Besides, you shouldn't worry. You're the hero now, remember?"

He laughed drily, but didn't say *no* again.

"Do you want a mask?" she teased, pulling the glasses from her hair and sliding them back onto his face. "Or will these do?"

Eli ran his thumb over his phone, hesitating for one last moment. And then he connected the call.

XI

LAST FALL
UNIVERSITY OF MERIT

SERENA Clarke lived alone. Eli could tell from the moment they walked in, when she slipped her shoes off by the door. The place was clean, calm, and unified. It had one cohesive taste, and Serena didn't look around for anyone before turning on him and raising the gun.

"Hold up," said Eli, shrugging his coat off. "This is my favorite. I'd rather not have holes in it." He took a small cylinder from the pocket, and tossed it to her.

"Do you actually know how to use a gun?" he asked.

Serena nodded as she screwed the silencer on. "Years of crime dramas. And I found my father's Colt once, and taught myself. Cans in the woods, and all that."

"Are you a decent shot?" Eli unbuttoned his shirt and took that off, too, draping it over the entry table with his coat. Serena gave him an appreciative head-to-toe-and-back look, and then she pulled the trigger. He gasped and staggered backward, red blossoming against his shoulder. The pain was brief and bright, the bullet passing straight through and lodging in the wall behind him. He watched Serena's eyes widen as the wound instantly began to close, his skin knitting back together. She gave a slow clap, the gun still in her grip. Eli rubbed his shoulder, and met her eyes.

"Happy now?" he grumbled.

"Don't be so sour," she said, setting the gun on the table.

"Just because I heal," he said, reaching past her for his shirt, "doesn't mean that didn't hurt."

Serena caught his arm in one hand and his face in the other, and held his gaze. Eli felt himself falling in. "Want me to kiss it?" she asked, brushing her lips against his. "Will that make it better?"

There it was again, in his chest, that strange flutter, like *want,* dusty and a decade old but there. Maybe it was a trick. Maybe this feeling—this simple, mortal ache—wasn't coming from him. But maybe it was. Maybe it could be. He nodded once, just enough to bring their lips together, and then she turned and led him toward to the bedroom.

"Don't kill me tonight," she added as she led him into the dark. And he never even thought of it.

∞

SERENA and Eli were lying together in a tangle of sheets. They faced each other, and she ran her fingers down his cheek, his throat, his chest. Her hand seemed fascinated with the place where she'd shot him, now only smooth skin shining in the near dark of the room. Her hand wandered, then, over his ribs and around his back, and came to rest on the web of old scars there. She drew in a small breath.

"They're from before," he said softly. "Nothing leaves marks anymore." Her lips parted, but before she could ask what happened, he added, "Please. Don't ask."

And she didn't. Instead, she drew her hand back to his unscarred chest and let it rest over his heart.

"Where will you go, after you kill me?"

"I don't know," he said honestly. "I'll have to start again."

"Will you sleep with that one, too?" she asked, and Eli laughed.

"Seduction is hardly part of my method."

"Well, then, I feel special."

"You are." It came out in a whisper. And it was true. Special. Different. Fascinating. Dangerous. Her hand slid back to the bed, and he thought perhaps she'd fallen asleep. He enjoyed watching her this way, knowing he could kill her, but not wanting to. It made him feel like he was in control again. Or closer to it. Being with Serena felt like a dream, an interlude. It made Eli feel human again. It made him forget.

"There must be an easier way," she wondered sleepily. "To find them . . . if you could access the right networks . . ."

"If only," he whispered. And then they slept.

∞

THE sun streamed in but the room was cool. Eli shivered, and sat up. The bed was empty beside him. He found his pants, and spent several minutes searching for his shirt before he remembered he'd left it by the front door, and padded out into the apartment. Serena was gone. His gun was still on the table, and he tucked it into the back of his pants and went into the kitchen to make coffee.

Eli was fascinated by kitchens. By the way people ordered their lives, the cabinets they used, the places they kept food, and the food they choose to keep. He'd spent the last decade studying people, and it was amazing how much could be gleaned from their homes. Their bedrooms, and bathrooms, and closets, of course, but also their kitchens. Serena's coffee was in the lowest cabinet over the counter, just beside the sink, which meant she drank a lot of it. A small black, two-to-four-cup coffeemaker sat tucked along the tile backsplash, another clue she lived alone. The apartment was far too nice for an underclassman, one of those lottery-only wins, and Eli wondered absently as he pulled out a filter if she'd used her talents to get this, too.

He found the coffee cups to the left of the sink, and tapped the coffeemaker, eager for it to brew. As soon as it did, he filled his cup and took a long sip. Now that he was alone, his mind was making its way faithfully back to the topic of how he was going to eliminate Serena, when the front door opened and she walked in, flanked by two men. One was a police officer, and the other was Detective Stell. Eli's heart lurched in his chest, but he managed a careful smile over his mug as he leaned against the counter to hide the gun in the back of his pants.

"Good morning," he said.

"Morning ...," said Stell, and Eli watched confusion spread through his features beneath a glazed calm, which Eli quickly recognized as Serena's doing. It had been nearly ten years, during which the Lockland case had gone stone cold, and during which Eli had constantly thought of Stell, casting backward glances to see if he would follow. Stell hadn't, but he clearly recognized him now. (How could he not? Eli was a photograph, unchanging.) Yet neither he nor the officer reached for their weapons, so that was promising. Eli looked to Serena, who was beaming.

"I have a present for you," she said, gesturing to the men.

"You really shouldn't have," said Eli slowly.

"This is Officer Frederick Dane, and his boss, Detective Stell."

"Mr. Cardale," said Stell.

"I go by Ever now."

"You two know each other?" asked Serena.

"Detective Stell was on Victor's case," offered Eli. "Back at Lockland."

Serena's eyes widened in recognition. Eli had told her about that day. He'd left out most of the details, and now, staring at the only man who'd ever even had reason to suspect him of foul play, potentially of *ExtraOrdinary* play, he wished he'd given her the entire truth.

"It's been some time," said Stell. "And yet you haven't changed, Mr. Card . . . Ever. Not at all—"

"What brings you to Merit?" cut in Eli.

"I transferred a few months ago."

"Change of scenery?"

"Followed a rash of killings."

Eli knew he should have broken up the path, the pattern, but he'd been on a roll. Merit had attracted an impressive number of EOs, by virtue of its population and its many dark corners. People came to the city thinking they could hide. But not from him.

"Eli," said Serena. "You're ruining my surprise. Stell and Dane and I, we've had a good long chat, and it's all been arranged. They're going to help us."

"Us?" asked Eli.

Serena turned back to the men and smiled. "Have a seat." The two men obediently sat down at the kitchen table.

"Eli, can you pour them some coffee?"

Eli wasn't sure how to do that without turning his back and his gun on the cops, so he reached for Serena instead, and pulled her close. Another small act of defiance. The motion had the easy movement of a lover's embrace, but his grip was tight. "What are you doing?" he growled into her ear.

"I was thinking," she said, tipping her head back against his chest, "about how tedious it must be, trying to find each EO." She wasn't even bothering to lower her voice. "And then I thought, there must be an easier way. It turns out the Merit Police Department has a database for persons of interest. Of course, it's not meant for

EOs, but the search matrix, that's what it's called, right?" Officer Dane nodded. "Yes, well, it's broad enough that we could use it for that." Serena seemed thoroughly proud of herself. "So I went to the station, and I asked to talk to someone involved with EO investigation—you told me, remember, that some of them were trained for it—and the man at the desk led me to these fine gentlemen. Dane is Stell's protégé, and they've both agreed to share their search engine with us."

"There's that *us* again," said Eli, aloud. Serena ignored him.

"We've got it all figured out, I think. Right, Officer Dane?"

The lanky man with dark, close-cropped hair nodded and set a thin folder on the table. "The first batch," he said.

"Thank you, Officer," said Serena, taking up the file. "This will keep us busy for a little while."

Us. Us. Us. What on earth was happening? But even as Eli's thoughts spun, he managed to keep his hand away from the gun against his back and focus on the instructions Serena was now giving the cops.

"Mr. Ever here is going to keep this city safe," she told them, her blue eyes shining. "He's a hero, isn't he, Officers?"

Officer Dane nodded. At first Stell only looked at Eli, but eventually, he nodded, too.

"A hero," they echoed.

XII

THIS AFTERNOON
THE FALCON PRICE PROJECT

DANE whimpered faintly from the floor.

Victor leaned back in the foldout chair, locking his fingers behind his head. A switchblade dangled loosely from one hand, the flat of the blade skimming his pale hair. It wasn't strictly necessary, but his talent was most effective when it amplified an existing source of pain. Officer Dane curled in on himself on the concrete floor, his uniform torn, blood streaking across the floor. Victor was glad Mitch had put some plastic sheeting down. He'd gotten a little carried away, but it had been so long since he'd stretched, so long since he'd let go. It cleared his head. It calmed him.

Dane's hands were still firmly bound behind his back, but the tape over his mouth had come off, and his shirt clung to his chest with sweat and blood. He'd given up the database's access codes, of course, and quickly at that—Victor had tested them on his phone to be sure. Then, with a bit more encouragement, he'd told Victor everything he knew about Detective Stell: his earlier days in Lockland, his transfer on the heels of a killing streak—Eli's work, no doubt—and Dane's own training. All cops these days, it turned out, learned an EO protocol, whether they were skeptics or believers, but at least one man in every precinct knew more than the basics, studied the indicators, and took charge of any investigation where an EO was even suspected.

Stell had been that man ten years ago at Lockland, and he was that man again here, and grooming Dane to follow. Not only that, but somehow, Eli had convinced the detective in charge of the investigation against him to *help* him.

Victor shook his head in wonder as he tortured the details out of Dane. Eli never ceased to amaze him. If he and Stell had been working together since Lockland, that would have been one thing, but this was a new arrangement—Stell and Dane had only been assisting Eli since last fall. How had Eli conned the Merit PD into helping him?

"Officer Dane," said Victor. The cop cringed at the sound of his voice. "Would you mind telling me about your interactions with Eli Ever?"

When Dane didn't answer, Victor stood and rolled the man onto his back with the tip of his shoe. "Well?" he asked calmly, leaning on the officer's broken ribs.

Dane screamed, but once the screams had given way to gasps, he said, "Eli Ever . . . is . . . a hero."

Victor let out a choked laugh, and put more weight on Dane's chest. "Who told you that?"

The officer's expression shifted. It was stern, but remarkably level when he answered. "Serena."

"And you bought it?"

Officer Dane looked at Victor as if he couldn't quite grasp the question.

And then Victor got it. "What else did Serena say?"

"To help Mr. Ever."

"And you did."

Officer Dane looked confused. "Of course."

Victor smiled grimly.

"Of course," he echoed, pulling the gun from his belt. He

rubbed his eyes, swore quietly beneath his breath, then fired two quick shots into Officer Dane's chest. This was the first person he'd killed since Angie Knight (if you didn't count that one man in prison, back when he'd been perfecting his technique, and Victor didn't), and certainly the first intentional *murder*. It wasn't that he shied away from killing; people simply weren't any good to him dead. After all, pain didn't have much effect on corpses. As for Dane's murder, it was unfortunate (albeit necessary), and the fact that a modicum of regret was all that Victor felt on the matter might have bothered him more, or at least been worth a moment of introspection, had he not been so preoccupied with bringing the dead man *back*.

Mitch ducked through the plastic sheeting and into the room at the muffled sound of the gunshots. He'd pulled on gloves, and already had a spare sheet of plastic tucked under one arm, just in case. He looked down at the officer's body, and sighed, but when he started taking up the plastic on the floor, and Dane with it, Victor held out a hand, and stopped him.

"Leave him," he said. "And go get Sydney."

Mitch hesitated. "I don't think . . ."

Victor spun on him. "I said, go get her."

Mitch looked profoundly unhappy, but did as he was told, leaving Victor alone with the officer's corpse.

XIII

LAST FALL
UNIVERSITY OF MERIT

SERENA ushered the detectives out, and returned to the kitchen to find Eli looking pale and bracing himself against the sink. Everything about him was coiled, the tension in his face something she hadn't seen, not in her presence, since the accident, and it sent a thrill through her. He looked *mad*. At *her*. She watched as he slid the gun from his back and set it on the kitchen counter, but left his hand on top.

"I should kill you," he growled. "I really, really should."

"But you won't."

"You're crazy. Those are my murders Stell's investigating and you just let him in."

"I didn't know about you and Stell," said Serena lightly. "Actually, it makes this even better."

"How so?"

"Because the whole point was to show you."

"That you've lost it?"

She pouted. "No. That I'm more use to you alive."

"I thought you had a death wish," said Eli. "And bringing back a man I've worked to avoid for a decade doesn't put you on my good side, Serena. Don't you think the cogs are turning in Stell's mind, somewhere past that spell you cast on him?"

"Calm down," she said simply. And sure enough, she could see the anger bleeding away, watched him try to cling to it as it thinned into nothing. She wondered what it felt like, to be under her influence.

Eli's shoulders loosened, and he let go of the counter while Serena flipped through the file Officer Dane had left for them. She plucked up a piece of paper, letting the rest fall to the table. Her eyes wandered absently over the page. A man in his twenties, handsome but for a scar that squinted one eye and carved a line down to his throat.

"What about your sister?" asked Eli, pouring more coffee now that his hands had stopped shaking.

Serena frowned, and looked up. "What about her?"

"You said she was an EO."

Had she? Had that been one of those confessions murmured in half sleep, the space where whispered thoughts and dreams and fears slipped out?

"Spin again," she said, trying to hide her tension as she nodded at the folder. She didn't like to think about Sydney. Not now. Her sister's power made Serena ill, not because of the talent itself but because it meant she was broken the way Serena was broken, the way Eli was broken. Missing pieces. She hadn't seen Sydney, not since leaving the hospital. She couldn't bear the thought of looking at her.

"What can she do?" pressed Eli.

"I don't know," lied Serena. "She's just a kid."

"What's her name?"

"Not her," she snapped. And then the smile was back, and she was passing the profile in her hands to Eli, "Let's try this one. He sounds like a challenge."

Eli looked at her for several long moments before he reached out and took the paper.

XIV

THIS AFTERNOON
THE ESQUIRE HOTEL

ELI sat waiting for the call to go through, and watching Serena as she crossed the hotel suite to the kitchen. Finally the ringing stopped, and a brusque voice answered.

"Stell here. What is it?"

"It's Ever," said Eli, taking the stupid glasses off. Serena was busying herself with the coffeepot, but he could tell from the way she tipped her head, the way she made so little noise, tiptoeing through the motions, that she was listening in.

"Sir," said the detective. Eli didn't like the way he said the word with a faint uptick at the end. "How can I assist you?"

Eli didn't know, when he dialed the number, if calling Stell was actually a good idea, or if it only seemed like one because it came from Serena. Now that he was talking to the detective, he realized that it wasn't a good idea at all. That it was, in fact, a very bad idea. For nine and a half of the last ten years, he'd been a ghost, managing to stay off radars despite his growing tally of removals and his unchanging face (the pairing of anonymity with immortality was no small feat). He'd managed to avoid Stell, until Serena involved him, and even then, everything Eli did, he did alone. He didn't trust other people, not with knowledge or with power, and certainly not with both. The risk here was high, probably too high.

And the reward? By indoctrinating an entire police force, he ensured both their support, with regard to Victor and his other targets, as well as sanction to continue his executions, his *removals*. But it meant tethering himself to the one person he knew he couldn't trust, and couldn't resist. The police wouldn't be listening to *him,* not really. They would be listening to Serena. She met his eyes across the room, and smiled, holding out a mug. He shook his head, *no,* a small action that made her smile. She brought the cup to him anyway, nested it right into his empty hand, and curled her fingers and his around it.

"Mr. Ever?" prompted Stell.

Eli swallowed. Whether it was a good idea or not, he knew one thing: he couldn't afford to let Victor get away.

"I need to set up a meeting," he told the detective, "with your entire police force. As soon as possible."

"I'll call them in. But it will take time for them to get here."

Eli looked at his watch. It was almost four. "I'll be there at six. And pass the word to Officer Dane."

"Will if I can find him."

Eli's brow furrowed. "What do you mean?"

"I just got back from the scene at the bank with your boy Lynch, and there's no sign of Dane. Must have stepped out for a smoke."

"Must have," echoed Eli. "Keep me posted." He hung up and hesitated a moment, turning the phone over and over in his hand.

"What's wrong?" asked Serena.

Eli didn't answer. He was able to resist answering, but only because he didn't *know*. Maybe nothing was wrong. Maybe the cop had gone on break, or cut out early. Or maybe . . . his senses tingled the way they did when Stell's words tipped up. The way they did when he knew he was following Serena's will instead of his own. The way they did when something was *off*. He didn't question the feeling. He trusted it as much as the quiet that followed his kills.

Which is why Eli dialed Officer Dane's number.

It rang.

And rang.

And rang.

∞

VICTOR paced the gutted room of the half-built high-rise and pondered the problem of Serena Clarke who, it seemed, was quite an influential person. No wonder Eli was keeping her around. Victor knew that he would have to kill her very, very quickly. He looked around the space and considered its potential and his options, but his attention drifted invariably back down to Dane's body, which lay sprawled in the middle of the floor on its plastic sheeting. Victor decided to do what he could to minimize the signs of torture, for Sydney's sake.

He knelt beside the corpse and began to straighten it up, align the limbs, do what he could to give the body a more natural appearance. He noticed a silver wedding band on Dane's finger—he slid it off, and into Dane's pocket—then placed the man's arms at his sides. There was nothing he could do to make the body look less dead; that would fall to Sydney.

Several minutes later when Mitch returned, holding aside a curtain of plastic and showing Sydney in, Victor was quite proud of the job he'd done. Dane practically looked peaceful (aside from the shredded uniform and the blood). But when Sydney's eyes snagged on the body, she stopped and let out a small sound.

"That's bad, isn't it?" she asked, pointing to the badge on the corpse's chest. "Killing a cop is bad."

"Only if it's a good cop," explained Victor. "And he wasn't one. This cop was helping Eli track down EOs. If Serena hadn't turned you over, this man would have." *So long as he was under Serena's spell,* he thought, but didn't say it.

"Is that why you killed him?" asked Sydney quietly.

Victor frowned. "It doesn't matter why I did it. What matters is that you bring him back."

Sydney blinked. "Why would I do that?"

"Because it's important," he said, shifting his weight from foot to foot, "and I promise to kill him again right after. I just need to see something."

Sydney frowned. "I don't want to bring him back."

"I don't *care,*" snapped Victor suddenly, the air humming to life around them. Mitch shot forward, putting his hulking form in front of Sydney, and Victor caught himself before he lost control. All three seemed surprised by the outburst, and guilt—or at least a pale version of it—tightened in Victor's chest as he considered the other two, the loyal guard and the impossible girl. He couldn't afford to lose them—their *help,* he corrected himself, their *cooperation*—certainly not today, so he drew the energy back into himself, wincing as he grounded it.

"I'm sorry," he said, letting out a low breath. Mitch took a small step to the side, but didn't abandon Sydney.

"Too far, Vic," he growled in a rare display of boldness.

"I know," said Victor, rolling his shoulders. Even with the energy grounded, the desire to hurt someone still coiled inside him, but he willed it to stay contained, just a little longer, just until he could find Eli. "I'm sorry," he said again, turning his attention to the small, blond girl still half-hidden behind Mitch. "I know you don't want to do this, Sydney. But I need your help if I'm going to stop Eli. I'm trying to protect you, and Mitch. And myself. I'm trying to protect all of us, but I can't do it alone. We have to work together. So will you do this for me?" He held his gun up for her to see. "I won't let the cop hurt you."

She hesitated, but finally crouched beside the body, careful to avoid the blood.

"Does he deserve a second chance?" she asked softly.

"Don't think of it that way," said Victor. "He only gets a moment. Just long enough to answer a question."

Sydney took a breath and pressed her fingertips to the clean spots on the officer's shirt. An instant later Dane gasped and sat up, and Sydney scrambled back to Mitch's side, gripping his arm.

Victor looked down at Officer Dane.

"Tell me again about Ever," he said.

The officer met his eyes. "Eli Ever is a hero."

"Well, that's discouraging," huffed Victor. He fired three more shots into the officer's chest. Sydney turned and buried her face in Mitch's shirt as Dane thudded back against the plastic-covered concrete, as dead as before.

"But now we know," said Victor, toeing the body with his shoe. Mitch looked at him over Sydney's pale hair, his face caught for the second time in as many minutes between horror and anger.

"What the fuck was that about, Vale?"

"Serena Clarke's power," said Victor. "She tells people what to do." He slid his gun back into his belt. "What to say, what to think." He gestured to the body. "And even death doesn't seem to sever the connection." Well, *the officer's* death, amended Victor silently. "We're done here."

Sydney stood very still. She'd let go of Mitch and now had her arms wrapped around her ribs, as if for warmth. Victor came over to her, but when he reached out to touch her shoulder, she cringed away. He sank to one knee in front of her so that he had to look up a fraction to meet her eyes.

"Your sister and Eli, they think they're a team. But they're nothing compared to us. Now come on," he said, straightening. "You look cold. I'll buy you a hot chocolate."

Her icy blue eyes found his, and she looked as though she had something to say, but she didn't get the chance, because that's when Victor heard the phone ring. It wasn't *his* phone, and he could tell by the look on Mitch's face, it wasn't his, either. And Sydney must have left hers back at the hotel because she didn't even reach for her pocket. Patting down the officer, Mitch found the device and drew it out.

"Leave it," said Victor.

"I think you want to take this one," said Mitch, tossing him the cell. In the place of the caller's name, there was only one word on the screen.

HERO.

Victor flashed a sharp, dark smile, cracked his neck, and answered the call.

"Dane, where are you?" snapped the person on the other end. Everything in Victor tensed at the sound, but he didn't answer. He hadn't heard that voice in ten years, but it didn't matter because the voice, like everything else about Eli Ever, hadn't changed at all.

"Officer Dane?" it said again.

"I'm afraid you just missed him," said Victor at last. He closed his eyes when he spoke, savoring the moment of quiet on the other end. If he concentrated, he could almost imagine Eli tensing at the sound of *his* voice.

"*Victor,*" said Eli. The word was a cough, as if the letters lodged in his chest.

"I admit, it's clever," said Victor, "using Merit's police database to find your targets. I'm a bit insulted that I haven't shown up on there yet, but give it time. I just got here."

"You're in the city."

"Of course."

"You won't get away," said Eli, the bravado dampening shock as it found its way back into his voice.

"I don't plan to," said Victor. "See you at midnight." He hung up, and broke the phone in two, dropping both parts onto Dane's body. The room filled with quiet as he considered the corpse, and then looked up.

"Sorry about that. You can clean up now," he said to Mitch, who was staring slack-jawed at him.

"Midnight?" growled Mitch. "Midnight? As in *tonight?*"

Victor checked his watch. It was already four. "Never put off till tomorrow what you can do today."

"I get the feeling that's not what Thomas Jefferson meant," muttered Mitch.

But Victor wasn't listening. His mind had spent the morning spinning, but now that it was set, now that there were only hours standing in his way, the violent energy quieted and the calm finally settled over him. He turned his attention back to Sydney. "How about that hot chocolate?"

∞

MITCH crossed his arms and watched them go, Sydney's short blond hair bobbing as she followed Victor out. When she'd taken hold of his arm, her fingers had been ice, and underneath the chill, she'd been shaking. That bone-deep kind of shiver that had less to do with cold, and more to do with fright. He wanted to say something, wanted to know what the hell Victor was thinking, wanted to tell him that he was playing with more lives than his own. But by the time he found the one word he should have said, one small, simple, powerful word—*STOP*—it was too late. They were gone and Mitch was alone in the plastic-shrouded room, so he did his best to swallow the word and the sinking feeling that went with it, then turned to the officer's body, and got to work.

XV

A LONG TIME AGO
VARIOUS CITIES

MITCHELL Turner was cursed.

Always had been.

Trouble followed him like a shadow, clinging to him no matter how much good light he tried to stand in. In his hands, good things broke and bad things grew. It didn't help that his mother died and his father bailed and his aunt took one look at him and waved him on, leaving Mitch to bounce between houses more like hotels, checking in and out, never putting down roots.

Most of his problems stemmed from the fact that people seemed to think size and intelligence were inversely proportional. They looked at him, at his hulking frame, and assumed that he was stupid. But Mitch wasn't stupid. In fact, he was smart. Very smart. And when you were that big, and that smart, it was easy to get into trouble. Especially when you were cursed.

By sixteen, Mitch had dabbled in everything from back-alley boxing to running books to roughing up thugs who owed money to people who liked money. And yet it wasn't any of those things that landed him his first stint in prison. In fact, he was innocent.

Mitch's curse, his *maldición*, as a Spanish foster mother had called it, was that bad things had a way of happening *around* him. The woman had never known its dark extent (she used the term to refer more to broken plates and baseballs through windows and tagged cars), but Mitch suffered from a cosmic case of wrong place, wrong time, and given his many, mostly illegal extracurricular activities, he didn't alibi out very easily.

So when a fight went wrong two streets over and left a man dead, and Mitch's knuckles were still raw from the back-alley match he'd won the night before, it didn't look good. He got off that time, but it was barely two weeks before it happened again. Another person died. It was uncanny and disturbing, and, though Mitch hated to admit it, a little thrilling. Or it would be, if Mitch didn't keep getting caught in the middle. It was becoming a problem, this trail of bodies, because even though he didn't make any of them, it certainly looked that way to the police, and by the third death, Metro PD seemed to think it would be easier to lock him up. Just in case. A hoodlum. A drain on society. Only a matter of time. The kinds of phrases tossed around by men playing catch with his life.

And just like that, with a curse and a rap sheet he didn't earn, Mitchell Turner went to jail.

∞

FOUR years.

He didn't mind it so much, prison. At least he fit in. In the real world, people took one look at him and tightened their grip on their purses, quickened their pace. Cops took one look and thought *guilty or going to be.* But in prison people took one look and thought *I want him on my side,* or *I don't want to mess with him,* or *he could crack my skull in his elbow,* or any number of far more useful thoughts. His size became a status symbol, even if it denied Mitch the perks of worldly conversation, and even if the staff considered him with skepticism when he checked out a book and was surprised when he used a word with more than two syllables. He spent most of his time trying to hack the prison computers' various safety settings and firewalls, more out of boredom than a desire to cause any real trouble. But at least his curse left him alone.

By the time Mitch got out of jail, he looked more the part than ever. The imposing teen had graduated into a towering adult, flecked with the first of many tattoos. Once out, he lasted a month and a half before the curse caught back up with him. He'd gotten a job in food distribution, mostly because he could unload four times the weight of any other guy on the truck, and because he liked physical work. He might be mentally cut out for a desk job, but he doubted he'd *fit* behind most desks. And everything was going smoothly—shitty apartment and shitty pay but all legally valid—until a man was beaten to death a few blocks from where his crew was unloading peaches. The cops took one look at Mitch and booked him. No bloody knuckles, and two coworkers to swear he had his arms full of fruit the whole time, and none of it mattered. Mitch went straight back to prison.

Good behavior and a staggering lack of evidence got him out in a matter of weeks, but Mitch, in a rare display of cynicism, decided that if he was going to go to back to jail (and given his curse, it was a matter of *when,* not *if*), he might as well commit a crime, since serving time on behalf of others wasn't an entirely satisfying use of his life. And so, Mitch set out to plan the one crime he'd always wanted to commit, for no better reason than it was the subject of books and movies, an archetypal affair involving brains far more than bulk.

Mitchell Turner was going to rob a bank.

MITCH knew three things about robbing a bank.

The first was that, because of his easily identifiable appearance, he couldn't actually go *into* the bank. Even if he disabled the security cameras, the people inside would pick him out of a hundred-person lineup (with his luck, even if he wasn't *in* it). The second was that, given the advances in security-based technology—many of which he'd learned about through observation in prison, but knew to be far more evolved in the private sector—a large component of the heist's success would lie in hacking the bank's systems and codes to disable the vault, which could be done remotely. The third was that he would need help. And thanks to the two prison stints he'd served so far, Mitch had developed a fairly extensive list of acquaintances, many of whom would be stupid, desperate, or otherwise willing enough to take up some guns and set foot inside the bank.

What Mitch didn't count on was that while his hacking would succeed without a hitch, the partners with guns would fail spectacularly, be promptly arrested, and drop his name faster than a hat. And somehow, upon seeing Mitchell Turner in all his physical prowess, the police would pin the gun-laden part of the robbery on him, and the hacking on the three smaller men caught in the actual heist and clearly discernible, even masked, on the security footage. And so Mitch's third strike landed him not in a prison for tax-frauders and info-leakers, but in Wrighton, a maximum security facility where the majority of the inmates had actually committed crimes, and where his size, while impressive, was no guarantee of safety.

And where, three years later, he would come to meet a man named Victor Vale.

XVI

SIX HOURS UNTIL MIDNIGHT
MERIT CENTRAL PRECINCT

ELI stood against the pale gray wall of the police conference room, and readjusted the mask on his face. It was simple, partial, black, running from his temples to his cheekbones, and Serena had teased him for it, but as more than half of Merit's police force accumulated in the room and took him in (the other half would listen in) he was thankful for the disguise. His face was the one thing he couldn't change, and as bad an idea as this was, it would be infinitely worse if the entire force had a chance to memorize his features. Serena stood at the podium and smiled her slow smile and spoke to the gathering men and women.

"What happens at midnight?" she had asked as they drove to the station.

Eli had gripped the steering wheel, knuckles white. "I don't know." He hated saying those words, not just because they were true or because admitting them meant Victor was a step ahead, but because he couldn't *not* say them, because the confession crawled its way up his throat before he thought to swallow. Victor had hung up on him with only the promise of *midnight*, and Eli had been left fighting the urge to throw the phone against the wall.

"The man behind me is a hero," Serena was saying now. Eli watched the eyes of the people in the room glaze slightly at her words. "His name is Eli Ever. He has been protecting your city for months, hunting down the kinds of criminals you do not know about, the kind you cannot stop. He has been working to keep you and your citizens safe. But now he needs your help. I want you to listen to him, and do as he says."

She smiled and stepped away from the podium and its microphone, urging Eli forward with a nod and a lazy smile. Eli let out a low breath, and stepped forward.

"A little over a week ago, a man named Victor Vale broke out of Wrighton Penitentiary along with his cellmate, Mitchell Turner. If you're wondering why you didn't hear about the break on the news, it's because it was not *on* the news." Eli himself didn't know about it until he got Victor's note, until he heard his voice, until he contacted Wrighton. They'd refused to tell him more, but had been happy to inform Serena, when he handed her the phone, that they'd been ordered to keep the escape quiet, due to suspicions about one of the convict's nature, suspicions that had been put aside until the man in question, a Mr. Vale, incapacitated a good chunk of the Wrighton staff without laying a finger on them.

"The reason you did not hear about the prison break," continued Eli, "is because Victor Vale is a confirmed EO." Several heads cocked at the term, torn between Serena's order to listen to him and their own varying degrees of belief. Eli knew that all precincts were given a mandatory day of training on EO protocol, but most of them didn't take it seriously. They couldn't. Decades after the term was coined, EOs were still largely a thing of myths and online forums, kept that way by incidents like the one at Wrighton. Fires smothered instead of spread. It was better for Eli, that cases involving EOs were so readily tamped out instead of made public—it gave him an unobstructed path—but he was constantly amazed by how eager the officials were to have incidents forgotten, and how eager the people involved were to forget. Sure, there would always be believers, but it helped that the vast majority of EOs didn't want to be believed in, and those that did, well, they'd saved Eli the trouble of hunting them down.

But who knows, maybe in another world EOs would have come to light by now, and the huddle of uniforms before him would have listened without a shred of disbelief, but Eli had done his job too well. He'd had a decade to cull the crop, cut the numbers down, and keep the monsters largely the stuff of stories. And so out of the crowd, only Stell, who stood at the back of the room, gaze trained on Eli, took in the words without surprise.

"But now," he continued, "Victor Vale and his accomplice, Mitchell Turner, are in Merit. In *your* city. And it is imperative that they are not allowed to escape. Imperative that they be found. These men have abducted a young girl named Sydney Clarke, and earlier today, they killed one of your own, Officer Frederick Dane."

The audience stirred at that, shock and anger spilling suddenly across their faces. They hadn't heard the news—Stell had been told, but he still looked gray with shock—and it got their attention. Serena could compel them, but this kind of report would do something different. Agitate them. Motivate them.

"I've been led to believe that these men are planning something *tonight*. By midnight. It is crucial that we find these criminals as soon as possible. But," he added, "for the hostage's safety, we must take them alive."

Ten years ago, Eli had faltered, and let a monster live. But tonight, he would correct his error, and end Victor's life himself.

"We have no photographic record for you," he added, "but you'll find physical descriptions arriving on your phones. I want you to blanket the city, block off the roads out, do whatever you have to do to find these men before anyone else dies."

Eli took a single step back from the podium. Serena came

forward, and put a hand on his shoulder as she addressed the room.

"Eli Ever is a hero," she said again, and this time the collected Merit Police Department nodded and stood and repeated.

"Eli Ever is a hero. A hero. A hero."

The words echoed and followed them out. Eli followed Serena through the precinct, as the words sank in. A hero. Wasn't he? Heroes saved the world from villains, from evil. Heroes sacrificed themselves to do it. Was he not bloodying his hands and his soul to set the world right? Did he not sacrifice himself every time he stripped away an EO's stolen life?

"Where to now?" asked Serena.

Eli dragged his thoughts back. They were cutting through the precinct garage to a side street where they'd parked the car; he pulled a thin folder from his satchel, and handed it to her. Inside were the profiles for the two remaining EOs in the Merit area, or at least *suspected* EOs. The first was a man named Zachary Flinch, a middle-aged miner who'd suffocated in a tunnel collapse the year before. He'd recovered . . . physically. The second was a young soldier named Dominic Rusher, who stood too close to a buried mine and landed himself in a coma two years prior. He'd come to, and vanished from the hospital. Literally. No one saw him leave. He sprang up in three different cities—no path, no trail, just there and gone and there—before appearing in Merit two months earlier. And as far as Eli could tell, he hadn't vanished again, *yet*.

"Victor mentioned the database when he called," said Eli as they reached the car, "which means he has access to these files, too. Whatever he's planning, I don't need him adopting any more strays."

"I want to come this time," said Serena.

Eli frowned behind his mask. He always did this part alone.

His murders, his *removals,* weren't like golf or porn or poker, some stereotypically male hobby that he didn't want to share. They were rituals, sacrosanct. Part of his covenant. Not only that, but the deaths were a culmination of days, sometimes weeks, of research and reconnaissance and patience. They *belonged* to him. The planning and the execution and the quiet after were his. Serena knew that. She was pushing him. Anger crackled beneath his skin.

He tried to spin the demand in his mind, to regain control. He knew he didn't have time to savor these particular kills. Chances were, he wouldn't even have time to wait for a demonstration. Today the rituals would be broken anyway, defiled.

He could feel Serena watching him struggle, and she seemed delighted by it. But not subdued. She took the file from him, and held up Zachary Flinch's profile.

"Just once," she said, the words tipping the scale.

Eli checked his watch. It was well after six. And there was no question she would expedite the process.

"Just once," he said, climbing in the car.

Serena beamed, and slid into the passenger's seat.

XVII

FIVE HOURS UNTIL MIDNIGHT
THE ESQUIRE HOTEL

SYDNEY was perched on the couch with Dol at her feet and the folder of executed EOs open in her lap when Mitch came in. The sun was setting beyond the floor-to-ceiling windows, and she looked up as he pulled the carton of chocolate milk from the fridge. He looked tired as he leaned his elbows—they were dusted with something chalkish and white—on the dark granite counter.

"Are you okay?" she asked.

"Where's Victor?"

"He went out."

Mitch swore under his breath. "He's crazy. The area is crawling with cops after that stunt."

"Which stunt?" asked Sydney, shuffling the papers in the folder. "Killing the cop or answering Eli's phone call?"

Mitch smiled grimly. "Both."

Sydney looked down at the face of a dead woman in her lap. "He can't mean it," she said quietly. "About meeting Eli at midnight. He doesn't mean it, right?"

"Victor means what he says," said Mitch. "But he wouldn't have said it if he didn't have a plan."

Mitch pushed off the counter, and vanished down the hall, and a moment later Sydney heard the bathroom door shut, and the shower snap on. She went back to reading the profiles, telling herself it was only because there was nothing good on television. The truth was, she didn't want to think about what would happen at midnight, or worse, what would happen *after*. She hated the *what-ifs* that crawled into her head the moment she lost focus. What if Eli won, what if Victor lost, what if Serena . . . she didn't even know what to think about her sister, what to hope for, what to fear. There were these traitorous parts of her that still wanted to feel Serena's arms around her, but she knew that now she had to run away from—not toward—her sister.

Sydney forced her eyes over the profiles in the folder, tried to focus on the EOs' lives and deaths—tried not to picture Victor's photo in among them, a black *x* across his calm, clear face—and guessed at what their powers were, even though she knew they could be anything. Victor had explained that it depended on the person, on their wants and wills and last thoughts.

The last profile was her own. She'd reprinted it after Victor took the first copy, and now her eyes wandered over the photo of her face. Unlike the other candid shots that filled the folder, hers was staged: head up, shoulders back, eyes leveled directly at the camera. It was a yearbook photo from last year, taken a week or so before the accident, and Sydney had loved it dearly because the camera had somehow, magically, caught her the moment before she smiled, and the proud upturn of her chin and faint crease in the corner of her mouth made her look *just* like Serena.

The only difference between this copy of the photo and the original was that this one had no *x* drawn through it. Eli knew by now that she was here, alive, and she hoped he felt sick when he'd heard about Barry's body walking back into the bank, when he'd put the pieces together and realized that it was her doing, that a few shots fired into the woods didn't equal a dead girl. Maybe it should have upset her, to see her own profile in the dead EO folder, and it had at first, but the shock had worn off, and the profile's existence in the digital trash bin, the fact that they'd underestimated her, assumed she was dead, and most of all the fact that she *wasn't*, made her smile.

"What's got you grinning?"

Sydney looked up to find Mitch freshly showered and dressed, a towel draped around his neck. She didn't realize how much time had passed. That happened to her more than she liked to admit. She'd blink, and the sun would be in a different position, or the show on TV would be over, or someone would be finishing a conversation she'd never heard them start.

"I hope Victor hurts him," she said cheerfully. "A lot."

"Jesus. Three days and you're already taking after him." Mitch sagged into a chair, ran his hand over his shaved head. "Look, Sydney, there's something you need to understand about Victor—"

"He's not a bad man," she said.

"There are no good men in this game," said Mitch.

But Sydney didn't care about *good*. She wasn't sure she believed in it. "I'm not afraid of Victor."

"I know." He sounded sad when he said it.

XVIII

FIVE YEARS AGO
WRIGHTON PENITENTIARY

THE third time Mitchell Turner went to jail, his curse followed him.

No matter where he went, or what he did (or didn't do), people kept dying. He lost two cellmates at the hands of others, one cellmate at the man's own hands, and a friend, who collapsed in the yard during the exercise period. So when the slim, polished form of Victor Vale appeared at the door of his cell one afternoon, pale in the dark gray prison uniforms, he figured the man was a goner. He was probably in for laundering, maybe a Ponzi scheme. Something heavy enough to make the right people angry and land him in max security, but light enough that he looked thoroughly out of place there. Mitch should have written him off but, still troubled by the death of his last cellmate, he became determined to keep Victor alive.

He assumed he would have his work cut out for him.

Victor didn't speak to Mitch for three days. Mitch, admittedly, didn't speak to Victor, either. There was something about the man, something Mitch couldn't place, but he didn't like it, in a primal, visceral way, and he found himself leaning vaguely away from Victor when the latter came near. The other inmates did it, too, on the rare occasions that first week when Victor ventured out among them. But even though it made Mitch uncomfortable, he followed the man, flanked him, constantly searching for an attacker, a threat. As far as Mitch could tell, his curse seemed firmly grounded in his proximity to people. When he was near them, they got hurt. But he couldn't seem to figure out how close was too close, how near he needed to be to doom a life, and he thought that maybe, if for once his proximity could save a person instead of somehow marking them . . . maybe then, he could break the curse.

Victor didn't ask him why he stayed so close, but he didn't tell him not to, either.

Mitch knew the attack would come. It always did. A way for the old to test the new. Sometimes it wasn't so bad, a few punches, a bit of roughing up. But other times, when men had a taste for blood or a bone to pick or even if they were just having a shitty day, it could get out of hand.

He followed Victor to the commons, to the yard, to the lunchroom. Mitch would sit on one side of the table, Victor on the other, picking at his lunch, while Mitch spent the entire time scanning the room. Victor never looked up from his plate. He didn't look at his plate, either, not exactly. His eyes had an unfocused intensity, as if he were somewhere else, unconcerned with the cage around him or the monsters inside.

Like a predator, Mitch realized one day. He'd seen enough nature specials on the common room set to know that prey had eyes on the sides of their head, were constantly on guard, but predators' eyes were forward-facing, close together, unafraid. Despite the fact that Victor was half the size of most inmates, and didn't look like he'd ever *been* in a fight, let alone won one, everything about him said predator.

And for the first time, Mitch wondered if Victor was really the one who needed protecting.

XIX

FOUR AND A HALF HOURS UNTIL MIDNIGHT
THE SUBURBS OF MERIT

ZACHARY Flinch lived alone.

That much Serena could tell before she ever set eyes on him. The front yard was a tangle of weeds, the car on the gravel strip of a driveway had two spares, the screen door was torn, and a coil of rope tied to a half-dead tree had been chewed through by whatever was once tied there. Whatever his power, if he even *was* an EO, it wasn't making him any money. Serena frowned, reconstructing his profile from memory. The entire page of data had been innocuous, except for the inversion—the Rebirth Principle, Eli had called it, a re-creation of self. It wasn't necessarily positive, or even voluntary, but always marked, and Flinch ticked off that box with a bold red check. In the wake of his trauma, everything about his life had changed. Not subtle changes, either, but full flips. He went from being married with three kids to being divorced, unemployed, and under a restraining order. His survival—or *revival*, rather—should have been cause for celebration, for joy. Instead, everything and everyone had fled. That, or he had pushed them away. He'd been to a slew of psychiatrists, and been prescribed antipsychotics, but judging by the state of his yard, he wasn't in a good place.

Serena knocked, wondering what would scare a man enough to throw his life away after he'd beaten death itself to keep it.

No one answered the door. The sun had dipped below the horizon, and when she exhaled it made small puffs of steam in the dusk. She knocked again, and could hear the sound of the television within. Eli sighed and pressed his back against the peeling paint of the siding by the door.

"Hello," she called. "Mr. Flinch? Could you come to the door?"

Sure enough, she could make out the shifting of feet, and a few moments later Zach Flinch appeared in the doorway wearing an old polo and a pair of jeans. Both were a size too big, making it look like he'd withered since putting them on. Over his shoulder she could see the coffee table littered with empty cans, the takeout boxes stacked on the floor beside it.

"Who are you?" he asked, dark rings beneath his eyes. There was a gruff tremor in his voice.

Serena clutched his dossier to her chest. "A friend. I just have a few questions."

Flinch grunted, but didn't shut the door in her face. She held his gaze so he wouldn't see Eli standing a couple feet to his right, still wearing his black hero's mask.

"Is your name Zachary Flinch?" she asked.

He nodded.

"Is it true you were involved in a mining accident last year? A tunnel collapse?"

He nodded.

She could feel Eli getting impatient, but she wasn't done. She wanted to know.

"In the wake of your accident, did anything change? Did you change?"

Flinch's eyes widened in surprise, but even as they did, he answered with a nod, his face caught between confusion and complacence. Serena smiled softly. "I see."

"How did you find me? Who are you?"

"Like I said, I'm a friend."

Flinch took a step forward, over the threshold. His shoes tangled in the stray greenish brown weeds that were trying to reclaim the porch. "I didn't want to die alone," he muttered. "That's all. Down there in the dark, I didn't want to die alone, but I didn't want this. Can you make them stop?"

"Make what stop, Mr. Flinch?"

"Please make them go away. Dru couldn't see them either till I showed her but they're everywhere. I just didn't want to die alone. But I can't take it. I don't want to see them. I don't want to hear them. Please make them stop."

Serena held out her hand. "Why don't you show me wha—"

The rest of the word was cut off by the gun as Eli swung it up to Zach Flinch's temple and pulled the trigger. Blood streaked across the siding of the house, flecking Serena's hair and dotting her face like freckles. Eli lowered the weapon and crossed himself.

"Why did you do that?" She spat, livid.

"He wanted to make them stop," said Eli.

"But I wasn't done—"

"I was merciful. He was sick. Besides, he confirmed he was an EO," said Eli, already turning toward the car. "A demonstration was no longer necessary."

"You have such a complex," she snapped. "You always have to be in control."

Eli gave a low, mocking laugh. "Says the siren."

"I just wanted to help."

"No," he said. "You wanted to *play*." He stormed away.

"Eli Ever, *stop*."

His shoe caught in the gravel, and stuck. The gun was still in his hand. For the briefest moment, Serena's temper got the best of her and she had to bite her tongue to stop herself from making him put the weapon to his own temple. The urge eased, and she stepped over Flinch's body and descended the stairs, coming up behind Eli. She wrapped her arms around Eli's waist and kissed the back of his neck.

"You know I don't want this kind of control," she whispered. "Now put the gun away." Eli's hand slid the weapon back into its holster. "You're not going to kill me today."

He turned to face her, wrapped his hands, now empty, around her back, and pulled her close, his lips brushing her ear.

"One of these days, Serena," he whispered, "you're going to forget to say that."

She tensed in his grip, and knew that he could feel it, but when she answered, her voice was even, light.

"Not today."

His hands fell away as he turned toward the car and held the door open for her.

"Are you coming with me?" he asked as they pulled out of the gravel drive. "To find Dominic?"

Serena chewed her lip, and shook her head. "No. Have your fun. I'm going back to the hotel to wash the blood out of my hair before it stains. Drop me off on your way."

Eli nodded, the relief written across his face as he gunned the engine, leaving Flinch on the porch, one lifeless hand trailing in the weeds.

XX

FOUR HOURS UNTIL MIDNIGHT
DOWNTOWN MERIT

VICTOR made his way back toward the hotel, a bag of takeout beneath one arm. It had been a pretense, really, this errand, a chance to escape the confines of the hotel room, a chance to breathe and think and plan. He ambled down the sidewalk, careful to keep his pace casual, his expression calm. Since the meeting with Officer Dane, the call with Eli, and the midnight ultimatum, the number of cops on the streets of Merit had gone dramatically up. Not all in uniform, of course, but all alert. Mitch had carved out any photographic evidence from the system, from Lockland University profile pictures down to the mug shots that were logged at Wrighton. All the Merit cops would have to go on was a stick-figure drawing, Eli's own memory (ten years out of date, since unlike him, Victor *had* aged), and descriptions from the penitentiary staff. Still, the police weren't to be discounted. Mitch's size made him terribly conspicuous, and Sydney stood out for being a child. Only Victor, arguably the most wanted of the group, had a defense mechanism. He smiled to himself as he strode within reach of a cop. The officer never looked up.

Victor had discovered that pain was a spectacularly nuanced sensation. A large, sudden quantity could cripple, of course, but it had many more practical applications than torture. Victor found that, by inflicting a subtle amount of pain on those in a determined radius, he could induce a subconscious aversion to his presence. People didn't register the pain, yet they leaned ever so slightly away. Their attention, too, seemed to bend around him, lending Victor a kind of invisibility. It served him in prison, and it served him now.

Victor made his way past the abandoned Falcon Price site and checked his watch again, marveling at the structure of revenge, the fact that years of waiting and planning and wanting would come down to hours—minutes, even—of execution. His pulse quickened with the thrill of it as he made his way back to the Esquire.

∞

ELI dropped Serena off on the Esquire curb with the sole instruction to pay attention and let him know if she noticed *anything* unusual. Victor was going to send another message, it was only a matter of when, and as the clock ticked away the minutes until midnight, Eli knew that his level of control would depend almost entirely on how quickly he got the memo. The later it got, the less time he'd have to plan, prepare, and he was sure that was Victor's intent, to keep him in the dark as long as possible.

Now he idled on the painted pavement of the drop-off square in front of the hotel, sliding the mask free and dropping it onto the passenger seat before reaching for Dominic Rusher's profile. Rusher had only been in the city a few months, but he already had a history with the Merit Police, a list of misdemeanors consisting almost exclusively of drunk and disorderly conduct charges. The vast majority of the trouble had emanated not from Dominic's shitty hole of an apartment in the south part of the city, but from a bar. One particular bar. The Three Crows. Eli knew the address. He pulled away from the hotel, just missing Victor and his bag of takeout.

∞

TWO cops stood in the Esquire's lobby, their full attention on a young blonde with her back to the hotel's revolving front doors. Victor wandered in unnoticed and headed for the stairs. When he reached the hotel room he found Sydney reading on the couch, Dol lying beneath her feet, and Mitch drinking straight from a carton at the counter while tapping out code one-handed on his laptop.

"Have any trouble?" asked Victor, setting the food down.

"With the body? No." Mitch set the carton aside. "But it was close with the cops. Jesus, Vale, they're everywhere. I don't exactly blend in as it is."

"That's what parking garage entrances are for. Besides, we just have to make it a few more hours," said Victor.

"About that . . . ," started Mitch, but Victor was busy scribbling something on a scrap of paper. He slid it toward him.

"What's this for?"

"It's Dane's ID and pass code. For the database. I need you to prepare a new flagged profile."

"And who are we flagging?"

Victor smiled, and gestured to himself. Mitch groaned. "I take it this has to do with midnight."

Victor nodded. "The Falcon Price high-rise. Ground floor."

"That place is a cage. You're going to get trapped."

"I have a plan," said Victor simply.

"Care to share?" Victor said nothing. Mitch grumbled. "I'm not using your photo. It took me ages to scrub it from the systems."

Victor looked around the room. His gaze settled on the latest Vale self-help tome he'd been inking out. He took it up, flashed the spine at Mitch, where VALE was written in glossy caps. "This'll do."

Mitch continued muttering even as he took the book and got to work.

Victor turned his attention toward Sydney. He carried a tub of noodles to the couch, and sagged onto the leather cushions as he offered it to her. Sydney set aside the dead EO folder and accepted the food, fingers curling around the still-warm container. She didn't eat. Neither did he. Victor stared past the windows and listened to the sounds of Mitch composing the post. His fingers itched to black out lines, but Mitch was using the book, so he closed his eyes and tried to find quiet, peace. He didn't picture sprawling fields or blue skies or water drops. He pictured squeezing the trigger three times, blood blossoming on Eli's chest in the same pattern it had on his, pictured carving lines into Eli's skin, watching them fade so he could do it over again, over and over and over. *Are you afraid yet?* he would ask when the floor was slick with Eli's blood. *Are you afraid?*

XXI

THREE AND A HALF HOURS UNTIL MIDNIGHT
THE ESQUIRE HOTEL

"**DO** you really have a plan?" asked Sydney sometime later.

Victor dragged his eyes back open, and said the same thing he'd said in the graveyard, when she asked if Wrighton Penitentiary had let him go. The same words and the same tone and the same look. "Of course," he said.

"Is it a good plan?" pressed Sydney. Her legs swung from the couch, boots grazing Dol's ears with every pass. The dog didn't seem to mind.

"No," said Victor. "Probably not."

Sydney made a sound, something between a cough and a sigh. Victor wasn't terribly fluent in her language yet, but guessed it was a kind of sad affirmative, the pre-teen version of *gotcha* or *okay*. The clock on the wall said it was almost nine p.m.. Victor closed his eyes again.

"I don't get it," said Sydney a few minutes later. She was scratching Dol's ear with her shoe. The dog's head rocked back and forth gently with the motion.

"What don't you get?" asked Victor, eyes still closed.

"If you want to find Eli, and Eli wants to find you, why do you have to go through all this? Why can't you just find each other?"

Victor blinked, and considered the small blond thing beside him on the couch. Her eyes were wide and waiting, but they were already losing their innocence. What little she'd clung to and brought with her down that road in the rain had faded in the face of Victor's pragmatic execution, his promises and his threats. She'd been betrayed, shot, saved, healed, hurt, healed again, forced to resurrect two men, only to witness the reassassination of one of them. She'd gotten tangled up in this, by Eli and then by Victor. She was like a child, but not a child, and Victor couldn't help but wonder if becoming an EO had hollowed her out the way it had him, had all of them—cut the ties of something vital and human. He wasn't protecting her, not by treating her like a normal kid. She wasn't normal.

"You asked me if I have a plan," he said, sitting forward. "I didn't, at first. I had options, yes, ideas, and factors, but not a plan."

"But you have one now."

"I do. But because of Eli, and because of your sister, I only have one shot to get it right. The first person to act sacrifices the element of surprise, and I can't afford to do that right now. Eli has a siren on his side, which means he could compel the entire city. Maybe he already has. I have a hacker, a half-dead dog, and a child. It's hardly an arsenal."

Sydney frowned and reached for the folder of living EOs. She held it out to him. "So make one. Or at least, make yours stronger. Try. Eli sees EOs—us—as monsters. But you don't, right?"

Victor wasn't sure how he felt about EOs. Up until he fetched Sydney from the side of the road, he'd only ever known one EO, himself excluded, and that was Eli. If he'd had to judge based on the two of them, then ExtraOrdinaries were damaged, to say the least. But these words people threw around—humans, monsters, heroes, villains—to Victor it was all just a matter of semantics. Someone could call themselves a hero and still walk around killing dozens. Someone else could be labeled a villain for trying to stop them. Plenty of humans were monstrous, and plenty of monsters knew how to play at being human. The difference between Victor and Eli, he suspected, wasn't their opinion on EOs. It was their reaction to them. Eli seemed intent to slaughter them, but Victor didn't see why a useful skill should be destroyed, just because of its origin. EOs were weapons, yes, but weapons with minds and wills and bodies, things that could be bent and twisted and broken and *used*.

But there were so many unknowns. Whether the EOs were still alive was an unknown. What their powers were was an unknown. Whether they would be receptive was an unknown, and while Victor possessed a compelling argument, since the other side wanted them dead and he had use for them alive, the fact remained that to recruit an EO would mean introducing unpredictable and unreliable elements into his equation. Add to that the fact that Eli was probably busy eliminating Victor's options, and it seemed more trouble than it was worth.

"Please, Victor," said Sydney, still holding out the folder. And so, to pacify her, and pass the time, he took it, and flipped the cover back. The page with the blue-haired girl had been removed, leaving only two profiles.

The first profile belonged to a man named Zachary Flinch. Victor had read through the man's page earlier that day, while waiting for Mitch's call, so he knew it was a dead end. Everything about the suspected EO was too ambiguous—an EO's ability seemed to have at least a tangential relationship to either the nature of death or the subject's mental state, but it was still a guessing game—and the fact that everyone had left in the wake of the accident suggested trouble. More trouble than Victor had time for.

He turned to the second profile, the one he hadn't gotten to yet, skimmed the page, and stopped.

Dominic Rusher was in his late twenties, an ex-soldier who'd had the misfortune of standing too close to a land mine overseas. The explosion had shattered many of Dominic's bones, and left him in a coma for two weeks, but it wasn't the coma or his newfound habit of disappearing that attracted Victor's attention. It was the brief medical note at the bottom of the page. According to the military hospital records, Rusher had been prescribed 35 milligrams of methahydricone.

It was a high dose of a fairly ambiguous synthetic opioid, but Victor had spent one rather slow summer in prison memorizing the extensive list of painkillers currently available via prescription, their purposes, dosages, and official names, as well as their medical ones, so he recognized the drug on sight. Not only that, but he felt sure that unless Eli had dedicated the same amount of time, he *wouldn't* recognize it.

Fate, it seemed, was smiling on Victor again.

With mere hours until his midnight meeting, he knew there was no time or place for building trust or loyalty, but perhaps these could be supplanted by *need*. And need, Victor had learned, could be as powerful as any emotional bond. The latter was neurotic, complicated, but need could be simple, as primal as fear or pain. Need could be the foundation of allegiance. And Victor had exactly what Dominic needed. He could supply, if Dominic's power was worth it. There was only one way to find out.

Victor folded the profile and put it in his pocket.

"Grab your coat, Mitch. We're going out."

"Car or foot?"

"Car."

"Absolutely not. Did you miss the memo about the cops? Last time I checked, that vehicle is stolen."

"Well, we'll just have to make sure we don't attract attention, then."

Mitch mumbled something unkind as he reached for his coat. Sydney ran to get hers from the bedroom where she'd abandoned it.

"No, Syd," said Victor when she reappeared, already tugging on her large red coat. "You need to stay here."

"But it was my idea!" she said.

"And it's a good one, but you still have to stay."

"Why?" she whined. "And don't tell me it's too dangerous. You said that about the cop, and then you dragged me in anyway."

Victor scoffed. "It *is* too dangerous, but that's not why you have to stay here. We stand out enough without a missing child, and I need you to do something for me."

Sydney crossed her arms and considered him skeptically.

"If I'm not back by ten thirty," he said, "I need you to hit the Post button on Mitch's computer, and upload my profile to the database. He has the window up and ready."

"Why ten thirty?" asked Mitch, buttoning his coat.

"Long enough for someone to see it, but hopefully not long enough for them to be prepared. It's a risk, I know."

"Not the biggest one you're taking," said Mitch.

"Is that all?" asked Sydney.

"No," said Victor. He patted down the pockets of his coat. His hand vanished, and then came out with a blue lighter. He didn't smoke, but it always seemed to come in handy. "At eleven, I need you to start burning the folders. All of them. Use the sink." He held out the lighter. "One page at a time, you understand?"

Syd took the small blue device, turning it over in her hands.

"This is really important," he said. "We can't be leaving evidence around, okay? You see why I need you here?" At last she nodded. Dol whined faintly.

"You're going to come back, right?" she asked when they reached the door.

Victor looked over his shoulder. "Of course I will," he said. "That's my favorite lighter."

Sydney almost smiled as the door shut.

"I get burning the papers, but why one page at a time?" asked Mitch as he and Victor were headed down the stairs.

"To keep her busy."

Mitch thrust his hands into his coat. "We're not coming back then, are we?"

"Not tonight."

XXII

THREE HOURS UNTIL MIDNIGHT
THE THREE CROWS BAR

ELI sat in a booth along the back wall of the Three Crows and waited for Dominic Rusher to show up. He'd checked with the bartender when he first arrived, and had been assured that Rusher came every night around nine o'clock. Eli had been early, but he had nothing else to do besides wait for midnight and whatever that would bring, so he'd ordered a beer and retreated to the corner booth, savoring the time away from Serena more than the booze.

The drink was mostly for appearances anyway, since regenerating negated its effect, and alcohol without inebriation was far less enticing (he'd been carded, too, and the novelty of *that* had long worn off). But the distance from Serena was important—vital, he'd found—to maintaining his slim hold on control. The longer he was with her, the more things seemed to blur, an intoxication Eli's body didn't overcome so easily. He should have killed her when he had the chance. Now, with the police involved, it was messy. Their loyalty was to her, not to him, and they both knew it.

A new city, that's what he needed.

After midnight and Victor and this whole mess was sorted out, he'd find a new city. Start over. Away from Detective Stell. Away from Serena, too, if he could help it. He didn't even mind the prospect of his old method, the time and dedication it took, the weeks of searching for the mere moments of payoff. Things had gotten too easy lately, and easy meant dangerous. Easy led to mistakes. Serena was a mistake. Eli took a sip of beer and checked his phone for messages. There were none.

Eli had hunted here once, a few years back, before Serena, when he was still a ghost, just passing through. The place was loud, and crowded, made for people who liked to surround themselves with chaos instead of quiet, ambient noise built of glass and shouting and music to which you could never discern the lyrics. It was an easy place to be invisible, to vanish, swallowed by the low light and the din of drunk and drinking and angry people. But even knowing that, Eli was neither bold enough nor foolish enough to perform a public execution. Serena might have secured him the police, but the people in the Three Crows weren't much for cops or conformity. A problem could escalate into a disaster in a place like this, especially without Serena to soothe the masses.

Eli reminded himself *again* that he was glad to be rid of her influence, both over others and over him. Now he could, out of want and necessity, do this his way.

He checked the time. Less than three hours until . . . until what? Victor had set the deadline to rattle him, put him on edge. He was disturbing Eli's calm, like a kid dropping rocks into a pond, making ripples, and Eli saw him doing it and still felt rippled, which perturbed him even more. Well, Eli was taking back control, of his mind and his life and his night. He drew his fingers through the ring left by his beer glass on the old wood table, before writing one word in the film of water.

EVER.

XXIII

TEN YEARS AGO
LOCKLAND UNIVERSITY

"WHY Ever?"

Victor posed the question from across the table. Eli had just died. Victor had just brought him back. Now the two were sitting in the bar a few blocks down from their apartment, buzzed from several rounds (or at least Victor was) and the fact they'd been lucky enough to survive an acute attack of stupidity. But Eli felt odd. Not bad, just... different. Distant. He couldn't put his finger on it yet. Something was missing, though, he could feel the absence of it, even if he couldn't deduce the shape. Physically though—and he supposed that mattered most, all things considered—he felt fine, persistently so, suspiciously so, given that for some time that evening he had been an inanimate object instead of a living being.

"What do you mean?" he asked, sipping his beer.

"I mean," said Victor, "you could pick any name. Why pick Ever?"

"Why not?"

"No," said Victor, waving his drink. "No, Eli. You don't do anything like that."

"Like what?"

"Without thinking. You had to have a reason."

"How do you know?"

"Because I know you. I see you."

Eli drew his fingers through a ring of water on the table. "I don't want to be forgotten."

He said it so softly he worried Victor wouldn't hear, not over the chatter of the bar, but he clamped his hand down on Eli's shoulder. For a moment he looked so serious, but then he let go and slumped back in his seat.

"Tell you what," said Victor. "You remember me, and I'll remember you, and that way we won't be forgotten."

"That's shit logic, Vic."

"It's perfect."

"And what happens when we're dead?"

"We won't die, then."

"You make cheating death sound so simple."

"We do seem awfully good at it," said Victor cheerfully. He lifted his glass. "To never dying."

Eli lifted his. "To being remembered."

Their glasses clinked as Eli added, "Forever."

XXIV

TWO AND A HALF HOURS UNTIL MIDNIGHT
THE THREE CROWS BAR

DOMINIC Rusher was a broken man. Literally.

Most of the bones on his left side, the side nearest the IED, were pinned or screwed or synthetic, the skin pocked with scars beneath his clothes. His hair—for three years buzzed to military standards—had grown out, and now hung shaggy around his eyes, one of which was fake. His skin was tan and his shoulders strong, his posture still too straight to blend entirely with the bar's regulars, and despite it all he was clearly broken.

Eli didn't need the files to tell him any of that; he could see it as the man walked up to the counter, slid onto a stool, and ordered his first drink. Time was ticking past and Eli's grip tightened on his own glass, as he watched the ex-soldier kick off his night with a Jack and Coke. He had to resist the urge to abandon the booth and the beer and shoot Dominic in the back of the head, just to be done with it. Eli did his best to smother the flare of impatience; his rituals existed for a reason, and he would—and had—*compromised* them on occasion, but would not abandon them, even now. To slay without cause would be an abuse of power, and an insult to God. The blood of EOs washed from his skin. The blood of innocents would not. He had to get Dominic out of the bar, had to get a confession, if not a demonstration, before he executed him. Besides, Dominic would make fine bait. So long as he was instilled at the bar, and in Eli's sight, he was as useful alive as he was dead, because if Victor came looking for the broken man, and made his way here before midnight, Eli would be waiting, and he would be ready.

∞

VICTOR drove, while Mitch lay sprawled across the backseat, as out of sight as possible given his mass. The city slid by, the greens and reds and office-window whites streaking past as Victor wove the car through the gridded streets, out of the downtown and into the old sector. They kept to the roads that curled through the side streets of Merit instead of the main grid that ran in and out of the city, avoiding any street that eventually led to a toll or a bridge or any other potential checkpoint. They watched their speed, pacing traffic when it went too fast because going slow would stand out just as much as speeding. Victor guided the stolen car through Merit, and soon the numbered avenues and lettered roads gave way to named streets. Real names, trees and people and places, clustered buildings, some dark, boarded, abandoned, and some bulging with life.

"Take a left," said Mitch, consulting the card-sized, shifting map on his phone. Victor checked his watch and ticked off the time it was taking to get to the bar, subtracted it from midnight to figure out how long they really had. He couldn't be late. Not tonight. He tried to find calm, find peace, but excitement rattled inside of him like loose change. He rapped his free hand on his leg and swallowed the whisper that this was a bad idea. It was better than sitting still. Besides, they had time. Plenty of time.

"Left again," said Mitch. Victor turned.

They'd spent the first half of the drive going over the plan, and now that it was laid out, and all that remained was to execute it, they drove in a silence punctuated only by Mitch's directions and Victor's restless tapping, and the roads rolling away beneath them.

WHILE Victor drove, Mitch wondered.

Wondered if he would survive the night.

Wondered if Victor would, too.

Wondered what tomorrow would bring if they both did.

Wondered what Victor would do to occupy his thoughts once Eli was gone. If Eli was gone.

Mitch wondered what *he* would do next. He and Victor had never discussed their partnership, its terms and termination, but it had always been about this. About finding Eli. There was never any mention of what would come next. He wondered if there *was* a next, in Victor's mind.

The moving green dot on his phone reached the red still dot that marked the Three Crows Bar, and Mitch sat up.

"We're here."

VICTOR parked in the lot across from the bar, even though it was crowded and narrow, and would prevent a quick exit, especially under pursuit. But with a stolen car and the cops on high alert, he didn't dare do anything that might stand out. He wasn't about to get picked up for a parking ticket on a stolen car. Not tonight. He shut off the engine, stepped out, and examined the huddle of bricks across the street that declared itself to be the Three Crows Bar, a trio of metal birds perching on the sign above the front doors. To the left of the bar was an alley, and as the two men crossed the street, Victor could make out the bar's side entrance set into the stained brick wall. When they reached the curb, he made his way toward the alley, and Mitch made his way toward the bar. Behind his eyes, Victor saw the pieces of his game lining up on the city-shaped board, chess and Battleship and Risk. His move.

"Hey," he called, as Mitch's hand gripped the front door. "Be careful."

Mitch smiled crookedly, and went inside.

XXV

FIVE YEARS AGO
WRIGHTON PENITENTIARY

"YOU want more milk?"

It was the first thing Victor Vale ever said to Mitchell Turner.

They were sitting in the cafeteria. Mitch had spent three days wondering absently what Victor's voice would sound like if he ever decided to talk. If he even *could* talk. Over the course of lunch, Mitch had actually taken to imagining that he couldn't, that beneath the collar of his prison-issued shirt some ghastly scar carved a smile across his throat, or that behind his curling lips there simply was no tongue. It sounded weird, but prison was boring, and Mitch found his imagination going to strange places more often than not. So when Victor finally opened his mouth and asked with perfect elocution if Mitch wanted another carton of milk, the latter was caught between surprise and disappointment.

He scraped his words together. "Uh. Yeah. Sure." He hated how stupid he sounded, how slow, but Victor only chuckled, and pushed up from the table.

"Keeps the body strong," he said before making his way across the cafeteria to the food counter. The moment he was gone, Mitch knew he should have followed. He'd spent three days shadowing his new cellmate, but the question had caught him off-guard, and now in its wake, he had a sinking feeling that he'd just sacrificed his chance to break the curse. He craned his neck in search of

Victor only to have someone slam him forward toward the table, and swing an arm around his shoulder. From across the room, the gesture might have looked friendly, but Mitch could see the sharpened metal in Ian Packer's hand, the edge angled toward his cheek. Mitch was twice the man's size but he knew the damage Ian could do before he'd be able to wrestle him off. Besides, Packer was one of those people who, despite his size, had power here, sway. Too much in a place this small.

"Hey, hey," said Packer, his breath foul. "Playing puppy dog?"

"What do you want?" growled Mitch, keeping his eyes on the tray in front of him.

"Been wanting you to play watchdog for my group for a year, been so kind and patient with your pacifistic shit"—Mitch was surprised (and a little impressed) that Packer knew the word *pacifistic*—"and suddenly this pointy prick shows up and you're all over the role." He tutted in Mitch's ear. "I should fuck him up just for wasting your time and talent, Turner."

A small carton of milk landed on his tray, and Mitch looked up to find Victor standing there, surveying the situation with mild interest. Packer's grip tightened on the sharpened metal as his attention flicked to the new man, and Mitch's heart sank. Another cellmate lost.

But Victor only tilted his head curiously at Packer.

"Is that a shiv?" he asked, bringing his shoe to rest on the bench, his hand to rest on his knee. "We didn't have those in isolation." *Isolation?* thought Mitch. "I've always wanted to see one."

"Oh, I'll show it to you close, you little fuck." Packer's arm vanished from Mitch's shoulders. He lunged for Victor, who did nothing more than set his foot back on the floor and curl his fingers into a fist, and Packer, halfway to him, buckled to the ground, screaming. Mitch blinked, confused by what had happened . . . and not happened. Victor had never even touched the guy.

The room broke into motion at the sound of the scream, the inmates on their feet and the guards on their way, as Mitch sat and watched and Victor stood and watched and Packer howled and writhed on the floor, hand bloody from clenching the sharpened sliver of metal as he twisted and screamed. There was a moment, before anyone else reached them, when Mitch saw Victor smile. A wolf's smile, thin and sharp.

"What's going on?" shouted a guard as he and another reached the table. Mitch looked to Victor, who only shrugged. The smile was gone, a faint crease of concern between his eyes.

"No idea," he said. "Guy comes over to talk. One minute he's fine and the next"—Victor snapped his fingers, and Mitch flinched—"just starts convulsing. Better get him checked out before he hurts himself."

The guards pinned the writhing Packer to the floor, and pried the blade from his shredded hand as his screams faded into groans and then into nothing. The convict had fainted. Somewhere between Packer attacking Victor, Victor dropping him with a look, and the guards reaching the scene, Mitch had extricated himself from the table bench, and now stood a few feet behind his cellmate, sipping his milk, and watching the events unfold, marveling in part at the scene, and in part at the fact that for once *he* hadn't been blamed.

But what the hell had happened?

Mitch must have whispered the question, because Victor honored him with a pale raised brow before turning back toward the cell blocks. Mitch followed.

"Well?" asked Victor as they made their way down the concrete halls. "Do *you* feel I'm wasting your time and talent?"

Mitch considered the impossible man beside him. Something

had changed. The discomfort, the aversion that he'd felt for three straight days had faded. Everyone else still seemed to bend away as they passed, but Mitch felt only wonder and, admittedly, a touch of fear. When they reached their cell, and he still hadn't answered, Victor stopped, rested his back against the bars, and looked at him. Not at his hulking shoulders or his meaty fists with their scarred knuckles, or the tattoos that ran up his neck, but at his face. He looked him in the eyes, even if he had to look up a bit to do so.

"I don't need a bodyguard," said Victor.

"I noticed that," said Mitch.

Victor let out a cough of a laugh. "Yes, well," he said, "I don't want everyone else to notice, too."

Mitch had been right. Victor Vale was a wolf among sheep. And it took a lot to make 463 hardened criminals look the part of prey.

"So what *do* you want then?" he asked.

Victor's lips curled into that same, dangerous smile. "A friend."

"That's all?" he asked, disbelieving.

"A good friend, Mr. Turner, is very hard to find."

Mitch watched Victor push off the bars and head into the cell, lifting a library book from his cot before settling onto it.

Mitch didn't know what had just happened back in the cafeteria, but a decade in and out of prison had taught him this: There were some people you had to stay away from, people who poisoned everything in reach. Then there were people you wanted to stick with, the ones with silver tongues and golden touches. And then, there were people you stood beside, because it meant you weren't in their way. And whoever Victor Vale was, whatever he was, and whatever he was up to, the only thing Mitch knew was that he did *not* want to be in his way.

XXVI

TWO HOURS UNTIL MIDNIGHT
THE THREE CROWS BAR

ELI tapped his phone awake, tensing when he saw the time. Still no Victor, and Dominic seemed to be an installation at the bar. Eli frowned, and dialed Serena, but she didn't pick up. When her voice mail kicked in, he hung up, eager to click End before her slow, melodic words could issue any instructions. He thought of Victor's threat: *It's clever, using the police database to find your targets. I'm a bit insulted I haven't shown up on there yet, but give it time. I just got here.*

Eli logged on to the database, hoping for clues, but it was after ten, and the only flagged profile belonged to the man currently stationed at the counter, nursing his third Jack and Coke. Eli frowned and put the phone away. His bait didn't seem to be drawing any fish. The seat beside Dominic emptied—it had been taken up and subsequently abandoned three times over the course of the hour—and Eli, tired of waiting, finished his beer and slid to the edge of the booth. He was about to make his way toward the target when a man appeared, approached the counter, and took the stool.

Eli stopped, and hovered at the edge of his booth.

He had seen the man before. In the lobby of the Esquire, and even though his presence here was less surprising—he fit in much better with the customers of the Three Crows than the suit-wearing clientele of the four-star hotel—his appearance still jarred Eli. There was something else about the man. He hadn't thought of it when he saw him before, but here, on the heels of the presentation to the Merit Metro Police Department, it seemed obvious. No photos existed of Mitchell Turner, Victor's partner in crime, but there had been generic thug descriptions: tall, burly, bald, tattooed. Dozens of men would fit the bill, but how many of them would cross Eli's path twice in as many days?

Eli had long since abandoned the notion of coincidence.

If this man was Turner, then Victor couldn't be far away.

He scanned the bar, searching for Victor's blond hair, his sharp smile, but he didn't see anyone who fit the bill, and by the time he turned his attention back to the counter, Mitchell was talking to Dominic Rusher. His hulking form leaned in over the ex-soldier like a shadow, and while the noise in the bar drowned out the conversation itself, Eli could see his lips moving quickly, could see Dominic stiffen in response. And then, mere moments after he sat down, Mitchell stood back up. Without ordering, without another word. Eli watched him scan the bar, watched the man's eyes pass blankly over him and settle on the sign that read RESTROOMS in neon yellow light. Mitchell Turner made his way, stepping between Dominic and the rest of the room, his massive form for a moment—a blink—hiding the man from view. By the time he'd finished the stride—crossed from one side of the ex-soldier to the other—Dominic was gone.

And Eli was on his feet.

The bar stool that had, for the better part of an hour, held his target was now suddenly empty, and there was no sign, to any side, of Dominic Rusher. *Not possible,* Eli's brain might have thought. Only Eli knew it was entirely possible, it was *too* possible. Where the man *went* took a backseat in Eli's thoughts to the question of *why* he went, and that was a question with only one answer. He'd been spooked. *Warned.* Eli's gaze swiveled across the room until he saw the door to the men's room swing shut behind Mitchell Turner.

He dropped a bill on the table beside his empty glass, and followed.

XXVII

NINETY MINUTES UNTIL MIDNIGHT
THE ESQUIRE HOTEL

SYDNEY perched on the desk chair, arms wrapped around her knees, attention flicking between the clock on the wall, the clock on the computer (the wall clock was a full ninety seconds faster), and the Post button glowing green in the open program on Mitch's screen. Just above the button was the profile they'd constructed. *Victor Vale* was typed in across the top, with *Eli* listed as his middle name. Where his date of birth should be, the current date was written. The space reserved for last known whereabouts was filled with the address of the Falcon Price high-rise project. Every other space—those reserved for background information, history, police notation—was filled with one word, repeated in every slot: *midnight*.

To the left of the profile was the photo, or the place where the photo would have been. Instead, the bold lettering of the book spine ran vertically, reading VALE.

The book they'd used for the picture, the one Victor had bought on their walk the day before, sat beneath the stack of papers Sydney was supposed to start burning soon, the blue lighter a spot of color resting on top. She slid the massive text out from under the folders, and ran a thumb over the book's cover. She'd seen it before, or one just like it. Her parents had a set in their study (spines uncracked, of course). Sydney opened the book, and turned to the first page, but it was a wall of black. Flipping through, she saw that every one of the first thirty-three pages had been systematically blacked out. The Sharpie nesting into the fold between pages thirty-three and thirty-four suggested that the only reason the remaining pages had been spared was because Victor hadn't gotten to them yet. It was only while flipping back through those thirty-three pages toward the front of the book that Sydney noticed two words exempt from the blackout.

For and *ever*.

The words were several pages apart, separated and surrounded by a sea of black. Not only that, but the word *ever* had been altered, part of a larger word, the *for-* preceding it blotted carefully out, which meant Victor was not trying to piece together the word *forever* from the text.

He clearly wanted it to be two separate words. Distinct.

For.

Ever.

She ran her fingers over the page, expected them to come away stained, but they didn't. Dol whined faintly beneath the desk chair, where he'd somehow crammed himself—or at least a good part of his front half—and Sydney shut the book and looked back at the clock. It was after ten thirty according to both the wall and the computer. Her index finger hovered over the screen.

She knew what it would mean to hit the button.

Even without knowing Victor's plan, she knew that if she clicked Post there would be no going back, and Eli would find Victor, and at least one of them would die, and tomorrow everything would be horrible again.

She would be alone.

One way or another, alone. An EO with a wounded arm and a sister who wanted her dead, with a sick, strange gift and absent parents, and maybe she would be running or maybe she would be killed, too—none of it sounded terribly appealing.

She considered *not* posting it. She could pretend the computer had crashed, could steal them another day. Why did Victor have to do this? Why did he and Eli have to find each other? But even as she asked it, she knew the answer. She knew because her own pulse still quickened defiantly at the thought of Serena, because even as reason told her to run as far from her sister as possible, the gravity of want drew Sydney back. She couldn't break the orbit.

But she could keep from falling. Couldn't Victor, just for a little while? Couldn't they all stay aloft? Alive? But then Mitch's warning echoed in her head—*there are no good men in this game*—and when she closed her eyes to block it out, she saw Victor Vale, not as he was in the rain that first day, or even as he was when she accidentally woke him, but as he was this afternoon, standing over that cop's body, pain crackling in the air around him as he ordered her to bring the dead man back.

Sydney opened her eyes, and hit the Post button.

XXVIII

SEVENTY-FIVE MINUTES UNTIL MIDNIGHT
THE THREE CROWS BAR

VICTOR was leaning back against the cold brick side of the bar's alley wall, consulting Dominic Rusher's profile, when a man matching the photo staggered out of nothing and into the narrow run between the buildings. Victor was impressed, especially considering the door to the bar had never opened, but did his best to hide it in the interest of maintaining the upper hand.

Dominic, for his part, took one look at Victor—he had a black eye and a blue one, and according to his file, the blue was fake—then staggered forward in pain, clutching his side, and crumpled, one knee cracking against the concrete. It wasn't Victor's doing. The man was in bad shape, and whatever disappearing stunt he'd pulled with the shadows hadn't helped his condition.

"You know, Mr. Rusher," said Victor, closing the folder, "you really shouldn't be mixing methahydricone with alcohol. And if you're this bad on 35 milligrams, a drink's not going to help."

"Who are you?" gasped Dominic.

"Where's my friend?" asked Victor. "The one who warned you?"

"Still in there. He just said there was a man—"

"I know what he said. I told him to say it. There's a man who wants to kill you."

"But why?"

Victor didn't enjoy persuasion nearly as much as coercion. It took so much longer.

"Because you're an EO," he said. "Because you're unnatural. Something to that extent. And I should clarify, the man doesn't just want to kill you. He *will* kill you."

Dominic struggled to his feet and met Victor's gaze. "Like I'm afraid to die." There was a stubborn intensity in his eyes.

"Well," said Victor, "how hard can it be, right? You've done it once. But being afraid and being unwilling are different things. I don't think you *want* to die."

"How do you know?" he growled.

Victor dropped the profile on top of a trashcan. "Because you would have done it. You're a mess. You're in constant pain. Every moment of every day, I'm guessing, but you don't end it, which speaks either to your resilience or your stupidity, but also to your wish to live. And because you came here." He gestured to the alley. "Mitch told you to come here if you wanted to live. You could have left and taken your chances, though how far you'd get given your condition, who knows. The point is, you didn't leave. You came here. So while I have no doubt you would face death again with all the honor of a soldier, I don't think you're eager to." Even as he spoke, he was picturing the game board, pieces shifting to accommodate a talent he'd only glimpsed, but already knew he wanted. "I'm giving you a choice," he added. "Go back inside and wait to die. Or go home and wait to die. Or stay with me and live."

"Why do you care?"

"I don't," said Victor, simply. "Not about you, that is. But the one who wants to kill you? I want him dead. And you can help me."

"Why would I?"

Victor sighed. "Aside from the obvious self-preservation?" He held out his empty hand, palm up, and smiled. "I'll make it worth your while."

When Dominic didn't take his hand, Victor brought it to rest on the man's shoulder. He could both feel and see as the pain left Dominic's body, watch it slide from his limbs and his jaw and his forehead and his eyes, which then widened in shock.

"What . . . what did you . . . ?"

"My name, Mr. Rusher, is Victor Vale. I am an EO, and I can take away your pain. All of it. Forever. Or . . ." His hand slid from the young man's shoulder, and a moment later Dominic's face crumpled as the pain swept back, redoubled. "I can give it back, and leave you here, to live in agony, or die at a stranger's hands. Not the best death for a soldier."

"No," hissed Dominic through gritted teeth. "Please. What do I have to do?"

Victor smiled. "One night's worth of work for a lifetime without pain. What are you *willing* to do?" When Dominic didn't answer, Victor clicked the dial up in his mind, watched the man wince, buckle.

"Anything," Dominic gasped at last. "Anything."

∞

MITCH stood at the bathroom sink, pushing the sleeves of his coat up to wash his hands. He turned the faucet on, and heard the door open over the sound of the water. His form filled the mirror, edge to edge, so he couldn't see the man behind him, but he didn't need to. He could hear Eli Ever cross the threshold, and slide the bolt on the bathroom door, locking the world out. Locking them in.

"What did you tell him?" came Eli's voice behind him.

Mitch turned the water off, but stayed at the sink. "Tell who?"

"The man at the bar. You were talking to him, and then he disappeared."

The paper towels were out of reach, and Mitch knew better than to make any sudden movements, so he wiped his hands on his coat, and turned to face the other man.

"It's a bar," he said with a shrug. "People come and go."

"No," snapped Eli. "He literally disappeared. Vanished."

Mitch forced a laugh. "Look, man," he said, walking past Eli toward the door as if he didn't notice the thrown bolt. "I think you've had a few too many—"

He heard Eli draw the gun from his coat, and his words cut off as his steps slowed, then stopped. Eli cocked the weapon. Mitch could tell it was an automatic by the metallic grating of the top half as it was shifted back and primed. He turned slowly toward the sound. The gun was in Eli's hand, the silencer already screwed on, but instead of being trained on Mitch, it hung at Eli's side. And that made Mitch more nervous, the casual way he held the weapon, fingers barely gripping it, not only comfortable with the gun, but in control. He looked like he felt in control.

"I've seen you before," said Eli. "At the Esquire downtown."

Mitch cocked his head and tugged one corner of his mouth up. "Do I look like I'd be caught in a place like that?"

"No. Which is exactly why I noticed you." Mitch's smile faded. Eli raised the gun, and took him in over the sight. "Someone swiped the visuals from the prison files and the police logs, but I'm willing to bet your name is Mitchell Turner. Now where is Victor?"

Mitch thought to feign ignorance, but in the end he decided not to chance it. He'd never been that great at telling lies, anyway, and he knew he'd have to make the few he needed count.

"You must be Eli," he said. "Victor told me about you. Said you had a thing for killing innocent people."

"They're not innocent," growled Eli. "Where is Victor?"

"Haven't seen him since we reached the city and split ways."

"I don't believe that."

"I don't care."

Eli swallowed, fingers drifting toward the trigger. "And Dominic Rusher?"

Mitch shrugged, but slid a step back. "Kid just vanished."

Eli took a step forward, settled his finger against the trigger. "What did you tell him?"

A smile twitched at the corner of Mitch's mouth. "I told him to run."

Eli's eyes narrowed. He twirled the gun in his hand, the barrel fetching up against his palm, and swung the handle hard against Mitch's head. His face cracked sideways, and blood poured from the gash above his eye, running into his vision as Eli brought his boot up, hard, and sent him sprawling backward to the bathroom floor. Eli spun the gun again, and trained it on Mitch's chest. "Where is Victor?" he demanded.

Mitch squinted through the blood. "You'll see him soon enough," he said. "It's almost midnight."

Eli bared his teeth, and bowed his head, and Mitch thought he could see him mouth the words *forgive me* before he looked up, and pulled the trigger.

∞

VICTOR checked his watch. It was almost eleven p.m., and Mitch still hadn't come out.

Dominic stood nearby stretching, rolling his head and shoulders and swinging his arms forward and backward and side to side, as if he'd just set down a heavy burden. Victor supposed that in many ways he had. After all, Victor knew pain enough to know how much Dominic had been in, and was frankly impressed by the man's threshold. But while he might be able to function in pain, his powers clearly didn't flourish under it. So Victor had taken it away. Taken it all away. He had, however, left as much *sensation* as possible, which was tricky, given how tightly the two things were intertwined, but he didn't need his newest asset accidentally bleeding out just because he didn't notice he'd cut himself.

Victor's attention flicked between his watch and the ex-soldier, who was busy examining himself. People took their bodies and their health for granted. But Dominic Rusher seemed to savor every painless flexing of his hands, every stride. He clearly understood what a gift he'd been given. *Good,* thought Victor.

"Dominic," he said. "What I've done can be undone. And for the record, I do not need to touch you to do it. That was for effect. Do you understand? What I've taken can be given back in a blink, from a city away, or a world away. So do not cross me."

Dominic nodded solemnly.

In truth, Victor could only influence a person's pain threshold if they were within eyesight. The farthest he'd gotten in prison was dropping a man from across the football-field-sized yard with only a finger gun. Once he'd managed to crumple an inmate at the other end of the cell block, only his hand visible through the bars, but still. Out of sight, and his accuracy quickly vanished. Not that Dominic needed to know any of that.

"Your power," asked Victor. "How does it work?"

"I don't exactly know how to explain." Dominic looked down at his hands, and flexed and stretched them as if working out a lingering stiffness. "Yea, though I walk in the shadow of the valley of death—"

"Biblical allusions aside, please."

"After the mine blew, it was bad. I couldn't . . . it was inhuman, that pain. It was animal and everywhere. And I didn't want to die. God, I didn't, but I wanted quiet and dark and . . . it's hard to explain."

He didn't have to. Victor knew.

"I felt torn apart. I was. Anyway. They brought me back but they couldn't seem to pull me through, not all the way. I spent weeks in a coma. All that time, I could feel the world. I could hear it. Swore I could see it, too, but it was like everything was far away. Murky. And I couldn't reach out, couldn't touch any of it. And then I woke up, and everything was so sharp and bright and full of pain again, and all I wanted was to find that place, that dull, quiet place. And then I did. I call it walking in shadows, because I don't know any other term. I step into the darkness and can move from one place to another without being seen. Without time passing. Without anything. It looks like teleporting, I guess, but I have to physically move. I could cross a city in the time it takes you to blink, but it would take me hours. I'd have to walk the whole way. And it's hard. Like walking through water. The world resists, when you break its rules."

"Can you take others with you?"

Dominic shrugged. "I've never tried."

"Well then," said Victor, taking hold of Dominic's arm, ignoring the moment when the man winced intrinsically away. "Consider this your audition."

"Where are we going?"

"My friend is still inside," said Victor, nodding toward the bar. "He should have come out after you. But he didn't."

"That big guy? He said he'd cover me."

Victor frowned. "From who?"

"The one who wants to kill me," said Dominic, frowning. "I tried to tell you, that guy sat down next to me and said there was a man who wanted to kill me, and that he was *in the bar*."

Victor's grip tightened on Dominic's sleeve. *Eli.* "Take me inside. *Now.*"

Dominic took a steadying breath, and put his hand over Victor's. "Don't know if this is even going to—"

The rest of the words dropped away, not fading out but plummeting into silence as the air around them shuddered, and split to allow the two men through. The moment Dominic and Victor stepped through the seam, everything hushed and darkened and stilled. Victor could see the man whose arm he was touching, just as he could see the alley around them, but all of it was cast in a kind of shadow, less like night and more like the world had been photographed in black and white and then the photo had aged, worn, grayed. When they walked, the world rippled thickly around them, the air viscous. It pressed in on them, weighed them down. When they reached the door to the bar, it resisted Dominic's pull before finally—slowly—giving way.

Inside, the photo world continued. People caught middrink, mid-pool-shot, midkiss, midfight, and mid-a-dozen-other-things, all stuck between one breath and the next. And all the sound caught, too, so that the space filled with a horrible, heavy quiet. Victor kept his hand on Dominic's arm like a blind man, but he couldn't take his eyes from the room. He scanned, searching the frozen faces of the crowd.

And then he saw him.

Victor ground to a halt, jarring Dominic backward. He glanced over his shoulder and asked what was wrong, the words mouthed, but never formed. And it didn't matter, anyway, because Victor didn't see his lips move. He didn't see anything but the dark-haired man caught midstride as he wove through the crowd, away from them and toward the front door, hand reaching out for the handle. Victor wondered how could he know that man without seeing his face. It was the posture, the broad shoulders and the arrogant way he held them, the edge of his sharp jaw visible as he turned away.

Eli.

Victor's hand began to slip from Dominic's arm. Eli Ever was *right there*. Half a room away. His back turned. His attention derailed and his body caught between seconds. Victor could do it. The bar was packed, but if he dropped every person at once, he'd have a shot—*No*. It took every ounce of focus for Victor to hold on to Dominic's sleeve. He had waited. Waited so long. He wasn't going to forfeit the planning, the lead, the control. It wouldn't work, not here, not the way it had to work. He dragged his eyes from Eli's back, and forced himself to search the rest of the room, but there was no sign of Mitch. His gaze swept through, and finally settled on the restrooms. A sign hung from the men's room. OUT OF ORDER in bold letters, a hand-drawn set of lines beneath to emphasize the point. He urged Dominic forward, through the heavy air until they reached the door, and went in.

Mitchell Turner was sprawled on the linoleum, his face stuck to the floor by a small puddle of blood emanating from a gash on his temple. Victor let go of Dominic's arm and winced as the room crashed into life around him all at once, a wave of color and noise and time. Dominic himself appeared a moment later, arms crossed, looking down at the body.

"Big guy," he said quietly.

Victor knelt carefully beside Mitch, and reconsidered his decision to leave Sydney at the hotel.

"Is he . . . ," started Dominic as Victor reached out and brought his fingertips to the gunshot hole in Mitch's jacket. His hand came away dry. He let out a breath and patted Mitch's jaw. The man groaned.

"Mother . . . fucker . . ."

"I see you met Eli," said Victor. "He's always been a bit trigger happy."

Mitch grunted as he sat up and touched his head, a bruise already blossoming beneath the drying blood. His gaze went to Dominic. "I see you're still alive then. Good choice."

He tried to stand, and got to one knee before pausing for breath.

"A little help?" he said, wincing. Victor's lips twitched, and the air hummed faintly for a moment before vanishing, taking Mitch's pain with it. The man got to his feet, swayed, and caught himself against the wall with a bloody hand before making his way to the strip of sinks to clean up.

"So he's like, bulletproof?" asked Dominic. Mitch laughed, and then pulled his jacket aside to reveal the vest beneath.

"Close enough," he said. "I'm not an EO, though, if that's what you're asking."

Victor wet a handful of paper towels and did his best to clean Mitch's blood off the floor and the wall while Mitch finished cleaning it off his face.

"What time is it?" asked Victor, tossing the ruined towels in the bin.

Dominic checked his watch. "Eleven. Why?"

Mitch snapped the faucet off. "Cutting it pretty close, Vic."

But Victor only smiled. "Dominic," he said. "Let's show Mitch what you can do."

XXIX

SIXTY MINUTES UNTIL MIDNIGHT
THE ESQUIRE HOTEL

SERENA toweled off her hair, holding strands up to the bathroom light to make sure Zachary Flinch hadn't stained them. She'd had to shower three times to get the feel of brain and blood off her skin, and even now, raw from scrubbing, with her hair probably damaged from the rinse repeat of it all, she didn't *feel* clean.

Clean was clearly not skin deep when it came to killing.

It was only the second execution she'd ever been to. The first had been Sydney's. Serena cringed at the thought of it. Maybe that's why she'd wanted to go, to wash the memory of her sister's almost-murder from her mind, replace it with some fresher horror, as if one scene could paint over the other.

Or maybe she'd asked to go along because she knew Eli would hate it—she knew how much his removals mattered to him, how much they *belonged* to him—and that he'd resist. Sometimes those moments when he fought back, when she could see the spark of defiance, were the only ones that made her feel alive. She hated living in such a limp world, every glazed eye and simple nod a reminder that nothing mattered. She would start to let go, and then Eli would fight back and force her to tighten her grip. She wondered with a thrill if maybe one day he would even break free.

Finally satisfied that the blood didn't stain, she dried her hair, pulled on a robe, and made her way into the living room, tapping the computer awake. She logged on to the police database, and filled out the "Middle Name" window of the search form with *ELI*, expecting it to return with no results, since Eli should have dispatched Dominic by now, but the search came back with two profiles. The first belonged to Dominic.

But the second belonged to *Victor*.

She read the profile three times, chewing her lip, then searched the room for her phone, which she'd lobbed onto the bed when she got in. She found it beneath a pile of clothes and towels, and was halfway through punching in Eli's number, when she stopped.

Less than an hour until midnight.

It was a trap. Eli would know it, too, of course, but he would go anyway. Why shouldn't he? Whatever Eli's enemy was planning, there was only one way this night would end, and that was with Victor Vale in a body bag. And Sydney? Serena's chest tightened. Her resolve had faltered the first time; she didn't know if she had the strength to watch Eli try again. Even if it wasn't really her sister, just a shadow of the little girl who'd clung to her side for twelve years, an imposter in her sister's shape. Even then.

Her fingers hovered over the screen. She could drag the file to the trash. Eli wouldn't find it in time. But it would only be a stay of execution. Victor wanted to find Eli, and Eli wanted to find Victor, and one way or another, they would succeed. She looked at Victor's profile one last time, and tried to picture the man who had once been Eli's friend, who had brought him back, made him what he was, saved her sister . . . and for a moment, as she finished dialing Eli's number, she almost wished he stood a fighting chance.

XXX

FIFTY MINUTES UNTIL MIDNIGHT
THE THREE CROWS BAR

ELI stormed through the front door of the Three Crows as he dialed Detective Stell and told him to send a cop over to the bar to clean up an incident.

"It was an EO, right?" asked Stell, and the question, as well as the shade of doubt that lined the officer's voice as he asked it, troubled Eli immensely. But he didn't have time to deal with the detective's resistance, not right now, not as the clock ticked down.

"Of course it was," he snapped, and hung up.

Eli paused beneath the metal sculpted crows on the bar's marquee, ran his fingers through his hair, and scoured the street for any sign of Dominic Rusher or Victor Vale, but all he saw were drunkards, and bums, and cars whizzing past too fast to see drivers or passengers. He swore and kicked the nearest trash can as hard as possible, relishing the blossom of pain even as it faded, whatever damage he'd done repairing, bone and tissue and skin knitting neatly back together.

He shouldn't have killed Mitch Turner.

He knew that. But it wasn't as though the man were innocent, not truly. Eli had seen the police records. Turner had sinned. And those who ally themselves with monsters are little better than monsters themselves. Still, he had felt no silence, no moment of peace, following the act, and Eli's chest tightened at being denied the calm, the assurance that he had not strayed.

Eli bowed his head, and crossed himself. His nerves were just beginning to smooth when his phone rang.

"What?" he snapped into the cell, heading for his car in the lot across the street.

"Victor posted to the database," said Serena. "That Falcon Price site. Ground floor." He heard the sound of the glass patio door sliding open. "It's right here, across from the hotel. Did you take care of Dominic Rusher?"

"No," he growled. "But Mitchell Turner's dead. Is the deadline still midnight?" His anger was cooling as he walked, focus knitting him closed the way his body knit together his skin. Things were on schedule. Not *his* schedule, but *a* schedule.

"Still midnight," said Serena. "What about the police? Should I call Stell? Have him send his men over to the high-rise?"

Eli rapped his fingers on his car and thought of Stell's question, his tone. "No. Not before midnight. Turner's dead, and Victor's mine. Tell them to be there at twelve, no sooner, and order them to stay outside the walls until we're done. Tell them it's not safe." He got inside, his breath fogging the windows. "I'm on my way. Should I pick you up?" She didn't answer. "Serena?"

After another long pause, she finally said, "No, no. I'm not dressed yet. I'll meet you there."

∞

SERENA hung up.

She was leaning on the balcony, and she barely noticed the biting chill of the iron rail under her elbows because she was too busy looking at a trail of smoke.

Two floors down and several rooms over, the smoke curled through a pair of open doors, wafting up toward her. It smelled like burning paper. Serena knew because in high school she and her friends would always light a bonfire on the first night of summer vacation and pitch their essays and exams in, casting the old year into the flames.

But nice as the Esquire rooms were, none of them had fireplaces.

She was still wondering about the smoke when a large black dog wandered out onto the balcony. It stared out through the bars of the railing for a moment before a girl's voice called it back.

"Dol," called the girl. "Dol! Come back in."

A shiver ran through Serena. She knew that voice.

A moment later the small blond girl who so many people had mistaken for Serena's twin bobbed onto the porch, and tugged at the dog's neck.

"Come on," coaxed Sydney. "Let's go in."

The dog turned and obediently followed her back inside.

Which hotel room? Serena began to count. Two floors down. Three rooms over.

She spun on her heel, and went inside.

XXXI

FORTY MINUTES UNTIL MIDNIGHT
THE THREE CROWS BAR

DOMINIC took hold of Victor and Mitch, and led them in silence and shadow out of the restrooms, through the bar, and into the alley that ran beside it.

Victor gave a nod and Dominic let go, the world springing back into life around them. Even the deserted alley was a cacophony compared to the heavy quiet of the in-between; Victor rolled his shoulders, and checked his watch.

"That was . . . weird," said Mitch, whose mood seemed to have soured considerably since being shot.

"It was perfect," said Victor. "Let's go."

"So I passed?" asked Dominic, still flexing his hands. Victor could see the fear in his eyes, the desperate hope that the pain would stay away. He appreciated how transparent Dominic's desires were. It kept things simple.

"The night's not over yet," he said. "But you're doing well so far."

Mitch grumbled about the hole in his jacket as they made their way to the mouth of the alley. Victor knew that it was the first thing Mitch bought when they got out, a well-made coat, lined with dark-dyed goose down that now leaked in small puffs as he stepped off the curb.

"Look at the bright side," said Victor. "You're alive."

"Night's still young," said Mitch under his breath as they crossed the street.

He said something else, or started to, but it was cut off by the sudden shriek of sirens.

A squad car tore around a corner and down the street toward them in red and blue and white and blaring ripples of noise. Mitch spun, and Victor tensed, and time slowed. And then, time *stopped*. Victor felt the hand come down on his arm a breath before the sound and color went out of the night. The cop car froze, suspended between moments through the film of Dominic's shadows. Dominic's other hand rested on Mitch's wrist, and all three of them now stood in the darkness of his in-between world, frozen as if they, too, were caught in time. Victor might have admitted—if he *could* admit, if his words could take shape and sound—how useful Dominic Rusher was turning out to be, but since he couldn't, he simply nodded in the direction of the parking lot, and the three men waded through the thick air across the street.

Victor knew that they had a predicament.

Dominic, while much improved, was in no condition to drag them across the city. They needed the car. But they couldn't use the car until they stepped out of the shadows, and the moment they did that, reality would resume and the squad car would continue down the street to the Three Crows. Victor led the way to the stolen sedan, the other two in a trailing line behind, and when they got there he gestured for them to kneel in the gap between their vehicle and the next on the side of the cop cars' frozen approach, which had before been a convertible and was now a considerably larger truck. He took one last breath, and said a quiet curse, which was as close as Victor came to praying, and then he nodded at Dominic, whose hand vanished from his shoulder, stripping the stillness and plunging his world back into chaos.

The cop car careened up to the bar's entrance, where it slammed to a stop, sirens blaring. Victor held his breath and pressed his body against the metal side of their sedan and peered through the narrow space between his front bumper and the truck's as the sirens cut abruptly off, and left his ears ringing.

Two officers got out, and met at the front doors.

One cop vanished inside, but the other stayed on the curb and confirmed their arrival on a radio. Something about a body. They were here for Mitch's body. Which was problematic, since there *was* no body, a fact that would soon become readily apparent.

Go inside, he begged the second cop.

The cop didn't move. Victor freed his gun and trained it on the officer, tracking up until it was level with the man's head. He had a clear shot. He drew in a breath, and held it. Victor didn't feel guilt, or fear, or even a sense of consequence, not like normal people. All those things had been dead—or at least dulled to the point of uselessness—for years. But he'd trained his mind to reconstruct those feelings from memory as best he could, and assemble them into a kind of code. Nothing so elaborate as Eli's set of rules, just a simple wish to avoid killing bystanders, if possible. It didn't feel wrong, resting his finger on the trigger, but his mind provided the word *wrong*. He lowered the gun a fraction, knowing that sacrificing a kill shot would also sacrifice the certitude of their escape.

He let out his breath just as the radio crackled, and even if Victor couldn't make out the message, he could hear the officer's response—"What kind of problem?"—and, a moment later, "What do you mean? According to Ever and Stell . . . forget it. Hold on."

And just like that, the second cop turned toward the door. Victor lowered his weapon and his eyes drifted skyward, where thick gray clouds weakened the black of the night. He'd never been one for God, never had Eli's zeal, never needed signs, but if there were such things, if there was Fate, or some higher power, maybe it had an issue with Eli's methods, too. The second officer followed the first inside, and Victor, Mitch, and Dominic were on their feet, and in the car before the front doors of the bar had even swung shut.

A yellow ticket flapped against the windshield, pinned beneath a wiper blade, and Victor leaned out the window, plucked it free, and crumpled it, dropping the paper to the ground. The wind instantly caught it, and the ticket bounced away.

"Littering," said Mitch as Victor started the car.

"Let's hope that's not the worst crime I commit tonight," said Victor as they pulled out of the lot, away from the Three Crows and the squad car and back into the heart of the city as the minutes ticked away toward midnight. "Call Sydney. Make sure everything's okay on her end."

An ambulance soared past them toward the bar. It wouldn't be necessary.

"If I didn't know better," said Mitch, dialing. "I'd think you care."

XXXII

THIRTY MINUTES UNTIL MIDNIGHT
THE ESQUIRE HOTEL

BURNING the papers took longer than Sydney expected, and by the seventh or eighth page, the novelty of ruining something had faded, replaced by a tedious sense of obligation. She stood at the sink, boosted up by Victor's book, and fed one page at a time to the flame of the small blue lighter, waiting until each was a layer of ash in the sink before she began the next sheet, and strongly suspecting Victor had given her the task just to keep her busy. She didn't mind so much. It was better than sitting still, staring at the clock and wondering when they'd be back.

If they'd be back.

Dol stood beside her, nearly able to rest his nose on the counter by the remaining papers, and whimpering faintly every time she touched the lighter's flame to a page. She'd wait as long as she dared before dropping the burning paper into the sink—a little longer each time—and then watch as the crossed-out faces of Eli's victims blackened and curled, watch as the fire ate away their names, their dates, their lives.

Sydney shivered.

The room was freezing with the balcony doors open, and Dol had already wandered out once, unsettled by the fire, but she had to leave them that way, because of the smoke. It drifted out from the charred remains, and Sydney spent the whole task waiting for the alarms to go off. She had to resist the urge to burn the folder's remnants in one go and be done with it, but her concern about the alarms kept her slow, methodical. The amount of smoke created by a single page appeared too little to disrupt the systems, but lighting the whole folder at once would surely trigger something.

Dol soon lost interest, and wandered out once more onto the balcony. Sydney didn't like him out there, and called him back, nearly singeing her fingers when she forgot to let go of the latest page.

A phone rang in Sydney's pocket.

Victor had bought it for her. Or rather, Victor had bought it, and then given it to Sydney after he saw what she could do. The phone was, in Sydney's eyes, an invitation to stay. She and Mitch and Victor all had the same models, and somehow that made Sydney happy. It was like belonging to a club. She'd wanted to belong to a club in school, but she'd never been great at sports, didn't care about student government (it was a joke in middle school, anyway), and after resurrecting the science class's hamster, she was a bit shy about participating in the after-school nature club. High school clubs would be more fun anyway, she'd reasoned.

If she could stay alive that long.

The phone rang again, and Sydney set the lighter aside and dug the device from her pocket.

"Hello?" she answered.

"Hey, Syd." It was Mitch. "Everything okay there?"

"I'm almost done with the papers," she said, taking up the lighter and setting fire to another page. It was the blue-haired girl. The same blue, almost, as the lighter itself. Sydney watched as the girl's face curled into nothing. "Are you going to think up more ways to keep me busy?"

Mitch laughed, but he didn't sound very happy.

"You're a kid. Just watch some TV. We'll be home later."

"Hey, Mitch," said Sydney, softer. "You . . . you're coming back, right?"

"As soon as I can, Syd. Promise."

"You better." She lit another page. "Or I'll drink all your chocolate milk."

"You wouldn't dare," said Mitch, and she could almost hear the smile in his voice before he hung up.

Sydney put her phone away, and lit the last page. It was hers. She touched the lighter to the corner and held the paper up so the fire ate its way along one side before swallowing the photo, the paper-thin version of the girl with short blond hair and water blue eyes. It burned right through her and then there was nothing. She let the fire lick her fingers before she dropped the page into the sink, and smiled.

That girl was dead.

Someone knocked on the hotel door, and Sydney nearly dropped the lighter.

The knocking came a second time.

She held her breath. Dol stood, made something like a growl, and put himself squarely between her and the hotel door.

The knocking came a third time, and then someone spoke.

"Sydney?"

Even on her toes, Sydney wouldn't be able see out of the peephole, but she didn't need to. She knew the voice, knew it better than her own. She lifted her hand and brought it over her mouth to stifle the surprise, the reply, the sound of breathing, as if she couldn't trust her lips with anything.

"Sydney, please," came Serena's voice through the door, smooth and soft and low.

For a moment, Sydney almost forgot—the hotel and the

shooting and the broken lake—and it was like they were home and playing hide-and-seek, and Sydney was too good and Serena had given up, or gotten bored, and was imploring her little sister to give up, too, to come out. If they'd been at home, Serena would have said she had cookies, or lemonade, or why didn't they go watch that movie Sydney had been wanting to see? They could make popcorn. None of it was true, of course. Even then, Serena would say anything to coax her little sister out, and Sydney wouldn't mind, not really, because she'd won.

But they weren't at home.

They weren't anywhere near home.

And this game was rigged, because her sister didn't have to lie, or bribe, or cheat. All she had to do was say the words.

"Sydney, come open the door."

She put aside the lighter and stepped down from Victor's book, and crossed the room, pressing her hand against the wood for a moment before her traitorous fingers drifted over to the doorknob, and turned. Serena stood in the doorway wearing a green pea coat and a pair of leggings that vanished into heeled black boots. Her hands were braced against the frame to either side. One hand was empty, and the other held a gun. The hand with the gun slid down the door frame with a metallic hiss before coming to rest at her side. Sydney cringed away from the weapon.

"Hello, Sydney," she said, as she tapped the gun absently against her leggings.

"Hello, Serena," said her sister.

"Don't run," said Serena. It never occurred to Sydney to do so. She couldn't tell, though, if the thought had been there and bled away at her sister's words, or if she was brave enough to have never considered running, or if she was simply smart enough to know she couldn't outrun bullets twice, especially without a forest and a head start.

Whatever the reason, Sydney stayed very, very still.

Dol growled as Serena stepped into the hotel room, but when she told him to sit, he did, back legs folding reluctantly. Serena strode past her little sister, surveying the ashes in the sink, and the carton of chocolate milk on the counter (Sydney had silently resolved to drink it—at least some of it—if Mitch didn't come back soon), before turning back to Sydney.

"Do you have a phone?" she asked.

Sydney nodded, her hand drifting of its own accord to her pocket and retrieving the one Victor had given her. The one that matched his, and Mitch's. The one that made them a team. Serena held out her hand and Sydney's hand held out itself, depositing the device into her sister's palm. Serena then walked to the balcony, where the doors were still open to vent the smoke, and lobbed the phone over the railing and into the night.

Sydney's heart sank with the rectangle of falling metal. She'd really liked that phone.

Serena then shut the balcony doors and perched on the back of the couch, facing her sister, her gun resting on her knee. She sat the way Sydney did, or rather, Sydney sat the way *she* always had, with only half her weight, as if she might need to dash up at any second. But where Sydney's perching looked coiled, Serena somehow made the act look casual, even lazy, despite the weapon.

"Happy birthday," she said.

"It's not midnight yet," said Sydney quietly. *You can come up and stay through your birthday,* Serena had promised. Now she smiled sadly.

"You used to stay up until the clock turned, even though Mom told you not to because she knew you'd be tired the next day. You'd sit awake and read and wait and when the clock struck midnight you'd light a candle you'd stashed under the bed, and make a wish." There was a coat draped on the back of the couch, the red one Sydney had thrown off after Victor told her she had to stay behind, and now Serena fiddled with one of the buttons. "It was like this secret birthday party," she added softly. "Just for you, before everyone else could join in and celebrate."

"How did you know?" asked Sydney.

"I'm your big sister," said Serena. "It's my job to know things."

"Then tell me," said Sydney. "Why do you hate me?"

Serena held her gaze. "I don't."

"But you want me to die. You think I'm somehow wrong. Broken."

"I think we're all broken," said Serena, tossing her the red coat. "Put that on."

"I don't feel broken," Sydney said quietly as she tugged on the too-big sleeves. "And even if I am, I can fix other people."

Serena considered her sister. "You can't fix the dead, Syd. EOs are proof of that. And besides, it's not your place to try."

"It's not your place to control people's lives," snapped Sydney.

Serena raised a brow, amused. "Who taught you to sing so loud? The little Sydney I knew could barely chirp."

"I'm not that Sydney anymore."

Serena's face fell. Her grip tightened on the gun.

"We're going for a walk," she said.

Sydney cast glances around the room, even as her feet followed Serena toward the door with the same simple obedience that had possessed her hands to offer up the phone. Treacherous limbs. She wanted to leave a note, a clue, something, but Serena got impatient and grabbed her sleeve, shoving her toward the hall. Dol sat in the middle of the room, whining as they passed.

"Can I bring him?"

Serena paused, and ejected the magazine of the gun to check the number of rounds.

"Okay," she said, snapping it shut again. "Where's his leash?"

"He doesn't have one."

Serena held open the door and sighed.

"Follow Sydney," she said to Dol, and the dog sprang to his feet and loped over, pressing himself against the girl's side.

Serena led Sydney and Dol down the concrete stairs that ran beside the elevator, all the way to the parking garage, an open-walled structure pressed against the Esquire's spine. The place smelled like gas, the light was dim, and the air was biting cold, a sideways wind ripping through in short, sharp gusts.

"Are we driving somewhere?" asked Sydney, pulling the coat close around her.

"No," said Serena, turning on her sister. She brought the gun up to Sydney's forehead, rested it against her skin, between her watery blue eyes. Dol growled. Sydney brought a hand up and rested it against his back to quiet him, but didn't take her gaze off Serena, even though it was a struggle to focus her vision around the barrel of the gun.

"We used to have the same eyes," said Serena. "Yours are paler now."

"I like that we're finally different," said Sydney, fighting back a shiver. "I don't want to be you."

Silence fell between the sisters. A silence full of shifting pieces.

"I don't need you to be me," said Serena at last. "But I need you to be brave. I need you to be strong."

Sydney squeezed her eyes shut. "I'm not afraid."

∞

SERENA stood in the garage with her finger on the trigger, the barrel resting between Sydney's eyes, and froze. The girl on the other side of the gun was and was not her sister. Maybe Eli was wrong and all EOs weren't broken, at least not in the same way. Or maybe Eli was right and the Sydney she knew was gone, but still, this new Sydney wasn't hollowed out, wasn't dark, wasn't truly dead. This Sydney was alive in a way the other had never been. It shone through her skin.

Serena's fingers loosened on the gun, and she let it slide from her sister's face. Sydney kept her eyes squeezed shut. The gun had left a mark on her forehead, a small dent where she'd leaned into the weapon, and Serena reached out and smoothed it away with her thumb. Only then did Sydney's eyes drift open, the strength in them wavering.

"Why—," she started.

"I need you to listen now," cut in Serena in her even tone, the one that no one—not even Eli—knew how to refuse. An absolute power. "I need you to do as I say." She pressed the gun into Sydney's hands, and then took her by the shoulders and squeezed.

"Go," she said.

"Where?" asked Sydney.

"Somewhere safe."

Serena let go and gave her sister a small push backward, away, a gesture that once might have been playful, normal. But the look in her eyes and the gun in Sydney's hands and the cold night hardening around them served as a vivid reminder that nothing was normal now. Sydney tucked the gun into her coat, but didn't take her eyes from her sister, and didn't move.

"*Go,*" snapped Serena.

This time, Sydney did as she was told. She turned, clutched the scruff of Dol's neck, and the two bolted between the cars. Serena watched until her sister was a speck of red, and then nothing. At least she'd have a chance.

A phone rang in the pocket of Serena's coat. She rubbed her eyes, and answered.

"I'm here," said Eli. "Where are you?"

Serena straightened. "I'm on my way."

XXXIII

TWENTY MINUTES UNTIL MIDNIGHT
THE FALCON PRICE PROJECT

SYDNEY ran.

She cut through the Esquire's parking garage and onto a side street that looped back around to the front of the hotel, and ended up a few yards to the left of the main doors. A cop stood several feet away, his back to her as he sipped a coffee and talked on his cell. Sydney felt the weight of the gun in her pocket—as if the hidden firearm would draw more attention than a missing girl in a bright red coat clutching the collar of a giant black dog—but the cop never turned around. It was late and the cars on the main road were sparse, the traffic clumping as the night wore on, and Sydney and Dol sprinted across the street, unnoticed.

She knew exactly where she was going.

Serena hadn't told Sydney to go *home*. She hadn't told her to run *away*. She'd told her to go somewhere *safe*. And over the course of the last week, *safe* had ceased to be a place for Sydney, and had become a person.

Specifically, *safe* had become Victor.

Which is why Sydney ran to the only place she knew Victor would be (at least, according to the profile he'd had her put up on the police database that night, the one she'd read through a dozen times while waiting and then working up the nerve to hit the Post button).

The Falcon Price high-rise project.

Down the block, the construction site was a spot of dark in the city, like a shadow between streetlights. There was a thin shell of wood surrounding the abandoned high-rise, two-story walls, the kind people loved to vandalize because they were both temporary and highly visible. The shell was plastered with posters and signs, tagged here and there by street art, and underneath it all, a few construction permits, and a building company logo.

Officially, there was only one way onto the construction site, through a front gate—also made of wooden sheeting—which had spent the last few months chained shut.

But earlier that day, when Mitch had brought her here to revive Officer Dane, he'd shown her another way in, not through the chained-off gate, but around the back of the building, through a place in the shell where two broad panels of wood overlapped slightly. He'd widened the gap between the sheets to let them through, the panels snapping shut again behind them. Sydney knew she could squeeze into the construction site without touching the walls, since even when the panels hung closed there was a small triangle of space near the bottom. She let go of Dol's neck, and worried the dog would bolt, but he didn't, only stood there watching Sydney crawl through the gap. Dol looked both distressed by Sydney's decision, and determined to follow her. When she made it to the other side and stood, brushing dirt from her pants, the dog crouched down, and squirmed through the gap in the boards.

"Good dog," she whispered as he stood and shook off.

Inside the wooden shell was a kind of yard, a large stretch of dirt strewn with bits of metal and plywood and bags of concrete. The yard was dark, shadows on shadows making the path from the wall to the building dangerous. The building itself towered, unfinished, a steel and concrete skeleton draped in layers of plastic sheeting like gauze.

But on the ground floor, several layers of plastic in, Sydney could make out a light.

It was diffused so much that if the yard hadn't been so dark, she might not have noticed it. But she did. Dol pressed himself against her side. Sydney stood in the yard, unsure what to do. Was Victor here already? It wasn't midnight yet, was it? She didn't have her phone, couldn't tell by the moon even if she knew *how* to read the moon because there was no moon above, only a thick layer of clouds, glowing faintly with reflected city light.

As for the light within the high-rise, it was steady, constant, more like a lamp than a flashlight, and somehow that gave Sydney comfort. Someone had set it there, had prepared, had planned. Victor planned things. But when she took a step toward the building, Dol barred her path. When she went around him, his jaws circled her forearm, and held fast. She twisted, but couldn't get free, and even though the dog was careful not to bite down, his grip was solid.

"Let go," she hissed. The dog didn't budge.

And then, on the other side of the building, beyond the thin wood shell, a car door slammed. Dol dropped Sydney's arm as his head snapped toward the sound. The noise, sharp and metallic, reminded Sydney of a gunshot, and sent her pulse spiking, the word *safe safe safe safe* pounding with the blood in her ears. She sprinted for the building, for the sheets and the steel and the shelter, tripping over a stray iron bar before reaching the hollow high-rise frame. Dol followed, and the two vanished into the Falcon Price as, somewhere, on the opposite side, someone dragged the front gate open.

∞

MITCH slammed the car door, and watched Victor and Dominic drive away. He'd planned to circle around to the back of the high-rise, pry open the loose wooden panel, and get in that way, but when he stepped up to the front gate, he saw it wasn't necessary. The chains had been cut, the snaking metal coiled on the ground at his feet. Someone was already inside.

"Great," whispered Mitch, withdrawing the gun Victor had given him.

Incidentally, Mitch had always hated guns, and the events of the evening hadn't made him any fonder. He pushed open the gate, wincing as the hinges screwed into the wood responded with a metallic whine. The yard was dark and, as far as he could tell, empty. He ejected the magazine on the gun, checked it, put it back, and rapped the barrel of the weapon nervously against his palm as he made his way to the center of the yard, halfway between the wooden shell of the fence and the steel skeleton of the high-rise, to a patch of dirt that was as open as possible.

A faint glow coming from the high-rise did little to illuminate him, but given his size and the sheer lack of other people, Mitch felt painfully confident he would be noticed, and soon. A stack of wooden beams, tarped against the weather, sat a few feet away, and Mitch sank onto them, checked his gun a second time, and waited.

∞

SERENA'S phone rang again as she crossed the street, making her way down the now nearly deserted block toward the Falcon Price high-rise.

"Serena," said the caller. It wasn't Eli's voice.

"Detective Stell," she replied. She could hear the open and close of a car door.

"We're on our way now," he said. The line was muffled for a moment while the phone's speaker was covered and orders were given.

"Remember," she said, "you're to stay outside the fence—"

"I know the orders," he said. "That's not why I called."

Serena saw the signage of the abandoned high-rise, and slowed her pace. "Then what is it?"

"Mr. Ever had me send officers to a bar to clean up after an incident. There was supposed to be a body."

"Yeah, Mitchell Turner's," she said.

"Only I get a call from the officers just now. There was no body. No signs of a body, either." Serena's boots slowed, and stopped. "I don't know what's going on," said Stell, "but that's the second time things haven't lined up and—"

"And you didn't call Eli," she cut in softly.

"I'm sorry if that was wrong . . ."

"Why did you call me instead?"

"I trust you," he answered, without hesitation.

"And Eli?"

"I trust you," he said again, and Serena's heart fluttered a little, both at the officer's small display of evasion, the defiance of it, and at her own control over him. She started walking again.

"You did well," she said as she reached the wooden walls of the construction site. And there, through the gap in the broken gate, she saw Mitch's hulking form. "I'll take care of it," she whispered, "trust me."

"I do," said Detective Stell.

Serena hung up, and pushed the metal gate open.

XXXIV

TEN MINUTES UNTIL MIDNIGHT
THE FALCON PRICE PROJECT

MITCH thought he heard something from the building behind him, but when he strained to listen, the sounds that made it into the yard were so broken and faint that they could have been wind through the plastic sheeting, or a loose pipe. He might have gone to see, but Victor's orders had been explicit, and even if he felt like challenging them, it was at that moment that the front gate that surrounded the bones of the high-rise groaned inward again, and a girl stepped into the yard.

She looked like Sydney, thought Mitch. If Sydney had grown a foot taller and several years older. The same blond hair curled down into eyes that were somehow bright and blue, even in the dark. It had to be Serena.

When she saw Mitch waiting, she crossed her arms.

"Mr. Turner," she said, stepping forward, her black boots weaving effortlessly through the debris of the construction yard. "You have an impressive resilience to death. Is this Sydney's work?"

"Call me a cat," said Mitch, pushing up off the planks. "I'm still working through my own nine lives. And just so you know," he added, raising his gun, "I like to think there's a special place in hell for girls who feed their little sisters to wolves."

Serena's face fell. "You should be careful, playing with guns," she said. "Sooner or later you're going to get shot."

Mitch cocked the gun. "The novelty wore off when your boyfriend played target practice with my chest."

"Yet here you are," said Serena. Her voice had a slow, almost lazy sweetness to it. "Clearly his message wasn't *impactful* enough."

Mitch tightened his grip on the gun, and leveled it at her.

Serena only smiled. "Let's point that in a safer direction," she said. "Place the gun against your temple."

Mitch did everything he could to keep his hand still, but it was as if it no longer belonged to him. His elbow softened, his arm bent, and his fingers turned, shifting position until the barrel of the gun came to rest against the side of his head.

He swallowed.

"There are worse ways to die," said Serena. "And worse things to do than die. I promise I'll make it quick."

Mitch looked at her, this girl so much like Sydney, and yet so much less. He couldn't look at her eyes—at once brighter than her sister's, but empty in a bad way, a dead way—so he watched her lips as they formed the words.

"Pull the trigger."

And he did.

∞

SYDNEY and Dol were halfway toward the glowing center of the high-rise's ground floor when she heard the sound of footsteps—not hers, or the dog's, but heavier—and froze in her tracks. She'd only been with Victor and Mitch a few days, but it had been long enough to grow familiar with the sounds they both made. Not just their voices, but the way they sounded when they weren't speaking, the way they breathed and laughed and moved, the way they filled a space, and traveled through it.

Mitch was huge, but his steps were careful, as if he knew his size and didn't want to accidentally crush anything. Victor was almost silent, footfalls as smooth and hushed as everything else about him.

The steps Sydney heard now through several layers of plastic sheeting were louder, the proud clip of nice shoes. Eli had worn nice shoes. Despite the cold and the fact that he was dating a college girl, and the fact that he looked like a college boy, he'd had on leather shoes beneath his jeans when she met him. Shoes that made a sharp sound when he walked.

Sydney held her breath, and slid Serena's gun from her coat pocket, clicking the safety off. Serena had showed her once, how to use a gun, but this one was a little too big for her grip, too heavy and ill-weighted from the silencer screwed on to the end. She looked behind her, and wondered if she could find her way back through the maze of plastic curtains and into the lot before Eli would . . .

Her thoughts trailed off as she realized that the footsteps had stopped.

She checked the curtains to every side for moving shadows, but there were none, so she crept forward, through another plastic sheet, the light brighter here, only a few curtains between her and the source. Victor should be here by now. She couldn't hear him, but that was because he was so quiet, she told herself. He was always quiet. And safe.

Sydney, look at me, he'd said. *No one is going to hurt you. Do you know why? Because I'll hurt them first.*

Safe. Safe. Safe.

She pulled aside the last curtain. She just had to find Victor, and he would keep her safe.

Eli was sitting in a chair in the middle of the room, a table made of wooden planks on cinder blocks displaying what looked like a set of kitchen knives, all gleaming beneath the light of a lamp. The lamp had no shade, and the bulb lit the whole room, from curtain to curtain, and Eli in between. A gun dangled loosely from his hand, and his eyes were far-off, unfocused.

Until he saw Sydney.

"What's this?" he asked, standing. "A little monster."

Sydney didn't wait. She raised Serena's gun and fired once at Eli's face. The weapon was heavy and her aim was off, but even though the blowback knocked the gun from her grip, the bullet still found Eli's jaw and sent him reeling, clutching his face, blood and bone between his fingers. She spun, and tried to run away, but his hand shot out and caught her sleeve, and even though he couldn't keep hold, the sudden change of course sent her stumbling to her hands and knees on the concrete.

Dol lunged forward as Sydney rolled onto her back and Eli straightened, jaw cracking and snapping and healing, leaving only a smear of blood on his skin as he raised his gun and pulled the trigger.

∞

CLICK.

One small sound after Mitch pulled the trigger, the sound made by the internal spring driving the firing pin to bypass the bullet and hit the mechanical stop. Because there were no bullets.

The gun was empty.

Mitch should know; he had checked it three times to make sure.

Now he watched the surprise spread across Serena's face, watched it turn to confusion, and begin to shift into something harder, but it never made it there, because that's when the darkness parted. The shadows behind Serena Clarke stirred and drew apart, and two men stepped into being out of nothing. Dominic stood, holding a red gas canister while Victor took a single stride up behind Serena, brought a knife to her throat, and drew it cleanly across.

There was a blossom of red, and her lips parted, but he'd cut deep, and no sound made it out.

"And Ulysses stopped up his ears against the siren's song," recited Victor, pulling the plugs from his own ears as Serena collapsed to the dirt lot, "for it was death."

"Jesus," said Dominic, looking away. "She was just a girl."

Victor looked down at her body. Blood was pooling beneath Serena's face, glistening and dark. "Don't be insulting," he said. "She was the most powerful woman in the city. Aside from Sydney, of course."

"About Sydney...," said Mitch, looking down at the dead girl. From this angle she seemed smaller, and with her face turned like that, her hair caught in the collar of her coat, the resemblance was disturbing. "What are we going to do about this?"

Dominic set the plastic gas tank on the dirt beside the body.

"Burn the body," said Victor, closing his knife. "I don't want Sydney seeing it. And I certainly don't want her getting her hands on it. The last thing we need is Serena coming back to life."

Mitch had just taken up the gas canister when a gun fired within the building, lighting up the bones of the high-rise like a camera flash.

"What the hell?" growled Victor.

"Looks like Eli got here first," said Mitch.

"But if I'm out here," said Victor, "then what's Eli shooting at?" He grabbed hold of Dominic's shoulder. "Take me in there. Now."

THE sound of Eli's gun rang off the concrete as Dol's body buckled, and even though he didn't seem to feel the pain of the shot, he fell onto his side, panting for air. His chest went up and down and up and down and then . . . stopped. Eli saw the girl reach for the dog but he recocked the gun and leveled it on her.

"Good-bye, Sydney," he said.

And then the darkness moved around her, and a pair of hands reached out of nothing and jerked her backward into nothing with them. Eli pulled the trigger and the bullet hit the plastic sheeting where the girl had been.

He let out a frustrated sound and fired two more shots into the space that had been Sydney. But she was gone.

XXXV

MIDNIGHT
THE FALCON PRICE PROJECT

SYDNEY felt someone take hold and pull her into the dark.

One moment she was looking down the barrel of Eli's gun and the next she was standing hand in hand with the man from the profile she'd given Victor. She looked around, but didn't let go. They were still in the plastic-sheeted room, and yet they weren't. It was like standing outside of life, stuck in a too still world that scared her more than she would ever admit. She could see Eli, the bullet from his gun hovering in the air where she had been, and Dol, lifeless on the ground.

And Victor.

He hadn't been there a moment before, but now he was, standing several feet behind Eli, unseen, one hand reaching slightly forward and out, as if about to rest on Eli's shoulder.

Sydney tried to tell the man holding her hand that she had to get Dol, but her lips made no sound, and he didn't even look at her, only dragged her through the heavy world, winding back through the curtains of plastic until they reached the place where the building gave way to the dirt lot. There was a bright light across the lot, casting shadows up against the metal bones of the highrise, but the man pulled her in the other direction, leading her to a darkened corner in the back of the construction site. They stepped back into the world, the bubble of quiet bursting into life and sound around them. Even just the sound of breathing, of time passing, was deafening compared to the quiet of the shadows.

"You have to go back," snapped Sydney, kneeling in the dirt.

"Can't. Victor's orders."

"But you have to get Dol."

"Sydney . . . it's Sydney, right?" The man knelt in front of her. "I saw the dog, okay? I'm sorry. It was too late."

She held his eyes, the way Serena had held hers. Calm and cold and unblinking. She knew she didn't have her sister's gift, her control, but even before, Serena got her way, and she was Serena's sister, and she needed him to see.

"Go back," she said sternly. "Go. Get. Dol."

And it must have worked because Dominic swallowed, nodded, and vanished into nothing.

∞

ELI emptied the gun into the air, but all signs of them were gone. He growled and ejected the magazine. It clattered to the ground as he dug in his coat for a full one.

"I watch you, and it's like watching two people."

He spun at the sound of the voice and found Victor leaning back against a concrete pillar.

"Vic—"

Victor didn't hesitate. He fired three times into Eli's chest, mimicking the pattern of the scars on his own body, the way he had imagined he would for the last ten years.

And it felt *good*. He had been worried that after so much waiting and so much wanting the actuality of shooting Eli wouldn't live up to the dream, but it did. The air buzzed around them and Eli groaned and braced himself against the chair as the pain multiplied.

"It's why I let you stay," said Victor. "Why I liked you. All that charm outside, all that evil inside. There was a monster under there, long before you died."

"I'm not a monster," growled Eli as he dug one of the bullets out of his shoulder, and dropped the bloodied metal to the floor. "I am God's—" But Victor was already there, burying a switchblade in Eli's chest. He punctured a lung, he could tell by the gasp. Victor's mouth twitched, face patient but knuckles white around the blade's grip.

"Enough," said Victor. Behind his eyes, the dial turned up. Eli screamed. "You aren't some avenging angel, Eli," he said. "You're not blessed, or divine, or burdened. You're a science experiment."

Victor pulled the knife out. Eli went down on one knee.

"You don't understand," gasped Eli. "No one understands."

"When *no one* understands, that's usually a good sign that you're wrong."

Eli struggled up to his knees, reaching for the makeshift table as his skin knit together.

Victor's gaze shifted to it, taking in the row of knives. Just like that day. "How nostalgic of you." He put a foot on the table and knocked it over, sending the weapons scattering across the concrete. The dog's body, he noticed, was gone.

"You can't kill me, Victor," said Eli. "You know that."

Victor's smile widened as he buried his knife between Eli's ribs.

"I know," he said loudly. He had to speak up over the screams. "But you'll have to indulge me. I've waited so long to try."

∞

A breath later, Dominic reappeared, half carrying half dragging a very large, very dead dog. He sank to the dirt lot beside its body, breathing heavily. Sydney hurried over, thanked him, and then asked him to get out of her way. Dominic sagged back, and watched as she ran a soothing hand over the dog's side, brushing the wound lightly. Her palm came away dark red, and she frowned.

"I told you," he said. "I'm sorry."

"Shhh," she said, and pressed her hands, fingers splayed, against the dog's chest. She drew in a shaky breath as the cold flooded up her arms.

"Come on," she whispered. "Come on, Dol."

But nothing happened. Her heart sank. Sydney Clarke gave second chances. But the dog had already had his. She'd fixed him once, but she didn't know if she could do it again. She pressed down harder, and felt the cold leeching something from her.

The dog still lay dead and stiff as the planks in the construction lot.

She shivered and knew it shouldn't be this hard as she reached not with her hands but something else, as if she could find a spark of heat within and take hold. She reached past the fur and skin and stiffness as her hands hurt and her lungs tightened and still she kept reaching.

And then she felt it, and took hold, and between one moment and the next, the dog's body softened, slackened. Its limbs twitched and its chest rose once, paused, fell, and a moment later rose again, before the beast stretched, and sat up.

Dominic scrambled to his feet. *"Dios mío,"* he whispered, crossing himself.

Sydney sat, gasping for breath, and rested her head against Dol's muzzle. "Good dog."

∞

VICTOR smiled. He was having a fabulous time killing Eli. Every time he thought his friend had given up, he pulled himself back together, and gave Victor the chance to try again. He wished it could go on awhile longer, but at least he was quite certain, as Eli's body buckled in pain, that he had his *full* attention. Eli gasped, and staggered to his feet, nearly slipping on the blood.

The floor was slick with it. Most of it was Eli's, Victor knew. But not all.

Blood ran down one of Victor's arms and over his stomach, both shallow cuts made by a wicked-looking kitchen knife Eli had managed to recover from the floor the last time Victor shot him. The guns were both empty now, and the two men stood bleeding, across from one another, each armed—Eli with a serrated knife, and Victor with a switchblade.

"This is a waste," said Eli, adjusting his grip. "You can't win."

Victor took a deep breath, wincing faintly. He'd had to turn his own threshold down because he couldn't afford to bleed out, not yet, and certainly not without noticing. He could hear the distant sirens of the cop cars. They were running out of time. He lunged for Eli, and managed to skim his shirt before Eli knocked the blow away and drove his own blade down into Victor's leg. He hissed as his knee buckled beneath him.

"What was your plan?" chided Eli, reaching out, not for Victor, but for the chair, for something coiled on it, something Victor hadn't noticed until Eli's hands took hold of it. "You hear the cops coming? They're all on my side here. No one's coming to save *you*."

"That's the idea," coughed Victor as his eyes focused on the thing in Eli's hand. Metal wire. Razor sharp.

"You and your ideas," hissed Eli. "Well, I've been planning, too."

Victor tried to find his feet, but he was too slow. Eli looped the wire in the air, and brought it down around Victor's wrist, the one with the knife, pulling hard. The wire dug in, slicing through skin and drawing blood, forcing Victor to drop the blade, which clattered to the concrete. Eli caught his free hand in a crushing grip, and wound the wire around that one, too. Victor pulled back, but the cord only bit deeper into his skin.

The wire, he noticed then, was threaded through the chair itself, which Eli must have fastened to the ground because it never moved, not during the fight, and not now when Eli yanked his end of the cord and the slack drew in, forcing Victor's hands toward the bars of the chair back. Blood ran down his wrists, too fast. His head was beginning to spin. He could hear the sirens now, loud and clear, and thought that he could even see the red and blue of the police lights through the plastic curtains. Color danced before his eyes.

He smiled grimly, and shut off the last of the pain.

"You'll never kill me, Eli," he goaded.

"That's where you're wrong, Victor. And this time," he said, cinching the wire, "I'm going to watch the life bleed out of your eyes."

∞

MITCH watched Serena's body burn, and tried not to listen to the sounds of gunfire coming from inside the high-rise. He had to trust Victor. Victor always had a plan. But where was he? And where was Dominic?

He refocused on the body and the task at hand until red and blue lights began to flash beyond the wood walls, colors cast up against the darkened building. That wasn't good. The cops weren't in the yard yet, but it was only a matter of minutes before they swarmed the place. Mitch couldn't risk the broken gate of the front entrance so he rounded the building toward the gap in the walls, only to find Sydney leaning over a half-dead Dol, and Dominic standing over both, praying silently.

"Sydney Clarke," he snapped. "What the hell are you doing here?"

"She told me I had to go somewhere safe," whispered Sydney, petting Dol.

She, thought Mitch. The same *she,* he guessed, that was burning on the other side of the building. "And you came *here*?"

"The dog was dead," whispered Dominic. "I saw it . . . it was deader than dead . . . and now . . ."

Mitch took Dominic's sleeve. "Get us out of here. *Now.*"

Dominic's eyes drifted up from the girl and the dog and seemed to register the flashing lights bouncing over the wooden walls and up against the high-rise for the first time. Car doors were slamming. Boots on pavement. *"Shit."*

"Yeah, exactly."

"What about Victor?" asked Sydney.

"We have to wait for him somewhere. Not here, Syd. We were never supposed to wait here."

"But what if he needs help?" she protested.

Mitch tried to smile. "It's Victor," he said. "There's nothing he can't handle."

But as Sydney took Dol, and Dominic took Sydney, and Mitch took Dominic, and they all vanished into the shadows, Mitch had a horrible feeling that he was wrong, and his curse had followed him all the way here.

∞

ELI heard the footsteps, the men shouting orders as they tore toward them, through room after room of the plastic sheeting. Victor slumped on the floor, the area around the chair slick with his blood. His eyes were open, but losing focus. Eli wanted this kill to be his, not the Merit Police Department's, and certainly not Serena's.

His.

He saw Victor's knife on the floor a few feet away and took it up, crouching in front of him.

"Some hero," he heard Victor whisper with his two last, labored breaths. Eli rested the blade carefully beneath Victor's ribs.

"Good-bye, Victor," he said.

And then he drove the knife in.

∞

DOMINIC buckled.

He went down on his hands and knees in an alley four blocks from the high-rise, a safe distance from the flood of cops and the burning girl and the guns. He cried out, and at the same time, Sydney clutched her arm, and Mitch rubbed at his bruised ribs. Pain swept over the three like a current, like a breath, something held back and now returned. And then, one by one, they realized what that meant.

"No!" shouted Sydney, turning back toward the high-rise.

Mitch caught her around the waist, wincing as she kicked and screamed and told him to put her down.

"It's over," he whispered as she fought. "It's over. It's over. I'm sorry. It's over."

∞

ELI watched Victor's eyes widen, and then empty, his forehead slumping forward against the metal bars of the chair. Dead. It was so strange that Eli of all people had thought Victor was invincible. And he'd been wrong. Eli drew the knife out of Victor's chest and stood there in the blood-slicked room, waiting for the telltale quiet, the moment of peace. He closed his eyes, and tipped his head back, and waited, and he was still waiting when the cops tore into the room, led by Detective Stell.

"Step away from the body," ordered Stell, raising his gun.

"It's okay," said Eli. He opened his eyes and let his gaze drift down over them. "It's over."

"Get your hands on your head!" shouted another cop.

"Put the knife down!" ordered another.

"It's okay," said Eli again. "He's no danger now."

"Hands up!" demanded Stell.

"I took care of him. He's dead." Eli grew indignant as he gestured to the blood-soaked room, and the dead man bound by wire to the chair bars. "Can't you see that? I'm a *hero*."

The men leveled their guns and shouted and looked at Eli as if he were a monster. And then it hit him. There was no glaze in their eyes. No spell.

"Where's Serena?" he demanded, but the question was swallowed up by the sirens and the shouting cops. "Where is she? She'll tell you!"

"Put the weapon *down*," demanded Stell above the noise.

"She'll tell you. I'm a hero!" he shouted back, throwing the knife aside. "I saved you all!"

But as the blade hit the floor, the cops rushed forward, and slammed him to the ground. He could see Victor's dead face from there, and it seemed to be smiling at him.

"Eli Ever, you're under arrest for the murder of Victor Vale . . ."

"Wait!" he shouted as they cuffed him. "The body."

Stell read him his rights as two cops wrenched him to his feet. Another cop hurried to Stell's side, and said something about a fire out in the lot.

Eli fought their grip. "You have to burn the body!"

Stell gave a signal, and the cops dragged Eli back through the plastic curtains.

"Stell!" shouted Eli again. "You have to burn Vale's body!"

His words echoed on the concrete as the detective and the blood-soaked room and Victor's corpse vanished from his view.

XXXVI

TWO NIGHTS LATER
MERIT CEMETERY

SYDNEY readjusted the shovel on her shoulder.

The air was cold but the night was clear, the moon overhead illuminating the broken gravestones and the dips in the grass as she wove through the cemetery, Dol trotting along beside her. It had been harder to bring him back the second time, but he flanked her now, as if his life were truly tied to hers.

Mitch followed close behind, carrying two more shovels. He'd offered to carry hers, too, but Sydney felt it was important she hold her own. Dominic lagged several yards behind them, buzzed on painkillers and whiskey and tripping every few steps on a clump of weeds or a bit of dislodged rock. She didn't like him this way—useless from all the liquor and mean from all the pain—but she tried not to think of that. She tried not to think of her own pain, either, of the gunshot still burning a hole in her arm as the muscle and skin slowly healed. She hoped it left a scar, the kind she could see, the kind that would remind her of the moment when everything changed.

Not that Sydney thought she'd ever forget.

She readjusted the shovel on her shoulder, and wondered if Eli would live forever, and how much of forever someone could reasonably remember, especially when nothing left a mark.

Eli, incidentally, had been a press field day.

She and Mitch had seen it on the news. The madman who'd murdered two people at the Falcon Price building, all the while claiming to be some monster-slayer, some *hero*. The press said he'd killed a young woman in the construction lot, and burned her body before torturing and then murdering an ex-con on the ground floor. The woman's identity hadn't been made public—they'd have to go by dental records—but Sydney knew it was Serena. She knew even before she made Mitch hack the coroner's reports. She could feel the absence of her sister, the place in her where the threads had been. What she didn't know was why Eli would have done it. But she meant to find out.

The members of the press weren't nearly as interested in Serena as they were in Eli.

Apparently Eli had stood there over Victor's body, covered in blood, still holding the knife and shouting that he was a hero. That he'd saved them all. When no one bought the hero line, he tried to claim it had been a fight. But since his opponent was shredded and he didn't have a scratch on him, that line hadn't worked so well, either. Add that to the papers found in the satchel in Eli's hotel room—he clearly didn't have Victor's foresight to burn anything that could be construed as evidence—and the profiles on his computer, and Eli's body count quickly jumped into double digits. The news never touched on the Merit Police Department's own involvement in a good number of the recent killings, but Eli was now awaiting trial and a psych evaluation.

There was no mention of him being an EO, of course, but then again, why would there be? All it meant for Eli was that if someone shanked him in prison, he'd live to have it happen again. If he were lucky they'd put him in isolation, like Victor. Sydney hoped they didn't put him in isolation. She thought that maybe if they found out he could heal himself, hurting him would become the most popular game in the facility.

Sydney made a mental note to leak that detail wherever he ended up.

It was too quiet in the cemetery, what with only the sounds of grass-muffled steps in the dark, so Sydney tried to hum the way Victor had when they'd gone to dig up Barry. But it sounded wrong in her mouth, eerie and sad, so she stopped and focused on finding her way by the map drawn in Sharpie on the back of her hand. She'd drawn it in daylight, but the Merit Cemetery, like most things, looked different at night.

Finally she caught sight of the fresh grave, and quickened her pace. The grave was unmarked except for Victor's book, which Sydney had set like a stone at the top of the patch of dirt that morning, waiting in the shadow of a stone angel for the diggers to finish and go away. That detective, Stell, had been there, too. He'd stayed long enough to watch the simple wood coffin get lowered down into the hole and covered with dirt.

Mitch caught up to her, and the two looked down at the grave for a moment before Sydney drove her shovel into the ground, and set to work. Dol wandered the plots nearby, but never let Sydney out of his sight, and Dominic eventually wandered over, and sat on a gravestone, keeping an eye out for trouble as the other two dug.

Thud.

Thud.

Thud.

They drove their shovels in the ground until the air seemed warmer and the night seemed thinner, and light grazed the far edges of the sky where it met the buildings of Merit. Sometime before dawn, Sydney's shovel hit wood, and they scraped the last dirt from the top of the coffin, and heaved the lid up.

Sydney looked down at Victor's body. Then she perched on the edge of the coffin, and pressed her hands against his chest, reaching as far as she could. A moment later, the cold ran up her arms, and caught her breath, and beneath her hands a heartbeat fluttered, as Victor Vale opened his eyes, and smiled.

ACKNOWLEDGMENTS

To my family, for not giving me strange looks when I told them what I wanted to write.

To my agent, Holly, for not giving me a strange look when I told her what I'd written.

To Patricia Riley, for loving every member of my motley crew (especially Mitch and his chocolate milk).

To Ruta Sepetys, who listened to me babble on and then told me very seriously to *finish this book*.

To Jen Barnhardt, for accompanying me to every comic book movie, even the not-so-great ones.

To Rachel Stark, for always asking hard questions, and for pushing me to do the same.

To Matthew Leach and Deanna Maurice, for the medical knowledge.

And to Sophie, for the term EO.

To my readers, for following me over moors and through dark halls and now into the heart of Merit.

And to my editor, Miriam, for making every step of this journey marvelous. From the first narwhal doodle to the last late-night discussions on morality, mortality, and villainy, I wouldn't have wanted to do this book with anyone else.

MORE

TOR

Read on for the *Tor.com* short story

WARM UP

IT had been 293 days since he locked himself in.

Now, as David stood facing the front door, he checked himself—keys, wallet, phone—savoring the small measure of control he felt at confirming each thing, and the small comfort at delaying the vital moment a few seconds longer. Shoes. Pants. Shirt. Jacket. He'd showered and shaved—not that he hadn't continued those rituals daily under his self-imposed seclusion; David had always been a creature of routine—and combed back his hair, which Jess had cut for him the week before.

I'm ready.

He reached out and brought his fingers to rest on the handle—it remained cool beneath his touch—and turned. He stepped through. Closed the door. Locked it. Took one step, then another. David made it to the end of the drive, through the gate, up the quiet road. Every block he paused and asked himself if he wanted to turn back, or keep going.

He kept going.

The Lanes' house sat only a mile or so from the city center, and as David walked, the street and path—both empty when he set out—began to fill. It happened quite suddenly, this populating of

Copyright © 2013 by Victoria Schwab

the world, and David soon found himself standing at an intersection crowded with people. His pulse quickened, and he hung back to let them cross while he composed himself, flexing his hands, reassuring himself that he was all right. A hedge decorated the corner behind him, and he plucked a leaf and held it in his palm. It didn't burn. He dropped it with relief, and crossed the street.

As he did, David had the feeling he was being watched. He scanned the other corners and found a handful of people—an older woman, a pair of teen girls, a young man—but none of them were looking his way, and he shook it off; nearly a year without prying eyes was bound to make the world seem full of them.

He kept going.

David passed half a dozen shops, a handful of restaurants, a bar. At the last, his steps slowed.

McKillan's, read the sign over the doors. Samantha despised bars, couldn't stand the noise and the smoke and the sticky floors.

David went in.

The world got smaller. The people got closer. He tried not to think about how easily the wooden shell of the place would burn as he made his way to the counter and climbed up onto the stool, lacing his fingers in front of him. He ordered a gin and tonic. And then another. And a third. He went to the bathroom. When he came back, a fresh drink was waiting at David's stool. A beer.

"From the lady at the end," said the bartender, pointing to the edge of the counter. "Said you looked like you could use it."

David twisted in his seat to see the woman. She had red hair and redder lips, and the darkest brown eyes he'd ever seen. Everything about her seemed . . . warm. David hesitated. And then he took his drink, and went to join her.

Her name was Christa. She touched his arm when she talked, and he leaned into her heat. After the first beer, he'd forgotten about the crowded bar. After the second, he'd forgotten about the days—weeks, months—of meticulous planning. After the third, he'd forgotten about his fear, and his power.

By the time David left, he could barely see straight enough to read Christa's number on the napkin. On the way out, he thought he recognized the young man in the corner booth. But he couldn't place him.

He ambled down the sidewalk, feeling better than he had in 297 days. The bar had been loud, but in the relative quiet of the street, David heard his phone beep. He had a message. He tugged the cell gingerly from his pocket and pressed the button, holding it lightly to his ear as he walked.

"Hey Dave," Jess's voice said, "just your baby sister here. I hope you made it past the driveway. Don't forget to check in. Love you. Be safe."

When he put the phone away and looked up, he realized his feet had carried him down a side street. He turned back and made his way toward the main road, and was halfway there when he snagged his shoe on a bit of alley debris and stumbled forward. Without thinking, he threw out his hand and caught himself against a restaurant's back door.

It only took a second. The surprise of the fall and the pain of the impact caught him off guard, and his control wavered. He pulled back as quickly as he could, but by then he'd singed a handprint into the wood.

Clumsy, growled David to himself as he straightened. He'd been doing so well.

He took another step toward the main road before he realized someone was standing in his way. The light in the alley was lower than that on the main street and at first the figure was nothing more than a fuzzy silhouette in David's far-from-sober vision.

And then the shape moved toward him, sharpening, and David frowned.

It was the young man from the corner booth. *And the street corner,* David realized. He was dressed in dark jeans and a long-sleeved shirt. He barely looked old enough to drink.

"Can I help you, kid?" asked David.

The stranger continued toward him with slow, measured steps, and David found himself retreating, even as he said, "Hey, I'm talking to you."

The young man reached the burned door, and stopped.

"The son of man," he said softly, bringing his hand to the wood, "shall send forth his angels, and they shall gather out of his kingdom all that offend." His hand fell away from the door. "And cast them into a furnace of fire."

The stranger's eyes glittered in the dark.

"What the hell are you talking about?" said David.

"David Lane," said the stranger.

David's blood ran cold. "How do you know my name?"

"You have sinned against God."

"Who are you?"

A knife appeared in the stranger's hand. "One of his angels."

David stumbled backward several feet, but his shoulders fetched up against a trash bin, and before he could get away, the stranger was there. "Wait, please—"

He didn't get the chance to finish. The knife slid between David's ribs. Pain, bright and hot—hotter than anything he'd felt in 297 days—tore through him as his knees buckled.

He grasped at the stranger's arm as he sank, tightening his fingers around the man's sleeve. The fabric burned instantly, and the flesh beneath began to char, and the stranger gritted his teeth, but didn't let go. David's grip began to weaken, until his fingers finally slipped from the stranger's arm. The knife slid free. Everything got quiet. Even the sound of his own body falling forward to the street seemed far away. He felt the cold then, not blistering as it had been beneath the snow, but steady, spreading through him as he lay there.

Warm up, he thought, but his hands rested uselessly against the pavement. *Warm up,* he willed, but only the cold was there to meet him. The cold and the quiet. They took hold and dragged him down, and the last thing David saw was the stranger crossing himself, the ruined flesh of his arm knitting back together.

And then the darkness came, and buried David Lane in a blanket of ash.

Read on for a sneak peek at
the sequel to *Vicious*

VENGEFUL

BEFORE

The night Marcella Riggins died, she made her husband's favorite dinner.

Not because it was a special occasion, but specifically because it *wasn't*, because spontaneity, the magazines insisted, that was the secret to love. That, and a home-cooked meal. Nothing too fancy; Marcus preferred a good steak, edges seared with black pepper, slow-baked sweet potatoes, a bottle of merlot.

But six o'clock came and went, and Marcus wasn't home.

She put the food in the oven to keep it warm, checked her lipstick in the hall mirror, fixed a stray curl, and smoothed the apron tied over her A-line skirt (he'd always liked the sight of her playing housewife). Her cherry red heels clicked across the wood floor as she set the table and lit each of the twenty-four tapers in the pair of standing candelabras.

Marcus gave her hell, but she loved those candelabras. With their long stems and branching limbs, they looked like the kind of thing you'd find in a French chateau. They made the home feel luxurious. Made new money feel old.

Copyright © 2018 by Victoria Schwab

She checked the time—seven, now—but resisted the urge to call him. The fastest way to kill a flame was to smother it. Besides, if Marcus had business, then business came first. That was the way of it.

She poured herself a glass of wine, leaned against the counter, and imagined his strong hands closing around someone's throat. A head forced underwater, a jaw cracking sideways, all of it done with calm precision. Control.

But as seven became eight, Marcella's arousal turned to annoyance, and by the time the front door finally swung open at ten to nine, annoyance was quickly hardening to anger.

"Sorry, darling." His southern accent always came through when he'd been drinking. It was the only sign. He never stumbled or swayed, his hands never shook. No, Marcus Riggins was made of stronger stuff.

Sure, his waist had widened a little (while hers had narrowed), his beautiful swimmer's body bloating a fraction every year, but his black hair hadn't thinned, and his blue eyes were still like chipped slate. He'd always been good-looking, though she wasn't sure how much of that was the tailored suit, the Glock holstered at his side, the heady scent of business—cash and gunpowder and cigars—she'd always found stronger than any cologne. The way he moved through the world, as if expecting it get out of his way.

It usually did.

"It's fine," she said, hating the edge in her voice. She turned toward the kitchen, but he caught her wrist, pulling her hard enough that she lost her balance and fell into him. His arms folded around her.

"You're gorgeous," he whispered, and she could feel the press of him, hungry against her hip. Another woman would let him take her right there in the hall. But Marcella wasn't another woman.

She reached up, nails dragging down his stubble. "You hungry, sweetheart?"

"Always," he growled into her hair.

"Good," said Marcella, stepping away. "Dinner's ready."

∞

A BEAD of red wine slid like sweat down the side of her glass, tracing its way toward the white tablecloth. Marcella had filled it too full, her hand made clumsy by her worsening mood. Marcus didn't seem to notice the spill. He didn't seem to notice anything.

He raised his tumbler of scotch.

"To my beautiful wife."

Marcus never prayed before meals, but he always made a toast. It didn't matter if he had an audience of twenty, or if they ate alone. She'd found it endearing on their first date. These days the gesture felt hollow, rehearsed. Designed to charm instead of genuinely charming. But he never failed to say the words, and perhaps that was a kind of love, a loyalty. Or perhaps he was simply a creature of habit.

Marcella lifted her own glass.

"To my elegant husband," she answered automatically.

The rim was halfway to her lips when she noticed the smudge on Marcus's cuff. At first she thought it was blood, but it was too bright, too pink.

Her fingers tightened on the stem.

It was lipstick.

Every conversation she'd had with Bethany or Hannah or Grace, all those prattling members of the second and third wives' club, came rushing back.

"His eyes start to wander yet?"

"Keeping his stick wet?"

"All men are rotten."

Marcus was busy cutting into his steak, and rambling on about Tony Hutch, but Marcella had stopped listening. Behind her eyes, her husband traced his thumb across a pair of stained lips, parting them around his knuckle.

She set down her glass. Heat was flushing her skin even as a cold weight settled in her stomach. "What a fucking cliché," she muttered.

He didn't stop chewing. "Excuse me?"

"Your sleeve."

His gaze drifted languidly down toward the bloom of pink. He didn't even have the decency to look surprised. "Must be yours," he said, as if she'd ever worn that shade, ever owned anything so tacky and *twee*—

"Who is she?"

"Honestly, Marce—"

"Who the *fuck* is she?" demanded Marcella, gritting those perfect teeth.

He finally stopped eating, and leaned back in his chair, blue eyes hanging on her. "Nobody."

"Oh, so you're fucking a ghost?"

He rolled his eyes, clearly tired of the subject, which was ironic, considering he usually relished any topic that revolved around *him*. "Marcella, envy really doesn't suit you."

"Nine years, Marcus. Nine. And *now* you can't keep it in your pants?"

Something flickered across his face, surprise, and it hit her—of course, this wasn't his first time cheating. This was only the first time he'd been *caught*.

"How long?" she asked icily.

"Let it go, Marce."

As if it were that simple. A rope she was winding around her fingers, when she was still standing on the ground. As if all that fear and anger were childish, unnecessary things. *Let it go.*

Her grip tightened. It wasn't the act itself—she could forgive a lot, in the interest of this life she'd made. It was the fact that others *knew*.

The look in Grace's eyes that she'd always taken for envy, Bethany's stoic warnings, the twitch at the corner of Hannah's smile—the realization that they knew, had known, for God knows how long, and she hadn't.

That made her burn.

Her hand closed around the steak knife, and Marcus had the nerve to scoff. As if she wouldn't know what to do with it. As if she hadn't listened to all his stories, hadn't begged for details. As if he didn't go on and on about his job when he was drunk. As if she hadn't practiced with a pillow. A bag of flour. A steak.

He raised a single brow. "What do you plan to do now?" he said, voice dripping with condescension.

How silly she must look to him, with those perfectly manicured nails gripping the monogrammed hilt of the blade.

"Dollface?"

Baby. Darling. Dollface. Was that how he really thought of her? As helpless, weak, a glass figurine designed only to shimmer and shine and look pretty on a shelf?

His gaze darkened. "Don't lift that knife unless you plan to use it. . . ."

Perhaps she *was* glass.

But glass is only brittle until it *breaks*.

Then it's sharp. Sharp enough to cut. Sharp enough to kill.

"*Marcella*—"

She lunged for him, and had the thrill of seeing his eyes widen a fraction in surprise, the bourbon spilling as he jerked backwards, but the blade barely skimmed his tie before his hand cracked across her mouth. Blood poured across her tongue, and her eyes blurred with tears as she tumbled back into the oak table, rattling the plates.

She still had the knife, but his hand was wrapped around her wrist, pinning it to the table so hard the bones began to grind together.

He'd been rough with her before, but that had always been in the heat of the moment, signaled by some unspoken pact, and she'd always been the one to signal it.

This was different.

Marcus was two hundred pounds of brute strength, a man who made a living breaking things. People. He clucked his tongue, as if she were just being silly. Blowing things out of proportion. As if she'd made him do this. Made him fuck another woman.

"Ah, Marce, you've always known how to rile me up."

"Let me *go*," she hissed.

He brought his face close to hers, ran a hand through her hair, cupped her cheek. "Only if you play nice."

He was smiling. *Smiling.* As if this were just another game.

Marcella spit blood into his face.

Her husband let out a long-suffering sigh.

And then he slammed her head against the table.

Marcella's world went white, then black—for several long seconds there was nothing—and when it flickered back, the room was cracked, broken. She was on the ground. Her head throbbed, and bile rose in her throat. She rolled over, vomited.

"You could have let it go," said Marcus.

Blood ran into one of her eyes, staining the dining room red as Marcus reached out and wrapped his hand around the nearest candelabra. "I always hated these," he said, tipping the pole until it fell.

The flame caught the silk curtains on the way down.

They were burning before the candelabra ever hit the floor.

She tried to get up, but the room swayed viciously. Something was wrong with her limbs. She felt like she was underwater. Slow, too slow.

Marcus stood in the doorway, watching. Just watching.

A steak knife gleamed on the hardwood floor. Marcella forced herself up through the heavy air. She was on her hands and knees when the blow hit her from behind. The second candelabra came crashing down, iron arms pinning her to the floor.

It was disconcerting, how fast the fire spread. It leapt from the curtain to a puddle of spilled bourbon, to the tablecloth and the rug. It was everywhere.

Marcus's voice, murky in the haze. "We've had a good run."

"I will kill you," she said, heaving against the candelabra. It didn't move. "I will crush you."

A voice through the smoke. "People say a lot of things before they die, sweetheart. I've heard them all."

Heat filled the room, her lungs, her head. She coughed, couldn't breath. "I will *ruin* you."

Nothing.

"Do you hear me, Marcus?"

No answer.

"I will ruin you!"

She screamed until her throat burned, until the smoke stole her voice. Until the world tipped, and fell. And even then, her voice echoed inside her head, her last thoughts following her down, down, down into the dark.

I will ruin you.

I will ruin.
I will.
I—

AFTER

Officer Perry Carson had been stuck on the twenty-seventh level of *Radical Raid* for the better part of an hour when he heard the engine rev to life and looked up in time to see Marcus Riggins's sleek black sedan peal out of the slate half-circle that formed the mansion's drive. It tore down the road, a good thirty over the suburb-mandated speed limit, but Carson wasn't in a patrol car, and even if he had been, he hadn't spent the last three weeks in this shit-heap eating greasy takeout just to bust Riggins for such a minor infraction.

No, the Merit PD needed something to stick.

He settled back and returned to his game, and cracked the twenty-seventh level just as he smelled smoke.

No doubt some asshole setting a poolside bonfire without a permit. He squinted out the window—it was late, half-past ten, the sky an inky black this far from Merit, and the smoke didn't stand out against the dark.

But the fire did.

He was out of the car by the time the flames flickered against the front windows of the Riggins mansion. Calling it in by the time he reached the front door. It was unlocked—thank god it was unlocked—and he threw it open, already composing his report. He'd say it was ajar, say he heard a call for help, even though the truth was he didn't hear *anything* but the crack of burning wood, the whoosh of flame sliding up the hall.

"Police!" he called through the smoke. "Is anyone here?"

He'd seen Marcella Riggins arrive home. But he hadn't seen her leave. The sedan had gone by fast, but not fast enough to leave any doubt—there was no one in the passenger seat.

Perry coughed into his sleeve. Sirens were already sounding in the distance. He knew he should go back outside and wait, outside, where the air was clean and cool and safe.

But then he rounded the corner and saw the body trapped beneath a massive coil of iron the size of a coatrack. The tapers had all melted, but Perry realized it was a candelabra. Who even *owned* a candelabra?

Perry reached for the iron stem and then recoiled—it was searing to the touch. He cursed himself. The metal arms had already burned through Marcella's dress wherever they touched her, the skin raw and red, but she didn't cry out, didn't scream.

She wasn't moving. Her eyes were closed and blood slicked the side of her head, matting the pale blond waves against her scalp.

He felt for a pulse, and found one that fluttered and then seemed to fall away beneath his touch. The fire was getting hotter. The smoke was getting thicker.

"Shit shit shit," he muttered, scanning the room as sirens wailed outside. A pitcher of water had spilled across a napkin, leaving it unburnt, and he wrapped the cloth around his hand and then took hold of the candelabra. The damp fabric hissed and heat shot toward his fingers as he heaved the iron bar up with all his strength. It lifted, and rolled off Marcella's body just as voices filled the hall. Firefighters came storming into the house.

"In here!" he wheezed, choking on the smoke.

A pair of firemen cut through the haze right before the ceiling groaned and a chandelier came toppling down. It shattered against the dining room table, which split and threw up flames, and the next thing Perry knew, he was being hauled backward out of the room and the burning mansion, and into the cool night.

Another fireman followed close behind, Marcella's body slung over one shoulder.

Outside, the trucks were splayed across the manicured lawn, and ambulance lights strobed across the slate drive.

The house was going up, and his hand was throbbing, and his lungs burned, and Perry didn't give a damn about any of it. The only thing he cared about right then and there was saving Marcella Riggins. Marcella, who had always flashed a wan smile and a pert wave to the cops whenever she was followed. Marcella, who would never, ever snitch on her crooked husband.

But judging by the gash on her head, and the house on fire, and the way Marcus peeled out of the drive, there was a chance her position had changed. And Perry wasn't about to waste that chance.

Hoses sent jets of water into the flames, and Perry hacked and spat, but pulled away from an oxygen mask as two medics loaded Marcella onto a stretcher.

"She's not breathing," said a medic, cutting open her dress.

Perry jogged after the medics.

"No pulse," said the other, beginning compressions.

"Then bring it back!" shouted Perry, hauling himself up into the ambulance. He couldn't put a corpse on the stand.

"Ox-sat levels tanking," said the first, strapping an oxygen mask over Marcella's nose and mouth. Her temperature was too high, and the medic pulled out a stack of cold packs and began to break the seals, applying them to her temples, neck, wrists. He handed the last one to Perry, who grudgingly accepted.

Marcella's heartbeat appeared on a small screen, a solid line, even and unmoving.

The van pulled away, the burning mansion quickly shrinking in the window. Three weeks Perry had spent outside that place. Three *years* he'd been trying to nail Marc "the Shark" Riggins. Fate had handed him the perfect witness, and he'd be damned if he was giving her back.

A third medic tried to tend to Perry's burned hand, but he pulled away. "Focus on her," he ordered.

The sirens cut through the night as the medics worked, trying to force her lungs to breathe, her heart to beat. Trying to coax life out of the ashes.

But it wasn't working.

Marcella lay there, limp and lifeless.

Perry's hope began to gutter, die.

And then, between one compression and the next, the horrible static line of her pulse gave a lurch, and a stutter, and finally began to beep.

Read on for an excerpt from the first book
in the Shades of Magic trilogy

A Darker Shade of Magic

I

Kell wore a very peculiar coat.

It had neither one side, which would be conventional, nor two, which would be unexpected, but *several,* which was, of course, impossible.

The first thing he did whenever he stepped out of one London and into another was take off the coat and turn it inside out once or twice (or even three times) until he found the side he needed. Not *all* of them were fashionable, but they each served a purpose. There were ones that blended in and ones that stood out, and one that served no purpose but of which he was just particularly fond.

So when Kell passed through the palace wall and into the anteroom, he took a moment to steady himself—it took its toll, moving between worlds—and then shrugged out of his red, high-collared coat and turned it inside out from right to left so that it became a simple black jacket. Well, a simple black jacket elegantly lined with silver thread and adorned with two gleaming columns of silver buttons. Just because he adopted a more modest palette when he was abroad (wishing neither to offend the local royalty nor to draw attention) didn't mean he had to sacrifice style.

Copyright © 2015 by Victoria Schwab

Oh, kings, thought Kell as he fastened the buttons on the coat. He was starting to think like Rhy.

On the wall behind him, he could just make out the ghosted symbol made by his passage. Like a footprint in sand, already fading.

He'd never bothered to mark the door from *this* side, simply because he never went back this way. Windsor's distance from London was terribly inconvenient considering the fact that, when traveling between worlds, Kell could only move between a place in one and the same *exact* place in another. Which was a problem because there was no Windsor Castle a day's journey from *Red* London. In fact, Kell had just come through the stone wall of a courtyard belonging to a wealthy gentleman in a town called Disan. Disan was, on the whole, a very pleasant place.

Windsor was not.

Impressive, to be sure. But not pleasant.

A marble counter ran against the wall, and on it a basin of water waited for him, as it always did. He rinsed his bloody hand, as well as the silver crown he'd used for passage, then slipped the cord it hung on over his head, and tucked the coin back beneath his collar. In the hall beyond, he could hear the shuffle of feet, the low murmur of servants and guards. He'd chosen the anteroom specifically to avoid them. He knew very well how little the Prince Regent liked him being here, and the last thing Kell wanted was an audience, a cluster of ears and eyes and mouths reporting the details of his visit back to the throne.

Above the counter and the basin hung a mirror in a gilded frame, and Kell checked his reflection quickly—his hair, a reddish brown, swept down across one eye, and he did not fix it, though he did take a moment to smooth the shoulders of his coat—before passing through a set of doors to meet his host.

The room was stiflingly warm—the windows latched despite

what looked like a lovely October day—and a fire raged oppressively in the hearth.

George III sat beside it, a robe dwarfing his withered frame and a tea tray untouched before his knees. When Kell came in, the king gripped the edges of his chair.

"Who's there?" he called out without turning. "Robbers? Ghosts?"

"I don't believe ghosts would answer, Your Majesty," said Kell, announcing himself.

The ailing king broke into a rotting grin. "Master Kell," he said. "You've kept me waiting."

"No more than a month," he said, stepping forward.

King George squinted his blind eyes. "It's been longer, I'm sure."

"I promise, it hasn't."

"Maybe not for *you*," said the king. "But time isn't the same for the mad and the blind."

Kell smiled. The king was in good form today. It wasn't always so. He was never sure what state he'd find his majesty in. Perhaps it had seemed like more than a month because the last time Kell visited, the king had been in one of his moods, and Kell had barely been able to calm his fraying nerves long enough to deliver his message.

"Maybe it's the year that has changed," continued the king, "and not the month."

"Ah, but the year is the same."

"And what year is that?"

Kell's brow furrowed. "Eighteen nineteen," he said.

A cloud passed across King George's face, and then he simply shook his head and said, "Time," as if that one word could be to blame for everything. "Sit, sit," he added, gesturing at the room. "There must be another chair here somewhere."

There wasn't. The room was shockingly sparse, and Kell was

certain the doors in the hall were locked and unlocked from without, not within.

The king held out a gnarled hand. They'd taken away his rings, to keep him from hurting himself, and his nails were cut to nothing.

"My letter," he said, and for an instant Kell saw a glimmer of George as he once was. Regal.

Kell patted the pockets of his coat and realized he'd forgotten to take the notes out before changing. He shrugged out of the jacket and returned it for a moment to its red self, digging through its folds until he found the envelope. When he pressed it into the king's hand, the latter fondled it and caressed the wax seal—the red throne's emblem, a chalice with a rising sun—then brought the paper to his nose and inhaled.

"Roses," he said wistfully.

He meant the magic. Kell never noticed the faint aromatic scent of Red London clinging to his clothes, but whenever he traveled, someone invariably told him that he smelled like freshly cut flowers. Some said tulips. Others stargazers. Chrysanthemums. Peonies. To the king of England, it was always roses. Kell was glad to know it was a pleasant scent, even if he couldn't smell it. He could smell Grey London (smoke) and White London (blood), but to him, Red London simply smelled like home.

"Open it for me," instructed the king. "But don't mar the seal."

Kell did as he was told, and withdrew the contents. For once, he was grateful the king could no longer see, so he could not know how brief the letter was. Three short lines. A courtesy paid to an ailing figurehead, but nothing more.

"It's from my queen," explained Kell.

The king nodded. "Go on," he commanded, affecting a stately countenance that warred with his fragile form and his faltering voice. *"Go on."*

Kell swallowed. "'Greetings to his majesty, King George III,'" he read, "'from a neighboring throne.'"

The queen did not refer to it as the *red* throne, or send greetings from *Red* London (even though the city was in fact quite crimson, thanks to the rich, pervasive light of the river), because she did not think of it that way. To her, and to everyone else who inhabited only one London, there was little need to differentiate among them. When the rulers of one conversed with those of another, they simply called them *others,* or *neighbors,* or on occasion (and particularly in regard to White London) less flattering terms.

Only those few who could move among the Londons needed a way to keep them straight. And so Kell—inspired by the lost city known to all as Black London—had given each remaining capital a color.

Grey for the magic-less city.

Red, for the healthy empire.

White, for the starving world.

In truth, the cities themselves bore little resemblance to one another (and the countries around and beyond bore even less). The fact they were all called *London* was its own mystery, though the prevailing theory was that one of the cities had taken the name long ago, before the doors were all sealed and the only things allowed through were letters between kings and queens. As to which city had first laid claim to the name, none could agree.

"'We hope to learn that you are well,'" continued the queen's letter, "'and that the season is as fair in your city as it is in ours.'"

Kell paused. There was nothing more, save a signature. King George wrung his hands.

"Is that all it says?" he asked.

Kell hesitated. "No," he said, folding the letter. "That's only the beginning."

He cleared his throat and began to pace as he pulled his thoughts together and put them into the queen's voice. "Thank you for asking after our family, she says. The King and I are well. Prince Rhy, on the other hand, continues to impress and infuriate in equal measure, but has at least gone the month without breaking his neck or taking an unsuitable bride. Thanks be to Kell alone for keeping him from doing either, or both."

Kell had every intention of letting the queen linger on his own merits, but just then the clock on the wall chimed five, and Kell swore under his breath. He was running late.

"Until my next letter," he finished hurriedly, "stay happy and stay well. With fondness. Her Highness Emira, Queen of Arnes."

Kell waited for the king to say something, but his blind eyes had a steady, faraway look, and Kell feared he had lost him. He set the folded note on the tea tray and was halfway to the wall when the king spoke up.

"I don't have a letter for her," he murmured.

"That's all right," said Kell softly. The king hadn't been able to write one for years. Some months he tried, dragging the quill haphazardly across the parchment, and some months he insisted on having Kell transcribe, but most months he simply told Kell the message and Kell promised to remember.

"You see, I didn't have the time," added the king, trying to salvage a vestige of his dignity. Kell let him have it.

"I understand," he said. "I'll give the royal family your regards."

Kell turned again to go, and again the old king called out to stop him.

"Wait, wait," he said. "Come back."

Kell paused. His eyes went to the clock. Late, and getting later. He pictured the Prince Regent sitting at his table in St. James, gripping his chair and quietly stewing. The thought made Kell smile, so he turned back toward the king as the latter pulled something from his robe with fumbling fingers.

It was a coin.

"It's fading," said the king, cupping the metal in his weathered hands as if it were precious and fragile. "I can't feel the magic anymore. Can't smell it."

"A coin is a coin, Your Majesty."

"Not so and you know it," grumbled the old king. "Turn out your pockets."

Kell sighed. "You'll get me in trouble."

"Come, come," said the king. "Our little secret."

Kell dug his hand into his pocket. The first time he had visited the king of England, he'd given him a coin as proof of who he was and where he came from. The story of the other Londons was entrusted to the crown and handed down heir to heir, but it had been years since a traveler had come. King George had taken one look at the sliver of a boy and squinted and held out his meaty hand, and Kell had set the coin in his palm. It was a simple lin, much like a grey shilling, only marked with a red star instead of a royal face. The king closed his fist over the coin and brought it to his nose, inhaling its scent. And then he'd smiled, and tucked the coin into his coat, and welcomed Kell inside.

From that day on, every time Kell paid his visit, the king would insist the magic had worn off the coin, and make him trade it for another, one new and pocket-warm. Every time Kell would say it was forbidden (it was, expressly), and every time the king would insist that it could be their little secret, and Kell would sigh and fetch a fresh bit of metal from his coat.

Now he plucked the old lin out of the king's palm and replaced it with a new one, folding George's gnarled fingers gently over it.

"Yes, yes," cooed the ailing king to the coin in his palm.

"Take care," said Kell as he turned to go.

"Yes, yes," said the king, his focus fading until he was lost to the world, and to his guest.

Curtains gathered in the corner of the room, and Kell pulled the heavy material aside to reveal a mark on the patterned wallpaper. A simple circle, bisected by a line, drawn in blood a month ago. On another wall in another room in another palace, the same mark stood. They were as handles on opposite sides of the same door.

Kell's blood, when paired with the token, allowed him to move *between* the worlds. He needn't specify a place because wherever he was, that's where he'd be. But to make a door *within* a world, both sides had to be marked by the same exact symbol. Close wasn't close enough. Kell had learned that the hard way.

The symbol on the wall was still clear from his last visit, the edges only slightly smeared, but it didn't matter. It had to be redone.

He rolled up his sleeve and freed the knife he kept strapped to the inside of his forearm. It was a lovely thing, that knife, a work of art, silver from tip to hilt and monogrammed with the letters *K* and *L*.

The only relic from another life.

A life he didn't know. Or at least, didn't remember.

Kell brought the blade to the back of his forearm. He'd already carved one line today, for the door that brought him this far. Now he carved a second. His blood, a rich ruby red, welled up and over, and he returned the knife to its sheath and touched his fingers to the cut and then to the wall, redrawing the circle and the line that ran through it. Kell guided his sleeve down over the wound—he'd treat all the cuts once he was home—and cast a last glance back at the babbling king before pressing his palm flat to the mark on the wall.

It hummed with magic.

"*As Tascen,*" he said. *Transfer.*

The patterned paper rippled and softened and gave way under his touch, and Kell stepped forward and through.

II

Between one stride and the next, dreary Windsor became elegant St. James. The stuffy cell of a room gave way to bright tapestries and polished silver, and the mad king's mumblings were replaced by a heavy quiet and a man sitting at the head of an ornate table, gripping a goblet of wine and looking thoroughly put out.

"You're late," observed the Prince Regent.

"Apologies," said Kell with a too-short bow. "I had an errand."

The Prince Regent set down his cup. "I thought *I* was your errand, Master Kell."

Kell straightened. "My orders, Your Highness, are to see to the *king* first."

"I wish you wouldn't indulge him," said the Prince Regent, whose name was also George (Kell found the Grey London habit of sons taking father's names both redundant and confusing) with a dismissive wave of his hand. "It gets his spirits up."

"Is that a bad thing?" asked Kell.

"For him, yes. He'll be in a frenzy later. Dancing on the tables talking of magic and other Londons. What trick did you do for him this time? Convince him he could fly?"

Kell had only made that mistake once. He learned on his next visit that the King of England had nearly walked out a window. On the third floor. "I assure you I gave no demonstrations."

Prince George pinched the bridge of his nose. "He cannot hold his tongue the way he used to. It's why he is confined to quarters."

"Imprisoned, then?"

Prince George ran his hand along the table's gilded edge. "Windsor is a perfectly respectable place to be kept."

A respectable prison is still a prison, thought Kell, withdrawing a second letter from his coat pocket. "Your correspondence."

The prince forced him to stand there as he read the note (he never commented on the way it smelled of flowers), and then as he withdrew a half-finished reply from the inside pocket of his coat and completed it. He was clearly taking his time in an effort to spite Kell, but Kell didn't mind. He occupied himself by drumming his fingers on the edge of the gilded table. Each time he made it from pinky to forefinger, one of the room's many candles went out.

"Must be a draft," he said absently while the Prince Regent's grip tightened on his quill. By the time he finished the note, he'd broken two and was in a bad mood, while Kell found his own disposition greatly improved.

He held out his hand for the letter, but the Prince Regent did not give it to him. Instead, he pushed up from his table. "I'm stiff from sitting. Walk with me."

Kell wasn't a fan of the idea, but since he couldn't very well leave empty-handed, he was forced to oblige. But not before pocketing the prince's latest unbroken quill from the table.

"Will you go straight back?" asked the prince as he led Kell down a hall to a discreet door half concealed by a curtain.

"Soon," said Kell, trailing by a stride. Two members of the royal guard had joined them in the hall and now slunk behind like shadows. Kell could feel their eyes on him, and he wondered how much they'd been told about their guest. The royals were always expected to know, but the understanding of those in their service was left to their discretion.

"I thought your only business was with me," said the prince.

"I'm a fan of your city," responded Kell lightly. "And what I do is draining. I'll go for a walk and get some air, then make my way back."

The prince's mouth was a thin grim line. "I fear the air is not as replenishing here in the city as in the countryside. What is it you call us . . . *Grey* London? These days that is far too apt a name. Stay for dinner." The prince ended nearly every sentence with a period. Even the questions. Rhy was the same way, and Kell thought it must simply be a by-product of never being told *no*.

"You'll fare better here," pressed the prince. "Let me revive you with wine and company."

It seemed a kind enough offer, but the Prince Regent didn't do things out of kindness.

"I cannot stay," said Kell.

"I insist. The table is set."

And who is coming? wondered Kell. What did the prince want? To put him on display? Kell often suspected that he would like to do as much, if for no other reason than that the younger George found secrets cumbersome, preferring spectacle. But for all his faults, the prince wasn't a fool, and only a fool would give someone like Kell a chance to stand out. Grey London had forgotten magic long ago. Kell wouldn't be the one to remind them of it.

"A lavish kindness, your highness, but I am better left a specter than made a show." Kell tipped his head so that his copper hair tumbled out of his eyes, revealing not only the crisp blue of the left one but the solid black of the right. A black that ran edge to edge, filling white and iris both. There was nothing human about that eye. It was pure magic. The mark of a blood magician. Of an *Antari*.

Kell relished what he saw in the Prince Regent's eyes when they tried to hold Kell's gaze. Caution, discomfort . . . and fear.

"Do you know why our worlds are kept separate, Your Highness?" He didn't wait for the prince to answer. "It is to keep yours safe. You see, there was a time, ages ago, when they were not so separate. When doors ran between your world and mine, and others, and anyone with a bit of power could pass through. Magic itself could pass through. But the thing about magic," added Kell, "is that it preys on the strong-minded and the weak-willed, and one of the worlds couldn't stop itself. The people fed on the magic and the magic fed on them until it ate their bodies and their minds and then their souls."

"Black London," whispered the Prince Regent.

Kell nodded. He hadn't given that city its color mark. Everyone—at least everyone in Red London and White, and those few in Grey who knew anything at all—knew the legend of Black London. It was a bedtime story. A fairy tale. A *warning*. Of the city—and the world—that wasn't, anymore.

"Do you know what Black London and yours have in common, Your Highness?" The Prince Regent's eyes narrowed, but he didn't interrupt. "Both lack temperance," said Kell. "Both hunger for power. The only reason your London still exists is because it was cut off. It learned to forget. You do not want it to remember." What Kell didn't say was that Black London had a wealth of magic in its veins, and Grey London hardly any; he wanted to make a point. And by the looks of it, he had. This time, when he held out his hand for the letter, the prince didn't refuse, or even resist. Kell tucked the parchment into his pocket along with the stolen quill.

"Thank you, as ever, for your hospitality," he said, offering an exaggerated bow.

The Prince Regent summoned a guard with a single snap of his fingers. "See that Master Kell gets where he is going." And then, without another word, he turned and strode away.

The royal guards left Kell at the edge of the park. St. James Palace loomed behind him. Grey London lay ahead. He took a deep breath and tasted smoke on the air. As eager as he was to get back home, he had some business to attend to, and after dealing with the king's ailments and the prince's attitude, Kell could use a drink. He brushed off his sleeves, straightened his collar, and set out toward the heart of the city.

His feet carried him through St. James Park, down an ambling dirt path that ran beside the river. The sun was setting, and the air was crisp if not clean, a fall breeze fluttering the edges of his black coat. He came upon a wooden footbridge that spanned the stream, and his boots sounded softly as he crossed it. Kell paused at the arc of the bridge, Buckingham House lantern-lit behind him and the Thames ahead. Water sloshed gently under the wooden slats, and he rested his elbows on the rail and stared down at it. When he flexed his fingers absently, the current stopped, the water stilling, smooth as glass, beneath him.

He considered his reflection.

"You're not *that* handsome," Rhy would say whenever he caught Kell gazing into a mirror.

"I can't get enough of myself," Kell would answer, even though he was never looking at himself—not *all* of himself anyway— only his eye. His right one. Even in Red London, where magic flourished, the eye set him apart. Marked him always as *other*.

A tinkling laugh sounded off to Kell's right, followed by a grunt, and a few other, less distinct noises, and the tension went out of his hand, the stream surging back into motion beneath him. He continued on until the park gave way to the streets of London, and then the looming form of Westminster. Kell had a fondness for the abbey, and he nodded to it, as if to an old friend. Despite the city's soot and dirt, its clutter and its poor, it had something Red London lacked: a resistance to change. An appreciation for the enduring, and the effort it took to make something so.

How many years had it taken to construct the abbey? How many more would it stand? In Red London, tastes turned as often as seasons, and with them, buildings went up and came down and went up again in different forms. Magic made things simple. *Sometimes,* thought Kell, *it made things* too *simple.*

There had been nights back home when he felt like he went to bed in one place and woke up in another.

But here, Westminster Abbey always stood, waiting to greet him.

He made his way past the towering stone structure, through the streets, crowded with carriages, and down a narrow road that hugged the dean's yard, walled by mossy stone. The narrow road grew narrower still before it finally stopped in front of a tavern.

And here Kell stopped, too, and shrugged out of his coat. He turned it once more from right to left, exchanging the black affair with silver buttons for a more modest, street-worn look: a brown high-collared jacket with fraying hems and scuffed elbows. He patted the pockets and, satisfied that he was ready, went inside.

Read the *New York Times* bestselling

Shades of Magic

Series

"Addictive and immersive."
—Entertainment Weekly
(Grade A) on *A Gathering of Shadows*

"Compulsively readable."
—NPR
on *A Darker Shade of Magic*

"Feels like a priceless object, brought from another, better world of fantasy books."
—*io9*
on *A Darker Shade of Magic*

TOR TOR-FORGE.COM